FIVE HARD BITES

Also by Grant Tracey

A Fourth Face

Cheap Amusements

Toronto, 1965: Cheap Amusements' Beat

Final Stanzas

Lovers & Strangers

Parallel Lines and the Hockey Universe

Playing Mac: A Novella in Two Acts,
and Other Stories

Five Hard Bites

Grant Tracey

A Collection of
Hayden Fuller Mysteries

Five Hard Bites Copyright © 2021 Grant Tracey
Cheap Amusements Copyright © 2016 Grant Tracey
A Fourth Face Copyright © 2018 Grant Tracey
Neon Kiss Copyright © 2021 Grant Tracey
Day of the Dragons Copyright © 2021 Grant Tracey
Shot, Reverse Shot Copyright © 2021 Grant Tracey

This is a work of fiction. Names, characters, places, and incidents either are the product of the author's imagination or are used fictitiously. Any resemblance to actual persons, living or dead, events, or locales is entirely coincidental. All rights reserved. No part of this book may be used or reproduced in any manner whatsoever without written permission except in the case of brief quotations embodied in critical articles and reviews.

Published by Twelve Winters, a literary project.

P. O. Box 414 • Sherman, Illinois 62684-0414 • twelvewinters.com

Five Hard Bites was first published by Twelve Winters in 2021. It is also available in a digital edition. The character Hayden Fuller and the phrases "A Hayden Fuller Mystery" and "Hayden Fuller Mysteries" are the property of Grant Tracey. All rights reserved.

Cover and interior page design by TWP Design.

Cover art copyright © 2021 Miles Wisniewski. Used by permission. All rights reserved.

Author photos copyright © 2018 Mitchell D. Strauss.

ISBN
978-1-7331949-5-2

Printed in the United States of America

For Effy,
daughter and amazing writer who has read and re-read every word put down here. Thanks for all the wonderful virtual coffee and writing sessions during a pandemic.

Acknowledgments

Cheap Amusements and *A Fourth Face* were first published by Twelve Winters Press. For this collection, the author made minor revisions and corrections to their texts. *Neon Kiss*, *Day of the Dragons*, and "Shot, Reverse Shot" are published here for the first time.

Contents

"The streets were dark with something more than night."

— Raymond Chandler

Five Hard Bites

Cheap Amusements

1965

The sky was black, clear, and speckled with dim stars, but it wasn't as cold as it should be for early December. Hayden Fuller was watching the sky, the tips of trees, the foamed frost of dark grass, ahead of him waiting, vaguely hoping. His breath twitched from his lips like small snakes. They had to find the girl.

The tip, a muffled voice, said the girl was holed up here. The voice called Hayden's office earlier that afternoon and Hayden wasn't sure if the tipster were a man or a woman. The one distinguishing feature to the cadence: the speaker said again like an American with the second syllable rhyming with Jen as opposed to the Canadian heavy emphasis on the second syllable "gain." Police Chief Sal Lambertino, who Hayden immediately called for backup, was chewing his lower lip and was worried. The picket fence of his beard had stiffened against his jawline. He let out a sharp gasp of air and huddled nearer a narrow slant of pine trees.

They had just passed a small grouping of cabins, empty, and there was one more cabin to go, a football field across from them, light flickering from one of the front windows. There were no human shadows in the cabin but the light danced as if there were a burning candle. Someone had to be close by. Where? Could be an ambush, the kidnapper lying fallow in the adjacent fields of foam, waiting for Hayden and Sal to cross the open expanse of tall grass and frozen cattails. "I don't like this—too much ground," Sal said.

"I'm not too crazy about it either." Hayden pulled his porkpie down along the tip of his ears. He wished he had worn a toque. Sarah Kerr, the daughter of his client Mrs. Kerr, had been missing for two days. According to Mrs. Kerr, the girl had allegedly received a phone call from her guidance counselor telling her to meet him at the coffee shop at the corner of Eglinton and Yonge to discuss her senior thesis. "Be home soon, Mom" were the last words she said. The counselor hadn't made the call. He had been in a meeting with fellow Castle Frank faculty at the time it was placed. Lambertino told Hayden not to hold out much hope. The girl was probably dead. Might never be found, but he had a full force of men behind him, loaded down with weaponry.

The window light danced with the rhythm of thin scarves on a downhill skier.

Suddenly bright lights filled the spaces around Hayden and Sal. Mounted high in trees, the arc lamps cut diamonds in the snow. It was so bright that Hayden felt his face tightening into a squint. Machine gun fire blurted from across the way, nicking spots of bark from the pine trees. Hayden dropped so low that snow filled his lower lip. Sal was on the ground too. The constables behind them and the RCMP returned fire.

It was a sharp attack like the fine stick work of a jazz drummer. The melody across the way was a robust ack-ack-ack. "AK-47," Sal mumbled. "A commie gun."

In the brief respite between gun bursts, a car engine slowly cranked. Even though the weather was unseasonably warm for early December it was still cold enough to play havoc with a car battery. Hayden motioned to Sal to their right and mumbled "getaway." Sal nodded and asked for cover as the two men broke across the tall grass. The sky and the cabin against it shook as Hayden closed in on the car, a Rambler, with a shadow of a man behind the wheel. "I see him, there, there, behind the wheel."

Hayden tried to get a shot off but hit the radiator. Steam hissed.

Sal opened up, spider webbing the windshield, the front end of the car drooping in sync with the man behind the wheel. Nothing was upright. Hardened leaves and bits of wood cracked under their shoes as they approached. Sal opened the door.

"What the hell?"

It wasn't a person. It was a bullet-riddled mannequin, a jacket around its shoulders. It didn't have a face.

"Fuck—"

And then they heard a second motor. A boat sludged across the slush of lake. It thumped up against chunks of ice, but it was definitely moving. It mustn't have far to go, Hayden figured, because there was no way it could get across a partially frozen lake.

The other police officers formed a curtain around the cabin and were already searching inside for the girl. "Captain—" one of them shouted.

Sal and Hayden rushed into the cabin, the fresh heat warming their faces. A carpet was kicked back from a trapdoor. They opened the door and followed the ladder to the cold, slapping water below. This was clearly the exit port. Sal's flashlight cut arc lines along the wood beams and hollow splashes of water. He shook his head, the flashlight creating rings a glass might make on a countertop. "We don't have anyone on the other side. Might as well radio ahead, but it's pretty pointless."

"He wanted us to come close without catching him. He wanted us to—" Hayden's stomach felt like it were full of rocks. "Let's check the cabin."

There wasn't much to see: a couch, three TV trays, a small transistor radio protected by a crocheted leather case, primitive bunk beds with threadbare bedroll, a bookshelf loaded up with *National Geographic* magazines, and charred wood in a stovetop fireplace. The room was warm and the candle was burning dim, flickers filling the room with Neolithic-looking shadows. In one corner was a huge Gladstone suitcase. It was heavy.

Hayden took another breath. He was afraid of what might be inside.

He was right to be afraid. Folded up was a naked blonde, a huge Christmas bow christening the top of her head. Her bloody parchment hair stuck to her shoulders, two bullet holes were behind her right ear. Sarah Kerr.

1

It was one of those days where everything is covered with layers of gauze, a kind of dusky twilight vibe, as if the world has stopped spinning and life's brightness is now layered in thin-veiled threads. I pushed back my porkpie, wiped tired eyes and swallowed, my voice catching. "So, how long she been missing?"

Another missing person case.

Like Sarah Kerr.

Kim Stabulas studied the lines in the hardwood floor. They ran parallel but every once in a while a wobbly knot suggested that rhythmic order could be knocked off its axis. "Two days."

No ransom note, no phone calls, nothing. Cathy had been working at the family store, when she said she had to meet a girlfriend at the corner of Yonge and St. Clair. This was at 6 p.m. on Saturday.

Yonge and St. Clair.

Yonge and Eglinton, 95 days ago.

It was now Monday, the last day of March, late afternoon.

The Stabulas mom and pop grocery had been in the family for over thirty years and was just below her bedroom.

"Who's the girlfriend?"

"She didn't say." Nick Stabulas, Kim and Cathy's father, crowded over my shoulder. "She wasn't one to, you know—reveal private matters." He had a wide-set face, bushy eyebrows, and a solemn expression that resembled a man squinting through a bright fire. "She's *very proper*. Never stays out late. Never speaks badly of anyone. She just isn't that kind of girl, you understand?"

Kim nodded, half-heartedly. "A saint, my sister."

The tone was slightly ironic and coated with regrets. I wasn't quite sure who she was sad for: herself or her sister.

"Three days ago, Cathy met with her guidance counselor. Well, he used to be her guidance counselor—" Kim looked away, eyes skimming details in the room.

"As in high school guidance counselor?" Cathy graduated four, nearly five years ago. I pulled on the brim of my porkpie. "She's still seeing her high school guidance counselor?"

"I'm not crazy about it either, but ever since the girls' mother died Landover has been a care provider, trying to talk Cathy into going to college. She has the smarts for it, he says." Nick shrugged apathetically.

Kim shot sharp edges at her father. "Yeah. This was one of those meetings. That was on Friday."

"Who is this guy? Did you say Landover?"

"Yeah, Landover Leeds."

Landover Leeds. The same guy in the Sarah Kerr case. He was her guidance counselor too. He was in a meeting at the time of her abduction. Toxicology reports on Sarah came back clean, but there were traces of semen. She had been raped, strangled, and shot twice behind the right ear.

Cathy attended Castle Frank High School from 1956–60, Sarah attended from 1961–65.

"She didn't have many friends." Nick shrugged with his big shoulders. "It was probably Lisa who called. Lisa Steinmetz—"

I wrote the name down in my yellow notepad. I had the spelling right the first time.

Nick had given me photographs of Cathy yesterday and it was hard to tell her apart from Kim. She and her sister were Irish twins. Kim born in January 1941; Cathy eleven months later in

December. Their faces and figures—long and lithe with athletic arms, modest breasts, and strong upper thighs—were very similar. Kim's hair, however, was sleek and black, like drawings in a four-color comic book. Cathy's hair was short, thicker and red, cut just below the ears, and even in still photographs you could tell that it bounced with a sassy energy. What was most striking about Cathy were her penetrating eyes, warm, with their dark black comfort. It was a mesmerizing yet odd combination for a woman in the predominantly English, Irish, and Scottish confines of Toronto: red hair, black eyes.

I stared into the bedroom. It was very polite, neat: twin beds with cover corners folded over in precise triangles; a bookshelf crowded with tight upright books; a small coffee table, a lamp, and a dozen or so jazz records fanned by a modest hi-fi unit.

"I shared this room with her." Kim pointed at the two beds. "That's before I moved out on my own at seventeen. Everything in here is hers, except a few clothes in the closet and that bed."

I made another note.

"She kept the bed, hoping I'd return, I guess."

There wasn't much else in the room but three Harold Barkley photographs torn from the *Star Weekly* hanging like pennants over the foot of her bed. I was in one of the photos, between the circles, wristing a shot over Terry Sawchuk's catch glove, one hole. Sawchuk, now a Leaf, was with Detroit at the time, and he looked like a display case mannequin as the puck tucked under the bar behind him. One and four holes (high catch glove and low stick side) were my favorite shots to make. I miss the game. Big time.

"Leafs fan?" I asked, pointing at the Barkleys.

"The biggest," her sister said.

"Twenty-two goals, your best season, 1958–59," Nick said, smiling.

I guess he was a big fan too.

On the dresser at the foot of Cathy's bed were a handful of

hockey programs done up in blue Art Deco lines with Tim Horton or the Big M, Frank Mahovlich, gracing the cover. On the back of the programs were ads for Dominion's grocery stores: "Mainly Because of the Meat!"

"Aww—" Nick groaned. "Goddamn Dominion's." They were putting him out of business. Three years ago the big chain opened just two blocks away, reconfiguring Nick's customer base to grandmas and kids. He shook his head. "You can't live on the baboes and the kids, you understand?"

"Sure."

Cathy couldn't have just wandered off, you understand, he said.

Ninety-five days ago, Sarah Kerr had received a phone call from someone pretending to be Landover Leeds. Meet me at the coffee shop on the corner of Yonge and Eglinton to discuss your senior thesis, the voice said. She went and her folded up body was found two days later in a suitcase in a cabin. She had been tattooed with cigarette burns and two bullets were placed behind the right ear.

"So Lisa Steinmetz, huh? It couldn't have been this Landover guy she went to see?"

"She wouldn't be involved with Landover or any guy over the phone. Like my father said, she was a quiet girl—" Kim shrugged.

Kim, by contrast, *was not* quiet. She wore a striking black-and-white jacket and medium skirt that vaguely resembled the vibrancy of a pop-art painting. The tight-sleeved jacket flared at the shoulders. The skirt was long with patches of white and black highlighting the curves of her hips and power of her thighs. She didn't quite fit in with her family. She was a realtor in a downtown office and had her own apartment. "You've seen her photographs. Does she look like the kind of girl that would run off with some guy?"

"I don't know." I shrugged.

I sure hoped that Cathy's fate wasn't like the girl's in the suitcase, and maybe I was doing too much thinking out loud, maybe it had something to do with all that gauze cluttering up the room and everything spinning askew, but when Nick's and Kim's eyes widened, I backpedaled and realized my thoughts were being spoken aloud. I do that sometimes. "I'm not trying to alarm anybody. I'm sorry. I just—I need something. A clue. A lead." I wiped the edges of my mouth. "You mind if I search her things?"

"No, no. Go ahead," Nick said.

I wondered if I could show her photographs to people.

Sure, they both said, and Nick pulled out a more recent one, a 3x5 from his wallet. It was slightly creased and taken two weeks ago. Cathy stood by the plate glass of the grocery store, head tilted, slightly shielding her eyes from the sun, a twist of a smile rising up from the corners of her mouth. It was as if she were retreating from something she really needed to share but was afraid to.

"Did she write a diary? Was she seeing anybody?"

"No. Like I said, she was a home girl, you know?" Stabulas rubbed at a bushy eyebrow and looked away. "She didn't date much. Worked in the store." He glanced over at Kim and I sensed disfavor at his older daughter's lifestyle and abandonment of old country ways.

"Tell me about Lisa Steinmetz—"

Lisa Steinmetz, a working girl. Not the sharpest knife in the drawer, Nick said. Occasionally, after the hockey game on Saturday nights, Lisa, Cathy and two others played bridge.

"Bridge?" That seemed just a little too English—not at all a Macedonian pastime.

"Lisa isn't Macedonian. German and English, I think," Kim said.

"She lives on her own." Nick again passed some kind of veiled judgment over female independence. She also didn't have a good relationship with her parents. "Her father used to hit her and drinks too much."

"She told you all this?"

"To me they talk, in the store," Nick said. "Lots of bad things in her home, you understand?" The heavy traces of his Eastern-European accent were more pronounced when he got excited. The rhythms gave him the dignity of experience.

"Yeah," Kim nodded, "Lisa's had it rough. And that's the extent of Cathy's social life. Bridge with a lost girl and hockey games in front of the TV on Saturday." Kim's lips were a terse line. "She also puts in long hours at the store."

Kim must have felt that her father hovered too much around Cathy's life, keeping her trapped in the home. As she spoke, she crossed her arms and shot him surly looks.

I wandered to the closet. Didn't find much of anything but simple, unflashy clothes: slacks and jeans and plain blouses and loose-fitting sweaters. On her tight bookshelf were novels by American and Canadian authors from John Steinbeck to Morley Callaghan. At the end of the shelf was a glass ball with a snow figure inside, a gentle reminder of childhood or a desire to hold onto a prior innocence.

"Oh, that's mine," Kim said. "That and the bed."

I nodded. I guess she was holding onto a part of her childhood too. I placed the glass ball back in front of the books and leafed through a dog-eared copy of Steinbeck's *East of Eden*.

"Cathy loved that book," Kim said. "Read it twice."

"Uh-huh."

The jazz records were classic hard bop, my favorites too: John Coltrane, Sonny Clark, Donald Byrd, and Hank Mobley. Scrapbooks were full of clippings from several Leafs games, including game one of the '63 finals in which I scored a goal and an assist. Cathy penciled across the headline in blue, "Way to go Fuller!"

It was weird. I suddenly felt like we had a personal connection. Just those four words and it was like we knew each other.

I never felt connected to Sarah. I never got to know her. She was an enigma and shortly after her murder I met with her mom once a week, pursuing new leads, asking for hints, anything. We don't get together much now.

But there was no diary. No sense of a sexual history. Not much to go on.

That was until we got to the dresser's bottom drawer. It wouldn't open.

The first two drawers were crowded with underwear and socks and T-shirts. But this drawer—

"I didn't know that drawer locked," Kim said.

Nick Stabulas pressed in closer. "Me neither."

I pulled on it harder, and then reached for my Buck knife. "Do you mind?" I don't know why I was asking for permission. Cathy wasn't a minor. I should be really asking her to look in her dresser, not her father, but for some reason I was asking him—Old World deference? I'm not sure.

He nodded and shrugged reluctantly. I jimmied it.

And the drawer stuttered awake.

On top was a Big Chief Tablet. "My writings" was scrawled about the Indian's head. Doodles of men's faces, crescent moons, a clown face in a homburg, and unbalanced stars (some of the points more open than others) filled the rest of the space.

The pages were slanted with left leaning prose. "She's a lefty?"

"Yes," Kim nodded. "So am I."

What were the odds?

I never did learn if Sarah was a lefty or righty. I never learned much about her at all. The suitcase she was found in was traced to Eaton's. It was a model that only they manufactured, and nine were sold in the four months before her disappearance: five on credit, four by cash. All of the credit purchases checked out: the customers still had their suitcases. The salesclerks couldn't recall any of the other buyers but one, a man with a heavy lower lip and eyes too close together. The sales gal didn't like him because he kept calling her "luv," and she was pretty sure it was a put-on

English accent to hide his real accent because the voice had too much bounce in it. "You should be a cop," I told her with a smile. "The guy was a real creep, Mr. Fuller. If he had a chance to he would've patted me on the fanny." He was a big man and his eyes were constantly removing her clothing. A real fucking creep, she said, covering her lower lip for swearing. Unfortunately, the lead about the creep led nowhere.

The Big Chief Tablet wasn't a diary. That was clear at first glance. It was fiction. Stories. In time, I would look these over. Maybe there was a narrative thread to follow.

Under the tablet were sheer nighties, frilly panties, bras without cups, a black leather strap with a ball to place in your mouth, latex gloves, whips, dildos, and other sexual toys that left me only speculating on how they might function.

Her father's eyebrows knitted together. "That's not hers." He shook his heavy head, his face and eyes darkening. She was always home. When would she have time for this? And why would she bring that filth into our home?

Kim smiled absently. "Maybe she wasn't only playing bridge on Saturdays—"

Nick slapped Kim, staggering her against Cathy's bed. It wasn't an open hand hit but it wasn't a full fist either. It was somewhere in-between. "You have a dirty mouth," he said. He raised his hand again. It was chunky like a cut of pork loin.

I grabbed him by the wrist, spun him, and pushed him back into a wooden chair that he knocked about. "Don't touch her again." The edges of my ears hurt and I felt my heart knocking in my throat.

"I don't believe it. This isn't her." Nick's fists rested atop his thighs. "And you should have more respect for your sister, you understand?" He pointed at Kim. And then he lit a cigarette, a heavy thick brand.

I didn't want to believe it about Cathy either, but I didn't know her or her third face. There's a face we show in public and one we show in private, but we also have a third face, the one that catches up with and scares us, the face that we didn't even know we were capable of until it appears in the rear-view mirror, hellhounds on our trail. But have we the guts to honestly acknowledge that face, or do we turn the mirror away?

I had experienced this face in hockey: bloody, brooding moments where I really wanted to hurt somebody or was so fixated on the game and excelling that I no longer knew or cared who I was. It was like I had become Art Blakey improvising on the skins and tins without any of the beauty.

Suddenly my head clouded with the spun gauze of dirty cotton candy. I could barely breathe. "I'll check with Lisa about the bridge thing."

Nick exhaled sharply off his cigarette.

I continued searching through the sex paraphernalia and found buried in the folds of a slinky nightie an 8x10 color photograph of Leafs president Steven Smith and Board of Governors member Calvin Bullard. Smith, the light in the room refracting off the lenses of his Lombardi glasses, had taken over ownership of the club in 1961 after his father, the Old Man, stepped down. The forty-something Smith was a playboy and often drank milk with his bourbon to soothe an ulcerous stomach. He sported a thin, Errol Flynn mustache.

"Pal Cal" was a buffoon, a fat, fast-talking guy who always had a king-size bag of chips in his hands and flecks of grease stains on the lapels of his double-breasted Brooks Brothers. His appetites ran toward curvy women and betting on the horses. After most road games he floundered in some downtown Boston-Chicago-Detroit-Montreal-New York pub. For home games, he knocked back brews in his Maple Leaf Gardens bunker, a haunt cut in the east end Blues of the building where he watched games with an unobstructed view.

In the photograph, both men had their arms around Cathy who looked slightly uncomfortable between them, pouring champagne into the lip of the Stanley Cup. She wore a velvety red dress that matched the color of her hair. The Greco-Roman architecture behind her and marble floors and Art Deco flourishes (parasol webbing on light fixtures) cued me that this particular snapshot was taken at the Royal York Hotel. The Leafs often stayed at the Westbury but we celebrated Stanley Cup victories at the Royal York. Smith's mustache, which he had only started sporting recently, dated the photo from '62 or '63. "I was at those parties, but I don't remember Cathy being there."

"Maybe you weren't. They won the cup last year too," Kim said.

My neck burned. I took off my porkpie, played with the short brim, and pushed it back on. I had been sent to the minors with 32 games remaining on the schedule and the Leafs went on to win the cup in seven over Detroit without me. I retired following the season. I didn't want to try to catch on with another pro team. I was a Leaf through and through. "Yeah. I missed that party didn't I?"

"Well apparently, she didn't." Kim fluffed up one of her puffed shoulders. "But what's the significance of the photo?" She touched the corners of her lips. "I mean, why else would she save this?"

In a locked drawer of all places—

"Good point." The photograph wasn't framed or hanging on a wall. Instead it was buried among a bunch of unmentionables.

I flipped the photograph over. A row of numbers: 44 20 0. 79 42 0. "What the hell is that?"

"It's not a phone number," Kim said. "Or Social Identification Number."

Nick inhaled his cigarette. It was two-thirds gone.

There was another row beneath the first one with more numbers: 79.5390 and 43.8430. And two words, "Canada's Bazaar." One final figure beneath all of that: "$568,000."

"Bazaar? What does that word even mean?"

Nick didn't say anything.

Kim reached for a dictionary on Cathy's bookshelf. "Market."

"Market? What kind of market? Do the numbers suggest a code of some kind? Market? And the figure price? Over half-a-million dollars. And then there's all the sex stuff—Market? Meat market?"

"That's not her," Nick trailed off, his voice losing energy, a tunnel of ash dipping from his cig. "It can't be, you understand?"

No, I didn't understand, not really, but what did I really know about Cathy? What would my third face have to say to the other faces in the mirror closing in behind me?

2

Landover Leeds was one of those athletic fellas gone to seed. His upper arms were full and strong, but his belly, from excessive drinking, strained the fabric of his sweater vest. His face, heavy with booze fat, made his eyes look small. But his hair was big and thick and had a bent back wave in front that was searching for a surfboard.

"Thanks for seeing me," I said.

"No probs, pard." He smiled. His lingo was fast and loose and a product of this era. He was a fifty-something hipster who wanted to fit in with the kids he counseled. On the walls of his office were prints of trees and rivers and some kind of diploma from the "Mind Control Institute" in Flagstaff, Arizona. To the right of his desk was a bulky console with levers and a microphone.

I told him about Cathy having gone missing.

"Troubled girl." Ever since her mother died Cathy had been lost. In high school, she attended his therapy sessions. They had had some breakthroughs in which Cathy found peace and calm and a sense of coming to terms.

"I know you can't tell me about what was said in here, and I respect that, but I was just wondering like how troubled?"

"Like way-out troubled, bro. Nuff said."

My porkpie rested on my knee. I don't know why but I had removed it out of some old-fashioned sense of politeness.

Landover had that vibe to him—old money, an Englishman whose ancestors probably went back to the Conquest of Quebec or the United Empire Loyalists and the War of 1812. "Uh-huh. What about Sarah, Sarah Kerr, you knew her too?"

"Oh, sad girl. Murdered. I had to answer a lot of police questions because my name was floated out there as the alleged contact person."

"It wasn't just floated. The girl told her mom just before she went missing that you had called."

"Well I didn't. I was in a meeting." He shrugged. "So whoever killed her knew me. Far-out, huh?"

I nodded.

"Look, I'll level with you, bro. I can't give you much skinny on Cathy, but—" Cathy needed to be free of her father, an old school fella; she needed to pursue a university degree and explore her creative side, he said. She was a very gifted writer.

I nodded again.

"I believe in relaxation exercises to free the mind of all that white noise, you know? Judgment?—" He climbed out of his chair and showed me the gizmo to the right. "I don't know much about electronics. McClelland Stuart got this wired up and running for me—" He pushed sliders and flicked a master switch, that looked like it could send a plane off into the sky.

"McClelland?" The voice of the Toronto Maple Leafs since 1924, McClelland was a pioneer of early radio and one of the great ambassadors for the sport.

"He's an old friend, like Ancient Rome, man. We were in the Old Man's militia together, drinking buddies, 1940–1945. Anyway—"

This cat was like a radio ad: talk fast and say nothing.

The electronic contraption was a jerry-rigged sound system. The student waited in the alcove—or what Landover called the Tangerine Room—headphones on, listening to soothing sounds of whales or birds or whatever. And then from his office Landover talked directly to the student, guiding her through the experience. He pointed at the next-door alcove. "You want to try it?" His eyebrows darted about, jigging to do a two-step, but his hair and kiss curl didn't move. They weren't in sync with the party.

"No thanks. Sounds a little too hey-wow for me."

"No, no." He held up a hand. "It works. It'll take you to a fifth dimension, man. Gets the students outside of their self-consciousness and loosens them up. They can face themselves."

"Relaxation exercises, huh?" I pointed at the diploma on the wall. "Is that what you learned at the Leonardo Da Silva Mind Control Institute?"

"It took me four summers in Flagstaff to get that degree." He smiled sheepishly. "Where would you like to go, if you could go anywhere in your imagination?"

"Outer space."

"Far out—" He paused, tapped his chin twice, and pointed at the toggles and sliders. "This takes you there. And I talk you through some exercises and you're with the stars, man, totally refreshed—"

"Totally." I smiled politely. "I don't mean to be indelicate, Mr. Leeds—but Cathy graduated four, nearly five years ago." I wiped the edges of my mouth. Light shone through his office window, leaving shadowed curtains between us. "Do you frequently maintain contact and advice sessions with students after they graduate?"

He sat down and placed his feet up on the desk, pushing his arms behind his head. Maybe I should put my hat back on. I did.

"Her father is Old World, man. Forget Ancient Rome, he's Stone Age. I'm trying to bring Cathy into the twentieth century, man, that's all." When he chuckled it was a little bit wet. "That girl shouldn't be tied up in the store and a sense of duty. She needs to get out and explore her own life." He shrugged. "I was just—a voice—trying to help her. Nothing more."

"Far out," I said.

He smiled.

I GET THESE HEADACHES. They start behind my eyes and then spread to my ears and the world winds up rotating about 25 degrees, not much, but enough to not spin the way it should, as events become dried-out swirls of spun cotton candy, and then I start saying things that I should keep inside (like about the girl in the damn suitcase). The headaches aren't that bad, more of a dull ache, but Dr. Abramowitz thinks they're from all the hits I took as a player—not just the dirty crosschecks to the head or Gordie Howe elbows along the glass, but the moment-to-moment, shoulder-to-shoulder bumping that occurs in the corners and at the front of the net. That "activity" (and he always refers to hockey as an activity with air quotes, like it's a bad thing or something to ever have laced up the skates, even though he admits to loving the game: "ballet on ice") caused bruising on my brain, spots of blood to appear and spread like lean fingers. So, whenever I feel off-kilter, I'm supposed to check in with doc. So here I was.

He's an older man in his late fifties, a chain smoker, with a stethoscope wrapped about his neck like a garter snake. His hair is a tight Brillo pad and he speaks with the cadence of a Borsch Belt comedian. His office is in the north-end suburbs, away from the Kensington Market where he grew up. Here marinara sauce is ketchup, local theatres show double-bills of B westerns, and strip malls sell flowers, one-hour dry cleaning, and donuts. Dr. Abramowitz's eyes have a wondrous mix of concern and the promise of letting you in on a really great joke. But like all comics, you can't trump him with any one-up jive. Don't even try. "You in a rush or something? What's with all the tapping?" He touched my leg, which even though I was propped on his examining table, was beating out a rhythm to an indistinct jazz score.

"Sorry. I don't have much time—I—" I had to find the girl.

"Make the time." He shook his head after looking into my

pupils with the pencil light in his left hand. "You didn't do so well on the eye chart, Hayden." The smell of Juicy Fruit filled the air, masking the layer of cigarette breath. "The fourth row. You might as well have been reading Hebraic. I figured you'd have the chart memorized by now." He smiled, his eyes crescent moons.

Back in my playing days I *did* have that damn chart memorized so that I wouldn't miss a game.

"Concussions are serious business. The medical profession isn't paying enough attention to them, not yet anyway. The research lags behind the need." He thumped heavy hands on the sides of his lab coat. "But you, my friend. Slow down, kid."

"I only know one gear, doc—" And it was fifth. He knew about the missing girl, and the urgency and all. I couldn't ride the brake on this one. I had to approach it like a hockey game—crashing the boards, bumping the opposition, and running the goalie.

"This one won't wind up like the last one," he said, eyes full of empathy.

"I hope not. Ninety-six days ago. I count the days, doc."

"Sarah was it?"

"Yeah."

He shook his head and mumbled something about why some of our species crawled out of the mud and couldn't have just stayed there. "No new leads on that case?"

"None. A dead file, cold case."

He nodded again. "This one isn't going to end like that one, huh? I just feel it." He graced my shoulder gently with a heavy hand. "You'll find her."

"We'll see."

He smiled, a lopsided grin. "Feeling any nausea?"

No. Just the gauze, that cement head mixer feel of everything tilted, off axis.

He knew I took target practice twice a week at the local police station on Bay Street. Was I wearing my headphones?

I laughed. "They're not headphones, Doctor A. They're called ear plugs. And yes I wear them and additional over-the-ear protection too."

He nodded a third time.

I don't use a big gun. A .45 has a lot of kick. I carry a snub-nosed .38. I know how to control the recoil to avoid any other damage.

"Good. That's good. Dizziness?"

"None."

"Dizziness." This time it wasn't a question.

"A little. When I bend over to tie my shoes."

He wrote something or other on his clipboard and mumbled something in Yiddish. "Bright lights a problem?"

"Only if it's the goddamn media wanting an interview."

"I'd laugh along with you Hayden, but this is some serious bullshit. Joke with your tailor, not me." He jotted down more numbers.

"Tailor? Do I look like I see a tailor? These threads came off the rack at Simpsons and Zellers."

"More jokes." He sighed. "Part of your dizziness might be anxiety over the Sarah case. And now this new case. And, I'm afraid the rest of your dizziness comes from the residual damage suffered from all the hits you've taken. I don't know what another serious hit might do to you."

"What are you saying?"

"I don't know. The headaches seem more frequent. More regular. That worries me." He glanced at his chart. Apparently, I now had more headaches a month than I did six months ago.

"Look, it's not like I'm going to jump out of rolling cars for fun. I mean—I'll be careful."

"In my right eye, you'll be careful. Always with the yakkety-yak jokes." He handed me some painkillers and told me to take life ten miles under the speed limit.

"That's good advice, Doc, but there's no highway signs where I'm going to be traveling."

ONE OF THE LAMPS stood in the far corner of the room, a hand on the hip, breasts sagging slightly, left leg flexed, dimples on knees and upper thighs. The shade on the lamp's head was pink and corrugated and resembled a fez.

The other lamp was to the left of Cal Bullard's desk, staring directly at me. Its aqua green hat was propped back with strands of blond hair twisting underneath like dying, yellow glass. Aqua Green's eyes gently pleaded, wanting the joke to stop. I nodded briefly, and then she looked off, through my shoulders. She was a shorter lamp than the other one.

Bullard grabbed a handful of potato chips and crunched, flecks fell on his desk blotter, the edges of his white shirt, and broad tie. He trapped a laugh along his upper lip. He rubbed his hands together and his eyes wrinkled as if he were our evening's impresario.

"So what did you want to see me about, again?" He cupped a hand by his ear, suggesting I needed to speak up. I was known as the Quiet Leaf during my playing days. "How many times you been slapped around, Fuller?"

I had had over twenty fights in my career, over fifty-five stitches across my face and hands, two missing teeth.

"'Cause you aren't listening. I told you, I know nothing about this missing girl. She probably went away on a toot. She'll be back." His eyes wrinkled again. "I'm also starting to wonder about your eyesight."

Steven Smith, the Old Man's son, leaned behind "Pal Cal" and laughed uncontrollably, stroking his Errol Flynn mustache as if it were its own on/off switch, regulating his moods and expressions. His slender white hands were so pale that they seemed to glow with phosphorus.

I glanced about the room. Over my shoulders were two brick

buildings filling up the space of the oak door. Lou Fortunado, ex-Ranger, was one of them. He led the league in penalty minutes for 1958-1959. We had rumbled a couple of times and I followed our Captain's advice, "Get in as close as you can and grab on. A big guy on skates can't hit you if you get in close. Just don't let go." I never did let go, but that didn't stop Lou from nearly biting my ear off. Lou's black hair was slicked with enough pomade to be a fire hazard. "What's with all the Dippity doo, Lou? I hope nobody lights a match," I said.

He grunted.

Next to him, hands in the pockets of his coal gray suit and leaning with sulky languor was Building Number Two, "Cool" Athol Leighton, ex-Bruin, and all around badass. He once busted up a woman's face in a Chicago hotel fracas. The details were sketchy and because she was a hooker nothing much came of the matter, not even a league suspension. He settled with the woman out of court for $2,000. As she took the payoff, her face was akimbo, like a primitive Picasso portrait: one ear lower than the other, the nose too far left.

By contrast, Cool Athol's face looked as if it had been splashed with cologne, as sprigs of perpetual sweat popped around his eyes. The skin across his cheekbones was stretched taut. He looked like Jack Palance, circa 1953. The only missing items were a dandified black vest, twin six-guns, and Shane giving him hell. Athol's eyes floated around the room like hovering dragonflies. They couldn't land or fix on a damn thing.

"Hey fellas." I waved. "I hear Warner Brothers is looking for some extras for their next gangster film—Jimmy Cagney's making a comeback. A sequel to *White Heat*."

Simultaneously, their arms crossed with command presence.

"Funny." Athol's eyes jumped from me to Bullard's desk to the blue carpet speckled with bits of off-white.

"Yeah. A regular riot," Lou said.

"Oh, Jackie Gleason. Even better. Bang, zoom. Things are

looking up, boys."

"Funny."

"I think you said that already. Can't we bring up the level of our conversation? Seen any good plays lately?"

"That's enough." Smith sat on the edge of Bullard's desk, one leg off the floor, his pants riding above his white socks. That killed me. I knew cops for seven years. The plainclothes detectives always wore suits with white socks. Smith was no cop. And his skin was so parchment thin I could see little rivers of vein pressing at the surface. But white socks. Really?

"They're only letting your sad attempts at comic banter ride because I haven't asked them to shut you up. So I'm being polite and now I'm asking. Shut up, wise guy." He pointed, his finger, a pale stiletto. And then he removed his glasses, wiped the lenses with a bit of cloth, and put them back on. They were brow line-style, like Vince Lombardi's, the bridge of the glasses low enough to show off Smith's eyebrows and neatly frame the eyes. But Smith's eyebrows were so faded that they resembled wet chalk lines.

"Come on, Steve." Bullard waved at the two lamps, his hands semaphore flags. "Let's keep things light. No need for overtures of violence. That's why these lamps are here." He giggled into his fleshy shoulder like a frat boy sneaking a cuddly girl into his dorm room at night.

I shrugged. "Cathy Stabulas. That's why I'm here."

"We already heard that melody," Smith said. "We don't know her. Get a new tune."

"Yeah. Never heard of that song," Bullard said, a little too quickly for my taste.

"Look at the fucking picture." I pointed with my porkpie.

"Language." Smith wagged another stiletto. His father, the Old Man, believed in decorum. Leafs season ticket holders, who sat in the Reds, Greens, or Blues, received an annual letter reminding them to wear a suit and tie to the games if they wanted to renew their season tickets. Hockey was a very upscale affair. My dad's seats were high in the Greys—that's where all the working people sat. None of us got an annual letter.

But fuck, there was nothing upscale about the son. Like Bullard, he was a good-time fella, a playboy. "I don't tolerate profanity," he said.

"Uh-huh." And what about the women in the goddamn room? This wasn't sublime, some kind of pop art collage; it was profane and crude, the kind of antics of spoiled rich kids, like pulling up all the flowers in a neighbor's garden. The women stood still, forgotten traffic signals.

"Is it bright enough in here for you?" Bullard reached the lamp standing next to him and tweaked a breast. "You want me to turn up the light? I think this one has three settings." He tweaked her breast again.

"Where did you get these girls?"

They were Gardens page girls or ushers, directing customers to seats or selling concessions. Eighteen years old. And they were getting a fine bonus for this afternoon's entertainment. Smith held up a flash of phosphorus, reassuring me that yes, they were of age. He pushed his glasses back against the bridge of his nose.

Yes, this is 1965 and we are all a part of the go-go generation, the new permissive society, but come on, man, this was way too much. I didn't see fat-ass Bullard or Skull and Bones Smith in long white go-go boots and pasties. And I expressed my feelings on this particular inconsistency. My censor was off and I said what I thought aloud.

"God, you're such a prude," Lou graveled behind me. "A regular crew-cut square."

My hair *was* shorn, buzzed. And if respecting the rights and dignity of others makes me a square, then give me my membership card. "Whattya going to do, crosscheck me in the back of the head when I can't see you, Lou-doo? That's how you played the game—"

"Keep talking, Crumpled Suit. You'll get yours."

"*Crumpled Suit*. I like that." I put my porkpie back on. Adjusted the brim. "That's a step up from Funny. Crumpled Suit. It has a certain gutter poetry. Crumpled Suit. I give it four smiley faces. Not quite five, but four."

The blonde looked at me pleadingly and her upper lip peeled back ever so slightly.

"And don't touch her again, Pal Cal. Nobody's paid enough for that bullshit." I smiled, a kind of sidewinder grin. "I mean it. Or I'll climb over this desk of yours and lay you out."

Bullard tried to laugh off my threat. "Boy, you were always so quiet as a player. I see retirement's done you some good. Made you more confident." He reached into his bag of chips and pulled out a handful that looked like it had an ear or two in it.

I pointed at the photograph. "She was at the Stanley Cup party two, three years ago. And now she's missing." I wondered if Cathy's drawer full of sex paraphernalia was tied into Smith and Bullard's choice of décor: human lamps.

"That's it. That's all the evidence you have tying us to this girl? A Stanley Cup party? Jesus Christ."

I made the sign of the cross and bowed my head penitently.

Smith was not amused. He leaned sharply forward with his shoulders. I don't know how he kept himself from falling off the desk.

Suddenly there were two gentle raps, and Brian "Spinner" Terrien, the Terrier to some, spun into the room. He was short, small across the shoulders, with tightly curled hair and eyes too close to the bridge of his nose. He weighed only 150 pounds and was probably too slight for the NHL, but he had this endless energy, like a spinning top, or a thousand firecrackers going off all at once.

He twitched his shoulders nervously, once, twice, and stretched a hand up over his head, an all-purpose greeting to everyone in the room without really landing on any one in particular. Spinner's pants were high-hipped, pleated, and dusky argyle socks completed the ensemble, granting him a perennially young-man-about-town appearance, or what they called in 1920s theatre, a juvenile role. All he needed was a tennis racket to fully look like a country-club regular. Brian was my age, twenty-nine, had been a call-up, eight or nine times when I was with the Leafs, but never stuck.

"Spinner, how the fuck are you?"

He nodded with appreciation. I was always good to the AHL guys. Many of my fellow Leafs shunned the call-ups because with only 120 jobs to go around in all of the NHL, they didn't want one of *those guys* encroaching upon their or a fellow veteran's roster spot. But Brian worked hard. He just didn't have the speed, toughness on his skates, or the hands around the net to last. He had a great first pass, however, which was very effective in getting the puck out of our zone. I liked the cat.

Smith wagged a fist of recognition at Spinner and pushed a button at the edge of Bullard's desk. A wall panel slid open behind a bookcase. Beyond the threshold were blue, corrugated floor-length curtains, lots of chrome, and spotless white bar stools. Brian smiled at me, before slip-spinning around the bookcase, and then, as quickly as it opened, the wall slid closed behind him.

Damn, the Gardens were full of secret, unchartered territories. You could hide a person inside this building pretty easily. Maybe Cathy was here. Somewhere?

Bullard, with Brian's entrance, now had enough time to look at the photograph and so did Smith. They both adjusted what they had to say. "All kinds of dolls go to our parties. So what?" Smith said.

"Uh-huh. And check out the numbers on the back. Any ideas what those might mean?"

"They're not a girl's measurements, that's for sure. Or if they were, that doll would break your bloody back," Smith said.

"Yeah, can you imagine an ass like that? 43.8430? That's some ass." Bullard licked bits of chips off fingertips.

That just cracked Smith up and he twisted his mustache again. He was laughing so hard I thought his glasses were about to slip off.

"How do you like being retired, Fuller?" asked Lou in his dark, gravelly voice. It was rocks sliding along the bed of a dump truck.

"Did you say something, Lou? I thought maybe it was feeding time at the zoo."

He plodded in my direction, but was held back by Pal Cal's upraised, stubby hand. "You never should have gone to the media with that Davis story last year. That's why you're no longer in the game," the man with the king-size potato chip bag said.

"Candy-ass traitor," Lou said.

"Yup, that's me, a regular candy ass." I shrugged. "Check my record, Lou-doo. I played in 458 consecutive games, three times as many as you. The only time you approached that kind of number was when you added up your penalty minutes in parts of three seasons."

He shuffled his feet and his hands hung in front of his thighs—an angry ape in repose.

"I was a regular iron man. Never missed a practice. Played with my ribs taped, my wrists sprained. Four or five times I suited up with concussions. I scored 107 goals in seven years. Won two Stanley Cups. But I'm a candy-ass, uh-huh, that's right."

"Nobody says you weren't tough Fuller, but you shouldn't have given Stana Younger that story."

"I didn't give her any fucking story." Now it was my turn to hold up a hand. "But enough about me. That was last year. New season, boys. What about the girl? Or that figure on the back, $568,000?"

Bullard grabbed the photo. That amount set something off.

His calm jocularity momentarily grayed. He turned to the lamp in the far corner of the room. "Isn't it a beautiful color? I think the pink shade is the cup duh grassie."

Bullard was always an asshole of an Anglophile, and maybe that's why so many reporters excused his atrocious pronunciation of French surnames (for Bullard, Richard lost all the "ree" of the first syllable and simply became Richard, as in the Second or the Third; Plante lost the long "a" sound of New England's aunt and became a green leafy thing, a plant; and Gagne, lost the "gone" of the first syllable and the long "yay" sound of the second and became a word emphasizing somebody literally choking on his knee). He still flew the British flag alongside the Canadian one at Leafs games, pronounced "territory" "territree," and had a framed portrait adorning his living room of Teeder Kennedy in his Leaf's white-with-blue piping shaking hands with the Queen.

"I don't remember the girl at all," Smith said. "But the number. That's interesting."

"How so?"

"It's just interesting." He rubbed at his chin, his eyes wet flames.

"Okay, play coy. But I think you know this girl. And you know why she's missing. Or have an idea."

"How many girls did you meet at parties or lay at various hotels? Do you remember them all?" Smith worked a piece of lint off his pant leg. "She's just a girl."

"When I get to the truth, I'm opening you two up and you'll bleed slowly." I leered at Smith and Bullard.

"Come on. Don't be such a clam." Pal Cal grabbed another handful of chips and patted one of the lamps on the shoulder. "This is a visual gag. It's funny."

"Funny? You know what I also don't find so funny? You got two bouncers: one an ex-Ranger, the other, an ex-Bruin. You couldn't even buy local. There's no ex-Leafs you could have hired? That's what I call a real fucking traitor." I moved toward the lamp at the side of his desk and handed her two twenties. She told me her name was Dawn. "Give the other one to your friend," I whispered, nodding in the direction of the far corner. "And put some clothes on. You're better than this."

3

Minutes later I was on my way rinkside to watch the boys practice when I ran into McClelland Stuart, the voice of the Leafs and hockey. He had just climbed down from the Gondola, a broadcast perch, suspended fifty-six feet over the ice surface. He was short, jaunty, wearing a long black overcoat and a tight-fitting homburg. Even though all of the rinks were now heated, McClelland insisted on the overcoat—it was part of his image, fashion élan, and gentlemanly style.

"Fuller, glad to see you, boy." He was always jovial. I never saw him cross. "Seeing the brain trust?" He rolled his eyes, and his chipmunk cheeks shuddered. He had a hawk nose, and a slightly quavering voice that sounded vaguely adenoidal. But the fans loved him. I couldn't figure out how his nasal twang was a voice suited for radio but McClelland was famous all across Canada. His catchphrase, "He shoots, he scores," had become industry standard.

McClelland didn't care much for Bullard or Smith. He missed the Old Man and worried about the future of the Leafs with their patriarchal figurehead gone. "You can't have playboys running a hockey team. You need men of character."

I nodded.

"You know those two clowns almost traded away The Big M for a cool million in '62?"

"Of course, everybody knows that."

"Well, I'll tell you what you don't know. We could have had Bobby Orr." He looked over both his shoulders, as if he were to let me in on some kind of top-level, RCMP secret. Bobby Orr, a phenom two years away from breaking into the league, should have been a Leaf instead of the property of the Bruins. In 1960, the twelve-year-old Orr wrote the Gardens telling them he wanted to play for the blue and white. Smith and Bullard wrote back, saying they don't look at twelve-year-old prospects. Talk to us again in a few years. The Next One was so put off by these two assholes and their lack of appreciation and attention that he went ahead and signed a contract with the Bruins. By the end of the decade, McClelland believed, "mark my words," the Leaf era of greatness will be over. "Bullard and Smith. All they care about is money." He listed what they made in concessions, and season ticket sales, radio and TV rights.

The figures were staggering.

I let out a sharp whistle. "$568,000? Does that mean anything to you?"

"How much?"

I repeated the number.

"No, not specifically. But I'm sure that amount can be found here. The Cashbox on Carlton Street, that's what Dick Bledsoe called this place. And it's true. That's all this is to those bozos. One giant cashbox." He laughed. In the past two years Smith and Bullard had watered down the syrup in the concession stand soft drinks to stretch their profits and dumped enough salt on the boxes of popcorn to force fans to drink the watered-down pop. "An S with a line through it. That should be the crest on the Leafs sweater."

Bledsoe was one of my favorite sports writers. He was funny, irreverent, and once wasn't allowed in the Gardens for two weeks after criticizing management for trading away Jim Thomson. Thomson was the Leaf representative during the Players Association fracas in the late '50s and wound up shipped off to

Chicago. Bledsoe questioned the club's ethics and was barred from the Gardens. In response, he called it the "Cashbox on Carlton Street." The man has integrity.

McClelland had the same integrity. He loved old-time hockey, talking about old-time hockey, and dreaded the advent of expansion (rumors abound that it would happen by 1967). McClelland argued that the game could only expand if the American hockey player got better. Right now there's nobody from the US good enough to play this game except maybe Tommy Williams and he's just average.

"Frankie Brimsek was pretty good."

"Yeah." McClelland nodded. "Quickest glove I ever saw." He sighed. "Mr. Zero. Six shutouts in his first seven games. Nobody will ever top that."

"Yeah." I was too young to have experienced the Eveleth, Minnesota, native's arrival in Boston, but when McClelland spoke of the past you felt as if you were there with him, witnessing, reliving it all.

And then I told McClelland about the case I was working on. He listened with his head tilted. He recognized Cathy's photograph. "I remember that girl. She was in their offices. Three, four times at least in the last few weeks."

"Really? They said they didn't know her at all."

He tightened his overcoat, adjusted his homburg. "They know her." He had seen her maybe just two, three days ago. Maybe even yesterday.

"You sure?"

"Does Bobby Hull use a curved blade? Yes, I'm sure." And then he leaned in toward me. He smelled of Clorets. "Be careful, Hayden. These guys play for keeps."

"Dangerous?"

"Very."

They weren't just getting money from the popcorn and pop either. There were rumors of connections with gangsters, drug dealers, and gamblers. “They also might be skimming.”

“Embezzlement?”

“Taxes, concessions. A lot of money’s going in, but I don’t see it all going out. It’s in their pockets. Or the Bolemac Corporation’s pockets.” He turned up his collar.

“Bolemac?”

“Yeah. It’s a concocted private company made up of Smith, Bullard and Toronto-area gangsters. Moving pots of money. Hiding it for investments.” Bolemac does all the repairs at the Gardens and their contracts, the ones Smith and Bullard sign off on, are outlandish. ‘Metal fastener, $200.’ You know what a metal fastener is?”

“No.”

“A screwdriver. A bloody screwdriver.” He laughed. “You should see those contracts. I have. Be careful.”

“I will.” I nodded.

He smiled and said he was heading to Mainly Drew’s, a tavern across Carlton Street for an open beef sandwich and a cup of tea.

McClelland, like me, didn’t drink. Never touched the stuff. And he hated to drive. Most play-by-play guys are kind of quirky and have their rituals and superstitions. McClelland wears the same blue and white tie whenever we play Montreal, because in 1963 he wore it and we won the series in five games.

But the driving thing was odd. It wasn’t a mere superstition. The practice of hating to drive came from a dark, very real place that he refuses to talk about.

I vaguely know the story. Years ago he was a passenger in some kind of horrible auto accident and hasn’t been able to get behind the wheel of a car since. He has to be chauffeured everywhere by friends or taxis, busses, and trains.

“The numbers on the backside mean anything to you?”

“Latitude and longitude lines, maybe?” McClelland fished up north during hockey’s offseason. He had his own boat called the

Kid Line and was kind of into nautical nuances. Timmins was a favorite getaway and its longitude and latitude lines were close to those on the photograph paper. “Sounds like northland numbers to me.”

“Latitude and longitude. Thanks, McClelland.”

He beamed.

Sarah was killed up north, about 65 miles from the city, in a cabin, by a small lake, more like a reservoir.

“Still no inkling as to what $568,000 might mean?”

“No idea.” But there were two safes inside the Gardens. And he had no doubt that one of them could hold that kind of money.

“Really?” An inside job? Somebody lifted money from a safe?

“Nothing’s been reported.”

“Yeah, right. And they don’t know Cathy, either.”

McClelland chuckled over that, his laughter deckled with edges of desire for more gossip. “Well, keep your stick on the ice.” He smiled at himself for using that old expression, the same one that my father and probably his father before him said goodbye with.

“I will.”

And then with a quick wave, McClelland jaunted off. He walked as if he were slightly prancing, like a small dog gently straining on a leash, his homburg shaking ever so.

I liked McClelland; he was charming, a man who enjoyed conspiring when he spoke, letting you in on secrets and a coveted space that just belonged to the two of you. But he was also a complex man, full of gray bigotry. One night, after a game in Chicago, we were in a bar, and I remember him saying, as if he were reading the evening’s stat lines, “Boy, there sure are a lot of niggers in this place.”

I SAT IN THE BLUES, feet up on the seat in front of me, watching the Leafs go through their paces.

Coach Hugh "Two-Fisted" Farrell, his voice echoing like stamping feet, had them skate through a repetition of two-on-ones. He was bald, with hair at the sides of his head like shorn hedges. His nose was long, his eyes intense blue marbles. "Faster to the puck. Hockey's a game of desire. It's a streetcar, boys, and you haven't caught it," he shouted.

He must've really liked that line because I heard it twice more in the span of ten minutes.

Next Coach scrimmaged them in royal blue versus gray mesh shirts. Small Bear, hair close-cropped, worked the corners, chipping pucks to the slot. His skating style was short, choppy, and deceptively quick. The Big M was gliding down the wing. Local reporters often mistook his loping stride for laziness, but the Big M was ready for the playoffs to start. He had scored 32 goals this year and twice his slapshots left Bower wincing in the net, forcing him from the crease to skate in small circles by the dashers.

Bower was in his late thirties and should probably have been wearing contacts and holding a walking cane instead of a goalie stick. I know for a fact that Bower can't pick up pucks by his skates. He loses sight of them there all the time. But contacts could fall out during a game and what would he do in a goalmouth scramble with one contact in and the other gone missing? He'd be seeing an avant-garde world through a dark glass.

Defenseman Tim Horton couldn't see either. He refused to play with glasses. We called him Mr. Magoo.

I loved those guys. Bower was just the nicest player, and Horton was so soft-spoken, never an unkind word for anyone. But he was a bit of a prankster and a strong son of a bitch. One time in a Montreal hotel, the pop machine ate his change and a pissed-off Horton hauled the whole damn thing into an elevator and sent it down to the main lobby.

And then there was Danny Davis, head high with arrogance, cutting tight little circles at center—never back-checking—waiting for the next breakout pass to fly with offensive fury at Sawchuk, the goalie at the far end.

I never cared much for Davis. He was a hedonist, a narcissist, and any other self-absorbed "ist" you want to throw in. He took Polaroids of topless girls, the mornings *after* he had slept with them. You had to stay "through the night" to get thus honored with your picture "taken," and then he'd flash them to us fellas on the chartered flights. I'd be in a poker game with the fella and suddenly in my hand were four cards and a Polaroid. I always suspected him of cheating. With his Polaroid distractions, he never lost at poker.

He was also the reason I was out of the league. Like Bledsoe being suspended in 1957 for questioning the league, you didn't question the integrity of the sport or its players in 1964. No reporters ever wrote about a player lacing up the skates hung over, or another player having an affair with a teammate's wife. At least no one had until Stana Younger.

Late in 1961, I got a Leica for Christmas from Stana. We had just started dating and were an item for the next three years. Anyway, I got pretty good at taking action shots. I pumped the *Star*'s Harold Barkley for technique tips and perfected his skill at mastering dim-lit photographs with an electronic flash. Eventually, in time, I had my own dark room and worked with infrared.

Some of the fellas even took to calling me the Kodak Kid and asking if I would snap glamour shots of their wives and girlfriends, all sexy and suggestive. I used filters and expensive umbrellas for bouncing the light and gave their sweethearts a sheen of stardust. All of this brought in a nice chunk of change. Kodak Kid.

Later, I bought a set of telephoto zoom lenses, pushing me closer to the action and after all that, one of my teammates, Bobby Ehle, a defenseman who twice was hospitalized with nervous breakdowns and joined me in retirement after the 1964 season, hired me to spy on his wife whom he suspected of fooling around with a physician who lived next door (she was). The physician was a plastic surgeon and at parties made a habit of telling people what "work" they needed done. I fucking hated the guy. I wanted to "work" his face over with my fists.

So, I snapped three rolls of film—infrared photography—of him and his baggy ass in private consort with her and made an extra $300 for my services. Maybe it wasn't as good as selling donuts, like teammate Tim Horton was doing, but I was making enough to get a better hi-fi and more jazz records. So it wasn't until late into my final season that my fourth surveillance case became my final curtain.

And this brings us back to Davis, the guy with the Polaroids and extreme good fortune at poker.

In February of 1964, the Big M was really down in the dumps. He was usually discussing some ballet he'd just seen or work of art he had admired (he was partial to A. J. Casson and the Group of Seven), but all season he wasn't talking at all. He was a recluse, holding up on the road in his hotel room with his turtle, Frankie.

Toronto is an Anglo city. Immigrants and their children struggle to be accepted. I'm a Jew; Mahovlich's bloodlines hail from Croatia. I can't tell you how many times people would ask me where I'm from. Toronto, I'd say. No, but where are you *from*? They were like placing me outside the group of "regular" Canadians. Russia, I'd tell them. Russia. My parents came from Russia. Oh, you're a commie kike? Yeah, I'm a commie kike. Uh-huh. How'd you get the name Fuller? My parents changed it, that's how. Oh, that's cool. Yeah, thanks, that's cool, l'chaim.

Anyway, one night over a couple of beers, a disconsolate Big M tells me that his wife suspects that Nancy Ehle, the wife of his best friend on the team Bobby Ehle, is at it again, sleeping around with Davis, who had recently been acquired from the Rangers.

"Have you seen any Polaroids of her?"

"Don't be stupid. Of course not. You think Davis would flash them around if he did sleep with her?"

She wasn't stupid either. Nancy graduated with honors in philosophy from the University of Toronto. Big M was sure that there'd been sexual hijinks. Nancy and Davis were seen at some jazz clubs and Nancy did tell Maclean's that she and Davis were good friends. He was a gourmet chef, or some such damn thing. Cooked up an awesome soufflé. Bobby can't talk about it, Frank said, but it's bringing me down. Well, I'm already down, but I'm more down. Bobby was Frank's roommate back at St Michael's.

So, as a favor to Frank and indirectly Bobby, I followed Chef Davis for two weeks. Taking pictures. He was seeing women at the ROM; at George's Restaurant on Queen Street; and at Mainly Drew's on Carlton. He had this ugly technique: he'd sport a pair of Ray-Bans, walk up to a woman at a bar, drop the shades ever so slightly, and shake his head with a dismissive no if they weren't pretty enough. If they were pretty enough, he'd raise an eyebrow and ask if they wanted to fuck. Seriously. Just like that. A lot of women said sure. I never photographed him with Nancy. Was he just being extra careful? I followed and followed.

Discovered he was having an affair with Nancy; also discovered that he was sleeping with Sharon, the slim-shaped blonde of our captain Benjamin Small Bear. Small Bear, an aboriginal from St. James Bay, upon hearing of my report from the Big M, punched Davis's lights out in a locker room skirmish. Super-tuned his ass as Big M later said.

Davis played that evening on *Hockey Night in Canada*'s telecast with two black eyes. Media speculated on his raccoon-like appearance. Ward Cornell wondered if Davis had fallen over a coffee table in his Scarborough home as had been reported by the *Star*.

No matter, Stana broke the true story in her column for the *Toronto Telegram*. Within minutes of that column's appearance, I was in Bullard's office and on my way to Rochester for *conduct detrimental to the team*. "Tawdry" I believe Smith garbled while rubbing clean his glasses and describing my moonlighting practices to the press. Or maybe it was "Lurid." He always had a way with words. I finished out the season in the AHL and promptly retired.

Stana apologized profusely after she heard of my dismissal from the club, but it didn't do any good. I was mad, unfairly so, but at the time there was no forgiveness in my heart. She didn't follow me to Rochester. Stana opted for advancing her career as a reporter. We were done. I still miss her.

But I miss the game more and that smell of the rink: a brisk cold chlorine slap mixed with the wet undersides of a hockey glove. I breathed it in, and then a puck zipped by my head, slapping off the seat next to me. I shifted and looked ice level.

There was Davis, forehead furrowed, gray eyes like gunmetal. He didn't move, just leaned at the blue line, fixated.

"Okay, okay. I promise." I raised my arms in surrender. "I won't put my feet on the furniture. No more."

Bower was smiling and gave a gentle wave with his blocker.

But not Davis. He did look kind of funny with his heavy eyebrows and hair neatly parted down the middle like Shemp Howard's, but there was nothing funny about the eyes. Absolutely nothing. They were full of burning leaves.

AFTER PRACTICE I strolled over to Mainly Drew's. I'm not quite sure why: maybe to touch base with old friends; maybe to get the feeling of being a hockey player back in my blood again; maybe to escape my feelings of loneliness. With my shoulders sore and a pain behind my eyes, I ducked in, feeling like that *Spy Who Came in from the Cold* guy. Shit, why did I leave the painkillers in my car?

Mainly Drew's is one of those typical taverns in Toronto, built with little architectural panache: lots of angles and squared lines that reflect the cold simplicity of Presbyterianism. I squinted my eyes, even in the dark glimmer of the tavern they hurt, and ducked under low hanging cedar beams. Steins graced the shelving behind the bar, and I wondered if I ought to be wearing a miner's hardhat with a glowing light.

That's how goddamn dark it was in there. A jazz combo played on a slightly raised stage, back of the bar. The alto-saxophonist was solid, taking us away from the shoreline on repeated, varied riffs, and then bringing us back. But I really liked the drummer. The cat was unobtrusive but driving the sound with rim knocks and the odd bright hits on his snare.

The afternoon editions had hit the street so I wasn't too surprised to see Stana sitting at her favorite table with one glass of Guinness. Just one was her limit. She was cautious.

And despite the pain behind my eyes, I became aware of an additional feeling: my heart pounding in my shoulders at the sight of her. I gestured.

She invited me to sit across from her. When we dated we sat side-by-side like high-school kids. That seemed so long ago.

Stana looked great, skin fresh, bright, and freckled. She had light features, delicate bones, and her blue, almost green eyes, what she self-effacingly referred to as dishwater beautiful, always struck me with their love light. Stana took you in for who you are and listened with exacting concentration and brightness. She was one of those people who were always present.

No shrouds of eye shadow, no fake lashes. She wore gray slacks, a beige blouse, and a pullover sweater, no sleeves. I ordered tonic water. "Any big-time news scoops?"

My dad was an abusive alcoholic. I don't touch the stuff.

She smiled awkwardly, asked how I was, and said that Montreal was ready to take us in the semis. The Leafs were three-time defending champs, but slipping. Two years ago was our best season, maybe the best of any Leaf team in history. We were the Prince of Wales Trophy winners for our regular season record and won the cup in 10 games, demolishing Montreal in game 5 of the semis, 5-0. The Habs wanted to get even. Last year we won game 7 on their ice, Davey Keon, our slick skating center, netting a hat trick. This year, Montreal was tougher, grittier with Ted Harris and John Ferguson entering their second seasons with the club.

I nodded at her assessments. "Trying to make me feel good?"

"No." She shrugged, her nose raised in the dark light. She was tall, angly, with square shoulders and freckles everywhere. Sometimes even her eyes looked freckled. "I just think the Leafs are ready to be knocked off."

"I like Ferguson. He's a cement head but not just a goon. He can put the puck in the net, unlike Fortunado and Leighton." I told her about my meeting with the two ex-NHL *pugilists* in Smith and Bullard's office. "That goddamn room is like a bunker. Secret passageways and everything." I looked at my fingers. "I feel like shit. You got any aspirin?"

"I always got aspirin." She reached into her purse, the size of a milk crate, and handed me two.

Bayer. I usually pop Anacin.

"Management doesn't give a shit about winning. It's just about money for them. The Cashbox on Carlton Street."

She smiled. "You seeing anyone?"

I looked away. "No." I dry-swallowed the pills and rubbed my hands together. "You?"

"No." She looked away. "Any leads on the Sarah Kerr case?"

"No. You hear anything?"

"No."

I told her how for a while there I was staying in touch with the girl's mother, giving weekly updates, telling her nothing new, but the case was always open for me. *I didn't tell her about all the nightmares I'd been having about a voice in a suitcase screaming to be let out. Sometimes I was the one in the suitcase, screaming, but I had no mouth, the noise a squawk of black crows.* And then the widow Kerr said talking to me was too painful and I didn't have to keep calling out of some sense of penance or responsibility, just call if I have anything new. When she first hired me, she gave me a $200 retainer. Two days later, we found the body. I never cashed the check.

"They'll never find that girl's killer—" Stana shrugged. It was what she hated about life, how it was so transitory and some mysteries were never solved.

"The final showdown. At the cabin? It was so flashy. Like the killer was making a big splash of it all. Amusing himself with his bag of tricks: searchlights, a mannequin, and then a motorboat stuck in the middle of a partially frozen lake." I shook my head. Lambertino plans to drag the lake at the end of this month, once the water's warm enough.

"Maybe the killer never got on the boat."

"What?"

"Maybe it was just a diversion. Maybe he was watching you guys the whole time."

"Hey," the Big M shouted in my direction. "Have a drink with us, Hayden." He was huddled around Small Bear and Bower. Their beers had high heads on them. The Big M was usually reclusive, alone with his turtle, but all that boisterous enthusiasm must mean he was feeling better emotionally. Fans in Toronto were tough and he was often targeted for "underachieving."

"How's Marie?"

"Awesome." He smiled broadly and flashed a thumb. Just last week, they had gone to McMichael's Art Gallery and at season's end were heading for a second honeymoon in Mexico.

"Fine. That sounds fine," I shouted back.

"Mexico? Do you remember our vacation there, two years ago?" Stana reached for my wrist.

How could I forget? We stayed in our motel room most of the time and when not making love ate tortillas, hiked, or lounged in the hot sun, she in a white bikini.

She squeezed my wrist. "I'm really sorry, if I had it to do all over again, I wouldn't have run the story about Davis and Small

Bear and Sharon."

"Bullshit."

"What?"

"I'm not being mean. Just being honest. If you had to do it again, you would still run the story." I touched her chin. "It was news. And you should run it. You're a professional." I looked at the rings crowding her glass on the table. "You really think he might have been watching us, the killer? I mean, just lurking?"

She nodded and apologized again for our muddy past. "It was a private utterance, between the two of us. You told me over our pillows. I—I had no right—"

"Small Bear? Christ. How did he get that name? He's one of the biggest wingers in the game. And strong—" I smiled at the irony life can give us.

"His name's Small Bear not Small Boy. A bear's pretty big, even a small one," she corrected, her eyes flashing with shifts of light.

"Good point." I tapped the tip of my porkpie. Small Bear was actually a pretty good name. Whenever Chief got coerced into a hockey fight, he bear-hugged his opponent, leaving the potential sparring partner gasping for breath, and ending any desire on the instigator's part to throw a haymaker. "You're a newspaper reporter. I was mad at first, but I respect it. It's who you are."

She smiled. "Thanks," she whispered.

She was a woman fighting for elbow room in an all-male bullpen. She couldn't afford to be sentimental. Sentiment would mark her as a "woman," placing love ahead of her profession. Around the other fellas of the press, she had to be tough and she was.

I told her about the new case I was working. Showed her the photograph, the numbers on back, and how I didn't want the Sarah Kerr outcome again.

"Cathy Stabulas?"

"Yeah—you know her?"

She leaned forward. "Do I know her? We were working on a story when she went missing. All about the shenanigans Smith and Bullard were pulling. Yeah, I know her."

"Tell me more. What story?" My voice suddenly sounded like McClelland's: adenoidal, scratchy, and full of a desire for coveted gossip.

Cathy was about to blow the lid off the Leafs organization. Skimming, cheating, drugs, but more importantly gambling. "She was going to give me a big story."

"Bolemac Corporation. Screwdrivers for $200—"

"Yeah." She was surprised by how much I knew.

"Was she working for you, undercover?"

"No. No." She looked down and spoke quietly, her fingers drawing lazy figure eights on the tabletop. "But what she saw sickened her."

"Saw? What do you mean? Where?"

"She'd gone to this club four or five times—very exclusive."

"How exclusive?"

"Very."

And then I asked if kinky sex were involved and told her about the drawer full of dildos and other toys and skimpy clothes in Cathy's room.

"That fits the profile of what she was telling me. But our focus was on illegal gambling mainly." Bullard and Smith were running some kind of exclusive gambling service. Very Q.T., high stakes, roulette wheels, poker, like right out of a goddamn 1940s film noir. "Hockey's a god here and in Montreal. The league, the media, will do anything to cover up this story, but I'm going to get to the bottom of it, and those two playboys are going to be spending time in the Don Jail." She shook her head with disapproval. "We had a couple of preliminary meetings, Cathy and I, and then she disappeared." She snapped her fingers for emphasis.

"Shit." That means she's either dead or in hiding. "Where's

this goddamn club?"

Stana's eyes squinted and danced with freckles. "I don't know. It's so exclusive, only a handful of people are invited or even know its whereabouts. But I know the moniker, Coughlins."

"Coughlins?"

She pulled a napkin from the boxy dispenser and drew the club's logo in stuttering blue ink. The marquee featured a homburg with a clown's face underneath.

"McClelland wears homburgs."

And then I thought about the doodles on Cathy's Big Chief tablet. There was a clown face with a homburg. She had been there.

"So do a lot of men. My father—"

But why a homburg?

Cathy had given Stana a few details but the biggest part of the story, the full confession was to follow. That was to have been unveiled later next week.

"Fucking great."

"One other tidbit that I think you'll appreciate: Davis is a regular at Coughlins." The four times Cathy was there she saw him. Playing the wheel and poker. "He wasn't winning. He seemed to lose every time."

"Hmm. I thought poker was his game." At least that's what I remembered from his days on the Leafs chartered flights.

"I've called him repeatedly for clarification, but he won't answer my phone calls."

"That fucker." I pushed back my porkpie.

There was another girl involved. Lisa Steinmetz.

"Why that's Cathy's friend, the one she was supposed to see the night she disappeared."

"Cathy said Steinmetz got her into the club. I can't get Steinmetz to talk to me either. I don't think she trusts women."

"Uh-huh."

"You think she'll talk to you?"

I nodded.

"You want to work together on this?"

"What the fuck—" It was Davis. He strolled in our direction, black wool coat swaying behind him like a cape. He started rambling, questioning my motives for being at practice, and why was I hanging out at a favored haunt of the players? Davis's neatly centered hair wasn't as sharp as usual. Two or three strands appeared to have broken off and defected from the flow of the pack.

Mahovlich and Bower and now Small Bear followed in the wake of Davis's black-coated prow. He was a tugboat that needed to be towed. Bower had a hand on Davis's shoulder.

"Get your hand off me, Johnny. This ain't your fight."

"There isn't going to be a fight, Danny," Bower said.

"Last I checked this is a public establishment and I'm allowed to do business here," I said. "With regards to the Leafs, I'm a stockholder. I have two or three shares of preferred stock."

"What?"

"Blue chip, I believe." I took off my hat, looked at the inside, enjoying the moment this pause was bringing.

Stana filled the gap. "Mr. Davis, would you care to make a statement about the missing whereabouts of Cathy Stabulas?"

She sure had a knack for calm utterances that were truly fiery salvos. I loved that about her. She had a way with irony too. I figured it was all the Jane Austen she read as an English major at the University of Toronto. She studied with Northrop Frye, a pretty big cat in the field. But her favorite professor was Hilary "Chip" Hampton. Later, she spent a year at Ryerson studying journalism. She was always smarter than me, and a smart-ass to boot.

God, how I hated playing Scrabble with her.

"And while you're at it," I leaned in Davis's direction, "Could I have your autograph? I'm such a fan—"

Okay, I'm a bit of a smart-ass too.

Davis didn't appreciate my zingers and shrugged off Johnny's pensive grip. Then, Davis shoved me and I shoved back, sliding my chair against his strong thighs. Before I could get up and push away from the table, Davis seized the back of my neck, squashing my head into the tabletop like a caved-in jack-o'-lantern. Wind chimes rattled behind my eyes, a light metallic tapping.

I tasted bits of salt and spilled vinegar.

Hockey players have strong legs and tuchuses—you need them, to push off and glide and accelerate quickly. So with my face tasting remnants of yesterday's fish and chips, I forced my chair back and to the left and went with the best of all cheap shots, the hockey slew foot. I twisted my right leg free, planted it behind Davis, and with a slow drag, as if I were wearing skates, nicked him behind the calves and an Achilles tendon, sending him thudding to the floor. He might have bounced a couple of times. He wasn't too happy about it.

He rubbed at the sides of his mouth, and then rummaged inside his coat pocket and came up with a blackjack that resembled a slick-heeled banana.

I pulled the snub-nosed .38 out of my side holster and directed it at him. "You have any other statements you'd care to make?"

"Come on, Hayden, put the gun away," said Johnny.

"You have a license for that?" asked Davis.

"Since when does a hockey player need a blackjack?" Stana said.

Big M and Small Bear weren't asking a thing.

"Yeah, I have a license for this. It comes complete with operating instructions, coloring book, and a coupon for Tim Horton's donuts." I pushed the seat sideways until I was propped against a wall. The wind chimes forming at the edges of my consciousness were now a slow rushing waterfall. "Beat it."

Davis dropped his arms at his sides and buried the blackjack in his coat. "Stay out of my business."

"Your business has become my business, pally. Where's the girl?"

"I don't know what you're talking about."

"Uh-huh." I smiled. I have a feeling there was something slightly off about my lopsided grin because Stana suddenly looked away. "How's Coughlins?"

"You talk too much."

"When I get answers to my questions, I'm going to talk a lot, pal. And then you and Smith and Bullard are going down."

"The girl should keep her mouth shut." His lips tightened into a terse line. He turned to Stana. "And that's off the record, bitch." He did up his jacket and strolled head high to the opposite side of the bar with his fellow teammates in retreat.

"Yours in Polaroids, pal," I shouted.

"What?" Stana's face was creased with worry. The freckles around her eyes were no longer moving.

"Inside joke." I exhaled. Maybe it wasn't that funny.

"You scared me just now."

"What, the gun? I've never fired it at a person." I shrugged. *Well except for that one time, sixty-five miles north of the city, the Sarah Kerr case. And that was a fucking mannequin.* "Twice a week, pistol practice at the cop shop. Head shots." I practice a lot. I did as a player, firing pucks at the four corners of the net, and I do as a detective, honing in on a silhouetted target with a bull's-eye. It keeps me in control, even-keeled. And frankly I like it. It's the only time, besides when I'm skating, that I'm not thinking. I'm just being.

"But why headshots? Isn't there more to hit in the chest area—less chance of missing?"

"Yeah." I shrugged. But if you land the head shot just right, the shooter goes down like a marionette with broken strings, I said.

"You know too much about this—"

“Sorry.”

“And the look on your face when you pulled your gun. I’ve never seen that look before. Even when you were playing hockey, I never saw that look.”

“What look?”

“A third face.” I had told her about the concept years ago. “That face was ready to use that gun.”

It was true. I re-holstered the weapon and took a deep breath. And then I pointed at the numbers. “Can you find out for me what those latitude and longitude lines precisely refer to? I mean, the exact spot of land—?”

She wrote the numbers on the napkin under the Coughlins logo.

“I help you, you help me. We find the girl. I get the story. Partners?” She reached for my hand across the table. Her fingers were slightly shaking.

“Partners,” I said.

4

"Tell me about Coughlins."

"What?" Lisa Steinmetz slowly sipped a cola at the El Mocambo. Potted palm trees swayed in the bar's crisp breeze and the table in front of us was a cold block of polished granite. I thought my fingers were going to get freezer burn.

"Coughlins. I know about it. And Davis and you and Cathy."

That wasn't completely true. I knew a little about it.

Lisa's face was wide, nose fleshy, eyebrows so plucked and streamlined as to be almost invisible. She tapped the table with chunky fingers. Her body was curvy, not heavy, but her fingers were porcine, the three rings on her left hand looking pinched and uncomfortable. "I called Cathy that night because I needed to talk?"

I wasn't sure of the hesitancy of her voice. Did it reflect intimations of danger or was she just that unsure of herself and insecure? She often ended sentences with questions. This was where she worked, waitressing. You figured she'd be comfortable in this setting. She was on break.

"What were you going to talk about?"

"Girl stuff."

"Davis? Come on, be specific." I pushed back my porkpie, took a deep breath. "Look, I'm not trying to pry and be an asshole here—I respect privacy—but I need some answers, real answers. A girl's life is at stake. That's if she's still alive."

I had already lost another girl in a missing persons case and I wasn't willing to play this case at practice speed. This was the Stanley Cup Finals. "Talk—"

"I think she's alive." She looked away.

"Why? Why do you feel that way?"

"This arrived in the mail this morning." She reached into her purse and pulled out a folded 9x12 envelope, heavily creased. Inside it was a black-and-white photograph.

It was Cathy. Her hair, heavy Cleopatra bangs, was unwashed and lay limp against her head and the sides of her face. Her eyes were flat too, lacking fervor. Her shoulders were curled in, stooped, and there were some small wisps of hair on her bare breasts. Suddenly I couldn't breathe again and the world was full of spun cotton candy.

"Was there a note? Ransom? Blackmail?"

"Nothing, Hayden. Just the picture."

"Jesus Christ." Davis? Who else had a fetish for this shit? Goddamn Davis. Sure, it's not a Polaroid but it's the same M.O., the handling of the photographic equipment suggesting the same lack of professionalism. The subject of the photograph was slightly off-center, the image a bit hazy, but not so far off as to be considered artsy, like playing with the horizon line in a landscape. This was just mediocre. "You need to go to the police, the press, with this story."

"I can't." If she did, she'd be dead, she said. These were powerful people. Even a Member of Parliament had been seen at Coughlins. She sighed and played with a thin necklace around her neck. The finish in places was chipped. "Okay, okay. What do you want to know?" She pushed strands of dusky blond hair over a shoulder.

"About Coughlins. What is it? How do I get in to find her?"

"You think she's there?"

"If she's alive, I think she's holed up there or in the Gardens."

I had spent a good part of the morning reading Cathy's Big

Chief tablet. The language of her stories was enchanting, bright with feeling. The heroines of her fiction were afraid to take risks and say how they felt to men—instead, they said how they felt to us, her readers, via a kind of confessional mode, but they said little in the worlds they inhabited. Some of the women worked in grocery stores and answered questions about bargain prices and specials of the day; others traveled lonely but crowded subways, hoping to be noticed, to be spoken to. I wanted to take these characters home with me, and tell them they were loved.

"Did she have a secret life that you knew of, a third face?"

"A third face?"

I explained the concept.

"No. I mean we all have secrets, right? Like right now, I can tell that you're looking at me, checking me out. You're too polite to say anything or do anything about it, but you're looking. And that's okay?"

I shrugged. "I guess you get a lot of that in your line of work?"

"Tell me about it? I mean, if I want a good tip, I got to put up with my ass being patted, you know?"

"What did Cathy put up with? Weird things at the store? Her father?"

"He's a jerk."

"Yeah. I gathered that might be the case. I saw him wallop Kim. It was a hard hit."

"They don't get along. At all."

"Yeah."

She paused, leaned back, and smiled. "I trust you. You're sincere."

"Thanks."

"I bet you're a good kisser, too."

I didn't know what to say to that.

"Because it just wouldn't be about you. You care about the other person?"

I took off my porkpie, to anchor me. I was short on sleep and that gauze of haze was swirling around again. I had to find the girl.

"Look. I'm sorry, I was flirting."

"It's okay," I said.

I did find one odd bit of social commentary in Cathy's Big Chief tablet that I didn't share with Lisa. Cathy had torn a full-page ad from *Life* magazine and stapled it to a page in the journal, folding to make it fit. The bizarre image was for Chase & Sanborn coffee. It featured a man in a hard wooden chair, his back to us. He wore suspenders. A woman, in heels, one leg raised, her slip and petticoat showing around her knees, was on his lap and kicking up a fuss as his raised, open hand, readied to spank her for not taste testing the coffee before buying it. The copy said something silly like, "If your husband finds out—"

I thought the ad was kind of sexy to be honest. The petticoat reveal gave the whole piece a peek into the forbidden. I don't believe in hitting women. I've never, ever, hit a woman, but the ad was titillating like tan lines up against the parts of a woman's body that don't usually see the sun. Apparently Cathy would totally disagree with me and give me holy hell.

Her commentary on the Chase & Sanborn image was a knife's edge, there was nothing funny or cute or sexy to this campaign. She was never (underscore twice) going to drink Chase & Sanborn "ever again." The ad men who concocted this were just cruel and into "male domination."

Men are pigs.

She wrote that fifteen times, on separate lines (I counted).

This tirade was a stunning piece of cultural criticism amidst all of the fiction and creative imagination on display. It did reveal how put upon she felt as a woman. *Men are pigs.* The lines got heavier and heavier each time she wrote that.

"Like I said, that night I just needed to talk. I was having a hard time with my boyfriend, so I invited Cathy for a drink—" She looked around the room and rubbed her full chin against her left shoulder. "That's all. She didn't show."

"Didn't that make you curious?"

"Yeah, yeah, of course." She had a few drinks alone and called Stabulas's Grocery the next day but never heard back from her. "I figured she was busy?" She raised her thin eyebrows.

I nodded. "If you don't mind me saying, you don't look like the bridge type—"

"Bridge?"

"Yeah. You know the card game?"

"Bridge? I've never played bridge." She laughed, pulled back, and tightened the cardigan sweater around her shoulders.

"That's not what her father told me. You and Cathy—"

She crossed her arms. "I wouldn't trust a word her father says." She slumped forward, chewed at her lower lip, and blew hair out of her eyes.

Maybe it was Kim who mentioned bridge and not the father. Now I wasn't sure, but they both agreed to that story line. Bridge.

Maybe I should check my notes. Shit, I didn't write that detail down.

"You see how hard he works her? Ever since their mother died—Cathy's become a second *wife* almost?"

Mrs. Stabulas died nearly ten years ago and since then, according to Lisa, Cathy kept her father's books for the store, cooked his meals, cleaned, and was the primary care provider.

"If not bridge, then what? Was it Coughlins on Saturdays?"

"Always after the hockey telecasts." She smiled wanly. "She was a Leafs fan."

"I know. I've seen her room, the Barkley photographs—"

Lisa tightened the cardigan. "You care about her, don't you?"

"I don't know her, but, yeah, I do."

"I can see it in your eyes."

Maybe Lisa could see the loss of Sarah residing there too.

"Coughlins. I got her into Coughlins. Somebody got me in."

"Where is it?"

"It's in the Gardens. One of the upstairs offices."

"The one behind a sliding wall?"

She nodded. It was that exclusive. Her guidance counselor, Mr. Landover Leeds, invited Lisa in on the party during her senior year.

"Leeds? The guy with the Tangerine Room and relaxation bullshit?"

Leeds. There was a connection to Sarah too. Leeds.

"Yeah." Her face darkened. "Pompous ass."

"What do you know about mind control and the Leonardo Da Silva Institute? Leeds has a diploma from—"

"Leeds couldn't call the room a simple color like red or green, oh, no, he opts for tangerine, because it had a 'far-out vibe.'" Anyway, Mr. Leeds, at this one afternoon appointment, handed Lisa a card with a silhouette of the NBC peacock, you know, and the words, *worship the cock* written under it. That made Lisa laugh and because of that laugh Leeds knew she was good material for Coughlins. "It was a great place to meet hockey players."

"I had never heard of it."

"I met Danny Davis there and Spinner—"

"Spinner?"

She shrugged at the mention of his name and readjusted her cardigan. It was that cold in here.

"I know him. Nice guy—so you were underage when you were first at this club—?"

"Yeah. Don't be such a square. I've known about sex since I was fifteen? How old were you?"

I shrugged. Fourteen. A hockey bunny, a middle-aged mom, snuck into the dressing room after a morning shoot around, and we did it after everyone else had gone home. I still had my skates on. Lisa was just seventeen when her guidance counselor pimped her out. I was going to have to have a follow-up with this Leeds fella. How many other girls did he pipe into Coughlins with his pithy business card test? So "Cathy was a regular there?"

"I wouldn't say a regular. But I got her in. She went some Saturdays."

I showed her the photograph taken of Cathy and two of the Maple Leafs Board of Governors.

"Yeah. That's the Coughlins crowd."

"This is the Royal York."

"Yeah, but Smith and Bullard run Coughlins." They skimmed and took a cut. A big cut, she said. "Man, there's nothing those guys won't stop at."

"Who are their partners? Who's fronting for them?"

"Migano."

"Babe Migano? The gangster?" The ex-Montrealer emigrated to Toronto in the post-war era and now flourished in drugs and the numbers racket. "Have you ever heard of the Bolemac Corporation?"

"Bolemac? No, I don't think so—"

Could Migano be helping to divert funds, divesting the Cashbox on Carlton Street to line all their pockets? "Bolemac does construction work at the Gardens. They ever talk to you about that?"

She bit her upper lip and shrugged. "Bolemac. No. Don't know Bolemac."

"Thanks for filling me in on Coughlins." And Landover Leeds and his Tangerine Room and "Worship the Cock" charm. It was time for some follow-up conversations. "This problem you had with a fella? Is he a hockey player?"

"Yes." She shrugged. "Was?"

I let out a sharp whistle. How could I be a detective and not know about this exclusive club? During my last two seasons with the Leafs, I did four surveillance jobs, finding out whose hockey wives were fooling around with other fellas, but I knew nothing about Coughlins.

And Smith and Bullard sent me to the minors. Fucking hypocrites. *Conduct detrimental to the team.* Please. They're running a sleazy escort service, a couple of real swingers, and are in league with a gangster like Migano and his Bolemac front. "It's an escort service, right. High end?"

"I never got paid for sex. But sex is a part of it. The girls hope to land a rich man. And the drinks are expensive. And the guys pay a lot for drinks so you got to put out." She held up a hand. "I'm not proud of it."

Bootlegging too.

She looked around for the fourth time. "I'm getting out. I'm leaving town?"

She was just waiting on her ex-hockey player to come get her. She wouldn't give me his name. He had a final deal to close or something.

"Deal?"

She shook her head as if she couldn't say anymore.

"Is it Spinner? I saw him at the Gardens. It's Spinner, isn't it?"

She nodded.

Were they blackmailing Bullard and Smith? "Blackmail can get you killed—"

"We're not blackmailing anybody," she said, not too convincingly. "We're just getting paid for services—"

"What kind of services, Lisa?"

"Services. It's not exactly legal or else I'd tell you? I can't talk about it. It's not stolen jewelry or something—"

"Something else stolen? Say $568,000?"

"Shit no. Christ, you're bringing down my good mood." She blew heavy air between her lips. "You're a real downer, you know that?"

"I want to find a girl before time runs out. If that makes me a real drag then write that on my tombstone." I breathed heavily.

How the hell could Cathy be a part of all this? It didn't sound like the woman who wrote such sad, beautiful stories.

A friendship with Lisa would always be about Lisa. But maybe they had something else in common, some shared secret? Lisa was physically abused by a drunken father. Did Nick slap Cathy around too?

I flipped the photograph over and showed her the numbers on the reverse side. "These mean anything to you?"

"Bingo? Results from a bingo game?"

"It's longitude and latitude lines. I just wondered if—does *bazaar* ring any bells?"

"As in weird?"

I laughed.

"Cathy needed some escape. Don't be too hard on her." Lisa looked furtively around. "Did you know that three years ago Cathy bought herself a new car, a '62 Ford Falcon, a modest set of wheels, but her father didn't think a girl should have a new car so he made her sign it over to him? Can you believe that shit? Talk about Old World values. Nick took it from her."

"Did she get any money for it, did Nick pay for it?"

"You kidding? No. So Nick's driving around in her car. Well he was. He now has another car. Traded the Falcon in a few months ago to get a new set of wheels. In-fucking-credible." She shook her head.

I couldn't believe the way Lisa spoke, crude and brittle. She just didn't seem like the kind of girl Cathy would hang with. But what did I really know about Cathy, or Sarah for that matter.

"Maybe she just ran away, you know?"

"But you don't think so?"

"Check with Smith and Bullard?"

"I did already. Treated the whole thing as a joke. Had two women dolled up like human lampshades—"

"Naked?"

"Yeah, except for the fezzes on their heads."

"Hell, they're repeating themselves. They did that gag at the club."

"What?"

"I was one of the lamps—wore a pink headdress—"

"Looked like a Fram oil filter—corrugated?"

"Yes?"

I wanted to believe Cathy just ran away from all the forced responsibility but knew that was no dice, not with that damn topless photograph.

I was thinking more and more that she was hidden somewhere in the Cashbox on Carlton Street. Maybe I was just hoping that she was. That was my only hope. "Did Cathy have encounters? Sexual encounters at this club? Weird, bondage encounters?"

Lisa laughed. That kind of stuff was available at Coughlins, but Cathy wasn't the type. "There's one woman who wears a dark mask. Nobody's seen her face. She's known as Starzz with two z's. She's wild. She'll do anything." She laughed again—a short angry burst. "I don't think Cathy was all that into sex?" She paused and laughed as she spoke. "I think she still might be a virgin—"

"Uh-huh."

Lisa pulled her shoulders back before smiling weakly and looking one final time in the direction of the bartender and the street outside. It was turning gray with late afternoon drizzle. A chestnut vendor was warming his hands over his pushcart. "I better get back to work. Things are picking up."

"Sure."

"There are some pretty crazy people who go to Coughlins. And I just hope—"

I nodded, thinking of that lower dresser drawer and the leather mouth strap with a ball.

"Wish me luck, huh?" Lisa now said. I had forgotten that she was still sitting there. Her face was pale in the green swatch of bar light and now her hair looked green too. "Spinner and I are going to head out west—start over—stay out of trouble."

She tapped the cold granite as if wishing herself luck or superstitiously trying to ward off evil spirits. "I guess, maybe the trouble's already started, huh? And it's following me?" Suddenly her eyes widened as if she were envisioning hellhounds on her trail and tongues of flame.

"Maybe," I said, looking away from the fire.

5

The sky outside my office window was gray and rain fell in penciled streaks. Stana and I sat on the floor poring over our notes. I was apologizing for forgetting that I had sent out my three office chairs to be refinished and they wouldn't be back until Friday.

"You always were disorganized."

"Hey, I've got a filing cabinet now." I pointed at the black cabinet and its four drawers. "Well, there are only five folders in there, but hey—"

"That's it. Five folders? No bottle of Canadian Club or a .45 with its shells rolling around?"

"That's only in the hardboiled novels."

"I thought you guys only existed in the hardboiled novels—"

I slyly nodded and shook my head. How many summer hours did I put in with the police force and at night classes at York University to acquire the training to get my license and become a peace officer? "Not anyone can hang up a shingle. The government monitors us detectives pretty closely."

"I know I was just joking." She leaned in and played with my shirt buttons.

I smoothed her hair. "So what do you think? This is it." I stretched out my arms and she took in the office: a filing cabinet; a wood desk with a lamp and a low-watt bulb; an ashtray full of Wrigley foils in one corner (a black phone was in the other); a blotter crowded with eccentric doodlings and dates circled on a calendar; on a far wall a Matisse print of what looked like a penguin on ice skates; on another wall an Export "A" calendar featuring my first pro team, the '57-'58 Leafs; a hat rack, sporting my porkpie and blue wool coat and Stana's black-and-white windbreaker; a bright basin with separate hot and cold taps; hardwood floors; and a window, with venetian blinds, overlooking Yonge Street.

"Spartan, but very, very disciplined. Like you were as a player. I guess that's why you don't have a swivel chair like most detectives. Instead hardwood chairs, three of them, all getting re-finished—while we get splinters in our asses."

"Be nice—"

"That's okay." She wiped the corners of her mouth and smiled, her eyes filling with light. We were sharing a greasy box of poutine. "Not having any office chairs makes it kind of romantic."

It was. "Yeah, all that's missing is a glare of sun, your white bikini, and spicy burritos."

She leaned in and kissed me.

"The burritos weren't that good," I said.

She laughed and touched my face. "For a guy who got over fifty stitches in his playing career, how come your face isn't all marked up?" She had once stepped into an elevator with Small Bear and Sawchuk and there were zippers of shadows everywhere.

"I always take my stitches out early, a few days before I should and treat the wounds with cocoa butter. It works—"

"Cocoa butter." She smiled. "I'll remember that."

We went over our notes again and how Lisa said that Coughlins was the exclusive club hidden behind Smith and Bullard's sliding wall. Maybe Cathy's hidden in there. "So how do we get in the Gardens to look? We need evidence."

"We'll need more evidence so the cops can get a warrant," she said.

After I had talked to Lisa, Stana contacted Castle Frank's guidance counselor Landover Leeds at his home. She mentioned Cathy Stabulas's name, my ongoing investigation, and rumors of moral turpitude (his, not hers). Playing it cagey didn't get her anywhere so she gave out with three little words, "Worship the cock." And there was a long pause, and then an even longer pause. "Let's talk, but not my home." His voice snick-snicked like a pair of hockey skates. "My office." His office was on Front Street, across from Union Station. He couldn't get there until later tonight. Nine P.M. He still had to work out at the gym: pump iron, run laps, maybe hit the bag.

A regular Jack LaLanne he was.

Stana also mentioned the $568,000 figure written on the photo's flip. "We'll talk about that too, but not on the phone." We were to meet him in a few hours.

"A second office? I don't get it. Why's he need a second office?"

Stana shrugged and dipped her chin. "It is strange—"

"It's not like he's an artist or writer or something—"

"You know what else I found?" She tilted her head and raised an eyebrow.

I removed a spot of gravy from her upper lip. "What?"

In 1957–58, Landover held a special Thursday night counseling service for a group of nine high school girls experiencing some kind of trauma.

"Yeah, I know. Cathy was a part of that group. Cathy's Mom died in 1955—"

"Yes, Cathy was a part of the group, but so was Lisa Steinmetz."

I nodded and felt rocks breaking in my stomach. "Could he have been recruiting this group for Gardens' bunnies? Human lamps?"

"I don't know." Stana wore a white dress with spaghetti straps and a shiny black belt. Around her neck was a thin chain with an ankh. This was the most feminine looking I'd seen Stana in years. And I liked it.

She reached into a black milk crate of a handbag and unfurled a rolled-up piece of paper with nine names listed. She got them, after much prodding, from Castle Frank's school secretary. The only names I recognized were Lisa and Cathy. "We'll need to look into this," she said.

"Uh-huh."

"Oh, and the longitude and latitude lines?" She squinted her eyes and they danced with freckles. "Barrie, Ontario." The other series of longitude and latitude lines were close to Vaughan, Ontario, but she hadn't found the specific location yet. A field, apparently, in the middle of nowhere.

A field apparently in the middle of nowhere. That's where Sarah Kerr had been killed, in a cabin, near Vaughan. A coincidence? "It's just so random—" It can't be a coincidence.

"What about this case isn't random?" Stana shifted against the wall, pushing her back away with the side of a hand. Rain pinged against my office window and the penciled streaks were now a lot heavier, creating dancing coins on the window's ledge. The sky too had darkened from gray to charcoal black.

Stana wondered if Cathy might already be dead. "She can't be dead. She just can't."

"What if Lisa were lying? The photograph angle just doesn't make any sense. Why would Davis send a photograph of a topless Cathy to Lisa?"

"To intimidate her?" said Stana.

"No. It's too easy and stupid. Davis is a lot of things but he's not stupid. Someone's setting him up."

"What?"

"Let's say Lisa's in on Cathy's murder or kidnapping. So to buy herself time and detract attention from herself out comes this convenient nudie. There's no note, no ransom, no nothing. Just a stupid picture. It's a stupid move. Davis won a scoring championship in 1957-58. He was Rookie of the Year in 1955. Stanley Cup champ last year. He's a winner. This is *not* a winner's play."

I dialed Steinmetz's number. The phone rang and rang and rang.

"What about the father? Could he have hurt Cathy?" Stana asked.

"He loves her. He was crushed when I opened that lower dresser drawer. He kept saying, 'That's not her. That's not her, you understand?'"

"Exactly. But what if he found out that *was* her, or at least a part of her? Could he have lived with that, reconciled that sexuality to his Old Country ways? Maybe he killed her? I mean, she told me some things in our interviews. He isn't a nice man. What if the kinky stuff drove him to murder? You saw the way he slapped Kim—"

"I did—"

"He took away Cathy's car—could he have taken away her life?"

"That's crazy." The rain now pounded and water trickled in through the window. "Absolutely crazy."

"There are patterns of behavior here." She laughed. "Sometimes you're so naive." She leaned forward and kissed my cheek.

"I always loved the smell of you." I touched her chin, and then slowly pulled her towards me and kissed her. She yielded pleasantly under my hold, tasted of salt and gravy, and then kissed back fervently and it was three years ago all over again. I breathed in the smell of her shampoo.

"I think the father's abusive. Kim got away. Cathy didn't," Stana said.

I didn't want to believe it, but then I started thinking about the slap. *Men are pigs.*

"Do you think I'm pretty? I mean—"

"What?"

"I mean, I know we were an item, and Mexico and everything, it's just—" It had been a long time since she had been loved.

"You're very pretty," I said.

She looked away. She hadn't felt as accepted, as confident in her body, since the breakup. With me, she enjoyed how I lingered, watching her prepare for bed, slipping out of her bra and into her pajama top or getting dressed in the morning, putting on her bra, as if that were one of the grand privileges of being in an intimate relationship, to be allowed to look at the nakedness of one another and to be accepted for who and what you are.

I leaned in and kissed her nose. "And I still love the smell of your hair."

She playfully punched my shoulder.

FORTY-FIVE MINUTES LATER I was at Kim's upscale apartment. I figured I should do this interview solo. Stana was streetside, waiting in my '63 Ford Galaxie, the engine running so she could stay warm. With Kim, my words rushed along like a slinky skater on a breakaway.

"Slow down, slow down," she said.

I took a deep breath. When Kim sat in profile, head slightly tilted, she looked an awful lot like Cathy: high cheekbones, fleshy jaw, and a pointed chin. It was a strange feeling of *déjà vu* that caught my breath, like one of those dreams you have when you're falling from a high window. They *could* be mistaken for twins, not just Irish, born in the same year, but actual twins.

"So tell me about Coughlins." I reached for the plastic mug in front of me. It was full of pens: blue with yellow lettering, Kim's name and the company she represented: Ogilvie and Beggert, Real Estate.

"Coughlins?"

"Your sister wasn't playing bridge on Saturdays. She was going to Coughlins with Lisa."

"What is it, a pizza place?"

I told her: an exclusive club, escort service, right in the heart of the Cashbox on Carlton Street. The whole S&M scene is a part of the package too, including some masked dominatrix called Starzz.

"You think that could be Cathy?" she asked.

Maybe. *Men are pigs*. Maybe it was her way of getting revenge?

Kim smiled incredulously and turned away in her pink, puffy chair.

"She never took you?"

"No. We went out for pizza. That's it. Boy do I feel naive." She blew a ribbon of dark hair off her forehead and tucked her knees up to her chin. She wore tight Capri pants and a white blouse, unbuttoned so that her raised clavicles showed. It was one of her striking features and she knew it.

Kim's whole apartment was done up in 1955 Eisenhower-era modernity: low slung coffee tables, hammock-style chairs with triangular leggings; framed Renoir prints, and a fireplace nestled inside a rock wall. Her television set was new, white, solid state, and broadcast, no doubt, a color signal. Most of us were still watching *Get Smart* in black and white.

She pulled on her cigarette. It was king-size with lipstick on the filter. "I don't know anything about this. That's wild." She laughed, almost as if she were admiring her sister's boldness. "I bet Dad will get a kick out of this."

"Kick? Like the way your father hit you? I bet that wasn't the first time."

She looked away, at a far corner of the ceiling. "It wasn't. But never Cathy. He never hit her. He loved her. I was the nuisance. The daughter he didn't want. The one that didn't obey—"

"Could he have hurt Cathy? Her lower dresser drawer shows her own *unique* streak of rebellion—"

"He didn't know about that."

"What if he did? I mean, what if he had discovered her kinky past—is he capable of murder—?"

"We're all capable of murder." She returned her gaze as I pushed back my porkpie. Her eyes darkened. "But murder his daughter? No."

I asked about the car, if Cathy bought a car that she had to sign over to Nick. Kim sighed and said that story was indeed true. She now blew smoke in the far corner of the room.

I rolled one of her Ogilvie and Beggert pens between a finger and thumb.

"So what's your next move?"

"I'm meeting with Leeds in an hour or so and then Davis. Get some answers. I need evidence to get a police warrant to search for Cathy in the Gardens—if she's still alive."

"My father took everything from her. I got out so he couldn't do the same to me." Two months working at Dominion's as a checker and then real-estate training and suddenly Kim made more in three months than her father made all year. "That really killed him. A girl making more than a man." She blew more smoke, and her thin lips grimaced. "Fuck that."

I was surprised at how easily Kim shifted from cool, detached realtor to brassy hard-edged working gal, to sexy hostess, who kept offering me drinks from her wet bar and was surprised when I settled for tonic water.

I had a stomach full of Dad's blue moods, his anger and combustible incoherence throughout my childhood, so I was an anomaly in my playing days: a hockey player who never drank Molsons. Ever.

One time when I was eleven, Dad locked me in our family car and visited the local tavern for two hours, tossing darts and drinking. On the ride home, I prayed and prayed that he kept the car between the white lines.

"What can you tell me about Spinner Terrien, Lisa's on-again, off-again boyfriend?"

"I don't know. Some ex-hockey player. Had a couple of brief stints in the pros. I heard he might be kind of funny." She held up a limp wrist. It looked like a dog's paw.

With only 120 spots in the pros there were a lot of players you could say had "brief stints." Hell, our goalie Johnny Bower didn't make the big time with the Leafs until he was 34. He was three-time MVP in the American Hockey League and had to wait his turn to stick with the six-team league. And if Spinner liked men or was bisexual that was his business. "Bolemac Corporation. Anything *funny* about that?"

"Excuse me?"

"Bolemac?"

"What's that? An expensive brand of Tupperware?"

I laughed. "No. A front, a construction company. Does work at the Gardens and may be a place to hide certain pots of money. Smith and Bullard are involved with it. So is a tough mobster, Babe Migano."

That made her sit up and straighten her shoulders.

"You recognize his name?"

"Who doesn't? He's big-time."

"He's a crook," I said.

"A woman doesn't always care about how a man makes his money. She cares about how he makes love." And from what she had heard from people at work and at parties, Migano was dynamite in bed.

"Great." I looked at my fingers and shook my head. Being great in the sack wasn't my strength. I was okay, but no MVP trophy winner. "What about counseling at the high school. Trauma counseling?"

"Oh, with Landover? Yeah, he tried to rope me into that. I wasn't too interested. Touchy-feely horseshit. Let's all hold hands and sing. Cathy went." She played with the bottom cuffs of her Capri slacks. "A lot."

"Did it help?"

"I thought the guy was kind of creepy and quit going after three or four sessions. Cathy stuck."

"I thought you described him previously as a helpful family *friend*—"

"I never quite said that—"

"Uh-huh." I told her about his calling card and *worship the cock*, and wondered if he had sprung that sales pitch on Cathy or Kim during one of their sessions.

"*Worship the cock*?" She laughed. "Doesn't he have it backwards? Women are the ones who give birth. The vagina, the womb?"

"How could you let this creep into your family."

"He was good for Cathy. He was trying to get her away from our father."

I rubbed an edge of my chin. "How often was he seeing Cathy?"

Kim looked away and filled her voice with fabric softener. "Not that often. Once a month maybe? To discuss her future."

What about the other girl, the one in the suitcase? How often did he see her?

"Landover was in a meeting the day she was abducted, remember?"

"Uh-huh. Convenient."

"*Worship the cock*. God, seriously? I think Freud's got it all wrong." The fabric softener edges returned to Kim's voice. "So does Landover apparently." She laughed and tucked her knees in closer to her chin.

She was confident in her position, eyebrows knitting with challenge as she tackled Freud's assumptions. No doubt, Kim could sell just about anything from her anti-Freud stance to products I should buy, like an Ogilvie and Beggert home.

I had read a couple of her ads in the Ogilvie and Beggert listings spread across the coffee table. Kim had a real talent for placing the reader in the heart of the scene and helping us feel the cozy comfort of the home on the market, even before experiencing the listing up close and personal. *Picture yourself next to a Bay window, as the sun dapples. . . .* Her prose was creative and inviting.

"It's all about enchantment," she said. "I'm the Hans Christian Andersen of Realtors."

"Speaking of fairy tales. This is a pretty expensive place." I looked behind her and felt underdressed in my porkpie. On the fireplace mantle were various Eskimo carvings, first editions, keys, and two cigars in cellophane. Cohiba. I recognized the brand. I smoked one myself after we won our second cup in '63. "How do you afford this?"

"I afford it. I make a lot of money."

I wondered who the man with the Cohiba was in her life and scanned the apartment for other indicators of his presence but all the chairs were pushed neatly against the dining table and no plates or abandoned bits of silverware were lying about. The careless presence of a man was absent.

Half a glass of what looked like flat Coke sat on the far edge of the mantle. The mouth of the glass had a lipstick stain matching the one on her cigarette filter.

She saw me spot the stains and lifted her cigarette. "You ever notice in the movies how you can never trust anyone with a cigarette holder?" She laughed. Three years ago, Kim smoked with one—it made the taste gentler, milder—but once she started selling homes, she quit the practice. Selling is about being open and attentive to the needs of buyers. A cigarette holder sends the wrong signal; it suggests not being quite Canadian, but foreign, continental.

She laughed again. "I also wear darker, conservative clothes now. Don't want to be too bright or show up the wives. You've got to keep the wives happy to close the sale. Men sign the check, but the women make the decisions. In my business it's ABC, Always Be Closing. That's the bottom line."

I nodded. There was a real no-frills, hard edge to her.

"And, get this, I wear men's deodorant. Can't have my perfume challenging what the women sport."

"That's strange." I laughed. "I swear I smelled Chanel No. 5. I—well, all good perfume smells like Chanel No. 5. It's the only perfume I know."

Kim took another puff off her cigarette. "Well, I'm not trying to sell a house right now."

"Oh." I looked down at the pen in my hand.

So she was wearing perfume.

"If you're interested, I'm interested." She leaned back in the puffy chair and smiled. Her upper lip was a little heavy. She wasn't just flirting with me like Lisa did. This was a real overture, a different kind of sales pitch. And she was a great-looking woman, but I was starting to be interested in Stana again.

"So how many houses do you sell a month?"

"Let's not talk business." She patted the spot on the couch next to the chair. "Sit here. I'll pour you another tonic water."

Her tone was a strange mixture of mockery and seduction. I wasn't quite sure of just how deep the irony cut, but even with the high cheekbones, fleshy chin, and supple curves like Cathy's I didn't find her appealing. I like a more muted, subtle approach. Shirley MacLaine, Teresa Wright, they're more my kind of woman. Not Marilyn Monroe.

"Okay. I see that you're going to be shy." She leaned forward.

"Look, I—"

"Sex can be invigorating—"

That's what Davis used to say, while flashing around his Polaroids. "Sorry—"

"Well, it's seasonal. Not the sex, the house selling." She laughed again. "Lots of homes sell around the start and end of the school calendar and holidays, but I average nine to ten a month."

I whistled. "Wow. Ten percent commission on that?"

She nodded. Toronto was in a housing boom. “Look at Richmond Hill. Right now, it’s cottage country.” But in ten years it will be a thriving suburb, its own city. West, east, north, the sprawl is on. From here to Barrie the land boom is happening.

Barrie. She mentioned Barrie. Was that some kind of slip?

If I had the money to invest, she insisted, I ought to buy houses, and sell them in a year or two. I’d make a fortune off the equity. Better yet, buy land north of the city and sell to future investors. Now’s the time to take the risks.

“I don’t have any money.” What I had as a hockey player—and that was never much—I spent. Seven years in the league, 458 consecutive games, and I averaged about $7500 a season.

“You sound bitter.”

“Not really. I just didn’t like the way it ended.”

“Yeah.” She knew about that. Most people did.

“You know your sister wrote to me, care of the Gardens, before I even took this case, 1964.” I looked at my fingers. “After I got canned and sent to the minors, she writes telling me that I was on ice for more goals scored by my team as opposed to against my team than any other player on the club. Cathy said I was the league’s top defensive forward and there ought to be an award for that. It’s funny, I didn’t think about that telegram and who wrote it until this morning—”

“So you have a prior history?” She smiled. “The two of you—”

“Well, I don’t know—it’s just a weird connection that’s all—”

“You really do want to find her, don’t you? You don’t even know her but you care—”

“Yeah.” I shrugged. I knew it wouldn’t take away the pain of having lost Sarah 96 days ago, but it might help, it might give me a little closure, but something else was emerging from all this, something that surprised me: the Cathy on display in the Big Chief tablets, her sensitivity, her vulnerability, that part of her, for a girl I didn’t even know, I was truly beginning to love, I think.

6

The rain hadn't let up. The driver-side wiper of my Galaxie needed to be replaced and instead of clear damp glass I was squinting through psychedelic scratches of rainbow streaks. In the shadows of Front Street, Leeds's office building was dark, and angry gargoyles were on two of its lintels. A heavy maple blocked most of the street's dim light, creating a greater aura of uncertainty. "What else can you tell me about this cat?" I asked Stana, as I pushed in the brake and clutch and threw the car into first, killing the engine.

Fifty years old; graduate of the University of Toronto, 1938; one year at the law school at Osgoode Hall; played varsity football, 1936–37; Olympic pole vaulter, 1936; guidance counselor for twenty-two years at Castle Frank. Ran for office twice, unsuccessfully, as a Conservative for an east side Toronto riding.

"Good work."

"That's not all. In 1942, he was in a car accident and killed a kid. No charges. The kid stepped out from between two parked cars. Guess who was in the car with him?"

I squeezed my eyes and pulled up my collar anticipating a fight with the rain. The left side of my jaw felt tight and a headache was coming on again. I reached for Anacin in the glove box and dry swallowed.

"You get a lot of headaches?"

"Sometimes. They just come on."

She wondered if it were playing-related. I shrugged. Stana's chiropractor friend was convinced that hockey was the worst sport ever. "A national disgrace" he called it. Right up there with football and boxing. Bad for your back, your head.

"Remind me to never refer that fella to anybody. *National disgrace.* Please."

"Did you ever have any concussions?"

"Yeah, of course." I had had a few; saw stars now and then after giving or receiving a terrific body check. Big deal. "I think it's the rain. It does something to my sinuses." I wasn't about to tell her about my off-and-on meetings with Dr. Abramowitz or his warnings for me to percolate ten miles below the speed limit.

"Sinuses, right. Jesus Christ, Hayden. How often do you get headaches?"

"Now and then. Relax."

"I don't know why you players don't wear helmets."

"You don't want to be a candy ass, that's why."

Stana mumbled something about macho horseshit.

"Okay, Popeye. Let's get a move on. Oh, and who the fuck was in the car with Landover? You thought with all these headaches and concussions I'd forgotten, didn't you?"

"McClelland Stuart." They both had commissions in the Old Man's militia, 1940–45, located off Church Street. "You know in case we were attacked at home or something? Old Man Smith had all of the Leafs, its employees, and broadcasters sign on for military training."

"Really?" That was interesting. "How did Landover fit in? What did he do for the Leafs?"

Stana shrugged. "But he and McClelland were driving home together after one such training session."

"Crazy."

Minutes later, after walking under drooping branches and fighting off water dripping down my porkpie, we were climbing toward Leeds's second-floor office. The light in the hallway was dead and so was the light at the top of the stairs. Both of the light fixtures looked like dirty tulips, full of smudges and dry fly flecks.

There were no other signs of upscale pleasures than those two tulips. Walls needed to be replastered and the lobby's carpeting was so threadbare as to display the hardwood slats angling through. The carpet's once blue pattern was now covered over with dingy gray from the weight of heavy footsteps.

On the frosted glass to Leeds's office door was a decal in the lower left corner. A line drawing of a man with Einstein hair and outstretched arms bouncing aloft two globes, eastern and western hemispheres, like atomic fireballs. "Da Silva Mind Control Institute" circled about the image.

And then I smelled gunpowder.

So did Stana. It was sharp and pinched the air.

The door to Leeds's office wasn't locked. It had only been pushed to and we nudged it open all too gently. The room was very still. A radiator thinly clanked now and again and there were Neolithic shadows of trees on a window. The roller blind was snapped up tight. Every desk drawer was open and in patches of black silhouettes, I saw a body slumped in a chair.

"Don't turn on the light." I stopped Stana until I pulled shut the blinds. "Now."

The small desk light splashed a cone of yellow across Leeds's face, his bulgy eyes open but strangely contented, as if in his last breathing moments he had resigned himself to death. A hand lay flat, palm up on his thigh, and there were powder marks on his shirt were the bullet entered. I pointed at the hole. "Look. Whoever did this got awfully close."

"A woman?"

"Maybe. Or a really good friend." I shrugged, covertly moving. "Someone he trusted. That smell is awfully fresh." I held an index finger to my lips, unholstered my snub-nosed .38, and quickly opened a narrow closet door. There was no one in there:

just five pairs of shoes, one of them a set of women's blue pumps. I picked them up. Four fedoras were ordered on the top shelf, all of their brims resting at the same point. On the rack were several coats and sweaters. Some of the sweaters had leather patches on the elbows.

"Is this Leeds?" she asked.

"Yup. Mr. Tangerine Room himself."

I sat on the front of the desk. On the blotter was a gym bag, with shorts and a T-shirt poking between the hard cut edges of the zipper. Across from Leeds was a polished wooden chair draped with a white towel. If this had just happened, why was there no commotion when we came in? Why didn't we hear feet trampling down stairs?

"Look at the shoes. The edges. They're wet," she said.

Small coins of water dripped from the low heel of one of the shoes. I snapped my fingers and ran back to the office's lone window, rolled up the blind, and raised the glass. Beyond the black fire escape, in a distant alley, was a woman running, her shoulders throwing her forward. Her body in the rain was a series of sharp angles caught in intermittent cones of streetlights. She wasn't wearing any shoes. "Goddamn it." And then, just as quickly, she was gone. Streaks of rain dimpled small puddles on the sidewalk.

I plunked the shoes on the desk. They were heavy. "Damn."

"You said that."

"No, I believe I said, 'God damn it.'"

Stana wondered if the assailant were a former student, a member of the special therapy sessions? Paying dividends? "Look at these drawers." Papers were strewn everywhere. One drawer was even upended and tossed at the foot of the corpse's office chair. A filing cabinet was toppled over, resting on its side.

Stana touched the corpse's neck. "The body is still warm."

"Right. But how warm and how long dead?"

Far from the fallen filing cabinet and fanned papers was a

solitary cubicle, like the one in Leeds's Castle Frank office. It had rippled glass walls, a padded chair, headphones, and a reel-to-reel contraption with a jet engine's console that resembled the rig I saw in his Castle Frank digs. *Tangerine Room Two?* "Check this out." There were seven or eight tapes in the cubby holes along the wall, featuring what appeared to be whale noises, loons on a still lake, and one session called "Mist over the Smokies, a Tennessee morning."

"He did relaxation sessions here?" Stana brushed up against my shoulder.

"Relaxation. Right." So he was a quack on the side, earning extra coin as some kind of mind healer, courtesy of Da Silva. I laughed briskly. In a far cubbyhole was a ledger with dates, numbers, and initials. It looked like hieroglyphics. CS. "If that's Cathy she was here four days ago."

"Four days ago? That was just before I was supposed to interview her."

"Leeds was running some kind of racket. But what?" I flipped the ledger's pages. In back, stuck in the ledger's creases, was a bright 5x7 photo: Landover in a turban, eyes brimming with comic mischief. Typed at the bottom, newspaper copy: "Appearing at Massey Hall, Lanzo the Great, Southern Ontario's Outrageous Hypnotist. Tickets $2, $2.50 at the door."

"Lanzo the Great?" Stana laughed, shoulders rising. "Lanzo the Great." She snapped her fingers. "Yes. I was at that show." She was just a girl; for her ninth birthday Dad took her to see the illusionist. "Lanzo, Landover, got people to bark like dogs. Dad said he couldn't be hypnotized, he had too strong a will, so at my urging he volunteered, and wound up putting on four jackets and some blankets because he was so cold—"

Power of suggestion. I wondered what he was suggesting in Tangerine Room Two? And for what purposes? What's his racket?

"Whoever got here wanted something specific. Something on paper." Stana turned back to the corpse.

"Not the ledger apparently—"

"Paper with linen in it?"

"$568,000?"

"Maybe." I tapped a finger at the edge of the desk. "Shit, shit, shit."

I dialed Lisa's number. She answered on the fourth ring. I told her that Leeds was dead.

"Wears a rug," Stana said.

"What?"

"Look at the weaves." She pointed. One set of lines waved left; another set of lines broke in a completely contrary direction.

"Wears a rug," I repeated to Lisa.

"He blamed God for his going bald. He mentioned that in our very first 'therapy' session," she said.

"Don't you see? His killing might mean you're in danger?"

She didn't see the connection.

"Leeds is connected to Cathy's disappearance. You're connected to Cathy. You're also connected to Leeds. You might want to lay low. When are you getting out of town?"

She didn't say anything.

"Lisa?"

"Yeah. I got it." All of the bounce was now out of her voice. She sounded like she had fallen in a well. "Got it." She promised to leave town soon.

I gathered the "deal" hadn't gone down the way she expected. She didn't answer my questions about that.

I hung up and picked up the shoes. Spots of water stained along the sides like small lakes. "Boy, did this gal have big feet."

"Be nice."

"I'm just saying. These shoes are a ten or an eleven. Maybe even a fourteen." I shrugged and now it was my turn to mumble like a disgruntled Popeye, "My cousin's feet expanded to an eight after her third child."

"I am's who's I am's," Stana said, talking out of the side of her mouth, scrunching shut one eye.

That cracked me up. "You know what's really sick, really random?" I pinched at the space between my eyebrows, trying to force the headache away. "We never even got to really talk to Leeds: one brief encounter with me, a phone call with you, and now the fella's dead. Gone. Like that. His life. Over."

"Lisa's a witness," Stana gently chided, reminding me. "Don't have her leave town."

"Her life might be in danger."

"Cathy's life is in bigger danger. We need Lisa around. Something about her story just doesn't add up—" She shook her head. "The whole Davis thing. It's a phony I tell you."

"Davis is a fucker—"

"Maybe. But that doesn't make him a killer or in on Cathy's gone missing."

"What about what he said at Drew's?"

"He was just barking. There was no real bite there. And you were the one who went all John Wayne with the gun and everything—"

She had me there.

Stana tapped the edge of her chin. "You know what would happen at this point in a hardboiled detective novel?"

"Do I really want to know?"

"Yes, you do. The detective would find an address written on the inside of the rolling papers the victim used for his cigarettes." She smiled, pleased with herself, her eyes dancing.

"That's just silly."

She reached for the corpse's toupee. "What if?"

"Wait. This is a crime scene. We don't want to contaminate—"

"Really, are you serious, says the man who sat atop Leeds's desk and lifted up a pair of shoes—"

"You got gloves—you had them on outside—"

She shrugged, slid them back on, and pulled off the toupee. The top of Leeds's head was stippled with swatches of sticky residue. Inside the hairpiece was a yellow-lined piece of paper taped to the cheesecloth.

"No fucking way."

Stana laughed. Scrawled across the paper were 402C and three additional numbers: 42, 23, and 7.

"402C? Some kind of safety deposit box, like at a bank?" I rubbed my chin again.

"Well, I don't think it's more of your ever-loving latitude and longitude lines—"

"Union Station's across the street. Maybe this is a number to a holding locker."

"Union Station doesn't have holding lockers with letters—"

"It doesn't?"

She dropped the toupee back onto Mr. Leeds. It didn't sit quite right. It now looked like a displaced whoopee cushion. I tried to adjust it but only made matters worse.

Stana moved to the far chair and snapped out a towel. "He said he had to go to the gym. To work out." She pointed at the unzippered bag. "There's his stuff." She studied the stretched towel. "Property of Hart House" was written in indelible marker on a small swatch of sewn-in fabric. She folded the towel back over the chair.

"I think we just found the thread," she said, pointing to the ink.

It didn't take us long to get to Hart House: Spadina to Harbord, and then I parked on Haskins. After walking through slanting rain we stood in front of one of the nation's oldest student centers. Built in 1919, the architectural style was Gothic, Stana said, capturing the dark mood of the country after the Great War. The windows were large, the exteriors round, one might even say downright stout, and the whole ensemble was cluttered with arches and vaults.

"Okay, you can quit making with the tour guide's report,"

I said. "Next you'll be talking about how it's wider than it is high—"

"No, I was going to say the building's contours are jagged." Stana blushed slightly and rubbed the back of a hand under her nose. In her third and fourth years at the university she led tours for prospective students and their parents. Chip had got her the job.

"Your professor, the one who wrote hockey and baseball books for kids?"

"Yeah. He also encouraged me to become a journalist." She smiled briefly. "The hardest thing about those tours was walking backwards and not tripping over anyone."

Hart House was immense and imposing. It looked like a giant Folgers can with added Gothic ornamentation.

Minutes later we were in the gym and its dusky brick walls and arched windows. We crossed a polished track and ducked down below the Art Deco swimming area with its light fixtures and marble tiling straight out of an Astaire-Rogers 1930s musical. Lockers were in back.

Some were floor length, some half-length. All were black with dented metal and slits at the top. 402C was a half locker at the end of a row, along a long wooden bench. Two discarded towels draped the bench that nobody stood by. Voices and shallow splashes echoed from the pool.

Inside the locker was a huge manila envelope with string slipped around a fastener in back. A dusty can of 8mm film was in the far corner of the locker. Probably about ten minutes of film.

The can barely fit into Stana's handbag. I don't know what else she had in there. A car's master cylinder?

"I don't have a film projector."

"I do. My parents do," she offered. I liked her parents. Her father worked at the TTC and her mother was a retired schoolteacher. They were honest, direct, didn't stand on ceremony, and hated entitlement.

We breathed heavily. And I kissed her. It was an impulse. I just followed it. My shoulders hurt with the weight of time.

The window on finding Cathy was closing. It had closed on Sarah 96 days ago.

She locked 402C.

I looked about again.

The envelope felt heavy, as if it were full of sand.

We slid away the towels, sat on the bench, and she smiled gently, pushing her lips together and made a big show of putting on her winter gloves. "Happy now?"

"Delighted."

She unfastened the bundle.

It was cramped with 8x10 photographs, five or so. All of the subjects were women. Naked. Medium shots: waist up and gritty grime haloed each image. "Looks like these were taken with a Speed Graphic, an f/16 setting, and shutter speed of around 200. Just guessing by the depth of field. Looks like about ten feet is in focus."

"Really, Hayden? Depth of field? Who cares?"

"Sorry, I was just showing off." I shrugged.

"A Speed Graphic? That's an old press camera, isn't it?"

"Uh-huh."

The fourth photograph featured Lisa Steinmetz. Her hair was darker than the dingy blond she now sports, her face much thinner. She was looking left, hoping to find an illusory moment of escape. Her eyes were vague, distracted, as if the cheesecake intentions weren't her idea. I'm pretty sure they weren't.

And then I noticed why the eyes were so distracted: they were caught in some kind of in-between space, as if the actions performed weren't of her own free will.

"Look at the background." Stana pointed.

Main lobby, Maple Leaf Gardens, Steinmetz parked in front of a photo of the 1947–48 Stanley Cup champs. I wondered what Syl Apps, Turk Broda, and Teeder Kennedy thought of Lisa being thus arrayed before their likenesses.

On the back of the photograph was scrawled: "LS. 4/14/59. MLG."

Stana couldn't figure out the point of the photograph. It wasn't erotic, she said. It had a punishing quality to it.

"Oh, I don't know, some guys are into punishment pictures. Like spanking a woman. Not that I'm into that, but for some guys that's a real turn-on. I think these photos are a depressed fella's idea of French postcards. I really do."

"You think these are sexy?"

"Well, yeah. I mean, yeah. I mean theoretically." Shit, I was about to get smacked in the shoulder again.

"These pictures are *dirty*."

"The craftsmanship displayed here is terrible—"

Now Stana *did* punch my shoulder. "Do you think Leeds took the photos?"

The fifth photograph: Sarah Kerr. Her blonde-white hair fell atop her shoulders like heavy snow. It was flat and the eyes were dull too, like she was under a spell. There was a mole between her small breasts. On back: "SK. MLG. 4/22/62."

I could never forget that date. On April 22, 1962, we won our first cup, 2-1 over the Blackhawks at Chicago Stadium on a late third-period goal by Dick Duff. And then there was that picture of Cathy, the one I found in her lower desk drawer: the Royal York with Bullard and Smith draping all over her like festive bunting. That was April 22nd, too, or most likely early on the morning of the 23rd after drinks and more drinks. She was at the Gardens the same time that Sarah was. And then I snapped my fingers. "1962, that's three years ago. Sarah was only 17 when she was murdered. That puts her at fourteen in this picture."

"What?" Stana grabbed a hold of it. "Kiddie porn?"

"Yeah." And Lisa Steinmetz, 1959. That puts her at 16 or 17.

"That photograph that Lisa showed you, the one allegedly

sent from Davis. Was it recent or was it taken on this date too, 1962?"

I don't know. I didn't know Cathy that well. I wasn't looking at the earlier photo close enough. *What else in this case wasn't I seeing?*

Stana's eyes furrowed. Lisa was lying. That photograph she sprung on me wasn't taken recently but was a relic from that Gardens party. "I bet you anything it's three years old."

It would be so easy to fool me, but now that I think about it, Cathy did look younger, the face more full with adolescent baby fat. I pulled out the folded print Lisa gave me the other day.

Davis had nothing to do with this, Stana mumbled. Lisa was trying to divert attention away from her to him. What's she hiding, why is she sending you on a false trail? "I don't think you can believe a word from Lisa—"

I shook my head. "This is three years old. Look at her hair. Bangs. She wears her hair out now. Fuck." I hated being a sucker. What *was* Lisa hiding? Who was she working for? "We've got to talk to her."

"We will."

"I told her to leave town—"

"We'll find her." Stana squeezed my hand. "We will. But first let's check out this film."

Her parents loved sharing home movies of Stana. When she was born, her father Clint got bit by the hobby and photographed everything from Stana's first bath, to *Early Morning outing at Jean Sibelius Square.* "By the time I entered second grade, Dad had tired of his hobby. So I guess, nothing's happened in my life since then." She smiled.

I kissed her nose.

Her parents' home was in the city's east end, Scarborough, off Eglinton, in a modest fourth-floor apartment.

I shuffled through the five photographs. They were all dated between 1958 and 1963. "Shit, I wonder if all of these girls were in that very first therapy session at Castle Frank."

"Probably," Stana said.

"The Tangerine Room. Landover Leeds," I mumbled. Lanzo the fucking Great. "Hey. I know this one too." DS, 3/12/63, MLG. Aqua green eyes, blonde. She was one of the human lamps in Bullard and Smith's office. In the photograph her eyes looked directly through the camera, unaware of any lingering stare on the other end. "She was wearing a pink fez." I had no idea what name was behind the initials. DS.

Stana reached into her handbag, finding the list of nine names. She cross checked the list against the 8x10's. Three of the nine girls from the 1958 therapy sessions were present in the envelope's pack of five, circa 1958–63. "Almost half of these young women are underage. You *still* think the photos are sexy?"

"No."

Stana shook her head and chewed at her upper lip. "Bullard and Smith. Fucking pimps," she said.

STANA'S MOM RENE was kind and didn't pry. She had never once passed judgment on our having lived together and she loved my sense of humor and the way I played hockey. She said I had integrity, didn't cheat anyone, skated every shift hard, back-checked, fore-checked, and scored when my team really needed it: in the close games, not the blowouts. She followed the team religiously and the day I got shipped to the minors a bit of her died. She got so mad at the Leafs that she almost became a Habs fan.

Rene wore a pink pajama top with big white buttons and her gray hair parachuted about her forehead and full face. Her eyes lingered with pleasantries, like she were about to share her favorite cookie recipes.

Her husband, Clint, loved to tell jokes and he was a die-hard Leafs fan too. He preferred listening to the radio play-by-play of McClelland Stuart over the television commentary of McClelland's son Bill, so, the nights Clint didn't work, he synched his radio to the television's pictures.

The nights he did work, the Wednesdays and Saturdays of Toronto's home games, the TTC ride to the College stop was a congested mess, full of elbows, bad smells, and tidbits of knowledge from the subways of hockey "general managers," suggesting trading away this guy or that guy for this one or that. The arrogance.

As far as Clint was concerned, Coach and GM Hugh "Two Fisted" Farrell knew what he's doing. Shut up, the rest of you, and let Farrell run the Leafs organization and me run this goddamn train.

"So we can't see this film, huh?" Clint's cigarette bounced on his lower lip, his T-shirt half-tucked in, half-tucked out, a suspender off a shoulder.

"No," I said. "For your own safety. The less who knows, the better." I had already mentioned the photographs to them, including the topless ones of Cathy, the missing girl. *And Sarah, the girl I lost 96 days ago*. "I don't know what we're in store for."

"You think the films might be *suggestive*?" Clint looked over at Stana.

"Don't worry. I've deputized her as a junior G-man. She can handle it," I said.

Clint wondered if we should be handing this stuff over to the police.

"Soon. I promise." But I wanted to look at it first and find enough evidence so that the cops could get a warrant and hopefully locate Cathy.

Rene hugged my left shoulder. "It's so good to see you, Hayden," and then she looked over in her husband's direction and then at Stana. Rene's eyes held a hopeful twinkle.

"You guys too. I missed you," I said.

Their apartment was on the frugal side of modest: a kitchen you could only stand in; a dining area with a small round table and three chrome-backed chairs (four wouldn't fit); a living room with a long coffee table, TV, radio, and a balcony off to the right. On the balcony were two lawn chairs and a small hibachi grill (not really much space for a block party). In back were a bathroom and two bedrooms. The hallway that led to the bathroom was squeezed with books and records. Clint liked Frank Sinatra and Johnny Cash.

"Well, we missed you, son." Clint seemed an inch shorter than I remembered and his shoulders sagged a little. He didn't have any plans to retire, but Rene thought he should once he reached thirty years with the TTC. "That's just two years away."

Stana wondered what the hell they were doing still awake.

"It's not late."

"It's almost midnight, Ma."

"Well, it's the weekend." They had been reading the latest Ed McBain when we arrived. They loved reading murder mysteries together. Instead of watching late night with Johnny Carson, they often fell asleep to an 87th Precinct novel. They took turns reading to each other and enjoyed the sounds of each other's voice. Rene was really good at taking on all the different roles, Clint said. "Should've been an actress."

"Oh, get out." Rene playfully smacked Clint on the shoulder.

"That's where you get it from," I pointed at Stana, and then rubbed my shoulder in sympathy with Clint.

They all laughed. There was something so gentle and romantic about the love that Clint and Rene had for each other.

"Can we get you anything before you start—you know—movie watching?"

"No, we're—uh—"

I cut Stana off. "Actually I'm kind of hungry. How about an egg sandwich—?"

Stana slugged me in the shoulder. "Hayden—"

"See what I mean?"

Rene laughed, her nose scrunching. "With some tabasco,

Hayden?" Rene's eyes glinted. She pushed strands of gray hair behind an ear.

"Yes. And maybe some green olives on the side? And chips or Cheezies?"

"Sure." She padded to the kitchen. She moved about a room lightly.

"You are shameless," Stana said.

"You want anything, hon?" Rene shouted from the kitchen. Her voice however wasn't light. All those years of teaching second grade taught her to project.

"No." Stana paused, tapping her chin. "Okay. Fried baloney. No bread. No tabasco. And definitely no green olives."

"Check," Mom shouted, the frying pan already spattering with a frying egg.

IT TOOK AWHILE to thread the film. It was delicate and broke a couple of times, but once we had it through the gate, it clacked and burped along the projector's tracking, catching and bouncing now and then. The images were relatively clear, but the camera was stationary, people moving in and out of the frame and it was pretty obvious due to lighting inconsistencies that the ten-minute roll was spliced together from several different parties. The exposures weren't consistent.

Corrugated curtains and the chrome finish to the wet bar and chairs suggested without a doubt that this was the space in the Gardens behind Smith and Bullard's office, the one you could only access through a button at the side of Pal Cal's desk, the one Spinner Terrien slipped into after a perfunctory wave. Spinner wasn't in any of the images. Neither was McClelland Stuart, the voice of Hockey Canada.

But Davis was there. He played cards or stood by a roulette wheel, watching, his face, especially his chin, shiny with sweat. Who knew how much money he was losing each night. But with hands hidden deep in his pockets he didn't appear ready, anytime soon, to donate to the March of Dimes.

"We got 'em," I said. "Running a common gaming house. That's enough for a warrant."

"Yeah," Stana said. "And bootlegging."

Smith and Bullard, however, were having a good time, engrossed in their own narcissistic, bon-vivant charm. They were chatting, highballs in hand, liquor splashing over the lips of their tear-shaped glasses. The two playboys sported homburgs and Bullard had a huge bag of chips in his right hand. He liked to eat with his left—probably to keep the dice clean. Smith moved his shoulders as he laughed.

At least I think he was laughing. The images were soundless.

Sometimes a naked woman could be spotted in the background, sitting on a couch, quietly smoking with long white gloves, nothing else on her person. Once in a while a naked woman danced off in a corner like a lethargic go-go dancer desperate for more bennies.

Kim Stabulas was never naked, but she was sitting on the arm of a chair in one brief stretch of film. She wore all black, including razor-edge stilettos and gloves that shined as if they were buffed with wax. She smoked a cigarette off a long slender holder. Her eyes were heavily made up, as were her lush lips. A white-haired sable collared her neck.

Babe Migano, the ex-Montreal mobster, smoked a cigar the size of a .45, and was by her feet on the floor. He was a big man and I was surprised that one of the kingpins of crime would sit by anybody's feet, let alone a woman's. His face was very prosperous, full of success and contentment. He never rolled dice nor worked the wheel. He was an observer and occasionally he and Davis would have a brief conversation, Davis leaning in with his head, the top of his hair uneven and needing more Brylcreem.

"She lied to us, too," I said.

"What?"

"Kim. She knew about Coughlins." I laughed bitterly. "She

told me she thought it was a pizza joint. Do you see any fucking anchovies in the room?"

This is dynamite, Stana said. "A grand jury will be looking into this." Check out the homburgs. What a perfect set-up for an exclusive club. Hold the party right in the Gardens pad. Who would know? An exclusive group of 10 or 15 guests could quietly party down after a hockey game or arrive in a limo at the Church Street entrance and nobody would be the wiser. "Our good friend Lisa's there too, I see."

I nodded. Lisa wore a black, low-cut gown. Her chin seemed perpetually tucked in, as if she were afraid of leading with it too much. Her body was displayed boldly, but her deportment—short, halting steps, slightly wobbling on heels—and overall fashion unease suggested a woman who didn't quite belong. She looked like a working girl, more comfortable waiting tables.

Migano's aloofness was one of choice.

"Who's operating the camera?" Stana asked.

"It's stationary." Could be on a tripod. Could be set up in a secret location, behind a two-way mirror. Few of these people knew they were being filmed. "They're too carefree, lacking in self-consciousness. None of them *look* into the camera. Usually a camera draws attention. Check out the guy obliviously picking his nose."

"Oh, my god. He represents my riding—"

"An M.P.?"

"Two term."

After a few more spliced chunks, and the film shaking, there was one odd forty-five second riff of Landover Leeds in dark dress pants, pleated, and a heavy sweater with patches at the elbows. He sat in a leather chair and a tall woman, full of lithe curves and sharp angles, sauntered toward him, her thin hips swaying.

She climbed onto his lap and thrust up, down, and around and he mewled, at least he appeared to be mewling, head tilted up, parted lips uttering pleasing sounds at the ceiling. The woman rolled her shoulders and arched her back like a cat. I think she was mewling too.

"Starzz. That must be Starzz. The woman in the mask Lisa told us about," Stana said.

"Really?"

"Look at the *mask*."

I hadn't noticed the *mask*.

Bullard and Smith, smiling, stood by the woman in the black dress. Flecks of chips fell to the carpet. Smith at some point applauded, took off his glasses, cleaned them, and then applauded some more. Davis was looking off at someone, probably Lisa or another well-endowed woman, outside the frame.

"I think they call that lap dancing," Stana said.

"Looks like fun, with the right girl."

I was surprised that Stana hadn't punched me. "Maybe later. At least a shower," she said.

"I can't see the woman's face."

"I'm telling you, she's wearing a mask."

And then I saw it. The mask was huge, with triangles around both eyes and feathers on the forehead. When Starzz arched back her head I could see the expressive playfulness behind the performance. The outfit would be perfect for Mardi Gras. "If I had beads, I'd throw them at her."

Really? Stana thought the whole act was too much.

We watched until the remaining lap dance footage bled into black leader.

And then we were quiet. The room. I stared at the bits of cold egg and baloney left on the plates Rene had served up.

There wasn't a TV on anywhere. I wondered if her parents had gone to bed.

I touched Stana's chin and lifted her face and studied the freckles that forever seemed to be dancing. "I'm sorry about last year. How I just shut you out—didn't return your calls, didn't—"

Suddenly my mouth was dry and my eyes burned.

"We've both made mistakes. Me at the newspaper—"

"We'll both try to do better." I crossed my heart and like a ten-year-old kid took her pinky, attaching it to mine. "Pinky promise." That made her laugh.

We had made out on this very bed many times over the years, keeping the noise down so that her parents wouldn't hear.

Stana must have been sharing my memories, because she was now leaning in, her nose catching my upper lip, while we both readjusted and kissed, and fell back on the bed. I pushed hair from her forehead and kissed her harder and then kissed her nose and both eyelids. "I love you," I said.

She tapped my chin three times. "Who do you think is the girl in the mask?"

I shrugged. "I'm kind of glad McClelland Stuart wasn't at these parties, living the life of the hipster libertine. I kind of like him—"

She sat up with her elbows. McClelland was a smart businessman. Owned his own radio station, CKMS, and had a lot of other investment interests including housing, land development, and sought to buy a piece of a CFL team. "But he's no saint." He was having an affair with his radio station manager.

"But he's married."

"Oh, sure. But when did that ever mean anything?"

Men are pigs.

"But the press just keeps quiet about it. It's hockey." She smiled thinly. "Excessive drinking? Wife beating? When does the press ever cover that? There's that star for the Blackhawks, fifty-goals-a-year-guy, who punches out his wife. Nobody touches that story. Nobody. Why?"

"Maybe it should be quiet?" My stomach was full of rocks.

"What?"

"Hockey provides young boys with dreams—"

"And what about young girls, and the women getting hurt?"

"You got me there—"

"McClelland has an ego and a need to feed it. His radio station? CKMS 1480. The last two call letters? Those are his initials: McClelland Stuart. 1480 on your dial."

I didn't know what to say, so I looked back at the remains of a sandwich and cold egg. "Let's call the police. Call in Leeds's murder. And get a warrant and kick Bullard and Smith's asses."

"Let's. But first—" She held a hand to her lips, my lips, and locked the door.

And we were quiet once again like we were four years ago, the first time we made love in her parents' apartment.

7

It wasn't a very good day, not for Pal Cal Bullard and Steven Smith. Not for the Toronto Maple Leafs. Not for the city. The Leafs had lost game one of the playoffs at the Forum in Montreal, 3-2. Jean Béliveau fed Rejean Bouldieu a slinky pass, and the fast, shifty winger split the Leafs D before beating Bower.

The Toronto hockey club played a thug fest last night, more intent on bashing the Canadiens than working the puck. Horton, of donuts fame, took a five-minute major and the Big M hit Terry Harper high and hard, giving the Habs rearguard a gash that required six stitches. "If you can't beat 'em on the ice, beat 'em in the back alley," the Old Man proselytized about the game back in the 1940s. I'd rather win on the ice, but, hey, that's just me.

For the city, their team's upper management was now under police suspicion and a warrant had been issued. "I'm lucky to still be standing." My forehead pinched with a raised eyebrow. "I thought I was going to break an ankle over all this damn police tape."

That cracked me up and I bent over laughing at my own joke. I mean there was black and gold tape by the lobby, the main office, and Smith's office. X's were everywhere, man.

But all joking aside, where the fuck was Cathy? I had hoped this bust would lead us directly to her or to a big enough clue to point me toward a resolution, but the longer this case went the more surprises and absurd twists confounded me.

"Smart-ass." Smith's tie and upper shirt buttons were loose, his hair dripping with alcohol sweat, his eyes unrecognizable behind flashes of light filling the lenses of his Lombardis, like sunspots.

For Pal Cal and Smith their office was full of police, reporters, and photographers. Bledsoe was jotting down notes like a jazz pianist, his fingers jittering. Stana crowded by Laurinda Mays and Dawn Stoukas—the human lamps from the other day.

Stana was stunning in dark slacks and a bright pink top, giving off a professional but warm appearance. She asked questions of the girls, on the side. Nick Stabulas, his eyebrows pushed together like the blade of a fat machete, was forced back by two constables, large patches of sweat under the arms of his off-white shirt and grocery store apron. The apron was soiled with food stains and splats of blood.

Chief of Police Sal Lambertino, my old pal who regularly received comp tickets from yours truly during my playing days, was conducting the investigation. He had a heavy jaw hidden behind the fence of a Hemingway fisherman's beard. His eyes were hard little stones. And when he spoke, it was his way, man, that's it, nothing else. I liked that about him. Direct.

"Yup. That's me, Smitty my boy. A regular smart-ass. And these gentlemen have, I believe, a warrant for your arrest." I introduced Sal and the five or six constables hunched around his shoulders. They all wore black hats with a thick red band. Their hats resembled a series of stop signs. The symbolism seemed appropriate.

Bullard reached into his bag for the biggest chunk of chips he could find. He looked disappointed.

"That's warrant, Smith. Not Wharram. Kenny Wharram? He plays for the Blackhawks. With Bobby Hull and Stan Mikita?" I laughed.

Sal shook his head, giving me the not-so-subtle high sign to scale things back a bit.

"We've done nothing wrong." Smith reached for a stout-shaped glass of milk with a chaser, in a smaller glass, parked inside of it. He sipped from the combination. "Nothing."

"Where's my daughter?" Nick strained, shifting his upper body away from the cops surrounding him, shouldering to get through the pack.

I was surprised that Kim wasn't here.

"Can he drink in here?" I turned to Lambertino.

He shrugged. "Sure. Let it go."

But I was enjoying it too much.

"I own the building, smart-ass," Smith said. "And you'll have a statement from my lawyer in the morning. This is all a misunderstanding—"

"What can you tell us about the Bolemac Corporation and hiding pots of money?" Stana asked, one hand on her hip, the other pointing her pencil like a thin microphone.

"I'm surprised you have the effrontery to ask me such a question, Miss."

"Well that's just me. I worry my *pretty little head* about such matters." Stana tapped her pencil against her lips and flicked red hair behind an ear. It was a gesture she had inherited from her mom, an eerie, yet attractive echo.

"I know nothing about Bolemac—"

"Didn't they re-design this office?" I glanced around. "Put in that secret sliding door behind you and the accompanying wet bar?"

Smith sighed heavily.

The arrogance of these assholes. Like a stripper removing a long glove, Smith teasingly showed me the secret sliding door and back room the other day. Did he and Bullard not think I'd follow up on that goddamn clue?

Bullard flecked specks of salt from his fingers. "It's a construction firm. What more do you need to know?"

"It's a construction firm that you own with your friend Babe Migano," Stana corrected, her eyes narrowing, the freckles about her face much brighter than the ones dancing on her upper arms.

That got the attention of all the reporters in the room. Everyone jotted words now. Migano was a gambling kingpin in the greater Toronto area. In recent years he had shifted much of his assets into a series of five-star restaurants, including White Heat, a place on Mt. Pleasant near my old ethnic neighborhood, named rather cheekily after the Babe's favorite gangster film with Jimmy the C. *Made it ma.*

"I resent the implications. We are not in league with gangsters. The Leafs have never—"

And then Smith, sipping *colored* milk, started in with something about no comment and contacting his lawyers (who suddenly had become more than one). I couldn't wait to read the statement in tomorrow's editions.

Stana, pushing hair over the other shoulder, worked on getting follow-up statements from Laurinda and Dawn. They were seated in blue chairs with silver chrome. Their posture and actions were identical, like the Doublemint twins: shoulders back, left leg crossed over right.

No, they hadn't felt totally mistreated for being human lamps. Right leg over left. Yes, it was degrading, but they got paid well, and Mr. Smith and Mr. Bullard made no sexual advances. *What about touching your breasts? Like the other day? Right here?* They shrugged, together, left leg over right. "He didn't mean anything by it," one of the two said after a long awkward pause. *What about the photographs of you naked in the Gardens lobby?* I don't remember anything about that, Dawn said. Seriously. Me neither, echoed Laurinda. It was like I was there but it's hazy. *"How old were you when you were in this haze?"* Seventeen. Right leg now over left.

"Underage—" I smiled my lopsided lupine look at Smith. I had flashed that grin a lot while skating truculently to the penalty box.

I still had no idea what Smith's eyes were doing. The sunspots across his lenses resembled soft yolks wobbling inside of poached eggs.

But his voice had climbed a ladder. He was shouting, and it was breaking up like radio static. The two activities aren't related: the girls' topless photographs and the everyday business goings on of the Gardens. Apples and oranges. Yes, the pictures were taken here, but we're not responsible for the pictures. "We, the Maple Leaf organization, don't sanction those pictures." He emphasized organization in all of its syllabic glory, slowly, like a 33 ⅓ LP on 16, to make his point, whatever that point was.

"Uh-huh," Bledsoe said.

"Uh-huh," I echoed. "What about Sarah Kerr, the girl that was murdered 97 days ago. Remember? The body in the suitcase?"

The room quieted, Bullard's hands quit rummaging for potato chips. Smith pushed himself upright, his lips a tense line.

"She was in one of the pictures. Topless. Fourteen years old." I pressed.

"Like I said," Smith nearly whispered. "Apples and oranges. We had nothing to do with—"

"Bullshit," Stana said.

"Answer the question," Bledsoe demanded.

"You want me to take your press pass away again, Dick?" Smith threatened. "And I can take yours away right now, Miss Younger."

"It won't be the first time," she said, winking at Bledsoe.

"I can get you a bail bondsman, Smitty," Dick quipped back. "Or a tailor who specializes in Brooks Brothers prison wear." Bledsoe's hat was nudged rakishly to the side and resembled a cap worn by a jester, cavorting about a stage, ridiculing Lear for his blind admiration for the fawning Goneril and Regan. Bledsoe's hair, streaks of which curled up and over the hat's felt brim, was gray, his green eyes mischief-riddled. But his eyebrows were the real gas. They wanted to do things on their own, like applaud over his wicked witticisms. "This is the hell of a circus show. All you need is an organ grinder and a monkey on your shoulder, Steve."

That cracked everybody up.

Lambertino smiled at me. I guess he liked Bledsoe's column too.

"This is a campaign of slander and misrepresentation," Smith intoned, his voice dropping back to its more regular rhythms, his knifing hands blurs of phosphorus. "I don't acknowledge this witch hunt. We've done nothing wrong and I don't understand why we're being arrested on such flimsy evidence."

"Let's just say, it's unlucky for you that the judge who signed off on this is a Habs fan." Now Lambertino was cracking wise. It was good to see.

I turned to the girls as Smith continued a litany of double-speak and denial. Apples and Oranges. Oranges and apples. Lions and tigers and bears, oh my.

Dawn's and Laurinda's legs were still crossed, and hands poised like tiny shelves propping up each chin. "Mister Smith might have a point," Laurinda said while Dawn nodded. "He was never present when the photos were taken—at least I don't remember him being there—do you?"

"No," Dawn echoed.

"He's 'Mister' now? You don't remember anything about the shoots?" I said.

"I remember Landover, I think—" Laurinda said.

"Was he wearing a turban? Was he made-up to look like his alter-ego, Lanzo the Great?"

"Lanzo the What?"

"Smith wasn't there, ever? Really?"

She looked away.

"Who was there?" Stana's face tightened, her freckled eyes flashing.

"Like I said, Landover Leeds, the guy in today's newspaper who was found dead on Front Street. He was the photographer."

"Why would you ever agree to this? To appear topless, to—"

"I didn't agree to it—it just happened—I don't even—" Dawn said.

"It's like you were hypnotized."

The Tangerine Room wasn't just for relaxation but mind control too. So was the second "room" in his office. In the 1940s, doctors used a little something labeled narcosynthesis, a kind of hypnosis as a curative power, releasing the deepest traumas of combat-fatigued veterans, helping them on the road to healing. But what if doctors used those curative powers to manipulate and abuse impressionable and traumatized young women? What if the Tangerine Room with its levers and headphones and Leeds talking to the girls ever so quietly, discreetly, were but a ruse to drip venom in their ears, a regular Claudius poisoning Hamlet's father, subliminal poison underneath the whale cries and breaking waves?

"Yeah, like I was hypnotized." Laurinda nodded. So did Dawn.

"Where's my daughter," Nick interjected, shoving closer to Smith. "Let's stop all the goddamn talk and boiler-plated bullshit and find her, you understand—" His face had reddened and for the first time I noticed his nose wasn't straight—it looked like it had been busted in a fist fight and it didn't quite mesh with all the square lines to his face.

"We have people looking right now," Sal informed him. "Settle down." There was a police posse searching the entire Gardens for the girl. All levels. Sal's voice was firm. Nick had better settle down or else he was going to get slapped with some cuffs.

Nick chewed his upper lip and the determined line of his

eyebrows became an even heavier machete. The image fit him: everything he said hacked and chopped and lacked subtlety or nuance.

Dawn said that they never agreed to the photographs. They were taking group therapy to liberate themselves from their low self-images, but this was never part of the package plan.

So Cathy wound up hypnotized too to appear nude. What about Sarah, *the girl I found in a suitcase?*

According to Dawn, Sarah always wanted to belong to their group. She was just a middle-schooler back then, always studying at the high school's library (because it had a better collection of resources), getting top grades, winning essay contests, and planning to become a doctor, but there was this side to her that wanted to be free of her mother's pressure. Kind of wild, you know? Like, there are stage moms, Dawn said, who force their kids into showbiz and then there are school moms who always want their kids to get A's and excel at learning. Sarah's mom was one of those. A crazy, demanding school mom. "We even suspected she helped write some of Sarah's award-winning essays. Like for Kiwanis Club and stuff? Anyway, Sarah was pushing back. Against all of it, you know—teachers, preachers, mama? She wanted to be sixteen, when she was twelve. You follow me? With the boys?"

I nodded. "Did she do drugs?"

"No, nothing like that," Laurinda said. "Just boys. A lot of boys."

And what about Cathy's lower dresser drawer and the leather mouth strap with a ball?

"I don't know. I don't remember Cathy at all," the two girls uttered in overlapping dialogue. Was she even at the Gardens? They remembered her from Leeds's therapy class. She was the eccentric chick, a little weird, always reading her own poetry about staring into the abyss of Lake Ontario. "All of her poems ended with her at a lake."

"I want my daughter back." Nick and his words slithered down a dark hole. To tell you the truth, there was something totally phony about his whole act, the overheated father, the rush of angst to bring matters to justice.

Smith took another drink of doctored milk and wiped the back of his mouth.

Dawn held out her hands by way of apology. The girls in Leeds's therapy sessions were all suffering from some kind of body self-consciousness. "I always thought my hands were too big. Anyway—"

"What was Sarah's hang-up?" I asked.

"She thought she was too skinny," Dawn said.

"Yeah. She hated being willowy. That's the word she always used to describe herself, willowy," Laurinda said.

"Willowy, huh?" But they couldn't remember anything else or how they all wound up posing nude. Collective amnesia. *Narcosynthesis. Lanzo the Not So Great.*

"Were drugs involved, any drugs?" Stana tapped her chin.

"Bennies maybe," Dawn said with an absent shrug. "I don't remember much in the way of drugs—" It wasn't prevalent, apparently.

What was prevalent was Leeds and his reassuring "relaxation." He may have convinced them that they were all beautiful and pointed a way for them to conquer their fears by becoming less inhibited, less clothed. And what did he get out of the pictures—kickbacks on kiddie porn, sales to minors, middle-aged men, and members of Parliament?

"That may be true," Dawn said. "But I never saw the photos before. You'd think I'd have seen them at school or something. If Landover was selling the work, it must've been a pretty discreet clientele."

"Coughlins Club discreet? What did your fellow classmates know about that outfit? Not much," Stana said.

Dawn nodded. "Landover wanted us to free ourselves from

judgment, but I don't remember any suggestions to free myself of my clothes—" They both laughed, left leg over right.

"Like I said, subliminal messages, that's how." Given commands that you follow without even knowing you're following them. Think of it as a form of exploitation, I said, mind control, chipping away your free will.

One of the girls laughed, "Mind control?" The other said, "Say what?"

He had some kind of diploma from some kind of institute in New Mexico, I said.

"Flagstaff, Arizona," Stana corrected, pushing pensive fingers and shrugging into a half-smile. "Come on, girls. Think. Think hard."

There was another guy, Dawn vaguely recalled. Burly, but she couldn't recollect his face. He sounded kind of English, but a phony kind of English. Too much "luv" and "mate" tossed about like tips at a diner's club.

Smith spewed more gobbledygook, a combination of legalese and self-entitled posturing. Bledsoe quit writing. "Are the Leafs going to win tomorrow night with all these distractions?"

"Damn right we're going to win. The boys owe it to this city—"

Right. Owe it to the city. More like the boys owe it to me to get my sorry face off the front page of three dailies.

"A burly fella, huh?"

"Yeah, he was big," Dawn said. "And he smelled of coffee, cigarettes, and licorice." But that was all she could remember.

"Where's my daughter—" Nick broke free of the two constables and jumped the desk, side-rolling across it, seizing Smith by the lapels and throttle swinging, one hand on Smith's turkey neck, the other slapping free the glasses.

Bullard, chips falling on the floor like bits of broken stone, cleared out of the way.

Nick's second punch landed on Smith's mouth, bloodying it.

"Why you big hypocritical phony," Smith shot back, shoving

and kneeing Nick in the groin, bending him, and then kneeing him again on the chin, sending him sprawling against the desk, knocking about a chair. Constables pulled the two apart, catching errant fingers and separated fists about their faces.

"Goddamn it," Lambertino shouted. "Arrest that man." He pointed at Nick who was immediately cuffed.

"If she's dead, I'll kill you, you understand," Nick promised Smith, his voice traced with hard frost.

"Get him out of here."

Two constables escorted Nick from the office and down the stairs. He was speaking loudly in Macedonian.

Stana tapped her foot, twitched her nose, and her eyes creased with mild amusement. She thought there was something phony about the whole scene too.

I shrugged. "The guy's no Marlon Brando."

"He's not even Mo or Curly Howard."

That cracked me up.

Smith readjusted his tie and wiped blood from his mouth with the tight triangle corner of a hanky. His eyes were red-rimmed from fighting and all the hard drinking he had been doing. He checked his glasses. The frames weren't bent and he put them back on, masking the raw exhaustion of his eyes.

"Okay, now for the cup duh grassy," I smiled in Bullard's direction. "There's a button on this desk. Voila." I pressed it and the bookcase behind Smith slid open.

We crossed the threshold. Blue corrugated curtains gleamed even in the dim light. I turned to Bullard and tweaked his nose. "Doesn't the light in here have three settings?" I tweaked his schnozzle twice more. Dawn laughed. "Oh, there we go."

Lambertino had turned on the actual lights. "Settle down, cowboy," he whisper-mumbled.

I turned to Bullard. "Where are your goons, Fortunado and Leighton? I was looking forward to some verbal sparring—or at least discussing the Dow Jones—"

"They'll meet up with you again," he vowed. "Maybe sooner than you think—"

"Great. I'll make sure to wear my interview tie."

The constables searched the room. Half-empty liquor glasses cluttered the wet bar and newspapers and magazines were fanned about, but it was fairly clean. A copy of Steinbeck's *Of Mice and Men* was on one of the coffee tables.

"Where did you get this?"

"I read," Smith said.

"Yeah. You read. Tell me about this book—" Cathy read Steinbeck, a lot of Steinbeck. *East of Eden* twice, according to her sister.

"A classic." And then Smith recounted the plot. I wondered if he had gotten a full report on the slender novel from Cathy. His summation showed no savvy for the beauty of Steinbeck's prose and craft. It was all this happened and then that happened and then, teacher, this happened.

"Uh-huh." I pointed to where the wheel was usually set up for roulette.

Bledsoe nodded. "I figured Bullard for craps myself." That got a few twitters from his fellow reporters.

"Gentlemen, ladies. Let's conduct ourselves with decorum." Sal held up a hand. "We are talking about an institution here. I don't like these guys either, but this is the Toronto Maple Leafs."

He had us there. The room quieted. I took off my porkpie and dropped my head, in observation of a moment of silence.

"Fuck you, Hayden," Smith said. "We don't gamble here. This isn't a common gaming house," he assured us. "I have friends over. We play some small ante poker. That's all. Some like to spin the wheel. Small stakes. Some of you, I'm sure, get together with friends for a friendly game."

"And drinking—" Sal removed his hat and clutched his sandy hair. "With underage girls?" He pushed the cap back in place and threw his hands on his hips. "I don't think many of us get together and do that." He rubbed at tired eyes. "We have it all on film."

"It's just a party, an after hours party." Smith raised a hand full of phosphorus. "Very exclusive. The guests arrive in stretch limos. But there's no hanky-panky."

"Naked girls? A woman in black dancing on the decedent's lap? That's not hanky-panky?" Sal was now giving Smith the stink eye.

"It gets a little wild, but I assure you the women are all of age—"

"Not the women in those photographs—" I said.

"As you undoubtedly have already heard. Landover took those photographs. I had nothing to do with that. Apples and oranges. Unfortunately, it happened here at the Gardens. I will have my people look into that. I promise."

"Apples and oranges," Bullard echoed. "Apples and oranges."

Just how was Landover not affiliated with the club? He was part of the Old Man's militia, 1940-45. Trained with McClelland Stuart and Syl Apps and all those boys.

"I know nothing of that," Bullard said.

"How did he get access to the Gardens?" Stana asked. "After-hours access?"

"Ask McClelland if they were such grand pals." Smith held up his chin. It was a real regal pose, a striking look that ought to be on a damn postage stamp or something. "God, that guy McClelland thinks he runs the Gardens. Saying how high the gondola should be off the ice. Inviting friends in. He's just a broadcaster—'he shoots, he scores.' Come up with some new catch-phrases for chrissakes."

"Is McClelland involved?" Bledsoe asked.

"I'll let you draw your own inferences."

Talk about passing the buck. "This is a side issue," I said.

"Talk to McClelland," Smith reiterated, for all the reporters to hear. They frenetically jotted it all down, heads tilted with feverish intensity.

"That spot right there, by the wet bar, Sal, that's where all the images were taken on the 8mm film." I glanced over my shoulder and snapped my fingers. "Which means the camera has to have been set up over here." The wall behind me was uncluttered: a couple of paintings and a gilt-edged wall mirror. I checked along the edgings and found another switch. I pressed it and the mirror's glass slid down, revealing a Bell and Howell camera.

"Two-way glass." Sal studied the camera. The casings on the front were smudged with a host of fingerprints that shined like melted caramel. "Get this dusted. Now we've got photographs of naked girls taken in the lobby of the Gardens and secret 8mm film shot in the very office of the president and his second in command." He pushed back his cap and rubbed his forehead again. "Game, set, match, Mr. Smith."

"They're not related. Apples and oranges," Bullard said.

"Oh, will you shut the fuck up," Smith said.

Bullard reached for another chunk of chips.

"GET IN THE CAR." The voice was dark gravel. Fortunado had a hand in the pocket of his tan overcoat. "The boss wants to see you." His lean eyes were the color of crisp bacon.

"The boss? He went thataway. Hi-ho, Silver." I pointed at the contrail of police cars that had just left the Gardens. Smith, Bullard, Lambertino, a bevy of photographers, reporters and various hangers-on were tooling to the cop shop, just a few stops west at College and Bay. "Away!"

"We're free agents. It's a different boss, Crumpled Suit."

"Uh-huh."

Lou-doo's face was patchy shadows. The sky was the blue of faded jeans, but Fortunado would forever exist in shadows. Even his voice sounded like a dark, demimonde whisper.

Next to him, brightly gleaming in a camel-haired coat and tight Oliver Hardy bowler was Athol Leighton, chin tucked in, readying to take a punch and kick back twice as hard. The skin on his face was stretched Saran Wrap. His lips were pressed as if he were fighting indigestion. "You heard him. Get."

"Hey—" Stana, thinking quickly, created a diversion, bumping Fortunado. Lou-doo shoved back, straight-arming her like an open-field running back, and then I shouldered him, jumping in tight, tying up his arms, and chopping down on the gun hidden in the hand in his pocket. Lou-doo screamed and slipped, stumbled, and stomped my toes—his feet were huge. The cat could float across Lake Ontario on those HMS's.

As Stana staggered behind me and righted herself, I head-butted Lou to the ground. He landed on his elbows and bounced a little. My gun was now un-holstered and in my hand.

"With your history of concussions, I don't think that head-butt was such a shit-hot idea," Stana said.

"Will you relax?"

I wondered what Dr. Abramowitz would say. *Slow down, kid.*

"Well, let's go to this powwow. I assume it was to be a friendly conversation?"

Cool Athol nodded and wiped back a belch. "Jesus Christ, Lou. I can't take you anywhere."

I asked for Lou's gun. He reached in and pointed the checkered grip toward me. I handed the .45 and my snub-nosed .38 to Stana. "Go to the paper. Type up your story." I motioned Stana away. The evening editions would hit the streets in a few hours. And what a story: Bullard and Smith arrested. The Gardens affiliated with underage drinking, gambling, and a high-end escort service. What did all of this have to do with the missing Cathy Stabulas and the murder of Sarah Kerr? The headlines would be screaming to know, tonight, in their 26-point font.

And maybe I would finally get some damn answers.

"We don't want the girl, right?" Lou-doo dusted off his elbows.

"You're not in a position to ask, pal," I said. "Get going, Stana.

I'll be all right. I'll call."

"Boss just said Fuller. The girl can go." Leighton tipped his hat, acting as if they were still the ones in charge and were doing us a favor. He pushed back his dandy of a bowler.

"You'll be okay?" Stana's eyes were wet.

"I'll be okay. I'll call when I'm done talking to Mister Big." I placed exaggerated air quotes around the name.

"You two can arrange your social calendar later." Fortunado shoved me toward a large yellow Buick. The glare hurt my eyes. Hell, it looked like it jumped off the pages of the Dick Tracy color comics.

My head was thudding, dark clouds forming behind my eyes. Stana was right about the head-butt. Stupid move, Hayden Ira Fuller.

The heavies, as they deposited me in the back seat, were surprisingly gentle, removing my porkpie and ducking my head so I wouldn't catch it on the car's metal frame. Lou got behind the wheel. Cool Athol sat by my shoulder. He popped a Tums and then another.

Cool Athol wasn't looking too cool right about now. "Bad clams?"

"Shut up."

"Well, don't tell me where I'm going, fellas. Surprise me."

They both shook their heads. Lou threw the big car in gear and gently nudged away from the curb. "You know, you're not nearly as funny as you think you are, pally," he said over his shoulder.

I never said I was Lenny Bruce but hey, bubeleh, I get by.

Babe Migano's stone home in Etobicoke was huge, spacious, with a slow-pitched slanted ceiling, and dark cedar wood trim. A fireplace smoldered and I wondered where to leave my poles and ski boots.

"Funny," Lou mumbled.

A swank cedar door, larger than usual, opened. Migano sauntered toward me. He was a big man, 240, 250, and moved like an upright cheetah, padding softly with clear, calculated steps. Light glinted off his shoulders as if he were a backlit movie star. "My study." He gestured behind him.

Babe's teeth were straight and even, and there wasn't a mark on his face. He was no Al Capone.

He smoked from a holder. On the lapel of his bathrobe was a pink rose. His face was more Irish puck than Italian, like Jackie Gleason if the Great One were like sixty pounds lighter. His hair was slicked back and his skin had that raw glare of a close shave with a hard razor. "I hope my boys weren't rough on you?" He smiled and straightened his cuffs.

"Oh, no. We went over what tie I should wear for the interview, skinny or regular-sized. Skinny seemed a more natural choice." I flipped the tie's triangular corner up and then back down.

"You got balls—"

"Thanks. Is Cathy Stabulas still alive?"

"How would I know?"

"You hear things."

"I didn't hear she was dead."

I nodded. "Fair enough." I smiled awkwardly. "Landover Leeds?"

"He got what he had coming. Exploiting young women—"

"Yeah, and a bunch of hypnosis right out of *Flash Gordon*. Any ideas who greased him?"

Migano shrugged. "Small change—I don't bother myself with small change—"

"What about Sarah Kerr?" I felt my face tightening. "She's not small change."

"The girl in the suitcase?"

"Yeah. Ninety-seven days ago she was murdered." I shrugged. "Found some nudies of her done at the Gardens. Seems to be a tie-in with Smith, Bullard, Landover and Cathy. I'm not sure how, but—"

"This is a business visit, Mr. Fuller. Nothing else. I assure you." He glanced at the far corner before dropping his eyes back on me. "I want to hire you."

He pointed me to a leather chair. On the desk between us was a drink, two fingers of scotch. My drink was tonic water with a small plate of rugelach.

Migano had done his homework. "Most people don't know I'm Jewish."

"I respect Jews. They had to fight for their piece of the pie. Like us wops. The cake eaters aren't going to give it to us. And when we first came to this country we had to climb the crooked rungs on the ladder to success."

It was the *only* way to get ahead for many from the Old Country. I sipped tonic water.

"My dad was in construction and had ties to the mob." He sighed and gestured with his hand, making a lazy figure eight. "Ran some liquor back in the day."

"Cake eaters? That's what my dad called the Anglos because they didn't put olive oil on anything."

"Right." He paused, taking a slow sip of scotch. "Didn't want it dripping off their chins. Wanted everything dry. Pizza practically with no sauce." He shook his head and the figure eights were now much wider, like the turn and banking of a Boeing 707. "Leafs got a chance against Montreal?"

"We got money players, but I don't know. The run might be done—"

"What about this Davis fuck?"

"What about him? He can score goals but he doesn't back-check."

"I think he stole my money."

"$568,000?"

Migano was impressed with how I knew the exact amount

missing. The money was kept in a safe at the Gardens. It was Migano's take from the Bolemac Corporation's handling of various accounts such as Coughlins (the hidden room behind the bookshelf).

Someone stole the money out of a Gardens safe before the funds were transferred to him.

"They always keep that amount on hand at the Gardens safe? That's a lot of chump change."

"Yeah. There was always some excuse to not get the money to me." He gestured away at an imaginary fly. "And then the money, it got got. I think it was Davis." He took another puff off his cigarette. "I got it on good authority that he was in league with Lisa Steinmetz and Spinner Terrien."

I nodded. "How good of authority?"

"Real good. This person's on the inside. In my pocket. Aces."

On the wall behind him were black-framed photographs of Coney Island. I recognized some of the iconic images: people crowded around the human roulette wheel as it spun and twisted you off its perch, crashing into walls below. Next to the wheel was another image from the '40s, men and women stumbling through the turning walls of the Barrel of Fun. A plump girl, face and body pressing the floor, had a guy straddling her, trying to help her up, or possibly thinking of joining her in her fall from dignity.

"Coney Island? I'm sorry I was distracted—"

"No, no. I loved Coney Island." Before arriving in Montreal his parents raised Babe in the mean streets of New York, Lower East Side, naming him after the Yankees all-star right fielder, the Sultan of Swat, and Migano and his family visited Coney every summer. "Cheap amusements. That's what us immigrants called it. Cheap amusements. Didn't cost much. Nickels, dimes, but it gave us hope."

"Cheap amusements," I mumbled to myself. That's what this case is, a series of false starts and turns, lies and double-crosses, and somebody was behind the curtain like the goddamn Wizard of Oz laughing over this shit, amused at my folly.

It wasn't the beach and the sun that made Coney such an attraction, Babe said. It was all about the rides. Some of them were kind of sexy, like the Barrel of Fun, where a guy could fall all over his girl, touching her ever so discreetly as they righted themselves and tried to stand. "I performed that maneuver. Even at nine."

"I bet it worked for you—"

"Oh, yeah." He shrugged proudly. "One of my best."

I never had fun at amusement parks. Everybody seems to be trying too hard to have a good time. There was a mass-produced plastic feeling to the way people played and laughed. "Cheap amusements? Not for me really." I glanced at my fingers. "But I played hockey. That's an amusement for millions in Canada. Maybe it's cheap too. I don't know."

"It's a way of life in Canada, pal. Nothing cheap about hockey. It's an honest game."

"Yeah." I smiled. "Thanks."

"So, you really don't like amusement parks?"

"They're not for me, no—"

He pondered that as if my opinion were worth considering. "Too old-fashioned?"

"No. Just too busy. I like things quiet now and then."

He shook his head. "Rollercoasters, on the other hand, that was all action, man, taking you somewhere."

He pointed at a much larger image over his right shoulder. "The Cyclone. It had an 85-foot drop at a 60-degree angle. My stomach would be in my throat." He laughed. "I guess we all long for some return to our youth and Coney's mine." Both of his parents had died recently: one from cancer, the other from an embolism following back surgery. "My best times with them were at Coney."

"I hear you. My dad never did much with me, flew kites now

and then, and listened to hockey on the radio, McClelland Stuart. Pop took me to my first game when I was four. I've been in love with it ever since—"

"I'd whack Davis. It would make it all easier." He shrugged. "But I want to wait until the playoffs are over." He laughed. "I'm kidding. Well, kind of kidding—" He laughed again.

I liked him. He was honest. "So you want me to find the money?"

"Yes, I want you to track Davis. That's all. I want my money. I need it. Davis had accrued quite a few gambling debts at Coughlins and at other, how shall I put it, Mr. Fuller, underground casinos. That's his motivation. I want my money, *all of my money*."

I could work his case in. "I have to find the Stabulas girl but this relates."

Just to my left the bright neon splash of the Wonder Wheel grabbed me, forcing me to look upon it. It was a yellow or gold Ferris wheel with rocking cars that nudged upright, touching the sky.

"I didn't take that girl. I know of your case and I know what you're trying to do. For your sake I hope you find her. I assure you, I had nothing to do with her going missing."

I believed him.

"And I didn't kill the other one."

"No, I didn't figure that for your style. It was too flashy, loud. An AK-47 and gunfire in the middle of a field lit up by search lights?"

He held up a hand, closed his eyes as if praying, and leaned back and said he didn't mess with women, ever. And he certainly would never fold one up in a suitcase. "That's just—wrong. Look at my business—" Construction, restaurants, gambling. "Sure I peddle H, but I have never touched prostitution. I got too much respect for women."

He leaned forward and spoke eloquently to the issue of how women were of a higher spiritual form. "Us guys will fuck anything. Women—they're nobler. Adam and Eve is such bullshit. Eve never reached for the apple. The guy did and then blamed her. Like I said, guys will do anything. Eve's the good one. And anyone who hits a woman is dead." He snapped his fingers twice, as if double-tapping a wife-beater behind the left ear. "Dead. That's my promise." He pointed with his cigarette holder.

If he respected women so much why did he have Cool Athol as one of his security detail, that creep punched the lights out on a Chicago prostitute, redesigning her face.

"He's married to one of my nieces."

I nodded, unaware that my previous comment had been spoken aloud. I guess my headache was getting pretty fucking bad. "So, Coughlins. That's not your outfit?"

"I get kickbacks for it. I put up the initial investment, but I don't party with them. That's Sicko Smith and Pal Cal's idea of a good time."

But I'd seen him on the 8mm film—him and Kim.

"The human lamps—you seen that bit?"

"Oh, yeah. Please. Infantile. They're a couple of arrested adolescents who never grew up." He smiled. "Spoiled rich boys, yacht-club set. They play tennis, for chrissakes. I mean what does a businessman like me really want?"

You mean a gangster. "More?"

"Well, yeah. But we want respect and acceptance." He poured himself another finger of scotch. "We want to be *legitimate*. I remember the signs. So do you. No dogs or—"

"Jews allowed. Yeah. I saw those goddamn signs." As a skinny kid in the early 1940s, joining my father for outings along Balmy Beach, and parts of Toronto East and the lakeshore, I saw them, boy did I see them. "No Jews allowed." We went to the beach anyway. My father would fight them if they tried to remove us.

"I want to shake things up, baby. Eventually, I'm going to leave that entire drug shit behind and make my money in more of the real chips, legit ventures. Like the restaurants and night-clubs—" He pinched his lips together. "You know what Wop means? Without papers. Well, I'm a Canadian citizen. I got my papers. I want in on the club, the action, the legitimate action."

Amen, I wanted to say, amen to that, as the immigrants on Coney's Parachute Jump fell through the sky, buffeted up by lean wires and promises of a better life.

8

irst there was the question about academics, and then the photographs.

I hated asking, but I had to.

I had been listening to jazz, waiting on a phone call from Stana to touch base on her findings, when Mrs. Kerr arrived, sat across from me, her eyes slowly darkening as I told her my recent findings, all about Coughlins, the Gardens, Landover Leeds's murder and the topless photograph of her daughter. She said she didn't believe any of it, of course, not a word, but I didn't believe her—not the way her hands were about to snap the brass clasp off her purse.

When I first took the case I had been led to believe that Sarah was just a studious gal who stayed home nights, applying herself, expanding her intellect, learning Latin outside of school via a correspondence course just for kicks, adding one more language to her mastery of French and Spanish. She was about to be the recipient of an Ontario Scholarship. Now, 98 days since her murder, a different Sarah was emerging. One who was boy crazy at twelve.

"Did she not like herself much?" I told her what Dawn said. Willowy.

"No." Her mother looked away. "She wasn't interested in boys."

"That's not answering my question. Did she not like her

looks?"

"Most girls struggle with their looks."

"Did she go out nights?"

"No."

"Could she have gone out without you knowing it?" Because I know she went out nights. They had lived on the ground floor of an apartment complex. Sarah's bedroom was also her study. "How do you account for the photograph? I'm not trying to hurt you. I want to avenge her murder."

Surely a "school mother," as Dawn put it, a woman who cared about her daughter excelling at academics, would have checked up on her late at night and peered into her bedroom, making sure she was sleeping. It only made sense. Mrs. Kerr had a hovering personality and would have known if Sarah went sometimes AWOL. "Come on, Mrs. Kerr. Level with me."

"I trusted my daughter."

"I know you loved her, but did you trust her? I mean *really* trust her."

The grip tightened. Yes, Mrs. Kerr had noticed that Sarah was missing some nights. They even talked about it, had a terrific row or two, and yet Sarah, to prove her loyalty to her mother, worked harder, got better grades, won more contests.

"Any boyfriends you know of?"

She shook her head.

"An adult boyfriend? *Think*. I think she knew her killer. I think the story she gave about meeting her counselor to discuss her thesis was a lie to cover herself. She went to a rendezvous point with a man she knew. To have sex. He killed her."

Her eyes watered and I handed her a Kleenex, and then the whole box. She was so upset that she was choking as she spoke. Sarah *was* sexually active. Mrs. Kerr nodded, the squeezed handbag now resembling a collapsed lung. Their family doctor had told Mrs. Kerr that her daughter was no longer a virgin. "But I know nothing of any specific man or Coughlins."

"Did you trust Landover Leeds with your daughter?"

"Yes. At the time." Sarah wasn't doing any of the therapy sessions that Mrs. Kerr knew of, and Mr. Leeds was always directing Sarah to new contests to apply to and encouraging her to become a medical doctor. "He believed in her. Or so he said."

"Uh-huh. What about Dawn Stoukas, Laurinda Mays, or Cathy Stabulas? What can you tell me about her relationships with them?"

Dawn was the heavyset gal always trying to get Sarah to wear lipstick and eye shadow, Mrs. Kerr said. She didn't know Laurinda, but Cathy came by the house now and then. When Sarah was younger, Cathy "babysat for me. Especially the nights I went curling. I also shopped at her father's store."

"You knew Cathy—"

"I never liked her father. He was a little too pushy, micromanaging Cathy all the time."

I smiled my lopsided grin. "How often did Cathy see Sarah?"

"Once, twice a week. She was really encouraging her to go to U of T."

They knew each other. Could Cathy have introduced Sarah to Coughlins?

"I told you I know nothing about Coughlins." She dabbed at her eyes with a Kleenex. "And Cathy wasn't that kind of girl. She was a sweetheart to Sarah. Caring. A role model. A real sweetheart."

I wondered if there was anything else she could think of or had in her possession that might help me with this case. She pondered and said no, everything had been turned over to the police. There were no diaries. Nothing.

"The police have everything?"

"More or less." She crumpled up the Kleenex and dropped it on the blotter. Oh, she said, after the police confiscated Sarah's things, Cathy visited one more time and left with a bundle of additional stuff.

"What kind of stuff?"

"Clothes, photos, knick-knacks—I don't know. Stuff the police didn't take."

"Stuff that they missed or didn't take?"

"I never thought of that distinction—"

"Stuff that was hidden?"

"Maybe. I really didn't check. It could have been anything. I just told Cathy to take whatever."

Take whatever. A leather strap or a ball to place in your mouth?

AFTERWARD, I dialed Stana at *The Toronto Telegram.*

"You were supposed to call me yesterday." Her voice wasn't quite as annoyed as she put on.

"I did. I called."

But it was so short, the conversation. I was supposed to call later, to talk longer.

My head ached with the punctuated stringy pops of Black Cat firecrackers. Goddamn Leighton with his clumsy gun-toting sidekick Fortunado. This morning, as I laced up my hard-soled shoes, I lost my balance. The glare of the sun nettled my eyes. Office lights were off, blinds drawn. I was a regular vampire.

"Well, that's a switch. The guy complaining of a headache."

"Yeah. It was pretty good last time," I said. "Not the headache, I mean the—Right?"

"It was sweet."

Sweet? "Yeah."

"You *do* sound *groggy*. What did I tell you about that damn head-butt?"

"I know, I know. I should wear a helmet the next time I get in a street fight—"

That made her laugh and I imagined her shaking her head at what she called "my insouciance." Like I said, I hated playing *Scrabble* with her. "Anything new on the Cathy front?"

"Yes. Landover and Da Silva Mind Control? The Flagstaff

group?"

"Yes?"

"It's an Esalen-type outfit," she said, specializing in helping people find ways to be more present in life. Through relaxation techniques, clients learn how to stay in the moment and discover the deeper truths hidden inside all of us—

"Far out," I said.

"No, really. It's a legitimate outfit. Nothing to do with hypnosis."

"Uh-huh. But you could use it as a cocktail mixer. Throw in some subliminal suggestions, and suddenly women are taking off their clothes—"

"Apparently so," she agreed, "but Da Silva's all right."

"Did you enroll?"

"Shut up."

"What else you got?"

Stana rattled off a short list of highly credible suspects: Leeds, the counselor; Lisa Steinmetz, the friend; Nick Stabulas, the father; Kim Stabulas, the sister.

"Her sister?"

"Why not? She was on that 8mm film. Coughlins. She lied to us. Big time."

I let out a hard whistle. "Yeah—"

"Her dad's still in jail by the way."

"Really?" That was interesting. Smith and Bullard were released on their own recognizance, but nobody posted Stabulas's bail. His friends or associates were letting him cool off. Or, maybe they were afraid of being seen springing him by the Fourth Estate and subsequently getting their photos splashed in the dailies. Maybe they were just vindictive assholes. How high was bail set?

She gave me the figure. It was pretty high for a working man.

"Hmm." I rubbed my tired eyes.

"By the way, Lisa has cleared out."

“I sort of figured on that.”

Stana, under the guise of a public health official, had broken into Lisa’s flat in the Kensington Market. Everything from the pad was gone, except twelve empty bottles of vodka on a small, stained table. The trim on the table’s edges was peeled away and pock-mocked cigarette burns cratered the tabletop.

“Why all these details? Just tell me the story. Get to the point.”

“There *is* a point. She was living in a dive, that’s *the point*.” Fingerprint stains were on the wood trim and smudging up the wall’s switch plates. Thin sheets covered bedroom windows. “I don’t think she had a lot of money. She was desperate for a better life, a life $568,000 could get her.”

Lisa had also been a no-show at the El Mocambo. She was scheduled to work yesterday. No sign of Spinner either.

“They better be careful. Migano doesn’t fuck around. Not with his money.”

“Yeah.” She paused. “And I’m not done. I got one more little bit of info.” She had done some other checking on Leeds: the car crash that killed the nine-year-old girl back in 1942, the crash in which Leeds was driving and McClelland Stuart was a passenger? There was something off about the whole damn thing. She had been going over the original police report and the two follow-up newspaper articles. Things didn’t jibe. Leeds’s statements weren’t consistent and some aspects were too consistent. On the report and in the articles, several details about the victim were too precise: the hat she wore was black with two red stripes; snow tented on both of her shoulders; and the cars she stepped between were big and bulky. But the detail that really mattered: how long was the interval between the girl’s emergence from between the cars and her getting hit, that was sketchy, listed on the police report as a jagged flash of lightning to an interval of two or three seconds in the newspaper reports.

“Mac and Leeds were at a scene of an accident together, Hayden.” Think about it, did this connect in any way with the topless girls appearing before a Speed Graphic camera?

Shit, Smith implicated McClelland in his closing rant at the Gardens earlier yesterday. It was clear that the brain trust didn't like the man who had been broadcasting hockey since 1924, but who had what over whom?

"I think we better talk to McClelland Stuart," I said and dry swallowed a painkiller Abramowitz had given me.

"I think we better," Stana said. "I already got us an appointment."

I TWISTED THE LAMP on the restaurant table away from me. It was a small lamp but the arc's glow cut like a Coast Guard searchlight. I blinked my eyes. The lids and lashes were sticky, bitten by specks of soggy cereal. I better see Dr. A soon.

McClelland Stuart, his apple cheeks puffy, his eyes sore with strain, smiled awkwardly while wiping gravy from the cramped corners of his mouth. He was eating a hot open-face sandwich and was in a hurry. The team and its support staff were readying to board the 11:30 P.M. train to Montreal. It departed in forty-seven minutes.

"I'm glad you took the time to see us," Stana said. "We appreciate it."

"I didn't have much of a choice, did I?" He shrugged, and then whispered in a low adenoidal whine, "It was my own fault." He nodded his head stiffly, the whites of his eyes pronounced like those on a jaunty dog, straining at a leash. His homburg sat next to him. He always removed his hat in the presence of a woman.

"So you know about the car?" McClelland answered our questions, nodding, looking as if he were about to be attacked by a pack of bigger dogs.

Stana adjusted the tablemat across from her, sipped her Coke, eyes dancing like diamond-backed snakes. "Yes. You didn't have much choice, did you?"

Her voice was new to me, jagged, broken. I'm not sure I liked it.

She reached into a purse that had rings for its handles. She slid Photostats from two 1942 newspaper articles toward McClelland. "The stories don't match, Leeds's details are off, out of sync with yours." She shrugged with her eyes. Important details, like how the girl was hit, inconsequential details like the make and design of the two cars she emerged from were too precise. "But as I told you on the phone, nothing has to come of this. Nothing."

"Right." He looked away, at the lamp, my tired face, back to the lamp. I think it hurt his eyes too.

Stana curved in with her shoulders. She wore a black blouse and dark slacks and an orange and black cardigan. It was the closest ensemble she had to 1940s Joan Crawford. She looked tough but still feminine. "It wasn't Leeds driving the car. It was you—"

He wiped the cramped edges of his mouth and his whole being appeared to be leaving the room, like air withering from a crumpling balloon. "How did you find out?"

"I have my sources."

This was the first I had heard of this. Sources, my ass. Gut instincts. She was right about Lisa's lies and maybe Nick and Kim's, and now the Voice of Canada's.

"Let us reset the scene. You were at Old Man Smith's militia with Leeds. It had been a hard session. You had to clean your Enfield or—"

"Climb the rope. I hated climbing the rope."

"Right, climb the rope."

He laughed nervously. "I loved boxing. I could knock people flat, but I hated climbing the goddamn rope."

"So to vent, let off steam, afterward you went to a local pub—"

"I had some drinks," McClelland acknowledged. "Three, four. Maybe more." He reached for his milk and slowly sipped. White waves painted the inside of the glass, and then slid back down as he returned the drink to his plate's side. The gravy on top of his lumpy remains of Texas-style toast hardened like cooling lava.

He hadn't had a drink since that night. But on that night nearly twenty-five years ago, he was on his way to the Gardens to do the evening's broadcast, when a girl flashed out from between two parked cars. "It was like a knife of lightning. She was bent low, chasing something, a ball, a toy, I never found out what—and she just was there, jagged lines in the night—"

Suddenly the car made a sickening double thump as the front end crumpled and the girl got tangled up in the under-carriage. "I'm pretty sure I wasn't drunk. Maybe buzzed, but I was afraid to take a chance, to own up to it."

"Buzzed, drunk, they're the same thing, McClelland," Stana said.

"Yeah, yeah," he acknowledged. At that time, 1942, he had a big endorsement deal with Bee Hive Corn Syrup. Sponsors were unheard of for sportscasters.

So, Leeds, who wasn't driving and only had a beer or two, says to Stuart, let's keep the Voice of Canada safe from scandal, and volunteers to take the fall, telling the police he was the one behind the wheel.

McClelland wiped his chin, his mouth cramping, emotion flashing across his eyes. "How did you find out?"

"That doesn't matter. What matters now is what am I going to do about it?"

"You're not going to run the story? Tell my listeners—"

"Can you imagine your final broadcast from high above the gondola? 'Hello, Canada. In 1942 I, McClelland Stuart, caused the death of a young child because I had been drinking too much—'" She let out a deep sigh. "No. No. I don't see it playing out that way—"

Stana was ruthless in pursuit of a story. She had sold out Sharon, Small Bear, me, and now Stuart. The "truth" was *everything* to her. Dusky cotton candy fuddled my head.

"What do you want?" He couldn't look at either of us.

I wanted him to put his homburg back on and look dignified.

"The truth," she said. "The answer to some questions so that we can get to the missing girl before it's too late."

Who would benefit from Cathy's gone missing? Who was she about to pull the plug on?

"I don't know," McClelland whispered, chin on chest. That night Leeds took the fall. Leeds *was* sober. Two beers, that's all. Under the legal limit.

The glass in the long windows behind us was stained with darting cherubs and splashing water fountains. The contrast in moods was striking. A loudspeaker listed a train number and said, "Boarding now for Montreal, Trois-Rivieres, and Quebec City."

McCelland eyed his homburg, stood, and slipped into his long overcoat with buttons that resembled anchors on a small boat. One of his arms got stuck in a sleeve. He struggled and elbowed on through. He looked like a little kid anxious for recess to start.

"But at what cost, McClelland?" Stana's eyes darted about, landing, holding his gaze, not allowing a furtive glance away.

"What cost?" For years, Leeds collected kickbacks. He got a percentage of all of Stuart's business investments. "Just one percent but it adds up."

"Sure it does," I said, my hands crossed, the pain behind my eyes hammock-shaped clouds, balancing above the horizon line, ready to drop.

"I got him access to the Gardens for his—"

"Photography sessions? Did you know about Coughlins or the photographs?"

"Yes, no. I mean—Leeds told me he was doing therapy there. It made the girls feel important to have their sessions at such a hallowed place, the Gardens."

"Was he doing Tangerine Room treatments there?"

"Tangerine Room?" McClelland looked down at his shoes, pensively. "You mean with the tape recordings and the—"

"—Relaxation exercises."

"Yes." He nodded his head slowly. "He was." Leeds had mentioned performing Tangerine Room activities at the Gardens and removing the girls' inhibitions, making them more confident. McClelland shook his head and played with the lip of his glass. "I wanted to believe him, that he was really helping them, so I chose to believe him, but deep down a voice kept telling me it wasn't right. The girls alone with him—there—"

"Something was creepy about it all—" Stana echoed, closing off his thoughts.

"Right. And because I chose not to mind what was going on, I'm responsible." He sat back down.

"Yes you were," Stana reminded him, her eyes roping him in. "So we're going to make some things right." She nodded. "Right here, right now."

Slowly his head nodded in rhythm with hers. He sat down.

"Leeds was blackmailing you and you let him into your investments. But the primary investment firm you worked with was Bolemac, right? The alleged construction company that was actually a subsidiary of Smith and Bullard?" Stana flipped through her notebook. The curled-over pages resembled a large sand dune.

He pushed his plate farther away and took another sip of milk, longer this time.

"What about the $568,000?" I jumped in. "The money Migano wants me to recover for him?"

"Migano needs it to keep up his end." He put on his homburg, buttoned his overcoat. Smith, Bullard and Migano were investing in land, north of the city. That's what those longitude and latitude lines were all about, south of Bradford in Vaughan, Ontario. Three-hundred and forty acres of land. They're going to build on it: houses, a whole city or suburb.

I let out a sharp whistle and played with the brim of my pork-pie. "That's a lot of land."

"A new housing development. It'll be worth a fortune."

That's where Sarah was killed, 98 days ago. On that expanse of land and the abandoned log cabins.

This business arrangement between Migano on one end and Smith on the other was supposed to be pretty much evenly divided, but Migano's now short and Smith wants to take on more of the principal, a bigger percentage for bigger profits.

"Did Leeds steal the money? The $568,000?"

"Yes. Probably with the help of Steinmetz and Terrien." He stood up. "I got to go. The train—"

"For who? Who did Leeds steal for? Smith?"

"Migano most likely." McClelland blinked his eyes. "He was the one short." You can check the records at City Hall. By the end of this month Migano was supposed to meet his end, otherwise Smith was going to buy up the open shares and the land balance would no longer be equal between them. "Migano stole it from the Gardens."

"He tells the story differently," I said. "He says someone, Davis, stole it. It was Babe's money, his part of the Bolemac arrangement. Kept in a Gardens wall safe."

"Davis." Stuart laughed. Davis was a gambler, a womanizer, but he was no criminal. "A liar, but no criminal. Migano stole the money. I'm pretty sure."

"That's Smith's story?" Stana said.

"Yes."

"Told over a game of golf at the links or hanging with his cronies knocking back Molsons?"

"He's not my friend." A trace of resentment glided behind McClelland's words. "We don't socialize. It's business." The effervescent pop to his world was gone. "I got to go." He was itching to catch his train.

"Well, I don't believe Smith's story," Stana said. "I don't trust that chauvinist pig."

"But let's say Stuart's version of the events is right—for argument's sake, Stana. That makes Leeds the middleman. He collected the money from Terrien and Steinmetz to hand over to Migano. And then he got *got*."

Someone's doing a double-cross. Who? Smith? Migano himself? And what about the woman with the heavy feet running away, the one I saw in slants of rain and conical light, the one known simply as Starzz? "That's Starzz with two z's, by the way, McClelland."

They announced boarding for Montreal again.

"I don't know Starzz," McClelland said. "Never heard of her." He stood up.

"Oh, come on. You're telling me you've never been to Coughlins, you've never—"

"I never go. I never drink anymore, either." He looked at his watch. It was a Lucerne with a Leafs crest emblazoned inside the crystal. "I better get going. You're not covering the game tomorrow night, Miss Younger?"

"No, I have a bigger story to follow."

He smiled awkwardly, looking a little nonplussed. For McClelland Stuart hockey was his escape, nothing was bigger. Hockey was Canada. "Davis had a thing for Starzz, or so I hear. You might ask him about her."

I nodded.

He glanced down at his check, adding up the amount, calculating the tip.

I took the slip from him and agreed to pay for it. It was the least I could do.

He appeared pleased, his eyes shiny coins. I had heard that he was a very frugal fella and there were many jokes at his expense. "Thanks," he said. "Well, keep your stick on the ice."

I laughed out of courtesy, his farewell greeting not quite as bouncy as at our earlier meeting. Traces of sad resignation filled in the edges of his words like a heavy, black curtain.

"The story of that night, 1942, remains with *us*," Stana promised. "Buried."

He nodded ever so slightly, eyes brimming. "There's one other thing," he said.

Stana and I leaned closer.

"There was a third person in that car." He wiped his chin and let out a short sigh, like air still leaking out of that withering balloon. "Nick Stabulas."

9

Nick wasn't too happy to see me. He didn't even get up to shake my hand. He was lying on his cot, still waiting to be bailed out, arms folded under his heavy head. He failed to answer question after question with anything but a perfunctory grunt or a disengaged nod of no, no, and more no's. What does Cathy's drawer of "toys" have to do with the nude photographs? Did Cathy know Laurinda and Dawn? Did you know them? What was your relationship with Leeds? How well did you know Sarah? She visited with Cathy, the grocery, your home. What was the connection between your daughter and Sarah? Nick's upper lip curled tighter under his front teeth, and I kept firing away, his eyes resembling dark lentils.

The jail cell was in the very old part of the building. The floors were thin slats of dirty hardwood. Concrete walls were chipped and scored and pocked. It had rained a lot the last couple of days and stains the shape of the Great Lakes ran along the wall closest to the outside. The room smelled of mildew and piss.

"This isn't about me. Find the girl." Nick's "you understand" was gone, so was the lilt. His argot now mirrored the streets of Toronto rather than the fields of Macedonia.

"Oh, so you quit acting. That's nice." I was trying to nudge him, push him to talk, my face taking on its lopsided lupine grin.

Beyond the high cell window, the sky was dark gray and the jail bars bounced shadowed piping across the lower end of his bed.

"Excuse me?"

"The Old World accent, the down-home charm. It's missing." In its place was a flat series of kidney punches. "You're no longer the male Anna Magnani, you understand, attempting to speak English, you understand."

He didn't like that too much. His bushy eyebrows knitted together, like a heavy snake waiting in tall grass.

"The question in this case? Why was Cathy kidnapped or killed? She knows something. What? And who's at risk? Maybe Cathy's disappearance is some kind of payback, payback against you—and maybe her disappearance has something to do with a girl found dead in a suitcase—"

"What?" He propped up on his elbows, a part of a leg crossed over a raised knee. "Smith's the one you want to find—he's the one responsible."

"What can you tell me about Sarah?"

He sighed and shrugged, his eyebrows a heavy machete. "She was a mousy kind of girl. Never said much."

"Uh-huh. It's not Smith, asshole. It's *you who's responsible.* I saw the way you hit Kim." He had no respect for women. And now McClelland has connected Nick to the car accident. You know Leeds. Leeds took photos of underage girls. Had them under hypnosis. "Maybe someone's punishing Cathy for something you did, I don't know, maybe something involving underage girls?"

"That's a lot of somethings. Hypnosis, really?"

"Sarah was only fourteen when her photo was taken, fucko."

He got off the bed and stood by my feet.

"Don't take a swing at me, Nick. I'm not Smith." I ground a fist into a palm. "Fifty-five stitches." I pointed at my face. I knew my way around.

He exhaled sharply, turned his back, and walked to the jail window. You couldn't see a thing but sky. "I didn't take any photos," he mumbled.

"You like licorice—" I said. It wasn't a question.

"What?"

"Just connecting some dots, Nick. Loose ends, you understand?"

"You are a smart-ass."

I repeated what I learned from McClelland, how Nick was a passenger in the car the night the nine-year-old got killed and I knew of the hold Leeds had over the Voice of Canada, and wondered what shared hold did Nick have—he too must have cashed in.

"I didn't cash in. I didn't—" He couldn't. Nick loved hockey. It was his way into the "Canadian cultural mosaic."

"Where did you learn that phrase?"

He said nothing.

"Uh-huh. What can you tell me about Dawn Stoukas or Laurinda Mays? They described a burly fella, who liked licorice—"

"Don't know them."

"They were friends of Landover Leeds—" Look, Landover got a hold of something and used it as leverage on McClelland, forcing his way into the Gardens. Leeds started taking dirty pictures of girls, under-aged, and I think you were in on it, Nick, a couple of Old Man's Militia pals. "You were there during the photo shoots. You were Leeds's second."

"That's ridiculous." He turned from the window, his face a nasty vicious leer. His third face could hurt a whole family.

"And that fight at the Gardens? That was a total phony." Why else would Smith call you a hypocrite? "Because he knew you had something on McClelland." Laurinda and Dawn had vague recollections, too, of a second person being present at their shoots. I had thought it was Smith. "But it was you, big man." They describe the person as bulky, but because of the mind control, they can't put a face to the form. "How's your English accent, guv'ner?"

"That's bullshit."

"Nick, you were so worried about them making you that you needed to make with a scene, a diversion, and suddenly *la voila* you make with the fancy roll across a desk and a half-ass fist fight that was about as real as a Whipper Billy Watson wrestling match at the Gardens."

"Fuck you. Guard!" His voice was flat and narrow. "Get this asshole out of here."

"Are you blackmailing Stuart? You were in the car the night of the accident. You are, aren't you? That's how you're staying afloat—you told me about the competition, Dominion's grocery chain, the big retailers, wiping you out—"

The guards escorted me from his cell.

On my exit, I asked if I could bring him anything next time. "Red licorice? Black? Cherry Nibs, or uh Goodies?"

"You take chances," he said.

"Goodies it is," I said. "Cheers."

WHEN I WALKED INTO KIM'S GROCERY Kim was behind the counter. That surprised me. Stana was surprised too. She gave me a look of genuine amusement, her mouth parting slightly, eyes brightening.

Ninety-nine days since I found the girl in the suitcase. Was I any closer to finding Cathy?

Stana and I hadn't shared much in the car ride over from the Don Jail. I was annoyed with how she treated such a dignified man like McClelland Stuart. Maybe I'm a little soft.

Maybe Kim's a little soft too. I knew she was quite a wheel at Ogilvie and Beggert and that she and her father had had a falling out when she was a teenager, and yet here she was, paying penance, manning the store, a pencil behind her ear, dark hair pulled back in a ponytail.

"Nick's still in jail, huh?" I said.

"He didn't want my money." Kim glanced away. A thin pulse

flashed along her jawline.

The pain was palpable. Kim was the neglected bad girl, the lost, forgotten daughter.

Sun, falling, filtered through the plate-glass window behind her, leaving a box of shadow in front of the counter. The counter shimmered with faint stains from past coffee cups and pop bottles.

Stana bit her upper lip. "I'm sorry," she said sincerely. "Busy?"

"Not really." With the children of Macedonian immigrants moving to the suburbs, neighborhood mom-and-pop stores like this one, she said, were suffering. I smiled slightly, having said something similar to her recalcitrant father just minutes ago. "Sure there are a few customers," and they kept her father barely afloat, "but all those damn discount stores selling canned and boxed goods at a fraction of the cost—sometimes taking a loss just to squeeze us out."

"Fuck the big chains," I said.

Old World loyalty didn't go very far, Kim noted. Some baboes, shawled and shuffling, tugging their portable pull carts on wheels, buy two- to three-days' worth of milk, bread, and the evening paper, but that was about all the business she had to handle. And of course there were the kids, buying candy or hockey cards or comic books. They were always polite.

She shrugged and straightened the three major dailies on the blue shelves behind her. The comics on the twirling pencil-lined rack were all leaning forward, the tops yellowed.

I picked up the afternoon editions of Stana's competitors.

The latest spin from Smith's camp was printed in the *Star*. This was all a misunderstanding, the Leafs CEO had said, his finger wagging in a medium close-up shot. These are two unrelated events that unfortunately appear connected. Lucky for all of us, Smitty dropped Pal Cal's apples and oranges refrain.

Smith reassured the public that he was innocent of all malfeasance and in a few days the real story would come to light.

This whole epic exaggeration was but the concocted petty results of an overzealous female reporter trying to make a splash in a male world and an ex-hockey player with an ax to grind against the organization that let him go for moral turpitude.

"Wow," I said, holding the folded paper in my hands. "There he goes again with the big words. I'm waiting for him to call the whole thing *lurid*."

Stana pointed a lean finger about three paragraphs down in the next column.

"Oh, well, there you go. Says right here: 'Lurid coverage. Yellow journalism at its finest.'"

The paper further reported what we already knew: Smith and Bullard were out on their own recognizance; Stabulas was still in the holding tank, proud and pouting.

I rubbed the edges of my forehead where my hat rested. My eyes weren't as sore as when we had met McClelland, but I was hiding in the perforated shadows, away from the sun. I tapped the papers on the edge of the countertop, next to the Beech-Nut chewing gum and Tums.

"Where's your sister?" Stana's eyes narrowed on Kim.

"No idea."

"I think you do. She's been in contact with you, hasn't she? You're too calm for someone whose sister is missing—"

Stana was all instincts. Maybe she should put on a homburg and learn a little dignity.

"Maybe I just don't like her that much? Ever think of that? Daddy's girl. Love of his life." Kim rubbed her chin.

I reached for and held it. "Don't play the hard-boiled dame. It doesn't fit you." I knew that under the mask of smoldering eyes was a sensitive, vulnerable woman. I let go her chin and she looked away, eyes watering. She wasn't wearing perfume, I couldn't smell Chanel, not a thing.

"I swear I know nothing of her disappearance."

"Lisa Steinmetz, then," Stana said. "It must be her. She and

Spinner."

I snapped my fingers. "Of course." Was Cathy involved in the missing money? Did she help Lisa and Spinner lift it from the Gardens' vaults? Did she abscond with it? Was she involved in the double-cross? Maybe she was going to head out west with them.

Two young boys, nine and seven probably, came in wearing heavy spring jackets and toques, wanting milk and popcorn in a box. A line drawing of a jolly circus elephant was on the box cover looking like it enjoyed popcorn too. The younger kid with a brighter toque bought two packs of hockey cards. "Hey—" He turned to me. "Aren't you?"

"I used to be," I said.

The kids left and a bell faintly rang.

The street outside looked like a hard disc. I rubbed my chin. "Why did you lie to us, Kim? About Coughlins. You've been there."

She played with her necklace, touched her collarbones, and smiled wanly. Sure she'd gone a few times, as a guest of Babe Migano's, but she didn't want Ogilvie and Beggert to know about it. Those visits were a part of a wilder past and now that she was a fast-rising star in real estate such associations could ruin her reputation and destroy her chance to climb into upper management. "That's why. Maybe my sister just wanted to get away. I know I wanted to. Christ, my father's not an easy man. Look, there was never a ransom note, nothing threatening."

"Too much has happened since then," I said. "Way too much. This whole thing feels threatening and I'm scared of losing her, like I lost another one 99 days ago."

Look, I told her, there had been a man murdered in his office chair; an unveiling of an escort service, nude photographs, and the sexual exploitation of underage girls; a movie camera in Smith's office; and a land grab involving the Greater Toronto Area's number-one mobster, Babe Migano; and a possible tie in with the Sarah Kerr killing. "Tell me about that relationship. I hear that your sister saw Sarah once or twice a week—"

"Yeah." Not much more to tell than that. Cathy was a mentor for the girl, proofed some of her award-winning essays, encouraged her to study pre-med at U of T, and gave the girl money every once in a while so she wouldn't have to work at Becker's to support her mom. Sarah was all about her studies—

"Is that what she was all about? I hear she was boy crazy at twelve. Never quite happy in her willowy body, but wanting to explore pleasure."

"I never saw that. Never. She was—"

"Mousy?" *That's what Nick said and I didn't believe him.*

"No. I wouldn't call her mousy. She was focused on school, but reserved in other ways."

"I think she might have also been a guest at Coughlins. A regular. You ever seen her there?"

"No."

"Your own sister?"

"No."

I rubbed the corners of my mouth and gave a lopsided grin, my lupine look. "What was your role at Coughlins?"

"Role?"

"You're on the film—"

"I told you, I went as a guest of Mr. Migano's. He asked me on a date. I'm alright looking, you know."

"Uh-huh. You'll forgive me if I don't quite believe you. I mean you are good-looking—"

"Thank you."

"However, before you said, and I quote, that you suspected Coughlins was a pizza joint and Bolemac an expensive brand of Tupperware—"

"Very expensive," Stana jumped in. "I checked with City Hall. Government lot line numbers. You represent Bolemac. You've helped Migano buy land in Vaughan. It's your name under the

Ogilvie and Beggert banner."

"It was a business transaction."

"Uh-huh."

"Bolemac has done major construction at the Gardens, at Smiths, and at your apartment, Miss Stabulas, in the North End. You're up to this to your dark eyes." Stana pushed against the edge of the counter.

"Uh-huh," Kim said, throwing my self-reliant refrain right back at us.

"Very good," I said. "That was good. Nice intonation. Rhythm."

The bell dinged and an old woman with a shawl on her shoulders, a cart by her left hand, and stockings wrinkled at the ankles, asked if there were any day-old donuts she could take home. There were: three for the price of one. Kim bundled them together in wax paper and placed them in a bag. The woman squeezed some fruit and bread and paid for the donuts and left.

I wondered why'd she have the cart with her if all she was getting were donuts? Some people have strange rituals or habits that can't be forgotten. It's another kind of cheap amusement I guess. Like me during my playing days, with all my damn superstitions: left skate and left glove first, and always the last player on the ice, the last to tap Bower's goalie pads before the opening faceoff, and the last to head into the dressing room for intermission. Cheap amusements.

"You and Migano look cozy on the film." I reminded her of the couch in Smith's office and Migano nestled by her feet.

"I help with his business interests and assets—"

"That's all—?"

"That's my business."

"What was Leeds to the family?"

"Leeds, the counselor?" She looked up at the tin ceiling. It was covered with riveted bumps. One of the tiles was loose and hung down like a flag. "I told you about him. A quack."

"Yeah, a quack, but—" Stana reached into her purse, the one with the rings for handles that resembled ten-pound weights on a barbell. She pulled out the photograph, Cathy nude, the eyes distant and sad.

Kim winced at the photograph as if she were looking at a Weegee crime scene photograph of a fallen gangster covered in a police sheet. "How'd you get this?"

"Lisa Steinmetz. She said it was sent to her in the mail."

Kim bit the inside of her lip. "Cathy's like twenty here. She looks stoned. Out of it."

I pushed back the porkpie, and then dropped my hands to my hips. "And she may have been hypnotized or under some subliminal spell—"

"Subliminal?"

"You ever hear of Leeds's Tangerine Room?"

"And that bogus relaxation shit? I never—volunteered—" She paused and her face lightened, the eyes were less heavy. "Yeah—control." She nodded and pressed her lips together. "But why?"

"Why, indeed," I said.

Nick knew Leeds. Did Leeds have a family connection?

Kim traced a small shimmer ring on the counter in front of her. The shadow carpet was gone. The sky outside: dark. The pavement: a wet lake. "Okay. I saw him now and then." At Christmas he'd give the girls dolls or clothes. "Always brought dad a fruitcake." She never liked the guy. A total phony. A hedonist. For him, the good life was wine, a good-looking woman, and a fast car. "I overheard him telling dad about the girls he balled or fucked in the ass. The pig."

Men are pigs.

"What about your sister? Did she like the cat?"

"Cathy trusted him." She was seeing him for therapy and career guidance, but Kim never knew about the photographs. "He took them, the photos?"

I nodded. And somebody else was witness to it, another

man. Dawn hinted there was a second man behind the camera on occasion.

"Not my father. Is that what you're intimating—"

"Is that what you thought I was intimating? I'm curious. Why did you think that?"

She pushed off from the counter and bit her lower lip. "I didn't think that. It's just—" She paused and played with a raised clavicle.

I looked away at the long row of canned goods along a far wall. Some of the goods had fly matter kissing their lids.

Cathy and her father kept secrets from Kim. The two of them went to hockey games together, listened to it on radio in the back alcove, shared dinners, and sometimes, after therapy sessions, they disappeared alone, on the town, restaurants, or so they said, for daddy-daughter quality time. "I never knew what they did. We never talked about it."

"Are you saying it's possible?"

"What? That my dad's a perv, that he took naked pictures of his own daughter or helped someone else take them? I—I—don't know. I don't know the man." She hit the counter with a fist and then slammed it again and again before crying into her shoulder. "He never wanted me. It was Cathy he loved—" Kim's mouth dribbled with tears. Stana motioned me away while consoling Kim, hugging her to her shoulders.

I asked if I could look around, see what I might dig up.

Neither of them heard me. They continued talking quietly, while I moved to the back of the store. Nick was involved. I was sure of it. The big rhubarb at the Gardens the other day, what with his tumbling dice roll across the desk and random punches and all, had an overdetermined artifice to it. It was all too fucking orchestrated for the reporters.

I shook my head, staring into the hardwood floors, searching for answers in the swirling grooves of wood grain. The floor needed to be refinished. Bubble gum was stuck in some of the knotted wood.

In back was a little room separated from the main space by a green curtain on a small white curtain rod. I pushed the curtain back, surveying the room for photographic equipment. There wasn't any.

There was however a stack of *Guns & Ammo* magazines against a small desk; a cot pushed up against cinder blocks with two flat pillows that needed to be punched up; a hot plate surrounded with several empty pea-soup cans, an ashtray packed with a pyre of ashen cigarettes; Bee Hive hockey photos and Export "A" calendars on the wall; and an old Crosley radio. I turned it on. The Leafs were already down 1-0. Habs forward Claude Provost, whom I admired and modeled my own game after, had scored. And the Leafs appeared tired, McClelland said.

We were all tired. I turned the radio down.

Shit, I figured the Leafs would have a little more giddy-up. Come on. Following game one, Montreal coach Toe Blake had said, "We expect to win four games, any four. But there's no doubt about it, the Leafs are not playing like they did last year." That should be bulletin board material, man. I shook my head and wished I could still lace them up for the blue and white.

Across from the radio was an openly displayed toilet. The porcelain was rust-stained with age. On the toilet's tank was a stack of books, mainly murder mysteries. A black pipe ran next to the toilet, up on through to the ceiling. The ceiling was exposed too—a drop hadn't been put in. Slats of wood, copper water pipes, and electrical lines bracketed the beams hovering above me, separating this room and space from the living space above.

Next to the Crosley was a small array of allsorts candy, an English blend made of sugar, coconut, fruit flavorings, gelatin, and of course aniseed jelly licorice. Square pieces, blocky layers, were stacked three high. Hard dotted nubs stood alone. Two pieces that resembled very small sidewall tires with fat axles in their centers had bites taken out of them. I called Lambertino's home. "Hey, Sal, I can't talk long. Do me a favor." I asked him to check into the bank accounts of Nick, Kim, and Cathy Stabulas.

If any of them were doing anything underhanded or were involved in blackmail kickbacks or porn rackets their accounts would show it. I couldn't access that info. He could. "Just a hunch." I rolled a piece of licorice between my fingers. "A pretty big hunch. I want to see if certain deposits in a high-dollar range have been made." I told him it had to do with one girl gone missing, the murder of another girl 99 days ago, and dirty pictures of underage girls and the Voice of Canada possibly being blackmailed. Oh, and licorice.

"Licorice, huh?"

"Yeah. And what can you tell me about the connection between Cathy and Sarah, the murdered girl? They were friends. Any evidence turn up when you collected stuff from the Kerr apartment?"

"I'll check the files in the basement—"

Leeds had a cohort. I was pretty sure it was Nick, but check the money, always follow the money. He swore at me and said he would and now could I please go away, he's watching the fucking hockey game. Some Leafs fan I was. "Sure, sure," I said and hung up.

Stana and Kim were quietly connecting in the next room. She was talking about neglect and feeling invisible and my head was suddenly pounding so I shut off the lights in the alcove, and lay back on the cot, fighting a shake of dizziness, and listened to the game. Ronnie Ellis was flying. So was Big M, but the rest of the club was plodding, as if they needed to sharpen the blades of their skates. Béliveau scored with about a minute to go in the period, damn him, and it was now 2-0.

In my time with the Leafs, I played a bruising style, hard checking. I didn't worry much about getting on the sheet. I averaged about 16-17 goals a year. My main objective was to stop the other guy from scoring and offer up opportunities for my guys to counterpunch. I was a reactive player. I didn't create on the ice so much as provide the time and space for other guys to create.

Damn, I missed it.

Béliveau. Now there was an innovator, a jazz improvisation guy, who constantly created new riffs with his easy-going skating style and smooth hands around the net. He was the deal. And could he pass the puck. Classy and cool like a John Coltrane tenor sax solo.

People always say there's a rivalry between the two cities, the solitudes of Canada: the English Protestant Toronto versus the French Catholic Montreal. That divide does exist, I guess, but I always respected Montreal, their freewheeling style, and how the entire province of Quebec was behind them. The Habs were a subset of the area's religious theology and mythology. And I'd like to think they respected us, the tight checking, center-man floating back, clogging up the middle style of play we harnessed. We were a thrifty and frugal bunch—very English.

The period was over and McClelland promised plenty of fight for the third.

Plenty of fight? Really?

The man with the homburg was a pioneer for the sport, a potential Hall of Famer in the Builders category, and I don't know, I still felt sad over how Stana and I treated him at the Via Rail restaurant. His eyes in that meeting were reduced to little coins and all of the feisty jocularity was gone. To have killed a child is a terrible thing, to live with the guilt every day, and our discussion did not release him of that pain. Instead it made it more pronounced and maybe that's why tonight, he too sounded tired, his promise of "plenty of fight" a mere pipe dream for himself and the club.

You never give up a goal in the last minute of a period and climb back into a game. It's a deal breaker, an unwritten rule from the hockey gods. And you never get over the death of a child. That's just an unwritten rule of life.

The darkness and smell of forgotten soup comforted me, but there was a veil of light, a thin shaft limning my shirt and part of my face. I lay there listening, the voices in the next room, and McClelland's over the radio, his adenoidal timbre giving us all a quick moment-to-moment, tape-to-tape reality that was as reassuring as the hurt that follows love lost.

But the light and its thin lines. I propped up on my elbows and moved in the direction of it. I couldn't reach the main line. It was lilting through the ceiling. I unfolded a metal chair slanted by the stack of magazines and climbed on it, my head filling with dizzy cotton.

I pulled at a piece of wood. It was loose, stuck in place with spots of Silly Putty. I pulled harder. Above me was another bathroom. Of course, the black pipe connected the two—simple plumbing design 101. From the chair, and the open space of missing wood, I could make out the edging of a shower stall against the far wall. Because the light was on in the bathroom above me, I could see the glass doors, and the towels with yellow trim hanging on a rack. From my space I could probably see a woman from her knees to her shoulders—that would be clearly visible.

Cramped and alone in the hidden shadows below, I could see into the shower stall.

10

My head was a black mass of pain behind my eyes. The painkillers were doing next to nothing for me, but I couldn't visit Abramowitz, not yet, no time, so I went skating as a kind of relief, a reset button to clear my head of its concrete clutter.

I enjoy skating, especially corner crossovers as one skate cuts over the other, shaving the curve close, and then tearing back up ice. I usually skate at the Gardens three mornings a week, 6 A.M. I love the snick-snick of my blades, the cool air on my face, and the openness of a white sheet before me, a sense of the infinite within the finite.

Lefty, the Zamboni driver, lets me in—seven years of signing hockey sticks for the cat built me up some goodwill—and nobody knows about the perk but us, but today, after firing off several rounds at the gun range under the police station on Bay, I was skating at a more routine 10 A.M. pace. Smith wasn't here to bawl me out as the Leafs had decided not to return home after Thursday's loss.

Too many distractions, Coach Farrell said to Bledsoe. The club was scrimmaging in Peterborough, Ontario, 85 miles northeast of the city, and they would not be returning until late tomorrow afternoon.

Before lacing up, I called Migano, explaining how I wasn't moving forward on the Davis front. First, he was in Montreal for a game and now he was holed up in Peterborough. I had work to do in Toronto.

"Priorities, Mr. Fuller?" His voice purred like a European car.

I had to find the girl, the one I hoped was in Toronto and still *alive.*

"I get that, but what am I paying you for?" A good-natured confidence permeated his words.

"Nothing apparently."

He laughed at my candor.

Then I told him what McClelland Stuart shared yesterday about the missing $568,000 and who stole the money from whom.

"That's twisted, Hayden. McClelland should just stick to calling hockey games and paying off his gambling debts."

"*He* owes at Coughlins?"

"Do Canadians love donuts? Yeah, he loves the wheel, and don't let him tell you differently, capisce? Always drinks a glass of milk. No booze. Bets black. Anyway, I never stole the money. It was grifted from me, or if you like the Bolemac Corporation, and I'm the Bolemac Corporation."

"You and Smith," I corrected.

"Smith? I'm the head kingpin. Smith?—he's an auxiliary member, if that. Get on Spinner and Steinmetz." He thought they were holed up on King Street near the waterfront. Some associates had seen them at a local A&P. "Get their story. When you find them, get me."

I didn't like the sound of that. I get them, and then what? Steinmetz and Terrien will get got that's what. "Associates? Can you elaborate?"

"You wouldn't want to know or if I told you, you wouldn't believe me. Legit guys. Politicos. Made guys in the non-Italian world, if you know what I mean."

I rubbed the edges of my mouth. "I'll track Davis after tomorrow night's game—"

"You do that."

I skated for another twenty minutes, trying to clear my head of Babe and his indirect threats and Cathy's disappearance and my sinking feeling that her own father was involved and killed her to cover up his twisted sexual preferences. Black licorice, and now the blackness behind my eyes was a light gray.

I skated and skated, seeking that space between conscious thought and involuntary action, the quiet zone of absolute stillness where nothing mattered and I was just mindlessly doing, no longer analyzing or fretting about what was to come next, but skating through pockets of silence.

Then I grabbed a bucket of pucks and my stick and skated to the slot and fired shot after shot: number-one and number-three hole, top shelf: right and left. It was a rhythm, the twine denting, me leaning on the lower part of the stick, gutting out leverage, the stick torquing with each quick wrist shot, faster, faster. I was doing pretty good. A few crossbars and the odd shot high over the net, but I was landing some beauties just under the bar.

I gathered up the pucks and moved from the slot to the left circle, and then the right circle. Same rhythm, same leverage, same dented twine. I was in a flow, the pockets of silence now filling me with grace. A few more pucks sailed over the net, a few more rattled the posts, but I was hitting my spots about seventy-five percent of the time. Flow. It was in me; I was in it.

I sighed, breathing in the Gardens air, and gathered up the pucks one final time and placed the bucket and my stick back in the penalty box, and then skated and skated and skated, pushing away Cathy and Babe and Nick. And the cool blue of the lines, the sharp checkered red of center, and the various circles, some filled in, others not, the boundaries of a game, giving everything a kind of order, and my heart, my strides, were in step, beat, step, beat, with those structures, aligned, and I felt a connectedness to the game, to the past, to this moment, to this time.

I skated with that feeling of assurance, trying to hold onto it, while pushing away an awareness of its very existence and suddenly all the doubt and despair spinning like dirty cotton candy webbed into my conscious space, and once you become aware of the freedom begot of stillness you allow it to be taken away from you by the penal colony of doubt, and those pockets of silence are gone and you have to find them all over again, the next time out, the next crossover, the next breath of air on the ice. And you *do* find stillness. You find it again and again and again.

I needed to find it now.

Cathy's father.

God damn him.

"Hey, superstar! Can we talk?"

It was Sal Lambertino, his voice a no-nonsense slap like a puck whapping around the glass.

I skated over to the boards, leaning in by the players' bench, my gloves slightly sliding down my hands.

"You could still play, couldn't you?" Sal tugged and massaged at the fenced edges of his Hemingway beard. "I saw you going top shelf. Pretty good."

"Thanks." I was pretty sure I could lace them up, even with a year away from the game, but unless Montreal called me I wasn't suiting up for anyone. I didn't respect anybody else. I had it too good for seven years. Why would I want to play for the Rangers?

"Maybe if the Leafs get new management you'll be back in blue and white?"

"Maybe." I laughed. "Any word on Smith?" I blew air between my lips and wiped sweat from my forehead.

"No. He was last seen at some charity event for Toronto's Sick Kids hospital."

"Swell. Nick?"

His account was dirty: $150-deposits a month, regularly, going back at least ten years.

"I knew it. Stuart. He's blackmailing Stuart."

"Leeds's account, the same story. I checked on that one too."

I let out a sharp whistle. Lefty and his Zamboni were now chugging up center ice, leaving a fresh squeegee streak that made the Gardens' overhead lights gleam against the ice like new china plates.

"Licorice? That was your clue, huh?"

"Well, yeah—"

"Well, I'll be damned."

"I think Nick was also present during some of the smokers at the Gardens. I think he was behind the camera."

"Probably. But I tell you, Smith's going to walk." The Leafs legal team is already covering up the story, Sal said, pushing back his stop sign of a hat. "And word on the street is that you guys—Stana and you—exaggerated the facts for your own agendas."

"Bull fucking shit."

"That's poetry. I like that. Bull fucking shit. Nice. And get this, the Old Man is going to take back temporary control of the club until the dust settles."

Not a bad idea. The Old Man has integrity, a leader who can be trusted. He might be in his mid-seventies, but he's mentally sharp and physically active. According to the paper, he plays mixed doubles every day for an hour. "I think Nick's a sick fuck and I think he's behind his daughter's disappearance."

"Blackmail's one thing, but that's something else." Sal looked down at the cuff of his police jacket. One of the buttons was missing. "How the fuck did that happen?" He held up his arm and studied the cuff more intently.

"I think Nick made Cathy pose nude. I think—will you stop looking at your fucking cuffs—"

"I'm sorry. I'm listening."

"Next you'll be picking your teeth with a toothpick—"

"I said I was sorry. Now don't get nasty. I mean picking your teeth in front of someone, that's gauche—and to suggest that I would ever do such a thing is just plain nasty—" He smiled.

"Sal, fathers aren't supposed to—"

"Incest?"

"Do I need to draw you a damn picture? Yes." I wiped the pain from my eyes. Suddenly I couldn't breathe. I bent at the waist, trying to clear my lungs.

Now it was Lambertino's turn to blow air through his lower lip. He removed his hat and scratched his sandy-haired head—it contrasted strangely with the gray of his Hemingway beard. "Wow. If that's true—" He scratched his head again. "I still need evidence—"

Men are pigs. "That's what Cathy wrote in her journal."

"Tell me something I don't already know."

"I think Nick raped her." I blinked my sore eyes. "And I think Nick may have killed Cathy. She was going to talk, tell her story to Stana. You didn't see Nick in the Don Jail. I did. A totally different cat. Brutal, all the Old World sheen was gone. The humility topos bit. Gone."

Chase & Sanborn. The coffee ad? The spanking ad?—Cathy wrote about it in her Big Chief tablet. Those were cries for help.

"Lots of inferences. No facts." He shrugged and reached inside his breast pocket, pulling out three or four folded photographs. "Found these in the case file."

It was Cathy inside the log cabin, the one out in Vaughan where Sarah was killed, 100 days ago. I recognized the candles on the table, the bunk beds, the threadbare bedroll, the dented carpet, and the stovetop fireplace. She was smiling, her head slightly tilted. Sarah was in another photo, standing by the wall, looking out the window as the tall grass bent with wind.

"They were out there together. They both knew this place before she was killed there," I said.

"Yes. Migano owns the land, but he said he thought the cabins were abandoned." Sal shrugged. "He knows nothing about anybody visiting out there."

"A Coughlins rendezvous point?"

"Maybe?" He rubbed his beard. "Migano said the cabins

would be plowed under soon as the land's converted into a new subdivision."

I don't know why I didn't tell Sal about the little shafts of light emanating from the shower stall above Nick's grocery store *office*. "So what's next? We talk to Nick?"

"If we can find him. Someone paid his bail. And he's missing."

"If he killed Cathy, I'm going to kill him," I said.

"I didn't hear that." Sal's eyes creased.

I didn't know what had come over me. I was no vigilante. I hadn't even fired a gun. Okay, at a target range two, three times a week, but never at an actual person, *except that time out at the cabin and all I did was kill a mannequin and hit a car radiator and make it hiss. And then we found the girl in a suitcase.*

Last night I dreamed I was in a suitcase. It was roomy, I could breathe and the air smelled of a pungent, sickly sweet odor, naphthalene, and I realized I was a dying moth, chewing on the suitcase's lining.

And somewhere outside my dad was laughing.

Firing pucks at a net. That's what I'm good at.

"Got one more little bit of information for you, pal—" Landover Leeds was killed with his own gun.

"His own gun? This is Canada—we have gun control laws. Why did he have his own gun?"

"Who knows? It was registered and everything. Kept it locked in a box in a drawer in his office. How did it get out of the box and he get plugged? You got me." His eyes squinted.

Jesus Christ.

Maybe Nick had something to do with Leeds and the photographs, Sal conceded. And he was probably blackmailing Stuart, but the incest angle and murder. That wouldn't hold up in a court of law without more evidence.

"I'll get the evidence," I said.

—

WHILE NOSHING A QUICK LUNCH (hot dog with cherry peppers, pickles, green olives, and mustard from a street vendor on Spadina), I called Stana from a phone booth to catch her up to speed. It was cold in Toronto, and I tugged at my jacket collar. I told her that Nick was now missing too, and I had a lot of other info to share, but I didn't want to talk over a phone. Could we meet in my office, 45 minutes? She said I was getting paranoid. Nobody was wiretapping us. She was working on a rewrite. Typewriters clacked in the background. She wanted takeout: egg rolls and moo goo gai pan. Forty-five minutes.

"Sure," I said.

Unfortunately, Stana said, Nick Stabulas was *not* the occasional ogler at Landover Leeds's Speed Graphic sessions. At least not with these two models. Laurinda and Dawn didn't recognize Nick's photograph, but Stana was positive that if we could remove the girls' mental block—placed there no doubt by Lanzo the Great—the girls would start talking and point to an even higher executive in the Leafs front office.

I reminded Stana of the licorice we found in the cordoned-off room to Nick's store.

A lot of people like licorice, she said.

Smith, I wondered?

"Why not Bullard, Hayden? What do we really know about him besides a fondness for fondling women's breasts and eating potato chips? He's my prime suspect. He craves attention and Bullard's clearly in Smith's shadows. Smith is brighter, a law-school grad, and the son of the former owner."

Good point, I said. "What else you got? I feel you're building to something big."

Her pencil clipped against the tip of her lips and the edge of the phone's mouthpiece. "$568,000 was put down on that slice of land out in Vaughan today."

"What? I thought the money was missing. Who put it down?"

"Who do you think? Bolemac. Migano and Bullard. Kim

handled it for Ogilvie and Beggert. Bullard's the partner, not Smith. They're squeezing Smith *out*."

"Wow. So Migano has his money? What's he need me for then?" In the background typewriters rat-a-tat-tatted like angry machine guns.

"To throw suspicion on Davis? But why?"

"Good work," I said. "The moo goo gai pan is on me."

"That's not all."

"Oh?"

"The zoning for the land? Bolemac got it changed. It's no longer residential, but commercial. They're building on commercial land—"

"Commercial?"

TWENTY MINUTES LATER I was climbing the stairs to my second-floor office two steps at a time, thinking about land in Vaughan, Ontario, and Stana and the takeout I was carrying and game three of the Leafs versus the Habs tomorrow night.

So I didn't notice that my office door was unlocked and two shadowy figures were sitting in my chairs; the one behind my desk had a gun in her hand.

"Hungry," I said, dropping the takeout on my desk blotter.

"So glad you could drop by, Mr. Fuller." It was Lisa Steinmetz. The gun was a pearl-handled .32. Lisa wore a short black jacket, long-armed gloves, and a tight-fitting dress. Her eyes were steady, calm, and darting right through me, the gun pointed at my navel.

"Sorry about this, Hayden." Spinner's tight curled hair looked like iron filings. He wore an open sport coat and a wrinkled off-white shirt. He raised his hands. "The whole gun thing ain't my bag. This was Lisa's idea." He apologized with his eyes.

"Uh-huh."

"I mean, you were always good to me, during all my call-ups. You're top drawer, man. Top drawer." And then he waved a hand at me, fingers fluttering as if he were a traffic cop wanting to get cars flowing again on Queen Street. "However, I must ask for your gun. You carry one, right? Side holstered?"

"Right. What happened to 'this whole gun thing ain't my bag,' baby?"

He shrugged and looked over at Lisa.

She told me to cool it, not with her eyes, but with two or three F-bombs.

Spinner looked slighter between the shoulders than he did when he played with the Leafs. Maybe I was used to seeing him in Cooper hockey pads, but I think he had lost weight. I handed him the snub-nosed, handle first.

"We got some info to sell—" Lisa leaned forward. The dim light in my office gave off a ghostly appearance. The halting rhythms of her voice were also gone. Question marks no longer ended each sentence. And her hair color was now Lucille Ball red. A disguise no doubt.

"Can I sit down?" I pointed at a hard, wood chair, the only other one in the room.

Spinner said sure, sure, and tucked my gun away in his belt. I flipped the chair around so that I could rest my hands and chin over the back of it. I pulled down on my porkpie. "It's your deal. Deal."

They wanted $1,000, in exchange for giving me some info.

"I don't have that kind of money—"

"$500?"

They were desperate and no doubt needed to get out of town. "Who did you guys double-cross and who's trying to kill you?"

Lisa sat up more firmly. Maybe she was anxious to speak and maybe her butt was just sore—all of the chairs in my office were hard: kept conversations short and moving along, no need to linger. I knew a fella once, Molson's exec, who held all his office meetings in a hallway, for brevity's sake. People don't talk as long when they're standing.

Lisa's face was troubled, pulled down by the weight of anxiety: cheeks, despite the blush, were heavy and drawn; lower lip, the red of a fire wagon, dropped like a sheet; and the mascara around her eyes was too thick, giving her a 1920s vamp reckoning.

"I can do $500," I said. "But it better be good. The info."

"It is. It's about Cathy Stabulas—" Spinner studied his fingers. "We've seen her." He paused and smiled, enjoying his moment. "She's alive."

"Where is she?"

"Where's the money?" Lisa's gun waving wasn't quite as level as I'd like it to be.

"Can you maybe put that down?"

"No."

I shrugged. She was direct at least.

"Go ahead. Eat. You guys must be hungry."

They reached for the stained bag and helped themselves. I asked permission to dial Stana for the money. Lisa said yes with the gun. I filled Stana in on the situation without mentioning Lisa's .32, and Stana said she'd dig up the cash, the newspaper had a pot of change for informants and other "incidentals" and since she was getting a big story out of all this, the *Telegram* could put up a large percentage and I could pay Stana back the remaining percentage whenever I got more solvent and above water. I think I had about two yards in my account. Fifteen minutes. She'd be here. "Oh, and bring more Chinese food," I said.

Twenty-five minutes then, she said.

"You got sweet and sour?" Spinner asked.

"Goes right to your hips." I laughed. "I never eat that shit. I got hot mustard—"

"Hot mustard? Come on, man. That's candy ass." He reached for a packet. "Well all right, if that's all you've got."

"Sweet and sour?" I requested from Stana, and then hung up.

Lisa wiped clips of egg roll from her lower lip.

"Okay. What do we do in the meantime while we're waiting? I like pinochle."

Spinner shook his head. "You were never that funny, Kodak Kid. Don't try to entertain us. We get the money, you get the info, we're out. Let's keep things light."

"Sure."

Spinner crossed one leg over another, like one of the Doublemint girls. It wasn't the casual lower leg, just above the ankle, pushed over the knee pose struck by most hockey players. "I suppose you have questions?" He placed a hand under his chin.

"I have a lot of questions. Who did you steal the money for, the $568,000?"

Spinner let out a deep sigh. "I guess $500 in coin entitles you to some answers." He smiled again and they admitted to taking the money, Spinner and Lisa, but he wouldn't name names. Leeds was the middleman. The fence. In twenty-four hours they were supposed to get a cut, ten percent, but when they arrived Leeds was dead.

Outside the sun was hidden in clouds and the sky a gray canvas curtain.

"I called you—that night from Leeds's office. I called you." I glanced over at Lisa, the barrel of the gun glinting arcs of light from my desk lamp. "You were already home. You couldn't have seen him dead—"

"I arrived. Just me. After you left, before the cops arrived—" Spinner was now sweating. He coughed and refolded his legs, left now over right.

"Were you the one outside the window?" I had thought it was a girl. I didn't tell him that part. "The one in the rain?"

"It was raining," he said, "but I don't remember noticing you at no window. I was gone pretty fast—"

"Did you kill him?"

"No. Of course not." He dried his forehead and then his eyelids and loosened his shirt collar. His white shirt could sure be pressed. It looked like a wrinkled paper bag. Even Spinner's upper lip was wet, resembling a perforated mustache. "*You* reported to the press that it was a woman you saw running away in the shadows of light. So it couldn't have been me you saw—"

Right, I did report that. Right, I said. Christ with these headaches I get, sometimes I forget who I told what to. And right about now my head was a drowning hornet's nest. "Starzz?" I rubbed the edges of my mouth. "How does she fit in?" Could she have been the shoeless woman I saw running in pencil-streaks of rain that night?

"Nobody knows who she is—" Lisa noshed on a second egg roll. "She wears a mask and she'll do anything, I mean *anything*, any fantasy."

"The management's been building up expectations, cause Starzz hasn't done her thing in a few months. Folks can't wait for her return," Spinner said. He mentioned something about S&M and a ball and a whip.

"Maybe three months, she's been gone. Visiting the Orient for, get this, 'new techniques.' That's Coughlins' spin on things," Lisa added.

"Kim Stabulas? She Starzz?" She had been to Coughlins.

"Is she in the Orient? Weren't you listening—?"

"Can't be Kim," Terrien said. "She's too classy."

"Oh, she's classy now." Lisa let out a short groan.

"So much for that character reference, huh?" I said, wagging a thumb at Lisa. "What about Cathy? Is Cathy Starzz?"

"Cathy?" Terrien shook his head. "No, no. Too sweet."

Lisa blew even heavier air between her lips. "Sweet?"

I turned to her. "You've been jealous of Cathy all along—"

She said nothing.

"You got her into Coughlins to, to, to destroy her—" I said.

"Yes."

Terrien looked again at his fingers, and the arc of light from my desk lamp seemed to have a frosty glow. Lisa glanced away at the blotter, absently taking in the words in front of her, the fingers of her left hand, tap tapping against my various appointments, the gun shaking even more noticeably in her other hand.

Leeds, the guidance counselor, had talked Lisa into the therapy sessions and following his "Worship the Cock" pronouncements introduced her to Coughlins. There she met some pretty interesting men, hockey players, and some even slept with her—recognizing her value, making her feel important.

Then one night, she took an orange pill and Leeds performed a relaxation exercise in which Lisa imagined herself on an island in the Caribbean. She just floated in the waters, feeling the sun on her shoulders, nose, the part in her hair, and then, she was naked, freely expressing herself for two men and their camera. She never knew how she got there. She was just there, like she were hypnotized or something.

"Or something? And yet you have some trace memories about it?"

"I know. I don't think I'm supposed to it's like a—a—"

"A world off its axis? Your head full of spun cotton candy?"

"Yes. Dirty cotton candy." Leeds was the ringleader, talking her through whatever paces he had her perform. He spoke very kindly. But there was another man. "Nick Stabulas."

"Nick. Nick was there—" I let out a sharp whistle and snapped my fingers. "I knew it."

"Yes." How dare he, she said. The sonuvabitch. How dare he. He knew that Lisa was Cathy's friend and how could her father be involved in something like this, just standing there, watching, as Leeds took several photographs.

"Did he speak in an English accent and smell of licorice?"

"I don't remember any accent, but the licorice, now that you mention it—"

"He had no idea that you'd remember. He was no longer the voyeur hiding in the closet, watching through slats, or lingering in shadows, peeking in windows. Instead—" I shook my head and looked at the splashes of dirt on my shoes. They resembled falling stars with teardrop ends.

It felt like *I* was crying.

Apparently, the Tangerine Room parlor trick of relaxation waves didn't quite work on Lisa. "It was a regular placebo with me, I guess." She smiled awkwardly, proud at herself for knowing such a word. "So I wanted to get even—"

"But not with Smith, just Nick. Smith's the real ringleader, isn't he? He's the one you stole the money for? It was Migano's money and you stole it for Smith. Leeds was the go-between. Migano found out and had him whacked. Starzz works for Migano." I breathed heavily, my lower lip giving out.

She shrugged. "You're way ahead of me."

"Starzz works for Migano. She killed for Migano. Got the money back for Migano." *Powder burns. A woman getting close. Maybe she even did a lap dance for the king of photography. She asked to see his gun and guns go off as guns will—*

All this Davis stuff was a smokescreen to send me off on yet another wild detour. This case was full of lies, mean side streets of deception: Migano in his maniacal quest for payback; Kim in her denial of ever visiting or knowing of Coughlins and the Bolemac Corporation; McClelland and his cover-ups over a prior connection to Leeds; Lisa and her dated naked portrait of Cathy, tossing unwarranted suspicions on Danny Davis; Lisa (again) and her alleged friendship with Cathy clouded over by jealousy and revenge; Davis himself, screwing other men's wives; and Nick Stabulas, playing the role of the loyal, desperate father who truly harbors in his heart an unhealthy desire for his daughters.

"Don't you see? Migano has *his* money. Stana told me. He put a deposit down on the land in Vaughan, and he has been running me around, distracting me. Migano's going to kill you—" I said.

Spinner fidgeted with his shirt collar once again.

"Yes. It *was* Smith we were working for." He was never at the photo shoots; however, she said. He did want the money, *Migano's money.* She nodded and her eyes misted. "Smith wasn't in on the land deal at all. It was Bullard."

Cal Bullard. He was making his move, independent big-time operator, independent of Smith, partnering with Migano and Bolemac for the land grab. Mr. Potato Chips was looking to be in a different kind of chips. "And Smith was jealous?"

She nodded. He wanted to wreck their partnership.

How could a lard-ass flunky like Bullard be in on something so big that would place his financial standing above me? I can't have that. That was Smith's line of reasoning. Another lie: their partnership, their running of Maple Leaf Gardens wasn't on as solid a footing as their smiles and Royal hand waves to us plebes would suggest. Phonies.

"Smith thought Bullard was a total ass, especially after a late night cocktail session in which the general partner tried to sell the Big M to Chicago for a cool million," Terrien said.

"Yeah, I know the story," I said. "Everybody knows the story."

"Yes. But after that event, Bullard was told to keep his nose out of hockey decisions. Stick to concessions and watered down sodas and salty popcorn." Terrien shrugged. "That punishment made Bullard want to get even, to one-up Smith. Thus the land grab—" Terrien shrugged again. "And Smith hates being one-upped."

So Smith took the money—because he knew Migano was short—and he was hoping to either destroy their partnership or buy his way into the operation. Become a trio instead of a duo—that's what Smith wanted. Right?

Spinner nodded this time.

McClelland Stuart had the story only half right, Spinner said. Yes, Migano was strapped. The $568,000 was crucial to his keeping an equal hold on the company. Smith stole from his own Gardens' safe to wreck Migano.

"What a needy fuck," I said. And I got to thinking again about the shift in zoning from residential to commercial. What was Migano really up to?

"Am I any different?" Lisa shrugged, placing the gun down in front of her. She had felt betrayed by Leeds and Nick. They had destroyed any vestiges of innocence she had and she struck back, luring Cathy there. "Revenge." She shrugged. "It's the oldest motivation isn't it? Goes back to Cain and Abel. It was just three or four times, I took her. That's all. The third time, I got her to take an orange pill and Leeds did his relaxation hypnosis bit on me and Cathy and Cathy took all her clothes off." Her lips became a thin line. "I eventually stole one of the photos from Leeds and mailed it to Nick."

"So what does Leeds do with his private collection of junk—blackmail—?"

"He rents them out, rented them out, to people who are into that—" She followed the lines in the ceiling and studied shadows in a far corner. "He had quite a collection, I hear."

"What about Sarah Kerr? Did Leeds rent out her photos too? She was underage. Fourteen, fifteen?"

"Sarah Kerr? I don't recognize the name—"

"A friend of Cathy's?"

"Nothing. Sorry." After the fourth or fifth time, Cathy quit going to Coughlins. She never knew about the nude photo session. No memory. "I told her about a lot of shit that went on, but I couldn't do that to her." She touched the tip of her chin and breathed.

"I see—"

But Lisa did make Cathy her confidant, telling her tales of what happened at Coughlins, the fucking in stretch limos, the $20,000 poker nights, the brawls over a dart game, and Starzz, the girl in the Mardi-Gras mask who would do it all. "How was I supposed to know Cathy wrote it all down?"

"What?"

"The debaucheries—all of it. In one of her Big Chief tablets." Cathy was planning to blow the whistle on the whole outfit to Stana, when they took her away.

"When they? Who's they?"

"I know." She paused. "When we see the money, I'll tell you—"

"*I*?" asked Terrien.

"*We*," Lisa corrected. "When we see the money."

"Did Cathy ever see Starzz 'perform' at the club?"

"Yes. Twice, I think."

"Why didn't they kill Cathy?"

She shrugged. "You got me. They chose to hide her instead."

"Where is she?"

"When I get the money—"

Quick, hurried steps were on the stairs behind me. Heavy, not as nimble as Stana usually is, but she was weighed down by bags of Chinese food, a lot of Chinese food, I suppose.

I turned to the frosted-glass door and they barged in, Fortunado and Leighton. They wore overcoats, gloves, and scarves covering part of their faces. The bigger guy, Leighton, was now holding the gun. Fortunado had been demoted. Leighton's eyes were narrow, his face determined. The gun gleamed in the arc of office light.

Lisa reached for the .32 but two quick shots hit her in the chest. She stuttered once or twice, fluttered back and then flopped on my desk, her eyes vacant. Blood was at the corners of her lips, the gun motionless in front of her.

My ears hurt from the gun blasts and I looked over at Spinner who held his fingers up before his eyes, hoping to disappear or stop another volley of bullets with his bare hands. Superman, he wasn't. My gun was still trapped against the belt of his pants.

It was all so damn quick—Lisa alive and now dead—like hammering a nail, and I couldn't think, no words, no actions, and suddenly I wanted to scream at Spinner, where's the girl, where is she, tell me, before they kill you, you dumbass, and maybe I said something or other to that effect, I don't know, but a gun flashed across my mouth, I felt blood and tin between my teeth, and then I dropped into a black pool. It was cold.

11

A glow of light skimmed over my eyes as the world went from dull red to darkness and back to dull red again. I tried to open my eyes against the pendulum splash of light and dark. I threw up in my mouth. It wasn't pleasant.

"What's that, Crumpled Suit?" I recognized the gravel crunch of Lou-doo's burr.

I spit out chunks of hot dog and olives and soda and looked for the moving light and found a bare bulb on a wire, hanging from a garage ceiling. The garage was brown, dusky. Corkboard and power tools draped one of the walls. The floor was coated with a giant plastic shower curtain. I was tied to a chair, my hands tight behind me. The bulb wasn't moving. It was as still as the '65 GTO parked to the right of me. I was the one moving, not really, but in my head, I was moving, all twisted up and dented.

I closed my eyes, but that only made those pendulum splashes of red and canvas black return.

I tasted tin, and traced my tongue across my teeth. One of them was sharp and chipped, another one was missing. I could taste the hole, the blood, the hole, and it hurt and my head hurt, but not as bad my eyes hurt when I shut them or as awful as the gurgle sounded, bubbling up to my left.

Strapped to an even bigger chair and tied down with heavier ropes was Spinner or what was left of him. His head hung over the chair's back and he gurgled some more, blood puffing out of his lips like a weak chewing gum bubble. The bubble got bigger and then popped and then there was another smaller bubble and another small pop.

His right eye was dislodged from the orbital bone and hanging on the side of his face. I don't know what it saw if anything. His breathing was very shallow and I didn't think he had enough left to make it.

"You okay?" A low, distant voice floated my way like heavy clouds.

And then the clouded voice broke up into the even-steady purr of Migano. He smelled of Old Spice and his hair looked great as always. "Sorry if my boys roughed you up." He smiled. "But I like you. That's why you're still alive." He pressed his lips together. "My apologies also about the girl. I don't like to hurt women, as you know. But she gave Leighton no choice."

I shrugged, the room still moving like a crazy teeter-totter. My head felt wedged in a vice grip and I threw up again, all over my suit and tie. It was a cheap tie. Zellers. I apologized for the mess.

"Hey," Migano motioned to Lou-doo. "Get him some water. Untie the ropes."

Fortunado nodded, touching the rear of the car, removing a pigeon-spot of schmutz with a chamois. Leighton was eating a sub sandwich. It was fat and I could see at least four types of cheese and even more slabs of meat. I wasn't hungry.

Fortunado ambled over to the water cooler next to the GTO, blue with chunky mag wheels on the back. I loved that car. I wish I could drive out of this fucking place in that lovely car. The cooler gurgled, bizarrely out of rhythm with the gurgles bubbling forth from Spinner. His mouth was dotted with spots of blood. The bubbles got smaller, less dynamic in shape. By contrast, the bubbles gurgling in the cooler were huge spots on the glass.

"What are you going to do to me."

"You're a smart guy. You didn't see any of this. We already cleaned up your office. These bodies will be buried somewhere, somewhere with a poetic touch." He smiled and laughed lightly. "I like poetry."

"I'm sorry if I can't join you in the gaiety, but I'll throw up again if I laugh—" Between a window and the closed garage door was a green Coleman lantern. It was probably plastic and fueled with a small bulb and wouldn't start much of a fire.

"You better have a dentist look at those teeth—" He shook his head apologetically and smiled. "Leighton, did you have to hit him so hard?"

He shrugged and waited to swallow. "There was a gun in the room. I had to act. And he carries heat."

"But not today." Migano pointed at my empty holster.

Not today. Last I saw of the gun it was adding panache to Spinner's fashion statement.

Dull red flashed throughout the room and my head, once again, was a drowning hornet's nest, buzz buzzing inside, and I couldn't shake the sound away. "Why kill him, why? He's nothing to you. You have your money."

"Oh, you know about that." He smiled again. "Yes, I have my money. All $568,000. But he disrespected me." He pointed in the direction of a gurgling Terrien. "And for that—" He shrugged. "Justice. Poetry. Now where to put the bodies?" He tapped his chin twice and raised an eyebrow. "Yes, of course. That's where."

"He's just small-time. You're bigger than this, man."

"When people hurt me, I hurt back. Capisce?"

I looked into his eyes and then the corkboard and a hammer and a power saw. I didn't know if I had the strength to access any of these to fight my way out of here.

"You, you haven't hurt me. You're alright, Fuller. I like you. Now Davis, that guy I don't dig. Him, I'd still like to whack. Just on principle. You don't fuck other men's wives."

Migano sure had a lot of rules. I wondered if anyone ever called him Ten Commandments Migano. Or Babe "Vengeance is Mine" Migano. Or—

"You're babbling," he said.

I didn't realize I had been talking out loud.

"At least you didn't call me King Herod Migano." He smiled like a movie star.

Lou-doo handed out a paper cup of water. It slipped off the lip, onto my hand, and it tasted cool and fresh and was the best water I'd ever tasted and the freshest and I wanted more of that damn water. I even drank the spot off my hand. So I asked, please sir, can I have more? And I got more. It was even better on the second go-around.

"Right, we're good here, right? You're not going to say a word about this to your reporter friend?"

I nodded and threw up again. I shouldn't have moved my head with such vigor.

"Clean him up." He held up his hands.

One of the guys took a quick chamois to my face. Me and the GTO—best buddies, equals, brothers in schmutz.

"It was Smith all along, wasn't it?"

Migano smiled and looked toward Spinner.

I noticed for the first time that Spinner was naked in the chair and his feet inside a large aluminum basin. They had subjected Spinner to some kind of water torture involving electric shock and a car battery, in an effort to try to discover that Smith had hired him to steal Babe's money.

"Fucking fruit," Fortunado said. "Goddamn gaylord."

"Hey, be respectful." Migano held up a hand. "The man is dying. Don't let the last words he hears be our derision."

Fortunado nodded and looked at some dirt under a fingernail. Leighton's hands were occupied with his football of a sandwich.

The room was spinning again, red and then black, a side-to-side spin. I felt lost in one of Migano's Coney Island fun houses.

"I don't care about a man's private life. I don't care. Does it matter?"

"No," I said.

Migano said he had an uncle who was a fag and nobody made fun of his uncle or else the Babe himself and his Louisville Slugger would knock him to shit. "He was a good man. Responsible. That's all that matters." He paused and looked over at Spinner. "This guy was a good man, too. A pretty good little hockey player."

I nodded. "When they gave him half a chance." I don't know how it is, but I remember stats, I do: twenty-seven career games, five goals, and nine assists. Feisty in the corners for a little guy. Let that be his epitaph.

Migano patted Spinner affectionately on the shoulder. His breathing was shallow, rippled tissue paper. "But he stole. From me. Or tried to steal from me. You don't do that." Migano smiled. "He got in with the wrong people. Smith."

"Right." I nodded with my eyes.

"I got another surprise." He held up his left hand. All of the fingers were covered in rings. Spinner was Starzz. "He owned up to it while my boys interrogated him. He was Starzz. Look at the film again. A guy in drag lap dancing all over Leeds, making him hard."

How did Migano know about the lap dancing? The papers said nothing about that. The press's words were *sordid behavior and goings-on at the Gardens.*

"Starzz killed Leeds. Shot him with his own gun, close range." Apparently Leeds knew the killer, trusted the killer. Leeds liked Starzz. Leeds liked men in drag.

I closed my eyes and thought about the figure running between slats of rain and conical light. The shoulders were a little heavy and the flats I found in the closet were big. Spinner *was* Starzz. *He was outside the window, dressed as a woman. One big masquerade.*

I think I said this latter point out loud again.

"Masquerade?" Lou-doo picked at more schmutz, a spackle on the side mirror.

"Why were they in your office?" Migano pushed.

"They were going to tell me where Cathy was—for $500."

"Did you pay them?"

"I didn't get a chance to."

"Did you find out where Cathy is?"

"Again, I didn't get a chance to." I looked over at Cool Athol. He shrugged twice. Fortunado's face was motionless as he rubbed off a third spot, this one by the GTO's rocker panel.

"Try Rosedale," Migano said. "Terrien said something about Rosedale." He shrugged. "Don't ever say I never tried to help you." He smiled again.

Rosedale was an affluent neighborhood in downtown Toronto full of old money and a bunch of ex-United Empire Loyalist types who enjoyed British theatre, tea and crumpets, and worshipped the Queen. They lived in ivy-walled houses with big bay windows and a pleasant view of Whitney Park across the way. Smith had a house in Rosedale, so did his lawyers and his father, The Old Man.

"Don't try to kill Smith," I said. He's a connected guy, not in the Italian sense of the word made, but a made guy nonetheless, and they'll come after you, old money, secret-handshake society fuckers.

He touched an eyebrow with an index finger and nodded thanks.

There was a gasp of a gurgle from Terrien, a bubble splat, and then no more bubbles.

"Is he?" asked Leighton, munching his sandwich, a leaf of prosciutto draping out of the back end. He wiped a spot of mustard off his lower lip.

Migano placed a finger by the side of Terrien's neck. He waited. “He is now.”

Leighton took another bite.

“I drive the car this time,” Lou-doo said.

I looked around the room but didn’t see any shovels.

Migano leaned over and kissed the top of Terrien’s head. “Goodnight, Sweet Prince,” he said.

THERE WAS WATER EVERYWHERE. Up to my ankles, past the cuffs of my pants. I sloshed along hardwood and water gushed from a filter fan or maybe it was an air conditioning unit or perhaps the back end of a dryer that was propped next to the stove. It bled in waves and sparkled like blue and white ticker-tape confetti.

Nick Stabulas pushed a broom along the floor as if it were a hockey stick and the water a puck he wanted to sweep into the corner of the kitchen. Whatever he was doing it wasn’t working, and he pressed his lips together in a determined grimace. Nick had less hair than I remembered and his eyebrows were gone.

And then my dad was there too, trying to help with a bigger broom, and directing me with his eyes to leave the goddamn room. “Help me here, Hayden,” Nick said.

“Get out, get out,” my dad said.

I was standing in the water but I couldn’t seem to move. My left foot felt like it was on a placemat in a bathtub and if I turned and stepped I’d fall off the world’s edge. My shoulders were sore from holding my pose for so long.

Water continued pushing through the wall, lean curled strips of taffy, and Cathy, her red hair pasted to her forehead, her nightie tied up tight to her neck, was screaming to shut the water off.

“I can’t,” Nick said. “We need the water. We need it.”

“Yes, we need it,” my dad echoed, tobacco-stained fingers pressed against the broom which was now a goalie’s stick. Dad was by a toilet that didn’t have any stall doors and water rippled from the top of the bowl all over the floor and onto his shoes, Nick’s shoes, white, low-cut canvas sneakers. Both sets of shoes.

The water wasn't clean.

"Shut it off, Hayden," Cathy said to me.

It never occurred to me that she could shut off the water.

She shouted again and then her red hair turned white blonde and the face filled with the sharp angles of Sarah Kerr's.

I slid and sloshed toward the wall, wondering how does one shut off water. "Maybe we should listen to your dad." Maybe we *all* need the water.

"Shut it off, please, please, please," said the muffled voice, a suitcase mumble.

"No, I need it," Nick repeated.

"You need it too," Dad said to me.

I FLUTTERED MY EYES and they felt coated with soggy cereal. I rubbed out the gunk and flashed my eyes again and adjusted to the bright sun filtering through the curtains. I was on a queen-size bed, functional sheets, a puffed-up pillow under my head. The gray dresser came with an attached mirror. A compact, tubes of lipstick, and a heavy upright purse crowded the mirror. The purse had huge rings the size of those circling Saturn. I was in Stana's apartment.

I groaned. My teeth still hurt. I felt the hole in my mouth with my tongue and wondered how I got here. My tongue was sore too. I must have bit it when I got pistol-whipped. I don't remember much of what happened after Spinner died.

A shadow filled the door's threshold. It was Stana, hooking an earring into her left ear and fluffing up her hair after having just showered and touching it up with hairspray. "I was starting to worry about you." She adjusted the clasp on her watch. "I can make you an egg sandwich? Carnation Instant Breakfast?"

"Sure."

She smiled and handed me some pills. Painkillers. She had her wisdom teeth pulled two years ago, and these were the remainders. She had also set up an appointment for me with a dentist for Monday. I'd have to see Abramowitz too.

"What day is today?"

"Saturday."

I tumbled to the side of the bed and slid into my pants. The room was too bright and I asked her to close the curtains.

"They are closed," she said.

"Can you close them tighter—" I was dizzy and leaned forward, hands on thighs to anchor me. "How did I get here?" I rubbed my mouth, smelled my hand. Geez, my breath was awful.

"Babe Migano." I was rather incoherent last night, and then passed out upright in the doorway standing between Leighton and Fortunado, she said.

"How do they know where you live?" My head was cluttered up with gauzed cotton candy, only now it felt like it was spun Plaster of Paris.

"I'm in the phone book, silly." She shrugged, hooking in another earring. "And I guess they know we're kind of an item."

I nodded, pushing my arms into my soiled shirt. It didn't smell any better than my breath. I took the shirt off and tossed it on a chair. I'd go with the T-shirt look, me and Brando and James Dean.

"Coffee?"

"Sure."

She left for the kitchen and I wobbled to my feet and stumbled into my shoes. Rosedale, Migano said. Rosedale. I had to get to Rosedale. Smith's house also had construction done by Bolemac and no doubt there was a sliding panel in a study somewhere and hopefully Cathy behind that panel. Rosedale.

I wandered to the kitchen, bumping the dresser on my way out, my steps surprisingly light. An egg was frying and the Carnation Instant Breakfast cooled my hands. I took a sip and struggled to swallow. I was a mess. And I didn't know what to believe anymore. I looked at my fingers. "You know, I was just wondering—Migano—right?"

"Right." Her eyes narrowed slightly as her hands gripped a coffee mug. Steam curled off the lip in backward S's.

"How did he know where Lisa and Spinner were?" Migano's men had come to my office. I thought it odd that it wasn't Stana with the Chinese food. Instead, it was Lou-doo and Cool Athol.

"I guess they had been tailing Spinner and Lisa from King Street. Remember you said someone saw them at an A&P on King. Followed them to your office—"

"No. Spinner was a skittish cat. He was too careful." I shoved my hands in my pockets. "I called you. I told you to bring the money—"

"Yes. That was yesterday—"

"Don't humor me—the money. You see. That's where you slipped up, Stana." I leaned against a chair in the kitchen and blinked my eyes, hoping to regain feeling in my face. "You forgot the money."

"Forgot?" There was just one S curling now, slow and steamy.

"I called you, told you to bring the money. You called Migano." There was no anger in my voice. It was just flat and dead, the way I felt . . . inside. "You called Migano."

"That's—that's—a" She plunked her cup of coffee on the Formica table. "You're starting to really piss me off. You know what—"

"Oh, am I? I'm pissing you off?" I pointed to the bedroom. "Go get your bag, your purse. The one that looks like a milk crate. If there's $500 in it, I'll eat my words. I'll apologize."

"I'm not going to get my purse. These accusations are—"

"Unwarranted? You never went to the bank. You called Migano and his boys showed up instead of you. Get your purse. Get the $500—"

"Do you realize what you're accusing me of—you—I love you—"

"Get it. Two more people dead, because of a phone call." I

kind of liked Terrien. He was a little guy, feisty, honest. "Show me the money." I rubbed my face again. Even my eyes felt numb.

"I already took the money back. There's no money in the purse—"

"It's Saturday. The banks aren't open." I slammed a chair against the table and headed through the kitchen and to her apartment door. "Did you think they'd kill me too? What did you think would happen?"

"I didn't *think* they'd kill you—"

"That's right, you didn't think. You were just protecting yourself and the next story you had to write. I'm just a *character* in one of your goddamn stories."

"Hayden—"

"Save it." It was cold outside but the sun was a burning egg and maybe it would get to be a better day.

I TOOK THE TTC TO MY OFFICE, and once I climbed the stairs to the second floor, I realized that I didn't remember a thing about the ride over on the subway. Who sat next to me? What books were people reading? Were they reading books? What was that conversation about between the young couple—her hugging his shoulders—across from me? Were they even talking?

I stumbled to the hard sink. It was next to my hat rack. I splashed my face with cold water and used the hat rack to steady me. Damn I didn't have my porkpie. I must've left it at Stana's. I stuck my head under the sink and the water ran and ran and ran. It was cold and felt good.

My .38 was lying atop my desk. That was real polite of Loudoo and Athol to leave me some artillery. It hadn't done Spinner any good, but maybe it could come in handy for yours truly. I visited the cop shop's indoor pistol shooting range twice a week, sporting both earplugs and over-the-head earmuffs, scoring nines and tens on the target's rings. I sighed and struggled opening the top desk drawer. It was stuck. But I finally shook it loose, grabbed some extra shells, and noticed that the chair behind me was dotted with two faint starbursts of blood. They couldn't clean it all away.

I breathed heavily. Rosedale.

The phone rang. Seven, eight, ten times.

It rang again. The receiver had smudges all over it. I'd clean it later.

Eight, nine, ten.

101 days ago, Sarah Kerr's body was found in a suitcase.

I left the office, my shoulders not as heavy, my mouth hurting like hell.

NICK STABULUS WASN'T AT HIS GROCERY STORE. Hadn't been seen since his bail. Kim wasn't there either. A neighborhood girl was manning the place. Because of my sore teeth, I passed up on buying some popcorn with the damn jolly circus elephant on the box.

Smith wasn't home either. I called and called. Moments later, I was tearing up the steps of the Gardens, looking for Pal Cal's bunker. I knocked on the door. It wasn't gentle.

"You trying to break my collectibles," Pal Cal said, with a big smile on his face, as he opened the door. "Oh, it's you." He wore a red robe, tied loosely at his generous waist. Wisps of chest hair poked out from the robe's pleated fabric. It was a bad look.

"Where's Smith?" He wasn't answering calls, he's not in his office, and Lefty, the Zamboni driver, said Smith's usually here by noon on game day.

"Probably out golfing, who knows?" Bullard shrugged. His face was craggy, and the lines around his mouth gave him the look of a marionette. He wasn't eating potato chips. There wasn't a fleck anywhere.

"Hockey season's not over. He wouldn't be golfing. God damn it. This is game day. Where is he?"

He held up a hand. It was covered with three Stanley Cup

rings. "I'm not his keeper."

"Migano's going to kill him, because he double-crossed the cat. He's going—"

Bullard blinked his eyes and took a step back. "Migano's not my concern—"

"Stop it. I know you're the brains behind Bolemac—he's your partner. Migano's your partner. You guys squeezed Smith out. I get it—"

"Well thanks." He crossed his arms and beamed, the robe bunching up even more by his portly waist. "It's nice to get recognized once in a while. Everyone thinks I'm some kind of clown, a buffoon. No, I'm smart. I have business savvy."

"You and Migano are buying up land in Vaughan. Building a city. Whatever. Smith hated that, being excluded, wanted in. You didn't let him in, right? Are you going to let me in your office?"

"Well, you see?" He shrugged, the corners of his mouth rising. A female voice behind him giggled. Through the space between his arm and hip, I saw Laurinda reclined along the top of a wet bar. Her legs crossed. She was topless. Flecks of chips were all over her breasts and belly.

"I'm kind of busy right now." Pal Cal smiled.

"Right." I should have known. I let out a sharp sigh. "You don't care what happens to Smith, do you?"

"Not really." He shrugged. He was ready to make the break from his partner and find his own independence.

"He stole from Migano and Migano's going to deep six him," I said.

"You need comp tickets for tonight's game?" Bullard laughed, looked over his shoulder and gave a gentle flutter of the fingers at Laurinda. His jowls shook as the door closed, separating me from his bunker house of fun.

—

I WAS AT ROSEDALE in less than ten minutes and parked out

front of Smith's palace. In terms of size, it appeared only slightly smaller than Maple Leafs Gardens.

Maple trees lined the pathway to the front door and vines and lush greenery covered the house's second-floor cathedral-style windows and arches like an inviting beard. The high windows were wide expressive eyes looking upon the curved driveway and the interloper below.

I shoved my hands in my pockets, glanced around and ran. Bits of stones and small sticks snapped and clicked as I reached the front door. The sun dropped below a line of big trees and Smith's place was awash in shadows. By contrast, his Rolls glinted in the glare. I pushed the doorbell. Nothing.

I waited. Tried the door. It opened.

It hadn't been closed all the way.

I wondered if this was all a trap and feared whether a fancy alarm system would be blaring in less than thirty seconds—I certainly didn't know what three-digit code to punch to deactivate the system—and the police could be wailing up the driveway any moment now. Swell.

I walked quickly past hard-edged furniture, a thick armoire, and crossed cutlasses above a shelf and some kind of African spear and giant mask in a far corner by a spittoon. I called Smith's name and looked about a room with an L-shaped couch and shag rugs. The line of the sun caused my watch to glow and bounce light on the ceiling. There was nothing on the ceiling, of course, but the bounce effect and sudden spot of glare made me spot another lens of light, caught by the sun at the foot of one of the couch's legs.

It was Smith's Lombardis. They were resting awkwardly on the side of their frames. One of the temple pieces was twisted and there was blood along the grooves of the hinge. Smith was probably smacked with an open hand or the barrel of a pistol.

I placed the glasses in my coat pocket and lifted my snub-nosed .38 from its side holster. I hurried past an open foyer area, with more couches, chairs, shag rugs, and portraits of the Leafs from the 1940s, including Syl Apps, Teeder Kennedy, and Harry Watson.

I hustled down a flight of short stairs to what was clearly an entertainment center. Three televisions were positioned high on the wall for simultaneous access to major area stations: CBC, CTV, and CHCH out of Hamilton.

The closest wall of the foyer was awash in terrariums, green speckled plants that looked like obscure species of octopus or artichokes. They rested in a desert setting or among smooth stones or dark moss and it was a strange mix—colors and shapes and climates that just didn't fit. There might have even been some orchids in the wall art, but I don't know, the whole shebang just seemed to be trying too damn hard. A roulette wheel was to my left, another straight ahead. A craps table was to my right and on the wet bar were a few eight-sided revolving poker chip racks. A bottle of scotch was next to them. Empty.

Migano? I guess a lot of fellas drink scotch.

I breathed quickly, hoping a secret alarm wasn't covertly sounding somewhere, exposing me. The sliding panel in Smith's Gardens office was behind a bookshelf. This room had no bookshelves. There wasn't a discarded Steinbeck anywhere.

I sighed.

Was Cathy still here? Was Smith dead?

I circled the roulette tables and found a switch on the farthest one. I toggled it back, and suddenly the wall across from the terrariums slid open, and sharp light cut a blocky path in front of me. I tightened my grip on my gun.

And in the glare, I saw the silhouette of a woman.

12

She walked intot the light, red and white flannel shirt, blue jeans, and tennis shoes: an Ivory Soap kind of purity. She had a strong, proud chin.

"Stana? What are you doing here?"

I holstered my gun.

"Your hat." She held out my porkpie. Her eyes were full of sadness, pulled down to resemble the tails of wasps.

I said nothing.

She played with the thin necklace around her neck. The ankh appeared upside down.

I pushed the porkpie back on my head and wondered again what the hell she was doing here.

She had heard me mention Rosedale several times in my sleep the other night and figured this was the next place I'd look for Cathy so she headed here, hoping we'd cross paths, and she could explain about, about—

"Letting Lisa and Spinner die—?"

"I didn't know he was going to—"

"Come on, Stana, don't be so disingenuous. What did you think was going to happen? They were going to play a wicked game of pinochle? Please. Don't bullshit me—"

"No, I—I—was scared—and I certainly wouldn't have sent you to your death—I—"

"I don't want to hear it. I'm tired. I want to find Cathy."

I quickly surveyed the room. Nothing. No perfume; no *East of Eden*; no jazz records. But it was loaded with more offbeat details. The floor was dull concrete; the walls cinder blocks on one side, wood paneling on the other. But what really got me were the accoutrements: eight or nine machine guns draped the wall, black flags on a different kind of golf course, black flags probably lifted from the Old Man's militia. They were vintage Tommys and AK-47s, with round cartridges and banana-curved. There were also hand grenades from Canadian pineapples to German potato mashers, tear-gas shells, and tear-gas masks. On a short shelf were stacks of money, positioned sideways. On a longer shelf were rolls and rolls of 8mm film in plastic cans.

There was a white space on the wall where a machine gun had once been. A missing AK-47?

"She's not here." Stana shrugged. "But—" She stepped aside and with a sweeping gesture announced, behind her, our guest, Mr. Steven Smith, President of the Leafs. A blue and white towel was firmly placed in his mouth. "Oh, and this note was pinned to a lapel."

Took you long enough.

Migano. Who else? What a genius. He didn't have to kill Smith, just truss him all up for us to find tied to a chair, and let us explore his secret lair and discover even more damage, the crucial chunks of evidence to nail his secret-handshake-society ass.

Smith didn't look so hot. His face had sharp cut lines and a shallow gouge by his forehead. There was a welt the size of a small potato where an eyebrow should be.

I moved toward the rolls and rolls of film.

AK-47. That's what was fired in our direction, 101 days ago, the day Sarah Kerr was killed.

Smith shook in the chair, his arms vibrating rapidly, his eyes straining. He was mumbling vaguely.

"Just stay the way you are, Mr. Smith. It's a good look for you."

His eyes darkened and both of his chalky eyebrows arched like angry cats as he rattled the chair. I thought he was going to pile-drive a hole into the floor.

I pried the towel from Smith's thin lips. "Who'd you loan the AK-47 to, Mr. People?"

"Fuck you."

"I reapplied the towel and turned to Stana. "Give me a hand here, will ya? Let's check these out." I pointed at the film cans and slowly twisted off a lid.

It didn't have the polish of good stag material or the charm of France's cinema vérité movement, but it was incriminating footage nonetheless, footage many of the subjects would rather see burned or buried.

As I slowly unfurled roll on roll, I unearthed offbeat images of women grinding on men's laps, prominent men playing poker, spinning the roulette wheel, tossing dice, or pinning the pasty on a naked woman wearing a haggard donkey mask. One of the donkey's eyes was missing.

Members of parliament were present, and hockey legends like a forty-goal scorer for Detroit and our own Danny Davis with a naked red-headed girl grinding away on his lap while another naked girl, big and blond, towels off with Davis's tie, shimmying about like a low-rent Chubby Checker.

No, it wasn't state of the art. The camera was stationary and the subjects often moved in and out of the frame, blurring lines between the seen and unseen, but this was incendiary stuff.

"Look at the background." Stana pointed at the corrugated curtains, the wet bar and the apparent blue and white chrome. The film was in black and white but this was clearly Smith's secret hideaway, the party room beyond the sliding bookshelf at the Gardens. "How you doing, Mr. People?" I smiled in Smith's direction.

He and the chair slowly fell sideways and his feet kicked the air like a scuttling crab.

"Blackmail, film to blackmail makers and shakers, no doubt?" Stana shook her head with disapproval.

"No doubt."

What we discovered in Leeds's locker matched up with this. It was a direct connect. Steven Smith, the Bell and Howell auteur, was the maestro, making these movies for his own twisted purposes: to exploit, to scare, to intimidate.

Smith mumbled and Stana laughed.

"So how did you get here exactly, Stana? Migano? Did he drive you here? Let you in?"

Yes, she called Migano, asking for the three-number passcode to disarm the alarm. She deliberately left the door open, for me.

"Oh." I nodded. "And how did you find this secret lair?"

She played with a collared corner to her red-and-white checkered shirt and rubbed under her nose with the back of a hand. "Migano told me where the switch is—"

"Migano again. Always with the Migano—"

"I want to explain about that, about—" She chewed on the collar corner's tip.

"I don't want to hear—" *Did one of Migano's men, Athol, kill Sarah?*

"You say you don't want to hear about it, but you do—"

I sighed dismissively.

There was no underage porn among our findings: no moving images of Leeds's therapy girls, no Lisa Steinmetz at sixteen or seventeen.

However, with foot after foot of the grainy images we did find, Smith could get what he wants when he wants. A zoning law changed so he can build or add to his empire: *no problem, Mr. Smith. Just don't show my movie.* A politician to back whatever side project would benefit the Leafs' Czar: no problem, Mr. Smith. Just don't show my movie. A Leafs hockey player who deserves a pay raise but is denied by upper management: *no problem, Mr. Smith. Just don't show my movie.*

Favors. That's what all these subjects on film owed him: favors. He was king of the cinema.

I dialed the cop shop and was patched right into Sal Lambertino. "What's the score of the game?"

"It hasn't started yet, asshole. Not for another six hours." He laughed.

"I know, I know. Just yanking your chain. But you're not going to believe this. Smith was getting beat up by some punks, they bloodied his glasses—I got the specs in my pocket—no, no he's okay—no, no, he can't talk right now, but you'll want to talk to him. After the hooligans fled I just happened to stumble onto Smith's secret lair. Like the one in the Gardens, and well, we hit the mother lode here, pal, the *Gone with the Wind* of evidence. One crime committed after another. All caught on film. Bring the vice squad."

Sal knew the Rosedale address, and I imagined him subtly scratching at his fence of a Hemingway beard. Would this find hold up since I didn't have a warrant?

"What warrant? I'm not a peace officer, Sal. Smitty was in trouble. I had reasonable and probable grounds to enter his domicile and to rescue him from the hooligans—no, they got away, no—can I help it if I happened to stumble upon this cache of smut?"

He said he'd get a judge's order fast, a warrant to haul in all of this and Smith's bony ass.

"Try to get that judge who is a Habs fan," I said.

That just cracked him up.

I hung up and turned to Smitty. "Well, Mr. People. Help's on its way."

Smith swore with his eyes, while his feet kept scuttling the air.

Stana nudged additional 8mm film into my fingers. McClelland Stuart, in his homburg, drank milk in a big chair while a curvy girl rubbed her breasts up against his face, and then drank his milk for him.

Damn.

And then after twenty or so minutes of unfurling additional film, I found footage of what I probably already knew but didn't want to have confirmed.

There was a woman with white blonde hair, her bare back to the camera, her shoulders angled. Tan lines were noticeable between the spaces where her bra should be and wasn't.

She turned slowly toward the camera. A Mardi-Gras mask was firmly in place as she walked closer and closer, placing her in a saucy medium close-up shot, hands on hips.

Her breasts were small, perky, not quite fully developed. There was a mole between them.

Suddenly I knew which girl was the elusive Starzz.

HOURS LATER, Kim must have still been out showing houses because I wasn't able to reach her about Cathy. Nick wasn't back at the store and his whereabouts were still unknown. Smith was in a holding tank downtown and the CBC was trying to figure out whether or not to break the subject on air tonight. Migano must have been laughing in his ski lodge at how this had all played out for his soon-to-be-ex-auxiliary partner. Stana was with me at Mainly Drew's, drinking a single Guinness. I was knocking back my second tonic water—probably not a good idea given the hole in my mouth.

"Okay, I'm ready to listen—" I cupped my hands together and turned sideways in the booth.

The hockey game was on the wall above me. The Leafs had some pop, especially Davis, who had missed a glorious chance from the slot. The puck hopped over his stick. Seconds later he missed another opportunity by the side of the net.

"Two people dead." I held up a V of crooked fingers for emphasis. "I stood by helplessly as both of them died. And I feel sick about it—"

Strangely, however, my head was actually doing much better: no dizziness, no foggy patches of memory, no feeling like I'm about to throw up in my mouth.

"God damn it." I pointed at the TV. Béliveau again on a screen shot—fuck. Bower had no chance, 1-0 Habs.

Stana nodded absently. She wasn't covering this game. She felt a greater need to come to terms with me. We had been lovers and now we're just friends. I had told her that we could never go back to being lovers again. A line had been crossed.

Even worse, there was no way to get Migano for the killings. We knew that. What evidence did we have? The bodies would never be found. And if they were, I'd be dead.

She twisted her shoulders and absently stirred her drink even though it wasn't the type that needed stirring. I wanted to yank the straw from her but opted to play this moment with blue-note cool, laid back like a Kenny Burrell guitar riff.

Stana paused, collecting her thoughts, two slender fingers caressing the side of her face. She wore a violet dress, stamped with red-shaped designs that could easily have passed for a hanging series of shoe insoles. The dress was high-necked, covering the clavicles, and the sleeves rested just above the elbows. She had four bracelets on her left wrist. They didn't seem to make a sound when she gestured. "Migano and I—" Her hand left her face and tapped the top of her glass.

"Yes?"

"Had a fling last year after you and me were done—"

"You and Babe Migano?"

"Yes."

I couldn't believe this. She had an affair with one of the kingpins, perhaps *the* biggest kingpin, in Toronto's organized crime world. Sure, he oozed style, élan, and cool. And yes, at least he had respect for women, unlike Smith and Bullard, but bottom line he was a kingpin.

Migano, with his connections to the Leafs, had hinted at getting Stana greater access to the players and perhaps even featuring her as the host for a new series he was creating with yet another pot of money he was shifting around.

Toronto After Dark would feature the Oscar Peterson Trio and air on an indie UHF channel. It would be all about hockey, player profiles, their lifestyles, and Stana would interview Leafs greats past and present, their wives and girlfriends. Their discussions would cover everything from politics to cooking to great books to read.

"You fell for that? Come on, Stana."

She played with her hands, the bracelets soundlessly spinning. "I was at a loss after you were gone—I—"

"Don't put this on me—" Yes I didn't return her calls and letters, but Migano the gangster? And then I thought about what Kim said days ago, *a woman doesn't care how a man makes his money, just how he makes love.* She was in love with him too. Everybody loved Migano. "You just wanted to get ahead and this was another one of your pragmatic moves, like running the story about Small Bear, his wife, and Davis," I said.

"I thought you forgave me for that—"

I looked at my fingers. "You're an opportunist—"

She turned sharply and leaned against the table, her shoulders throwing her forward. "*Smith* photographed me and Migano, making love in the CEO's office. The camera was running, the one behind the two-way glass. I had no idea."

"You were at Coughlins?"

"No. It was a date. Migano took me to Smith's office to discuss business and one thing led—"

Didn't I see? She and Migano were *victims*, subjects to be ruled by King Smith's blackmail threats, she said. Only this time Migano got proactive. He learned the alarm code to Smith's Rosedale residence, broke in, and after hours of searching the film's library, found the damaging 8mm evidence. He probably also lifted a few other gems, ones he could use for leverage against the CEO and president, maybe even a gritty little ditty featuring Starzz dancing on Leeds's lap. Maybe an AK-47 to boot.

"You did *it* in Smith's office?"

"I didn't *do it*. I made love. Yes."

"How was he? I bet Babe was real good—"

She looked away.

"Right."

And once Migano got the film back he decided to go after the blackmailer through indirect means, she said.

"Very indirect," I said. "What did Migano want from you in return for this film he stole?"

"My allegiances, my help, a favor." She still couldn't look at me.

"How long have you been in his pocket?"

"*Pocket*? That sounds so dirty—"

"Well, it is dirty—he said he had someone inside—'Aces.'" *His words, not mine.*

"A while," she cut me off.

"How long?"

"Months," she admitted.

How much information about this case was Migano feeding me through Stana? What about the toupee and the note hidden under the cheesecloth? "That was a set-up, too easy, too convenient, wasn't it? That note, the combination numbers, everything, and you knew it and directed me to planted evidence at Hart House."

I snapped my fingers. "Of course. You knew Leeds was dead before we even went over there. You checked in with Migano while I was interviewing Kim and then drove alone in the Galaxie to Leeds's office, checked his corpse, and planted evidence. Then returned in plenty of time before I got done with Kim."

She looked through my shoulder.

"Who did Migano say killed Leeds? And don't tell me Terrien. That's just another smokescreen—" *Another lie, another cheap amusement.*

She played with the lip of her glass and tears slowly splattered on the tabletop. "Kim. He said, Kim. But don't quote me, that's—"

"*Off the record*?"

"Don't be like that—"

"Please." Kim was too cool during our interview to have just killed a man. But maybe she did do it, and that's why she made all those damn overtures at me, to distract herself. I sighed sharply. "The stuff in that locker wasn't even Leeds's—right?"

"Not the 8mm film, no," she said. "That was Smith's. But the photographs were Leeds's." She shrugged and didn't touch the tears of her eyes. It was an arresting tableau, one I didn't feel at liberty to fix.

"Apples and oranges, huh? The apples are Leeds's photos. The oranges are Smith's films, and Bullard's not as stupid as everybody thinks. The two *aren't* connected. Apples and fucking oranges." I threw my hands up with disgust.

"I can't look at you when we talk about this—"

"You better look at me. You didn't have to look at Lisa and Spinner as they died. Lisa went over very fast. Two shots, like hammering a nail. Dead." I snapped my fingers.

"Please—"

"Spinner took a lot longer to die. Blood bubbles kept popping from his mouth and his eye was out of its orbital bone—"

She covered her mouth with her hands and her eyes crowded together.

I never thought I'd tell her what I had seen in that garage, but I wasn't feeling like Hayden Fuller anymore. I was somebody else. "Well, Stana, all of this—us, the case, Lisa and Spinner, Smith and his films—is fucking messy. Look at me—"

Her eyes were red-rimmed, the mascara unbalanced

star-pointed smears.

"And then there was Cathy. She was about to spill the whole thing. The works about Coughlins, her father, maybe even Babe Migano. But then she found out you were in cahoots with the Babe and she couldn't trust you and she got real scared. Would you turn her over to the Babe? Would he kill her? Rather than give you an exclusive she had to go hide. She's in exile because of you—"

"That's not true."

"Bullshit." I grabbed her by the chin, my voice calm, but my face itching like I had a mask on with a dirty string rubbing at the back of my head, around my ears, and a third face was emerging, one part avenging angel and another all hellhound. "He called in the favor, right? Give me Cathy. And she caught wind. Maybe from Kim—she knows Babe. Heard him talk. Warned her sister. Loves her sister despite the pain of her father's love for the one and not the other. Loves her sister even more than she loves Migano, who she has a thing with."

"No."

"Come on, the truth. He wanted you to give her up."

"I wouldn't do that—"

"Sure you wouldn't." I tapped my fingertips together. "Babe did say give me Lisa and Spinner, didn't he? I'm curious. How did he ask? Was his voice a polite carnal purr of a European car?"

I let go of her chin.

"You son of a bitch," she mumbled, her mouth full of tears. He just wanted to talk to Lisa and Spinner. "I didn't think he'd kill them. Maybe rough them up a little—he wanted information, he wanted to know—"

"He also wanted to *talk* to Cathy didn't he? Goddamn it, tell me the truth. No fucking lies."

"Yes."

"He wanted to hurt them, hurt them all—that's all—there

was nothing else behind his motivations. Nothing." I waved her and her explanations away with a quick hand flip and we didn't say anything for five or so minutes.

I couldn't even follow the damn hockey game. My face was aflame, my eyes cindered.

I wondered how I could ever have loved her.

Another five minutes passed.

Rosedale. We didn't nail Smith the first time with the evidence Migano planted in Leeds's locker, but the second go-around sure did the trick. The second tip explains everything—Migano's desires to vaporize Smith from the goddamn planet. Cathy was *never* at Rosedale. Another false lead. *Another cheap amusement.*

She tapped her glass of Guinness. I looked into my glass of tonic water, the bubbles flat.

From a phone booth, I called Kim again. No answer. Nick: nothing. Before the end of the second period, Small Bear tied up the game on a wrist shot that slithered through Lorne "Gump" Worsley's chest protector.

When I returned to the table, Stana was gone. I finished my tonic water and decided it was time to honor the dead.

THE RIDE TO VAUGHAN on Highway 400 North, the old Toronto-Barrie run, took me just over an hour. I had the windows wide open, and the air was crisp and cool and reminded me of flying kites with my dad.

We never did a whole lot together, my father and me. He was often sleeping the hard rest of the drunk on a couch or hitting my mother, but every now and then he took me to a hockey game or helped fly a red kite at Wilket Creek Park, letting out more and more string as the kite rose and flapped, and appeared to hang still in the sky like a spot of mercury, a wobbly iris.

For a second, the glare off the overhanging streetlights blazed streamers on the windshield that reminded me of my kite tail, swimming with sky.

After inching down a long skinny road that turned from pavement to gravel to dirt, I was at the site, the huge acreage of land that Bullard and Migano had bought up. I shut off the lights and walked and walked and walked.

I saw thin spots of cabins, like discarded dice, in the distance. Sarah and the suitcase. 101 days ago.

There were sentries of CAT machines and bulldozers parked next to the cabins. The discarded dice were to be demolished, forgotten.

The sky was full of silver: the stars and moon creating pockets of silence for me to slide into. A red flag marked one corner of the property. The expanse between me and where black sky touched ground was a hard disc. I couldn't see any other flags.

Migano said he was going to do something poetic. What would be more poetic than to bury the bodies on this hallowed place where his dream would be built?

I walked further, my hands in my pockets, my head no longer hurting, my eyes on the stars, and I spoke, mumbled, some words, incoherent but a mashed-up narrative nonetheless. About Lisa, I lamented how she had been given a tough break, an abusive father, another man, the father of a friend, who betrayed and manipulated her, and how that hurt made her want to hurt back, and that there was a sadness to her, a sadness that nobody, except maybe Spinner, really wanted to extinguish. She was forgotten, but not for me.

And then I said an epitaph for Spinner, how he was a guy underestimated by many and deserved better than he got and I think he was good for Lisa. I could see it in their eyes—I think they really cared about each other. Gay or not, he loved her.

And I stood there under the stars. Breathed and understood.

I wanted to curse the heavens and not cry, but I did cry, for them, myself, for Stana. For all of us.

It was an act of mourning.

And then I heard it. Chains click-click-clicking as wheels slowly climbed the sky, and then voices, thousands of voices screaming—joy and pain—as wheels, hundreds of them, thudded and pounded wooden tracks.

And a giant wheel, and another, and another, spinning not together, but in different arcs, to my right, to my left, full of bright lights glowing slowly, as cars twisted, and more joyous voices rained down.

And below the Ferris wheels, people on the boardwalk, eating cotton candy, talking, kissing, running, lost in funhouses, barrels spinning, floors turning faster and faster, as crowded folks fall from the human roulette wheel and huddle and bunch and grip together like a charm bracelet of bodies.

And somewhere a kid with a red kite enjoys all of this, standing back from the midway's attractions, drinking a cola. Afterward he tosses balls at wood bottles and thinks that this bazaar, this wondrous place that Babe Migano has built, this is indeed Canada's Bazaar, and it is indeed pretty glorious.

13

It didn't take long to get back into the city. Most of the traffic was going the other way after the Leafs' overtime win over Montreal. I had listened to what was left of the game on the radio. Davis scored the tying goal midway through the third—the crowd had been booing him all night. Maybe they were upset over the point-blank chances the ex-scoring champ had missed, or maybe they had caught wind of Stana's ongoing investigation and how he was about to be named as a frequent guest at Coughlins. In less than an hour, I'd have even more of a story for Stana.

I dry swallowed another painkiller.

The gang was all there at Kim's apartment. Cool Athol and Lou-doo filled the door behind me, arms folded with command presence. Lou's hair, liquid napalm, had enough pomade to burn a town. Athol wore his Oliver Hardy bowler and his hands were on his hips, flaring his jacket so that I could see that he had a side-holster too. His eyes flitted about like hovering dragonflies.

Babe Migano wore a dark suit, a jaunty pink rose in the lapel, and he slowly sipped scotch. "Salut." He raised the shot glass. "Nice job on Smith."

"Thanks, but right now I have bigger fish to fry." I tipped my porkpie.

I smiled, my legs, shoulders and arms loose like a pool hustler ready to pocket a tricky combination shot. The headaches were gone. The room quieted. A clock that looked like a cat's face stuttered, eyes moving left, right.

Kim pulled her legs closer to her chin. She was sitting in her big comfy chair. I didn't smell Chanel. She twisted hair behind one of her ears and sighed.

"All right, you ready for the big finish?" I planted myself in front of a coffee table and rubbed hands together. I smiled my lupine lopsided grin, the same smart-ass leer that's riding on my private investigator's license.

"How about those Leafs, huh?" Lou-doo interrupted, a clumsy attempt to loosen the tension his boss and his girlfriend were feeling. "Keon in overtime. That guy's money."

I nodded. McClelland's radio play-by-play had suggested that Big M's forecheck forced J. C. Tremblay to cough up the puck, and then Keon corralled the pass, broke in on Worsley, and beat the Gumper stick-side with a backhand. Programs splashed down as the home crowd let out a pent-up cheer of relief. The Leafs were back in the series.

"Money," Lou-doo repeated.

"Shut up, Lou." Migano smiled at me. Even his pink rose appeared to be smiling. "It's your floor, shamus." He looked at his watch. "But I do want to catch Peterson's final set at the White Heat, so pick up the pace."

"Sure, anything for jazz." I smiled back. "It took me a long time to figure this case out. What with all the lies and double-crosses." I held up a finger. "There was one constant. Love, people helping and covering up for others out of love. With every case, I ask that central question. Where's the love? Why was Cathy abducted and who did it? Simple, huh?" I laughed. "But it wasn't that simple. Cathy wasn't abducted."

I rubbed the edges of my mouth. Kim tucked her knees in tighter. She *did* look wonderful in Capris. Giant hoop earrings caught the light and enunciated the flash line along her lower jaw.

"Cathy found out that Stana is on your payroll, Babe. So she couldn't trust her. The story she was about to break about Coughlins and all the shenanigans going on at the Gardens, forget about it. She feared the story would never break and she'd wind up a corpse buried out on that big subdivision you're building an amusement park on."

That got a response. Migano leaned forward and Athol's hand moved closer to his pistol. "Leeds was the key. He wasn't killed by Terrien. That kid couldn't have harmed anyone." I lifted Kim's chin and smiled. "You know where Cathy is." I walked to the stonewall and thumbed the lip of the ledge.

Kim no longer looked at me. She was worrying the inside of her mouth.

"Look, Landover was killed by someone he knew. There were powder burns on his chest. Close range." I shoved my hands in my pockets. "For some reason, Babe, you thought Kim did it. Why? Because she told you she did."

"What?" Babe was no longer looking at his smiling flower.

"Stana told me, although she swears that comment's off the record." I shrugged. "You love Kim, Babe, and when she told you what she allegedly did you tried to cover for her. You sent Stana over there to plant evidence. The toupee and the hidden 'key' to a locker full of smut. And let's not forget the trumped-up Terrien angle. The fucking shoes."

Babe looked back at the flower in his lapel and smiled slightly. "What about the girl you saw in the street without shoes on?"

"Oh, Stana told you about that. Your ace, huh?" My lips formed a tight line. "I saw a girl all right, but she was wearing shoes. I expected her not to be so I projected—"

"Bullshit," Athol said, eyes narrowing.

I turned and slapped hands over the front of my shirt. "What color's my tie?"

"Huh?" Migano's face creased like an avant-garde painting.

"Answer it."

"Black like the skinny one you wore for our first meeting." The tents around his shoulders puffed up again.

"That's right," Lou-doo said. "Black like the Ace of Spades."

"He's not wearing a tie," Cool Athol said, his fingers gracing the gun's checkered grip.

The way his eyes danced around every area code but this one, I figured the cat wasn't taking in anything, but I was wrong. I made a note not to underestimate him.

"Right." I pointed at Athol, revealing my open-collared tieless look. Cool Athol was on his game. "But two of you seemed to think there was one there. Our eyes play tricks all the time—that night I saw what I wanted to see." I started laughing and I couldn't quite stay on top of it. Maybe I wasn't quite the relaxed pool shark that I thought I was. "It wasn't Kim that killed Leeds. It wasn't Terrien either dressed up as Starzz. What a reach that is. Starzz was Sarah. The first girl killed, 101 days ago. I've seen the film. The mole on her chest. Cathy was Sarah's friend, and Nick was involved with Sarah. It's all hunches of course, but detectives go on instincts. The night of Sarah's murder she had been raped. Someone's going to pay for that." I touched stone ridges, feeling for a toggle switch. "Cathy tried to protect Sarah. Sarah ends up dead. Nobody's seen Starzz in three months. The Orient? Really?" I laughed. "With her friend murdered, Cathy wants to get even, spill the whole Coughlins story to Stana, but Kim loves her sister and warns her about you Babe and the reporter on your payroll. So what does Cathy do? Goes underground." I looked over at Kim. "Right?"

Kim nodded at her knees.

Athol took a step forward.

"As a matter of fact, Kim loves her sister so much that she's willing to take the rap for her." I started laughing again. It wasn't how I wanted to play this.

Kim rushed from her seat, as if she were going to hit me, and then changed her mind. She stood before me, her lower lip wobbling. "I'm glad you didn't hit me, or else I'd have to hipcheck you into that chair." I smiled. "Sorry, I'm an ex-hockey player. Some habits die hard."

She smiled slightly. She didn't want to, but she did. She sat back down.

"Cathy's hiding is really a kind of voluntary seclusion, courtesy of Kim. Kim's no warden, she gives her sister the freedom to come and go as she pleases. One night, Cathy goes and visits Leeds, convinces him, for old times' sake, to open his gun box, and he lets her even play with the gun for a while, and guns go off as guns do—"

"My sister never killed anyone—"

"This time she did. You convinced Babe that you did it to get back the $568,000, but it was Cathy."

"How about that Keon," Lou-doo mumbled with glee.

"Shut up, Lou," Babe said, his voice low, easy.

"She did it for Sarah. She knew about Leeds, the Tangerine Room, the therapy sessions—"

Someone had to pay for Sarah and her death, 101 days ago.

"Boss, you want me to shut this guy up." Athol's fingers tightened along his gun's checkered grip. His eyes hovered over me, then back to his boss, and then the shag rug and maybe parts of downtown Toronto. He had a hard time staying in the vicinity. I wasn't even sure he was in the 416 area code.

"No, no. Let him rave. I admire his chutzpah. That's a Jewish word fellas, for balls."

"More or less," I said with a shrug. "But women can have chutzpah too." I turned to Lou-doo. "How about that Keon."

He nodded proudly. "Keon's money, man." And he wasn't just talking figuratively. Apparently Fortunado put down $200 on the game and Keon's goal helped put Lou-doo in the coin, big time. "I couldn't believe the odds I was getting," he said.

"I'm happy for you."

Lou-doo smiled like a ten-year-old.

Cool Athol's fingers twitched, awaiting instructions.

I studied Kim and her Capris. "The powder burns." I took a breath. "It was someone Leeds knew who he thought he had control over. . . . You got a glass of water?"

Migano poured me one from a pitcher crowded with ice.

Next, the bathroom at Stabulas's Grocery and the dislodged piece of wood, and the light streaming in from above. "Nick had a fetish for underage girls, looking at them, wanting them. He was involved with Leeds in their sick habit and somehow Cathy had become a victim of this porn ring. And let's not forget the dash of hypnosis right out of a fucking Buck Rogers serial. When did it start—the rape?"

Kim glanced at Babe, and hurried her look away. Athol's eyes hovered about me, and then over ten different locations before returning to yours truly.

"When I was twelve." She sat at the edge of her puffy chair, hands level, her voice a flatline. Nick would come into the room Kim shared with her sister and place a hand over Kim's mouth and say she was beautiful.

"He never touched Cathy?"

Her voice maintained a flatline. No. Never. But Nick made the Irish twin listen. Cathy was ordered to turn the other way and face the wall, but she heard it all. "For years my sister has been sexually inactive, a *saint* because of this."

"And then when you got too old, he wanted Sarah, didn't he? He wanted younger girls. She was Starzz at fifteen."

"Yes."

"Cathy knew about this too. That was another secret she was about to reveal, but you tried to talk her out of it." It would blow the lid off the whole thing. Starzz, Sarah, Coughlins, repeated rapes. "What would it do with your standing at Ogilvie and Beggert? What would it do to your relationship with Babe? He believed in the purity of women. What would he think of a woman who had been thus sullied?"

Kim's eyes watered and she covered her face.

"You take too many chances," Babe said.

"If I didn't take chances, I wouldn't be here now." I shrugged sluggishly. "Cathy loved you too. She wanted to make amends. Tell her story as an act of healing. Help her sister."

Babe moved closer to Kim.

"I didn't think Babe could live with what had happened to me—"

"I can." Babe kissed Kim, caressing her shoulders, holding her.

"And that brings me back to Cathy. The stuff in the drawer wasn't hers. It was Sarah's." Cathy, according to Mrs. Kerr, had gone back to the apartment after the police confiscated a bunch of possessions. Cathy found the hidden stash of S&M material and locked it in her drawer to protect her friend, or maybe use later as evidence.

Kim nodded.

I sat down, rubbed the corners of my mouth.

My shoes were lined with black dirt, Canada's Bazaar. "The first time I was here, I smelled Chanel No. 5. A pleasant enough smell, Kim. I thought it was yours. I shouldn't have." I stood up, pushed back my porkpie, and returned to the stone wall, the one displaying the color television and expensive ivory art carvings by Eskimos. "Bolemac did construction at the Gardens, at Smith's, and here. Two of the three had secret compartments, sliding walls, hidden lairs." I blew air slowly between my lips and felt along the wall's edgings, fingers slithering for a switch. "Third time a charm?"

Embedded in one of the crease lines of stone was a button. I pushed it. The wall silently shifted from left to right.

There on a plush couch sat Cathy, her red hair brimming with backlight, and Steinbeck's *The Grapes of Wrath* on the long, low coffee table in front of her. I waved. It was a weird gesture. I was kind of at a loss for words, but I was so glad to see her and the crumbling rocks returned to my stomach but in a good way.

Her lips were pinched tight, her shoulders tense and upright.

But despite the bodily tension, she smiled back with her whole face and eyes.

Next to her on the couch was the reason for Cathy's stiffness—Nick Stabulas. He wore green work pants, suspenders and a V-neck T-shirt. He was coring an apple with a rather large knife. He did not look at me or smile in any way.

Of course he'd be hiding here. Mr. Exploitation. Where else would he be but desperately using his daughters to get by? A master manipulator, Nick had no qualms over calling in a favor from daughters he had abused repeatedly.

I stepped into the lair and tipped my head to Cathy. "Did you hear everything? Do I need to say anything again?"

"You don't need to say anything again."

And then I heard it, the American pronunciation, the gen as in Jen instead of the Canadian strong "gain" on the second syllable. "You were the one who tipped me? 101 days ago about Sarah."

She nodded, hands on thighs. She wore white pants with the zipper in the back, a black scarf around her neck, and a bright shirt full of pastel-colored circles. It gave her an upbeat tempo. I hoped that mood would win the day.

"Am I right? About the past events—am I? You weren't really a prisoner here. You were free to come and go. And one night, you killed Leeds. I don't really give a damn about that. He was an asshole. Exploited you and Sarah, got you both into the porn ring, but Sarah liked it, didn't she?"

Cathy looked away.

"She felt empowered. The mousy girl, the willowy one full of sexual allure. Sex was a drug for her."

"I tried to get her free of it," Cathy said.

"She needed to be free of her mom." I shook my head. "Leeds was the lowest of the low and deserved to get got. I'm not turning you in, Cathy." I guess, in a way, Migano and me had some things in common. We liked women.

Cathy nodded again, her eyes brushed with happiness.

I stared at Nick and his cocky, self-assured leer, as he rotated the apple with the large knife sticking in it around his thumb and forefinger as if it were the world spinning on an axis that he controlled.

"And what about me?"

"You, Mr. Fucko. You're not so lucky. Why'd you kill Sarah?"

"What?" Kim said.

"I didn't," Nick said.

"Sure you didn't. Did you wait around the woods and watch me and the police standing about like schmucks as an empty motor boat broke across the ice?"

"You can't prove it."

"What did Sarah ever do to you?"

"She laughed at me, said I had too many hang-ups. Nobody laughs at me."

Kim let out a short gasp.

The spin of the apple was slow and Nick's eyebrows meshed again into a long machete blade. "So she allowed me to punish her." He smiled an angry leer. "What are you going to do about it, tough guy?"

I had seen that anger before, when he slapped Kim around.

"Well, since you asked." I gestured and rubbed the back of my neck. "Take you in. Arrest you. Throw away the fucking key." I shrugged, pulling back my jacket, revealing the snub-nosed at my side.

"I don't think so," he said.

"I don't get you. You killed Sarah. You—"

"Spare me the speeches. Willowy? That's tough. Maybe I was feeling empowered when I killed her, huh?" His head sunk into his raised shoulders and combined with his mood gave off the gloaming of an unrepentant toad. He wasn't placing blame on anyone. No victim card. He owned up to his evil—Iago of the Year Award Winner, 1965.

I held up my hands as if to say okay and wondered how many people were in on his and Leeds's little photograph racket.

"A lot. You'd be surprised. What with the blackmail kickbacks from Stuart, and the sales to middle-school boys, enough to keep my storefront in business."

"Well don't brag about it. I was just asking out of politeness—"

"Look, there were older men too. Middle-aged men. Just as some men prefer veal instead of steak, other men prefer—"

"Shut up—" The gun was now in my hands, leveled at him.

"I made some nice money." He leered, oblivious to right and wrong. "It was good. Fun."

"Let's go." I waved with my gun.

"I don't think so."

"Think again. You have no hold on anyone anymore." I wiped the edges of my mouth again. "Isn't that right, Babe?"

He looked into his pink rose and then squeezed the tops of Kim's shoulders. "That's right."

"If you take me in, I'll talk." Nick's cool don't-give-a-damn demeanor wasn't cracking. He was just laying out his case, but the Old World accent, the one filled with traces of humility, was so far gone as to have been part of another lifetime. Now, he sounded like any other Anglo punk.

"You're finished, creep."

"I'm finished, when I say I'm finished." He looked at his fingers. "Look, I'll tell them about Coughlins, about the Gardens, about Babe's tie-in with the deaths of Lisa and Spinner—" His eyes were lean, his face a still mask: his cheeks, his lips, barely twitching as he spoke.

Athol pulled his gun and aimed it at the back of my head.

"I'll tell how Smith tried to create sex scandals with people in power. How Bullard was involved with an underage escort girl,

Starzz, a.k.a. Sarah Kerr. What will that do to your land deal, Babe?" He smiled darkly. "Bolemac. You're tied in to all of this. Don't forget what I know."

I let out a sharp whistle and turned around. Athol's eyes were hovering in the direction of Montreal, Cambridge, and Barrie, anywhere but in this room, and me, this moment in Toronto. He was an unsteady mess. "Athol, put the gun away. Babe—" I breathed deeply.

"I'll tell them Cathy killed Leeds." Nick's smile grew bigger, like a big wobbly bubble.

"I can't have that," Kim said. "Him talking about my sister that way. They'll lock her up."

"I can't have that either. You got to keep harmony with your woman," Babe said. "Athol, take the fuck out."

"Which one, boss? Who do you want taken out?" Athol's eyes and gun flashed between me and Nick and Montreal and Saskatchewan.

"Oh, for chrissakes," Migano said, but it was too late by then.

In the indecision of the interim, Nick had seized Cathy in a rock-hard headlock and yanked her towards him. The sharp-edged knife was still in the goddamn apple on the coffee table. Instead, by Cathy's temple was a much more dangerous weapon, a Smith & Wesson .38. Where did the gun come from? I was spending too much time following the spin of the knife to be looking for a gun.

"I'm getting out of here." Nick tugged Cathy closer, his finger whitening on the gun's trigger guard. "I got nothing to lose. If I go, she goes." He shrugged, his jaw and chin jutted forward.

"Don't, Babe," Kim pleaded. "Let him go. Just let him go—please, please, please."

"Boss?" Athol's gun was poised like a sharp flag.

"You better kill me, Dad," Cathy intervened, "because I won't lie for you. No free passes. Give yourself up. I'm telling everyone what you did—what you did to my sister, to me, to Lisa—and

Sarah, who I loved as a second sister." She couldn't look at him. "And I'm not saying a word against Babe. Because of my sister." She could only look at Babe. Her voice was a husky whisper. She didn't smoke but the timbre sounded as if she did.

"What about your love for your father, huh? Where's all that love?"

"I lost that sometime ago." She took a deep breath. "I'm going to tell my story. With truth comes healing." This time she was looking at him.

With truth comes healing. I wondered about that. With truth comes healing.

"Where did you read that? From a fortune cookie at Sai Woo's?" Nick clamped a forearm under Cathy's chin, silencing her. The leer deepened. "I'm getting out of this room—"

"You might want to stand up then." I leveled my gun at him. "Give yourself a fair shake."

"What?"

Athol's gun was now trained on me. So too Lou-doo's.

"Boss—" Lou-doo's usual gravel was now replaced with wet mud. "Boss—"

"Be money, Lou," I said. "Just be money. I got this." I wanted to catch Nick off guard so I threw quirky tidbits his way. I told him how hockey nets were four-by-six and right now, with you seated like that, Nick, your head is about four feet off the ground, top-shelf. I practiced top-shelf shots all my life and this was a top-shelf moment.

"This isn't a goddamn hockey game."

No, but the focus and commitment I brought to hockey I bring to everything I do, I said. At the police station, twice a week, I take target practice, headshots, Nick.

He smiled. "You shoot me, my reflexes kill the girl."

"No. A bullet in the right place and the assailant goes down like spaghetti, loose limbed, one dead marionette. Let go of Cathy. I'm counting to three."

"You were never that good. Top-shelf, my ass."

"I really think you should stand up. I won't have as good a chance with you standing—it evens up the odds—"

He refused.

"Boss—" Lou-doo asked.

"Boss?" Athol seconded.

"Babe, stop him, stop them—" Kim screamed.

"I always said the kid had chutzpah." Babe's voice was bold and confident. "Let Hayden skate with this. Play it out, kid—"

Athol and Lou sighed and I sensed they were lowering their guns behind me. And I slid back between pockets of silence, calm, relaxed, the infinite space becoming finite. I feared nothing.

"One."

Nick's fingers moved from the trigger guard to the trigger.

"I scored 107 goals," I said.

"Most of them were low and to the stick side. I watched you play."

He wouldn't let the girl go. He knew what he was doing. Nobody in prison likes a guy who rapes twelve-year-olds.

Short eyes, they call such perpetrators. Short eyes.

"You were never that good," he challenged.

"I did all right."

He laughed. "You're no Bobby Hull."

"No."

Cathy's eyes didn't widen with fear. Sure her mouth parted slightly, but she remained calm, she had skated into those pockets of silence with me. So had Kim. She was no longer screaming. I heard her breath catch, like right after a referee's whistle, before play starts up again.

Nothing was breaking my flow, the pain, everything, was gone. My shoulders, arms, and legs: loose. "Let Cathy go."

"Prove it, hotshot."

Cathy nodded with her eyes, *do it.*

"Two."

"Prove it. I don't think you're that good. You were never that good. A marginal player at best, a third-line guy."

"Drop the gun—"

His hardened trigger finger was white phosphorus. "Prove it. Prove it, you motherfucker, prove it, you candy-ass."

And I did, right under the bar.

A Fourth Face

1

"They think I did it."

His voice was buried shells on a beach, thin creases, full of sand. I didn't recognize it at first.

I squeezed my eyes in an effort to open them more fully. They were caked with cereal crust and the shadowy figure before me was a series of rocks floating by the side of my bed. I propped myself up on my elbows.

Thin traces of moon lit his shoulders and the tips of his chin and hawk nose.

"Bobby?"

He opened his mouth without speaking. The clock on the nightstand glowed 3:40 or 8:17. It had to be 3:40—it was too dark to be morning. My face was hot but my forehead was cool and the ceiling fan twisted with a slight rattle.

Anyway, I hadn't been sleeping well. My therapist says I got shit to work out. That's how she talks, "shit to work out." The 1960s is a progressive time.

I have this recurring dream: I'm trapped in a musty suitcase, full of moths, my father's bourbon-soaked voice yelling, "get out, get out." I'm never sure, in the dream, if he's imploring me to fight and free myself from the suitcase or to extricate myself from his life. Get out.

"I saw her. A plastic bag." Bobby dropped his forehead into his shoulder, his voice taking on more sand. "I didn't do it—"

The rattle of the ceiling fan was louder than I expected it to be. It was as if some of the sand had slipped inside its bearings.

Bobby Ehle was an ex-Leaf defenseman, and tonight his face was full of little scratches like he had fallen down an ivy trellis or some such damn thing. There were deeper marks around his Adam's apple and along the tops of his hands. His hockey story: at the start of the 1964 season, after being a seven-year pro, three-time Stanley Cup champ, and second-team all-star the prior season, he retires, leaving training camp in Peterborough, Ontario, having had it with my ex-coach Hugh "Two-Fisted" Farrell, a regular resident philosopher. "Hockey's a game of emotion, Ehle, it's a streetcar named desire, and I don't think you've ever caught it."

Two Fists sure loved that line. He said it to Big M, me, Billy Harris. He should get a patent on it or one of them registered trademark things. You know with the R and the circle? Anyway.

I think Gordie Howe has one next to his name. Really.

You can look it up.

I'm kidding. Who the hell would do such a thing? He's known as Mr. Hockey, but he's not full of himself, and Bobby was known as the Pest, the Intimidator, and the ever so pithy moniker Little Shit. The latter was only uttered behind opposing teams' locker room doors, a shared space that the press had limited access to.

I guess Bobby eventually caught a different streetcar than the one coach was riding. I don't know what he'd been doing the last year or so. One time, I saw him in back of the Gardens, near Church Street, smoking a cigarette, signing autographs. It looked like the last place he wanted to be, but there he was, shoulders hunched, chin on chest.

As I adjusted to the shadow light, the marks on Bobby's hands became more apparent. The skin around the fingernails was nicked up, gouged, and flecked with dried blood.

And his voice. It wasn't the same. The fast rat-a-tat-tat he had as a player was now full of beach sand and much slower than I remembered.

The real reason Bobby walked away from hockey? He was depressed. His wife Nancy had cheated on him with a plastic surgeon, Cliff Airedale, a tall angular guy with a baggy ass and a hitch in his walk, a guy who should carry a tennis racket wherever he goes, a guy who thinks a goatee makes him Beat Generation–cool.

I took the pictures of their "interludes" with a Leica and fast film so I know how baggy his ass is.

Bobby had hired me. It was my first "case." Before snapping covert pix of Nancy and Cliff I took mainly photos of the fellas' girlfriends and wives, sexy snapshots to keep in a cedar chest or the far recesses of a desk drawer. The Bobby case helped pay for my new Hi-Fi. Unfortunately, the dividends didn't outweigh the full cost. The story of the affair broke when my girlfriend at the time, Stana Younger, reported it in the pages of *The Toronto Telegram*, and I wound up drummed out of the NHL for "moral turpitude." Bobby played the rest of that season without me, and then hung up the skates after a few weeks of training camp, summer 1964.

It was now a year later. Summer, 1965. July. Nancy Ehle had returned to being Nancy Drouin. And I had the feeling Bobby wanted to hire me again. Something about the sand in his voice.

"Plastic bag?"

"Yeah. It was on her face." He grinned a troubled corkscrew leer, like he couldn't get things to add up in his head. He always had that look as a player, in practices, during games, while playing cards on long train rides. It was a look inhabiting a vacant parking lot and at the same time an intense stare filled up with crammed cars, stories he couldn't share. Now the voice was heavily medicated.

"She's dead?"

He nodded. Slowly.

"And you—saw her?"

"I was following her." He looked away. A scar, the chunk of a golf divot, was a small river creasing his lower lip, and the skin around his eyes were puffy leeches, the face of a boxer. Bobby was tough but he was dirty. He led our team in penalty minutes every year, scrapping with the likes of a Lou Fortunado, and one night at Madison Square Garden, Lou-doo tried to tomahawk Bobby's hair from his scalp with sharp clutching hands and razor-like forearms, and Bobby knocked him cold with an overhand haymaker, but he didn't take off his gloves. You don't fight with your gloves. Hockey code. But Fortunado had treated Bobby's hair as if it were an unwarranted accessory, and Bobby just lost it. Did he do the same thing with Nancy? Did he hit her with gloves on?

"You had a restraining order." I reminded him of what I read in the dailies, Stana Younger's column. Every goddamn day. "You're supposed to be nowhere near her—" He had been previously arrested, including sixty days ago, but Nancy dropped the charges.

She did that on more than one occasion.

"I know, I know." He shrugged, his left ankle turned awkwardly. "I wanted another chance—" He rubbed at deeper scratches on his left cheek. There were sharp, parallel lines, three tines on a fork. He scrubbed his tan-colored hair, trying to remember something.

"She's not your wife anymore—"

"I know, I know. I got the memo, okay?" His chocolate-brown eyes filled with remnants of a corkscrew leer. "To be honest with you, I don't know how I got to her apartment. I was just there." He leaned his forehead into a flat hand and steadied himself. "And I saw her—"

There were lots of things he couldn't remember anymore. Too many concussions. "Who was number 15. On the Leafs," he asked. "Fifteen?"

For some reason it was important to know this, now.

"Billy Harris," I said. Our fourth-line center.

"Four?"

"Red Kelly." Our best backchecker, next to Keon. Shut down Béliveau.

"Seventeen?"

"Me." I smiled, my face hurting a little. "Hayden Fuller." Drummed out of the league for a "hobby."

"Right, right." He remembered his "D" partner, Bobby Baun, and our goalie Johnny Bower, and the Captain, Benjamin Smallbear, but their faces, and highlights from various games, like the overtime winner he scored in '61, were all disappearing, shallow puddles lifting up from a hot sidewalk.

I don't know if it were because I only had two hours of sleep, but suddenly the whole room was full of sand, in my eyes, behind my eyes, in my mouth, in my head, on my skin. It swirled about like a dust storm. It stuck everywhere. I felt like I was in Oklahoma, 1934.

"What's with the scratches?"

He shrugged. "Barroom scuffle? Habs fan?" The joke wasn't getting any play. Maybe the timing was off. He delivered the line two beats too slow.

"Look at your hands. The scratches around your neck. Someone was fighting back. Desperately." One of the fingernails on his left hand was torn off.

I was now circling him. "Why were you following her?" My knees hurt a little.

"I wasn't *following* her."

"You just said you were."

"I misspoke. I was just. There. Like. There."

"What suddenly you're Tinkerbell now, floating through keyholes, magically appearing in people's apartments? C'mon Bobby, level with me."

"I don't remember."

"Did you kill her?"

"No." He shrugged.

The ceiling fan needed an adjustment or two.

"I was worried about her, I guess, so I wanted to see. Her."

"Worried. What do you mean?"

"Airedale's bunch. She's mixed up with them."

Well, she had been sleeping with him, the guy in need of a tennis racket.

That ended a while ago. They were still friends, Bobby said. Imagine that guy being. Your. Friend? "I've seen them at his clinic. Guys with gloves on their hands."

"Gangsters?"

What was Bobby doing at the Queen Street clinic?

He couldn't remember the name of the clinic. Neither could I.

"Hitmen," he said, nodding. Slowly. "That's the kind of guys who wear gloves." He raised his shoulders. "Did you hear about that publishing house in Montreal, the one that publishes literary novels that nobody reads?"

Literary. When did he learn that word? In his playing days all Bobby ever read were comic books and racing forms. He really liked Hawkman. Said they had similar beaks.

"Yeah." I read the story. A fire burned down half the building, delaying the release of several titles, including a new collection of poems by Leonard Cohen.

"Nancy overhead Airedale's crowd vaguely. Talking about. It. Taking sideways credit."

"Uh-huh."

"Nothing specific."

"Right."

"And then there was that English paper in Montreal—"

"*The Citizen*?"

"Yeah."

A small bomb was found in the lobby with a threatening note attached, something about those who tell the stories having the power. The bomb squad rushed in and uncovered three or four faux wires, discovering it was nothing but a smoke bomb, a variation on a mild teargas canister.

"Same outfit?"

"Maybe."

My stomach was full of cold rocks but everything else about me was gritted with sweat and sand. I needed a shower.

"Believe me, Hayden. I never hit her. Ever." He reached into his shirt pocket and dry swallowed some pills. A lot of pills.

And those hands. A fingernail missing.

"That's not what the papers said." I was still circling. "The scratches? Those are fresh—" The lower part of my back was on fire. I leaned left, right, stretching. Maybe I needed a new bed.

Stana last week ran a three-part feature, an exclusive story with Nancy Drouin, detailing Bobby's depressed moods as a player, his melancholic outbursts, his intense jealousies whenever Nancy talked to another man. He'd punch her again and again and yelled, "Don't you ever disrespect me. You hear what I said. Don't you ever—"

"We'd scuffle a little. In the past. That's all."

"What about tonight?"

"A little." He pushed a hand against his forehead. "I think. I'm not. Sure. God, I think. My head hurts—"

"You remember 'scuffling'?"

"I think so."

"Your head? That's what the pills are for?"

"Yeah." Like I was telling you, *Hayden, concussions*. He'd had a lot of fights in the pros, and sat out a dozen or so games each season with excruciating pain, black dogs barking about in his head. One time, the pain was so bad, that before a game Bobby was lying on the locker-room floor, his head resting against the cool concrete.

Coach stepped over him as he rattled on about desire.

The ceiling fan whirred like a helicopter. I was still circling. "C'mon Bobby—the truth—"

"I was just there. And the plastic. Bag."

"You were just there? Scuffling." I wondered if he'd take a lie detector.

"Hell, yeah. Lie detector. Fuck. Yeah. Wrestling. That's all. Scuffling. I never, ever, punched her. I pushed her sometimes when she got a little crazy, slapped her back when she slapped me, but I never punched her. You got to believe me." The whirring got louder.

I looked up at the ceiling fan. "What the fuck's with that?" I wasn't very good at fixing things. Toasters, lamps, light switches, forget about it. My pop never passed on basic electrical skills, or carpentry or masonry, nothing. I was good at making phone calls.

It wasn't the goddamn fan, he said. "Helicopter." *That really cracked him up. You think a fan can get that noisy, Hayden? He was still laughing, crumpling over. Maybe it was helping with his headaches.*

"In my backyard? A fucking helicopter?"

He was heading to Oslo, Sweden. Oslo's in Norway, I told him, and he said he always sucked at geography, but the place in Sweden sounds like Oslo, it has an "O" in it anyway, a lot of O's, but for now the helicopter was taking him somewhere up north, bush country, and from there he was going to make his way to Sweden to coach hockey. "They want us Canadians over there. They say Terrien's there too."

Brian Spinner Terrien was buried in a plot of land about to become an amusement park. But only I and a handful of people knew that. Stana knew.

"Sweden. They have extradition, Bobby—"

"This will all blow over by then."

He'd be in *Oslo, Sweden* in less than twenty-four hours.

"I'm hiring you to find out who killed her. The real killer." He shook his head again. "A plastic bag, man." He popped another pill, and the laughter stopped, a match puffed out.

Was she seeing anybody?

No. He nodded. "Well, maybe Terry."

"Who's Terry?"

"Some fucko she met at the clinic. Terry Quinton."

I wrote it down on a yellow pad by my nightstand, next to the clock, and my .38, in its holster, loaded.

Bobby's shoulders suddenly shook. Nancy's death eyes, man, were shiny coins, he said. Bright and much bigger than they should have been. He absently touched one of the tines on his cheek. "I don't know if I can take these headaches much longer. Sometimes I figure—"

I handed him a glass of water.

"I loved her."

I bit my lower lip.

Blades whirred.

My mind drifted to the suitcase and my father, yelling.

Shit, I don't know how the helicopter even landed in my backyard without waking the whole fucking neighborhood. I live in the suburbs, a kind of Toronto Levittown, where every fourth house is the same. Fortunately, some of the houses around me haven't been finished yet. The house to my left needed sheet rock added to the upstairs frames, and the two houses to my right were on bald brown dirt, awaiting the additions of mats of grass. But my yard was a different story. A helicopter sat like a huge black dragonfly filling up space, kicking up puffs of dust. I hadn't mowed in weeks. It looked like South Vietnam out there.

I could make out some markings on the copter, KEY. It was black and white and the front windows tinted. Who was the pilot? Bobby couldn't even drive a car. He was the worst, taking his hands off the wheel, frequently, to make whatever point he was bloviating about. "Who's flying the bird?"

"Was I really a second-team all-star my final year?"

"Yeah."

He nodded, his lips pushed together, and he looked away, his voice dropping. "A friend. Flying the insect." He handed me five hundred dollars. Slowly. They were crumpled and resembled fat worms. "That's all I've got." His face was boyish, bashful, as if he were afraid of being in trouble. "Don't be mad at me."

"I'm not mad. Who's flying the bird?"

"You look mad."

"I'm just trying to figure things out."

"That's just for starters. The money? What do you call it?"

"A retainer?" It was more than generous. My fee was $40 a day and expenses.

"Yeah, that. Retainer. Will you look into this?" He crushed a hiccup in a big shoulder. "Help me?"

"I got to tell you, Bobby. It doesn't look so good. The evidence, I mean?"

I'll take a lie detector. In Sweden. Send it to you. He wanted so much for me to believe in him. He was like a little kid. "You're really not mad at me, right?"

"No, Bobby."

"You sound mad."

"Jesus Christ. I said I wasn't. I'm not. Who's flying the oversized dragonfly?" I pointed to the helicopter.

He reached for his pills. They were tiny bird bones in his big hands. "I didn't do it." He dry swallowed.

Maybe it was the headaches. I get them too. Maybe that's why I decided to help him. "How will I get in touch?"

"You won't. I will." He took down my number. Here and at my office near Yonge and Bloor.

"Okay." Look, I told him, I had to play this cautiously. Not make a big ruckus. I was trying to get back into the NHL. The Montreal Canadiens had invited me to their summer tryout camp; GM Sam Pollock had even visited my house and we talked about art; he too was a big fan of the Original Seven and A. J. Casson, but NHL President Clarence Campbell didn't care much for Pollock or Montreal or Casson for that matter and blocked my ability to play anywhere in the NHL next season. However, Soupy said if I continued to keep my nose clean he'd reevaluate my chances for reinstatement later this summer.

"The Habs?"

"Yeah."

Bobby shook his head. Slowly. "I'd love to have played. For the Habs." He was from Laval, a Montreal suburb.

My getting banned from the league wasn't quite on the level of the 1955 Rocket Richard case or any reason to riot, but the Montreal fans sure were kicking up a great big noisy fuss saying the NHL was once again pitting itself against the French Canadian team and everything French Canadian. I guess I had become a bit of a celeb for solving the Stabulas, missing girl case. Got good press notices. Even Stana wrote me up a two-page spread in the *Tely*.

Got some good business out of it too: a woman whose cat, yes Felix, had gone missing, and a fella who thought his wife was cheating on him. She was. With another woman.

Bobby had read the *Telegram* spread. That's why he was here. He liked how I operated.

I reminded him that I didn't even know how to fix light switches.

"Bilingualism in Canada has always been about being French and having to learn English," Bobby reminded me. "It's never the other way around." He shrugged. "You speak French?"

"Un petit peu."

"Je me Souviens? That's the name of the outfit that Nancy knew about and runs with Airedale's crowd. Was. Running. Or Airedale was. Taking credit for? Shit, I'm not sure. Je me—no. That's not quite the name. Something like that."

I remember. Bobby couldn't remember much of anything.

The floor creaked as Bobby ambled to a dresser and looked at himself in the mirror. He wiped his tired eyes and didn't like what he saw. And then he traced his face in the glass with his fingers, or hand, at least that's what it looked like from where I stood in the angular lights of moon. He was writing words on his face, trying to erase his face with words, but there were no words on the mirror. Nothing.

Just his face: vulnerable, sad. That's something, my therapist argues that I struggle with, being more present in my feelings. I was supposed to be taking a rest cure. On my last case, I had killed a man, a miserable fuck who raped young girls and exploited women, and everyone felt like *I needed time alone, to heal.* My therapist said I wasn't dealing honestly with my emotions, my past, my relationship with my father (why is it always about the father?), and I needed to truly listen to that voice of discontent that tells us all is not good, but I wasn't hearing any such voice, not even late at night when I couldn't sleep. "Vulnerability is the key," she said, *let go of things and admit what hurts. Face the past. For it is never fully forgotten, she said, just obscured.*

Maybe I needed a new therapist.

And what was there to admit anyway?

I guess I should tell her about my recurring dream, the one with the damn suitcase.

"Yeah, I read about that too," Bobby said. Slowly. "You blew him away. Head shot. He got got. Got what he deserved. Abusing women. That guy was a real lowlife."

I don't know if he saw the possible connection to himself.

Irony is not a strong point with hockey players.

Bobby was definitely bigger than I remembered, his pants hitched under his round, hard belly, his belt a notch too tight. Certain meds can slow you down and pack on the pounds, I guess.

"The scratches, Bobby? From Nancy? Before you killed her?"

"Look, Hayden. You're my friend. Would I ask a friend for this kind of favor, if I wasn't speaking the truth?"

"You would if you were desperate."

He moved from the mirror, his face disappearing into the shadows of moonlight. "I *am* desperate, damn it. After Stana's articles, who's going to believe that I didn't do it?" He hitched up his pants and returned to the mirror. Maybe he saw other faces there that I couldn't see.

"Hey, she's just doing her job," I said.

After all that happened during what the papers labeled the "Cheap Amusements Caper," Stana's lies, and her tie-in with Babe Migano, being his undercover ace in the deck, and eventually being the cause for the inadvertent deaths of Terrien and Lisa Steinmetz, I just don't know why I still have a soft spot for, why my body chills with expectant desire for her, a throbbing buzz buzz.

"I'm sorry. You're. Right. I forgot you two had a thing."

Yeah. Had. But the two-page spread in the Tely *was nice.*

"Look into Airedale, the doc, he's running some kind of racket and I think he killed her."

"What kind of racket?"

"Maybe that publishing house. I don't. Know. Nancy hinted at some things—Cassel for chrissakes." He shrugged, looked at his fingers, and smiled his perpetual corkscrew leer.

"Drugs?"

And then he mumbled something about blue pills.

"What kind of pills?"

The ones he was popping were white. I noticed. Tiny bird bones.

"Damn." He screamed, his voice a short burst from a .45. His head wasn't working right, goddamn it. He couldn't remember the name. But blue was the color of the pills, and at least some of his migraines were blue. Like. The. Pills.

"You said something about Cassel, Lenny Cassel, Detroit kingpin? Did Nancy tell Stana about Cassel and his possible involvement with Airdeale?" *It was probably her next big story, just like the Cathy Stabulas case, young women wanting to blow the lid off abusive power and corruption. I'd have to see Stana again and get the skinny to follow the thread.*

Maybe I'll return the photos. I have a couple of nude art photos, okay five or six, I took of her back in '62, when I was learning my craft, and we had a thing going. I still look at them, occasionally.

"Yeah. Damn straight. Lenny Cassel. Detroit mobster."

He was a sick, scary fuck. A slight man, thin in the shoulders, but the eyes, burning snakes, Bobby said. Lenny had disappeared three-four weeks ago after a witness testified to the feds that she had seen him kill a prominent politician and reporter in a black, shaded alley. He used a machete. Chopped the shit out of them and tossed chunks of limbs into green trash bags. Lenny thought he was alone but a restaurant owner, tossing a different kind of refuse into the trash, saw the murders. Lenny has been hiding since. Reports had him spotted in three American cities and two in Canada. "Nancy saw Lenny at Airedale's clinic."

"You're sure?" Maybe he was involved on some kind of drug front, I said. The blue pills.

"Maybe. Nancy. Told. Me. She saw him."

I nodded.

"I used to go to Cliff's clinic. He does some kind of hydrotherapy. Water treatments and electric shock."

"And blue pills."

"Yeah. The pills helped. For. A. While." They calmed him down, relaxed his headaches.

"I thought Airedale was a plastic surgeon?"

"He's a doctor, ain't he? Has his hands in a lot of, let's say, projects." Airedale's clinic specializes in out-patient procedures, the removal of moles etc., and also electric shock and hydrotherapy for depression, Bobby said. "He's got a ton of famous clients, including actors, that guy on that TV western with the spotted dog—and the sidekick who wears a top hat? Always says cheerio?"

"Uh-huh." Bonanza–lite that show. "I thought you hated Cliff."

"I do." But Nancy had gone there. "You know he worked on her nose? Yeah. Took the bump out of it—"

"I see—"

"And that's when I saw all those men with gloves on. Something's going on there and Cassel's involved."

"Could Cassel have placed a plastic bag over a woman's head?"

After all, he had hacked two people to death with a machete. What could he do for an encore?

"Anything's possible with that cat." Bobby smiled, his corkscrew leer. "Nancy talked to Stana. Told her things. See the reporter."

Stana. I wasn't looking forward to the idea of seeing her. Maybe I should wear new shoes.

The blades whirred louder.

Stana. My stomach still had this empty space in it, like a hole, over what had happened before, my last case.

Stana. In a way I did want to see, if, as my therapist suggests I was really being honest with myself, and my complicated feelings toward Stana, new shoes or old shoes.

Bobby waved goodbye and before I knew it, the slow walking Ehle was under snapping blades, the yellow moon a slice of lemon.

He never did give me the name of the damn pilot.

And then the nose of the dragonfly came back towards the earth, up, down, and lumbered, over fences, houses, and I wondered if it would ever stay above the horizon line.

On to Oslo; Sweden that is.

Jesus Christ, that just cracked me up.

2

The pictures weren't pretty. Eight-by-ten's. Black-and-white. The focus off, a little messy. Police crime photographers weren't high-end shutterbugs, but there was enough sick evidence here to hammer home the point: Nancy Drouin was beaten repeatedly, horribly. Exhibit A: dark half-moons under her eyes, a split lip, and a hard hockey puck rising up out of one of her cheeks; Exhibit B: two chipped teeth and an open cut from a ring's sharp edge along her chin; Exhibit C: hair shorn away from above her left ear, like a patch of torn carpet gnashed by an angry Rottweiler. These weren't autopsy pictures. These were post-domestic abuse exhibits, beatings courtesy of one ex-husband, Bobby Ehle.

"How can you be working for this fuck?" *Stana.* Her voice, a fallen icicle.

How indeed.

It wasn't some moral code. I believed my client, in the emotions behind the words. Sure the evidence wasn't stacked in his favor, but in my line of work talking to people is more than just reading words, it's about reading psychology, and my instincts were telling me to have some reasonable doubts.

Stana huffed, shuffled the photos, her eyes sharp freckles, the lines on her hands raised. She was wearing a long brown skirt, a dark blouse, and a cardigan with diamond-shaped buttons. A small scarf traced about her neck like a feminine bow tie. A pencil was behind an ear. The fragile lines of her face were almost translucent, bare china against such fine bone structure.

She tapped the tip of her chin.

Top Cop Sal Lambertino was nodding along with Stana's tip-tapping. He apologized for being unable to get us access to the crime scene photos, yet, but, man, once I saw those I'd be "puking through my eye balls. They're disgusting. I've never seen such a beating." He leaned up against Stana's desk and played with the fringed off fence ends of his Hemingway beard.

Stana's desk was cluttered with loose paper, memo pads, pens in a glass, flowers in another glass, and seven or eight ceramic coffee cups. One of the cups was red, green and brown and had an Aztec vibe.

Sal let out a short breath, raised an eyebrow, and wondered if I was a dumbass or what. *How could I be helping such a person?*

"Sal, I've already heard that melody, huh?"

"Well, you're going to hear a lot more, pal."

He was also pissed at me for not reporting Bobby's visit—the absurd helicopter rendezvous—at my house a lot sooner. "What were you thinking, Hayden?"

"Apparently I wasn't," I said.

I thought I was being ironic. They read it more as an abject apology. I guess in a way it was.

I wanted to tell them both about the dream of me and the damn suitcase.

Sal must have gotten promoted after our last missing girl case, Cathy Stabulas. He was now a plainclothes guy: gray flannel suit, white shirt, gray tie, gray fedora, a regular Sloan Wilson.

"I like the new look, Sal. Very Joe Friday."

"I'm not in the mood for jokes."

"Just the facts, huh?"

"You're pushing it—"

"Sorry."

"From what you told me about Bobby's hands, the missing fingernail, the spots of blood, those are clear indicators of someone who probably just killed somebody else." He shrugged absently. Lit a Rothman's. "Or super-tuned them really fuckin' bad." He blew smoke in a far corner of the room.

One of the overhead fluorescent tubes needed to be replaced. It was blinking dimly.

I couldn't disagree with their feelings.

But somehow my instincts were telling me that the killing was much more complicated than it appeared, that Bobby, despite his record of domestic abuse, may not have been fully accountable for what happened. Those damn blue pills. His memory loss. How did that figure? Hell, he couldn't even remember Bobby Pulford, one of the greatest two-way Leafs ever. Number 20.

After my client left, I couldn't get back to sleep. So I wandered the dark lonely streets of Toronto, my heart punching my chest and shoulders, as rain fell in gentle perforated streaks. I ate a donut or two. That didn't calm me down. So I ate a third donut. And a fourth. Cream-filled. And then I came here. To Stana.

And now I needed her help. Again.

I didn't bring the photos. The ones I took in '62. I thought about it. Really.

And I thought about Mexico, 62–63, and making love, and playing cards, Scrabble, and walking hikes and searching through ruins, and talks about faith, hers more than mine, and our belief that we are wired to do good, and her belief that our purpose is to be better than we ever imagined, and my fears that I could never live up to that, not after all I had been through. My father. An alcoholic.

"We're looking into that helicopter pilot. Nothing so far." Sal shrugged. There was loose thread in the suit's weave, the crease where the shoulder meets the sleeve. "Jesus Christ, who lands a helicopter in a backyard?" He laughed. I wanted to tear away the thread.

"I know, right?" I laughed too. My face hurt a little. I had eaten two donuts too many.

I needed Stana's help on my last case. Three months ago. I wondered if she were still on Babe Migano's payroll.

"If I didn't like you so much, Hayden. I'd run you in—for sitting on that as long as you did." Sal jabbed a finger into my chest. It hurt. I think it was intentional.

I gave him my lopsided, lupine grin. My head was full of spun cotton candy, a world slightly thrown off axis. Shit, I wish I had some of Bobby's white pills.

A water cooler gurgled and typewriters clacked and paper scratching across platens filled the silences between our words. The fluorescent tube still blinked dimly. I pushed back the brim of my porkpie. "Where were you taking the story next, Stana?"

"I didn't have a next." Her fingers curled along the rim of an adjacent coffee cup. It was the "Aztec" one, the one I had bought for her in Mexico in 1963.

Men, in the open-doored office behind us, spoke in rushed voices. The Leafs had just traded Danny Davis for Marcel Pronovost. In the offseason, Davis had complained that Hugh "Two Fisted" Farrell had overworked the boys in daily scrimmages and they were "too tired" to beat Montreal in last year's semi-finals. The Leafs lost in six.

"That's too bad, huh?" I pointed to the adjacent office door. My face had a sneer to it. I hated Davis. He had an affair with our captain's wife, Sharon Smallbear, and he had a habit of dropping Polaroids, topless photos of the women he'd slept with, into his winning poker hands: three kings, two eights, two boobs.

Stana looked away from their office and rubbed the edge of a wrist. She was no longer interested in the sports pages. She too, like Sal, had been promoted, writing hard-hitting features, focusing on the lives of women. Two weeks ago the emphasis was on unequal pay in the workforce. This was the week before the Nancy Drouin abuse story.

"The paper wouldn't let me run the photos." She shrugged and reached for a cigarette. Parliaments. An English cigarette. Her favorite beer was Guinness. Irish. Something seemed at odds there. *Like her personality, full of quirky contradictions. Could I trust her, again? Could I?* "The publisher said no photos. Surprise, surprise, huh? Another fucking cover-up, mustn't explore truths that would shine a negative light on the wonderful sport of hockey."

Stana tossed the photos in front of her. The stack fell apart and crumbled across her desk blotter. She flipped hair behind the ear without the pencil.

"What did you expect?" There was no challenge in my voice. Shit, Stana worked for *The Toronto Telegram*. It was a conservative paper, with ties to Imperialism and England, I said. The *Tely* always endorsed the Conservative Party. Every goddamn election. Is it so surprising that they wouldn't want to print such photos? Too salacious, the higher-ups would say. Such photos challenged patriarchy, the very system the *Telegram*'s editorial staff and publishers reinforced. "Maybe you ought to work for the *Star*?"

She shot me a sulky look. The *Star* wouldn't offer her enough money.

"I'll get you the autopsy photos, Stana, once I get the green light from upstairs." Sal's eyes were lean. "Nice guy this Bobby Ehle."

It wasn't like I wanted to stare at the photos before me, but it was hard not to. Nancy's eyes looked blackened, forever wandering in the dark, like me this morning, lost, walking heavy in the light rain. It was as if whatever optimism she had once believed in could no longer be summoned up.

I feel like that a lot.

Stana sighed heavily as she exhaled. "Nancy wouldn't press charges." She shook her head in disbelief. It was an ongoing pattern, women blame themselves, she said. "How fucked up is that?"

"Pretty fucked up." Lambertino shoved his hands deep in his pockets. He'd seen it over and over again as a cop. The worst call to respond to was a domestic disturbance. Any cop will tell you that. "Shit, I got a knife in the shoulder one time—from a wife. I had been subduing her husband who was whacking her with a hockey stick." He rubbed at the phantom wound. The loose thread of his sleeve was gone.

Scuffling, Bobby said. These photos didn't back that story. This wasn't scuffling, wrestling, or slapping her down when she slapped him. This was full-fledged fisticuffs and maybe yesterday he went too far, maybe he just might have killed her. But his voice, the tears. They were so sincere. I wonder how he'd do with a lie detector test?

And the plastic bag? That little rhetorical flourish wasn't Bobby. No way.

"When we found her body, hours ago. She had been beaten to death. And then the plastic bag was placed on her head." Sal's fists tightened inside the pockets of his trousers, pushing against the fabric like an outcropping of moon rocks.

"You mean the bag was—"

"Post-mortem. Some kind of special effect. A calling card. I don't know." *She was already dead, Hayden.* Sick fuck.

I wasn't sure if he was referring to me or Bobby.

"Any chance it could be Lenny Cassel?" *He had a way with machetes and trash bags. Did he add plastic bags over faces to his repertoire?* "I hear he's in town. Nancy saw him—"

"She never told me that." Stana's eyes were full of freckles.

"Bobby said—"

"And you believe what Bobby said?"

"I'm with Stana." Sal leaned further into the desk's edge.

I'm surprised his thighs didn't have splinters.

"I wouldn't trust anything a man who beats up women has to say." He shook his head. "Besides, does he remember anything accurately? From what you told me, the guy's brain is fried." He took a short drag.

Fried. I wasn't crazy about Sal's choice of words, but Bobby sure couldn't think like he used to. And he couldn't remember much either.

"Look, Hayden, you yourself said the scratch lines on his face were fresh. He didn't get those in a bar fight," Stana said, leaning in with her pencil. The eraser was worn, gray, nearly scuffed away.

"No."

"And the torn fingernail—"

"Right."

"So how did he get like that?"

Bobby never did directly answer that.

What if I got him to take a lie detector test and he passed? Would it help muddy things a little? Would it point the arrows of this case in different directions?

It might, Sal said, but he didn't think Bobby could pass a polygraph here or in Oslo, Sweden. I had told Sal that joke twenty minutes ago and he, no doubt, thought it was worth repeating. Bobby would be overseas in a few hours. "Under Nancy's fingernails we found traces of skin, blood, and hair. We'll get a match. Trust me."

"What about Airedale? What's his racket? Curing depression with hydrotherapy. Electric shock. Bobby looked like he was fucked-up on meds to me."

"How so?"

Typewriter keys rat-a-tat-tatted like coins slapped on counter tops.

"Everything he said was really slow. Like he had to think before he could walk or nod his goddamn head." And the words full of sand. The voice, *the whole room*, full of sand. I felt like I was walking in his sand, right now, that I couldn't get up hill. "And he kept muttering something about blue pills."

"That's interesting—"

"Why?"

Stana took another drag. "Yeah, why?"

Sal placed his hands on Stana's desk, and leaned across, both eyebrows raised. I could smell his Old Spice aftershave. The police *had been* looking into Airedale's clinic; there were rumors from two different informants of mind-altering experiments involving LSD Blue 27, a special hallucinogen that takes away pain, but slows people down. You no longer have any inhibitions but you no longer have any desire either. The competitive edge is gone. The drug hasn't been licensed, but the Canadian Army had been experimenting with it to help returning vets combat battle fatigue and maybe Airedale got a hold of some. He had served as a medic in Korea, 1952. "Right now these are just rumors, so don't print this shit. Stana, you read me?"

She smiled. It was good to see. "Right." She doffed an imaginary cap his way.

I was glad she had kept the coffee cup I had got her in Mexico.

The early '60s was when the drug was first introduced, Sal said, a French-Canadian scientist invented it. Sal couldn't remember the name. He took off his hat and scratched his sandy-haired head.

"Hey." I looked at my watch. "It's my birthday." July 17th.

I just said it without thinking. I do that sometimes.

Sal smiled. "Congrats." He laughed. "We were working the day watch out of Bunco. The captain is Stana Younger, my partner is the Birthday Boy. My name's Lambertino."

That just cracked me up. His Webb-like intonation was impeccable.

"Don't ask me to do that again. I mean like ever." He straightened the cuff of his left sleeve. "My birthday gift to you."

"Thanks."

Stana nodded, her imaginary cap now doffed in my direction. The lone fluorescent tube still blinked dimly, announcing its separation for the bright track lines of the rest.

"So you think Nancy knew about this, the blue pills, and they killed her?"

"*He*, Bobby Ehle, killed her," Stana corrected me. Her jaw was tense and her hands looked like sharp flags.

"It's a possibility. I'm not ruling it out. The blue pills are the wild card," Sal confirmed.

"Could Bobby and Nancy be partnered in something, something illegal, something—maybe involving LSD blue 27?"

"Nancy and Bobby? Fuck no." Stana took another sharp drag and crushed what was left of her cigarette in a shallow ashtray. It was a sign that my allotted time with her was running low on minutes. Subtle.

"Oh, and another thing about your alleged client." Sal stabbed an even stiffer, stubby finger into my chest. And it hurt more than the last one. "Remember when I said if you saw the autopsy photos you'd be puking through your eyeballs?"

"Yeah. The whole puking through my eyeballs thing? Not an expression I'd care to re-visit, Sal."

"Whoever slugged Nancy, used heavy fists, breaking the orbital bones around her eyes and arranging her nose so it no longer would fit her or any face. It was as if the assailant wanted to lift her whole head off her shoulders with his fists. A guillotine with his hands." He shook his head. "You like Picasso?"

"Not particularly," I said.

"A goddamn Picasso painting," he said. "That's what she looked like. Abstract art."

Sal's not one for hyperbole.

How could someone on the calming effects of LSD Blue 27 do such a thing?

"He'd done all these other beatings." Stana's hand hovered over the brick of photographs crowding her desk. "It's a pattern—"

"Yeah, but he was slow last night. His reaction time. If he was on LSD Blue 27—"

"Maybe he took the hallucinogens after killing her, to numb the pain—" Sal said.

Typewriters clacked. A water cooler in the far corner of the bullpen still gurgled. *But the pills he took after were white. I saw them. Little bones of birds.*

"So what do you want?" Stana blew smoke from a freshly lit cigarette into a near corner of the room. "Why are you here, Hayden?"

"Help. That's what I want. Look, I'm just doing my job, Stana."

"He did it, Hayden. Look at these pictures. That's his third face." She stared me down, her blue eyes darkening with anger, becoming almost green, and then threw a photo at me and said Bobby's third face was on full display. Photos don't lie. "That's a man who can kill and did."

She sat back in her chair, hands behind her head, arms two triangles, a tense pulse line running along her jaw. "Maybe what he said sounded so real to you, so sincere, but—" She piled the photos, corners lining up. "You ever think, Hayden, there might be a fourth face?"

"Huh?"

"The three faces you told me about. There's the one we have in private, the one we have in public, and the one we don't even know we ever had, the one that emerges and shocks us under extreme conditions like combat or insane psychical obsessions. And this friend of yours is obsessed."

"That doesn't make him a killer."

"You hockey players sure stick together—"

"That's not fair."

"Blood brothers for life? Is that it?" The water cooler was no longer gurgling. "A fourth face denies what the third face ever did and convinces faces one and two and the world that the third face was a part of someone else, another time that doesn't matter. A fourth face is a face of denial, a fourth face counteracts the third face, proving the lie that you can run from yourself, hide from who you really are." She pressed her hands deeper behind her neck. "Bobby truly believes he didn't do it, even though he knows he truly did because that Bobby is not the real Bobby." Her thin smile stretched into a sad line. "You killed a man, Hayden, and feel no guilt about it whatsoever. You told me as much."

"I did." My upper lip trembled slightly. *The man abused his daughters.*

"What's that but your fourth face denying what your third face did?"

Jesus Christ. "Maybe." I shrugged. "You might have something there."

"I think you should fire your therapist and hire her, birthday boy." Sal shadowboxed my shoulder and chin with soft air punches.

"You see a therapist?" Stana lowered her eyes.

"Yeah." I shrugged. "Of course."

My confession got her to smile slightly.

"Me too," she said. "Things I've done that I feel guilt over, things—" She rearranged the company of pens in her coffee cup. They resembled a set of various country's flags at the UN. "Something I can forget, forgive about myself—"

Does the therapy help?

"It makes me more honest with myself." She rubbed fingers along a clavicle. "More forgiving, I guess, of others." She shuffled the pens some more and smiled briefly.

I like it when she smiles, her whole face and eyes take you in. *Damn, I thought I never could feel for her again, I said it was all over, we could never go back after a line had been crossed, a line of trust, after she used me, to get a story, and now some of me wanted to go back to Mexico. Damn.*

Yes I needed her help but I also wanted it, wanted to need it, wanted her to need me.

"Any idea on who was flying the helicopter?" She tapped the pencil against her lower lip.

"No." I smiled, my lopsided grin. I told them about the letters KEY on the side. That's all I could make out. There was just too much sand. "You have any ideas?"

"I'm not going to be your partner—"

"You want to get Nancy's killer, don't you?"

"You let him get away," she said.

I smiled.

And maybe, just maybe she was right.

3

I bowled a few games to clear my head: 120, 163, 155. I throw a straight ball. Never could figure out how to put a hook in the damn thing. Get more action with a hook. Anyway, after three games, I grabbed a hotdog, with mustard, yellow peppers, and kosher pickles, from a street vendor, ate on the run and belched my way up the stairs to my office.

I love Hebrew Nationals but they always do that to me.

Thank god I passed on the onions and a side order of roasted chestnuts.

Outside my frosted glass door was a girl with a pixie cut, blue jeans, and a checkered flannel shirt. The first time I saw her, three months ago, she was a human lamp, wearing nothing but a fez.

"Dawn—"

"Hello, Mr. Fuller—"

"Dispense with the formalities, Dawn. You can call me, Hayden."

She smiled awkwardly, her teeth denting her lower lip.

I unlocked the door and let her in. I wondered why, in this humidity, she was wearing a long-sleeved shirt.

"I know it, but the AC inside offices—"

"Obviously. You've never been in my office." I flipped on a desk fan and opened a window. Traffic from Yonge Street bled into the room. "AC? I don't even have plush chairs."

She slid into a wooden chair and quickly propped her elbows

on my desk blotter and smiled across from me. Small specks of lipstick marked her teeth. I tossed my porkpie toward the hat rack in the near corner, behind the door, and it bounced off a stem and to the floor. I tossed it a second time, hit the target on a third. "I'm no James Bond."

She laughed.

People don't always get my jokes. I like it when they do.

I too sat down. "What can I do for you?"

Since my last case, I heard she was turning her life around, no longer ushering at Maple Leaf Gardens as a page girl. She was taking correspondence courses toward her GED and working at the downtown Eaton's. Toy department. "You look good," I said, trying to keep my eyes on hers.

She smiled. "You look tired. You must be working on a case."

"I am."

"Bobby Ehle?"

"Yeah."

Wrinkles formed at the corners of her eyes and her voice was a rush of worries. Bobby Ehle was her boyfriend, and he skipped out, not because he killed Nancy, but because he was running from the mob. They wanted to kill him for a bad drug deal, she said. "You see, Mr. Fuller, I was making a delivery for a Dr. Airedale, well actually his associate Dr. Williams. Well, I was making it for Bobby. He was feeling sick and—"

"Slow down. Who's Dr. Williams?"

Gillian Williams was another plastic surgeon who co-owned and performed out-patient surgeries and hydrotherapy sessions at Adora Borealis, the Queen Street clinic. Her specialties: breast reduction, tummy tucks, and face lifts.

"Adora Borealis." I laughed.

It was such a cornball name.

"You want to know the real kicker." She smiled. It's ad slogan was "the Northern Lights of Beauty."

That just cracked me up. It was tastelessly Canadian.

"So Dr. Williams sent you on a drug run? You sure?"

"I think so. I don't know. I didn't look in the canisters." It was a long train ride from Toronto to Montreal. Three canisters in a suitcase. She saw the canisters placed there. Bobby placed them there. She repeated how she never looked in the canisters.

"Bobby was too sick?"

"Yeah. Sometimes he gets—" She looked away and bit at one of the corners of her shirt collar.

Outside the traffic chatted like folks in a theater lobby, between acts, smoking cigs. A jackhammer mildly thudded, and rock music climbed up from a passing hack that had its windows lowered. A street vendor shouted the day's headlines. Something to do with de Gaulle and his take on Expo '67. A wasted extravagance. Quebec for Quebecois. I closed the window.

"I didn't look in the suitcase. But it must have been drugs." Anyway, the drop happened and the real shipment wasn't delivered. They, the folks on the other end, never got what they asked for, whatever that was, "but I figured it was drugs. I mean, I didn't know what it was at the time, but I was getting a hundred for the delivery, and what else could it have been?"

Blueprints for a new hydrogen bomb, body parts packed in ice, vials full of flesh eating viruses? I mean, come on, this case had taken a weird turn once LSD Blue 27 was thrown into the gumbo, I joshed.

I leaned forward. The light from the street was an amber glare that had Dawn shielding her eyes. "Gillian Williams, directly, she, asked you to do this?"

I wondered about Williams's possible involvement with LSD Blue 27.

"Well not directly. Bobby was in contact with Gillian, I think, and asked me to make the drop for him and I traveled the train." Dawn blinked her green eyes. There was a flaw in one of them, a slight scythe in an iris, resembling a floating eye lash. I wondered why I'd never noticed it before.

"But you never saw Dr. Williams or Dr. Airedale handling the canisters?"

"No."

"And Bobby was too sick to make the delivery himself?"

Sometimes the meds make him immobile. He can't even get out of the apartment or change the channel on the TV.

"Does he work?"

"Construction. Occasionally. This week. Construction."

"Uh-huh." I doodled on my desk blotter. A hockey net, gloves, a puck. "Who was on the other end? Of the drop?"

"Some guys, wise guys I think." She smiled nonchalantly. The touches of red lipstick that daubed her teeth were distracting, strangely sexy. I kept telling myself I was thirty.

When not leaving lipstick accents on her teeth, Dawn chewed on the triangle tip of one of the ends of her collar. She was such a kid. No wonder she and Bobby connected so well.

"What did they look like?"

Sharp chins, lean faces, gloves on their hands. Wise guys, you know?

"Yup. Sounds like wise guys. And they say they didn't get what they were supposed to get?"

"Yeah. One of them was kind of bookish. Wore a black lambskin hat and very mod clothes."

"Did you get his name?"

"Dennis. Well, Denys. He's French."

"I figured that."

She smiled and shook her head, slightly embarrassed. "He also had a birthmark, like a club, like in a deck of cards—"

"A three-leaf clover?"

"Yeah."

"It wasn't a tattoo?"

"It might have been. But who gets one on their face?" The marking was under his left eye, and almost looked like three tears.

"Maybe it wasn't a clover, but tears?"

"Maybe." She gently tugged on the gold necklace around her neck. It was a gift from Bobby.

Tears. Crying over what? And what was a nice girl like Dawn Stoukas doing with a lost soul like Bobby Ehle, a lost soul who couldn't even change the channels on his television? "It could be a double-cross. They're lying. Or, Bobby made the switch before you boarded the train."

"No. He wouldn't do that. He loves me." She couldn't look at me. The amber lights of Yonge Street were bright but not that bright. She played with a crease line in her jeans. The jackhammer, with the window closed, had become a dull pound. "He wouldn't set me up."

"Oh, he wouldn't would he?" I'd seen some nasty photographs authored by my virtuous client, I muttered.

"No, he wouldn't." The crease on her jeans must have been a thin creek by now, the way she was working it. Soon it would be a river.

She absently looked up at me, smiled weakly, and edged at the crease more furiously, and then pounded her leg with a closed fist, the rhythm of her hits in step with the jackhammer outside.

"Your leg okay?"

"When I get nervous or stressed it twitches. Throbs." It starts with a thin tremble, then starts throbbing. "Bobby, double-cross me?"

She tried trapping tears behind her mouth, and then her voice was full of them. "It's not like that—"

"He's a desperate man. He may have killed his wife."

"I don't believe that either—"

"Uh-huh."

"You don't believe me?"

"No, that's not it, Dawn." I smiled. "I just like saying 'uh-huh' when I get stressed."

That made her smile and laugh. It was a little wet.

This was the first time I had heard of Bobby's great love for Dawn. He hadn't even mentioned her at my house. I reached for her hand. Her fingers were strong. And like her leg, trembling. "How long you two been dating?"

"Two months." She unclasped the gold chain from around her neck. It looked a little dusky and lumpy in my hands. "That's a friendship bracelet," she said.

It was gold-plated. Their anniversary was last Friday, the day before Bobby may have killed Nancy. She shrugged. They ate an anniversary meal at Bassel's. Had hamburgers. "It's a nice restaurant."

"Yeah, I know. I've been there," I said. *Used to take Stana there, once every three weeks or so.*

She had never dated a man for more than two weeks before. This felt different. Like when you really care, like really really care, she said.

I nodded and handed her back her necklace. A fleck or two of gold dust slivered my fingers. "And when did this drop not happen?"

"Three days ago. And now the mob's trying to kill me. Well, Bobby, mainly. But I'm his accomplice. Everywhere I go. I can't—" She struggled with the clasp and asked me to snap it back in place. Her hair smelled of flowers.

Like the other day at the R.O.M., for instance—she goes there to relax and write poems—anyway, she felt she was being followed. There was this real creepy guy, tall, and heavy set with a jaunty little bowler on his head.

"A lot of people go to the R.O.M. Not all of them to write poems." I smiled. "Dinosaurs are popular with the kids these days."

"I know, but this one guy, he was creepy. A girl knows all about creepy looks, you know? He was slinking along the fern plants. Following, watching me. It felt like he was touching my tits with his eyes."

It surprised me how quickly she could move from innocent

ingénue to tough-talking dame.

"I'm sorry I shouldn't have said tits. But I guarantee you that he knew my measurements and cup size."

"Sure, sure." I think I was blushing a little. 34B.

And his face, Mr. Fuller, was real tight.

"Like it's wrapped in Saran Wrap?" Jack Palance without the black vest and fringe and Shane giving him hell.

"Yes. Like Jack Palance."

She sure knew her movies.

Athol Leighton. Cool Athol, ex-NHL'er and Babe Migano's hit man. A brute. *Once he beat up a prostitute in Chicago or maybe it was Boston, I can't remember, but he re-designed her face, shifted her nose into Picasso territory. Could he have attacked Nancy, made her too into his idea of abstract art?* "Where else you seen him?"

"Yesterday. On King Street. The cigar store." She tented her fingers and they pressed about like an accordion. "I lost him on the subway exchange."

"Athol Leighton is his name."

"Asshole? Really?"

I laughed. "Athol. A-T-H-O-L. It's British. But Asshole fits." I laughed again. "Yeah. It fits real fine." I doodled across my blotter, a smiley face, a circle with a dot in the middle, a maple leaf, a horse. I draw terrible horses. Mine always look like a drunken moose. What was I going to do with Dawn? She needed protection, but I couldn't take her on a case this hot. And it was going to get a lot hotter.

Athol Leighton meant Babe Migano, the ex-Montreal kingpin and now Toronto-area gangster, was thrown into this criminal gumbo with its domestic violence, LSD Blue 27, and unsavory plastic surgeons. Migano said he had wanted to go legit, open a chain of restaurants, get in the good, fast money, but perhaps the drug part of this case, LSD Blue 27, was too enticing a piece of the action to cut himself out of. "You saw Bobby before you boarded the train? He gave you the package?"

She nodded. "Packages. They were in these cylinders. They looked like they'd hold lenses for a camera or something. Long lenses."

"Uh-huh."

The phone on my desk rang. I apologized and answered. Stana.

"Terry Quniton. He's the pilot. You were on the right rack with KEY. He didn't report to CKEY this morning. You know, 590 on your dial? Everyone's doing traffic reports these days. He does their traffic report. Helicopters."

"He call in sick?"

"No. Nothing."

"Shit, Stana. Thanks. I appreciate this."

"The dispatcher says that two days ago she saw him talking to a fella that fits Bobby's description."

"Wow."

"He's probably the one, huh?" She paused. I heard her pencil clack-clacking against the mouthpiece of the phone. "I'm in. I'll help—"

I imagined her tapping the pens curled in her Mexican mug.

"Thanks. I got a client. We'll talk."

"Sure. And happy birthday. Thirty, huh?"

"Yeah. I'm no longer the same age as Clark Kent."

"I'll call you later, Superman."

"Thanks, Lois." I placed the receiver on its holder and felt a buzz, a warm rush through my upper back, shoulders, and the tips of my ears.

"Terry, huh?" The line on Dawn's forehead, between her eyebrows creased, resembling the fold in a daily.

"You know him, Dawn?"

"Yeah. He's Bobby's friend. They grew up in Montreal together. Watched hockey at our place, Saturdays—"

Bobby called him a fucko, said fucko was fucking his ex.

Her eyes wandered, her mind shifting to something she should have recalled earlier. Terry has a tattoo on his left shoulder, a fleur-de-lis. One time he was in a T-shirt, drinking beers, and she asked him about it. It looks a bit like the clover on Denys's face, she said.

"You think the clover might be a fleur-de-lis?"

"Maybe. A fleur-de-lis that's crying?" Denys's version sure looked like tears.

"Interesting."

"It was definitely crying." She smiled, pleased.

I tapped my fingers on the blotter. "You ever hear of LSD Blue 27? Did Bobby ever say anything about that?"

He did. And it wasn't LSD Blue 27, Mr. Fuller. Just Blue 27. That's what it was called on the streets.

"There's a lot of this on the street?"

"Some."

Bobby was taking it, but it wasn't helping that much, she said. At first it made the headaches go away but then it started making him forget things and, well, she didn't really want to talk about it, but in bed, it made it difficult for him to get intimate, you know, like all the desire was gone. He couldn't stay—

"Interested?"

"Yeah. That's a good way to put it, Mr. Fuller. *Interested*." And he hated not being his old self and, you know, that's important with men, the whole proving yourself in bed thing.

"Yeah." I smiled absently. I was no MVP in the bedroom.

And that shit only seemed to be getting worse.

Anyway, he started putting on weight, and that frustrated him even more. He refused to get new jeans, cramming himself into the old ones, his belt tighter and tighter around his waist, trying to hitch his pants in place. And, Mr. Fuller, he sought out other solutions, too, for the weight, eating only one meal before supper, a can of soup, and for the headaches, hydrotherapy. Electric shock.

"When did he last take the blue pills?"

"Off and on. I'm not sure he ever stopped. He just cut back. Tried other things." Her accordion fingers played a new melody. "I mean the headaches were so bad."

"Yeah." I rubbed the edge of my chin. "Did he ever hit you?"

"No, no. Never. He never even got mad. Ever. If anything I'd like to have seen him get mad—"

"No you wouldn't."

I didn't want any woman to ever look like Nancy again, hair missing from the left side of her head, just over an ear. A faded human carpet.

"Well, I just mean in terms of sexual energy." They had even tried incense, rare resins from Mexican plants, special oils at the back of his neck, and fondue. I'm not sure how melted cheese would help, but Bobby was a big fan. Anyway, Dawn said that the blue pills transformed Bobby into that old tom cat, you know the one you wait too long to fix, and then when you do he just sits on top of the TV and stares at you?

That just cracked me up. I really shouldn't have been laughing but she didn't seem to mind.

I wondered if she'd ever gone to the clinic, the Northern Lights of Beauty, what did it look like on the inside? "What was the setup?"

"Small staff. Two or three nurses. Three doctors."

"Three?"

"There's Stangl. Dallas Stangl. He works in the lab." She shrugged. There's also a lot of white rooms, she said. The hydrotherapy room was all white: walls, tile, and long angular windows with bars on it. The bars were even painted white. Bobby would rest there, covered in some kind of hydro blankets, earphones on his head, listening to jazz music, while the water around him pulsed and pushed and rippled and did whatever hydrotherapy does.

"You don't believe in it?"

"Was you ever bit by a dead bee?"

Another movie reference. And a pretty good one at that.

"Anything else you saw?"

A lab in back straight out of those freaky Frankenstein films with beakers and Bunsen burners, test tubes, vials, scales, and machines with a lot of lights. Green lights and red. And rooms, like hotel suites for overnight clients, she said.

"Bobby ever stay overnight?"

"Sure. Lots of times." She stayed with him three or four times. They were given filtered water. Told to drink it. A lot of water.

"Filtered water?"

"Purity to fight the body's impurities. They were big on that. Lots of filtered water, 24–7."

"He *never* hit you?"

"Never."

But he might have double-crossed her. The diamond necklace he got Dawn was straight out of a Crackerjack box. God-damn four-flusher. I didn't tell her that but sure as hell wanted to.

"He's probably in Sweden, huh? You think Terry went too?"

"I'm not sure."

"There's one other thing. One time I was at Adora Borealis, like last week, with Bobby and I saw him. A man no-one has seen for weeks. Months."

"Who?"

"Brian 'Spinner' Terrien."

The back of my neck and arms throbbed. *Spinner was dead. I saw him die. Him and Lisa. Vaughan, Ontario. Two shots. She went down, like hammering a nail.*

It was a guilt Stana and I carry, share. She for being naive; me for being silent.

I didn't repeat this aloud to Dawn. At least I don't think I did.

She read my incredulity, however. It was him, she insisted. The angular shoulders. The walk. She had seen him plenty of times at the Gardens during his up-and-down playing days. He was living in one of the back rooms at the clinic. She said hello, but he hesitated, smiled briefly and slunk away to an adjoining room. She leaned forward. "It was the same hair from his playing days, looked like—"

"A Brillo pad?"

"Yeah. A Brillo pad. It's like he's hiding out there or something."

"Or something." How long ago was this?

The last time Bobby got a treatment. Three days ago.

Spinner died in a garage, one of his eyes hanging away from the orbital bone, resting against a cheek as intermittent bubblegum bursts of blood puffed from his lips.

"Will you protect me?" She didn't have much money but she didn't know where else to turn. Her father was dead and her mother wanted nothing to do with her. *Like I said before, it always comes down to trouble with the fathers doesn't it?*

And me trapped in a suitcase full of drying moths.

I got on the blower. Dr. Abramowitz, a good friend of mine out in the north-end suburbs. He took care of me and my concussions during my playing days and has ever since. He asked if I were having any dizzy spells and I lied, said I was fine, and then told him the whole story, the death threats, and Athol Leighton, and Bobby Ehle wanted for murder, and he said sure, bring the girl over. Oh, and he said one other thing, "Slow down kid."

It was a standing joke between us. He knew I only had one gear and it was revving in fifth. I'd bring the girl over in the next hour or so. I smiled at Dawn. "How much you have?"

She reached into her back pocket for a tiny pink wallet. It took her awhile to get it out of her back pocket. Her jeans were tight. Youth. "Fifty?"

"Give it to me."

She did.

I handed her back all of it but two tens.

"That's the amount you gave me three months ago." She smiled. "That time in Cal Bullard's office and I was a human lamp."

"How old are you, Dawn?"

"Twenty. I turned twenty last week—"

Bobby was thirty-something. I was thirty.

I needed a girlfriend, age appropriate, of course.

"I know what you're thinking. I'm too young to know what love is, but I love him, Mr. Fuller." She didn't know how to explain it—it was just a part of her like breathing or waking or walking. It was walking light, she said, feet not fully grounded, and it was wonderful. "Like the whole world's full of helium, you know?"

And that's a good thing?

"You don't think about it, you just do it. You love. I love."

I had felt that way too, once, back in 1962–64, with Stana. *Christ that was some time ago. Back then I smiled all the time and we sat side by side in restaurant booths.*

"It hurts to love the way I love." She looked down at her leg and tapped her thigh's tremors. They were ebbing, becoming a trickle. "Shit, sometimes I wonder if I'll ever grow up." She felt like a kid, needing help reaching for the damn drinking glasses on the top shelf of the kitchen cabinet.

"I keep asking myself that question too." There was so much I didn't know and the older I got the more I realized it.

She smiled and it filled her green eyes, turning teal from the amber light off Yonge Street. "The whole life experience thing—sucks."

"It gets easier."

"Really?"

"No." I smiled and laughed at my previous lie. "I wish it were true."

We both shrugged.

"I guess we're even now." She crossed one leg over the other.

"I guess so."

"I mean I'm returning the twenty." The smile that had stretched to her eyes now flowed through her, all the way to her hands and fingertips. She was no longer trembling. "I can cook for Dr. Abramowitz. I can. Well not much. Eggs, pasta, peanut butter and jelly—"

"That's not cooking. Peanut butter and jelly's not cooking."

"With a glass of milk it's a complete meal. Especially if you use whole-wheat bread," she said.

I gave her a doubtful look. "He'll order out. I'll pay him. And I'll see if I can straighten things out about Athol with Babe Migano."

"Did you know Bobby was selling hockey sticks in back of the Gardens to get by?" She shifted in her chair. The sun was now a bar across her shoulders and chest. One of the triangles to her collar was a darker color than the rest of the shirt. The jackhammer was still quietly pounding. "He had no money left from his hockey days and being too tired to work construction was selling broken practice sticks, autographing them for the fans."

I nodded. Bobby would be in Sweden soon. What was in those damn canisters? My money was on Blue 27. Or maybe something more potent, something cooked up in Airedale and Williams's lab on Queen Street, the Adora Borealis.

The Northern Lights of Beauty.

Give me a fucking break.

4

Something didn't feel right as soon as we hit Yonge Street. There was a crew crushing up concrete, but the technique of the main guy jackhammering the sidewalk was all wrong. He was using a lift assist, but the way he hovered, with his full belly over the jackhammer's handles, didn't allow the lift assist to do much assisting. I had an uncle who could not only change light switches but worked construction and he always said keep a safe distance from you and the jackhammer, the list on the left hand side, and allow it to make you more efficient. Sure this guy had a lot of fat and muscle, torquing up shards of road, but it was all misplaced energy.

And then there was his hard hat. It didn't quite fit his head. It was too loose and rode up in front like a springboard, like he was more concerned with getting face time in a W.W. II action film than just doing his job. The fella next to him was even more wrong. He was holding a paper bag. A typical Yonge Street rummy, with his early afternoon shadow, crumpled sport jacket, and stained khakis, but the shoes, the damn shoes. Too clean. Not quite business casual but too damn new. Always start with the shoes when building a character, an actor friend once told me, and these fellas knew nothing about character.

Dawn was saying something or other about mac and cheese and how most people made it with sharp cheddar but the key ingredient was the hard yellow cheese, gruyere, from Switzerland,

and she could whip that up for Dr. A, damn straight she could, she'd forgotten how good she was at making that dish, and I said swell, thinking about peanut butter and jelly and the guy's belly over the jackhammer handles, and how he seemed to bury the bit too deeply into the ground, when Skid Row reached inside his crumpled bag for something other than a mickey.

That's when I reached for my snub-nosed.

The black checkered grip of his gun peeked over the bag's lip, but my. 38 was already barking.

The first shot hit him in the cheek and his mouth wobbled like a wave. The second broke off a whole set of front teeth and he stumbled and fell and choked and died, gray matter and grits of bone on the sidewalk. The crumpled bag was at his feet, the gun still gripped in his left hand.

I quickly shoved Dawn aside, sending her to the curb's edge and into an adjacent parking meter as I waited for the other fella to reach behind his belt for a hidden gun, but he came at me instead with the damn jackhammer, stabbing at my legs, blasting up bits of concrete around my feet, forcing me to fall back on my ass.

I avoided the bit, twisting left, then right, before firing into his belly. Three rapid knocks. He fell hard, writhing, bouncing a little, his body the shape of the letter C.

A gut-shot is not a nice way to checkout of a building.

He was moaning, his voice the sound of a small dog with a broken leg. His moans slid into seven or eight Hail Marys.

I hoped he had enough left to hold on until the ambulance arrived.

He didn't. I smelled shit.

Workers crowded around us, one guy, in a cut-off gray sweatshirt, acted like he was going to make trouble, but I flashed my PI license and gave him a surly snarl, shouting these guys are Lenny Cassel's hitmen, and he backed off.

Dawn called the police from a nearby Beckers, and then we

sat on the sidewalk and waited and waited for Sal Lambertino.

Dawn didn't scream or yell. I was surprised at how cool she was.

She kissed my cheek, hair smelling of flowers.

I guess I had saved her life.

"That's not Athol," she said.

"No, that's not Athol."

"Neither's the other one."

"Nope."

People crowding around us kept their distance. The guy in the cut-off grays had his hands on his hips, eyes focused. On me. They were full of black flies.

I looked at the flaw in Dawn's iris, the tiny scythe, and wanted to kiss her. I did. The gun never left my hand.

THEY WERE DETROIT-AREA MOBSTERS. Johnny "Red Eye" Thompson, nicknamed for his penchant in delivering late night hits, was the guy with no front teeth. He was a handsome guy at one time: blond hair, big teeth, cleft in his chin, a regular playboy. I bet he slept in a circular bed. The other cat was Danny "Lazy Legs" Langois. Buzz cut, aquiline nose, eyes too closely set. Both were on their way to the morgue in the basement of Wellesley hospital.

At least I hear it's air-conditioned.

"Cassel muscle no doubt about it," Sal said, rubbing at his Hemingway beard. It had just come in over his radio. Rap sheets as long as a city block. "Jesus Christ, cowboy, you're getting a little too good at this killing thing. Three is it now?"

I shielded the sun from my eyes. The tips of my shoulders hurt. I wondered who Johnny Jackhammer replaced on the construction crew. The teamsters are unionized. You don't just step onto a crew. Even if you have Cassel credentials. Somebody didn't check into work today. Let's follow up that thread and find that somebody.

"That's a pretty big hunch."

"I know, I know." I kicked at bits of candy wrappers and crushed coffee cups curled along the curb. "How else did Thompson become a member of that crew, on this day?"

Sal barked into the microphone snaking around his rearview mirror, telling them to check into the list of workers on that particular crew. He rubbed at the top of his sandy-hair head. Like me he sported a buzz cut. We were a couple of 1950s cats adrift in the 1960s. You'll never catch either of us in Nehru jackets.

"I'm no cowboy, Sal. They never gave me a choice." I shrugged. Shit, I really wanted to bowl a few more frames or listen to some jazz to calm the edge off my shoulders and arms. My trigger hand still trembled. Dexter Gordon, Hank Mobley, Freddie Hubbard. Those cats could help, right about now, take the tremble out of me.

"They really gave Hayden no chance," Dawn echoed, her long legs crossing their way to the street's edge. We were doing the initial interview right here on Yonge, the sun a sharp edge of light. Spindly trees grew out of squares in the sidewalk.

Dawn was in the clear, after she told her story of the drop gone wrong. She wasn't seen as an accessory nor was Sal sizing her up for any criminal misdemeanors or felonies. She truly didn't know what was in the canisters and he believed her. I think he felt a little sorry for how she was all mixed up with a wrong guy like Bobby Ehle. And that pixie cut and green eyes. With a flaw in the iris.

When it came my turn to talk, I wasn't getting any Dawn light and easy treatment, uh-uh. Sal thought I was just a tool, not thinking straight. "The guy's a fucking lowlife," he mumbled, when Dawn's shoulders were turned.

But we weren't done with the interviews. Sal wanted us to go downtown to make a full report, and, no, we couldn't get a warrant issued to Airedale and Williams's clinic. There just wasn't enough evidence.

"What do we need for chrissakes?" Dawn was terse, impatient.

He turned to Dawn. "Did you ever see these two killers at the clinic?"

She shook her head dejectedly.

"Did you ever see them or Dr. Williams or Dr. Airedale involved with LSD Blue 27?" He pushed back his gray fedora and dropped his hands on his hips.

"Blue 27," Dawn corrected. The only stranger Dawn had ever seen at the clinic was one Brian Spinner Terrien, five eight, 145 pounds. Hair sharp like a Brillo pad. The same Spinner I and Migano and Stana and a few others knew had said the long goodbye long ago and was buried in rolls of black dirt out in a field near Vaughan, Ontario.

Okay, Sal said, even if Dawn saw Spinner that wasn't enough grounds for a warrant. He's not wanted or connected to any crime.

I nodded. *No, he's not wanted for much of anything but a decent burial.*

"The guy's probably taking a respite."

Some respite.

More squawk on the call box. Sal ducked his head through the passenger window to listen.

Drugs cost money. Street money. Junk like Blue 27 isn't covered by Canada's HIDS Acts Program. It's not part of universal health care. How much was this junk costing him? Did he ever write a check?

"What are you babbling about?" Sal returned from the recesses of his car, a '64 Pontiac Catalina. One of the hubcaps was missing.

There I was doing it again. Talking out loud. A by-product of hockey concussions. Bobby was taking a lot of those blue pills. They cost money. Look into his bank accounts. See if he routinely wrote checks, big checks to Airedale and Williams, I said. If he did, and I was betting on it, and if they can't account for large sums of money brought in from a poor, destitute ex-hockey player, then we probably have reasonable and probable grounds to go in and search the joint.

The Adora Borealis. The Northern Lights of Beauty. Flop house for fallen stars.

"I'll get my people on it."

I waved my hand, flashing away the frayed edges of the sun, and that's when I realized the sun wasn't that bright. There was a pain cluttering behind my eyes, in my head, spun cotton candy. When Lazy Legs bounced me to the sidewalk it jarred my neck and back enough to trigger a post-concussive aftershock. I stared down at my shoes and felt dizzy. Shit. So, I moved to the shade of a spindly tree. A lot of fucking good that did.

"Can you get anymore fucking pretentious than Adora Borealis," Sal philosophized.

"The Northern Lights of Beauty." Dawn laughed in disapproval.

Sal pointed a finger at me. "The radio call I just got. The other construction worker. The one who didn't check in today?"

"Yeah."

"Bobby Ehle."

After we filed our reports at the Bay Street Station, Dawn was taken into police custody for her own protection.

They didn't tell me where they were holding her.

I was worried with her out of the mix, Bobby's contact person was bottled up, denying me, in turn, access to him.

From a street corner, I called Dr. A. and filled him in. Two more people dead. "You sure you're alright?" I nodded, but he couldn't see me, and then he asked when was I seeing my therapist? She had called. I had cancelled last Tuesday and Dr. A and her were friends. "Don't skip out again. See her, Hayden."

"Okay, okay."

“I’m not asking—”

The man had such gravitas. He was a Holocaust survivor. So was Dr. Jeanette Cohen, my therapist. You listen to and pay respect to people like that.

I dry swallowed some pills, ate another hotdog, and at 3:45 called Stana from a different drugstore phone, told her what went down outside my office, and asked her to look into any ties Cassel might have with Montreal and Migano. She hesitated, but assured me she was no longer on Migano’s payroll, was no longer aces in the kingpin’s pocket. “I quit after the death of Spinner and Lisa.” I wasn’t sure if I could believe her or not. For the time, I decided I’d roll the dice and take the risk. And then I told her about “Terrien” being spotted at the Adora Borealis by Dawn. “He” was hiding in one of the back recovery rooms. Stana’s voice caught, and the silence filled the space between us, like the brief pause after a referee blows his whistle and just before he drops the puck.

“But you saw him die—”

I was pretty sure I did. Yes, I had been pistol-whipped into a daze, but I saw Spinner quit breathing, I saw the eye hanging from the orbital bone.

“I got a key,” she said.

“To the clinic?”

“The Northern Lights of Beauty? Yeah. I have a key.” Nancy had given it to her along with some other personal effects Stana hadn’t turned over to the police.

I was going in the front doors, for now. A little conversation. I might need the key later on.

“Right,” she said.

Before she signed off she reminded me that a disguise or cover story wouldn’t work, they’d recognize me as soon as I walked through their doors. Remember, I’m the ex-Leaf who took photographs of Airedale’s baggy ass back when he was fucking Nancy.

"Baggy ass, indeed," I said.

THE OFFICE WAS DARK, a narrow edge of light burning through the slight fissure in the drawn curtains.

I requested it to be that way. Sonny Clark was on the turntable, "Cool Struttin." I requested that too.

I lay on a couch that smelled of wool and fabric softener. One low watt lamp burned next to Dr. Cohen. She had helmeted hair, thick and coarse, and a round face full of a sad optimism. She was fortyish, and leaned back in a swivel chair. Pince-nez glasses propped up along the front of her nose, giving her a distinguished appearance. She looked a bit like Emma Goldman. A tabby cat, with a scratch over its left eye, perched behind her. The cat was licking a paw, as if removing leftover bits of fish bones. Dr. Cohen really didn't care much for cats, but this one had wandered in out of the rain one day and had chosen to adopt the good doctor. So, she took it in. I don't think it had a name.

Dr. Cohen wore a plain black dress with a Peter Pan collar. Did she ever wear anything but black? She once joked that it fit all her moods.

I guess, at some of our sessions the roles get kind of reversed and she tells me of the depression she suffers from, the survivor's guilt for being the one still standing. She lost her mother, father, sister and uncle at Auschwitz. Occasionally, limping with remorse, she finds herself drifting toward the Prince Edward Viaduct, peering down below, and imagining letting go, tumbling, falling through the sky, over and over, never hitting bottom, just forever falling, like tumbling dice. These feelings don't consume her, much, but when they do nudge through her defense mechanisms, they are bright flames, a fallen jet burning in the woods. It's a fight to not become a part of the debris.

Black anchors her, "keeps me level-headed," she says.

After such confessions, she smiles, and in a heavy, full and yet melodic voice praises herself for being so present before me, opening up, allowing the vulnerability to show. Why can't I reciprocate her intimacies with some of my own? That's how it's supposed to work, Hayden. I tell you what hurts me. And then you return the favor. What hurts you?

So I shrug and laugh nervously.

Nothing hurts me. Nothing.

I can't let it hurt me.

So nothing does.

It's like a script, a mantra, I repeat it again and again whenever I start feeling too much or a heavy rain falls. Water—bathtubs—taffy—

I can't talk about him, my father.

So we're talking about Stana. You still like her, maybe love her, Dr Cohen had asked. And I said, I guess so, I don't know, but a line had been crossed, I said, and she said, what line, show me this line, you define the line and you can remove it if you wish.

But she caused the deaths of Spinner and Lisa.

Weren't they already dead? They just didn't know it yet, the doctor said. Wasn't it just a matter of time before Migano closed the book on them? They had double-crossed him, they were the walking dead. And I've read Miss Younger's columns, she cares about justice, protecting women against injustice, domestic battery, do you really think she would have really given Cathy Stabulas over to Babe to be hurt? Would Babe, who is now engaged to Cathy's sister Kim, have hurt Cathy? That part of the narrative doesn't add up, Hayden. Stana cared for Cathy. Do you really think she would have betrayed her?

I don't know.

Yes you do. Answer the question.

I shrugged.

I shrug a lot during our sessions and talk circles around what's really bothering me, my asshole father, my conflicted feelings, my desire, still, for Stana.

Dad used to hit me with the belt for mixing his drinks the

wrong way. You put the ice in first, then the drink, not the other way around. I never could figure that out. What difference did it make? But when he saw that I didn't remember correctly, the belt came off.

I just can't open up. I can't tell her these things. I believe in getting by, keep your head down, do your job. No point crying over what I can't change. Let's move on. Punch the clock. What am I going to do today and tomorrow? Forget the past. Live in the now.

"There are no clocks here," she often says. "If we have to stay longer, we stay longer. This is not work. This is a free space to express."

And she wanted me to open up, to let go, so that I could live in the present more freely.

Talk about Stana, talk about my father.

I can't let go. I can't open up. And some days I can't even tie my shoes. The headaches.

And Sonny Clark hits a run on the keys, and the rush of notes soothes, heals. Somehow jazz speaks to me, filling in the holes of my hollow moods.

So today, she told me a story, one that I'll never forget. When she was in Auschwitz, you lose all of your "inner-directedness," your identity, self, living for food, for enough to sustain you through the next minute, hour, day. You're reduced to an animal. One woman, Leah, had been a dancer back in Germany, and she now only looked down at her lap and her flipped-up hands. One day, as she and several others were being led to the gas chambers, one of the SS officers, laughed, saying weren't you at one time a dancer. He named the cabaret. Let's see you dance. And she did.

I said nothing.

Was she motivated by other-directed choices, trying to please them? That's what they *all* thought, but as she danced, she pirouetted closer to the officer, removed his gun, and shot him, through the heart. She of course was immediately killed by his fellow officers, but this act was a free act, her last one. Through dancing she had re-claimed a part of her lost identity, her autonomy, her inner-directed self. Isn't that what detective work is for you, a chance to claim your lost autonomy?

"I guess so," I said, not looking at her.

"How are you not free in your everyday life?" *How are you a part of the lonely crowd, guided by the approving nods, commands of others?*

"You're getting kind of theoretical now, aren't you, doc? *Lonely Crowd*?"

"I use a cross-discplinary approach to my work." She smiled tightly. "David Reisman," she mumbled. A sociologist.

Honestly, there are things that I'd like to tell you, doc, but I can't. I just can't. I shrugged. "I really didn't feel anything over the man I killed, the one in the last case."

"Nothing?"

I inhaled wool and fabric softener. The little doilies on the arms and head rests of the couches and chairs must be washed daily. It just smelled too good in here. Reminded me of my grandma's basement. I took in another breath. "No, doc."

"Hayden. Don't call me doc." She shifted in her chair, tissue paper crinkling. "Call me Jeannette or Dr. Cohen. I have a name. Don't diminish me."

"I'm sorry, Jeannette."

"And what was the name of the man you killed?"

"Johnny "Red Eye" Thompson—a real handsome fucko—"

"Do I detect a note of jealousy?"

"He was one of those made guys, you know? Thought the world was his? Blond hair, capped teeth. Entitlement, you know?" I was Jewish. I had to fight for everything.

"What about the other one, the other man you killed, the last case?"

She wouldn't say his name. She wanted me to. I wouldn't say

it either.

"Iago of the Year Award Winner, 1965. The human toad?" The guy who had raped his daughters and killed Sarah Kerr, a young woman I had found crumpled up in a suitcase, two bullets behind an ear?

She wrote something on a yellow note pad. "You can't even acknowledge him."

"What's to acknowledge?"

"Own up to it. He was a human being."

"Was he?" I still wouldn't say his name. I'm a stubborn son of a bitch.

"You told me your father was an alcoholic—"

"Still is."

"Your mother, dead."

"Yes. Died when I was eight." Tears pushed behind my eyes. I wasn't going to show it though. And I sure as hell wasn't going to talk about it.

"Your father used to take you to the bars and keep you parked outside while he threw darts, for how long, two-three hours?" She flipped pages, her notebook resembling a yellow sand dune. "Three hours, I wrote down, three. How did that make you feel?" She removed her glasses and massaged the two little dents, mini-Frankenstein feet, at the edges of her nose.

"How the fuck do you think it made me feel?"

The gap in the curtain seemed narrower.

"You're still angry."

"Damn right."

I breathed in fabric softener.

"Are you still angry at Stana—"

She's not my father. No.

I shrugged, *I'm disappointed but not angry. I'm confused.*

You like her.

Love her, I think. I didn't think I did, anymore, but maybe I am moving that line, or rubbing it away, or putting some perforated marks in it, I don't know.

Good.

But my dad. Yeah. I'm still pissed.

"Was some of that anger being transferred to the—"

I sat up on the couch, rocks breaking in my stomach. "What are you saying? That when I killed that man, blew away his brains, I was really killing my own father?"

"I'm suggesting maybe it was a free act—a response to something else—" She smiled and wiped dust off a sleeve of her dress. "Maybe we're dwelling too much in the past. You obviously have a lot of feelings trapped inside you, Hayden. And when you're ready to deal with them, you will."

I shrugged.

"You're minimizing again—"

I looked sideways. Clark was on another run of notes, filling the hollow spaces.

"Shrugging is minimizing—it's a default setting keeping real feelings from being expressed. You need to be more present, mindful, aware—"

"My shoulders ache from old hockey injuries so I shrug—"

"Don't bullshit and joke—"

"Sorry."

"So how do we move forward?"

"Forward with what?"

"You? Your life?" She placed her glasses back on. "What can you do now, to ease the pain, to reintegrate—" *What can you do about Stana, your father?*

"Well, like you said, there's always the next case, that's what keeps me going, the next—"

"So, you find meaning in this kind of work—?" She shifted again, poised fingers tenting together.

"Yeah. When I'm helping people like Dawn. Damn right I do. Yeah." And then I told her how after killing those two men, my gun hand shaking so, I just kissed Dawn, not on the cheek either, on the lips, full, in front of all those people, construction workers, bystanders, through traffic. It wasn't a sexual kiss. I didn't want her. Yes, I was attracted to her, but it was a relief, a need, a—

"An affirmation—"

"Yeah." I looked at my shoes. One of the laces was undone.

"An affirmation that you are alive. Like me, you are a survivor."

I hadn't thought of it that way. *She fucking scares me sometimes. She can see right into the secrets of my heart.* "I guess so. Yeah."

"So you really have it backwards, don't you, Hayden?"

"What?"

"They *help you*. Your clients give you purpose, meaning." She pointed at me, herself. "I'm going to role play, imagine the screen of your mind": My relationship with Stana is over and my life is somewhat empty, but rather than surrender to the void—

Are you saying that relationship is over? For good?

Didn't you tell me it was?

But, I can't get it back?

Do you want to?

I want answers, not more questions—

You have to find the answers. That line and what you do with it, it's up to you.

I—

Talk to her—

I'm trying to—there's so much to overcome—

Hmm.

Hmm? What's that mean?

Hmm, means hmm. But back to role playing—

I'm you. My life is somewhat empty, and rather than surrender to the void, give in, fall from the Prince Edward Viaduct, forever falling, falling forever, the work gives me hope. The work justifies existence. There are people a lot worse off than I am.

I deal with them every day. I may live a lonely existence, but the work bolsters me up, saving me from loneliness's glare and alienation.

"You sure you're not talking about yourself, doc, Jeannette?"

She was all right. I liked how worked up she got trying to help me, open me up, make me vulnerable and truthful.

Dr. Cohen smiled and tapped the arm rests of her chair, the notebook nestled in her lap. "I guess I am." She wrote a note, and scribbled some more. "Fuck, I guess I am."

5

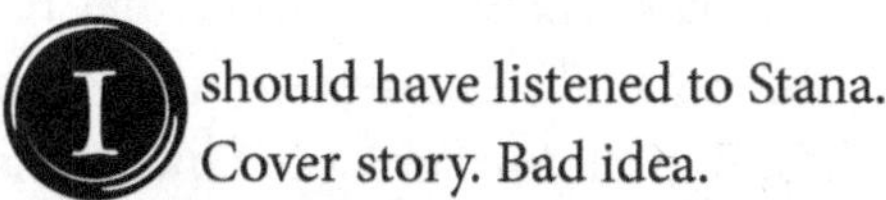

I should have listened to Stana.

Cover story. Bad idea.

But I'm stubborn and Airedale was nowhere to be seen and I went with a story that was so covert that the *Spy who Came in from the Cold* cat would want to get tips from me.

Check it: I was Hawley Walker, thoroughbred-owning cat, seeking restorative powers for a troubled, ailing mother. Anyway, Dr. Williams, while nodding compassionately over my mother's "plight," sure drank a lot of water. I guess all of the staff at Adora Borealis and their clients did. They were big on that. There were fountains everywhere along the L-shaped building, but Dr. Williams only drank water from the various alcoves, partially hidden recesses. There the water was filtered. And in pitchers. Water was the key to hydration and beauty, it removed all of the poisons from your system, she said. "It is the first step to better health."

"Uh-huh," I said, or something equally unimpressed. I'm a bit of a smart-ass.

But she sure was pretty, a surreal beauty. I couldn't look at her directly for fear of being caught staring, breaking professional protocols, so I would catch furtive glances, every now and then, taking in her thin those, the blue eyes set wide apart, and the skin, fresh-scrubbed, porcelain smooth. She had alert eyes, listening to all. Her breathing was a steady, calm rhythm.

You couldn't hear much of anything else going on in the clinic: few clients, few staff. Adora Borealis was fairly empty. I guess it was 5:46, close to closing time. I had no idea what was going on behind adjacent doors, but one woman, in the lobby, was finishing up with some kind of facial, restorative treatment, her face caked with muddy cream. She was about twenty-seven and like all women in no need of that junk.

We began my "tour" for my troubled mother in the lab. White walls, blue composite counters, and white shelving full of beakers, bottles, test tubes, vials. There were scales that resembled Hobarts right out of the Stabulas's corner store grocery. Microscopes and petri dishes. Bunsen burners. I felt like I was back in eleventh-grade chemistry, dying to get to English class. In case you haven't guessed, I hated chemistry. Never could get the results of the various experiments to line up like they were supposed to: my litmus paper always turned red when it was supposed to turn blue.

The latter got a laugh out of Dr. Williams. Her voice was husky and her face, when I caught a glimpse refracted in the glass of the cabinet doors, reminded me of a young, platinum blonde Barbara Stanwyck, a combination of expressive eyes and an almost frozen inflexibility. When she spoke, her lips barely moved. They were like the crinkly tied off end of a balloon.

A man hunched over a microscope at the far end of the blue counter. He was fiftyish, bald, his eyes when he looked in my direction were a sharp, inviting hazel. Dr. Dallas Stangl. He was working the cosmetics end for Adora, perfecting new facial creams.

"I thought you performed surgeries. Plastic—"

"Well we're expanding our base of operations to include cosmetics. Dr. Stangl's perfecting a blemishing cream for women." And then Gillian leaned forward and whispered in my ear how he was also working on a lubricating gel for post-menopausal women to help them get lubricated during sex. With age, some women struggle. Sex hurts.

It sure does.

"The gel warms the body within seconds." She smiled. It had some kind of Brazilian extract, aphrodisiac in its composition.

"Interesting," I said, unsure of what else to say. I wasn't quite sure of why I needed to know this, or why her breath against my ear tickled. It wasn't unpleasant.

Dr. Stangl smiled awkwardly. I don't think Dr. Williams was adept at whispering.

I nodded, and then he peered back into his microscope. He kept both eyes open.

We lingered for a few moments. I picked up two or three beakers, but saw no traces of any kind of powder, Blue 27 or otherwise.

"Shall we go to the hydrotherapy room." It wasn't really a question. Dr. Williams hooked her arm around mine and ushered me from the lab.

She floated as we flowed down the narrow halls, the track lighting bright above us. It made her platinum hair look a little bit green.

"So tell me, what do you miss most about the game?"

My back story or cover, the thoroughbred angle, also involved an ex-hockey player joining the family biz. I loved my handle: Hawley Walker. It sounded English, stuffy, and hoi polloi enough.

"But surely, horses aren't enough, you must miss the game." She leaned ever closer, smelling of Chanel No. 5.

I wasn't sure if hockey was the only game she was talking about.

"I bet you had a lot of pussy during your playing days."

I wasn't expecting her to say that.

I coughed nervously.

"I had some women, yes." I looked away and the cough stretched into a shallow sigh. "The first breakout pass, I miss that." I smiled awkwardly. The quick pass from your own zone that gets the puck moving up ice and on a counter attack. When you execute that well, there's a kind of simplicity and poetry to it. Don't hold the puck long. Look up, and stick to stick, get it to a man who is moving. Don't pass it to a man standing still. Too easy to get it taken away by their forwards. Look for the man moving. "Stuff like that, I guess. It's simple but smart hockey. I miss rituals, the unwritten rules. Hockey has order, you know?"

"Yes." She leaned even closer, bolstering up her arm in mine. One more nudge and she'd be bolstering my back pocket.

I couldn't help but think of her breath in my ear.

"And you like that?"

"Yeah. Who wouldn't?" So much in hockey makes sense.

She was ethereal, that's for sure. We floated further down that hall. Her steps were like curtain edges lifting gently in a slightly open window. I'm a product of the 1950s. I like curvy women with an ample bust line and big hips, and Dr. Williams may have been very petite, her breasts slight, her hands and feet small, but I found her and her fresh-scrubbed face strangely attractive. There wasn't a blemish, a line, a crow's foot, anywhere.

And if you looked long enough you felt like you might catch a reflection of your own face in her porcelain glow.

She had to be mid-to late thirties. She looked twenty-five. Next to her, with my slight scars from 55 stitches, hockey fights, I was Methuselah.

"Howe or Richard?" Her blond hair glowed with backlighting.

"What?"

"Who's the greatest player of all time, Howe or Richard?"

"Is this a test of some kind?"

"Howe or Richard?"

"Doug Harvey." I loved puck-rushing defensemen.

"Doug Harvey?" She laughed. "Well that's outside the box."

"Montreal doesn't win all those cups without Harvey." Seven-time Norris trophy champion. But between Richard and Howe, I had to go with Richard, I said. Even though he had retired in 1960 and Howe was still playing, the Rocket was the best money player ever. Over 80 playoff goals, multiple overtime winners, and from the blue line in he was the fastest to the net I'd ever seen. "Richard, no doubt."

I always thought Howe was a bit of a doofus. For years he kept all of our salaries low because he allowed himself to be underpaid. My rookie season, I had been a member of Ted Lindsay's Players Association seeking a fair cut of the profits the owners were raking in with their TV money, watered-down pop, and season ticket prices, and hoarding from us. Lindsay played the game the way I did, tough in the corners, gritty, but he scored a helluva lot more goals, much much more. Next to Claude Provost of the Canadiens, he was my idol.

Jim Thomson of the Leafs was also part of the association. When the Old Man, Steve Smith's father, heard about it, he banished Thomson to the then lowly Blackhawks. To me, a second year guy, the Old Man was more forgiving, haranguing me in his office, a twisted finger in my chest, *behave yourself if you want to stay here.* I behaved until 1964 and the photos I took of Ehle's wife Nancy and Baggy-Ass, and then later, another set of photos of Danny Davis and Sharon Smallbear, our captain's wife, messing around in a hotel room. The Old Man was retired by then. His son and Pal Cal Bullard canned my ass.

And now they were awaiting trial for running a common gaming house, bootlegging, tax evasion, and prostitution.

Dr. Williams stopped. "I'm surprised. I thought you'd say Howe."

"Because I'm English?" Now I figured out the subtle off-Ontario accent. She was French, something about the "e-u" sound in her yous.

"Yeah."

"I'm not, I'm a Jew."

She nodded.

"Besides, lots of English Canadians love Richard. His nickname is English after all. The Rocket. He's not known as La Fusée."

She tapped her chin. "You're right. That's a good point." Her blue eyes glinted with a dusky veil. "Dormiras tu avec moi?"

"I know what that means, doctor."

She laughed, parts of her lower teeth showing. "Of course, you do." Her voice sounded as if she smoked a pack of cigarettes an hour.

I wasn't sure of what to make of all of her overtures.

The expanse of her eyes probably gave her great peripheral vision and created a boundary line between the sublimely stunning pushing up against the edges of the slightly profane. A couple of genetic tweaks and her brittle porcelain mask would crack, fall, to the other side of the beauty equation. It was a surreal balance between the known and oblivion.

And yet, I couldn't stop looking at her, furtive glances and all. Hell, she needed to be on a poster for Oil of Olay.

"You're French, I gather?"

"Oui." She came to Toronto two or three years ago and opened this office with Cliff in 1963. She missed Montreal. Nobody could make croissants like the French, and she thought the architecture of T.O. sucked, bland, too many straight lines and arches, too much Presbyterian righteousness to everything. Boring complacency.

"What about the new City Hall they're building?" It was just a few blocks down from her office and set to be inaugurated soon.

"Just fine, but who landed the spaceship in the middle of it?"

That cracked me up.

Dawn sure was right about the joint's whiteness. Everything in this L-shaped compound was a radioactive full on glare. The walls, the tiles, even her very short lab coat, slacks and shoes.

White.

I felt like a slalom racer fighting the snow blind.

Dr. Williams drank more water at one of the many stations along our tour. "You should have some—"

"Uh-huh."

"It's not poison."

I laughed. "It just isn't for me, Dr. Williams. I mean I like water and all but I don't need a drink every ten minutes."

"Call me Gillian."

I liked the name. "Gillian." In my playing days, doc, we were taught to eat steaks before puck drop and spit out the water we drank *during* the game, I said. Don't want to get waterlogged.

That's ridiculous, you need water to replenish. "Hockey players are so barbarian."

I couldn't disagree with the latter part of her assessment. We are barbarians on the ice, especially when we slip into our third faces, but the whole water fetish felt like some kind of goddamn pagan ritual. Any second, I expected to see someone tossed into a volcano.

I only hoped it wasn't about to be me.

More on my clever cover story: Mom (who in reality died when I was eight—gas-oven type suicide) had been in a terrible car accident and was in need of care, the kind of hydrotherapy I hear Adora Borealis specializes in. She gets these terrible headaches.

Hence the tour, the lab, the first-name basis bit. The comical flirting. The whisper in the ear. The pleasant Dr. Stangl overhearing but acting like he didn't. Yet despite the friendly hijinks, Gillian wouldn't let me see what was behind door number one, two, or three. There wasn't even a curtain with Carol Merril.

Clients. Privacy, you know, Dr. Williams said, and we were now floating through some large white doors, the handle looking like one of those wheels that closes a hatch on a submarine.

It too was white. Bleached, bone dry, brighter than chalk.

The hydrotherapy room on the other side glowed like phosphorus.

It was a strange room. The building itself was one story, but this room was two, possibly two and a half stories high.

Even the bars on the windows glowed, just like Dawn said.

I wish I had worn sunglasses.

To the left, high on the wall, ran blocks of glass windows, twelve by twelve with steel reinforcement between them. The glass was tinted and there was probably enough space behind there to host the Toronto Maple Leafs. It reminded me of those hospital dramas on TV where doctors watch other doctors performing surgeries. I waved. Nobody waved back. At least no one I could see.

The room was crammed with tubs and its accompanying accouterments of nozzles and whirlpools and foam guns. A nurse, with one eye higher on her face than the other, greeted us and smiled briefly at me, before looking down at a black lemon scuff mark on her white shoes. She was in her mid-thirties and fleshy in the arms, a little plump. Her face, pale; her hands small. The hair breaking under her white cap was auburn. The violet-colored lipstick she wore made her face even paler, like a member of kabuki theater. I liked her. It was just a feeling I had. I liked her.

"This is Leila. One of our best nurses. She'll probably be working with your mother." Gillian finished introductions, smiled. "She's in charge of our hydrotherapy ward."

We exchanged handshakes. One of Leila's fingers gently pricked my palm like the broken off nub of a rose stem. She looked down once again at the lemon scuff as she prepared to wheel a client away.

"When you're done with her, you're free to go Leila."

"Thank-you, Dr. Williams." Her voice rose from the bottom of a tunnel.

The client, fiftyish, was in a one-piece swimsuit, her knees pointed up, thin hair matting her eyes. She kept nodding her head at everyone. I said hello. She couldn't stop nodding.

Leila wheeled her away. A wheel caught, over and over again, seemingly screaming, stop, stop.

"You better call CAA and get that thing towed somewhere."

Gillian shook her head, her lips pressing into a thin bemused line. "You have a very good sense of humor, Mr. Walker."

"Thanks. It's part of the new school of comedy, urban smart-ass."

She laughed.

"That gal that left, she okay?"

"Leila can be a little moody—"

"No, I mean the client. With all the nodding and stuff."

"I can't talk about our clients, Hawley."

But she could talk about Leila. Anyway, the Hawley Walker bit was cracking me up. I'm a regular riot all right. *Hawley Walker. Shall we visit any botanical gardens today, luv? Hilarious. Biscuits and clotted cream? Strawberries too?*

"Privacy." She smiled sincerely, her face a shiny new coin.

"Of course."

I wondered if the woman with the yen to listlessly nod had been taking too much Blue 27. She sure was lethargic. She nodded in half-time. And that's when I asked Dr. Williams if Dr. Airedale had more radical treatments. I wasn't sure that hydrotherapy would be enough for dear old Mom. The headaches were severe. She was talking suicide.

Gillian tapped her chin, smiled, and said something reassuring.

I told her about my good friend Bobby Ehle, the cat wanted for murder, and how he told me Dr. Airedale had really helped him out with some kind of experimental treatment involving Blue 27. I made it sound like I really believed in the good doctor, a regular Albert Schweitzer Dr. Airedale was.

Maybe I overplayed my hand.

"I don't know what you're talking about. Blue 27? This is a place for cosmetic surgery and relaxation therapy, not an episode of *Flash Gordon*."

I nodded. "I'm just repeating what Bobby told me. Blue 27. Works wonders, he says."

"You should read more racing forms and less comic books, Mr. Walker."

Like I said before—my cover story, not a good idea. It hadn't fooled her one bit.

I checked out the switches and levers by the hydrotherapy tub, looking under the rubber sheets to the nozzles along the side that let out jets of water. This looks cozy, I said, to say something.

I turned the handles, worked the tap trigger. Squeezed. Foam spilled from the gun, like the broken bits of puffed flowers that coated cattails.

"So are you interested in, perhaps, bringing your mother by, to check out the facilities?"

"Sure." I rubbed the sides of my mouth and pushed back my porkpie. "Sure. This might be a good fit." I rubbed at the edges of my mouth and smiled my lopsided lupine grin.

And then she shrank to another alcove, for another glass of water. She drank quickly, seeking to knock away my humor. One last sip. Gillian never finished any of the glasses. I asked why.

The bottom of the cup, Mr. Fuller, is full of your saliva, your impurities. It doesn't do your body any good to put those *back* in the system. "I never finish my drinks."

She had called me Mr. Fuller. "When did you know?"

"When you walked in." She smiled. "I read the papers. And your hat is a noticeable affectation."

"Affectation?" *Stana had said the same thing during our first case together, Cheap Amusements.*

Lights flashed above, on the other side of the tinted glass. Our long shadows, resembling narrow birch trees, spread behind me and Gillian. "Yes, asshole, affectation." It was the inestimable Dr. Airedale leaning against the upstairs glass. I recognized his thin voice, even if it were distorted, bleeding and bouncing all over the room through an intercom system he must've purchased for ten dollars at Canadian Tire. He had been tracking the whole conversation, watching with a kind of god-like gaze from above. Mr. Opticon.

"You going to come down here to talk, or do I have to keep looking up, your Highness." My neck was getting sore and I couldn't read his facial expressions. He was a silhouette painted on glass.

"Fuck you."

More distortion, static over telephone wires.

"Yup, definitely Canadian Tire."

"Go take a flying fuck at a rolling donut—"

"A man of few words, I see. And donuts liven up any party." Beer and donuts: the Canadian way.

He dropped another F-bomb.

"Your boys, Airedale, or Cassel's boys, I should say, are dead. Thompson and Lazy Legs? Gone." I snapped my fingers for emphasis. "They've taken their final taxis, the long goodbye. Can you pass the message onto Cassel? As in Lenny, Mr. Machete? I think he's just down the hall—an expert in tossing people's remains in trash bags. Your kind of guy."

The upper window lights dimmed back to black.

"I wouldn't push it with him." Gillian leaned closer to me. Her voice was painted with concern. "Watch yourself."

"Uh-huh."

"I assure you—" Gillian spoke softly. "There's no Mr. Cassel here." She tapped her chin once or twice, her lips parting while her face appeared immobile.

"Then let me check."

"I can't—"

"Right, right privacy."

"And you don't have a warrant—"

"No. No warrant." I forced a smile. It hurt my face.

She smiled. "I liked blowing in your ear. We should do more of that," she whispered again.

And that's when her hand patted my ass. I have an okay functional ass for a hockey player, helps with power skating, but I was a little embarrassed by the whole deal.

"Come." She had changed her mind. Maybe my ass is better than I give it credit for: she was going to show me the rooms after all.

There were eight of them, small, nicely furnished. The only one occupied, number five, housed, the woman with the nodding grin. The other seven rooms had no windows, no television, two lamps, a dresser, a small bookshelf, a comfortable queen-size bed, blue carpeting, blue walls, a closet, and a private bathroom. Room seven was crammed with pulp novels. I recognized Georges Simenon, Jim Thompson, and Elliott Chaze, *Black Wings has My Angel.* In the bathroom cabinet were several over-the-counter remedies for an upset stomach.

"We haven't cleared this room yet. Our last client left last night."

I wondered if it were Cassel. For a hood he had good reading taste. "Uh-huh," I said. "Who was in here?"

She smiled, her lips barely moving, her blue eyes filling with charm. "An actor. I can't give you his name."

"Is he on a western and says cheerio a lot?"

"I couldn't say." She smiled, the tip of her chin glinting in the low level of light.

Airedale, with a hitch in his walk, huffed into the room, his left leg limping slightly, shifting his body into a wobbly I. "Oh, there you are."

"Here we are," she echoed, her tone mocking, annoyed.

Airedale was very thin, his goatee and hair white, his face sharp angles, ears cuts of pork that didn't fit his narrow face. He wore wool pants and a double-breasted blazer with a crown on the left pocket. He exuded country-club ease, a regular descendent of the United Empire Loyalists.

"Hey, Baggy Ass."

"Fuck you."

"Can't we bring up the level of conversation? I thought doctors appreciated fine wines, abstract art, and discussing the lifetime work of the Durants—the story of civilization series?"

He glared. His face blotchy, mismatched puzzle pieces.

Gillian suppressed a laugh and covered her mouth. "Will and Ariel, Cliff?"

I guess she had read them too.

He hadn't and that really pissed him off.

We moved out of the room, Cliff getting between the two of us, asserting what little authority he had. As we crossed white lines of light and tile, Airedale shot her surly looks. She wasn't minding her place. I guess as the senior partner, he was the big Kahuna. "I told you not to fuck with this guy."

And then she laughed, a husky laugh, one that matched her cigarette-tinged voice, and stripped him of his threadbare machismo. "Don't play hardboiled, Cliff. It doesn't suit you. You're no tough guy."

I guess the big Kahuna had suddenly become chum for sharks out in the Pacific.

His eyes sharpened. "I warned you about trying to *play him*."

"Play? I enjoy playing. Playing gives me pleasure. Something I haven't experienced in a long, long time."

I assumed there was some sex stuff going on under all that "play" talk, like telling me all about female lubricant, whispering in my ear, and wondering how much action I got as a hockey player. Maybe Gillian and Cliff were one-time lovers. There was something peevish and petty about their exchanges that suggested a washed-out love.

Airedale's eyes now filled his voice with blades. "He's a wise-ass and we don't need to be amused by him or amuse him. He has no authority here."

He stopped at one of the alcoves and poured himself a drink of water. It was smooth. There wasn't a bubble in it. "Get rid of him."

"Since when do you run things?" She turned politely toward me, assuring me that Bobby Ehle was a client; took hydrotherapy treatments, that's all.

"Can you show me the books, the payments he made?"

She said nothing.

"I think you better be going, asshole." Airedale again, always on point.

"What about dear old Mom? She had such hopes for this place."

"Next time, Gillian, you make a choice to 'entertain' a guest. Consult me—"

"Don't tell me how to behave, Cliff. I don't like it." She crossed her arms over her chest. "And I like him, I like Hayden Fuller, and I'd like to see him." She shrugged, raising an eyebrow in my direction, her face sultry, a little insolent.

"Sure, Gillian, but my social calendar's a little busy right now. The murder of Nancy, Blue 27, Bobby gone missing, and, oh, yeah, a certain crime czar named Lenny Cassel, who at one time was hanging out in a certain little hamlet known as the Adora Borealis. And let's not forget two gangsters lying on a slab who tried to kill me and another client, Dawn Stoukas. But, hey, my people will call your people." I winked at her and headed to the door.

One of the buttons on Airedale's double blazer had loosened, opening up the jacket like a bent corner of a paperback. "Cut the comedy, shamus. You're no Soupy Sales."

"I was always partial to Lenny Bruce, bubbie."

Airedale rubbed his hands as if removing chunks of dirt. "Bruce was provocative. He was never funny." He was proud of his pronouncement, a regular Nathan Cohen. "Get out Fuller. Your so-called zingers *bore* me."

"Yours in Blue 27—"

"Get going—"

I spun around, and once again flashed my lopsided lupine grin, the same one splashed across my PI license. "How about Terrien? Either of you seen him around? Ex-hockey player? Small guy? Five foot eight. Hair like a Brillo pad?"

They quit glaring at one another and Airedale took a step back and Gillian's breath quickened. Her shoulders tightened too.

That told me enough.

I pushed back my porkpie. "Where's the tennis racket, pally? You don't look quite at home without it."

He dropped another F-bomb. This time it was an unexploded bomb, lacking conviction.

"We'll do lunch sometime," I said to Gillian.

"Till then." Her face was a fresh sheet of ice, no hairline scratches at all, just clear skin and lips and eyes full of possibilities.

SHE WAS WAITING for me in the car.

Leila. Her breaths were like her voice, coming from a tunnel far away.

Her pale face glowed dimly in the glimmer of the early evening sun splashing red in front of my '63 Ford Galaxie.

"I needed to see you." Her fingers twisted about a large manila envelope.

I tossed my keys onto the dash. "I figured that or you were really into muscle cars." It had a 427 engine.

Leila looked younger without her nurse's cap. Her auburn hair was done in a pageboy cut.

And her eyes were more evenly level than I had initially thought.

The edges of the manila envelope were worn by the dusty oil of nervous fingers, the clasp in back broken.

I adjusted the car's rear view mirror, and then shifted about in the bench seat and looked right at her, my voice low. "You don't need to be scared of me." The inside of my palm still itched a little from the scratch she had served up a few minutes ago.

She wore a light blue jacket over her scrubs. Her red hair was pulled along the tops of her ears with the assist of two tortoise-shell barrettes. Her face was anxious, lips pressed tight, but her eyes were sliding into trusting me.

"And you don't need to be scared about anything else either." I flipped back my blue blazer, flashing my snub-nosed, side-holstered. I had an additional .45 in the glove box. After my tangle with Cassel's goons, Thompson and Langlois, I was packing extra heat.

She nodded, lips loosening into a broken rubber band.

Besides, Leila, I'm parked under a tree, I said, and nobody's around to see us in this car. Toronto wasn't exactly New York. I don't know if you noticed, but this city *does* sleep. We have blue laws. Bits of loose paper and a Styrofoam cup or two kissed the bottom ends of closed-up offices.

But how did she find my car? *Know it was my car?* Before I could ask, she opened the envelope, the tip of her tongue peeking from a corner of her firm mouth. Her lips were heavy, full. Her nose had a little Bob Hope lift to it. I wondered if she'd had it fixed, like Nancy's. The design looked awfully similar to Nancy's before her face became a Picasso.

Leila slid out an 8x10 photo, black and white. The focus was sharp. Five people on a street, all smiling. The sky behind them black, turning slightly gray from hazy lines of smoke. They stood in front of the Montreal Forum and people ringed about, laughing, hollering, celebrating. There were names written in thin magic marker under the five principals.

Denys, the one on the far right of the frame, was not looking into the camera, but off to the left. He wore a lambskin hat, black. I couldn't make out any crying fleur-de-lis on his face. Maybe it was on his other cheek, the one not quite visible. He wore jeans and a blazer. He was obviously the self-appointed "artist" of the group, separating himself from the pack, looking in a different direction from their victorious stares. Next to him, a young Bobby Ehle, probably just before his call up to the Leafs, head slightly tossed back with jocularity, comb behind his left ear. Back then, his tan hair wasn't buzzed, it was slicked back, rockabilly style. He wore a white T-shirt and Cuban-heeled boots. Badass. The Beatles before Hamburg. Leaning into Bobby's shoulder, Terry. Also wearing the same get-up as Bobby. He had a comb in his right hand, a big fallen placard in his left, and his pompadour had broken slightly, loose strands twisting across one of his eyes. He looked pouty and sulky, as if he needed a glass of milk before going to bed. A step or two away was Lenny Cassel, the Detroit-area mobster. His hair was charcoal black, his beady eyes pieces of led, and his face stiff, the lips downturned. He was slight, small between the shoulders but he radiated menace. I had no idea that he'd been to Montreal, ever. For five months in 1955, Leila said, Montreal had been his home. Bobby had told her that back then Lenny was running from a narcotics rap. The last fella, on the far end, lost in a loose-fitting blazer and jeans, a bookend for Denys, was *Guillame*. His hair was buzzed, but it looked like iron filings, prematurely gray or white. His hands were in his pockets. And his face wasn't exactly heavy, but his cheeks sagged and his nose was like mine, somewhat generous. The look on his mismatched face was faraway, not quite radiating the same level of anger as the rest of the posse. *N'oublie jamais* was scrawled above the photo in heavier lines.

N'oublie jamais. Je me souviens. Similar but different. Is this the outfit Bobby was trying to remember? N'oublie jamais.

"Cassel speak French?"

"No." Leila laughed. The photo was taken in the wake of the Richard Riot. "You see the smoke in the background?"

I did. I also saw a line-drawing of a pig and the name Campbell written above it on the placard in Terry's left hand. It pointed down near the ground.

All but two of the participants were smiling: Cassel, the sadistic mobster, and Denys, the artist.

"*Never forget.*" Leila translated the French.

"Yeah, I know."

"You speak French?"

"*Un petit peu.*"

"*Un petit peu.*" She looked away. "That's what this group was against. Second class. French equality."

I nodded. I kind of got the point. I'm a Jew. I know what it means to be an outsider. *Where you from Fuller? You don't look like us. I'm from Toronto, asshole, I was born at St. Mike's. But where you from, your people?*

And then I thought about the fleur-de-lis, the crying one that Denys sported. And then I got to thinking about the half-burned down publishing house in Montreal, and the "bomb" in the newspaper offices of *The Citizen*. It was starting to make sense. Maybe.

"Bobby always said that bilingualism in Canada means being French and having to learn English. It doesn't work the other way around," she said.

"Yeah." It never has worked the other way around. *The English didn't lose at the Plains of Abraham, 1759 or the siege of Montreal, 1760. Conquest of Quebec.*

Bobby was involved in that, the Richard Riot, Leila said. Bobby threw eggs at Clarence S. Campbell. "Campbell was a prick, suspending a French-Canadian hero, and then having the gall to show up at the next Habs game. A real fucking creep."

"Uh-huh." A major fucking creep.

I only wished the creep would let me back in the NHL, revoke my life-time ban.

We're all walking contradictions, I guess.

Leila wasn't at the Richard Riot. She's an Etobicoke girl. But if she were there, she too would have thrown some eggs. Richard was her favorite player. And her father's, even though they were Leaf fans.

Was being a Richard fan a prerequisite for work at Adora Borealis?

That made her laugh, wrinkles at the corners of her eyes. "No, Mr. Fuller." Her boss admires Richard because he makes you proud to be French.

I could get that.

We all need heroes. *I was always looking for Jewish ones. When I was a kid, my dad went on and on about Barney Ross, the boxer, being one tough Jew. He loved the cat. I too, sought out members of our tribe, cheering for Hank Greenberg in the 1945 World Series. He'd just got back from the War and he kicked ass.*

My father was never my hero.

"You have me at a disadvantage, Leila. I don't know your last name but you know mine. So call me Hayden, huh?" When did women start treating me so formally? I was always Hayden or Hays on the ice. Pretty soon people are going to start calling me hon, like I'm an old man buying postage stamps. Jesus Christ.

Anyway, in 1955, Campbell suspended the Rocket the rest of the regular season and all of the playoffs for attacking an official. Richard would eventually lose the scoring title to teammate Bernie "Boom-Boom" Geoffrion and Montreal would go on to lose the cup to Detroit that spring in seven games. Montreal fans protested, feeling that this was yet another example of English colonial rule. Richard was often viewed as a Christ-like figure by the French media, sacrificing himself game after game, beaten down by the shields and spears of his opponents. They yelled slurs at him: "frog" and "hey, pea soup." I'm proud to say, I never called the Rocket any of that, not once, but I did hit him hard, every chance I got, because, damn it, he was great. Once in a while one of my elbows would ride up a little high, and cut open his face, right under the eyes. I shut him down some games, but more often than not he got the better of me, scoring a goal or two. One night a hat trick. Another night: four goals. Several coaches sent goons over the boards, sticking the Rocket with high cross checks from behind in every area of the ice. Not just the corners. He had to take matters into his own hands, and during one such after-the-whistle fracas a linesman inadvertently held Richard's arms back allowing Bruin's defenseman Hal Laycoe a clear path to knock Rocket's lights out. Rocket regained his footing, hit the official over the head with his stick, and did a number on Laycoe. Fair-minded people felt the social injustices Richard endured, night after night, but most of English Canada thought Campbell's sentencing was far too light. *Kick him out for a whole season!*

French Canada felt differently.

Bilingualism means being French and having to learn English.

"Denys was the one who threw the canister of tear gas."

"Really?"

"So he says." She shrugged.

That tossed canister forced Montreal to forfeit that night's game against Detroit and Campbell to leave the fabulous Forum under police protection.

Could Denys also send a "tear-gas bomb" to the offices of The Citizen*?*

Bobby had given this very photo to Leila. The last time he visited. "He wanted me to have it." She looked over her shoulder into the red shadows of the street. "I don't know why." Now Leila wanted me to have it. "I don't know the why of that either." I guess, she didn't think he'd killed Nancy. The drugs made him too tired to do anything, she said.

The Richard Riot, the fleur-de-lis, Denys on the other end of the drug drop gone bad. Did this have anything to do with Expo

’67? Airedale’s crowd was taking “vague credit,” Nancy said for what happened to that literary publishing house.

Leila didn’t know. Her eyes narrowed.

And who’s Guillame? I pointed at the photograph, the little guy with iron filings for hair.

She spoke quickly, her voice still resonating a faint tunnel echo. Guillame had disappeared in the late ’50s. He’d be about your age now, Hayden. Maybe a little older. He was a scientist. Chemistry. There was a car accident. He almost died, and afterward he had enough with science and all, and went onto Copenhagen, Denmark. That was around 1962, Leila said. No, 1963.

She never met Guillame, but Bobby swears he was really strange. Never dated, never interested in girls, or boys for that matter. Maybe boys, Leila said. “At least he was always more comfortable with them. Slight boys. You know, the Nancy boys.”

She made a face as if she’d found spiders in her shoes.

“Nancy boys. You mean gay men?”

“Yeah. Anyway, Bobby says Guillame always sat away in the far corners of the booth at the bistros they congregated at. His chair, in the cafes, was the farthest from the table.”

“Uh-huh. So he was shy?”

“Chronically. But when he spoke. So much quiet, brutal confidence.” She crocheted her fingers together and her face was still, following the crawling steps of spiders.

“How so?”

Guillame was the designer of the Richard Riot, she said. He made an impassioned plea at a secret meeting in a dank corner of a Montreal wine cellar and then orchestrated the tear-gas attack. It was all about the birth of a new Quebec, one no longer dominated by old world Catholic values, the Catholic church, and lazy-thinking politicians tied into the conservative hierarchy. “It was time for a quiet revolution, a change was a coming. They were no longer going to be the white niggers of Canada.”

“Really? He went *there*?”

It was such bullshit. I couldn't say that word, the one that started with N. For me it was the worst word, ever.

"He went more than just there. He wrote-up a whole manifesto: *The White Niggers of Canada.*" It might have even been published, she said, by an underground press.

Probably not the press in Montreal that burned half-way down.

"That's how Guillame saw all of French Canada, indentured slaves of the English." Her fingers tightened into a heavy web.

I nodded again. "So this was the first step in the revolution?"

"I don't know." She looked out the back window of my Galaxie, sighed, and shifted, pushing herself up against the door and its handle. "There hasn't been another step in their revolution in ten years."

I didn't know about that. Blue 27 could be part of the plan but how?

"Blue 27's a drug that never worked right," she said, her voice falling through a long tunnel.

I disagreed with her about there being no new "steps" in the revolution. A quiet revolution was taking place. Quebec is ready for change. "Pierre Elliot Trudeau's a fast rising French-Canadian star in the Liberal party and he talks quiet revolution rhetoric, moving French Canada out of the shadows of Catholicism and a system of kickbacks and payouts."

The Duplessis era is dead. Political appointments, kickbacks, conservatism.

Leila liked Trudeau. A lot. "He's sexy."

"So I hear."

Guillame's vision may be more incendiary, but he could still be on the loose, I suggested. Orchestrating things from Denmark? "I take it he's still there?" *A chemist? What's he mixing up?*

"I guess so." She shrugged. No one in Canada had heard from him in over two years.

"Uh-huh?" Maybe Guillame and Denys were behind the need for those three canisters, the ones Dawn was supposed to deliver to Montreal. *Maybe Bobby broke up that delivery. Why? Could Guillame be plotting a more sinister form of rebellion? A new kind of Blue 27?*

Leila had no idea what I was talking about. All she'd seen of Blue 27 was nothing that would cause any kind of revolution. Dr. Stangl, the chemist working for Airedale and Williams, couldn't bake a cake. He was no real doctor, just ex-army, working in radar, she said. "What did he really know? Besides, Blue 27 wasn't a weapon—it just slowed you down, made you less inhibited but also took away all initiative." Bobby couldn't even get it up, she said, embarrassed as soon as the words tumbled from her mouth.

"He told you that?"

She looked away. "I'm a nurse. People tell me things."

I wasn't about to tell her about my father.

"Will you testify to this? To the police. About the distribution of illegal drugs—"

"It won't get us anywhere." And it would only get me killed, she said. Again she looked over my bench seat, into the red streets. The sun filled the sky with the luster one expected in autumn. "I just want to help Bobby." She looked away, eyes misting.

"You're in love with him—"

She nodded. But he wasn't her boyfriend. He didn't even notice her.

I knew a thing or two about that. I reached into the glove box, and pulled out some tissues nestled against my .45. I unfolded the tissues and handed her a couple. "Had Bobby given up?"

I was starting to have my doubts about Oslo, Sweden.

"I don't know if he's given up," Leila said. But she was worried he had. He'd given her one of his Stanley Cup rings.

"Really?"

I'd also have to get Stana looking into Copenhagen, Denmark and the whereabouts of this loose rebel cat, Guillame. I had a feel-

ing he was loose in Montreal. "This Guillame got a last name?"

"Clausen."

"Clausen?"

"It's Danish."

"Danish, huh?" Of course, that's why he fled to Denmark after the auto accident. *Guillame Clausen, chemist.*

"I don't know if Bobby's still alive." Her cheeks were spritzed with light tears. On the last day that she saw him, the last session, on his last dose of Blue 27, falling asleep as he stood up, he handed Leila this photo. "Use it," he said. "I can't."

"Maybe I can," I said. "Maybe I can."

6

Why is it that the people we've made love to and lost, the people we need in some ways to move away from, never ever really leave us? At least for me, a part of myself, my head, my heart, longs to hold onto that younger self that was a part of a life with somebody else. Stana. Her skin still danced with freckles and I remember the feel of her arms, her lips, her hip against mine, the musicality of it all, like drum fills sliding rapidly into a roll, vibrating quickly, her skin pulsing with the blur of two sticks becoming several sticks flashing across a drum head, flash flak rhythms, her rhythms, never the same patterns to her lovemaking, always varying it up like an Art Blakey drum break, her own kind of jazz.

And those eyes, still soldering with commitment to whatever she was working on. And she was working on this case. Helping me.

I wanted to talk about the past, the Stabulas case, the deaths of Lisa and Spinner, our shared guilt, and forgiveness.

I mourned over their deaths.

She did too. Dr. Cohen insisted, Stana must have mourned. Mourning is in every word she writes for the Telegram.

I trust Dr. Cohen.

Her insights.

I want to trust Stana again, but how, how do we talk about this?

"You're not going to believe what I got for you, today. In fucking credible." She smiled, eyes dancing.

Back then, in a bar, during a Leafs playoffs game, I said our relationship was over, a line had been crossed. Her betrayal had ended things, and yet a part of me, the part that resides in all the little parts of me, the corners of my elbows, the top of my closed eyes, the back of my knees, wanted her, wanted to take back, revise what I said, but I'm no wordsmith, no goddamn writer, she is. And she looked great this morning, wearing an orange paisley dress with white beads and a black beret slanted to the left. She tapped her chin with the edge of a pencil.

I tried not to let my interest in her show. I looked at the hardwood floors of her office, the nicked-up baseboard, the dusky shoe prints of her colleagues, the lines in the wood. I imagined myself skating between those lines, into pockets of silence.

I wondered if she knew that I was skating to find the words.

"Hayden, focus."

"Sure, sure."

Terry Quinton was back in town, she said.

He had been beaten up pretty badly, but he was okay enough to give a statement. He met the police with a lawyer, a fancy high-brow orator who loved quoting John Donne. Maybe someday he'll become mayor.

His testimony: Terry flew Bobby up to Vaughan, Ontario, dropped Bobby off at an open field up there. Two cars arrived. One took him away.

A black sedan. A yellow Buick.

"Like out of Dick Tracy color comics?"

"Huh?"

I had been in that car, the last time around, the Stabulas case. Babe Migano. And that was probably his field, the one he was building an amusement park on. Canada's Coney Island in Vaughan, Ontario. *For worms, brave Percy. Fare the well, great heart.*

I too can quote famous writers.

Stana nodded, her pencil no longer tap-tapping. "Where Lisa and Spinner are buried." She knew what I was thinking.

The secret we shared.

I wondered how the pickup with Babe Migano went down. Did they laugh, smile as they led him to one of the cars or did Bobby's shoulders fall, full of resignation and fearful of imminent death? Was Terry Bobby's friend or betrayer?

"His Judas?" Stana leaned forward, seeking clarification.

"Well I'm Jewish. I don't usually go there."

She smiled, freckles dancing in her eyes, pencil tapping, once, twice.

I'd have to see Migano, soon.

Was Migano hiding Bobby or burying him in a field some place, next to Terrien and Lisa Steinmetz?

Somehow I'm pretty sure Bobby Ehle never got to Oslo, Sweden.

Stana was thinking the same thing. "I only hope he's still alive." He may be guilty of domestic violence, but he's still a human being, she said.

Anyway, she announced that Terry was back with 590. His story was full of a bunch of nothings. He told the police he thought the early morning flight was all a lark, prep school hijinks, Bobby being Bobby, wanting to be weird, like in his playing days, when he painted the visiting locker room at the Montreal Forum blue and white, Leafs colors.

"How did he get beat up, then if it's all a bunch of goddamn hijinks?"

"Rolled by a drunk, he said."

"When did he have time to get rolled?"

Stana shrugged, the beret dangling motionlessly. It was a great look for her: arty, liberal, sexy. *Why was she working for a conservative rag like the* Telegram?

"How could Sal let Terry off the hook so—"

"I think he's having him followed, hoping he'll lead us to something bigger. He's playing Terry."

I nodded. "Of course."

Typewriters clacked in the background. Did they ever stop? And the teletype, a slower, less rapid pounding, was ticking away in the left corner. It was 11 a.m., the sun shrouded in clouds, the office a bit dim. Only half of the overhead lights were on.

Terry swore on his rosary beads that he didn't know that Bobby was fleeing a murder rap.

"Uh-huh." I looked at the lights.

Migano also knew Cassel, she said. She had looked into it. Old pals. When Babe was an up and comer in the Montreal gangs, Cassel and he had crossed paths during some drug runs between Montreal and Canada.

"Crossed paths how?"

"Cassel is the godfather for his niece. The one who married Athol."

"Swell."

I also wondered what went down between them in 1955, the five months Cassel hid out in Montreal. I told Stana about it. Narcotics rap.

Maybe Babe had Cassel holed up in Adora Borealis. I don't think Mr. Machete is still there. I told Stana about my tour of the rooms. *But the room with the pulp novels? I wonder*. Why did Cassel's men try to kill Dawn? "I guess, Dawn's not on Babe's team—" I was thinking out loud.

Stana smiled. "I guess not." She put down her pencil and traced her fingers on her desk blotter around a line drawing of a kite. "Just what do you know about her, about Dawn?"

"What do you mean?"

"Dawn. You seem smitten with her."

"I'm not."

"You like her, I can tell."

"She's twenty-years-old."

"Right."

"I care about her, that's all."

"You care to take a lie detector?"

Jesus Christ. Was Stana jealous? I'd kind of like it if she were. "Dawn was in love with Bobby—I believe that about her. Those tears in my office—"

"Bobby, huh?" Stana paced, the shoulders of her dress tenting slightly every time her pencil missed the blotter and tapped the desk's wood finish. "She's in love with Bobby. Uh-huh." If that's so true, Hayden, why did Nancy never tell me anything about that, huh? I interviewed her. Hours and hours of tapes. She opened a lower desk drawer and pulled out three reel-to-reel tapes. Several of the boxes, with the plaid Scotch brand, were dented in the corners. Rusty tape held lids in place. "Nancy said Bobby was depressed, never having got over losing her, that's why he continued to stalk and beat her. He wanted her for himself and no other woman would do. Did he have another woman? If Dawn were that woman, and his alleged girlfriend, why did he not say a word about it to you—"

"I don't know. I trust her—"

"You trust too many people."

She looked away. Typewriters clacked. I traced my fingers around the lip of a coffee cup. The ceramic edges were cool.

I topped it off. It was a little sludgy. I made a face.

"I'll make a fresh pot," Stana said.

"Tell me where the stuff is. I'll do it."

She pointed at a cork board cabinet over a rusty sink.

I poured in the Nescafe and boiled water while talking out loud. So Athol was trying to kill her on Migano's orders because she was betraying Migano? Or Migano, in league with Cassel, was doing the latter crime czar a favor. But what did Dawn have to do with Cassel? She never saw him at the clinic. She saw Terrien, or the presumptive Terrien. Maybe the hit was ordered because Dawn had stolen Cassel's drugs? Migano's drugs? No, the drugs were the exclusive property of The Northern Lights of Beauty. *I couldn't figure it. Why the attempted hit?*

"Maybe Dawn knew what was in those canisters and stole it for herself. From Bobby, from Adora. And Adora has friends. Cassel." Stana leaned forward, her eyes narrowing. She always had good instincts. "Dawn's trying to make a big score."

"Ransom? Some kind of leverage? I don't know—"

"Dawn never loved Bobby." She returned to the lower desk drawer and threw another manila envelope my way, my second in less than twenty-four hours.

"What about Denys? Who's he in league with?"

"Denys?"

"The guy in the lambskin hat?"

And how did the whole N'oublie jamais crowd fit in, if they did at all?

Stana's eyes were dancing but she wasn't following. "Open the damn envelope. In fucking credible."

"The Richard Riot. The Quiet Revolution?" I waved a hand. "Never mind."

"The envelope—"

Stana lit a Parliament.

I slid out a series of photos: Dawn, lips parted, a man's face buried in her neck, nuzzling her ear, a hand on a left breast, a fleur-de-lis over his left shoulder. Dawn and Terry Quinton, sitting inside Bassel's Restaurant eating hamburgers the size of hubcaps and drinking Molson's, his right hand atop her left wrist, laughing at some event happening outside the frame; Dawn and Terry sitting in his helicopter, awaiting takeoff—she has a clipboard on her lap; Dawn and Terry in Allen Gardens outside the Palm House, a Victorian style building shaped like a Queen's crown, squinting into the sun; Dawn on top of Terry, his bald spot resembling a small, white yarmulke, as her shoulders pull back, her breasts thrust out, and his hands play with her upper arms and a sheet bunches behind her back and nests on top of his lower legs.

"Shit—"

"Does that look like a person in love with Bobby?" The pencil hit blotter, then wood, blotter.

"It looks like I need to talk to Dawn." And Migano. And Terry.

And Bobby. If I ever hear from him. If he's still alive.

"Yeah."

The water boiled. I poured it in the pot, let it percolate.

I pulled down my porkpie and asked Stana to look into a Guillame Clausen. I spelled the name for her. "He was a chemist. Part of the Richard Riot. Wrote a manifesto with a crazy, offensive title." I couldn't repeat those words so I wrote them down for her. "Disappeared around 1963. Copenhagen, Denmark. Check with Interpol, whatever, but find this person."

Her face creased into an abstract painting.

I poured us each a cup of coffee, added one cream and two sugars to hers.

"Maybe check phone records from Adora Borealis." Stangl was no chemist. Guillame was. "Ma Bell might lead us to a contact in Montreal that'll lead us to Guillame." I sipped coffee. The slight burn felt good going down.

She figured she could get the phone records from Sal. She smiled demurely, breathing in the warmth of her cup. "I think he likes me—" She sipped.

"He's married." Two kids, a dog, an above-ground pool.

"I know. I'm just saying—"

"Well, don't say—"

She smiled slightly. Maybe she was getting my drift.

And maybe she was making me jealous. Deliberately. Maybe these were the words we were using to heal. Maybe.

"I think Guillame's in back of this whole thing, somewhere, mixing up Blue 27, planning a possible attack of some kind."

"A hunch?"

"A feeling I have in my gut, and it still feels like shards of dissolving rocks—"

She nodded. We both had good instincts.

I shuffled through the photos of Dawn. They were done by a professional, the images crisp and clear, the resolution full of deep-focus detail. This person knew how to work expertly with low levels of light.

"Blacks Detective Agency out of Hamilton," Stana said.

"Who hired Blacks?"

They came in the mail. Today. Special delivery from Denise Drouin. Nancy's sister. She had hired Blacks to spy on Bobby, find proof to nail his ass for killing her sister, she said. "Their leads led to Terry and from Terry to Dawn and Terry. And from there—"

"Denise Drouin, huh?"

"Along with the photos, Denise sent a letter long enough to read like a host of UN resolutions, listing her grievances, explaining her motivations." Stana tossed it my way.

It was written by hand. I read it, most of it, quickly. The penmanship was a bit messy, hurried. Denise was a schoolteacher, taking time off to see justice served. She truly believed that Bobby stalked and killed her sister. She was using all of her resources to "bring him down." She repeated that in the letter seven times. I counted.

"Is she legit?" I asked.

I had wondered where Nancy's family was. Usually when someone's brutally murdered family members show up, full of angry tears, demanding justice. After her death, not a voice of protest, of sorrow, nothing. Nancy's parents were deceased. Bobby never spoke of a sister, but then again Bobby rarely spoke at all when we suited up for the blue and white.

"I know, right? *Bring him down*. Like she's out of a movie, with her own catch phrase, and not a very good one at that."

"No, no. I was referring to the sister angle. Nancy had a sister?"

Nancy never mentioned her to me, not once, Stana said. All those interviews. No mention of Denise. Stana's pencil tapped out a new rhythm.

"Background—does it check out?"

Stana's lips pushed together. The Department of Motor Vehicles in Montreal confirmed a registration for one Denise Lucerne Drouin, born October 14, 1933. She also has a registered Social Identification Number and her Birth Certificate checks out. Party affiliation: Liberal. No children. No husband, Stana said.

"Wow." I sipped more coffee. "Find out what school she teaches at in Quebec. Talk to the Principal. What does he think of her?"

When I was five my school principal thought I was mildly retarded from an early bout with mumps and rubella. I was just chronically shy and didn't talk much back then, but he had sent me to a special school for a week. When I got out, my parents got me a dog.

"You owe me dinner," she said. "And none of those damn street corner hotdogs that you're so fond of."

I like fried chicken, pizza, a hamburger with onion rings.

"We're not talking lo-fi, Hayden."

She was talking like it was a date.

"George's?"

"George's." She agreed.

Maybe she too missed a little of what we once had and both lost. I can dream, can't I?

I'VE NEVER BEEN A BIG FAN OF HEIGHTS. When I was a kid, like four or so, my dad, smelling of Molson's, thought it was real funny to hang me upside down over a balcony at my uncle's place, the one who works construction. It was out in the Scarborough bluffs, near our home on Gradwell, and we were fourteen fucking stories up. My uncle and Ma were yelling at my dad to put me down, afraid to rush him, just in case such a choice might startle Pop, so they all laughed nervously, and I just prayed that my feet wouldn't slip out of my Keds. They weren't high tops.

No wonder I was so shy in kindergarten.

Like a dog was going to solve *everything*. Christ.

I never told Dr. Cohen about this episode. Maybe I should, next week.

Anyway, I had just called the good doctor about my meeting with Stana, and the thoughts kicking around inside me, and Jeanette thought, like I thought, that maybe the line between Stana and me was thinning, had become perforated, that the teasing, the small bits of flirtatious jealousies were breaking down the barrier between us. I told Dr. Cohen thanks and that I'd pay for the quick over-the-phone advice but she said, no worries, she was bored with the damn crossword she was working on.

Now, here I was, years after the father-son balcony incident, atop another fourteen or fifteen story building, legs shaking with wind, my porkpie hat threatening to lift off.

Terry Quinton, face full of booze fat, lower lip a small football, was working out some minor kinks and repairs to his 590 CKEY helicopter. He had a wrench or something like it in his left hand and was knocking and pinging about on something down in the nose. My hands were in my pockets, anchoring me in place, at the edges of the landing pad. The high winds puffed open my unbuttoned blazer, flashing glimpses of my side-holstered .38.

I liked the look. It was a good one for me.

I don't think Terry was too impressed. "I don't have to talk to you, Fuller. You're not po-lice." He came out from inside the nose and stepped down, joining me on the landing platform. The air was brisk, the clouds thin ribbons.

I pushed my hand more firmly atop my porkpie, holding it in place. "No, I'm not the po-lice, but I got the pix, that might interest the po-lice. Dig? Bedroom pics." I was no beat-generation cat, but sometimes when I get mad I slip into a voice full of ersatz jazz.

He pushed his sunglasses against the bridge of his nose. They were aviator style, and even under the tint lenses his eyes were puffy.

"You and Dawn."

The wrench quit moving.

And the wind opened my blazer even more.

He moved his feet slowly as he walked a small half-circle. The landing mat that the copter rested against was gold and the central design was the Expo '67 logo, a leaf composed of eleven triangles. At least I think it was a leaf. It looked a little like the variation on the Star of David. *Right. Star of David. Uh-huh.*

I shrugged, holding the manila envelope, with the six photos, out toward him. I told him what I knew. He wasn't only involved with Dawn but also involved in double-crossing Bobby, my client. "You dropped him in a field. That's what the log reports say and the police report. A field in Vaughan, Ontario. That's land owned by Migano, the Toronto-area gangster—"

A land he dreamed of building an amusement park on.

"I don't know no Migano—"

"Right. And I don't know who won the Stanley Cup last year. Come on." I pointed at him. "Your lips are two footballs and the sunglasses can't hide the raccoon eyes. Who laid you out and why? Bobby? Migano?" I wiped the edges of my mouth. "And don't give me no bullshit about getting rolled by a drunk."

He pushed the glasses farther back against the bridge of his nose and exhaled sharply. "You're still not po-lice."

I held up my hand. "You got me, I'm not." I wanted to erase his half-circle steps, push him up against the copter's skids, get him to talk. "I guess I better go to the po-lice."

I headed toward the exit door. Green. Thank god it wasn't white and didn't glow. And no one was offering me a glass of goddamn water on the way.

"Wait."

I smiled and loped back to the nose of the helicopter, one hand still on my porkpie. The wind was gusting. "Smart," I said. Look, the police may have believed your story about flying Bobby around on some kind of lark, Bobby being Bobby, but when they see these photos they'll think differently. You had a reason to get rid of him. "You loved his girl."

"Dawn was never Bobby's girl." His eyebrows stretched into a sharp line, a small snake. "They slept together but she was never *his* girl."

"Then why did she tell me she was?"

"I don't know."

I grimaced, my teeth hurting. "What was in the canisters? The ones Dawn delivered that didn't have in them what they were supposed to have in them, the ones Denys was a little angry about?"

"Denys?"

"Yeah. A friend of yours. Richard Riot. 1955. Lambskin hat. Threw a tear-gas bomb. He was on the other end of the so-called drugs-gone-wrong drop. He wasn't too happy."

He might also have tried to burn down a publishing house.

He was surprised I knew about the tear-gas. "I don't know anything about any canisters."

The mention of Denys made him jumpy. His hands twitched at his sides.

"Here's what I think—" I pushed back my porkpie. The wind had died down. Bobby was a courier for Adora. I figured Terry and Dawn pulled a double-cross on Bobby. Took the stuff he was pushing, substituted it with something else, and left him holding the bag, wanted by Migano and Cassel's bunch. "You set him up. And now you've got the bundle, you and Dawn. Whatever the bundle is and are waiting for a payoff."

"That's *your* story."

"A pretty good one too. It's no Maltese Falcon but I give it three out of four smiley faces."

"I loved Bobby. We were like brothers—"

"Yeah. And you led him right to his executioners—"

"I didn't. We were brothers—"

"And now those executioners are going to come for you, the lambskin hat guy. Denys. Your brother."

He said nothing.

"He's got a fleur-de-lis tattoo thing going. Just like you. But why's his crying?"

"Because the French demand justice. N'oublie jamais."

"How come Bobby never got a tattoo?"

"He didn't like needles—scared shitless by them—"

"Of course. So he takes Blue 27 in powder form, right?"

"Yeah."

I had him.

"No, no, Blue 27. What? I know nothing about—"

"It was Blue 27 in the canisters wasn't it? And that's why you stole from him. You and Dawn. A couple of extortionists."

He laughed bitterly. "There's no market for Blue 27. Blue 27 doesn't work." He sat on a workbench covered with flecks of pigeon shit. He rubbed his forehead with a dirty cuff of his coveralls. They were stained with enough oil and grease to heat a subdivision. "It just makes you tired. That's all." He shrugged. Sure, it briefly eliminates pain but it takes away all inhibition and desire. An awkward combination. You feel free to try anything but you have no energy to carry it off. He smiled, his chubby pressed lips resembling a crab's claw. "Nobody wants Blue 27."

"What do they want? Something was supposed to be in those canisters. Something important."

"I know nothing about canisters, okay?"

"What really went down with you and Dawn and Bobby?"

"Nothing." He said something about her being good in bed. The sun reflected off his glasses, filling his eyes with clouded ribbons.

"We had a threesome going. A couple of times. That was it." He smiled. It wasn't pretty. "A ménage a trois, as the French would say."

"Uh-huh." Mr. Culture.

So he really didn't love Dawn either. You don't talk about a girlfriend that way. No wonder he gave her a gold-plated necklace, goddamn four-flusher phony.

I pushed down my porkpie and smiled my lopsided lupine grin.

"So why's the mob trying to kill her? What's the real story? She's not Bobby's girlfriend, she's not yours, apparently. What's the real story?" The edges of my shoulders hurt and my eyes were stinging. Dawn made it seem like it had something to do with Bobby, something to do with the canisters.

"Dawn *thought* I was her boyfriend. So did Bobby. Maybe he knew about us and was setting her up. Ever think of that?"

"Bobby made the switch?"

"Yeah." He looked at his shoes, white sneakers, covered in mud patches of oil. "Yeah. Set her up to get got."

"So Dawn had two boyfriends. Bobby and you?"

"Yeah? Ménage a trois. That's what it means." He looked away and shrugged. "It's 1965. Grow up."

"If that's true, why did he allow you to fly him to safety—if you were in competition for the same girl?"

"It wasn't a competition."

I was confused.

"Besides he never allowed me anything. Allow? He forced me to fly him that night."

So it wasn't a lark.

"He—he—" Terry removed his aviator's glasses. Heavy pouches under his eyes made him squint slightly. The right eye was a series of fish scales. He couldn't see a damn thing out of it and never would again.

"Bobby did that?"

Terry nudged the glasses back in place. "Now, I'm a mechanic. No longer a pilot." His depth perception was all off. He picked up the wrench. "Bobby has a temper, a wicked one. He found out about me and Dawn—"

"I thought it wasn't a competition—"

"Found out about the drugs. Supertuned me. Look, he killed Nancy. No matter how you cut it, he did it."

I exhaled sharply.

Everyone was telling me Bobby did it. I'm funny about things like that. When a narrative gets overdetermined, I distrust the narrative.

"I'm sorry." I didn't know what else to say. "Bobby has the drugs?"

Terry said nothing.

I held onto my porkpie and envisioned pushing my father over the edge.

Blue 27 was created by Guillame Clausen, back in 1959, Terry said.

The chemist, the one that fled to Copenhagen, Denmark?

Terry nodded. He was the guy in the photo with the narrow shoulders and loose-fitting clothes, looking a little lost, or above the fray. He worked for MacMillan Pharmaceuticals in Montreal, seeking out a new kind of Anacin tablet to top all migraines, Terry said. He started toying around with barbiturate compounds and various antipsychotics and hallucinogens and discovered Blue 27. The military tried it out with Canada's NATO forces. "It didn't work. Sure, it cured pain, temporarily, but it also took away all initiative. Not what our fighting forces want."

Of course not.

1961. Why did Guillame leave Canada?

A car accident.

"That doesn't make people leave their homeland. Come on."

Terry rubbed at one of the hinges of his sunglasses. "Okay,

okay, okay." He shielded his eyes from the high sun and said that there was another passenger in the car. It rolled and that passenger, Guillame's lab assistant Gray Davies, wasn't wearing a seatbelt. Dead at the scene. Body mutilated beyond recognition. The car had caught fire. Anyway, Terry snapped his fingers for emphasis. Like that. Done. Here. Gone. "Anyway, Guillame didn't report the accident for several hours and the police suspected he was running from a drunk-driving rap." Guillame said he was disoriented after the crash and drifted listlessly about the streets of Montreal, clueless as to who the fuck he was. Amnesia. The foggy forgetfulness eventually cleared and Guillame returned to the scene and called the police. By then the body had been carted away and the gendarmes speculated on pressing charges. An MD testified on Guillame's behalf, saying, after interviewing him, that he believed Guillame's temporary amnesia story. The police, however, were still considering legal proceedings. In the interim, while the gendarmes decided on their next move, Guillame fled to Denmark, telling friends, in a series of postcards, that the sex there was pretty good.

"I heard he wasn't that much into sex. Boys or girls."

"That's true. But Denmark, you know?"

I didn't know.

"Anyway, Guillame's father is Dutch so the kid had dual citizenship."

"Isn't the Dutch thing like the Netherlands?"

"Oh, yeah. Right. His father was Danish."

Next he'll be telling me Guillame made a stopover in Oslo, Sweden.

"You been in contact with Dawn—"

It wasn't a question.

He couldn't look at me.

Of course she'd contact him, police custody or not she'd find a way. She loved him, no matter how much he diminished her in my eyes.

I wanted an address.

He gave it to me.

Nice fella.

Don Mills. Another one of them goddamn high rises. This one a hotel, fourteenth floor. Don Mills and Eglinton.

I handed him the envelope with the photographs. Maybe I should have hung onto them for evidence but it felt like the right thing to do. He smiled meekly.

"Tell me more about N'oublie jamais—"

A bunch of creative young people, artists trying to change the world, he said. "Denys was a playwright. Wrote four or five experimental shows performed in Laval." Terry, at one time was a painter in the Renoir mode. Lost interest. Didn't have lasting talent. Bobby was the artist who painted with his skates. Guillame was a scientist, but he was also the brains, the one who wrote up the manifesto, *White Niggers of Canada*, asking for Quebec for Quebecois.

But the title emphasized Canada, so I guess he wasn't a hard-core separatist.

Terry couldn't disagree with that. Guillame did love Canada or the idea of what Canada should be. "You ever notice," Terry pointed a crooked finger, "the street signs in Montreal? They're in French and English."

"Yeah."

"They aren't bilingual in Toronto. Melville, Saskatchewan? English only."

I nodded.

"Being bilingual in Canada means being French having to learn English—"

Bobby had said the exact words to Leila a few days ago, words that must have been memorized as part of the manifesto.

"What about Cassel? He was at the Richard Riot?"

"An interloper. Fleeing some kind of Detroit rap."

"Narcotics?"

"I think he beat up a woman. Broke her nose."

Did he make her look like a Picasso painting? Did he make Nancy look like one?

"So you still in contact with Guillame? Heard anything lately?"

Terry firmly nodded no, his face hard. No postcards, nothing, since summer, 1963. "The same year I quit being interested in hockey." He dropped his hand from the sun.

"1963?"

"The year Montreal traded away Jacques Plante. Broke my heart."

I nodded. "You wouldn't know anyone following me in a silver Chevy Corvair, would ya?" It looked a little gray in the bright sun.

"Can't say I do, 'cause I don't."

Someone was following me. I felt it all afternoon. "Jacques Plante, huh?"

"Greatest goalie ever," Terry said. "The Gumper and Charlie Hodge, forget about it. They're no Jacques Plante."

I guess that would be Terry's answer to the Howe or Richard debate. Jacques Plante, the first goalie to roam from his nets, to wear a mask permanently, to bark orders to his defensemen. The Innovator, the press labeled him.

"This Denys guy, king of the lambskin hat. He got a last name?"

"Denys? Sure he does." He smiled. It filled his face with malice. "But you ain't no po-lice."

7

 don't think Top Cop Sal Lambertino was too pleased to see me.

"What the fuck are you doing here?"

Maybe I should have brought a dozen donuts.

Sal filled the door frame, hands on hips. When Sal was on duty he was a lot bigger than when he was off duty. It was a presence thing.

His mouth worked a piece of gum the size of two jawbreakers.

"Hiya, handsome." I pointed at his puffy lips. "You look like you're hoarding acorns for the winter—"

He shook his head, unimpressed with the wit and wisdom of one Hayden Fuller.

I told him quickly what I heard from Terry about Dawn and Bobby, a threesome, and how Dawn may have lied to us and how I had to talk to her, like right fucking now.

Sweat dotted the top of his forehead, and he quickly looked beyond me into the hallway. He tapped my shoulder and I went in.

Dawn sat on the edge of a couch, hands in her lap, flipped up. She wore dark dress pants and a blue and white middy blouse with crisp shoulders. She looked as if she were about to give a presentation to IBM or christen a ship. When she saw the anger in my face, she spun the bracelet on her right wrist. It became a jet turbine, twisting with enough torque to crash through Mach one. The table was covered with magazines, *Macleans*, *Life*, a small vase crowded with blue dahlias, a *TV Guide*, and a cassette recorder, red with white trim. I noticed because I was so mad I could no longer look directly at her.

The tape recorder wasn't new. A chunk of plastic was missing from a corner and I saw a contact and an edge to one of the batteries.

The tape recorder reminded me of Sal's Pontiac Catalina with the missing hubcap. With their budget these cops could never eat at Bassels.

"It wasn't Bobby you were in love with but Terry. You work for Terry. You stole from Bobby—for Terry—"

Dawn shifted on the couch, her hands twitching slightly, her clavicles pressing against her middy blouse. The sky in the window behind her was high, bright, cloudless.

"I love them both," she said.

"How did you get this address?" Lambertino side-holstered his weapon. He must've drawn it when I knocked on the door. I hadn't noticed.

"Quinton."

The jawbreaker slid to the other side of Sal's face. He had figured to have Dawn all sewn-up, protected. Twelve or fifteen people came in and out of this room. All police. Part of the detail. All with credentials. Dawn never left the room. She was never alone, Sal said. The phone was tapped. Jesus Christ.

"Did somebody come clean the room?"

Sal nodded, so did the young woman, thirtyish, sitting across from Dawn. She wore a red-checkered shirt and blue jeans, her hair pulled back severely. Eyebrows lightly penciled and lipstick was drawn from Dawn's fashion élan: 1950s–era bobbysoxer in candy-apple red. None of the lipstick left chipped marks on her teeth.

And her lips were full, like the rooftop of a '49 Mercury.

Officer Sarah Linney was made-up as Dawn, a character in a play. Only I hoped this wasn't a tragedy, because she'd be a hit man's first target.

I gently saluted her with two fingers.

She smiled back, her eyes seizing hold of me, warm, deep dark green, like right after it rains and the sun has yet to return from behind clouds. *Petrichor, I think. Oh, what do I know. Stana's the Scrabble player.*

Stana. Even now she was crowding my heart.

"Dawn must have slipped the cleaning lady a note, with a phone number on it, and a ten-spot attached, telling Terry where she is, and Quinton gave up her location. That's the only way it figures," I said, staining to focus.

Sal glared at Dawn. "It figures."

"Twenty," she mumbled. "I gave her a twenty."

"And if Quinton gave up Dawn's whereabouts to me he'll certainly give it up to someone else. Someone with more muscle." I punched a fist into an open hand crushing my fingers like cigarettes in an ashtray. "You better move her to another room. Now."

Sal huffed, the fist of gum now on his right side. He dialed the front desk. It was a fast conversation. He snapped the phone back in place. "Give them ten minutes," he said.

I exhaled sharply and told Dawn the truth, as far as Terry tells it. It wasn't Bobby you were in love with but Terry. I got the goddamn surveillance photos from Blacks, a detective agency out of Hamilton who were working for Denise, Nancy's sister.

"I told you. I loved them both."

Right. This is 1965. The so-called permissive society. Go-go dancers and head shops on Yonge Street. Massage parlors. I get it.

The bracelet was now moving counterclockwise.

"Nancy had a sister?"

"She did."

I wondered if the bracelet left a dirty, dingy stain on her wrist? Another *gift* from Terry?

A French song buoyed softly across the room from a portable Hi-Fi, the music more on the high end, a little tinny, but I liked the song's folksy strum, and the plaintive lyrics, something about a girlfriend who doesn't have to be a starlet or wear sunglasses and the speaker loves her and she works at the factory. Something like that. "Terry's song. Yours and Terry's?"

She nodded. "Jean Ferrat. From France. Terry was big on him."

"Uh-huh."

Standing in front of the picture window, backlit with blue denim sky, was a guy in brown: pants, jacket, fedora, with a white shirt, black tie. He complained about having to hear that damn fucking song over and over again. Dawn must've had the stereo's arm set on repeat and this fella was getting queasy from the three-four beat. He was Sgt. James Moffat, hands deep in his pockets, reaching, I guessed, for some Rolaids.

"Oh leave her alone," Sarah said. "It relaxes her. Let her relax."

"Right, right." He waved Sarah away with a long-fingered hand. He and Sarah were partners and both seemed a little tired of one another.

"It has been over forty plays," Sal said, flat-lining the words. "Forty."

"Are you going to start in on the kid too?"

"No, Sarah. I'm just saying—"

"Twenty-seven." Sarah's eyes had a slight crease to them. "Twenty-seven. Soon to be twenty-eight."

The arm circled left, back right, and then hit the vinyl groove with a carbonated hiss and pop.

I pushed back my porkpie. "Quit spinning the bracelet." It was hurting my eyes, my head, and I was afraid I was going to slip into a seizure or something. I still felt a little dizzy from my mix-up with Lazy Legs. "Why'd you lie to me?"

"I didn't. I said I loved Bobby. I do. But I love Terry more."

"You work for Terry? You stole for Terry, from Bobby."

Lambertino leaned next to my left shoulder, his chunk of gum working its way back over to the other side of his face. It took a lot of effort to get it there.

"We deserve some honest answers. I risked my life for you." I pointed at the officer across from her. "This woman here is risking her life for you—"

"And I believed you too, believed in you." Sal's jawbreaker was trapped under his upper lip, big as a tortoise shell.

The tall angular Moffat, pushed down a crinkle or two on his shirt and moved from the window. He pushed the record button on the cassette player, and gave me the go signal.

"That's why she's wearing your clothes." Sal pointed at Sarah. "She believed in you too."

Dawn looked down, hands twitching like flippers on a pinball machine.

I seized her face and made her look at Sarah, at me, at Sal. "These people are responsible for you, you're responsible to them." It wasn't Bobby who made the switch, but you, I said. You and Terry wanted to make a big score, but Bobby found out, didn't he?

She nodded again, the light from the window cutting a wide bar across her forehead. She squinted slightly.

Thin ribbons of white were returning to the sky. A stuttering thrush of a helicopter whirred faintly beyond the ribbons. North York General was nearby. Probably a patient being rushed to emergency. There was a pile-up on the Gardiner Expressway. I had heard about it on the radio, on the way over. At least one dead at the scene.

And then there was the silver Corvair, gray in the sun.

"You know anyone in a Corvair, Sal?" I had been followed twice today, a 1964 Corvair. The driver was pretty cagey, keeping three or four cars back, pulling ahead for a while, and then slipping behind. All the way up the Don Valley Parkway to the Eglinton exit the Corvair moved about like that. The driver had dark hair, sunglasses.

Sal said no idea.

It didn't have a license to go on, but vague dealer plates. I gave him the number. He said he'd check with DMV.

Sal had, however, followed up on Bobby's checkbook. And there were many checks, for big-time dollar amounts, written out to Adora Borealis, big enough amounts to raise some questions about fair-trade practices and have a follow-up interview with Drs. Airedale and Williams.

"Great." I rubbed the edges of my mouth. "You wearing a vest?" I asked officer Linney.

"Yes."

I nodded.

She had been on the force ten years.

I introduced myself.

"I know who you are, Mr. Fuller." A smile spread through her dark green eyes.

I smiled back.

"Game two, 1963 against Detroit you scored the winning goal. Second period, high under the bar."

"Yeah." I scratched the back of a hand against my lips. That was my favorite shot to make, under the bar, tight. "You like this kind of detail?"

"I do my job."

She was a professional.

Dawn said she didn't steal anything from Bobby. She stole from Nancy. Terry knew Bobby and thus had an in at the clinic. And Terry knew Nancy from their Montreal salad days. She was a regular at bistro hangouts in the 1950s when the two attended McGill. Nancy was also at the Richard Riot, throwing eggs, and Terry had slept with her before he met Dawn and knew Nancy was planning on lifting the stuff for "N'oublie jamais," an outfit in Montreal who believed in a free Quebec. She was the one on the train, not Dawn, the one who had to deal with the anger over the double cross.

Why did Dawn tell me she was the one who made the drop? To get my sympathy? Why?

"Did they kill her?"

"Maybe." Dawn shrugged. "They were awfully mad." Terry had substituted sugar and baking powder for what Nancy was supposed to deliver and Bobby found out and beat the shit out of Terry, knocking out one of his eyes with his Stanley Cup ring. The one he wears on his left hand. And then he took the goods with him.

He didn't have the ring on his left hand when he visited with me in my bungalow three days ago. I wonder if that was the one he gave Leila.

And no wonder Terry struggled to keep the over-sized dragonfly above the horizon line that first night at my place, he was flying with one eye.

"Bobby took the goods. To sell on the open market?"

Dawn didn't know.

"Did he do it to protect Nancy, to protect her from committing a treasonous act?"

She didn't know about that either.

"So nobody was ever trying to kill you—"

"No." She fought back an urge to cry, gasping without opening her mouth. The threat of death, that part of the story was true. She did see Athol stalking her, after the bad drop.

"Athol wanted you dead?"

"Yes."

So Bobby was in league with Migano?

Athol also had a connection with Cassel. The Detroit area mobster and master of the machete was the godfather to Athol's wife or something or other. I'd have to re-check my notes.

"When Terry made the switch, who was he going to leverage

the drugs with? Was it Migano? Or Cassel?"

All she knew was a pair of heists took place: Terry and Dawn from Nancy; Bobby from Terry and Dawn.

All for blue 27? It was a goddamn drug that didn't even work. At least not that well. "I don't buy it, Dawn." My face slipped out of my lopsided lupine grin. "What was supposed to be in the canisters that Nancy was delivering to N'oublie jamais?"

She looked at the floor. A small patch of carpet was covered with bits of candy wrappers that resembled giant chunks of popcorn.

She had been eating assorted truffles.

"Who are these Never Forget people?" Sal tossed his chunk of gum into a nearby trash bin. It thudded, a heavy meteorite.

"I know nothing about N'oublie jamais," Dawn said.

Nancy knew something, some vague credit the Airedale clinic was taking for a half-burned out publishing house, I muttered. "Not sure who they are," I said. They wrote a manifesto, one Guillame Classen wrote it. Find him. He's supposed to be in Denmark. "I think he's here. In Canada. Most likely Montreal. He helped organize the Richard Riot."

I filled Sal in on the photograph with the Campbell placard and how three of the five players (Bobby, Denys, Terry) from the then Richard Riot were all present and accounted for in this caper. Two from the infamous photograph: Guillame, the little guy with the large nose and iron filings for hair, and Cassel, a modern-day Houdini, were somewhat less accounted for. Was Cassel ever at Airedale's? Nancy said she saw him there and then Nancy got got.

Dawn wiped her hands on the sides of her hips, and pushed up from the couch, moving to the Hi-Fi. Apparently, she was tired of the song. I hoped that maybe it suggested that she was tired of Terry too. The way Terry talked about Dawn and Bobby and him, the sideways nasty smile, the self-satisfied leer, the disparaging underbelly to all he said, made him an unrepentant toad. He and his threesomes.

"I'll get it," Officer Linney offered. "What do you want to hear?"

"Sinatra. Ballads. Anything sad." Dawn sank into the cushy center pillow of the couch. The lines in her blouse crisp, freshly pressed.

"I haven't forgotten my original question. What was in the canisters, Dawn?"

"I don't know."

"I don't believe you—"

She couldn't look at me. Detective Moffat rubbed at his stubble, filing it down with the edge of a heavy hand, and then a distant whir-whir cluttered the room, like my rattling fan with the loose ball bearing, hammering a thousand timpani's together, and then a short burst, followed by a longer burst and triangles of glass splintering the room, and a dotted checkered shirt, falling, and I pushed Dawn from the couch, banging the side of my face on the coffee table, and the room became louder, whirring, spinning with ten thousand timpani's. A hundred thousand. A million.

I looked up.

Officer Linney, eyes filmy, her body torn, lay on her side, face to face with me, and Sal crouched low, hands gripping his gun, firing out the window. The helicopter dipped and then rose, and hovered left and away.

Sal kept firing through broken glass.

He reloaded.

Wind rustled the room.

Sal didn't stop until his gun was empty.

WE WERE IN A DIFFERENT ROOM. This one had less windows and smelled of cigarettes and cleanser. It was blue, from the curtains to the carpet. Even the cedar trim that covered half the walls was blue in the dim light.

Minutes ago they had taken Sarah Linney out in a body bag. The bullet-proof vest wasn't enough.

"I wish I could've thrown you out that broken window, bitch." Moffat raised a tired arm and then dropped it, his voice sinking with the gesture. "That was my partner, you got killed." Tears filled his voice. He pinched at his eyes. "My partner. Do you hear me? My partner."

Nobody said a thing.

Terry Quinton was also dead. Sal had just got the call from HQ that Quinton was found on top of CKEY's office building, his throat slit wide, and "N'oublie jamais" scrawled with his blood all over the Expo '67 logo. The helicopter was gone. Who flew it? And who fired the rounds of machine gun bursts? Two different people.

And neither of the two was Terry Quinton. The ME said that the decedent's body temperature indicated he had been dead too long to have been doing much of anything during the timeframe of the attack on Linney, who was supposed to be Dawn.

My money was on the guy with the lambskin hat and crying fleur-de-lis tattoo. Denys with no last name.

Dawn was spread across the bed, on top of the covers, her legs on the floor, her arms folded on her chest. Tears crowded her eyes.

One of the medics wanted to give her a sedative but Sal waved him and his damn suggestion away. He wanted answers. Now.

Moffat was mumbling on about Sarah, her husband, two kids. He said something about ten years. His left hand trembled as he wiped at the filed-down stubble and hardened blood on his chin. I think one of his fingers was broken. It dangled at an acute angle.

Dawn stared at the lines in the ceiling, locking on the hexagonal shaped light fixture, and the broken off pieces of flies and bugs netting the fixture's center with shallow ashes. "I didn't want this to happen to her." Her voice was nearly an inaudible whisper. "She was a good person."

"She was," I said.

"Goddamn window. I should have pushed you out of it." Moffat was full of sulky languor. "I still might."

"That'll be enough," I said. "Enough. Who left the goddamn drapes wide open?"

Nobody said a thing.

"Fucking bitch." Moffat again, leaning, lifting a bent, tired arm that resembled a broken curtain.

"Did you hear me?"

He took a step or two back, his eyes lean, unmoving, his hands hanging at his sides still trembling. His chin was full of pepperoni blood.

You should get that finger looked at, I said.

He muttered an f-bomb.

I sat next to Dawn on the bed, touching her face, pushing wet hair from her eyes. "I'm sorry about, Terry. I really am."

Tears slipped away.

I still cared about that girl I gave twenty dollars too, the girl whose mother had disavowed any connection to following her involvement with dangerous men and sex parties, the girl who liked to listen to Jean Ferrat, the girl who, like the singer praises, doesn't need sunglasses or a movie star's face to be beautiful.

"He doesn't quite say that." She laughed. Her wet matted hair resembled discarded pick up sticks. I wanted to kiss her, tell her that she was loved.

"I need your help, Dawn. Please."

Sgt. Moffat, his hat twirling in his right hand, reluctantly moved toward the coffee table and punched on the tape recorder. The back of his hand was raw from where he scraped it on some broken glass.

"That finger needs to be set," I said.

He shrugged. "It can wait."

"Dawn what really went wrong with the drop?" I wanted her

theory. I didn't care if it was totally right, what do you really think happened, no bullshit. I smiled a watered-down version of my lopsided grin and removed another tendril of hair from her face.

She smiled awkwardly, teeth touching.

I kissed her nose.

Nancy did do the drop. That's for sure, Dawn said. That's what happened. Dawn wanted nothing to do with it all. At first. But Terry kept asking her. It was like he needed her to do this, to prove her love for him. He kept pushing that idea, how much do you love me, really, and so she did it, switching out the drugs with sugar and baking powder. The original drugs were in small red packets that looked like those condom packages you'd pick up at a lonely out of the way gas station.

"Red? Red packages."

"Yes."

"Not Blue 27."

"No."

"Something else?"

"Probably."

"How many of these packages were in each canister?" Sal huffed, his face unreadable, eyes heavy.

"Two, three hundred."

Sal let out a low, sharp whistle.

Adora Borealis was behind the manufacture and pushing of the drugs. They cooked them up in a lab at the clinic, but not in the lab I had seen, that, with its pristine blue cabinets and scrubbed white tiled floors, was a dummy for the public. "There's another lab," she said.

"Where?"

Next to the hydrotherapy room. Between the second and main floor. "You know with the mirrored glass?"

"Yeah?"

"There's a lab under that." A section of the building had a

dropped floor or a half floor like the stacks in university libraries. That part of the building wasn't two stories but two and a half.

"A hidden floor?"

Yes, she said. And you had to keep your head low. The girls were okay, but the fellas were always having to duck, to keep from bumping up against the ceiling.

"Girls? How many working in the lab?"

Seven or so, Dawn said, and they were all naked, covered with spots of powder, little constellations, as they mixed up and cut the drugs and put them in the red packages. It was Airdale's idea to have all the girls naked. It prevented individual pilfering. "That's what he called it. Individual pilfering. A total ass—"

What can you expect from a hipster who dresses for Wimbledon?

"But I suspect he just liked looking at our titties." She smiled weakly. She said our. I didn't miss that.

Dawn squinted at the ceiling, as if counting each ash in the light fixture.

"I thought you worked at Eaton's, the toy department?"

"That's what I tell people."

Dawn, lab worker. For a couple of months, anyway, while working on her GED. It was good money, and Terry, one of Airedale's couriers, flying junk up to northern Ontario, was always there, kibitzing with her, saying he liked her eyes, while looking at the spots of powder on her tits and navel, and they had a good laugh about that, and then he asked her out, and that's when she found out all about Nancy, and Terry's scheme to double-cross her. Bobby was at the lab a lot, too, picking up his fixes of Blue 27, and patting Dawn on the fanny, saying how good it was seeing her naked again, and this time without a fez on her head. It was funny what he could remember because he had forgotten so much, but the fez, that he remembered. At first it was just staring and teasing, but Bobby eventually opened up about being Bobby. "I guess I have one of those faces that people want to share things with." She shrugged. He shared about his headaches, his pain, his problems with his ex, his inability to sustain an erection, and how Blue 27 was a temporary fix, relieving pain but taking away his ambition. "One day, he kissed me. And then he did it again. And then Terry saw and suggested he join us. In bed."

"Uh-huh."

It didn't go well. The threesome.

"Bobby pushed up against me, my hip, touched me, kissed, me, but he couldn't get hard, and he watched Terry and I finish up, and then Bobby cried. For twenty minutes." Terry had tried to console him, but the bawling Bobby punched Terry in the solar plexus, winding him, leaving the room. Two days later Terry wanted to get back at Bobby and Nancy and make a big score. She wiped the tears at the corner of her eyes. "But there was something we never counted on."

"What's that?"

"The merchandise had changed." They were no longer pushing Blue 27. The red packages weren't like the blues at all. The reds were crammed with something new, much more dangerous. Her eyes zeroed in on the light fixture. "We didn't know what it was—"

"A new drug?"

"Dallas Stangl discovered it—"

"I doubt it," I said. "That guy couldn't find his car in a small parking lot. Guillame was a chemist. He's back here. He's working on this shit."

Dawn knew no Guillame.

Sal wanted to know more about the new drug.

It wasn't a pain reliever, Dawn said. The opposite actually. It was made to inflict pain, but that's all she knew.

"Was Bobby in on this new drug? Was he on it?" I wondered if he used it to kill Nancy.

"I don't know."

I rubbed Dawn's left shoulder. It was tight, full of sand. I rubbed harder. "Could he be?"

"Maybe."

Dawn had no idea.

Bobby may have been the test case. They got him to take the drug. He killed his wife and then they, whoever they all are, knew it worked wonders.

Maybe whoever killed Terry and Sarah was also on this junk. Could it be Bobby?

"Is Airedale the top man? Is he the one in charge of this racket?" Sal's jaw jutted forward and his eyes were locked tight. "Or is it Williams?"

Dawn only saw Airedale, he was the one always there in the lab, getting a good look at the naked girls, copping a feel now and then for laughs, always touching.

"Is Williams involved in trafficking?"

"Yes." Well, she then said, she wasn't 100% sure. Eight-five per cent. Dawn rolled sideways and then on her back, arms straight at her side as if she were standing at attention while lying in bed.

"You never saw her in the lab?"

She didn't. But how could she not know, Dawn wondered. She shared the office with Baggy Ass.

And Gillian Williams wasn't carrying his tennis rackets. She was a smart woman.

And then I thought about Cassel and the day I got to check the rooms there, the room with the pulp paperbacks and Pepto-Bismol. Was Cassel whisked away, hiding out in the half-floor of the lab? Nancy had seen Cassel there. My feeling was that he was still there. Why hadn't he left? That was the bigger question.

"So, if Bobby took the drugs from you and Terry, what did Bobby do with them and where are they now?" Sal placed a hand on top of the television.

"A bigger question," I offered, "How much more of this new

drug are they going to produce?"

"We'll get that stopped," Sal promised. He got on the phone and called the judge in our last case, the one who's a Habs fan.

"Migano," I said. "Bobby took the stuff to Migano."

"We're green lit." Sal smacked the phone back in place. "We'll have the warrant soon." He paced and let out a slow breath that was a skinny skip of air. He picked up the phone. It was time to call the Linney family.

Dawn returned to counting ashes.

8

It didn't surprise me at all that we didn't find a damn thing at Adora Borealis. There had to be a leak somewhere, someone who was always tipping off Airedale and Williams, making us a step late, slow. I'm not a paranoid person, but this case had me convinced that the bad guys had moles, television monitors, and wiretaps everywhere. Maybe I ought to check back in with Dr. Cohen.

Anyway, we had our warrant, yellow police tape, X's, everywhere, and all the rooms, except for the woman who nods, were empty. The hardboiled paperbacks were still in room seven, but it appeared unoccupied and Cassel was a no-show. What struck me odd about room seven this time were the switch plates, four of them, low on each wall. They weren't outlets, but more like a path for sending a signal, like a closed circuit TV signal.

The lab? It was low-ceilinged, but not a drop of powder blue or any drug-related evidence: balancing scales, beakers, nothing. Instead, the cramped room, which felt like a crumpling cave, was full of uneven shelves, old *How and Why Wonder Books*, turpentine and paint cans, white of course. During the course of our explorations, Dr. Cliff Airedale repeatedly raised his fists and shouted how we were infringing upon his civil liberties. He wore a different colored blazer but it had the same crown on the left breast pocket.

Sal kept banging his head on the low ceiling and letting out

57 varieties of expletives.

Cliff drank water, a lot of water. Stopping at every alcove. The water was so clear as to not be water. There were no blemishes, no bubbles, nothing. It was mercury in a thermometer without the red tinting.

I still wanted to hand him a damn tennis racket.

Dr. Gillian Williams, her face impassive, lips forever parched it seemed, also drank a lot of water, while floating two steps behind Police Chief Sal Lambertino, who was rubbing his noggin. She tilted her head left while showcasing the hydrotherapy room and its seven tubs and their nozzles and foam guns. She even let us in on the room behind the mirrors. It featured a long, narrow conference table, punctuated by seven or eight phones, and ashtrays for everyone. A blackboard ran along the opposite wall and was full of ideas for marketing their new projected products, including "Jouissance," a female lubricant. I guess Stangl really was working on that.

Jouissance. I kid you not.

Off to the left of the command office's conference table and fleet of phones was a pale green door, not white, but this door had an equally big handle like you'd find on a submarine hatch, that led to the half floor and rags and paint and paper towels and cleaning supplies. A waste of space, a total phony, that half floor room. Something much more important had to have been going on there. What was tossed in appeared hurried and it showed. *The How and Why Wonder Books* was the tip-off. Those were for grade school kids. And the cans of paint: ten years old.

They wanted to make it look like an unused junk room, an elaborate closet, but I wasn't buying. Maybe they should have thrown in a beat up trap set and broken-stringed guitar for the convincer.

Gillian smiled a lot, sipping water during our "tour," leaving one-third empty glasses everywhere, nodding quickly, answering questions. And she moved like she had taken ballet lessons:

shoulders back, head up, feet balanced. Barbara Stanwyck in *Double Indemnity.*

Once or twice she made a point of nudging next to me. There was a clear agenda behind how her body touched mine. The first time she apologized; the second time she smiled; the third time, breasts against my chest and arm, her lips parted.

What about the checks Bobby had written for such astronomical amounts? Sal cited some of the totals and Gillian looked at Airedale who was still citing a list of breached civil liberties and she said, I guess it's okay to tell you, Cliff won't mind, but Bobby was a regular who believed in our product and was buying into the business. Those checks signified down payments to join their team. Bobby was going to be one of their partners. She could send the police the paperwork in a few days if they wish. Sal wished.

"This new drug, in red packages? Was that part of the business Bobby was buying a piece of?" Sometimes Sal lacks all nuance.

"I don't know what you mean."

Sal twirled his hat in his hands, lips pressed tight. "I think you do—"

Airedale raised his fist again, prattling on about police persecution.

"Lenny Cassel, the gangster. Nancy saw him here."

"Well, Nancy's dead. God rest her soul. Perhaps she suffered from some form of hysteria. Lord knows she had hang-ups." She smiled in the direction of Airedale, then at me, her teeth perfect.

I wondered if she knew about my hang-ups?

Everything about Gillian was too, too perfect, from her petite-balanced figure to her delicate nose and wide set, soulful eyes. The only thing off, the hair. The platinum glow looked a little too green in Adora Borealis's track lighting, like she'd been swimming too long in chlorine.

But it was the smile, slight, full of a whimsical distance, a

Mona Lisa Smile. Sexy, arty, and unintentionally intimidating.

It kind of got to me and kept me away simultaneously. Her whole presentation to the world did that, an inviting mix of beautiful glam with a tinge of the macabre and offbeat.

"Terry, one of your associates, we understand, ran drugs—"

"If you got that information from Dawn, who can trust her?" Airedale smiled.

His face wasn't full of whimsical distance. Instead, there was a bit of a sneer to his smile.

"We know she posed nude for art photos," he said, imagining the sessions taking place before him, now.

That was my last case. The one involving Maple Leaf Gardens. And Dawn was hypnotized when she did the posing.

She wasn't responsible for posing nude, asshole.

Stana posed nude for art photos too. Private ones. A free choice of love. Just for me. 1962–63.

"That girl, Dawn, even had a fez on her head. No clothes, just the fez. I wouldn't trust any testimony from such a character. Wait til my lawyers—"

How did he know about the fez?

Did Bobby tell him?

Did Airedale run with the Coughlins crowd, a secret gentlemen's club that was part of my last case: gambling, drinking, and underage sex at the Cashbox on Carlton Street.

"You better get some lawyers, pal," I said. "What about Denys? Lambskin hat?"

"Who? I thought the hipsters went out with the Beats in the '50s." He laughed. It was a little tinny.

"Get those lawyers ready, asshole. We're going to keep an eye on this place," Sal promised, pointing his hat as if it were a stiff Billy club. I guess there was still a little blue in all that Sloan Wilson gray. "Who comes in, who goes out."

"That's harassment," Airedale shouted.

"That's police work," Sal said.

I'm not quite sure that came out right. Anyway.

"Let's go," Sal said.

His team followed him out the main doors of the lobby. A couple of fingerprint men remained, dusting. I didn't expect they'd find much of anything.

On my way out, Gillian's shoulder nudged up against mine for the fourth time, and she put a little more breast into it. She whispered, "Dinner tonight?"

I paused, pulled down my porkpie. I was supposed to go to George's with Stana.

She gave me her slight, Mona Lisa smile, whimsical, playful.

"Cassel *was* here," she said. "But that's off the record." She drank from a fresh glass of water. "I need to talk."

"So, he's not here, now?"

"No. *Cassel* isn't."

I was wondering if she was wanting to broker some kind of deal. "Tonight then—"

"Where?"

She smelled great. Northern pine trees. "George's?"

I felt like a heel for suggesting such a thing.

"George's," she said, her nipples pushing through the bra she wore, pressing against the fabric of her blouse.

"George's," I repeated, my affirmation full of wandering steps.

THE CEILING WAS HIGH, VAULTED. The fireplace, a stone circle, topped with books, briefcases, and newspapers. Babe Migano's upscale home in Etobicoke resembled a ski lodge and I wondered where I should park my boots and poles.

"Can't you get some new material?" groaned Athol Leighton, the bowler plunked tightly on his head.

I forgot I made that joke last time I was here.

"Jesus Christ." He shook his head, his left hand inside his sport coat. He grimaced. Athol reminded me of Napoleon with indigestion.

"Bad escargots?" This was a "French" case so I was being relevant, making with the French-flavored zingers.

He shook his head and belched.

"Linguine, definitely linguine, heavy on the alfredo. Can I recommend the salad next time?"

"Shut the fuck up. Wait here."

He lumbered to the room at the end of a long hall, his shoulders pushing him forward, a hand still inside his sport coat.

A huge cedar door, the size of two, opened, and Babe Migano with a raised eyebrow nod, crossed the room, his face freshly shaved, a red rose in the lapel of his pinstripe suit. "Hayden Fuller, the boy with the chutzpah. Mazeltov, my Jewish friend."

He was a big man, 250 pounds or so, and moved like a cheetah.

"Thanks for agreeing to see me, Babe."

"Nonsense." He smiled, took me by the arm and led me to his office, a low-lit room, full of rare first editions and a faint haze of blue cigar smoke. A glass taboret stacked with fine bourbon and three shot glasses was by the side of his oak-top desk. A series of photographs of people having fun at Coney Island, circa 1920s, was on the wall behind him. Cheap Amusements. I pointed at the photographs. I wish I too were falling from the sky on thin wires like those of the parachute ride.

"I stare at them all day long," Babe said, acknowledging my stare. Sometimes he wished he could be a kid again and then he wouldn't have to deal with all the messes that come with being a restaurateur.

How go the plans for the amusement park, I asked.

He was building one near Barrie. It was kind of a secret but Stana and I knew all about it from our last case together, and he had just finished buying up land, taking ownership of Bullard and Smith's holdings. With their upcoming trial for gambling, bootlegging, and human trafficking at the Gardens, they felt it best to divest of their other "business" interests.

It's still a mess, but moving forward, he said with a big, lollygagging wave of a hand.

"What about other messes?"

He stared into his rose. Spritzed it with water. "Such as?"

I sat across from him. My chair was kind of big and made me look small. His chair was a little smaller and made the big man look even bigger. On several fingers were rings.

"Drugs that come in red packages?"

He had heard of them. He looked at his fingers. "Three missing canisters—"

I was taken aback by his directness. "You don't have them?"

Of course. People talk. He didn't know where they were, but he knew of them. And if he did know where, he wouldn't sell them on the open market, ever, that's for sure. The jag-offs pushing this stuff weren't patriots. This was a new Canada and he was in on the party. The libre Quebec crowd could kiss his Dago ass. They were messing with his livelihood.

He waved Athol away.

A hand, inside his blazer, Athol belched quietly on his way out.

"Salad, buddy, keep pushing the salad."

"Shut up, Fuller."

"How do you feel about Expo?" Babe leaned forward and poured himself a glass of Blanton's bourbon. He poured me a seltzer and dipped in a wedge of lemon.

I didn't think about it one way or the other. "It's okay." In 1967, Canada would be 100 years young, and the city of Montreal was hosting the World's Fair. The Expo exhibit was labeled "Man and his World" and Canada had been awarded the bid in 1962 after the Soviets backed out. In 1967, the Soviets would be celebrating fifty glorious years of communism.

Irony intended.

"Some people don't like it. Some of Airedale's crowd," Babe said.

"What do you mean?"

"Nancy hinted to Bobby and Bobby acted—quickly and with extreme prejudice."

"She tell him about vague hints and the publishing house fire?"

"That and other things. The detractors of Expo hated the whole show. They feel the city of Montreal didn't have the real-estate to host such an event. Damn, they needed 64 city blocks. So what does Mayor Drapeau do? He built the habitat right on the St. Lawrence River. Brilliant."

It was. Drapeau and his team created an amusement-park island. It figures Babe would love that. So far 25 million tons of silt had been dumped into the St. Lawrence to build the land mass. Twenty-five million. Some think they'll need fifteen million more to touch-up the project.

"But some parts of French Canada, Hayden, aren't too big on celebrating what feels like another example of English colonialism."

The Conquest of Quebec, 1760.

He leaned back in his chair, smiling. "They think the money can be spent on better things: education, infrastructure, making Canada more French."

"Uh-huh."

"So they got themselves a weapon. Red 45."

"Red 45?"

"The drugs in the canisters. That's the street name." Bobby had told him all this.

"You've seen Bobby?"

"Of course."

"And he's still alive?"

"Please. Don't make me sensitive." He knocked back a finger of bourbon. Poured another glass. It was a dark amber gold, burned honey. "Of course he's still alive." He smiled. "I'm a businessman." Another smile. "Most of the time."

"What kind of weapon and who are they?"

Kids from the old neighborhood, disgruntled. They weren't able to figure out the Canadian dream. He knocked back his second shot. He knew them all, operated a candy shop on St. Catherine's Street years ago and some of these kids ran small errands for him, collecting for the numbers racket. Bobby was just ten then. Harmless, cared about the community, shoveled sidewalks for his neighbors, made some extra money to put food on his mother's table. Bobby didn't have a father. Terry. He was a little shit even then. Never shoveled sidewalks and didn't always return all the cash he received, a regular goniff. "You like the Yid word, Fuller? I'm speaking your language, paisan. Anyway, Terry would short me, nickels, dimes and I'd have to smack him around a little. Capiche?"

I nodded. "Bobby brought you the—"

"No. He didn't bring me the canisters. He hid them somewhere—"

"So you're holding him prisoner to find out where this junk is?"

"Would I do that?" He pulled out a small plastic container from his pocket and spritzed the rose once again in his lapel. "You're making me sensitive again."

Right, you're a businessman.

"I can hear you. You're thinking out loud, Fuller."

"Sorry."

I do that. With all the concussions I suffered as a hockey player I often find my censor's checked out, playing golf somewhere.

Bobby's a patriot, Babe said. He cared about the kid. He was giving him refuge until this whole thing blows over and the truth comes out.

"What if the truth comes out not in his favor?"

"Then I'll send him somewhere."

"Sweden?"

"Somewhere." Look, Babe said, Bobby may have run with

those Quiet Revolution folks, but he was a federalist, a union guy. “Of course this is all off the record, shamus. You understand?”

I sipped my seltzer. “What do these people want? How are drugs going to hurt Expo ’67?”

“Want? I’m not even sure they know. Really. They think they’re bringing France to Canada. The people of France don’t really even like us. They think we’re too undignified for them, lacking in clear, plain-speaking argot. We’re the bastards of their republic.”

“I thought de Gaulle’s behind the Quebecois.”

“Anything for a headline. de Gaulle. Please.” Look at the mess he made with Algiers.

I forgot that Babe, by association, felt he was part French. He had lived in Montreal for years.

Those canisters contained anywhere from 600-900 packets of Red 45, I figured. “If you have them, you should turn it over to the authorities.”

“I don’t.” He reiterated how Bobby had hid them someplace. Babe opened the drawer to his desk, and jacketed a round into the chamber of his .45. He dropped it on the desk blotter. “I’m going to take down Airedale. That fuck’s gotta get got.”

“He’s behind all this?”

“That’s why I got this.” He pointed at the piece. “They, this crowd, want to mess up the party, Expo ’67.” And Red 45 was a hell of a shit disturber. It acts on anger. It makes people want to kill without being aware of what they did. Like Blue 27 it has a forgetting component, amnesia, but it moves people beyond their consciences, outside of judgment, he said.

I exhaled sharply. No remorse, no regrets.

Could Bobby have been a test case? Could they have got him to kill Nancy?

“How are these people going to use Red 45 to start a revolution?”

"Well let's call it a diversion, shall we?" He took another sip. "Revolution? Not likely. Diversion, yes. You heard about the 'bomb' at *The Citizen*?"

"Yeah."

"Chump change. Their idea, it seems, is to drug Mayor Drapeau with this shit and other followers of the old Duplessis regime, Members of Parliament. Mess up the House of Commons. A variation on Guy Fawkes day."

"Uh-huh."

"And then. This makes more sense." Babe smiled. It was a little bit wobbly. "Get the powders, Red 45, and spread the stuff through water."

I whistled. "Fuck."

He poured a third shot. "Uh-huh."

"Water filtration plants. Fuck up a lot of people. Divert attention, pull focus from Expo."

People killing people. Indiscriminately. That's what this drug allegedly makes you do, Babe said. If you have a deep-seated hate, that part of the brain triggered for anger, your oxytocin receptors, get overstimulated to the point you act out that anger, hate.

I said nothing. I'm no scientist, but I got the gist. *Flash Gordon Conquers Expo.*

The hands on the small clock of his desk stuttered. "Who's Denys, Denys something or other? Got a crying fleur-de-lis on his face."

"Denys Goyette, the Brain, they call him. Not much of a brain really. I mean who the hell puts a tattoo on their face?"

"What about Guillame?"

"The fairy?"

"The chemist."

"He's in Holland, isn't he?"

"Denmark."

"No idea."

"I think he's here and behind all this."

"Could be." He knocked back the shot. "What do you want from me?"

"Leave Dawn alone."

He laughed. "Dawn?"

"Dawn Stoukas."

"Yeah, I know who Dawn Stoukas is. The chick in the fez."

"Yes, the chick in the fez. Leave her alone."

"I didn't know I was pursuing her. I'm practically a married man." He smiled. Kim Stabulas.

"How's Cathy?" Stabulas. The girl I rescued from a cruel father in my last case. Kim's sister.

She's decided to go into teaching, he said. Secondary. High School. She's enrolled at the Ontario Teachers College.

I nodded. "Call off Athol."

Babe's face turned to crumpled-up paper. "What about Athol?"

"He followed Dawn with intentional malice all through the R.O.M the other day."

"Those weren't my orders."

"Whose orders was he following then?"

Babe's eyes narrowed. He opened the desk drawer again, took out a small wedge of paper and wrote a note and scrawled his name. He handed it to me. "My marker. That's my promise not to hurt Dawn." He held up his hand as if preparing to take the witness stand.

I pocketed the note. "Cassel's no longer at Adora?"

"I don't know anything about Cassel either."

"Isn't he your pal?"

Babe made a jerking off gesture.

"Something about a nephew or a niece—?"

"Cassel's got no hold over me. I hate his punk ass."

Christ, I guess times had changed, niece or no niece.

"Bobby?"

“He’s alive.” He adjusted the cufflinks poking from the arms of his pinstripe jacket and snapped his fingers. Athol returned, rolling in a cart with a huge machine on the lower shelf. The machine looked like a mini Hi-Fi. It was a videocassette recorder, Babe said, three-quarter inch tape, the kind used by CBC to archive hockey games. They film the games right off the TV screen with 16mm cameras and then store the material on videotape.

I wondered how he got his hands on such advanced technology.

“A guy lost a lot of money in a poker game at White Heat,” Babe’s high-end restaurant. He smiled. He nodded sideways at Athol and Athol slid a tape, the size of a porterhouse steak, into the machine. Snow appeared and then an image: Bobby from high above, sitting upright in a chair, coiled rubber tubing around his chest, wires flowing from a few fingers. He was taking a polygraph. I recognized the guy administering it. He worked at the Bay Street police station.

Babe had connections.

The questions were straightforward and simple. What’s your favorite color, what was the name of your first dog, did you kill your wife?

It looked, by the cedar trim, and high ceiling, like it was filmed in Migano’s living room. At one moment, when the camera pulled out for a wider shot, I thought I saw a corner of the stone circled fireplace.

And my ski poles.

Question after question. The tape ran for twenty, maybe thirty minutes. Bobby passed with flying colors. There were very few blips on the polygraph paper. Only one: did you hate your wife? “No?” Bobby answered the question with a question. When asked again, he said no with a more robust tone and the lines spiked. But when asked if he killed her and answered no, the graph didn’t spike.

The expert held up the scores for the camera, and said that

in his opinion Bobby Ehle truly believes he didn't kill Nancy Drouin.

However, he did hate his wife. For the record, the expert said. Full disclosure.

"A polygraph doesn't mean much, Babe." Let's face it, I said. Red 45 makes you forget. So does Blue 27. Maybe he just doesn't remember and truly believes he didn't do it but truly did. Maybe, in time, he will believe he did it.

"Maybe." Babe lit a cigar. "Maybe." But Babe believed him. He knew Bobby as a kid. He was a gentle person. Bobby insisted on the lie detector. "He did it for you. He wanted you to believe in him." Babe shrugged nonchalantly.

"Sure—" But all those concussions, the years of marital discord, the abuse of Blue 27? What if Stana's right? Bobby's fourth face denies the actions of the third, refusing to acknowledge its violent history. I'd seen the photographs. Nancy's disfigured face. I told Babe about those photographs, that history.

"Nancy was a good woman, a good-looking woman. Bobby shouldn't have done what he did. Never hit a woman." He played with a bulky ring on a pinky. "But he didn't kill her—"

Athol was looking away at the golf-ball like dimples on his Florsheims.

"What if Bobby's memory returns and he discovers—I mean, what if—"

"If that happens—" Babe looked into his empty glass of bourbon, twirling in his right hand. "If that happens, Bobby couldn't live with that kind of truth."

"The final taxi?"

The glass stopped twirling. "Huh?"

"A suicide, a hearse, a funeral."

"Right." He laughed. "Final taxi. I like that. It's the one ride we don't have to pay the fare."

"So how long can you keep him locked in a candy store?"

Babe smiled. He wasn't sure, but he cared about Bobby, and

he wanted to keep him safe. He was there at Bobby's confirmation, his first hockey game, his wedding.

"And you're trying to get his cache of Red 45?"

"I'm a businessman, Hayden. I don't deal in that kind of business." He believed in putting Canada first. This was a young country, a great country. "Bobby's protecting all of us from ourselves by hiding it."

A patriot, huh?

I smiled my lopsided lupine grin.

"You wouldn't have someone in a silver Corvair, looks kind of gray in the sun, following me, would you?"

"I wouldn't drive a car like that or let any of my friends behind the wheel. They don't handle well. They're not safe."

I guess, he'd test-driven a few.

"How are things with Kim?" Kim Stabulas was a feisty woman, a survivor, I liked her.

"She's excited about the wedding, you know, arrangements and shit. Petersen's going to play, and Julie London is going to sing at it." Babe smiled, his rose shaking slightly. "I got connections." Babe hadn't posted the banns yet because all the troubles with Bobby had him preoccupied.

"I don't know if you can protect him, Babe." I thought Bobby should come forward, turn himself in, get medical help, psychiatric help. If he killed Nancy, I said, the extenuating circumstances will set him free.

Extenuating circumstances would not give Bobby his freedom but a death sentence. So for now, he feels like he didn't do it, Babe said. "Let's keep it that way."

"Is he really heading to Oslo, Sweden?"

"Oslo, Sweden?"

"Inside joke."

"I can't say where he's heading but he's heading somewhere." And it was neither Norway or Sweden, Babe assured me.

"You really love Bobby."

"Was there ever any doubt?" Babe smiled. His flower seemed to be smiling too.

9

Gillian Williams looked awful good. She wore cream-colored slacks and a blouse with a brown sweater vest. Her shoes were two-toned—tan brown with white looking doilies for the inlets and laces. Her purse was brown. Her lipstick and nail polish cream-colored. She knew how to accessorize.

Me, I wore a blue suit, a powder-blue shirt, a new tie, and left my porkpie at home.

It was my gentlemanly look, de-accessorizing.

We sat at a back table, a red and white checkered cloth giving our space at George's an added intimacy. Gillian had escargots with her meal. I noshed on Italian bread with garlic butter.

A candle, with a strong angular flame, burned yellow between us.

And I felt guilty as hell. I was supposed to have taken Stana here, tonight. Instead I was sitting across from Gillian, staring into gentle candle flames.

And she looked awful good.

"So what's on your mind?" I folded my arms on my chest, leaned back.

She pursed her lips tight, in a French way, and smiled whimsically. Cassel was on her mind. Her blue expansive eyes glanced around the restaurant, taking in strangers, quickly darting about for anyone who may be an enemy. I guess pushing drugs can do that to you, if she is pushing drugs. I wasn't quite sure how deep her involvement in trafficking Blue 27 and working alongside Cliff Airdale went.

But I was sure of one thing. She was no ingénue.

And that certainty led to a second one: be careful, this might be a setup.

I stole furtive glances at her beauty—the fine line of her cameo-style neck, her delicate cheekbones, pencil thin eyebrows, full sassy hair—afraid of having my look captured and contained by her.

She peeked over a left shoulder, right. The 1950s were all about bust lines, hips, and curves. She was 1960s beautiful.

She sloughed an escargot from its shell.

It wasn't done with malice but a gentle, quiet gesture. If I weren't stealing looks I wouldn't have noticed.

Worm for sale.

Kids on a softball diamond down by the Humber River. The sun bleeding across a low horizon line. I'm eleven or twelve, pounding a fist in my mitt, listening to them poking fun at French Canadians and their struggles with English, dropping the "s" in plural constructions, worm for worms. Big joke. Worm for sale.

How do you think your accent would sound to them if you tried to speak French, dickhead?

Me, I don't have an accent, Fuller, they'd say.

I couldn't stop talking about it. Worm for sale. Instead of peeking over shoulders, I was peeking over my past, apologizing to her and all of French Canada for the sense of social injustice that occurred daily throughout my childhood.

"Am I trying too hard to tell you I'm not like those other kids on the softball diamond?" I admired the French, what they had to put up with, all the English businesses in Quebec hiring their own over French people, and I have a soft spot for chocolate croissants.

"Your love for French culture makes me think I might have a

chance with you."

I didn't look away fast enough. I was caught in her eyes. "I, uh—"

She liked the vulnerability in me. My eyes lived there, in that space, she said.

I smiled. What would Dr. Cohen have to say about that, huh? For the last six months, Dr. Cohen had tried to get me to express my vulnerability, to open up about the past, my troubles with my father, my troubles with intimacy. *Vulnerability, Dr. C, vulnerability. That's what Gillian said. I swear it.*

Be on your guard Fuller. Could be a setup.

"So much pain—"

"I get by." I watched the candle's flame stretching taller.

She smiled, teeth perfect. "Doug Harvey, huh? You really think he's the greatest?"

"Yeah."

Richard for her, was the ambassador for French Canada, no doubt. She too was there at the infamous Richard Riot. "Over the years the amount of people at the Forum that night has grown to a quarter of a million. But I really was there."

With Cassel.

"Come again?" Cassel was an American but his mother's family was French and he'd often visit Montreal. "Isn't that Tim Horton over there?"

It was. All the Leafs came to George's Spaghetti House on Dundas and Sherbourne. It's not far from the Gardens. It was their hangout, away from Hugh "Two Fisted" Farrell and his streetcars.

"What were you going to say about Cassel?" Was he the person in the Corvair tracking me, watching me? The Corvair's dealer plates were a phony according to Sal. The car was never registered.

Cassel was at Adora Borealis. And still is.

I stopped pushing a twirl of spaghetti against my spoon.

"What?"

She slid a key in my direction. It was green, a Yale brand, with a gray putty smudge on its top edge. It nudged under the rim of my plate and stayed there. "Room 7."

But don't call the police, please. She didn't trust them. There had to be a mole. On the police force. If I brought Lambertino and his men over, Cassel would surely disappear.

And she'd be dead.

"That sounds like high-blown melodrama," I said. "How would you be dead?"

"Trust me." Her eyes held mine, filling me with her detached whimsicality.

I couldn't possibly understand how Cassel could still be hiding there. We knew all about the half-floor and we searched and searched—

"The mole gave us plenty of time to relocate him."

"Uh-huh."

She wanted to broker a deal. She'd give up Cassel if I'd agree to put in a good word on her behalf with the police. Her involvement in this case was extenuating. If the police barge in, her life could be in jeopardy. She wiped gently at the corners of the mouth. She was tired of it all. Room seven. The one with the pulp novels and cabinet full of over-the-counter relief for indigestion.

"What's Airedale got on you?"

"It's not him. It's Cassel."

"What's he got?"

Gillian knew Lenny in Montreal back in 1954–56. Cassel played in the AHL with the Providence Reds. Won the Calder Cup in 1955. He was a decent two-way forward, feisty, but never got the call-up to the NHL. Anyway, because of his French-Canadian Mom, he often visited the area in the off-season, sometimes during the season. He knew the whole gang: Denys, Gillian, Terry. "Palled around with us all."

"Uh-huh."

"His best friend was Guillame."

"The chemist?"

She nodded. Some people thought Cassel was a little funny on Guillame, had a thing for him. Kind of a crush. She looked toward the back exit, the front door. Her fork gently tapped her plate with a trace note or two. "Cassel was taken with him." Her face was an immobile portrait. "In love—"

"I see."

"I never liked Cassel much. Too brash. Typical American. Loud."

I nodded.

"But he knows me." She rolled spaghetti against her spoon. Her lips pinched together into a pouty French-shaped circle. "And when the troubles in Detroit started—"

"Troubles? He hacked two people to death with a machete—"

"When that mess hit the proverbial fan he came to me for help. Pulled on our prior friendship."

"Blackmail—"

"No, no a favor."

"A favor? You mean blackmail."

She ate her crushed circle of spaghetti. Her wide-set eyes glinted.

So she agreed to help him because of a connection the two forged over ten years ago. Airedale, being the asshole that he is, insisted that Cassel earn his keep, $50,000. Cassel obliged.

I let out a low whistle. "That's a lot of keep."

"Airedale's a bastard."

"You don't like him much."

Her porcelain face remained impassive. Only her eyes moved, revealing the glare she felt toward him. "No," she whispered. "No." She touched up her lipstick. "No."

That was one more "no" than I expected. She really did hate him. "So, why the change of heart? Why come to me?" I couldn't figure this. She does a favor and now she is turning Cassel over. And I wasn't sure about the no police part of the equation either. Something smelled like a big fat phony and I wasn't about to be a patsy.

She pushed aside her spoon and fork. We'd both lost our appetites. "Nobody knows this." Her chin dropped slightly, her lipstick glistened. There wasn't a blemish on her face. "Nobody knows this, nobody." Her fingers tented together. "They'll have no record of her disappearance."

I knew someone else like that. Dead and no one knows. Brian "Spinner" Terrien, buried in a field.

"Leila. She's dead."

Leila, the woman with the heavy face and autumnal hair, the one I promised to protect.

"She found out who he really was—"

Was there ever any doubt? He was front-page headlines on every paper from here to Montreal.

"We did some work on his face. Airedale and I." Slight, she said, but enough to make him a new person.

"A fourth face," I mumbled like Brando. That's the only language, besides English that I speak fluently. Marlon Brando.

"A fourth face?"

"A theory." I explained it, how Stana had christened it. I talked some more about what a good reporter she was, but I didn't confess to how Stana's not being here made the back of my neck and shoulder blades tingle with guilt.

Nor did I confess to how catching glimmers of Gillian through angular light made the guilt even worse. I'll have to send Stana fifty flowers to make this right. Maybe even a new pair of pumps, Maple Leaf blue. She always looked good in blue.

So Cassel could now board a plane to Sweden. He and his fourth face. "And let me guess, coach hockey?"

Her lips parted and the lines around the top of her eyes appeared slightly downturned. "Yes, how'd you know?"

"What does Bobby have to do with all this? He was going to coach hockey in Sweden too."

"That's right," she said. The plan was for Bobby to get plastic surgery while over there. And then join Cassel as fresh talent from Canada. Of course they'd change their names to some obscure forgotten players. AHL types that no one remembers.

"So how did Cassel kill her. Leila?"

I'm not sure why I needed to know, but I did.

"His hands." Gillian wiped at her mouth with the back of a small hand. She grimaced, her chin wrinkling, the lines forming into an upside-down horseshoe. "I liked her." She looked at her discarded spoon, spots of dark marinara hardening in its center.

"Me too."

"Oh, you had a conversation with her?"

"Un petit peu."

Another smile. After the killing, which was so pointless, Gillian had enough with harboring such a sociopath. Cassel didn't have to kill Leila. He enjoyed the excuse that allowed him to do so. As he strangled her, Cassel claimed he counted the seconds, seven, it took for her to die. It was just a game to him, a crazy game. A cheap amusement.

"And I don't quite get your game." I pointed a fork at her. "Why can't the police just go in and bust his ass?" Take some guns, take him out.

The leak, the mole. I told you. The mole. In the police department. Inside. That mole would tell Cliff and he'd figure me for the traitor, she said. Cassel would get hid and after the police found nothing Cassel would add one more victim to his killing floor. "With me, he'd probably use the machete."

"Why's the fuck still holed up in your place?"

They were waiting for the plastic surgery to heal and he was almost set to leave, but after he killed Leila and she scratched his face with her hands, they had to do some touch-ups. It would be a few more days before he'd leave Canada with a fourth face.

"Who's the leak?"

Gillian didn't know. If she did, she'd tell me. It was someone on Lambertino's staff that's all she could figure.

Sarah Linney's death at the high-rise hotel took place in a room full of five people: Lambertino, Linney, Moffat, Stoukas and me. Five of us. Who left the goddamn drapes open? What did I know about Sgt. Moffat? Of course, there were a lot of other people on that particular detail who came in and out of the room. Twelve-to-fifteen, Sal said. When the shots were fired, however, it was just us five.

And the drapes were open. Wide.

Christ. I wish I would've thought to have closed them.

Gillian shook her head. She knew no Moffat.

Neither of us could touch our food. Rocks were dissolving in my stomach. Gillian, as always, was composed, her face a calm lake.

There are a lot of other people on Sal's staff, people I didn't know. Any one of them could be Airedale's go-to.

And what about the person following me in the Corvair? Silver, gray in the sun? Could that be our mole?

I couldn't see Cassel driving a Corvair. Too much ego. A Cadillac. Black, she said.

I sipped seltzer water, Gillian pale beer. The tan color matched her purse and shoes.

Gillian pulled out a compact, powdered a spot on her chin. "If it wasn't for this case and me being on the other side, I could go for you."

I can't sleep with someone unless I love them, I said. I'm old school. Squaresville.

"But wouldn't it be fun to mess around?" This was the 1960s. It wasn't our mothers' time, Hayden. Join the permissive society.

She reached for and touched my hand, fingers full of fire. "We could make love, once, no strings. I would never tell anyone about it—"

The words were wrong, forbidden words, a secret kind of love.

"What time tonight do you want me to fish out Mr. Machete?"

Just after two a.m. The nurses switch shifts then. I could sneak in during the interim, she said.

"Airedale won't be there?"

"You kidding? The guy has banker hours. Ten a.m. to 3 p.m."

She was still holding my hand. I motioned for the check. "Back to my earlier question." I pressed my hands together. "What does Cassel have on you?"

"What do you mean?"

"To do such a favor." I rattled off a list: harbor a fugitive, perform minor plastic surgery, help get him into Sweden. Shit like that. "This isn't about friendship. You don't even like this sociopathic cat."

No, she didn't like him. Much. Anymore. It was about Guillame Clausen. "My best friend." Cassel, at one time, was crazy over Guillame. "If I didn't help Cassel, he was going to expose Guillame as the chemist, the mastermind behind Red 45."

"The plot to poison the water filtration plants around Montreal and pull focus from Expo?"

Gillian was surprised over what all I knew.

Did she know that I knew that Bobby had 600-900 packets of that shit hid somewhere?

Cassel and Gillian, back in the mid-1950s went to Beat poetry readings and shared a passion for French politics and the burgeoning need for a quiet revolution. "I was smitten. But he never could see me."

"Cassel knows where Guillame is?"

"Yes."

"Where?"

"Close by."

"Montreal?"

"A suburb there. In Montreal. That's their base of operation."

"Look, you got to go to the police. You give them this information, they'll give you a goddamn medal. All charges will be dropped."

She couldn't do that. She cared too much about Guillame.

The waitress in a black turtleneck and slacks returned with the check and a phone with a long chord on some kind of gold platter. She placed them on the table. "For you, Miss Williams." She handed her the receiver.

Gillian smiled absently. For the first time her sexy whimsicality had become awkward, every gesture losing its sharp focus.

Tentatively she spoke into the phone. "Yes—thank, you—" She turned sideways in her chair, one leg over the other, the phone caught like an errant Frisbee, between shoulder and ear. "No, I don't think so. No. I can't—yes—a guest—"

I tried focusing on the candle, but I couldn't help overhearing. It was my job to eavesdrop.

"That's not a good idea. You need—no—Guillame, listen—"

Guillame. The voice bleeding out of the dial was slightly elevated with a nervous, adenoidal whisper.

I leaned forward in my chair, huffed sharply, the candle between us puffing once or twice, and then it continued burning a longer flame.

"We'll talk later. I don't think—Guillame—listen—no—later—"

She held out the dead receiver.

"Long distance?" I heard her start the conversation by accepting the charges. "Collect?"

"Yes—Montreal." She couldn't look at me.

It was him, she confessed, eyes on her hands, still holding the dead phone. Guillame wanted to put his plan into action, now, yesterday, the day before yesterday. He was impatient, and she was trying to talk him down. He was a troubled person.

"The plan? The water filtration plan?"

"Yes."

He often called for advice, particularly when he was in a manic phase or a terrible blue mood, as he called it. "He's a genius, but moody. Very moody." She looked through my shoulder.

"Moody enough to unleash Red 45?"

She nodded. "I told you he was a troubled person." Her calm face was the very cup of trembling. There was no absolution possible for Guillame and possibly for all of us, she said.

"What about all the troubled persons who'll drink water tainted with Red 45?"

She was aware of that. It took a subtle approach when talking to Guillame. Always subtle.

"How did he know you were here?"

"They have ways." Her blue eyes had lost some of their stillness.

"They?"

"They. N'oublie jamais."

"Is Denys, Lambskin Hat, part of this outfit?"

"I don't like him—"

"You've seen him?"

"He knows Cliff." She held up two fingers curling together. "Tight."

"How big's the organization?"

"I'm being followed. Constantly." She figured maybe the Corvair was a part of their outfit.

She pushed her hands together, played with the collar on her blouse, adjusted the lines in her sweater vest. Her goal was to keep Guillame calm, work on his better side, and reach his conscience.

I wondered if Sal had those phone records yet from Adora Borealis. They surely should lead right to Dr. Frankenstein. In Montreal.

"You got to turn him in. It's your duty."

"I'll turn in Cassel. To you. And we'll see where that leads." With time Guillame would soften. "The way he talked now.

Manic phase. He's always talking extremes when in that stage, but he'll come out of it, soon." She was sure of it. Her face lost its calm trembling.

Soften? What if Bobby's not the great patriot Babe makes him out to be and has plans to return Red 45 to Guillame, or, even worse, sell it on the open market? How much more of that junk could be cooked up by Guillame and shipped onto the streets of Laval and Montreal?

"Do you know why Guillame went to Copenhagen, Denmark?"

"Sure. Relatives." The seltzer was too warm.

The waitress retrieved the phone with the long cord and I handed her my Diner's card.

The call was long distance. When it comes in, charge me, I said. She nodded and left.

Relatives? In Denmark? No, Hayden, that wasn't it. Gillian took in a deep breath and ice cubes clacked in her water glass. The water here was nowhere near as good as the filtered stuff at Adora Borealis, she said. But she drank some anyway. The cubes were noisy chipped marbles as she parked the glass to the side of her plate.

Guillame, according to Gillian, wasn't happy in his own skin, in trying to be a man. His hands were too small, his feet dainty, the distance between his shoulders slight. Yes, he had a man's nose, a rather generous one like yours, Hayden, but Guillame always felt like a woman trapped in a man's body. Denmark is one of the leading places in the world for sex reassignment surgery. That's why Guillame went there. Not to be with relatives, not to escape the gendarmes, but to be re-made, re-modeled. He was placed on the reassignment list, underwent psychological evaluation, even had his nose adjusted, thinned, but in the end couldn't do it. Instead of being re-made he remained. A man with a new nose, a more feminine nose, but still a man.

"Wow." I was Brando again, inarticulately looking down at

my plate, the spaghetti drying.

Cassel loved Guillame, but not as a man. He wanted the sex change. It's complicated, Gillian said, because Guillame wanted it too, and openly shared this with Lenny, his desire to become a woman, even taking on early hormone treatments, but as the surgery loomed, he had doubts, and those doubts got more desperate as Guillame feared losing his relationship with Cassel. He wrote several long letters to Gillian explaining his confusion, his desire to be both sexes, but he ultimately decided to remain what he was born with: a Nancy-boy fella who was constantly teased and ridiculed for not being manly enough.

"And your loyalty to Guillame is such that you feel a need to protect him and thus were willing to go along with Cassel's demands?"

"Yes."

"To coach hockey. In Sweden."

"Yes."

It sounded so ludicrous. A Detroit-area mobster, a machete wielding czar, turned hockey instructor and coach. "I'm telling you, turn this info over to Sal's team and they'll give you a medal."

"I can't. I think I'm in love with Guillame too."

"I see."

She smiled, her lips a thin wave. Guillame is a very mixed-up man, unsure of his identity in a rapidly changing world. "I mean some men are now growing their hair out, looking like women."

My smile joined hers. I still sported a buzz cut.

She shrugged, one shoulder rising higher than the other. "I had to help him."

"Of course."

I pocketed the key. Room seven. Two o-five a.m.

"I'll leave the light on," she said, and then winked.

—

I WASN'T TOO PLEASED when I got back to my bungalow in the suburbs. Someone had tossed the joint. The mattress was ripped off the bed and slit down the middle; the pillows on the couch were gashed with a serrated knife, chunks of foam spilling out of jagged slits like dropped intestines. Jazz records, abandoned and tossed, slipped from their sleeves and were discarded akimbo hubcaps. My filing cabinet was upended and loose-leaf papers ran across the dining table and over the top of record jackets. Plates and glasses were broken in the kitchen.

And to think, I was planning to sit down and read for a couple of hours.

Mickey Spillane. *The Girl Hunters.*

What were they looking for?

Stana's topless photos from 1962–63 were still there. In a manila envelope. The clasp broken.

I didn't know if I should be offended that they hadn't taken them. They were low-key noir images, shot with an ISO of 100, a 1/200 shutter speed, the F stop set at 1.4. I was proud of the work. Stana was beautiful.

She still is.

Shit. I placed the photos back in a lower desk drawer and cleaned and oiled my gun, re-aligning the firing pin. Then I loaded it, snapped shut the chamber, and dropped an extra six shells in the pocket of my red windbreaker.

I scrubbed my hands clean with Comet, and turned to the fridge and made myself a quick Swiss pastrami sandwich on rye with mayo and a side of kosher dill pickles. Glass of orange juice.

The spaghetti dinner at George's just didn't sit well. I was supposed to have been there with Stana.

I got ready to call her when my phone jarred loudly.

Gillian.

"Hey, what's up?" I already felt I'd spent too much time with her. I wanted to talk to Stana.

"Well, that doesn't sound too friendly—" Her words purred

like a Peugeot.

I switched the phone to my left ear. “Sorry. I had just sat down to a bite—”

“George’s wasn’t very appetizing?”

“I was tense the whole time—and I can’t eat when I’m tense.” There’s a lot of things I can’t do when I’m tense.

“I know what can help you unwind—” The purr to her voice had popped into a higher rev.

“I’m too tired—I’ll—”

“Raincheck?”

“Maybe.”

There was a long silence, the phone’s static light snowfall.

“I want to rest up before—”

“I can be a great sleeping pill.” The purr was Mona Lisa whimsy.

“Do you have any idea who might have broken into my home—rifled my files—”

“It was broken into?”

“While we were dining at George’s.” *Coincidence?* “Come on. Don’t bullshit me. Did you set me up?”

“No.” Static snow swirled between us. “I tried telling you they were watching us. They knew—”

“I got to go. My sandwich is getting cold.” I like pastrami cold.

“That’s not the only thing that’s cold right now.” The purr of her voice had become grinding gears.

“I’m sorry. I—”

“Good luck tonight.”

She kissed the receiver.

It smacked my ear.

I wasn’t sure if she were being ironic.

I ate half the sandwich and called Stana. Her voice was distracted. I wondered if she had company, a fella.

“I call at a bad time?” What business is it of mine if she were on a date?

"No, no." She had just nodded off watching TV. "What is it?"

I told her about my conversation with Gillian, not the latest one, the one at George's, and the part about Guillame and Copenhagen and the possible sex change operation. He got his nose fixed, but that's about it. "Can you look into it? Fact check?"

She could.

There was also a Corvair that was following me.

Yes. Silver. Looks kind of gray in the sun? Apparently, it was following her too. This afternoon, as she left the *Tely*'s Front Street office, the Corvair tagged behind her to a local A&P where Stana bought an apple and some brie. She hadn't been eating too well lately either.

I promised to make it up to her. Bassel's in a day or two?"

She wanted George's.

I didn't dare confess that that's where I took Gillian.

I also didn't confess to Stana about Gillian's human sleeping pills pitch.

I did tell her about Denys. Gillian's slim connection, how she didn't like him much. A paint thinner glaze of hate coated her eyes when she spoke briefly of him.

Oh, Stana said. "Yeah. That guy. The one in the lambskin hat, Denys Goyette?" He's not just a former playwright but a hit man, she said. Two newspaper informants, an ex-mobster turned politician and an associate of Migano's who insisted on anonymity, knew of at least four hits in the last six months claimed by Goyette.

"Who's he work for?"

"Freelance." Her voice parachuted to a whisper. "Goyette was probably the gunman in the helicopter."

"That makes six," I said. "Six kills in six months." Terry and Sarah.

"Yes," she said, all of her words falling slowly. "No doubt he's mixed up with that Red 45 crowd. Guillame hired him."

"Yeah." Guillame. I wondered what he looked like now.

"Probably heavier with a thinner nose," she said.

Did Denys kill Nancy?

"Not his style. He doesn't use his hands." Stana was still convinced that that murder was Bobby's.

"Look, if you don't hear from me by noon tomorrow—"

"What?"

"Never mind."

"You can tell me, Hayden." Her words were no longer softly falling.

I guess I wanted to tell her or else I wouldn't have called in the first place. Two a.m., I had a key, Adora, going to get Cassel.

"He's there?"

"Yes."

"Don't do it alone."

Like me, she thought this might be a setup. Stana didn't buy Gillian's rationale for a covert op. "Bullshit, bullshit, bullshit" was all she had to say on that subject.

"I love you," I said, my voice now dropping like a parachute. I was afraid she didn't feel the same. "I just wanted you to know in case—"

Static gently buzz-buzzed between us.

"You hear what I said, Hayden? Don't go in alone."

"I got my friends, Smith and Wesson."

"Don't be a smart-ass." She figured this setup for a real phony, better call Sal.

So I did.

WE SYNCHRONIZED OUR WATCHES. My Galaxie was parked on a deserted side street from Adora. A trash dumpster was to our left and the black alley, away from the lights, was charred black logs. 1:46 a.m.

I gripped a smudged key in my left hand. It was supposed to unlock a back door. I toyed with the tacky substance atop the key, by the Yale name.

"What about the room, room seven?"

I didn't have a key for that.

"Christ, Fuller." Sal shook his head and rubbed at the traces of his Hemingway beard. "Details aren't your bag—"

I laughed. "No. I guess not."

"Shit. Details. I didn't bring my badge."

We didn't have a warrant so he wasn't a cop anymore. Just a fellow citizen, helping a friend.

I nodded, grateful for his company.

Unlike Stana, Sal figured there was some truth to Gillian's yarn. If he brought in a full platoon of cops, word would get out and we'd be playing button-button with Cassel. There most definitely was a leak and it was under his watch and that pissed him off. After Linney's death, he wasn't sure who he could trust.

"Who opened the curtains in Dawn's room, the day Sarah got shot?" I pushed back my porkpie. It was good to have it on again. I felt naked at George's.

Sal had no idea. Like he said before, twelve to fifteen personnel went through that room. Could have been anyone. Could have been Dawn herself. "But I doubt it."

"What if Dawn wasn't the target?"

"I don't follow?"

"What if Sarah were the target all along?" I pulled on the brim of my porkpie. "We're getting tripped up because she was wearing Dawn's clothes, but what if the killer knew that?"

Sal pushed himself back in the bench seat and the color of his face turned to ashes.

"What was she working on?"

"The Stoukas detail." He shuffled a Rothman's from his deck of smokes. Lit it. "The other day I saw her talking to some high ranking officials, upstairs, behind a frosted glass door—"

"Internal Affairs?"

"Looked like RCMP."

He asked Officer Linney about it later and she said it was a cold-case file they were following up on, something about the Marilyn Cozart case, the sixteen-year-old girl who disappeared from Toronto four years ago and was last seen in a lakefront bar in Buffalo.

What if she were blowing smoke, Sal, and it was this case, this one right now?

Sal nodded, taking a long, slow drag.

I suggested that when we get done with Cassel that we go through all of Linney's files, everything, all the cases she was working up.

"Yes. Let's." He took another drag and tossed his cigarette through the open window. It arced and sparked when it bounced along the pavement.

I checked my side-holstered weapon. My hand shook. "I appreciate you being in on this with me, Sal. It means a lot to me."

"You need a hug or something? I got Lifesavers."

That cracked me. "Let's go."

The alley's shadows were full of Neolithic monsters and splashes of conical light. We darted through the darkness.

THE HALLS OF ADORA, with its faint red runners glinting instead of the bright fire of the overhead track lighting, looked narrower. We wore PF Flyers, giving us quiet stealth. Quickly we moved through the hall to the L part of the building, the wing away from the hydrotherapy unit and the drop floor. A central-air system, pumping coolant, hummed off and on.

I couldn't control my breathing. It kept catching and I felt as if I were about to drown.

Around the elbow of the L, voices, women. One nurse was replacing the other. The accent of the older woman was crisp, clear, bright leaves on an autumn afternoon. The other voice was faint, lost in the rumble of a subway tunnel.

Leila.

She wasn't dead.

I'm pretty sure that was her voice, beyond the building's elbow. Leila.

I jotted a quick note and handed it to Sal.

He couldn't figure what the fuck the scrawl meant.

I neglected to fill him in on the alleged murder of Leila at the hands of one Lenny Cassel, machete-wielding sociopath. I didn't tell Stana about it either. Sometimes my head works as slow as Bobby's.

Sal jotted on the back of the note: abort the mission? *We being set up?*

Probably. But we didn't have time to get out of here quick enough without being detected. What the fuck, let's get Cassel and shut this place down.

A dark line was at the bottom of the door to room seven. I grabbed my flashlight, my gun was in my other hand.

A faint cigar smell bled from under the door.

It wasn't fresh.

And the voices beyond the elbow. Moving. Our way.

Sal nodded, motioned toward the door handle, nodded "no," locked, then he held up two fingers. He was going in first. I was to follow.

His right foot bashed the door back.

Arc light flashed the room, the shelves, pulp paperbacks, an ashtray, two crushed cigars, on a nightstand, a face.

Tight curly hair, like a Brillo pad. Eyes closely set. The space between his shoulders, slight.

Terrien. Brian "Spinner" Terrien, the man I saw die, an eye hanging from its orbital bone, his last breath, bubblegum blood.

"Hello, Hayden. Taken any good photos lately?"

The voice wasn't quite right. But it was close. Real close.

"Where's Cassel?" Sal said.

"Where indeed." Terrien smiled, his signature grin, the corners of his mouth turning up at the ends. "I thought you were coming alone." He was slightly annoyed, but the edges of the words were filled with pleasantries. Another Terrien trademark. Gentleness.

There were bandages and gauze along the lower left side of his face and part of an ear.

The door clicked shut behind us and then gas streams, thin waves, flushed from the switch plates of the room's four walls.

I couldn't see. My eyes filled with bee stings. The door was locked.

I wanted to blast my .38 but I was afraid of hitting Sal. Couldn't see him.

"What's going on? Terrien where are you?" Sal's voice was full of shadows.

"Nose filters," Terrien said, his voice drifting away from us. "Nose filters."

And the room got heavier and heavier, my lungs hurting as if blankets of flame were burning inside me.

And that's all I remember.

10

The world was off its axis and the spun cotton candy clotting my head had turned red. Red lint limned my eyes. The room was a dark, dark red and I wasn't sure if I was in a chair or even sitting down.

Terrien.

Gas.

Where was Sal?

Dr. Stangl, a hypodermic in his right hand, his eyes bright red coins, stood with his other hand inside his blood-colored lab coat. His face was hard to read in the clutter of reds that looked like a kid had let loose with his Spirograph.

I couldn't think right.

It was as if the walls in this room were made of dust.

"Where is it?"

Gillian's voice. All of the soft, whimsical edges dissolving into hard elbows. When her lips moved I saw small coral snakes.

I was in a hardback chair. My hands and legs were free, but I didn't feel like I could lift them. "Where's what?"

The red clay walls turned dark, earthen footlights. More Spirograph swirls.

"What Bobby left you." This time it was Airedale, his voice terse and thin, like a pack of weak firecrackers, not the kind that could blow off your hand. "Tell us—" He wasn't in a lab coat like Gillian. He was still the dedicated United Empire Loyalist in his blazer, now heavy red, with the three-pointed crown on the left breast. Behind him, looking at her shoes, was Leila, chips of hair peeking like angry birds from under her cap.

This was some fucking party.

And I had a killer hangover.

Not that I've ever been drunk. My father was an alcoholic, wearing sunglasses on days he was in a good mood, and I'd seen enough of his foul moods to never want to touch the stuff. But this felt like what a hangover must feel like. My head hurt like I'd fallen hard at center ice. And behind my eyes, a dull constant ache. Anacin wasn't going to help this shit. I blinked. The ache intensified.

"Where is it?"

I wasn't sure who asked this time. Did it matter?

The floor was a flood of red snakes.

I swam with their current.

WATER TRICKLED FROM A FAUCET like pulls of soft taffy. I was eight, maybe nine, mother had recently died, and it was my Saturday night ritual, a bath before the Leafs broadcast on radio with McClelland Stuart.

And then my father walked in, naked, hard in his hand.

The water looked like taffy.

"WHERE IS IT?"

That game again. I fluttered open my eyes, but the red was still there, flashing, bright, heavy, darker than the cherries on a police cruiser. "I don't know what you're fucking talking about."

Gillian leaned in, her breath full of coffee, dabs of Paris perfume on her neck. "The canisters? Three of them." Her face was an immobile mask.

That's why my house was broken into while the good doctor and I ate spaghetti at George's. "You owe me a mattress."

"Terry told us that Bobby left the bundle with you." I guess my client had brought them with him when he and the helicopter landed in my yard.

This was the first I'd heard of it. "So Terry was working for you too, huh? Why'd you whack him?"

"He had served his purpose." Airedale rubbed scruffy ends of his goatee.

"Who killed him?"

"No one you know." Airedale shrugged and pulled on the lapels of his blazer.

Gillian swallowed a half glass of water. I think it was water. It was odorless, but the color was a little off.

"No one I know, huh? Denys? Denys Goyette?"

Airdale rocked back slightly on his moccasins. It was a strange combo: the blazer, the wool pants, and moccasins with no socks. I started laughing about the no socks thing. I couldn't help it.

"Denys doesn't use his hands," Gillian assured me, a thin smile creasing her lips.

I nodded. Denys. "A class act. He's got principles."

"Shut up." Airedale slapped me hard. As his hand knifed the room it resembled five flags flying in a hard wind. None of the flags were Canadian.

"Look, if Bobby left the junk with me, he didn't tell me." The cotton candy in my head was now bleeding through my nose and eyes. They must have pumped me full of Red 45, but if one of the side effects of the drug is forgetfulness why ask me to remember something that I've probably forgotten?

It takes several doses or an extreme dose for that side effect to kick in, Gillian said, assuring me that what they gave me was minimal, just enough to loosen my inhibitions and get me to talk.

I had been talking out loud. Again. "Your version of the truth serum, huh?"

"Yes, a truth serum." Airedale, bored.

"Where's Terrien?"

Gillian's sexy charm and whimsy no longer had any fabric softener to it. She too was bored.

I guess I was a real pain in the ass. There I was drugged up, in a chair, listless, seeing all kinds of amoeba-shaped hallucinations, and I'm asking the questions.

"Yes, Fuller, you are a pain in the ass." Airedale rubbed the edge of a hand. I guess he hurt it when my face hit him.

"Terrien's resting comfortably." Gillian nodded.

Stangl, over her left shoulder, did something or other to the hypodermic, and it perspired. Leila was still studying her shoes. There weren't any snakes crawling across them. Gillian's shoes, on the other hand, were covered in thin snakes.

I think I hated her at that moment.

"Bobby didn't leave me a thing, except the conviction that he hadn't killed his wife. A conviction I share."

"Where are the canisters?" Airedale's goatee had turned to red dust.

When I was walking the half-light of consciousness, when I was reliving bathtub memories of my father and taffy, I heard overlapping words, a slapping rush and fall of frustrations. It seems the formula to Red 45 was lost or its original conception had been an accident, the compounds that went into its making forgotten. Some components came from rare South American extracts and plant resins. They could create new powders from the prototype, but the perfected mixture was impossible, it seems to re-attain. Guillame didn't take very good notes, apparently. Those 800 or so packets of Red 45 were the pure stuff. Everything else pales and lacks the killing power N'oublie jamais requires. Guillame was trying to find the right amount of elements, reinvent the old formula, but so far his efforts to recreate his work of accidental genius were limp. Bobby had stolen the best of what Guillame had to offer and they wanted it back.

"I'd rather die than give it to you fuckos."

That got me another slap.

This time from Gillian. She hit a hell of a lot harder than Baggy Ass.

If they didn't have the number-one stuff, the prime Red 45, what was this version doing to me?

"It may be watered down and not as potent, but it will let us know what we need to know," Gillian promised, her lips barely moving.

I inhaled, lungs full of flames. "Leila. What are you doing here? You're too nice a person to be mixed up with these yahoos."

She looked at her shoes. Now, they too, were covered with snakes.

The snakes slithering from my nose and mouth shifted sideways across the floor toward her shoes.

I closed my eyes. I hate snakes.

"Bobby didn't kill Nancy, did he, Cliff? Did he, Gillian? It was Terrien. That's why he had those bandages on his face when the gas spilled into that room. He was recovering from Nancy's counter punches. And she got in some good licks before she died." I smiled, eyes closed, breathing deeply, flames lashing my chest. "Only Terrien's not Terrien is he? Oh, no." I opened tired eyes, readying for more snakes. "Terrien was beaten to death three months ago in a garage. I was there. Saw his eye hanging out of his head, saw him take a last breath of bubblegum blood. Dawn saw Terrien but it wasn't the real Terrien, and that's why you wanted Dawn dead. Terrien's Cassel. You made him look like Spinner—you—"

It was rather simple, actually, Airedale gloated, playing with his goateed chin, left eyebrow raised like the back of a cat. "Their body structures were very similar." He paced behind my chair, hands locked. He smelled of Aqua Velva, the kind of aftershave I expected a cat like him to wear, swinger wannabe. The cool, mature cats like Migano wear Old Spice. Airedale bragged on and on about his work, his skill as a surgeon, how because they were both slight men with close-set eyes it was easy. Yes, the chin, the nose needed a lot of work, and some restructuring around the hairline, but overall it was a good match. And he was a great surgeon, highly skilled, top of his class at the U of T. Did I already tell you the highly skilled part? He must have mentioned it like eight times.

"And the voice." Gillian smiled. She couldn't resist joining the conversation. Doctors and their egos. Spinner had been interviewed twice on *Hockey Night in Canada* in the early '60s. They got Cassel archival tapes and had him practice the sound, rhythms, to Spinner's voice.

A regular Method actor he was.

Did Migano supply the archival tapes? He did win a video recorder in a high-stakes poker game. The person he won it from worked for the CBC.

CBC archived old games.

So, Cassel got himself a fourth face. Terrien's dead and Cassel was going to use Spinner's face to begin a new life in Oslo, Sweden.

"Oh, those plans have changed." Airedale missed my joke. "He's going away. Tomorrow. But he's not going there—"

"Quiet," Gillian chastised. "You're saying too much."

"Who cares, he won't live through the evening—"

"That's right." Gillian's kabuki face was faraway, all of its distanced artistry lost in Spirograph amoebas. "You should have—when I called you—you should have—said yes—"

"I don't live in should haves."

I did learn something from my therapist. The present is what matters, what I can do now. Don't live in the past.

Gillian looked over at Leila who was still studying her shoes. "We should keep our plans on the down-low, Cliff. There are other people present."

I wanted to re-tie Leila's laces.

I'm not sure why my mind went there but I wanted to untie and re-tie, untie and re-tie.

I started laughing again thinking about those laces. They looked like they belonged on the feet of a girl, a little girl.

And then I wanted to draw with Spirograph. I was a real mess. "Why did Cassel kill Nancy?"

"She knew too much about our operation." Airedale's voice was bathed in shrugs. "After she did that exclusive with that reporter, we couldn't take any more chances with follow-up conversations."

I blinked my eyes. The red wouldn't go away.

Talking to Stana numbered Nancy's days. If she could rat out Bobby, disclosing all of his sordid moments of domestic violence, what was to stop her from disclosing the secrets of N'oublie jamais? After all, she knew all of the players of this drama during her undergrad days at McGill. She was a Montreal girl. And from what I could gather, she didn't care for the whole lot of them.

"Yes. She was expendable and untrustworthy." Gillian folded her arms across her chest.

"She wasn't much of a lay either." Airedale smiled and motioned to Stangl.

He closed in. The tip of the needle perspired.

"I know nothing about the goddamn canisters—"

"The only reason you're still alive are those three canisters." Gillian's voice was full of blood.

"Where's Sal?"

I think I was screaming after that as the needle hit a vein and I hit the floor, my head landing hard at center ice, again, like taking a stick up high, a careless crosscheck, and I smelled wet leather, the undersides of hockey gloves, wet leather—

I STAGGERED ABOUT ON MY FEET, unsure of how I got there or how to move my feet.

I kept talking to my feet. Move, damn it. And they did, like a baby walking for the first time, halting steps.

The hydrotherapy room.

And it wasn't white.

I didn't feel like a slalom skier fighting snow glare, because everything was red, but not the dark red of tinctured maple syrup, instead this was a brighter color, the landscape converted into Andy Warhol pop-art.

Sal stood across from me. His arms swung in front of him, swaying axes. The ends of his beard were the red of a hot sun slipping beyond the horizon.

We didn't have a thing on.

Sal's arms kept swaying, as he leaned forward, the lower part of his face loose and jutted as if his jaw were unhinged.

Nobody else was in the room. They must have been in the paneled windows above us, looking down, taking notes. Maybe they were even filming the event for Wide World of Sports.

Airedale's voice squawked across the intercom. It was the caw-caw of a crow with laryngitis.

Trust him to be unable to shut the fuck up. Mr. Soliloquy.

The doors were locked, he said. There was no exit.

And now Airedale too was quoting John Donne. Talk about the power of an attorney.

I surveyed the room. A high ceiling, windows with bars, six tubs, with foam guns and nozzles for whirlpool comfort. Four shower stalls, open with sliding glass to our left, and the two locked exits with door handles that resembled submarine hatches.

He was still quoting Donne. He finally stopped. In five minutes, Airedale full of faux stentorian glee, said the Red 45 they had shot us full of will have taken effect and we will be transformed to our primordial ancestors and we will kill each other, like the story of the frog and the scorpion going across the lake and the scorpion needs the frog to get across but he stings him anyway and the two drown.

"I know the story," I shouted. Jesus Christ. Shut the fuck up.

"They drown, and when asked why? The scorpion said, 'Because it's my nature.'" He laughed. He just couldn't resist finishing stories. Some guys are real control freaks. "Your nature is to hunt, to gather, to kill. To tear off each other's faces."

That's what he was looking forward to, from this freak show that we were a part of. He laughed, caw-cawing as if fighting a cold.

To tell you the truth, I'd rather hear him quoting Donne.

But my thinking was solid. I hadn't reverted to an animal. I was still so cerebral, less instinctual. "I think we've come a long way since frogs and scorpions ruled the earth," I said.

"Droll, very droll. Mr. Fuller. Let's see who's laughing in five minutes."

No doubt, this was an experiment to see how potent their new improved Red 45 was.

Sweat formed across the top of Sal's upper lip and he snarled, the sounds coming up from deep inside him, and he lumbered toward me.

He definitely wasn't cerebral anymore.

I moved quickly, dancing, avoiding, running to the glass doors, then away from them, and toward the hydrotherapy tubs. I couldn't understand why Sal was transforming beyond a third face to a fourth, that of the primordial. Me, nothing much was happening to me. My reflexes were still slow, I saw pink roses, and my arms weren't swaying.

At least the Spirograph amoebas were gone.

Sal tackled me and I fell hard, jarring my left shoulder, wincing from an old hockey injury. Sal was on top of me, fingers gouging my eyes. I twisted away from a stubby pressure that felt like the thumbs of heavy boxing gloves. I punched him hard on the chin and he fell to the floor before springing back up.

My punch ought to have done more damage than that.

Shit.

He came at me again, the curled hairs of his chest matted to his skin, those arms swaying axes.

Why wasn't I filled with hate?

He was? Why not I?

We grappled with the back of each other's necks, his hands hooks, scratching, tearing, tine fork lines across my skin, like Bobby's face, and pictures of Nancy, and I tried talking to Sal, we don't have to do this, but his rational id had punched the clock, breaking it, minutes ago.

His hands stiffened around my neck.

My lungs were tongues of flame.

And I felt my father's hands on my neck, as he pushed my face into the bed, and told me to stay quiet, this wouldn't hurt, and this is how we show our love, a secret kind of love, the room full of beer and cigarettes, his fingers like Sal's fingers, boxing gloves, and a shuddering stickiness against my hip and thigh.

"Sal." I stomped on the instep of one of his feet. He let go, and then I kneed him, hard, in the crotch. He collapsed like a heavy canvas feed sack. I ran for the hydrotherapy tub. A foam gun. Shit, I hope the water's turned on. It was.

The foam gun jittered in my hands.

Sal clambered to his feet, arms swaying.

He raced toward the gun.

I fired. Foam, ropes of soap suds, arced the air and he stumbled and fell, tangled in the slippery mess.

With my other hand I reached for the spray gun and alternated blast after blast of the two weapons, at his chest, propelling him back, farther back, and he toppled, hitting his head on the edge of one of the tubs, ropes of foam all around him.

He wasn't moving.

I swayed and fell in the foamy suds and laughed. I laughed. And laughed.

And then I wondered who it was who was laughing because

it didn't feel like me anymore.

I WOKE UP AND I COULD SMELL IT. Turpentine. Paint.

There was no chair. Just me and a mattress. I was in their secret lab, the one on the drop floor. Where was Sal?

A door opened followed by light that glinted and then died.

The red was almost an orange and yellow now. My eyes didn't hurt as much when I blinked them or held them shut.

Airedale, his blazer now a completely different color, the three-crowns on his breast as pointed as ever, wobbled into the room, limping like a twisted letter I. Behind him, Leila, carrying a tray with two hypodermics, cotton swabs, gauzes and tape.

"Well, that didn't quite go as we expected, now did it?" He was talking as if giving yet another soliloquy. He was no Edmund.

But I was feeling a little bit like Lear. "Sorry to disappoint." I guess, the new Red 45 wasn't up to the old standards, I said.

"Both of you should be dead."

"It's nice to see I have clothes on today." It was the first time I noticed. I was in hospital scrubs.

"Your resistance interests me, Mr. Fuller. Sal turned primordial. You didn't? Why? What kind of will power do you have?"

"Willpower? Shit. I never finished a crossword puzzle in my life—"

"Let's see how strong your will is."

"Another test?"

He pointed at the tray in Leila's arms. Two needles. One full of enough Red 45 to turn me into an ape-man, possibly causing me to kill myself, as if I were the scorpion and the frog rolled into one. The other needle Heroin. Pure. Uncut. Mainline that and I'd be dead within minutes. Which of the two will I choose? He tapped his chin, grinned and nodded. His nose looked slick in the orange light. "I'm providing you with a possible exit strategy." He threw back his head and laughed.

I suspected that the heart of this experiment was to see if a person under enough Red 45 could actually tear himself to death.

The way these sickos got their kicks.

"Yes, kicks." Another laugh. He smiled. "Think over your options. I'll be back in five." He laughed again and told Leila to watch me until he returned. He left the room.

Leila pulled out a gun. It was my snub-nosed .38. I recognized the grip tape on the handle and nick on the barrel's edging.

I sat on the mattress.

Leila held the tray. Option A or B.

"What would you choose to do," I said, thinking myself a regular smart-ass.

"Fight. And get out of here."

"Huh?"

She smiled, her lips parting slightly, and she nudged close the door behind her. The Red 45 she had been administering to me was a low, low dose. It was primarily a saline solution.

"That's why the red migraines haven't been as dark as—"

She nodded.

The room was yellow-orange right about now. But Sal, he had been given the full treatment.

"Yes," she mumbled, looking away. "I never thought they'd have the two of you fight." She shook her head. "I'm sorry I put you to such a disadvantage." Her voice was no longer a whisper lost in a tunnel.

"Is Sal still alive?"

He was. After finishing with me, they were about to make him the same offer. Only Sal wasn't in his right mind. He was lost, full of primordial wanderings and incomprehensible mumbling. And he couldn't remember a goddamn thing.

By contrast, the low dose of drugs caused me to come to terms with things I had conveniently repressed, forced away, incidents with my father that I wanted to confess to her, encounters that ended once I reached puberty and got stronger, excelling at hockey.

The game gave control over my body.

"You're nowhere as weak as Cliff expects you to be," she said. "Use that to your advantage." Yes, the hypodermic on the left of the tray was a suicide bomb, pure heroin, but that on the right wasn't full of Red 45, but enough of a knockout elixir to render someone unconscious for hours. Her plan: when Airedale returns, stab him with the hypo.

"What if he has company?"

She pointed at the gun in her hand.

"Why not just give me the goddamn gun?"

"Because it's empty." No one else knew the gun was empty but Cliff. "Cliff didn't trust me with a loaded gun, but he figured you wouldn't risk it."

"This is fucked up."

"You want to know what's fucked up?"

I was surprised by her language. I liked it. "What's fucked up?"

They filmed our fight, mine and Sal's, from the Opticon room upstairs. All the time, Dr. Williams sat forward in her chair, fingertips by her mouth as if she were anticipating a car wreck at Indy, like Sad Eddie Sachs, remember, dying in a ball of flame?

I remembered.

They filmed murder to get their kicks.

"Where's Cassel?"

He had left the country. And he wasn't going to Sweden, she said. Some other undisclosed place was his destination where he could begin a new life with a new identity. Argentina, Brazil, maybe? Singapore? She wasn't sure. She'd been listening for hints but Airedale and Williams were pretty closed-mouth about it all.

I gave her a look. "Is he really gone, this time?"

She nodded.

"You ever see Denys? The guy in the photo you showed me, the guy with a fleur-de-lis tattoo under his left eye. Lambskin hat?"

All the time. Comes in often around closing. Talks to Gillian, possibly plotting the next moves for N'oublie jamais, she said.

"Did Bobby tell you what he was going to do with the canisters?"

"I hoped you would tell me."

"Is that why you're helping me?"

She reached into her lab coat and flashed her credentials. "I'm RCMP. Undercover." Anne Chevalier was her real name. She was from Quebec City and had been infiltrating N'oublie jamais for months. She was the one in the silver Corvair, gray in the sun, following me. It was also she who fed me additional information about Dawn Stoukas, sending photographs of her and Terry to Stana's *Toronto Telegram* location.

"All to get me to help you, to be part of your mission—"

"Yes."

"I don't like the games the RCMP plays, Anne. I could've got killed."

"A whole lot of other people could get killed, if not for—" Look, we need those canisters, to stop them from falling into enemy hands, she said. They can't duplicate the formula, but what they have created, and Bobby may have hid, those lost prototypes are deadly. Yes, she used me, but for the greater good. She had tried to minimize the risks.

"Minimize? What do you call those low-risk hijinks in the hydrotherapy room, a friendly wrestling match?"

"That was a variable I didn't see coming."

But if I had been pumped full of Red 45 both Sal and me would be dead, faceless, I said.

"Yes. I wasn't sure what side you were on. If you had the canisters would you sell them?"

"You don't know me very well," I said.

"What I'm getting to know, I like." She smiled. It was pretty and disarming.

Airedale re-entered the room. He had a jaunty appearance as if he had just got laid. Maybe he had. "What did you decide?"

"Red 45? What else?"

"Good." The other option, massive cardiac arrest was too easy. He appreciated how I entered into the sport of it all, my fight, my willingness to not be conquered but accept defeat nonetheless. It was another damn soliloquy.

He motioned Leila to administer the hypo and adjusted a loose button on his blazer, undid it, tucked in his shirt, hitched his pants, re-adjusted the blazer. He *did* just get laid.

Leila lifted the hypo from the tray and stabbed Airedale in the chest with it. His hands stuttered and his eyes turned filmy as he reached for her face, thumb in her mouth, hand slipping on her shoulders, and as his fingers flitted, he flopped down her hips, to the floor. I smelled shit.

"Well, that's rather unfortunate," I said.

"God, he would never shut up," Anne said. "I'm going with you."

"I figured that once you went all John Wayne with the needle."

I also figured it was my fight, but Anne figured differently. These were scientists. How long before they realized the switches she was making in the doses she administered to me? How long before they figured out the knockout hypo? It was too risky to stay undercover.

I smiled and said let's find Sal.

"Room six," she said.

Airedale snored loudly into his shoulder. He was a frayed serpentine belt.

We hurried down the long, low-ceilinged lab to the green door at the end. Green. I actually saw the color. Green, not yellow-orange. I was coming out of it. "You know we did background checks on you, Nancy's alleged sister?"

"When the RCMP gives you a cover story it's a good one."

"You're a good actor, Anne. I mean, mousy girl, all retreating and shit, and now the voice of confidence, a kickass professional who just gave Baggy Ass one hell of a sleeper move. Look out Whipper Billy Watson."

She looked at me.

"Professional Wrestling?"

The look intensified.

"Never mind."

We ran down the hall. It was dim and the runners faintly bled red.

Anne gave me back my empty gun, but I really wanted my porkpie.

I'll buy you a new one, she said.

I stumbled against her shoulder and over her feet as we darted along the walls. Her feet looked like a twist of red snakes. I guess the after effects of the drugs hadn't completely worn off.

Sal was in a lot worse shape than me.

If his injections were at the same low level as mine, Gillian and Cliff would surely have gotten suspicious and Anne's cover would be blown. But Sal. In his purple room, with a bookshelf, bed, chair and lamp, just sat limp in his chair, shoulders slumped, eyes unfocused, mindlessly staring.

"Sal, Sal."

I wondered if his world were still filled with red footlights.

I nudged and pushed, but I couldn't get him off the chair he was anchored to. His scrubs had dried spittle on them. A line of sweat, perforated licorice, dotted his upper lip.

"Let me." Anne injected Sal with whatever was in the hypo in her lab coat. He collapsed into her chest within seconds. She eased him to the floor, and seizing the back of his collar, dragged him down the narrow hallway, the runner lights blinking black, every time Sal's massive form passed by.

We got to the end of the hall, the door. It opened soundlessly.

The side street was dark with conical light splashed here and there. It was cool for July, the night air brightening my face. I was drowning in the air, a good kind of drowning, I gulped in more of it.

She glanced up and down the street and said something or other about having a gun in her car. "Wait here."

"What did you mean before when you said you weren't sure you could trust me?"

"What?"

"Back in the lab. You said, you weren't sure you could trust me—"

Well, I did make a name for myself taking photos of people having affairs, didn't I, she said. "It's kind of a dirty business. Divorce work."

I nodded.

"And all for what?" She exhaled sharply. It had got me drummed out of the NHL didn't it? "Why do it, why?"

"A Hi-Fi unit," I said.

Her smile was slightly broken off. She promised to be right back.

I breathed in more deeply, the flames in my lungs losing some of their tongues. Leila. That was her fourth face. A reticent, scared woman, vulnerable, the kind of woman I feel a need to protect. But Anne was strong, in control. Knew her shit.

Cassel. His fourth face was Terrien. I'm sure he had Terrien's social identification card, readying to take on the identity of a person so unlike himself, a kind person, a person who had to scratch and fight for every chance he ever got in the NHL. And now Cassel was somewhere in South America. Or Singapore. Cassel. As a kid, the myth was that the RCMP always got its man. I sure hope they catch up with that creep someday.

Anne was six cars down, leaning into her Corvair. The dim light from a nearby Becker's backlit her shoulders.

The sky was black asphalt. Sal was crumpled up against my knees. He looked odd and lost in his hospital scrubs. I wanted to get him back in his Sloan Wilson grays.

I don't have a lot of friends.

Sal was one of the few.

From the shadows emerged a tall, lanky form, Sgt. Jack Moffat, his brown fedora pushed back rakishly.

"Moffat—"

He reached inside his brown blazer and two shots, sounding as if they were one, nails hammered rapidly, had Moffat falling sideways to the street, his hat tumbling, landing upside down on a manhole cover.

Anne walked into the light, breathing heavily, her pistol low on her right side. She stood over his body. Gray matter was on the street. "He was the mole," she said. "He was going to kill you. You and Sal."

There was a gun next to his cold fingers. She was a hell of a shot. Moffat went down like a marionette that had its strings cut.

Moffat had killed Officer Sarah Linney, his partner, Anne said. Linney had been working undercover for the RCMP, digging up dirt on Moffat, filling file folders with information on his ties with N'oublie jamais.

"Moffat? Isn't that an English name?"

"You don't have to be French to be a traitor." Anne re-holstered her pistol.

I nodded. Sirens filled the sky.

Moffat, Anne said, had set up Sarah for the hit. He was the one who opened the curtains. He was the one who contacted Goyette with her location. She was the target all along. It was never about Dawn.

The sirens overlapped, concussing through the night's stillness.

Soon the curtain would fall on Adora Borealis.

Fall?

I wanted to burn down their whole fucking theatre of operations. God knows they had enough turpentine and paint in that place to make it burn. All of them inside, including my father, laughing, while burning red, burning bright.

Christ.

And I started crying.

Anne hugged me.

She smelled of the night. Flowers blooming at night. I guess that's what her name means in Hebrew, night, and something about that made me laugh a little through the tears.

She strengthened her hold.

I hadn't been loved this way in a long, long time.

11

I was out for three days and then, I was back.

No more migraines.

And Stana was with me.

She fed me soup, helped me get to and from the bathroom, and listened to my teeth chatter as I went through withdrawal.

My body was always cold and my skin looked like a fish's underbelly.

I slept on the couch.

Adora Borealis was shut down. The police and the RCMP found enough stuff to indict Airedale, Williams, and Stangl on more charges than the Leafs had Stanley Cup rings. Kidnapping, attempted murder (mine and Sal's), sedition and trafficking. Dawn Stoukas and a host of other "lab workers" agreed to testify against the clinic and its manufacturing of illegal drugs. The RCMP found traces of black market hallucinogens in both labs. A chemical analysis revealed that the powders were made up of a compound of LSD and several rare components from plant life. Only five of the eight elements in the drug samples could be identified. No wonder, N'oublie jamais wanted those 800 or so packets back. They had no idea what some of the rare elements, resins and extracts were. A search of Airedale's office uncovered a half-ass outline of Guillame's plans for Expo '67, including a rather elaborate analysis of how Montreal's water filtration operates, and just how much Red 45 would be needed to mess up the system.

Cliff Airedale and "Dr." Stangl were in police custody awaiting their preliminary hearing. Indictments would follow.

Dr. Gillian Williams was a no-show. A dragnet had been dropped on the city and somehow she had slipped through. N'ouble jamais had her, in hiding, somewhere between here and Montreal.

Sal was still in the hospital, suffering from some kind of form of combat fatigue.

He couldn't remember a damn thing involving the last two weeks of his life.

Anne Chevalier had checked up on me a couple of times in the past three days to see how I was doing. Both times she wore Capri pants, a tan-colored blouse, and moved about my living room with long, brisk strides, as if she were just finishing up eighteen holes of golf. Her face was fresh-scrubbed, no makeup. I wanted to ask her out for a cup of coffee, but she was probably due to get re-stationed someplace, like the Yukon or something, chasing Dangerous Dan McGrew.

And Gray Davies, the guy who died in the car wreck, Guillame's lab assistant? He lived with Guillame for two years, in an apartment they shared, Stana said.

"Bachelors or lovers?"

"It could go either way—"

"Wow."

"You look better." Stana's hair was pulled back in a long ponytail. She wore slacks and a blouse. She lit a Parliament.

"I feel better. Lots better." A red blanket covered me. I was still a little cold. My feet in wool socks were up on a low-riding coffee table.

"I guess I should get going pretty soon. Back to work. Tomorrow maybe." A trace of lipstick dotted the end of her cigarette.

It was late in the afternoon, my backyard a shimmer of blue lake.

I reached for her wrist and gave it a pat. "I appreciate you being here. Watching over me."

She smiled. "I want to stay your friend—"

Maybe we *could* gain on the distance between us and close it. "You are my friend."

"I know we can't go back to where we were before but—"

But? It's one of those great words that can end a flow of thought or add to it with a fresh set of conditions. But. I was hoping in our case it was the latter. But. "Friends?" My voice had a hesitant catch to it.

"Friends." She took another drag and smothered a short laugh. "I guess I should have asked if I could smoke before I lit up—"

I shifted on the couch, part of my ass was numb, and my left shoulder, from my fight with Sal, was no longer as tight as it was yesterday. I could at least raise my arm above my head. "It's fine." I always liked the smell of cigarettes, the heavy curtain of Rothman's, which my father and Sal smoked, to the lighter varieties, the moody Venetian blinds of an Export A or a Parliament.

"Sal should be leaving the hospital today," Stana said.

"Good. He's all right?"

She shook her hand, fingers stuttering. "Comme ci, comme ca."

I loved the freckles to her eyes, the line between her eyebrows that furrowed when she concentrated, the stern set to her jaw when she's mad, the gentleness of her full lips. "I was abused—"

I just said it. I didn't think. I just said it.

She knew about the abuse, how my father loved to hang me over a balcony in Scarborough, fourteen floors up from the street, or how he left me abandoned for several hours in a car, window cracked, while he tossed darts in the neighborhood bar, or how he smacked me about for whatever he failed at in life: work, marriage, being a father.

We flew kites together, watched hockey, strolled Balmy

Beach. Those were the good times. There weren't many.

Stana knew all that. She placed her burning cigarette on the lip of an ashtray parked next to a folded-over copy of *The Hockey News.*

"No. I don't mean just that way."

We didn't say anything. The smell of the cigarette lingered, suddenly pungent.

And now she really knew.

She moved between the coffee table and couch, hugging me, tears warming our faces.

I guess I needed her to understand that that was why, or possibly why, there was a part of me that held back in our relationship, that couldn't give my all. During sex I feared letting go, as if giving of myself completely to her would be a surrender. I needed to protect myself. Always. There was so much armor covering me, a heavy chain mail of jokes, ironic quips, smart-ass zingers, keeping me from being totally present and mindful. And maybe the abuse accounts for why I was so mediocre in bed.

"You weren't mediocre." She looked away.

"You can't even look at me when you say it. I wanted our love to be passionate. Not sweet." She told me it was nice, sweet, the last time. "B+. That's the best I could ever do with you, B+."

"Don't reduce yourself to a letter grade."

"B+."

"Okay. That seems about fair." She smiled and kissed me on the cheek. "but that's a really good grade." She laughed, wiping tears from the corners of my eyes. Then she kissed my forehead. I wiped tears from her face. She kissed me gently on the lips. "I'm so sorry this happened to you—"

And then we both cried.

"Hey, hey—" I reached for her hands. "It was a relief to tell you."

"How long did it go on?"

"I'm not sure." I looked at my fingers. One of the nails was torn, just like a nail on Bobby's hand after whatever happened on the night Nancy died. "I was eight, nine, ten." I shrugged. "After a while, I didn't count."

She wondered if I were going to confront my father about this. He was living somewhere in Scarborough.

I planned to.

See Dr. Cohen first, talk it over with her, seek her advice, Stana recommended.

I planned to do that too.

"Oh, Hayden—"

She rested her head between my shoulder and neck.

It made me happy.

And we stayed like that for forty-five minutes or so, watching the early newscast on CBC.

I shifted once again.

"You need to pee?"

She'd got me one of those cylinder things from a hospital so I wouldn't have to walk to the bathroom as often. It was difficult to move, my back still felt like it was wrapped in chains. "No, no. I'm good." I smiled. It was pleasing to smile when you knew someone cared about you. "Lower desk drawer. Left hand side."

Stana moved a lot like Anne: brisk, compact, athletic.

The drawer stuttered and she lifted the manila envelope, undid the clasp, and pulled out five 8x10s. She studied them as if looking at an American cousin who only visits Canada every two-three years. "Wow. I was something."

"You still are." My lips were rubber bands, loosening. "I want you to have them back—"

She wasn't ashamed of these photographs. I had captured the fun, playful, sexy side to her, a side that wasn't very present these days. "Keep them, Hayden."

I'm not sure that that was what I wanted to hear.

Mementoes weren't for me. "Sure, sure."

"God, I was so young back then." She took a quick puff off her Parliament. "And my ass hadn't started to fall—"

"Your ass is great—"

"And you, obviously, aren't fully recovered. You're still seeing a lot of red."

"Don't make me laugh or I will need to piss."

"Go ahead."

So I did, sitting on the couch, spraying into the container. When I finished she took it away.

The way I keep desiring a return to Stana, wanting her to come back, to love Stana. Is that a sign of someone who suffers from sexual abuse? An inability to let go and move on, just like I felt I needed my father? Is it healthy to still want Stana after what happened in the prior Stabulas case?

She returned and we watched *Combat!* on ABC. I couldn't wait for the new fall season to start, *Honey West.*

"You just like Anne Francis," she said.

"What's not to like," I said, and then I looked down at my half-torn off fingernail from my fight with Sal and I knew why Bobby, on the night I saw him, looked like he had fallen into a barbed-wired fishing net.

TWO HOURS LATER, AROUND NINE P.M., the sky outside was a dark harvest red, and Babe Migano strolled into my living room, jousting on the balls of his feet. He wore a pin-stripe suit, and the rose in his lapel was jousting too.

"I don't usually make house calls, shamus, but Stana called me. Said you wanted to get a message to Bobby." He sat by my side in a leather chair, removed his hat, and balanced it on a knee. He smelled of Old Spice. None of that flashy Aqua Velva shit for him. "How you doing, Stana?"

"I'm good, Babe." She wasn't afraid of their past. Her glance wasn't awkwardly avoiding him.

"Good, good. That article you wrote about unfair wages for

women—" He pointed a ringed finger that resembled a scorpion's tale. "My niece loved it. Said it was about time. A real woman's libber, that broad." The seven or eight rings were soundless.

"How's Athol?" I interrupted, a slight edge to my voice.

"You're being a little salty, shamus. And you're making me sensitive again." He smiled, his face glowing with the confidence of a music-hall impresario. "Just to ease your mind. There's nothing going on between me and Stana. That's over."

They had been partners in the past, planting evidence, setting me up to discover overdetermined outcomes. False leads under a toupee.

Stana nodded, her looks at me, him, steady. "Over." It was a very quiet utterance full of mild conviction.

"Athol?" Babe shrugged. "Let's just say he's no longer driving the yellow Buick." That car was a block and a half long.

"He's dead?"

"No." Babe wiped away a laugh with the back of a hand. "Like I said, he's no longer driving the car. It's all Lou, 24–7."

Lou Fortunado. Babe's other bodyguard. "Where's Lou?" I missed our fine chatter about the latest plays in Toronto's burgeoning theatre scene.

"He's in love. Typical fella. Head over heels about some doll and the boys never see him anymore. Doesn't shoot pool. Doesn't bowl—"

I nodded.

Athol, bowler in his hands, had apologized to Babe for moonlighting, making side money. He knew Cassel in the American Hockey League. They played in Providence, for a while, roommates on the road, before Athol got the call-up with Boston. Anyway, while holed up in Adora Borealis, Cassel got in touch with Athol, and one conversation led to another, and Athol confessed to beating Brian "Spinner" Terrien to death, on orders from me, Migano, and how they threw his body in a field, and that's when Cassel decided to become Terrien. They had similar bone structure, Bab said.

Drs. Airedale and Williams agreed and performed the plastic surgery and now Cassel's walking this land as Terrien.

Just great. Terrien becomes a fourth face for a sadistic piece of shit like Cassel, I said.

Migano shrugged. "I know it."

But it was a guilt we all three have to carry. We know the truth. I saw Terrien die. Stana, accidently, set up the death. Neither of us could report it because Babe would kill us. So all three of us keep breathing, living this horrible lie, while a faux Terrien walks, possibly, alongside us.

"It doesn't seem right. A nice guy like Terrien inhabited by Cassel," Stana said.

"Right or not that's how the dice rolled," Babe said. He leaned forward in his chair. The leather squeaked a little. Hank Mobley with Philly Joe Jones on drums was playing the last set at White Heat. He had to catch it, so let's hurry things along.

"Hank Mobley?" I was jealous. I wanted to join Babe for the set, but Stana said no, I was still pissing in a container. I was in no condition to go out.

"Well, you two sure have got comfortable with one another again." Migano glanced back and forth between us.

"We're just friends," she said.

"And I'm just a businessman." He laughed and pointed the finger crowded with rings at me. "It's funny when I make that joke. You make it, Hayden, and I get sensitive." He laughed again. "Ever find that cache of Red 45?"

"No," I said.

"What message do you want me to get to Bobby?"

"Tell him he didn't kill Nancy. Cassel did. Airedale and Gillian practically admitted as much when Cliff was threatening to shoot me up with Red 45." I rubbed the edges of my mouth. "You know how people get when they think you're about to take your final taxi? They bloviate, go on and on."

Airedale was a pretentious set of bagpipes.

Anyway, my teeth were sore and my body cold. I pulled the blanket around me tightly. You, see, Babe, it was partial payment for the surgery, a kind of sick experiment, I said. They wanted to see how powerful the drug was, how much it loosened up inhibitions and filled our receptors with enough anger and hate to bring about action. Nancy was being difficult and she knew too much. She'd become expendable after she'd talked to Stana. Maybe she was going to tell Stana more than what they wanted out there. The kicker. They filmed it. I'm pretty sure. Gillian's into that, she gets her sexual kicks out of hurting, killing people. If I could just get my hands on that film. Anyway, Bobby, medicated on Blue 27, must have stumbled on Cassel's kill at Nancy's apartment. Remember now, Bobby out of his own sickly obsessions or need to protect Nancy had been following her. On the night she was murdered Bobby stumbled upon Cassel, out of his mind on Red 45, killing Nancy, that's why Bobby was all cut-up, his fingernail torn off. He didn't get those wounds from Nancy warding him off to save her own life. No, he got those wounds from Cassel, fighting Bobby off, trying to save his miserable life. I held up my broken fingernail. "I got this from tangling with Sal, and we hardly grappled at all. Bobby's fight with Cassel lasted a while, a long while. Unfortunately, Bobby has no memory of the night in question, a side effect of the drugs, but once he experiences some recall, lookout!"

"Shit." Babe exhaled sharply, his shoulders slightly shaking.

"Cassel killed Nancy. But in a way Gillian did. She made Cassel into an experimental hit man." And they were there. Filming it all.

"You won't be able to prove it unless Bobby's memory returns," Babe said.

I touched my forehead. It was cold. "Or unless I get that goddamn film. But that's how I see it."

"You've proved it to me," Babe said.

"It sounds pretty convincing," Stana agreed. *When all the arrows of a case point in one direction, chances are you need to break some of the arrows and twist them so they point elsewhere.*

That's my theory and I'd been sharing it with her all afternoon. "Tell Bobby." He can quit living with fear, guilt.

"I will." Babe patted my shoulder. I could sit in his hand—It was that big. "This will make him happy." He stood up. "You feel a little cold, Hayden, you okay?"

"Yeah, yeah." It felt like winter in here for chrissakes. I wanted a second blanket.

"Me and Stana may have had a brief thing a while back, but she always talked about you. When she was with me, she was with you." He lifted his black fedora from his knee, put it on, and was gone.

"Oh, hell, hell." Stana ambled toward the desk, resting a hip against it. She picked up the manila envelope. "I can't be this person again, Hayden. She's gone."

"Who says I even want you to be that person?" I couldn't follow her to the desk. I wanted to follow, to hug her, kiss her, but I was too cold to move. "That person is a part of you now, but you're no longer her. I love both of those people—"

"Your teeth are chattering—"

"Must be love." I laughed weakly.

She brought me another blanket, and a third. She tucked it around me, the freckles in her eyes, sad.

I smiled meekly and slipped into a rigid lake, my face trapped for air somewhere between the black cold beneath me and the layer of ice above.

When I awoke, Stana sat next to me, her face, what I could see of it, full of concern, her lips downturned. "Maybe I should stay a couple of more days." She laughed gently. She could go to work but come back in the evenings. I wasn't doing so hot.

I was actually feeling a lot better than a few hours ago, but I didn't want to ruin any suggestion that would keep her around longer. She made even watching Ed Sullivan fun.

"Yeah. That would be great." The room was dark. Slight shadows from streetlights filled out a corner of the coffee table and the side of Stana's face. A pulse line ran through her jaw.

"What was it you liked about me, the first moment you saw me?" She touched my arm.

"Your freckles." They had this random chaos, like so many atoms moving at once, glowing, suggesting all kinds of contradictions and fun possibilities, I said. There was an energy to Stana that I was drawn to, still am, an uncertainty to the movements of her freckles, suggesting that no one moment would ever be the same. I tried to put all that into words and since she was smiling I figured I had said something nice and complimentary. My mind wasn't working so good, and I couldn't express myself as clearly as I usually could.

"I noticed in my pictures, the freckles, you always brought them out."

I nodded. "Like I said, I have a thing for freckles."

She laughed. "I can't believe you talked me into posing."

"Yeah." I laughed faintly under her words.

"You wanted to test out the equipment, see how well it works, before you started working cases—"

"Right. All very reasonable."

"Right, reasonable. Uh-huh. And you needed me naked to—"

"To, uh, make sure I had the contrasts set right." Filming a woman in clothes was much different, in terms of lighting, from filming her naked. After all, I was working divorce cases. Skin tone, right?

"Right. I'm sure the variables between shooting clothes and the human body are different." She turned, her shoulders backlit with streetlight. A smile filled her eyes. "And do you remember that crazy idea you had to shoot me in infrared? That was just a little too kinky."

It was a kind of a gimmicky lens, sentimental. Stana had a point, but—

I pinched my eyes shut. "Infrared—"

"What—"

Bobby, when he was last here, looked a couple of times in the mirror, world weary, tracing the lines of his tired face, unhappy with what he saw. But what if he were tracing something else? "Help me get to the bedroom."

She guided my steps as if we were crossing a rickety, roped bridge in some South American dictatorship. I grabbed my camera from between the wall and bed, set the f-stop to 1.4, and twisted in place the infrared lens. I motioned for her to shut off all the lights.

Bobby *wasn't* tracing the lines in his face.

Bobby was writing words, dry soapy streaks, scratched against the mirror.

In the bald grass.

I motioned for Stana to look through the Leica's viewfinder.

"In the bald grass," she repeated. "What the fuck's that mean?" She turned on the lights. The words disappeared. "Invisible ink?"

"Invisible ink," I echoed. Bobby did bring the Red 45 here, not on my premises, but the house to the left, the one with no grass, *bald grass*, I said.

"Why didn't he just give you the shit?"

"I don't know." He didn't trust me, I guess, not completely, so he was speaking in a metaphoric code. Maybe if he gave the stuff directly to me, I'd make the wrong choice, too soon. Getting seeped in the case, got me thinking right.

I slid into a pair of Keds and breathed deeply. The flames had left my lungs.

Stana did up the top buttons on my pajamas and kissed me.

"I also liked how you care about people. That attracted me to you, Stana. The stories you wrote for the *Telegram*. You write about underdogs. Women being mistreated. You write about our shared need for social justice—"

This time I kissed her.

She seemed to like it.

But I wasn't going to allow myself to get confused over our relationship. If only she'd have agreed to take the nude photos. That would have been a sign that we could move forward romantically, that she wasn't leaving me with leftovers to remember her by.

I better talk to Dr. Cohen, make sure, in light of the sexual abuse I had experienced from my father, if this rush of feelings for Stana, weren't another pattern that I needed to free myself from.

There's a lot of things I need to be free from.

I played with her ponytail, lifting it from the back of her neck. "You want to find a treasure?"

"Yes."

We grabbed a flashlight.

It took only twenty minutes.

There was a patch of earth, not as dry and gray as the rest. We dug black dirt with our hands. I'd forgotten a shovel. The earth pushed and nudged under my fingernails.

All three canisters were there.

We unscrewed the lids. Condom-like packages pressed up against the insides of the cylinders. It was like a red sky and it was all you could see.

I squeezed her arm, between her wrist and elbow. The moon above us was a flipped omelet. Two or three lights were lit on the block. "We got it, Stana, we got it."

"Easy, Hayden, you're hurting me."

"We've got it. Goddamn it, we've got it."

12

The air circled my face, cool then warming, as I came out of a light sleep, sensing some presence in the leather chair next to me.

A bundle of formless rocks breathed gently in the shadows. The mass gently rubbed its chin. Bobby.

“Hey, shamus.”

My eyes were sewn open.

The clock on the coffee table read 2:10. It’s fifteen minutes fast. I pinched my eyes shut and blinked away bits of grit. Stana was off in the bedroom. I heard gentle sighs, rising and falling.

I couldn’t see much of Bobby’s face. The night was a series of darker and darker triangles, diagonal shadows, that only revealed a corner of the coffee table, an arm on the leather chair, a spot on the floor. The marks on Bobby’s right hand, the one gripping the chair’s armrest, had more or less healed over.

“Babe told me you wanted to see me. Something to do with Nancy’s death.” He repeated what I had told Babe. Bobby’s nose in black-angled light looked different, smaller, the bump of a hawk, gone.

“Yeah. That’s exactly what I told him.” Not quite, but I wasn’t going to quibble over a few minor details.

“I knew something wasn’t quite right.” He took in a deep breath. He struggled to fill his lungs. I wondered if he were still feeling the after effects from his fight with Cassel.

"What do you mean?"

Aside from the plastic bag and Nancy's bulging eyes, he couldn't remember a single detail of the scuffle. But much later, as of two days ago, small little pockets of memory filled him with dread, as he remembered sitting on a loveseat in Nancy's apartment, Gillian and Airedale, leaning into each other's shoulders while telling him the horrors of what they saw, how Bobby had tried to lift Nancy's head from her neck. They had it all on film and he better take the boarding pass they handed him to a boat bound for Sweden. They knew a captain of this merchant ship. It was docked in Montreal. "'You don't ever want to see that film,' they told me."

"Why were they in the apartment, Nancy's apartment in the first place?"

He stretched his fingers. They were spiderwebs. "Getting her reaction on film to a new drug—"

"Jouissance?"

"Yeah."

I didn't say anything else.

"It was supposed to be a woman's drug or something—"

Or *something*. "I'd like to see that film." I sat forward on the couch. "It was Cassel. They lied to you, Bobby."

A cheap amusements of lies, everywhere I turned in this case. An uncertainty of facts, a litany of half-truths, and false turns and double-crosses.

"How can you be so sure it was Cassel?"

"The lines on his face. That's how." I placed my hand by my pillow. My snub-nosed .38 was a stretch of fingers away. "Cassel's need for follow-up plastic surgery. That's how. And Airedale confessed as much, suggesting Cassel was the killer, when he thought I was about to checkout, tear off my own face and die from an overdose of Red 45."

He nodded, the bottom half of his face rearranged, sunset puzzle pieces fit into puzzle pieces for a cool lunar surface.

"Think about it, man, think about that night. What really happened? Not that story they concocted and brainwashed you with—Think back—" Cassel was in the room, attacking Nancy. You were following her, came upon the attack, tried to stop it—

He smiled, lips raw liver, heavier than I remembered. "That makes a nice story. Me as hero, trying to rescue her." He shook his head. "But I'm no hero. She died. And even if I didn't kill her, I could have easily done it all those other times I had beaten her with these fists." He held up his hands. They were no longer full of barb-wire scratches. "I'm guilty all the same."

He had created an environment of abuse he said.

Yes, I nodded, you had. The photographs Stana tossed my way a week ago, the ones with Nancy and chipped teeth, swollen face, pouchy eyes, and missing hair corroborated Bobby's presumption of guilt.

"That's what happens when you have time to think, Hayden. I hurt her. Again and again." He cried gently, his mouth quavering. "You find the stuff?"

"Yeah. I gave it to the RCMP." I lied. I had three cylinders hidden in my bedroom closet, in a hockey duffel bag, full of old gear. My snub-nosed .38 wasn't visible, but I could seize it if need be. "Why didn't you tell me about the cache of drugs a week ago?" I rubbed at the sides of my mouth.

Bobby tented his fingers together. Arc light from a passing car flashed across the living room, lighting up the new lines in Bobby's face. It was completely different. Except for the eyes, no-one would recognize him.

"You work divorce cases," he said.

"Yes, I work divorce cases." I shifted, my body no longer cold, my face and eyes tingling with heat. "Divorce. You hired me for one such divorce case." A case that was closed from the evidence I had on Airedale and Nancy. The Ramada Inn. Room 401.

"I know, I know. You got the evidence." He looked away. "But it was all so dirty."

Jesus Christ. What did he want? Pictures of them playing canasta? I sat up, my legs stiffening, The gun close by.

He reached into the lapels of his chocolate-brown suit. The shirt was off-white. He left five hundred dollar bills on the side of the coffee table. The case was dead for him. He was dead. The new face he wore meant a new beginning. "There you go." He pointed at the bills.

Car lights, brighter this time, arced through the living room once more. The whole bottom-half of his face was new, the cheekbones heavier, the chin shorter.

Bobby had a fourth face.

"Bobby—"

"I'm no longer Bobby." He was now Jean Paul Gendron. Advertising man. He had a social identification card, fake birth certificate, everything. Bobby, now call me Jean Paul, had chutzpah. Look, he said, the new face gave him a chance to start over, to find himself, the better part of himself.

"The Road to Damascus, huh?"

"I thought you were Jewish?"

"No harm in keeping up with other people's stories."

He tapped his short chin three times and agreed.

I wasn't so sure about his becoming a better person. Do-overs happen on the playground: hopscotch, tag, hide and seek. I kept thinking about that damn story with the scorpion and the frog and all of us being true to our natures.

"At least I want to try." He stood, hands in pockets. "I didn't like who I used to be—" That person, the old Bobby, should have died with a plastic bag over his head instead of Nancy, he said, and smiled.

And then I got to thinking of that son of a bitch Cassel walking the earth as Terrien. I was pretty damn sure that he wasn't trying to become a better person.

"Thanks for everything—"

He patted my shoulder.

I wondered what they'd done with his fingerprints. Acid?

He pushed himself up from the leather chair, stretched heavy arms over his head. "Would you have used that gun on me?" He pointed at the pillow.

I guess he had frisked me and searched the room before I awoke.

"If I had to, yeah."

How was I supposed to know which Bobby I was getting? What if he'd held back some Red 45 for himself?

"I figured as much." He frowned, his mouth clicking with disappointment. "Maybe you need a new face, Fuller."

"A fourth face? No thanks." I was happy dealing with the three that gave me hell.

He moved in shadows and crossed over to and through the front door, his shoulders, legs, and the back of his head, briefly glinting through triangles of dark.

I waited.

There was no helicopter.

STANA COULDN'T BELIEVE IT when I told her about Bobby call me Jean Paul's visit.

"Why didn't you wake me?"

I shrugged. I guess I didn't want him to be part of any story, to be interviewed for a story. He was so forlorn, resigned and yet hopeful, and I wanted to preserve his dignity.

Stana huffed under the striped towel covering her face. She was drying the ends of her wet hair, readying for work. She set the clasp on her watch and pushed a bracelet in place on her other wrist. "What's your plan now?"

"I don't know. I'm making this shit up as I go." I wanted Guillame, the ringleader, and maybe they, N'oublie jamais, were willing to throw him over for 811 packets of Red 45. I counted the batch. Twice.

Stana handed me the Ma Bell records she had got from Sal's

office. She'd been holding onto them, waiting for me to feel better. "Call the Montreal numbers. Maybe you'll hit the mother lode."

There were several calls made from Adora to five Montreal area-code numbers.

She sat across from me, notepad on lap, hair still dripping from the shower.

I dialed. Breathed in and blurted, "I got the stuff."

The first person paused and tossed a series of French expletives my way. I assured her it wasn't a pickup line. More F-bombs.

The fourth person to answer was the one.

His voice paused, breath catching, like that quiet interval before the referee drops the puck for a faceoff. "What stuff?"

There was something vaguely familiar about the voice. Manly but a kind of whisper as if the speaker's vocal chords had been burned by acid. I wondered if it were Denys Goyette, the man in the lambskin hat. Something about the timbre of the voice is what I expected to hear in the tones of a hit man.

"Red 45. 811 packets. That stuff."

Another pause, and his voice steady, a regular metronome. "You have it?"

"I have it, pally."

"What do you want for it?"

"Guillame. The chemist—"

"I'm afraid that's not possible."

"I hear you lost the formula. I've got what's left of the 'noble' experiment. Irony intentional, pally."

"No can do."

The way he said it, the accent, the emphasis on the first word, was all wrong. "Come again?"

"I'm Guillame."

I smiled over the phone to Stana. It was a nasty smile, and she looked at her pumps but sat forward nevertheless so that she could hear anything else the pieces of torn tissue paper had to say.

"I guess your little Guy Fawkes Day isn't going quite according to Hoyle, huh?"

"I don't play poker, Mr. Fuller."

"How did you know who I was?"

"We have our operatives. All over Toronto. We know you're in contact with your supplier of Red 45, Bobby Ehle."

"Is Gillian one of your prime operatives?"

He said nothing.

"Can't recapture the original formula, huh?"

"No." Another pause. This one longer, his breath catching. "What do you want for those packets? You can't possibly expect me to give myself up. $100,000?"

"Sure." I winked at Stana. "In tens and twenties. And I want the girl. Gillian, your Toronto agent and prime manufacturer of your wonderful product."

I was just trying to keep the conversation rolling. Gillian wasn't my ultimate target. Guillame was, but I had to get in a room with him to bring him in. It was fun to pretend that I would ever take that kind of payoff.

Think of all the jazz records I could own. Art Blakey, baby.

"Gillian. That's my asking price." Everyone should play the bad guy every once in a while.

"Gillian. That might—be arranged."

"You arrange it, pally."

Funny how quickly card-carrying terrorist creeps give up their own.

"I won't meet you in Montreal. We meet on my turf," I challenged.

"Who said we were going to meet?"

"We don't meet, we don't deal."

Another catch to his breath. Toronto is six and a half hours, he said, somewhere on Wellesley between the Riverdale Zoo and Parliament. "I'll give you the address once we arrive. I'll expect you to arrive in twenty-five minutes of my phone call. It should only take that long from your home on Houston Crescent to the Don Valley and the Bloor-Danforth exit. If it takes longer. The deal's off."

I was surprised with how well he knew my city and where I lived. "I'll wait for your call."

"Do, pally."

That just cracked me.

Six and a half hours to kill. Maybe I'd finally get around to reading *The Girl Hunters*.

"Oh, can we throw in a bonus?"

"You ask too much, Mr. Fuller."

"I am a covetous son of a bitch, huh?" Always pressing, that's how I played hockey, on the forecheck, backcheck, banging my opponent into the boards. "I want the film, the one that shows Cassel killing Nancy Drouin."

"I know nothing about Nancy Drouin—"

"Bullshit. Gillian's into that shit. She gets off on watching people die. She threw me and my best friend at each other, shot full of Red 45, hoping to see us tear away at each other's faces."

"She really got to you, didn't she—"

"We're not talking about me. We're talking about you and your cause. You want the stuff. I want $100,000, the girl, and the film."

He couldn't do that. Cassel's cover would be blown. The world would know he's walking the planet as Terrien, and that the "new" face is the face of a murderer, he said.

I smiled, my third face's lopsided leer, at Stana. She wrote down what she heard.

"I understand—"

"See you later this afternoon, Mr. Fuller."

"Yours in drugs," I said and hung up.

I still didn't have a plan.

But Stana had a story. She wrote feverishly. "I got to get this to the *Telegram*."

I nodded.

Once the story was in, she wanted to go with me to Wellesley Street, but I said it was too dangerous. What about that extra gun, the .45 in your glove box, I could use that, she pleaded. I could be your partner. No, I said.

"Call Sal. Make sure you've got backup. Don't go in there alone."

I promised I would. She kissed my forehead and gathered her stuff, the handbag that looked like a milk crate, and some loose papers from atop the desk in the living room. She rushed from the room, fluttering her fingers behind the back of her head.

I dialed my therapist. "This is Hayden." "Hayden, yes?" I pinched my eyes. My lips trembled, and the room dropped from cool to colder. I wanted to discuss my father, my past, things I hadn't told anyone but Stana. "Hayden—?" I exhaled sharply, the phone a heavy gun in my hand. Stana. I didn't know how I felt or if it were appropriate to feel the way I did, still did, about her. The phone hurt my ear. I could feel my heart in my shoulders. "Hayden—?"

Was it okay to love her. Again. Was it okay?

My therapist had told me before that such complications were a part of every life, but what about the pattern of my having been sexually abused, how does that rubric fit or counter this new pattern with Stana?

My inner monolog remained a secret.

I hung up.

And paced and paced and paced.

Twenty minutes later, I called Sal. He picked up on the second ring. "Jesus Christ. My nuts are still sore from where you kicked me."

"I thought you can't remember a thing—"

"My nuts remember."

I gave him the whole setup, the deal I'd brokered with Guillame. Sal promised backup, at least three unmarked cars all along that stretch of Wellesley, right now. Once I got the location, call and they'd move in closer. And then he patched me through to the RCMP and Anne Chevalier.

I got put on hold.

It took a while.

In fucking credible.

Anne Chevalier's voice was breathy as if she had just run eight city blocks to reach the phone. I gave her the setup. I had the cylinders. I wasn't taking them to the meeting, but if she could come get them after I close out this deal, they were hers. I was really close to bringing in the head terrorist, I said.

"You've got 48 hours."

I thanked her for her confidence in me. And, I don't know, maybe because I wasn't sure if I ought to be having any feelings for Stana again, I wondered if maybe Anne would like to go out with me for coffee sometime.

"Sure," she said, her voice full of bleach, making everything bright.

"Maybe lunch too?" I admired her energy, her courage, and I liked her looks: curvy, full-figured, a little plump. I like that. A lot.

I didn't say that part out loud. At least I don't think I did, but my head was sore.

"Hayden—" There was an awkward pause. "I'm not on the same team."

She liked girls. Usually when men asked her out, she'd go on an obligatory date or two, and then let the connections drift away, but with me she felt she could be totally honest, dropping her cover.

"You seeing someone?"

She was. A girlfriend of two years. It was all very quiet. The RCMP frowned upon—

"I understand."

"I knew you would."

"Before you said you weren't sure you could trust me."

"I was wrong."

That made me smile and the back of my eyes hurt with tears.

She promised to stay with this detail and back me up on Wellesley Street. She really, really liked me, she said.

"Thanks."

When I hung up, the smell of Stana's strawberry shampoo and Parliament cigarettes lingered.

I shrugged my shoulders, fought back more tears, I was a fucking mess from that Red 45 shit, and put on some Hank Mobley, *Roll Call.* I hummed along to "The More I See You."

From my duffel bag, I pulled out one of the cylinders and removed three packets of Red 45. I placed two packets in the pockets of my blue blazer, and one in the corner of my wallet.

From the refrigerator I grabbed a Coke. No ice.

I couldn't sit down, or read, my head and fingers were jittery, stuttering with thoughts, emotions, love, anger, betrayal. Maybe I'd wash dishes. I gathered up yesterday's cups and plates.

The manila envelope with Stana's nude photos was no longer atop my office desk. It wasn't in the drawers either.

She had taken it.

13

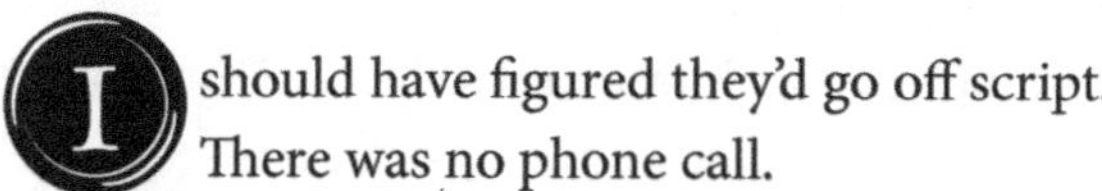

I should have figured they'd go off script.

There was no phone call.

Around 5:15 they arrived at my house in Toronto's north end. Guillame wore a gray hat and heavy overcoat, tied tightly, much too tightly for a hot warm afternoon in July. Denys Goyette, who introduced himself with a big flutter of manicured fingers and the terse pronouncement, "I'm the guy who deep-sixed that nosy cop," sported striped pants, a size too small that highlighted his thick thighs, and a fluffy shirt with Edwardian cuffs and collar. He wore white shoes, heavy curved Carmen Ghias for the feet. He smelled of cologne. On his right wrist was a Rolex so that meant he was a lefty. His black lambskin hat was pushed so far back on his head as if to be in another province, maybe even Newfoundland. The fleur-de-lis on his face was crying.

He smiled. There were shadows between some of his teeth.

He wasn't collecting for the newspaper.

Between them was Stana, hands, lower part of her legs, roped. A small tea towel was crushed into her mouth and duct taped in place. The tape was wound three times around her head and hair. It was going to hurt like hell to remove. Her right eye was a pulpy, swollen peach. Denys had acknowledged with an insincere abject nod that he had done much of the preliminary work on her. So much for not working with his hands.

"Can we come in?" Guillame was all politeness, doffing his

fedora to reveal a head full of iron filings. The hair was a phony, a low-budget wig cast off from the Harpo Marx collection. The curls just had too much polyester bend to them. Guillame's eyes were dark, chocolate brown. His nose generous.

I thought he had it fixed in Denmark.

Denys pushed the long barrel of his Smith and Wesson against my chest and I backed into the breezeway, then the living room, tripping up over the edge of a welcome mat and some discarded shoes. In Denys's other hand was a tripod. Over his left shoulder a bulging tan bag.

"Planning on shooting more home movies? The right profile? It's my better side."

He motioned with the gun, forcing my arms high, and then removed my snub-nosed .38, cracked open the chamber, and let the shells fall, dancing across the coffee table. I didn't like the heavy rain that accompanied their steps. He dropped my empty gun to the floor. A hollow thud, sand in a heavy envelope.

"I got screens, reflectors, in my bedroom closet. Help you bounce the light. Infrared? We can do infrared—"

"Just keep talking smart-ass. You're running out of minute." He smiled and pointed me toward the living room couch. I sat. His accent was French, but the way he dropped the "s" in "minutes" struck me as a masquerade of sorts, like he was giving the Anglo Jew-boy the kind of a Frenchman we outsiders expected to see.

But he didn't know about that young kid who played baseball on the Humber River and cared about social justice.

They shoved Stana into the leather chair next to me, she toppled chest first and tried to right herself. It was hard to do with her feet and arms tied. She flipped about like she were at Sea World.

The rope was white. Nylon. Slick. Easy to slip out of.

Stana shifted some more, rolled in place with her hip, and slouched low in the chair, her one good eye on me.

One side of her blouse was torn, a shoulder strap to her bra visible. I shot her a quick reassuring nod, telling her I had a plan.

Right. The only plan I had was to pay some overdue Hydro bills. Plan.

Guillame plunked a heavy metal box on the living room's low-riding coffee table. The lid snapped open as if it were a bigger version of an attaché case. Inside the box were four glasses, polished brightly. He placed them on the table, neatly. And then he hauled out a huge beaker that looked like a desk lamp of frosted glass. On top of the beaker was some kind of cap, a white plastic gizmo with a camel's hump. Atop the hump were slits, three lines. Under the slits were carbon-silver filaments, reminding me of the inside of a light bulb.

"Filtration." He smiled. Apparently Gillian Williams got her water fetish from this cat. "This filter takes out impurities. You pour the water through the filter and it drips down slowly in the beaker. Like slow drip coffee, only better for you."

"Uh-huh." I kind of liked coffee, water not so much.

"Uh-huh, uh-huh." His voice, a shadowy whisper mocked me. "Don't play the tough, cool cat with me, shamus. I'm here to break you." He smiled again and motioned Denys away to fill the contraption with water.

"And don't try to rush me." He smiled, the teeth small, tight, perfect. "We've got two operatives outside, watching. Anything happens they've got their orders." One of the operatives had a rocket launcher, or bazooka, or some damn thing. The other an old-fashioned Tommy, Al Capone style.

Sure enough the blocky shadow of a T-bird was visible through the shroud of the living room curtains.

Guillame held up one of the drinking glasses to the light, twirled it about, and approved of its spotless clarity. His hands were rather small.

"The glasses look new."

"They are. Every time I drink, I like using, when convenient, a new glass."

Guillame removed a small piece of paper from inside his coat, the belt hanging like a limp beaver's tail. I don't know how he wasn't sweating. "9:46 a.m. Stana Younger leaves the residence of Hayden Fuller." He wagged a finger between us. "4:35 p.m., we abduct Miss Younger from the offices of *The Toronto Telegram.*"

Water rushed in the kitchen.

"You didn't have to hit her," I said.

"Oh, but we did. She's feisty." He gave Stana a patronizing tap on her bare shoulder. "I like feisty."

Denys returned with the filtered pitcher. It perspired on the sides. Guillame poured a drink. Drank. Denys did the same.

I declined the invitation to join them.

"I'll have a Coke when you leave."

"Droll, Mr. Fuller. Very droll."

"Yeah, droll," Denys said, teeth full of shadows.

"Surprised we knew your every move? We've got operatives watching your house, watching you—" He pointed through the breezeway to the front door. "We even know that the girl's been here for three days." Another finger wag. This time he threw in a clicking sound of disapproval from the back of his mouth.

"Hydration is the center of good health," Denys said, the French accent coming and going. He laughed through his nose and drank some more.

"Needless to say—" Guillame held up a crooked finger for emphasis. "You can't have Gillian."

"I figured on that when you brought Stana—"

"And the story she was going to print?" He reached inside his tight overcoat and pulled out a longer piece of paper, this one smudged with typewriter ink and spits of blood. He read a choice paragraph or two from her column, and then crumpled the paper and tossed it beyond the far end of the couch, where it rested, a fallen planet, on some Dexter Gordon sessions recorded in Paris.

I smiled over at Stana, my lopsided lupine look.

She bravely smiled back.

"No $100,000, Mr. Fuller."

"No $100,000," Denys echoed, his laughter hollow thunder, eyes a dark sky.

"No girl."

"No girl."

"We got here first."

"We got here first." Denys's thunder was now an erratic drum fill.

Guillame drank more water. "Where are the cylinders?" His eyes darkened.

"I give them to you, will you let the girl go?"

"Her. Yes. You. I have other plans for." The bemused glow to his face forced his lips to press against one another.

It wasn't pretty.

I think Denys might have broken a stick because his laughter now was like playing the drums with one hand.

"You ought to bottle that and sell it to the networks. I think they can find a place to use you on their laugh tracks."

Denys pushed down his hat, over his forehead, his face filling with downturned angry wrinkles. He was no longer laughing.

It was somewhat an improvement.

"Where are the cylinders?" Guillame's voice was a set of dull knives.

"I hid them in the basement." I rifled through my wallet, making like I was looking for a secret combination. "In a safe in the basement." I kept looking, through cards, while palming, from under my birth certificate, a red packet that had been peeking out of a wallet's corner like a treasured, unused condom. "No, no. I'm wrong. I didn't put it in the safe." I didn't even own a safe. My hands were now on my hips and I slid the red packet in a pocket. I smiled, tearing an edge of the packet with my finger and thumb. "That Red 45 you people gave me sure fucked up my memory—"

"It will do that." Guillame smiled patiently, awaiting my answer.

So damn polite.

"They're in the bedroom closet. Inside a duffel bag." I snapped my fingers, making like my faulty memory was clearing up. I told you I spoke a fluent Brando, a regular actor I was. "That's where—duffel bag." More finger snaps. "Wow," I mumbled. *Wild One* Brando.

My left hand worked the packet, opening the lip wider.

Denys left the room in a rush. He had a low center of gravity, his shoulders moving left, right, as he hustled.

Guillame unzipped the camera bag, pulled out an 8 mm Bell and Howell, placed it on a wooden chair, his back to me. He raised an arm, wagged a finger. "Don't try anything. Remember. My boys outside."

He was arrogant, over-confident. He ought not to have taken his eyes off me, ever, but the camera, filming, was an obsession with him, his narcotic.

With his attention focused on just the damn tripod, Guillame adjusted the legs, unscrewing each, trying to get the three to match up. While he tightened the first leg, I quickly lifted the lid off his elaborate Kool-Aid container and sprinkled enough dust in there to kill a corn field.

A second leg tightened in place.

I had already returned the lid.

The third leg was just where it needed to be. Guillame turned back toward me.

Denys sauntered into the room, three cylinders clutched to his chest.

His pants hurt my eyes. Those stripes belonged on a barber shop pole.

"Got 'em?" Guillame wasn't really looking at anything but his tripod.

"Got 'em."

"Attach the camera—"

Denys nodded.

Guillame set aside the small remains of one glass of water and grabbed a clean glass, doing the same bit, holding the glass up to the light, searching for spots, twirling it, before pouring himself a fresh drink. The liquid was clear, the dusty drugs dissolved. Within seconds half the glass was gone.

He topped off Denys's glass.

Denys too drank half a glass.

Good for him.

"I see you looking oddly at me, Hayden. You've seen this all before, haven't you? The unfinished glasses?"

I had. Adora Borealis. The Northern Lights of Beauty.

"I believe your moniker for that visit was Hawley Walker—"

Shit.

Guillame quickly stepped toward me, stopped, knees touching mine, a smile curving his lips into a twisted snake, and then the trench coat slipped off his shoulders.

Her shoulders.

Naked. Beautiful. Small breasts with pert, pointed nipples. An outy belly button, and a golden hump of blond brush over her privates. "You like what you see?"

It was a bit of a freak show to tell you the truth. That wonderful body with Harpo Marx's hair.

"I am Gillian."

Another fourth face. Bobby Ehle became Jean Paul Gendron, re-born, Saul call me Jean Paul. Anne Chevalier was the mousy Leila. Lenny "The Machete" Cassel was now Brian "Spinner" Terrien. And Gillian Williams lived the life of identity confusion, switching behind the mask of her alter-ego, Guillame Clausen.

Or was Gilliam Williams the fourth face for Guillame Clausen? Who was the alter-ego? Bruce Wayne or Batman? My money was on Mr. Mxyzptlk.

"Fourth face?"

I was talking out loud again. I should have figured on the connection between Guillame and Gillian. Guillame is William in French. Dr. Gillian *Williams*. Dr. Gillian, Guillame. Jesus Christ. Criminals, when they pick aliases for themselves, often don't stray too far from their origins. A Julie Benton becomes Jennifer Boudreau. That's what I learned in my criminology classes at York University, the ones I needed to get my P.I. license. Shit. I guess I should have attended more classes. I got a B in the course. Gillian Willams. Guillame Clausen.

It was as clear as the prosthetic nose on his, her face. "That's a phony, too." I pointed.

She removed it. "A little theatrics." She shrugged. She figured if I saw her real nose I'd spot her, dead away. "I enjoy playing, play acting—" She dropped the nose, a mix of putty and wax to the floor. It rested up against my gun.

"Here's the deal." She moved, spinning around briefly like a runway model, her body free of wrinkles, her ass, dimple free.

She was too perfect. Her skin taut, tight, stretched smooth, as if her very body were sealed up in Tupperware.

She'd had a lot of work done over the years, that's why her face was so immobile. "You're going to make love to me." She hadn't liked how I had tossed her aside at the clinic, and at George's, and later on the phone. Repeatedly. Rejection, doesn't sit well, Mr. Fuller, she said.

"Make love," Denys gleamed, the one-handed drum break returning. He drank the rest of the glass. Poured another.

Drink up, friend.

He sure had pretty fingers. All manicured and all.

"If I like your performance, you live. If you don't give me an orgasm—" She shrugged.

"You die," Denys smiled, as if he knew of my troubles in the bedroom.

B+ with Stana.

And the topper. Gillian was going to film the whole thing. "That's how I get off." She said this so directly, unashamed. Orgasm or not, she enjoyed re-living the experience, again and again. Later.

"I figured that."

"Take off your clothes." The words were a shadowy whisper, as if Gillian were re-adopting the Guillame voice, the one I heard on the phone, from whimsy to whispers, the two faces of Guillame/Gillian.

Denys pointed his gun at me. "Clothes."

I undressed, taking my time, hoping the Red 45 would soon seize hold of their logic and break them down, animals with less intelligence, giving me the space in their impending irrational chaos to act.

My pants and their heavy buckle thudded against the hardwood floor. Pain rushed behind my eyes and the tops of my shoulders.

You already know the nose was a prosthesis. The hair too is fake, a wig, Gillian said, the female voice returning.

There was a charm-school undercurrent to the voice, no doubt practiced for hours in front of the Wicked Witch's mirror.

Her polite charm was as real as her brown eyes: colored contacts. She didn't remove them. Gillian was always a woman. She had passed as a man for years, covering up her breasts with rolls of Ace bandages. How else could she be taken seriously as the leader of a political revolution?

"This isn't about revolution," I said. "That's just a smoke screen. Revolutionaries don't carry around their own beakers of filtered water, for chrissakes." She and her pals liked comfortable things, bourgeois things. "You're a goddamn poser. What's the Red 45 really for? To blackmail the city of Montreal? At what price?"

"You're a smart man, Mr. Fuller." The male voice resurfaced, filling in the spaces of the female with a heavier thump. "Quit stalling. Take off your clothes."

My briefs stuck to my thighs like a pair of wet swimming trunks. But I finally rolled them away from my skin.

I was naked.

"Not bad," she said, one of her eyebrows raising. "I can see that you are, indeed, Jewish."

"Yeah. And I really like rugulech." I smiled. "Manischewitz wine, not so much."

"You don't seem all that excited to see me."

My skin was covered in goosebumps, but the rest of me, limp.

"Remember, I have to come before you. If I don't, if I don't come—" Her nipples were hard.

I tried to think of Stana, naked beneath me, moving together, moaning, she now on top, me underneath, but those substitution strategies were getting me nowhere, all I could feel was my pounding heart and the seismic shakes of my legs. Sweat coated my upper lip like a layer of fast drying paint.

And there was nothing happening down there, at all.

"Maybe this will help."

She doffed her wig in Stana's lap.

Gillian's bald head, beautifully shaped, round, was contoured with no awkward bumps or ridges. She had suffered scarlet fever as a child and lost her hair. It never grew back. She smiled awkwardly to fight back the tears crowding her eyes. "Hair's important," she said. "Especially for girls. It defines our femininity. It—" Shortly after the illness she started thinking of herself in a new way, taking on a new identity, passing for male. "That's where the power is."

Unfortunately, I couldn't disagree with her.

This might be the permissive society, but it was still pretty much a man's world.

"How about this? Will this help?" She placed my hand on

her breast, and guided it there, her wrist over mine. As she was touching herself with my hand, she talked about the past, placing herself here and there. Cassel, Gillian said, knew. Right away. He saw through the mask, knew Guillame was a woman, but he wanted her as a man. "And I wanted him." So she went to Copenhagen for sex reassignment, but ultimately couldn't go through with it. As much as she loved Cassel, she wanted to love him as a woman, not as a man. But he liked boys. To spite him she got a nose job. "It made me girly."

"Uh-huh. I suppose he still likes boys?"

"He still does."

Boys. Fourteen, thirteen.

"He saw me as a boy. He wanted me as a boy. That's why I couldn't go through with the surgery." Her eyes brimmed. "How I did love him—"

Christ. What Cassel was now doing in the name of Terrien sickened me. He was probably on a sexual tourism jag, picking up kids in Singapore.

My hand cramped up under the pressure of her grip, but she kept guiding me, toying with the edges of her breast's nipple.

I felt like a family practitioner, not a lover.

I wondered if I should check her tonsils.

"It was all very confusing, Mr. Fuller." When she returned from Copenhagen, she was two people. Gillian, the Toronto plastic surgeon, and Guillame, the French Canadian chemist. "A quarter of a million dollars is our asking price for Red 45—"

She dropped my hand.

"I knew it," I mumbled. "Posers."

"We're business men, people."

"Right. Giving Canada the business—"

"Today, I embody both aspects of who I am. A woman and a man."

Her voice slid easily between genders, high low, canaries in cages and torn shadowy whispers. She laughed. "Well, shall we roll film?" The voice, male, again.

I shrugged. I just wasn't into this.

Gillian now sat next to me. Her perfume smelled of a sandy beach, and thoughts of water dripping from a faucet like pulled taffy filled my mind as she toyed with me, down there, along the shaft, around the head, under the head. Her hands were cold.

"There we go, starting to get a little jump—"

"Little jump," Denys echoed.

The film in the camera snick-snicked, catching now and then, before continuing its ticking purr.

Stana closed her eyes.

Gillian slapped Stana's knees. "You have to watch. You don't—get to leave the room—"

Stana opened her eyes. We were across from each other. My lips loosening as I was getting hard in Gillian's hand.

My body was letting me down, doing in my heart what I didn't want it to do. I felt like a bowl of soggy cereal. "Wait, wait." I had to stall, anything to stop this. I pushed myself to the other end of the couch.

"This isn't time for pillow talk."

"Who was Gray Davies? What's the real story there?"

"Come back here."

I slid toward her, her hand, cold, returned, pushing against and around the head. "Maybe we need lubricant?"

Denys tossed her some.

What was he, a walking drug store?

She squirted a glob in her hand. "Davies, huh?"

"You lived with him two years—lovers?"

"Yes." What she was warming in her hand was, indeed, Jouissance. It worked on men too. Brazilian resins, extracts, aphrodisiacs. "It'll do wonders." "Great," I mumbled, my Marlon Brando lingo resurfacing. Davies, her lab assistant, saw Guillame adjusting his wig one day, and knew that the man was a woman passing as a man. "Don't ask me how he knew, but he knew." She shrugged, a hand full of lubricant warming me.

I was responding.

"In two years he was my double—when I needed to be both Guillame and Gillian. He would take on one of those identities. Family outing and a meeting with my fellow scientists—get it?"

"Uh-huh."

"Denys now fills that role. When I'm Gillian in Toronto, he can pass for Guillame in Montreal—"

"The phone call—"

"At George's. Yes." She smiled. "I apologize for the dramatic subterfuge, but I needed to be in two places at once. You were getting too close. Denys was Guillame—" Her smile was full of funeral ashes.

"So why'd you kill Davies?"

She drank more water, pressing her lips with satisfaction. "It doesn't really matter, does it?" Another shrug. "Suffice it to say he tired of his role and wanted—"

"More?"

"More."

"Like you and a quarter of a million dollars?"

"Something like that." Another smile of black crepe.

So she killed Davies, overdose of, "well, it doesn't really matter, does it?"

Keep talking.

In his dying moments Gray Davies's mouth frothed. It took nine and a half minutes to let go.

She captured it all on Super 8. In color.

The first death she filmed.

The car accident was later rigged to hide the real evidence.

I looked over at Denys. "This little story doesn't bode so well for you, does it?"

"Shut up."

"What happened to the French accent, pally?"

Gillian laughed. Denys was originally from Kirkland Lake,

Ontario. His father was a coal miner. Denys attended McGill because he had great grades in high school. "He's an honorary Frenchman."

"Bunch of phonies—"

The lubricant had me there more or less ready.

"She'll tire of you just as she did of Davies." I snapped my fingers in Denys's direction. "And then one morning, you'll be brushing your teeth and your mouth will froth over because of some compound she put in the toothpaste. Your days are numbered, pally."

He glanced at Gillian, eyes filling with burning leaves.

"Don't listen to him—" she said.

"You better listen to me," I said. And then I told of a prior conversation, one at George's, and how Gillian confessed that she didn't like Denys.

"I was acting," she said.

"Uh-huh. Acting. You'll get rid of him when you tire of him. Toothpaste. That's my bet—poison toothpaste—"

"Shut up," he said, but the smoldering amber of his eyes was still burning. *I had him. It was the Airedale/Williams setup all over again. Deep down, these two also hated each other. I was counting on that. The oxytocin receptors and anger and hate mixing with Red 45, a killer cocktail.*

"Let's get with the program—" Gillian's eyes colored with impatience.

God, I hoped my people wouldn't be watching over me soon with a lighted shiva candle.

"I'm not doing it. I—I—" *I couldn't allow this, not again, not like before, years of it, three years of it, my father pushing my face into pillows that smelled of beer and sweat.*

"Your mind says one thing, Hayden, but your—" She touched the tip of me. "The little head. It says something else. Let it do your talking."

"No—"

Stana's one good eye was imploring me to go through with it. *Save myself. Whatever it took Just survive, goddamn it, survive. No shame, no judgment. Survive.*

Like I had done before. Like I will always do. Like Dr. Cohen did in Auschwitz.

Denys's long-barreled gun was aimed at my forehead.

Stana's eyes and face were telling me "do it, do it." Buy more time. Just a little more. It's okay. I care about you. Do it. No judgment, no judgment.

"Okay, okay." I huffed, lungs once again full of flames.

Gillian lay back, a couch pillow propped behind her head, the twisting smile telling me now.

The camera snick-snicked, skates gliding across center ice, but something about Denys's face was wobbly and needed straightening. He quickly reached for what was left of his water, drank it, hands shaking jackhammers. The glass fell to the floor, a bowling ball exploding through pins. The gun followed, slapping the coffee table as the last pin of his control toppled. I got up quickly and kicked his gun away. It skipped and slid under the couch.

"Feeling a little funny, Mr. Kirkland Lake?"

I leaned into the punch and he staggered back to the bookshelf, knocking about a floor lamp. Three books shook loose, hitting him on the head. One was Bernard Malamud's *The Magic Barrel*. Something about that title seemed appropriate.

He clambered to his feet, grunting, knocking over the tripod, arms swaying in front of him, heavy axes, his attention, hate, on Gillian.

"How long does it take for Red 45 to kick in, doc? I poured a whole packet of that magic dust into your little old Kool-Aid kit."

She pushed up from the couch, glanced at her watch.

Suddenly she looked very small in my living room. Her shoulders were rounding in on her, her face pulling down the last of her twisted smile.

"That's right, doc. You're the one running out of minute."

Her lips parted, but she was unable to speak.

"You know what it does, don't you, doc? You've filmed it before. Filmed Cassel killing Nancy, only you gave Cassel a small dose, I gave you a whole packet. Look at Denys. Will he tear off your face? Or will you tear off his? Look at him. That's you in a matter of seconds." I smiled. "I know you dislike me, but you *hate* him, being *indebted* to him, the Davies pattern all over again—"

"I hate you, you, and—" She shouted French expletives that quickly slid into a groan of inarticulate babblings, as words suddenly failed her. All of her rational brilliance and scientific know-how had slipped into the primordial ooze.

Her arms now swayed like Denys's.

Before she jumped me, he jumped Gillian.

I grabbed Stana, yanked free her ropes, the slick nylon sliding loose easily.

Denys punched at and tore off one of Gillian's eyebrows. Blood washed over the smooth porcelain of her face.

Harrowing animal mewling, jungle cats let loose in my house, filled the room. Thousands of jungle cats, padding, hissing, clawing.

I pulled Stana from the leather chair and we stumbled, barking our shins on the coffee table. I grabbed my .38, my pants, and we hurried to the kitchen. On the way I stepped over a top of an ear tossed to the floor. And a chewed-off finger.

I didn't know whose ear it was. The finger was Denys. I recognized the manicure.

They snarled and grappled behind us. Chunks of furniture yawped and cracked. More glass shattered. Screams escalated.

I undid the heavy tape wound round Stana's head and mouth. It hurt.

She told me make no mind, no apologies necessary. Instead

she was kissing me repeatedly.

I found extra shells for my .38 in a kitchen drawer. Loaded it.

With much difficulty.

I slid into my pants. I couldn't get the belt buckled. My hands were shaking.

Stana reached behind me and buckled the belt.

We parted the curtains over the kitchen sink. There were two shadows in a car in front of the Cerlon house. The windows of the house were open. Aldo and his wife Sharon wouldn't be home for another forty-five minutes. The shadows in the car had Tommys. I didn't see a bazooka or rocket launcher.

I called Sal. My voice a rush, high and breathless. I told him to get his fucking motherfucking ass to my place, fucking pronto. They'd pulled a switch and our lives, mine and Stana's, were in a goddamn sling. Hurry. And watch yourself. Two boys in a '64 Thunderbird, carrying Tommy's.

I wiped the edges of my mouth.

"On my way. Hang in there."

The RCMP was coming too, he said. I hoped Anne Chevalier could write me up a commendation, send it to Soupy Campbell, get me back in the NHL.

Hayden Fuller, Canadian hero.

My mind wanders sometimes.

Anyway, the yelling, beyond our sight lines, were now guttural screams, a million drums rat-a-tat-tatting, pound-pounding, and then a crack of bones like the tearing apart of a Thanksgiving day carcass. And we quickly got the sense that somebody was no longer moving and never would again.

More grunts. Pleasing. More bones breaking, separating, tearing of skin, muscle from bone.

Stana leaned into me, an arm around my shoulder. My right hand gripped the .38.

We sat at the kitchen table, her hand in mine, fingers crocheted together. I hoped that whoever out there had devoured the other was wanting a nap after dining.

Soon I might have to kill whatever thing was still out there.

Then I'd shower and put on some fresh clothes.

But for now we waited, Stana and me, and waited and waited for Sal Lambertino.

Neon Kiss

Pre-Game

 don't know why I'd thought he'd be there.

When had he not let me down before?

Two Green seats several rows up from the Habs bench. Vacant.

Stana Younger sat in the row behind, a new set of hoop earrings glinting in the glare from the ice. Her shoulders were thrown forward, experiencing every rush, every hit, every pass, shot and save as if she were on the ice herself. It's what I admire about her. Commitment.

It was great to see her.

But those two other seats.

I quickly flexed my fingers inside my gloves and skated half-circles by our goalie, Charlie Hodge.

"We got this, Hodgy," I said.

His eyes focused passed me, lost in the meditative realm of projected successes: a save, the clock winding down, a clear and breakout from our end, and the puck sliding over the checkered line across the way.

The crowd at the Gardens was wobbly rocks whumping around inside a hubcap.

I glanced over my shoulder, water dropping from my chin, tight coins. Near the end Blues, set into a wall like a private WWII bunker, were my former bosses, Leafs owners Steven Smith and Cal Bullard. Both of them were facing trials for illegal gambling and embezzlement. Things were even worse for Smith, who was up on charges of extortion and racketeering. How could they still show themselves in this grand old barn that once housed the likes of Syl Apps, Max Bentley, and Teeder Kennedy? Bunting draped from their bunker, red and white, with a cluster of inlaid poppies asking us to remember sacrifices made.

It was November 11th. Remembrance Day. My father had a cousin who died at Vimy.

The eleventh day, on the eleventh hour of November, the Great War ended. There are Canadians buried in fields all over Europe, Belgium mostly.

I took in a deep breath.

Flexed fingers once more.

The whump-whumping was a rhythmic wash of loud, louder, loudest, and then silence, followed by a slow winding rush of loud, louder, loudest all over again. I wiped the corners of my mouth and smiled in the direction of Jean Béliveau. Far post, he pointed.

I nodded.

Before the game the 48th Highlanders played "The Maple Leaf Forever." Bagpipes never sounded so damn good.

It was great to be back in the place I once called home.

From his bunker, Bullard hunched, readying for the faceoff, absently reaching into his large bag of potato chips, pulling out chips that looked like an ear or two. Sharp flecks dripped from his chin and speckled the inlaid poppies with grease stains. Christ.

Smith, a blur of white phosphorous, his skin parchment thin, slouched back, belching into a skinny hand. He'd been in the hospital last month for bleeding ulcers. Looked like he'd lost forty pounds.

I guess I should have sent him a get-well card.

Their trial was set for January, 1966. And Perry Mason isn't a real cat so these guys are fucked.

I parked in front of our far post, cutting the ice in half, giving the Leafs less room.

Fifty-two seconds to go.

After my last case, involving N'oublie jamais, Red 45, and a plot to poison the water filtration system in Montreal, Anne Chevalier and the RCMP implored NHL President Clarence S (as in Soupy or Shithead, you decide) Campbell to reinstate me, with the Habs. And he did. *Bless his heart.* In the South, such a phrase, bless his heart, can be ironically inflected.

I'm intending the inflection.

Bless his heart.

Anyway, this was our ninth game of the season. Our record: 4-2-2: my stats: three goals, four assists, three fights on the season. Potted my third tally of the year, the go-ahead goal, midway through the second, high stick side on Bower, just under the bar.

Also, assisted on the first goal: Cournoyer on the power play. And, earned five minutes for fighting to start the third. A Gordie Howe hat trick.

I don't know why we call it (a goal, an assist, a fight) that. Howe only has two in his career and the last one was in 1954 for Chrissakes, but the guy's like a regular registered trademark: "The Gordie Howe hat trick."

I'm surprised he doesn't have his own line of hockey sticks.

Béliveau was waved out of the circle for cheating, leaning in. He skated a loose-lined lariat around the linesman and then dimly smiled at me. "It's all yours."

The Leaf net at the other end was empty.

Coach Hugh "Two-Fisted" Farrell had a foot up on their bench, shouting something about streetcars and desire.

Some things never change.

I shook my head, and then set myself behind the dot. Boos rattled, waffling over the whump-whump of cheers. I gave Pully my lopsided leer. He didn't say anything. I had five stitches in my chin from our fight and a bitter taste of tin in my mouth. My stick hit the ice, then his stick, then the puck.

But I didn't go for the puck. I went for Pulford and his stick, tying him up, knowing the refs wouldn't call it, keeping him from drawing the puck back, and J. C. Tremblay picked up the biscuit on the dot, backhanded it behind our net, and Jacques Lapierre cleared the zone.

Horton quickly retrieved it at center and rushed up ice, dumping it back in. Pully crashed the boards behind our net, gathering in the puck, but I wedged my stick between his legs, up against his left skate so he couldn't move. I locked my hand on his sweater. There was no way he'd fall and draw a tripping call, and our Captain Le Gros Bill scraped up the leftovers, saucered a pass to Tremblay, who alley-ooped one to Claude Provost who lumbered over the blue line to center, and rifled a shot into the middle of the Leaf net. 3-1.

I shrugged and smiled at the crowd as the whump-whumping flattened into waffling notes, and then a warbling waterfall.

Two vacant seats.

Stana stood, applauding, the purse on her wrist the size of a large milk crate. She wore a brown pantsuit and a sandy pillbox hat.

The Leaf fans around her were giving her the business, thumbs down, mouthing off, and she mouthed off right back at them. I waved in her direction and then their thumbs were thumbing me down.

Programs waltzed and curved my way, sharp-edged Frisbees.

They weren't asking for autographs.

Béliveau tap-tapped my shin guards. "Heady play, mon ami." He ruffled my buzz cut. "I always told you, you'd like playing for Montreal."

Damn straight.

Béliveau was my roommate and the nicest cat I've ever suited up with. "Merci," I said.

Bullard crumpled his bag of chips into a large rock and threw it at the ice.

I think it bounced off the head of an usher, two aisles down.

Class.

As I left the ice, the timekeeper tapped me on the shoulder and said McClelland Stuart, the voice of the Leafs on radio, had selected me one of the game's three stars. I hung around in the tunnel, fans jeering, shouting frog lover, pea soup, and I just breathed and breathed and looked off in the direction of my father's empty seat.

My shoulder pads felt heavy. My left leg shook. Why was I scared of a curtain call?

Ladies and Gentlemen the third star: Hayden Fuller.

Okay, yes, it was my first game back at the Gardens, and I guess I wasn't expecting a parade or some damn thing, but I wanted to be respected, and the fans were actually cheering me, many of them. Sure, there were some boos, but there was a greater mix of appreciation, and it filled me with thankfulness, and I smiled, pointing an index finger, acknowledging the crowd, our past connection. Nine years I was a Leaf, 458 consecutive games, 107 goals, two Cups, before those assholes, those arrested adolescent playboys Bullard and Smith bounced me to the AHL for "moral turpitude"—I had taken nude photos of a cheating wife, divorce case, for one of my teammates, Bobby Ehle.

At twenty-nine I retired. At thirty I was back.

But not with the blue and white, but with the bleu-blanc-rouge.

My dad's seat: empty.

Bullard crunched back in his bunker, eyes hard, hands across his chest, face dour. Smith slithered in his seat like a long white worm, his Lombardi glasses resting on top of his head as if he were some kind of famous general at the Plains of Abraham or some damn thing.

And then I did it.

I always was a smart-ass.

They had fucked me over. I was a Toronto kid, listened to the games on radio throughout childhood, stood in the standing room only section of the Greys as the Leafs won the Cup in 1951 on Bill Barilko's goal. They took that away from me.

Moral turpitude my ass. Their idea of fun was having naked women pose as human lamps in their office. I was there for such a display of morality. Great guys.

I skated in the direction of their bunker, and their bunting, and their bullshit, imagining it a kraut pillbox, and took a phantom grenade, pulled the pin with my teeth, and with a straight arm gesture lobbed it in their direction.

The crowd really liked that. Standing. Applauding.

They weren't booing anymore.

AS YOU CAN IMAGINE, the post-game Canadiens dressing room was raucous; Coach Blake gave me a strong slap on the back and said something in a combination of French and English about that's why we got you Third Star, to help us beat Toronto. He was excited. Usually he talks to me in English.

I shrugged sheepishly, the edge of my shoulder pads no longer itching my chest, my legs no longer shaking.

I like Coach Blake. No nonsense. Tough guy. But unlike Farrell and his streetcars, Blake wasn't into mind games. He doesn't go to the media and trash-talk us and prattle on about grit and fists. Short, quick passes, *always be moving*, that was his philosophy. Sure, he trashed the other team, but never his guys. Before this game, he said the Leafs weren't as strong as in the past, their run was done. Montreal was the team to beat. Cup winners last year, and planning on being Cup winners again. Hell, Chicago was better than Toronto, Blake said. Maybe even Detroit was better than Toronto.

Coach Farrell responded like a drill sergeant with a run of words the papers couldn't print. Loose translation: "We'll see who has the last laugh tonight."

Yeah, we did see, didn't we?

Dick Bledsoe of *The Star*, his King Lear Fool's hat a triangle wedge pushed down on his forehead, asked me about the grenade toss, his eyes dancing.

It was a spur of the moment thing, Dick. I shouldn't have done it, I got caught up in getting even with the fellas who let me go. It was wrong.

Shit it was Remembrance Day. And what about the honored dead, in hallowed Flanders Fields?

"It was great theater," Bledsoe corrected, his hands gesturing with enthusiasm. He hadn't seen such pyrotechnics since "Terrible" Ted Lindsay fired an imaginary machine gun at the fans back in the 1950s.

"I got nothing against the fans," I said.

"No. And they still like you." Bledsoe smiled, a warm genuine expression that invited you to join him in a beer. He figured the fans wished they'd thought of it, the grenade thing. "Believe me, Fuller, if the Gardens ushers were handing out hot pineapples instead of felt poppies tonight that bunker would be under rubble right now."

"Yeah." I rubbed at the dirty adhesive bandage pinching my chin. There were spots of blood on my sweater. Five stitches.

Then some other reporter asked how it felt beating my old team.

I love the fans of Toronto, love this city, I said. "I guess you can tell how I feel about management."

That got quite a few laughs.

"Hmm." The lanky reporter, with some kind of fraternity pin in the lapel of his blazer, tapped his heavy lower lip with a twisted finger.

I didn't recognize him as a regular beat writer; he was new, and wasn't I rubbing it in, with the grenade toss? I mean, real people, young Canadian men, died in Vimy, and Ypres, all through the dirty trenches of war in Europe. "Yes, I know. You're right."

"It was a grandstand play." He refused to let my indiscretion go. This cat, with his pinched lips, blue eyes, was old school, a United Empire Loyalist, a lover of decorum, blue laws, secret handshake society shit.

And he smelled of money. You really can smell money. It's there in the starch of freshly pressed clothes, and the high-priced cologne behind the ears.

This guy sported both.

"Strictly American Hockey League hijinks. Bush league." His fraternity pin glinted.

"Oh, come on, Franklin." Bledsoe was having none of Franklin W. Whitfield's remarks. I caught the name after squinting at his press pass, a lanyard around his neck. I took a second look. It really was Franklin W. Whitfield II. Who puts Roman numerals after their name? Christ.

He wore a crew-neck sweater vest over a razor-sharp dress shirt. *The Toronto Telegram*. His outfit. Surprise, surprise. With a name like Franklin W. Whitfield II he might even have some American plantation owners kicking about in his storied past.

"Those two crumbs should be in jail, and you know it." Hayden was expressing how we all feel, well, all of us who don't work at the *Tely*, Bledsoe said, his hands flashing about as if juggling three or four pins. "I mean, God bless the Queen, the Empire! Rule Britannia!"

None of the pins hit the floor, but the room filled with a crash of laughs.

And then the laughing stopped.

Sal Lambertino, my old pal, Toronto's top cop, who I hadn't seen much of since signing with Montreal, stood with a felt hat in his hands, eyes full of sadness, Sloan Wilson grays sagging his shoulders. Stana Younger, my first real love and a woman I still loved—we had only spent a couple of weekends together since my time in Montreal and the start of the season nearly three weeks ago—was full of an equal sadness, standing behind him, the freckles of her eyes invisible beneath the pillbox hat and locker room light.

And I knew.

Dad.

Dead.

First Period

The small house on Gradwell had three little trees in front of it, a lawn that was balding, and shutters on the windows that hung crookedly. Inside, it was dank and full of soiled food and decay.

The windows were open, letting in cold air, and an ME, with slicked-back hair and early 60s fashion (black pants, white shirt, skinny tie), stood over the tangled-up corpse, sheets bunching like errant snowballs around legs and arms, glassy eyes full of vague ceiling reflections. Dad had been dead for about three, four days, the ME figured, latex gloves on his hands, a syringe in his right. "Looks like drugs. An overdose." The ME placed the syringe in a plastic bag, sealed it.

"Can't you guys cover him up. At least—"

Stana gasped when she saw what I had seen on the living room couch: Dad naked, left foot touching the floor, lower extremities exposed, a rocket-sized erection knifing the air.

As a prepubescent eight, nine-year-old, I had seen such erections. After mom died.

Sal, biting his upper lip, snapped his fingers, and they covered up Dad, the sheet tenting.

Stana seized my shoulders, hands a heavy, worn fishermen's net. And then she cried. "I'm so sorry, Hayden."

I had been trying to work out things about my father with my therapist. She told me I needed to talk to him about the past, about what he did and why, and I was no longer a victim because I could talk to her about it. That was a first step. My troubled relationship with my father was connected to the man I killed in my first real case, blew his head off. Now there was no time to work out a fucking thing.

Sorry, the ME said. Sam Ross was his name.

We shook hands. His latex fingers felt full of Silly Putty.

And then he spoke quickly about what I'd seen, about methane gas, and how because Dad had been here for a while, gas had escaped up his legs, engorging his penis.

"How long would you say he's been here?" Sal scratched at his uneven Hemingway beard.

"At least three days. Judging by—"

I sighed. "The size of—"

"Yeah." Ross looked away.

"My dad never did drugs."

Ross held up the bagged syringe. Needle marks, inside on his left arm. Fresh. "A deadly dose of heroin, most likely." He shrugged. "Probably uncut."

"Were there other marks there? On his arms? Any sign of a habitual user?" Sal.

"No." Ross rubbed the edges of his mouth. "Probably a first-time experiment."

"Experiment?" Stana shook her head violently, her teeth denting her lower lip. "Hayden's father was in his sixties. Experiment? He wasn't the kind of guy to wear Nehru jackets and hang out at head shops."

"She's right. He was a chain-smoker, a beer drinker." I smiled dimly. All around the living room couch were empties of Molson Canadian. I pushed back my porkpie hat.

On the coffee table was also a copy of *Playboy*, Hemingway's *The Old Man and the Sea*, and Morley Callaghan's *More Joy in Heaven.* When did Dad start reading? He never read. Except the sports page and Mickey Spillane's *I, the Jury.*

Dad wouldn't touch drugs. That shit's poison, he'd say, blowing a river of cigarette smoke into a far corner of the room. Poison.

Ross shrugged at the evidence, the room. There were no signs of struggle, nothing stolen, no cupboards left open. Nothing.

"He has forty dollars in his wallet," said a blue-eyed cop, hanging over Sal's shoulder. "TV's still here. The radio."

"The washer and dryer—"

"No one takes a washer and dryer, Hayden." Sal corrected.

"I know. I'm just saying, I'm being ironic." I shrugged. "He was murdered."

The house may not have been rousted for goods, but it was a fucking mess. Dishes in the sink weren't done, piled high, covered with hardened bits of canned meat, broken triangles of grilled-cheese sandwiches, and three bottles of Coke and an Orange Crush. Dad didn't drink soda pop. Ever.

His choice of poison was Rothmans. The tiled floor in the kitchen needed to be washed, grungy scuff marks smudged the walls, and a filmy layer of gray streaked the inside of the windows. Ashtrays were full of cigarettes.

"Who found him?" Sal asked.

Someone from Silverwood's. A Bob Waterman. Dad was a milkman for them, making deliveries in the McGowan Road area of Scarborough, and when he didn't show for work Saturday, Monday, or Tuesday, Bob dropped by, smelled decay, and came in.

I wrote the cat's name down in my yellow notebook.

It was now almost Wednesday, November 12th.

Sal, holding his gray fedora, sighed. "No other marks? On his arms?"

Nothing. Just the fatal dose.

Three burly fellas slid Dad slowly into a black body bag.

"He was murdered," I said. "Dad was left handed. The needle marks, if he shot himself up, should be on the inside of his right arm."

Ross looked over at Sal. "A lefty—?"

We all nodded.

Sal clamped his hat back on his head. "Start dusting for fingerprints, fellas. This is a crime scene."

"A lefty. The killer didn't know that—" I said.

"Neither did I, apparently," said Ross.

FORTY-FIVE MINUTES LATER, Stana and I were walking down Gradwell Street toward a Becker's on the corner, its green sign glowing. I could use a donut. Maybe three.

Dad wouldn't be buried in three days. There would be an autopsy. Saturday funeral. Maybe.

There were shallow puddles on the sidewalk. It had rained a lot the last few days, and I walked on through them, recalling being a kid, my boots on the wrong feet, stomping about in the splashes of fun. At four, I never could figure out how to tie shoe laces, so I loved wearing boots. One time, Dad got so mad at me for not tying my shoes right—I always made two separate loops before joining the laces and that just never could work out—so he walloped me again and again, saying I had to get it right before kindergarten started. *For fuck sakes, get it right, dummy.*

"What are you going to do?"

"Find who killed him."

"You don't owe him anything." Her pillbox hat dipped to the left, the freckles in her eyes dancing. "Nothing."

"He's my father. Doesn't matter what I thought about him—"

"Or what he did to you—"

"He's my father. Good or bad—" *There were some good times: flying kites on lazy afternoons; walking along the sand of Balmy Beach; listening to the Leafs and McClelland Stuart on radio.* "I *do* owe him."

"It sounds good in theory, Hayden, but what about the Montreal Canadiens?" She stopped and turned my face toward hers, kissed my nose. "You got a good thing going. You owe them, the Habs, for giving you a second chance." Her lower lip quivered. "You owe the NHL the best you can give the game."

And I played great tonight. A goal, an assist.

"A fight too." She lifted the tip of my porkpie.

"That was stupid," I admitted.

"It was."

"Pulford called me a traitor for playing for the Habs. I couldn't let that go."

"You couldn't let that go? What are you ten years old? With your history of concussions—" A thin line skated between her eyebrows. "How's your chin?"

"It burns a little."

She peeled back the bandage. "It looks infected."

"It's nothing—"

"Maybe tomorrow. See a doctor."

I smiled my lopsided grin and pulled her toward me, kissing her.

She kissed back.

"You want me to stay with you tonight?"

Part of me did. I still owned my home in Willowdale on Houston Crescent. *Another part of me sought loneliness, isolation.* "No. Thanks. I just need to reflect, to—but stay with me for a little while."

"Sure." She smiled, and then reaffixed the bandage and kissed my chin. "I love you." She laughed inwardly. "I don't say it enough, but I do."

"Yeah."

I love her too. I think. Dr. Jeanette Cohen, my therapist, however, told me to be careful and not rush things. Victims of abuse live their lives inside a triangle: the abuser (my dad), the victim (me), and the bystanders (my rabbi, my school teachers who couldn't read the signals, who didn't acknowledge how much I hurt, how my shyness and solemn retreat from the world was a signal of trouble, of painful trauma; they all should have known better, they should have *been listening*).

And as a victim of abuse gets older, Dr. Cohen said, they manifest all three sides of the original trauma in their later relationships with others. *Face it, Hayden, at times, as a detective, you become the abuser, bullying clients, manipulating others to get what you want.* I guess, in my first case when I blew the head off of a rapist, I was exacting revenge, abusing him for abusing others. "But he wanted me to do it," I said in her office on a particularly dreary afternoon, the rain spitting pencil streaks. *You did it because you wanted to. You wanted to exert the same power over someone that your father exerted over you.*

Maybe so.

How am I a victim? Now? How am I?

Perhaps in going back to Stana, perhaps you feel this is what you deserve. She hurt you. Maybe you want to be hurt again? And all those donuts you eat—

Okay, okay.

You certainly are a bystander in your relationship with her, refusing to acknowledge her betrayal, to address it.

We've addressed it.

How?

We have. Trust me.

"I really think you need to think about all this, Hayden," Stana now said. I had been out of the league for a year. Montreal was a good fit for me. "I've never seen you happier."

I nodded.

The Habs played Detroit on Friday. That was less than three days away. I promised Mr. Pollock, our GM, that I'd be there for that game. He gave me a temporary leave from the team, to sort things out, but I needed the team, I told him, the safety, the clear rules that the game of hockey provides. Hockey makes sense. My father's murder? "Please don't make me sit," I told Pollock. He smiled with his eyes. A man never forgets the day his father died, never, Pollock said.

"So, you have three days to solve a murder?" Stana now said.

"Something like that." I shrugged.

"What if you don't solve it?"

"I'll be back with the Habs."

"Will you?"

I didn't answer. My PI license didn't expire until the end of December. I hadn't thought of re-upping until now. Shit, I had work to do. "Yes. Yes. My commitment's to Montreal."

She glanced down at her hands, flipped up on her thighs.

I lifted Stana's chin. Dr. Cohen said that me and Stana had a lot to work through, and because my love for her made me feel good and her good, then that love *was good*, and I shouldn't feel ashamed all the time; however, because of her past betrayals involving Lisa Steinmetz and Spinner Terrien, and my vulnerable condition, I might not be ready for a fully healthy, sexual relationship. I laughed when she said that as the pencil streaks continued to fall outside. *When have I ever been sexually healthy?* I can't make women come. Sometimes, but it's rare. *A lot of men have that problem, she said, not just men who have been abused.*

Yeah, well, I never feel that I completely give of myself when making love. There's always a part of me holding back.

That's the victim in you. Feeling unworthy. I know of all these levels, Hayden. I live them every day. I saw my siblings, my uncle, my parents, killed at Auschwitz. I survived. There isn't a day that goes by where I don't feel like a bystander, someone who should have done more.

Should have? You couldn't do more, Doc. Surviving was what you did. You should be proud.

Please don't call me Doc. But your empathy for others is a good first step in healing yourself.

I admire you, Dr. Cohen.

Let's not get maudlin.

Uh-huh, I said.

And we laughed. She doesn't laugh a whole lot, but she did that day.

It was a sad kind of laughter that made you want to cry.

And I think we both cried, truth be told.

I squeezed Stana's hand and told her she and Sal and Doc Cohen were my only friends. It's weird to call your therapist a friend, but, yeah, she's in the club. All those years playing hockey and my three closest friends aren't hockey players.

I had taken Stana to a couple of sessions with me, to discuss us, and my fears of sex, of really being present, there, for the other person. Why was I so afraid to just love and be loved? *Not every moment of intimacy was a test, like the final 52 seconds of a 2–1 hockey game. God, I was good tonight.*

Anyway, we walked into Becker's. The lights hurt my eyes, and I didn't say a word about it to Stana because she'd just give me shit over that damn fight with Pulford in the third period. What was I thinking? I felt a little dizzy, nauseous, and figured nothing a donut or two couldn't fix. I found a couple of cream-filled chocolate frosted ones from Margaret's, and a box of fresh bandages. Stana bought a deck of Parliaments.

I wish I had worn sunglasses.

The cashier had dark eyes and a brown beard that didn't quite match his black hair.

"You didn't get harassed by a fucker with a beanie cap, did you?" He huffed as he spoke. His lower teeth, crooked. He wore a white butcher's coat over a dress shirt and black-knit tie. The cuff on the left sleeve was pulled back.

"Huh?"

"Outside. Crazy guy. Beanie cap, goggles, green coat, long. Pushing pamphlets for some kind of church down the street."

"No, didn't see him."

"Called the cops on him four times this past week." He bit his upper lip. "He's disturbing my business."

His anger was palpable. There was a backstory here.

I asked him if he knew my father, Ira Fuller. Molson Canadian, Rothmans, looks a lot like me but thirty years older.

"Oh, yeah. Ira. A regular. My name's Gus by the way. Gus Carhart. Ira. Yeah, comes in every night around six for the paper. *The Star.* A pack of smokes and a six pack. Rothmans. Yeah, that's his brand. Rothmans. Good old Ira."

"Yeah, well, good old Ira's good old dead. He was murdered."

Gus gasped and looked down at his fingers. They were dirty, and along his right index finger were black, greasy marks of a butcher's pencil. There were marks also dotting his left wrist. "What happened?"

"He was killed in his home. Drug overdose. But he didn't give it to himself. Wrong arm."

"Huh?"

"He's a lefty. Needle marks were on the left arm. Wrong arm. He was killed."

"Who'd want to kill Ira?"

I didn't say anything, but boy did I want to.

"Did you see him come in here with someone strange or—" Stana cut in.

"No. The only strange cat I've had to deal with is that beanie-cap guy, talking about giving up all your possessions for the kingdom of heaven. A regular nut." He shrugged again. "I'm trying to run a business and he's talking to my customers about giving that business to a church."

"Yeah."

"Down the street they are. Anyway, who gives up everything for the kingdom of heaven?"

"Some people do," Stana said.

"Sure, sure. This is a democracy. To each his own. Love your neighbor and all that, but Christ, not in front of my store."

I nodded.

He apologized, mumbled something about so sorry for your loss, and I asked him again if he was sure he hadn't seen Ira with anybody recently.

Ira. Ira Fuller. I have his middle name. Hayden Ira Fuller. It was mom's idea.

"Did he buy any soda pop? Coke, Orange Crush."

"Yeah. Six or seven bottles the past week."

"The past week you say?"

"Yeah."

I turned to Stana. "Dad didn't drink pop."

She nodded.

"Never saw Ira with anyone?" Stana asked Gus.

"No, always by himself." He looked up and then locked eyes with Stana, like he had something to share, just with her. "The last time he was in, though, he bought something kind of odd."

"Uh-huh?"

A box of Tampax, he whispered.

STANA AND I SHARED A SMOKE (I don't know what was the matter with me, I never smoke), walked along the edge of a park to a dirt path above the Scarborough Bluffs, and looked over Lake Ontario, and up, up, the stars, sharp points, the water a black disc with painted spots a deeper black. "Maybe, now's not the time," she said, "but I want to stay with you tonight."

We don't have to sleep together, she assured me, but I'll give these next three days over to you to help you. Before you head to Detroit.

Over to you. It sounded biblical.

"Maybe tomorrow," I said. But tonight, I want to be alone.

She nodded. Her eyes filled with black paint.

I smoked a second cigarette, my head spun cotton candy, the Lake a dark mass of uncertainties.

THERE WAS YELLOW TAPE EVERYWHERE and the smell hadn't changed, even with two windows left open. The house had stilled. I was surprised that the clock on a low coffee table was ticking. I had expected it to be stopped too, like my dad. It was next to a row of beer bottles and an empty of Orange Crush and read 2:17. I couldn't sleep.

The police had left the scene and I had climbed through the kitchen window.

I had to be here. I said it was to find a clue, but I suspect I was here as a son, looking for what a father leaves behind. For a son.

I strolled through the kitchen. A ceramic sink was chipped, the marks resembling small leeches. A cupboard door was partially ajar. Behind the door was a dumbwaiter with small pulleys, wheels, and ropes that I used to play in, pretending I was an astronaut, the basement below Mars.

I pushed back my porkpie and picked up a bottle of Rémy-Martin that was parked by the sink. I don't drink, but in honor of my father, I poured two fingers, knocked it back.

It burned going down.

Goddamn it. *There were things I wanted to say to the son of a bitch that I can't now. So many things.*

I found a half-empty Tampax box under the sink in the bathroom.

No other signs of a woman: no perfume, no air fresheners, no intimates, no pink toothbrushes. Nothing.

But in the bedroom: a large portrait of a blond, blue-eyed Jesus, haloed with enough radioactive afterglow to burn out your retinas. Shit, Jesus wasn't blond; he was swarthy like me, and Dad was a Jew, I'm a Jew, so I don't know what's with the goy Jesus at the foot of the bed.

This had to belong to the woman with the Tampax box. So, she also belonged in his bedroom? Who is she?

And the box was half empty, and if the tampons were bought just a few days ago that meant the woman wasn't planning on coming back right away, if at all.

I plunked myself down in the living room, in Dad's slick leather chair with its worn-down arms and the heady smell of cigarette ashes and beer sweat.

I could still see him there, knifing the air, eyes darkened glass.

The phone rang. I wasn't sure I should answer it.

Béliveau.

"How did you get this number?"

"Information. Where else would you be but at your father's?"

"My relationship with him was troubled, Jean."

"We don't need to—"

"You're not prying. It's—how the fellas?"

The team had just arrived in Montreal, and he was calling from the train station. He wanted to know how I was and assured me that if I needed more time to take the time, the team will get by.

"Jean, Jean, I need you guys, man. I'll be there in Detroit." We had a home and home, Friday, Saturday against them. It was a four-hour drive from T.O. "I'll be there."

"Okay, mon ami. You played great tonight."

"Thanks." I sighed. "The reporters been asking questions about me, my absence?"

"They don't know yet. We covered for you."

"Sure. Thanks for calling, Jean. How's Coach Blake about this whole thing?"

"He's not happy, but he understands. Me and Provie set him straight."

"Great. It means a lot to me." I'm totally committed to the Habs, I said. This was the happiest I'd ever been as a player.

"I know. I wasn't calling to check up on your loyalties, Hays, I was just worried about you."

"I know. I'm doing as well as can be expected."

Am I? Smoking cigarettes. Drinking Rémy-Martin? Breathing in stale tobacco ash and wishing I could have one last conversation with my father. Am I, really?

"Sure. Call if you need anything."

After he hung up I collapsed down in the chair, breathing in the darkness and the dirt, and wondering why Dad didn't take better care of himself, this place, and what's with the blonde Jesus, and then I saw it: the switch plate across from me, there was a sliver of clean wall, bleach white, above and around all sides of the plate's rim. It was an odd detail, but quirky enough to be important.

I snapped my fingers.

Dad had removed the switch plate recently and when he replaced it he over tightened the plate in place sinking it into the plaster, allowing some of the previously hidden wall to show.

But did he just replace the light switch? Or—

I grabbed a screwdriver from the silverware drawer (that's where he always kept that shit) and unscrewed the plate from the wall, pulled out the switch with its three wires, and wedged behind was an envelope.

I opened it.

Why did Dad hide this? Was this some kind of keepsake? Blackmail? Did he know he was going to die?

It was a photograph of a young woman, fifteen or thereabouts, with caramel-colored skin, high accented cheekbones, ragged black bangs, and green eyes. There was a space between her two front teeth and her face was vaguely amused at having her picture taken. It was as if my father wanted me to find it, knew I would.

But why? *To find her?*

On the outside of the envelope was written *11/14/65, Midnight Mass?* A Friday night mass. Where? What mass? What church? And why the fucking question mark? *Midnight mass?*

Moreover, who is the girl?

I really wanted to listen to some jazz right about now: Jimmy Smith, Kenny Burrell, Art Blakey. But Dad was more of a Johnny Cash, Marty Robbins, Hank Williams kind of guy.

I sank into the chair, removed my hat. Closed my eyes. The girl, the mass. This was the goddamn clue I needed, but what did it mean?

UNDER THE COFFEE TABLE, red with yellow trim and smelling of smoldering cigarettes and rubber cement, was a scrapbook. The pages were crammed with stories of yours truly: my first write-up in *The Star*, after making the Leafs, summer of 1957; an article from *Maclean's* on how I'm a new kind of forward, the defenseman as winger; pictures of me potting my overtime winning goal, game three against Chicago, 1962; a chatty piece on how I like steak and noodles with parmesan and olive oil before every game, and chocolate-chip cookies and milk after; a photo of me and the fellas, gathered around the Stanley Cup on a card table, center ice, 1963; my dismissal, 1964, from the league and Dad's heavily scrawled lines: bullshit, bullshit, bullshit. Bright, angry ink.

I didn't know he kept a scrapbook. I didn't know that he followed my career that closely.

Or cared.

The cigarette-rubber cement smell quickly diffused into a kind of perfume, sandalwood, and as the smell took over the room, scrapbook pages blurred into broken chips of ink and slivers of pulp latticed my fingers.

Auburn hair. Freckles. Stana's face. A bemused smile. "Sleep well?"

She wore a short red jacket, red hat, white gloves, and black slacks. Jackie Kennedy had nothing on her. Nothing.

Me, in my crumpled slacks and blue blazer, felt like I had been folded up into a suitcase. My arms, knees, the back of my shoulders ached.

"I thought I'd find you here." She tossed me my gun, snug in its side holster. She had retrieved it from my home on Houston Crescent. "I also thought you might want this." My license didn't expire for six more weeks.

The clock said 6:37.

I shook my head, ran a tongue across the front of my teeth, my mouth feeling as if a towel were in it. I looked at my hands. There was no goddamn scrapbook.

All that was under the coffee table were old copies of *TV Guide*, *Playboy*, and other men's magazines, featuring nudists playing volleyball and then having romantic interludes all over the beach. Of course, they did it on over-sized towels the size of swimming pool tarpaulins.

"Some legacy, huh?"

"Huh?"

"Never mind." I rubbed the ledges of my lips. "Shit. I dreamed Dad kept a scrapbook. Of me. Instead, look what I find." I tossed the frolicking beachcombers on the coffee table.

Some of the pages stuck, pressing the magazine in the air as if it had hind legs. Stana picked it up, quickly fanned pages, and glanced at the volleyball players twisted about like taffy. "That looks really uncomfortable."

I waited for her to close the magazine and then reached into my back pocket and handed her the photo I found. I wondered if she recognized the girl. Was she listed as missing or anything?

"She's Indian. Métis maybe. The green eyes?"

"Yeah—"

Stana nodded. Looks like a runaway. We should have Sal check with CAS, but the face looked familiar. She stared at it again, eyes squinting. "Ellen Reynolds." She pushed back her red hat. Snapped her fingers. "Yes. Saskatchewan girl." She tapped her lower lip. "Regina. No, wait. That's where they took her."

"Who?"

"The police. Took her from her Mom. She has no father. Put her with a white woman."

"The police just—"

"A knock at the door—yes." Stana shook her head, face set in a tight grimace.

Ellen Reynolds *was* Métis. After living with a white family for several years she ran away from them. But she didn't head home. She knew better. The CAS would only take her back to them so she ran to the big city of T.O. and just disappeared, swallowed up in bath houses and shoe-shine parlors. The dark side of the streets. Fourteen then, fifteen now. "Probably a victim of abuse. White parents wanting to 'beat the red devil' out of her. That's what gets them to run. Often."

"Uh-huh."

Stana had wanted to write an article on the failure of residential schools in Canada, but the editors at the *Telegram* nixed the idea. "Some say Ellen became a child prostitute. Here." Stana nervously pulled at the fingers of one of her gloves. "At least that's the rumor, innuendo, dirty hearsay, who knows her real story." Her white parents had been trying to find Ellen for fourteen, eighteen months. "I'm sure that's the girl in the photo." She shrugged. "It wasn't my story, but I remember editing some copy for another columnist."

"Sure."

Trying to find herself in the city. Maybe she found Jesus. Or was just into kitsch.

"Oh, they probably beat Jesus into her. Literally," I said.

"Why's your dad have her photograph?"

"I don't know."

I wagged my thumb in the direction of the bedroom. "Check out the wallpaper."

Stana walked quickly down the hall, pushed open the door, and said nothing. For a while. "Really? A blond Jesus."

She returned smothering a laugh.

"Yeah. A gasser. I think she was here. Ellen."

"I think you're right."

I told her about the Tampax box I found, the bottles full of half-drank flat pop, the library books. *She was living here.* "I think he was protecting her."

"Or fucking her—"

"Stana—" Ellen's photograph wasn't a nudie. It was just a picture. Evidence. Of some kind. "There was a date too on the envelope the photo came in. 11/14/65. Midnight mass?"

"What's with the question mark?"

I laughed. "You got me. Either the time of the mass is in question or whether or not the mass itself qualifies as a mass."

"The time *better be* in question. Is there such a thing as a midnight mass in November?" She tapped her lower lip and quickly shook her head. The Catholics do midnight masses on Christmas Eve, she said. Not on November fourteenth.

"Yeah, two days from now."

"What's going to happen at midnight?"

"I don't know." I shrugged. "Dad was an ethnic Jew, not a religious one, and he sure the hell wouldn't go to mass." *Well, maybe, if the deal got him laid.*

"But he wrote it down?"

"It's his handwriting. Yeah."

She paced, pulling off the other glove. "A portrait of Jesus?"

My shoes needed a shine. And one of the laces was frayed. "Yeah. Overlooking the bed."

"I guess it's okay to fuck if Jesus is watching over you—"

"A goy Jesus." I shrugged again. "I don't get it. He has blond hair and is backlit by a halo the size of a hula hoop."

"Do you think?" She looked away. "Don't get mad, but let's not give up on the sex angle. Maybe your dad was keeping her, the Reynolds girl, abusing her, and she killed him?"

"What? No."

"Why not?" She crossed her arms and returned to working the fingers on the other glove. "We know what he did to *you*."

She couldn't look at me. "How did your dad feel about the Métis?"

"My dad was a lot of things but a bigot wasn't one of them. He hated Nazis."

She nodded.

I was now the one pacing behind the couch, reaching into my shirt pocket and pulling out two sticks of Juicy Fruit. Christ, my breath was awful. I handed Stana one. "I think he was trying to help her."

"When did he ever help you?"

"People change."

There was a long pause. The clock on the coffee table stuttered and ticked. "I guess so." Her eyes were wet. "But this case is really about you, your relationship with him."

"We're not talking about me." A knife's edge slid over my words.

"This whole case is about you."

"It's about finding my father's killer—"

"It's about you—"

I said nothing, breathing in, out. *Breathe. In. Breathe. Out.* The clock stuttered and ticked again. "Maybe it was *his chance* at redemption." I smiled my lopsided leer and she knew the double meaning to my words, that I was talking about us, my last case, and how Stana made amends for the wrongs of the prior one. "You believe in redemption, right?"

"Yeah." She still couldn't look at me. "Yeah. I guess so." She played with the edge of her hat. It looked like a giant steering wheel in her hands.

"We've got to find this girl." Maybe she knew what was going down with this so-called mass and hid and got away. Maybe she was responsible, indirectly, for what went down with my dad. Whatever the case, what did she know that cost my father his life?

"The mass?"

"Maybe. I'm just thinking out loud."

Stana figured we should check back at Becker's, the pizza place next door, and see if anyone had any leads about the girl and Dad. Show the photo. I didn't have that last night.

I stretched my neck. Shit it was stiff. I adjusted the side holster to my belt. "Yeah." My lower lip trembled and pain returned to my eyes. "Good idea." Suddenly my mouth was full of tears. *Everything was making me cry. I wasn't sure I was really fit to be doing this. Avenging the father shit. Leave that to mopes like Hamlet.* "I wish the scrapbook were real."

Stana lit a parliament as we approached Becker's, dead leaves crinkling under our steps, and exhaled sharply. There was a guy standing out front in a long green jacket. On his head was a beanie cap with a propeller, across his eyes, aviator glasses from the First World War. He was the kind of cat if you smiled at him he'd start talking to you, so I didn't smile.

That didn't stop him from talking.

Under the glasses: his eyes appeared dipped in honey.

"Do you believe in giving up everything for heaven's pearl?" His breath, despite the ragged clothes, was Listerine fresh. On his long-tattered jacket were bumper-sticker placards and buttons of various US presidential hopefuls, creating a walking billboard of "I Like Ike" and "Ban the bomb" sentiments. My favorite: a large red button, the size of a plate, with a line drawing of Emma Goldman that said: "If I can't Dance, I don't Want to be in Your Revolution."

This cat was some kind of religious hipster.

"I believe in getting another donut," I said. "Maybe a coffee. Black."

I can be such a smart-ass.

He was not waylaid by my words. Instead, he staggered my steps by humming a tune, plaintive, that startled me with its raw sadness. The song wasn't pretty, but its minor key held Stana and I in its sway and carried us to some quiet place of dissonance. The gaps between the notes were long, as the song's sadness crawled into our skins with its desperate desire to scream. It didn't feel holy, holy, holy the way a hymn should or a poem by Allen Ginsberg. Instead, something was slant about it.

Then he stepped sideways, slightly blocking my way to the store, arms raised scarecrow style.

He was no longer humming.

"The pearl is the way."

Poor Gus. I could see why he'd been calling the cops on this cat. He was hurting biz.

The fella un-scarecrowed his arms, dropping them to his pockets, and hauled pamphlets with the image of a bright sun glowing against the steeple of a church, The People's Way to Christ. I wasn't sure if that was the name of the church or the pamphlet's clarion call, a manifesto on how to live one's life in accordance with letting go.

He smiled. His teeth were straight and a thin mustache dotted his upper lip. The amber lenses to his goggles sealed his eyes tight to his face, making him look like a man walking in a desert sun, and the pockets of his green coat were ballooning with even more pamphlets, folded over like thin newspapers. Thousands of them.

His eyes, I couldn't tell because of the amber lenses, appeared brown. His nose, a bit pulpy.

And then he started talking as if nothing could stop him, as if his very words would change our lives, now, today.

There's this story, see, of this man, and he wanted a pearl, it was for sale, at a market, and the man, a rich man, offered a fair price for the pearl, but the merchant said no, that's not enough. So, the man doubled the offer. No. No sale.

Stana huffed on her cigarette and gave me a look suggesting that she was getting fucking cold. Her gloves were wafer thin.

So, this fella, he goes home, see, and he tosses and turns all night and he can't sleep. He wants that pearl, you know?

"Yeah. We call that addiction," I said.

"Or being horny."

Stana's a smart-ass too.

He smiled awkwardly, pushed back his beanie cap, the propeller slightly turning. "I don't like the man in there. Horny. I don't like a lot of people. People who make fun of other people. Listen in and mock—"

Where was this coming from?

He paused, aware that he had gone away for a few seconds, and smiled awkwardly. "Where was I?"

"Fella going home, tossing and turning. Pearls," Stana said.

"Right." *So, the guy, get this, sells everything, his home, his possessions, all of it, to get the pearl—*

"I'm not giving up my jazz records—"

The pearl is the kingdom. The merchant is Jesus or God. In Matthew *19—*

"It's actually Matthew 13: 45–46." Stana smiled. "I was a Catholic girl. Holy Communion and all that."

"That's right, that's right. I don't know how I got them mixed up. Matthew 13:45–46. Very good. Now, Matthew 19, however, has the best advice, 'Sell what you have and give to the poor and you'll have your treasure in heaven'—"

Two shots, underwater firecrackers, pock-pocked the early morning light. I pushed the guy and his pamphlets aside, told him to take cover, and unholstered my .38. Crouched, and waited for the shooter to hit the street.

Seconds.

The sound of a bus on a distant street.

The smell of coffee.

Nothing else.

"There's a back door," the guy with the beanie said. "A back door."

"Fuck. Jesus Christ."

I apologized to him for taking the Lord's name in vain and he took that as a sure indication that I needed a pamphlet. The People's Way to Christ. The outfit was located on McGowan.

"Thanks."

What else do you say to someone who's that earnest?

I ran along cyclone fencing, down the alleyway, kicking up curled dead leaves, heard a rush and pound of footsteps, a rattle of bumped-up against trash can lids, but saw no one. I ran and ran and ran. He must have climbed behind Becker's and cut through someone's yard.

There were a lot of yards. Seven I could see.

I threw my hands on my hips and breathed.

The back door to the store was still open.

I was afraid of what I'd find.

Stana was already shadowed over the corpse, calling the police.

Sure enough, it was our friend from last night. Gus. Two bullet holes in the back of his head. Brain matter, bone, and remnants of an ear splashed across his lower shelving and the cash register.

Sal Lambertino was on his way.

I asked Stana for a cigarette and we waited.

Our friend had left with Heaven's pearls.

SAL THOUGHT THE ENTRY WOUND and accompanying blood splatter indicated a heavy gun like a .45 at close range. "Bullets probably cut. Dum-dum style. Makes a mess."

I nodded.

The morning light, even for 7:30 a.m., felt like the liminal space of dusty twilight, between night and day, gray with little black scratches in the edges of sky like worn-down car tires.

"Dum-dum bullets, huh? Can I quote you on that," shouted Franklin W. Whitfield II, his blue blazer crinkled at the bottom and a scratch from a razor marking his upper lip. His aquiline nose was straight and his blue eyes intense bits of cobalt. He pushed his way through the crowd, pen poised like a microphone. There was a thumbnail of shaving cream in his left ear.

"What are you doing here, Deuces?" Sal said.

There were two other *Toronto Telegram* reporters on the

scene. No newspaper had three there. *What was he doing here?* Trying to make a name for himself, to be something more than just Deuces.

Deuces. That cracked me up.

"The name's Whitfield the Second, not Deuces, Chief. Police radio. Got one in my car." His father, he boasted, could afford it.

Deuces and his father. I bet they have skeet shooting in his backyard before tea at three. They're pushy people; they don't wait till four.

Yesterday, while we were at the Bluffs, Stana filled me in on Franklin's backstory: he wasn't a star columnist, but what the biz called a stringer, one of those extra staffers the *Telegram* carries so they could fill in wherever the press needed them, and Franklin, apparently this morning, aggressively pursued this story, wanting them to need them, to notice him. "Out on another case, Fuller?" He smiled cryptically. "No Red 45 on this one, I hope. People eating each other. Right out of *EC Comics*." He laughed. "Aren't you supposed to be back in Montreal?"

Before I could say a thing, Sal was between us, his shoulders leaning forward, a vein under his left eye throbbing slightly. "His father was just killed. Give him a break." Sal's voice was barbwire.

"Yeah give Hays a break," said a burly guy in a big wool jacket and garden gloves with holes in the thumbs. A twisted baseball cap perched to the left of his heavy head and flour dotted the bill like a cluster of constellations.

I thought I saw Orion.

Definitely, Taurus the bull.

"Thanks, pal." I shook his hand.

"Tony De Luca. I run the pizza joint. Next door."

"Hayden Fuller, hockey player."

"I know who you are. 107 goals as a Leaf." His head dipped, almost preparing to have himself knighted for his hockey knowledge. "You played great last night, you bum. Why the Leafs let you go?"

"Because they're assholes." Stana's shoulders lifted slightly, crowding her face.

"Oh, I like her." He pointed at Stana. "They are assholes. Hope Smith and Bullard wind up in the big house." He had no idea, listening to the game on radio last night what I'd done on the ice during the three-star festivities to cause such a commotion. Radio play-by-play man McClelland Stuart didn't describe my lobbed hand grenade in the most lucid light. Instead, he referred to the toss as obscene dumb-show pyrotechnics.

"*Dumb-show*, he said that?"

"Yeah." De Luca nodded and spit into the street. "He did." He shrugged. "I think he should just stick to 'he shoots, he scores.'"

Stuart's legendary call.

"Dumb-show was about right," Franklin offered, his hands dancing spider webs. "I thought it was obscene and about what I'd expect from a guy who should still be in the American Hockey League."

It had been a hard couple of days. Dad dead. I still needed to make burial arrangements. And now this crack—

I shoved Deuces.

Franklin staggered and balanced himself against a trash can. A slight smile crossed his mouth. "You see that, Lambertino."

"Yeah. Wind's picking up. Watch your step."

"Don't push your luck, Fuller. I'm not a bunch of lame French terrorists."

I adjusted my porkpie, pulling it down tighter across my forehead and grabbed a cigarette from Stana's deck, lit it, and sharply exhaled.

The so-called terrorist thing was my last case, the one that got me reinstated into the NHL. "They weren't terrorists. They were just thieves posing as terrorists. A dumb-show, if you will."

"Funny," he sneered.

A spot of dried shaving cream was on one of the lapels. "They wanted to ruin Expo," he reminded me. "They were terrorists."

That was the copy presented in the fine pages of the *Telegram*: "Libre Quebec Anarchists" in size 36 font. I wondered if Franklin had ghost written some of that shit.

"You got your bearings, Deuces?" Sal asked. "The wind just died down so you should be okay. Hold tight to the trash can if you need to."

Sal was in rare form.

Anyway, Toronto's Top Cop summarized the initial findings: looks like robbery; $77 taken from the cash register; dum-dum bullets, so whoever did the shooting was probably angry; initial dusting indicates the likelihood of two perps, one gun; found a bloody shoe print, size nine, at the foot of the cash register; all the beef jerky was gone.

"Beef jerky?"

"Who eats that much beef jerky?" Tony twisted his ball cap back in place.

"Yeah. Dead over $77 and beef jerky," Sal said.

"Sounds like kids." Franklin wrote hurriedly. "*Beef jerky*? You think it has anything to do with the Fuller killing? That happened just a block away."

"No comment."

"That means yes."

"No comment means no comment, Deuces."

"Don't call me Deuces."

"How about shithead? You like that better?"

Sal was no Shakespeare, but he sure knew how to turn a phrase. American Hockey League, he mumbled.

"Look, there was over $40 in my dad's wallet that was still there when they found the body. He wasn't robbed, motherfucker."

"Okay, okay."

He took more notes.

The beef jerky angle sure was an odd quirky detail and I got to wondering if it were but a false lead, something to distract the cops from a genuine hit that took place. Gus may have been targeted but for what? He seemed like an okay fella. Was he connected to my father? The missing girl? I took another drag. Exhaled.

"When the fuck did you start smoking?" Sal's eyes were gray ashes.

"Yesterday." I pushed back my porkpie.

Franklin turned to Sal and pointed in my direction. "Is his license still valid?"

"Can't believe you're playing for the Habs." De Luca sighed at the unreality of it all, the instability of a hockey life. You were always one of my favorite players, he said. "Shit, you look just like your dad."

"Yeah." *I get that a lot. I hate hearing it. I was now looking at my shoes. Still needed that shine and a new set of laces.*

"You didn't answer my question, Sal."

"What's that, Deuces?"

"About his license."

I still have my office on Yonge and Bloor, and Sal informed Deuces that my credentials were valid up through the end of December.

"I somehow think it's tied into the Fuller kill." He returned to writing more notes. They looked like the wheels of trucks.

Additional bystanders crowded around, staring solemnly at police tape. They wore mufflers, heavy coats, gloves, and expressions of disbelief. Gus was well-liked.

"What about this guy with the goggles and pamphlets?" Franklin asked. "I been hearing talk about some guy with goggles and pamphlets. A real nutter."

"What about him?" Sal was growing impatient, his right eyebrow arching like the back of a cat on a midnight fence. No one would ever call Sal Mr. Sociable.

"Suspicious character. He'd been chased off a few times—I

hear."

"Harmless, Franklin. Harmless."

"Your Dad, every Tuesday ordered a pizza. Pepperoni and black olives. And not those canned olives you get at Dominion's. Kalamata. Well, the last two Tuesdays it was half and half. Half pepperoni and Kalamata olives and half pineapple and green olives." And, Tony said—

I didn't hear what he went on to say, my hands shoved deep in pockets, mind wandering to a tenth birthday, and Dad tossing pizza slices off the edges of my face, the sticky cheese burning, because I forgot to put his damn twelve-pack of Molson's in the fridge. Nobody wants warm beer at a birthday party. *Christ, don't you know anything?*

Stana bobby-pinned her hat in place with a left hand. Yellow police tape stretched across the store's plate glass on the accompanying wind. "Gus didn't think this guy was so harmless—"

"I told you," Deuces said. "Follow up on this guy, Lambertino. He might be the key to it all."

"Goggles? Beanie cap?" De Luca asked.

I nodded. "Yeah."

"Always wears a long green jacket stuffed with pamphlets for The People's Way to Christ?"

"That's him."

"Hangs around my storefront, too, days, wanting free slices of pizza. I often gave him one so he'd go away and quit pushing his pamphlets."

Sal smiled. "We had to run him off a couple of times last week." He shook his head. "Earnest but not very bright."

"I'm not so sure about that, Sal. The way he quoted scripture and created a possible diversion. What if he was the lookout to the killing or something?"

"Lookout? The only thing you need to look out for with him is that he gets his Bible verses right," Sal said. "He thought the Beatitudes were in *Acts*. They're in Matthew."

Stana laughed, recalling our Matthew 13 versus 19 discussions, then she tapped her lower lip once. "What's this about pizza?" She moved toward Tony, pulling him aside.

"Half and half."

"As in, for two different people—" Her eyes narrowed.

"I guess so."

"You ever see him with anyone." She flashed the photograph of Ellen. "This girl?"

"No."

"Who's she?" Deuces crowding between them, pen filling his notebook with wobbly circles, trucks in the margins. They really were trucks and umbrellas and circles with dots in their centers. "Indian chick, huh?"

"Yeah. An Indian chick." Stana's words dripped with freezing rain.

"Routine police matter," Sal said.

"Never seen her." Tony removed his cap and went on about what a regular riot my father was, always making with the jokes. "Hell, after Hayden got sent to the minors, your father quit rooting for the Leafs. Said they were a bunch of bums."

"I didn't know that—"

"And when you signed with Montreal he became a Habs fan. Every Tuesday he came to the pizza parlor wearing a Habs toque."

I didn't see it in his home on Gradwell. "A Habs toque?"

"Yeah. Oh, there's the truck, pulling up back. Got to go."

The truck was one of those big green boxy things often packed with furniture.

Tony shook hands again and re-iterated how much he missed my tight, checking, defensive game. Hell, your dad was really looking forward to seeing you on Tuesday. That's all he could talk about. "How you were going to kick some Leafs ass." He smiled, waved at the truck driver, telling him he'd be released from the police soon. "And don't get me started on what he thought of Smith and Bullard, the club owners, a couple of assholes. Excuse my language. That's what he said. A couple of king-size assholes."

That sounds like my dad. He had a way with words.

I thanked De Luca again, and then he was talking to some guy with a clipboard and a handcart loaded down with crates of canned sauces and packaged cheeses.

"What next?" Franklin rubbed his hands, the pen behind his ear, like a kid playing at being a reporter. "Track down this beanie-cap guy?"

"Beat it," the three of us yelled, and he did.

The wind picked up, the police tape stretched tighter.

Sal rubbed at the edges of his Hemingway beard, the left side of his face a little ragged. I wondered if he'd just woken up when he got this call about Gus.

"What can you tell us about this church?" Stana readjusted her hat with an additional bobby pin.

"Not much." The building was just a few blocks down, next to a giant Army Surplus store. In the 1930s, the church was a dance hall known as the Neon Park Ballroom. "Held all sorts of soirees, dance marathons, mainly." He smiled. "It was always lit in oranges and greens, reds and blues, and was known as a great place to make out because of the lighting. It was some kind of dream world."

"A neon kiss, huh?"

"I guess so."

"And then by the 1950s it was passé, an empty Emporium. It re-opened in the early 1960s as a church."

He shrugged. Seemed they had a whole compound behind the church, little cottages or log cabins, of twelve or thirteen families, loyal to the church's principles. "People who gave up all to become part of the family."

A cult? Goggles was offbeat, to say the least, his humming edgy, haunting, a sort of plaintive hymn in a minor key that made the hairs on my arms bend back. His singing wasn't at all faithful, almost profane, as if he were one of the damned.

Stana showed Sal the photo of Ellen so that he could take a closer look.

"Where did you get this?"

I told him about the switch plate.

He bent at the waist, laughing. There was a heist case he was involved in years ago that hinged on putting together pieces of a cut-up photograph, a treasure chest if you will. One key piece of that map Sal found inside a floor lamp, hidden under a light bulb.

"That's pretty cool."

"I thought so." It was his first breakthrough as a detective. His first big success. He put all the missing photographs together. Found the treasure buried by the Gardiner Expressway. "You think this girl is connected to your dad's killing?"

"Some way. Yeah. At least that's what we want to know."

And then I told him about the life-size portrait of a blond Jesus. And the books. And soda pop.

"She was with him, we think," Stana said. "And she got out or got taken."

"Kidnapping, huh?"

"Maybe."

"I hope she got out," Sal said. Métis girl. He remembered the story. Ran away from her white mother. "Now there was a piece of work." Sal had talked to foster Mom on the phone. "Thought the girl had gone to the devil. If she said that once she said it a thousand times, 'Gone to the devil.' Couldn't see her own goddamn sins."

"Amen to that," Stana said.

Brother Durgana repeatedly called us brother and sister, even though I'm a Jew and Stana was raised Catholic, and I have no idea and I wasn't about to ask, figuring I might be in for a two-hundred-page sequel to the Sermon on the Mount, as to just what kind of denomination The People's Way to Christ really were. But Brother Durgana didn't seem to mind our lack of attention to such matters. He was giving us a guided tour of the church's interior, regardless. The offices had sixteen-foot-high ceilings and the main sanctuary looked like the inside of a prohibition speakeasy: red brick walls, heavy cedar wood beams, and hexagonal lamps attached here and there.

Close by each of the lamps were mounted cameras, closed-circuit security. The cameras were gray, the size of cigar boxes, and pivoted slightly when we moved. I wasn't sure why the church needed so much security, but I counted at least twelve or thirteen of them in the rooms we passed through.

But the oddest detail: instead of stained-glass windows, or any windows, The People's Way to Christ was full of neon kitsch: blue watery cherubims and red, wet angels and yellow ascension light above and dark blue burning pentagrams below. A red-haired Christ held aloft his heart on one of the walls, smiling, as a green Thomas poked a finger in his side. Across the way, a yellow Jesus was talking to a bunch of orange and green children, sitting within waving fields of grass. Orange. Grass.

There were no windows, no natural light.

Just neon light. And it glowed brightly.

And cameras. And they pivoted, stiffly.

Durgana, hair curly black and wet, full of holy oil, incense, and the smell of fried eggs.

I was getting hungry. I might even eat some peameal bacon.

Besides fried eggs, the sanctuary smelled of mold and fresh flowers.

Kneeling in the sanctuary before an empty cross, an ornate lectern, and a large curtain scrawled with obscure Latin: "Amissum quod nescitur non amittitur," were thirteen or so men and women, bent over, hands gently slapped against the floor. Ten others were standing about, quietly carrying a cross above their heads, moving in half-circles, forward and backward. Save for our whispers, there wasn't a sound. And nobody was looking at anyone, just quietly centering, eyes opened or closed, thoughts inward. Even from our distance of half a football field away, it was clear that beneath their uniformed clothing they weren't wearing underthings. I saw shadows of pubic hair, curves of breasts, dangles of johnsons. The church's followers were gussied up in low-rent hospital gowns.

They even had the requisite loose strings in back that barely kept a gown in place.

Brother Durgana caught my look. "We believe in order to get closer to God, one must free oneself, be in a natural state of grace to feel the presence of God everywhere."

I nodded.

Durgana was wearing a three-piece suit.

And had feasted on fried eggs.

His followers were fasting. No food until noon. It was 10:15.

I guess it was good to be the king.

"I assure you," he whispered, his voice barely audible. "We don't dress this way all the time. Just during three hours of devotions, meditations, in the morning."

I wanted coffee. And a donut. "And you walk around like that too? In transparent robes? For devotions?"

He smiled, his teeth a little too large for his mouth. His eyes black. "Yes. The body is a temple. I'm not ashamed of my body."

"Sure."

I was. Ashamed. I always had been. Hockey gave me some feeling of power over my body's imperfections, its failures to protect me, its moments of betrayal when I didn't want it to respond the ways it did. With my father.

"How many followers are there?" Stana asked as he ushered us out of the quiet room into a lobby covered with brutal neon depictions of biblical trauma: the red severed head of John the Baptist held aloft; the fall of a blue Sodom and Gomorrah; green unbelievers and infidels drowning in the dark red of Noah's flood; a yellow David standing over a green Goliath, a blue foot on his head; a black green and blue plague of locusts, faces covered with boils.

Again, there were no windows. Just red brick, the faint smell of mold, and a sweet, flowery fragrance.

Two cameras, positioned in opposite corners of the room, tracked me.

I waved at one of them. "I can get you tickets to the game in Detroit, Friday night. Interested?"

The camera shifted left and stilled.

"If you don't mind me asking, Brother Durgana, how do you pay for all this?"

Stana was always direct.

The neon art alone, although no Roy Lichtenstein, wasn't cheap.

And the architecture, the sixteen-foot-high ceilings. This place was at one-time a huge fucking music hall. The Neon Park Ballroom. "That's what is was called back then—"

"Well, we're now a church." He blessed himself or maybe he was flashing me signals from third base, asking me to lay down a bunt.

I had a headache right now and I dry swallowed some aspirins.

Stana gave me a worried look.

"Pulford," I mumbled.

Brother Durgana held up a sharp hand like a flag. "We have fifteen committed families, totaling thirty-three members. And we have roughly 70–85 folks who attend regularly who have yet to transition—"

He played with his left ear, in the crease by the lobe. I wondered if he had a bug bite, but it was November.

"Transition?" Stana was tapping her lower lip as she took notes.

"To total commitment. Matthew 19:26. 'With God, all things are possible.'" But in order to seize upon the possibilities one must give up everything.

"And the Latin? On the curtain? 'The Loss that is not known is no loss at all.'"

"Yes." He smiled at Stana, his upper lip quivering slightly. "Very good."

"I'm a retired Catholic."

"Retired?"

She sheepishly shrugged. "Yeah. Retired." Stana considered herself a spiritual person, a believer; she just didn't believe in all of the church dictates (anti-abortion, anti-divorce) or in a Pope decoding God's word for her. "I don't need a man telling me how to think."

Durgana raised a skeptical eyebrow.

The Latin phrase was their mantra, their manifesto. One has to have lived a certain life to surrender from that life, surrender from pleasure. "In there is real power. To accept simplicity."

"The pearl. Heaven, huh?" I smiled, the pain behind my eyes lessening.

"Yes."

I told him about the guy with the goggles, the green coat, beanie, and all the buttons, including "I Like Ike" and Emma Goldman's positive spin on dance and revolution. The latter were sentiments I can get behind.

"Brother Thompson—"

"Where is Brother Thompson?"

"Working the Yonge and St. Clair area today."

Stana pulled out Ellen's photograph from her milk-crate of a purse. "Ellen Reynolds. Recognize her. A follower?"

He tilted his head slightly right and studied the photograph as if an important quiz were to follow. He raised a different skeptical eyebrow, like he was holding back from saying something he might regret.

From the neon sanctuary, a rumbling chant filled the spaces between us. It began in dissonance and then built into a breathy hum, the chant not so much filled with words but notes, a song, like the one Brother Thompson was humming when we first came upon him. And as quickly as the rush of sounds made sense they became dissonant once again.

"What's that?" I asked. "That song?"

A lament, Brother Durgana said, massaging at his ear once again, in honor of our Latin mantra, a sad regret of a way of life that's no more, and the uncertainties about the new adventure to begin. In order to begin anew, one must acknowledge with some honesty the sadness of what is lost: lust, gluttony, envy. With his mantra on lamentations, I drifted to tyke hockey, first game, seven goals, and Coach giving me a pair of tickets to a Leafs game. Dad and I went, and it was on me, me, and it felt good to have that kind of control. This was just before Mom died. We drank Cokes, ate popcorn, and Dad didn't yell at me, not once. The Leafs won the game 3–1, Apps a goal and an assist, and afterwards we held hands walking out of Maple Leaf Gardens. Dad smelled of Old Spice and Rothmans. It was probably the best moment of my childhood.

The seven deadly sins, Durgana said, the wants that are like obesity to our bodies, unhealthy appetites that we crave but know we must reject in order to exist in a true state of oneness.

"And this oneness—what is that exactly?"

"Peace. Contentment. It is an experience that gives you stillness, a feeling of wonder and joy free of the stimulant derived from drugs and sex."

It was a natural, spiritual stimulant. Meditation contains the sparkle of life. With prolonged meditation, he had even found sex null and void. "Oh, I still think about sex, Brother Fuller, Sister Younger, but I don't crave it. Need it. I've moved beyond it."

"And that's a good thing?" Stana wasn't buying it.

His black eyes glowed with some kind of half-life of truth I couldn't quite get a handle on. "It makes life simpler. I have a much simpler life."

He smiled. It was a good look, a face on an election billboard. But there was something about that smile, that he could take it away as quickly as he granted it. "You've both been in love. With each other. How's that worked out for you?"

How did he know that?

Stana and I said nothing, looking at each other, and then the walls and neon boils and orange grass filled my thoughts.

"Life is so much simpler without the trappings of romantic love."

Simpler? Brooks Brothers suits? Diamonds on his fingers? And attaining oneness. That seems simple enough. "This oneness? Some kind of nirvana?" I asked.

"Well, that's a little too mystical for us—"

I bit my upper lip, hard, to keep from bending over at the waist and cracking up.

Stana couldn't help herself. She *was* bent over, laughing through fingers, cracking up. "I'm sorry. It just seems so—so—"

"Absurd?"

"Yes. Frankly." She shrugged. "Jesus was divine but he was also a man. I'm sure he had sex."

"I see why you left the Catholic church." He tented his fingers together. "Biblically speaking, there's no proof that Christ had sex—"

"Can we at least agree he masturbated?"

What would the Pope say to that?

By contrast, Brother Durgana said nothing, lips tightening. His skeptical eyebrows were now incredulous.

"Midnight mass. 11/14/65? Mean anything to you?" Stana leaned forward slightly, angry freckles returning to her eyes.

"Midnight mass. We're not Catholic. Mass?" He tented his fingers, three, four, five times, rubbed at his ear. "Friday, huh?" It's not even Christmas, he said. There are no other midnight masses that he knew of.

I told him about the envelope I had found in dad's wall: the photograph of Ellen Reynolds and the brief note. "Did you know Ellen? Ellen Reynolds?"

I pointed at the photograph that Stana was now holding.

He played at his ear once again, smiled limply. "I must have slept on the wrong side of the pillow last night." He gently tugged at his ear once more.

"Sure."

"Wasn't she a prostitute or something? Got mixed up in some bath houses or sleazy shoe-shine parlors on Charles Street?"

"That's one story." Stana's eyes were full of flames. "She's the kind of girl Christ would have sought out, spoken to, worked with."

"Point taken." He smiled. "We get those types here, too, but—"

Those types?

He didn't recognize the girl in the photograph. Or his own lack of Christian charity.

The bloody head of John the Baptist appeared to be peaking over my shoulder so I shifted a few feet to my left. Now I had the deadly plagues enveloping me, my face full of boils. "She was never one of your disciples?"

"*Followers*. No. She wasn't." He held the photo closely. Just looking at her eyes, he said, he could see it. The lack of contentment, the inability to find personal solace. "She is guided by pleasure."

"How can you tell that just by her eyes?" A line formed between Stana's eyebrows, and her shoulders narrowed in on herself. "Come on."

"I read faces. You two are skeptical." He pointed at me, traced the curve of an ear. "You are troubled. Something in your past haunts you and you seek answers. But first you must forgive yourself."

I said nothing.

"You—" He looked at Stana. "Carry guilt and anger in your shoulders. There's much injustice in the world you want to fix, but first you must fix your relationship with him. Guilt is in your eyes."

Stana now said nothing.

The girl might have arrived one time, weeks ago, sat in the back, but no, not a regular, and he knew nothing of her personal life.

Only what he saw in her eyes.

The chant-sing hum buzzed around us with a discordant beat that felt slightly behind the 3/4 rhythm. Or maybe it was ahead of the beat. Either way, no one was on the same musical page.

"What's Mr. Thompson's connection—how long's he been here, how—?"

"Two months." He held up both hands, rubbed them together. "He took to our practices right away. He's an excellent singer. And a respected member of our congregation."

Thompson had no earthly possessions to give; he was homeless before arriving, so he pays his way by sweeping floors and dusting the sanctuary and laundering the spiritual robes.

Spiritual robes. Threadbare sheets.

"When he returns I want to talk to him," I said.

"We can arrange that."

"Do."

Stana gave him the number at *The Toronto Telegram.*

"You've never seen this girl?"

"No." He shrugged absently.

"Her looks are striking—you'd remember—"

"We've had Cree, Ojibway tribe members drop by—drop in—and decide we're not for them. She might have dropped by—I don't—" He shrugged again.

"My father ever visit here?"

"What?" He laughed. "No. Your father strikes me as a man who saw his life as too practical for simplicity."

What did he mean by that? His words were full of riddles. It felt like a crack. "You knew my father? He was here?"

"I can read auras. I don't need to be in the presence of someone to know them. Through you, I know him." Auras, he said, were like books. If Steinbeck's *Grapes of Wrath* was influenced by the poetry of Walt Whitman, then while reading Steinbeck you were also "reading" Whitman. In reading my aura he could read my father's.

"Auras huh?" I pointed at all the boils and the neon surrounding us, a circle of menace. "Cute pictures."

John the Baptist's severed head was still staring me down.

And David wasn't wearing sandals. I think one of the laces on his blue sneakers was untied. PF Flyers. Seriously. PF fucking Flyers, his footwear of choice.

"A vengeful God. Vengeance is mine?"

"Darkness allows for the utterance of a simpler life." He smiled again. "Life is dialectics. There is no Jew without the anti-Semite. There can be no good without the accompanying evil. We must know the darkness to know the light."

"Sure." That's a lot of knowing. I smiled. "Do you know where I can get a donut?"

AFTER AN EARLY LUNCH of a hot open-faced beef sandwich at one of the diners along McGowan, Stana lit a cigarette and said she was going to check into Durgana's background. How does he run his operation? Who's backing him?

"His followers give generously just to hear him speak."

"Uh-huh," she said.

That cracked me up. "And see what you can find out from the folks that live in those little cottages in back of the church." *Quonset Huts to Christ.*

"On it. Already on it." She wrote down some notes on the back of a napkin.

We saw nine or ten of those huts made of some kind of fiberglass, sort of igloo-cubed Quonset huts. Small, cozy, rimmed in a circle so that they all could keep their eyes on each other. Perched high on two of the streetlights overlooking the compound were mounted cameras. They followed us as we moved about.

"Sure." She picked a strand of tobacco off her lower lip. "They'll be reticent, but I'll come up with an angle."

"Future follower—" I offered.

"*Followers.* I'm going to pretend you're my husband."

"I like that."

"Me too."

We both looked at our plates, listening for sounds round us.

A short-order cook barked back the waitress's orders, ham and rye on dark, hold mustard, as silverware clattered against hard plates, and hamburgers spit on an open grill. The diner was a mass of black countertops, chrome, and coffee-colored walls. The smell of grease and look of 1950s–style waitresses, curvy women with short sassy hair and bright lipstick, floated around us. "The sandwich was a good choice." I didn't know what else to say. *I wanted her, Stana. I want you.* Hot open-faced sandwiches were the diner's specialty since 1933.

"Not now." She patted my hand and blushed slightly.

"I said *that* out loud?"

"Yes."

"Sorry." Christ. All that talk of nirvana and Durgana's notions of simplicity were putting other ideas in my head. And all the damn concussions from hockey. I have no internal censor sometimes.

"Don't worry, I'm not moving *beyond* sex." She played with a huge hoop earring.

I laughed.

"What did you make of the no-window look? There were none in the sanctuary."

"Or lobby," I said.

"Creepy."

"I think they want to keep the distractions of the outside world outside, to attain oneness within."

"Or to keep us outsiders from seeing what the brothers and sisters are up to."

"Yeah." *Like a midnight mass in two days?*

"I'm not giving up on this 11/14 angle either. I'm going to ask the folks in ice cubes about it." She patted my hand and took a short drag. "This afternoon."

The shoes of one of the waitresses squawked across the freshly waxed tile, breaking the romantic kismet between us. And the short-order cook in back was now singing Sinatra.

"I mean," she said, "the place used to have windows but now they're bricked up. The red bricks in the former windows were a brighter color than the red bricks of the original walls."

"You'd make a good detective."

The short-order cook wanted to play among the stars.

After the interviews with the ice-cube people, Stana planned to follow Brother Durgana. Tail job.

"That's dangerous."

"I'll be careful."

"Take my .45." I had extra heat in the glove box of my Ford Galaxie.

"I don't have a permit." She played with the other earring and shook her head, bemused. "I don't trust the guy. A total phony. He was wearing a Brooks Brothers suit." She exhaled sharply off her cigarette and blew a wisp of auburn out of her eyes.

"I noticed."

"Did you also notice the pentagram in one of the neon tableaux?"

"Yes."

More dishes clattered and one of the waitresses laughed at the sexual overtures of a customer who said she should be on television or on a billboard or on the couch in his living room, wearing nothing but his necktie.

Whatever.

"I bet Brother Durgana's got a swimming pool, a circular bed, and throws swinging parties."

That sounded more like Bullard and Smith, the yacht-club set that owned the Leafs. Christ, Bullard used to pour potato chips over naked women, his idea of foreplay fun. And Smith had got his kicks filming people through a two-way mirror at Maple Leaf Gardens parties: lap dances and blow jobs. Playboy set. Gambling. Stuff he'd be up on trial for in less than sixty days. Brother Durgana was much more subdued than those cats, or so it seemed.

From the phone book, Stana had already retrieved Durgana's address, a home on Walmer Road.

Those were old modest houses, I told her, turn of the century, near Sibelius Park, with short postage-stamp lawns and wooden fences. I knew the area. Had a cousin who lived there. "Just be careful."

"I will."

"You got a good book to read?"

She didn't say anything, her fork tapping by the side of the plate. "For a phony, he sure is charismatic."

"Yeah. It's like he looks into you and sees things you don't want revealed."

"Yeah."

And he takes his time before speaking, waiting on the right words. He's like on a time delay, she said, wanting to be precise. "Never shoots from the hip. Very controlled."

"Yeah."

My plan for the afternoon was to go to Silverwood's on Danforth, the company Dad was a milkman for, and check his call sheets and see if he had any upset customers or conflicts that might erupt in violence and murder. It was a long shot, but maybe it would get me another lead. We'd check back with each other later in the afternoon. My place on Houston Crescent. Six-ish. I planned to take a shower, nap, and change my clothes. My mouth still felt like it had a towel in it.

"Sure, sure. Your phone number's still active?"

"Yeah."

"Christ, Hayden. I—I—" Her eyes filled with tears. She did carry guilt in her shoulders and eyes, like Durgana said, guilt over her past, and how I nearly died at the hands of Babe Migano's men, and how Brian "Spinner" Terrien and Lisa Steinmetz did die from their hands. "I didn't want you to get hurt. I didn't think they'd kill them, I just didn't think." And the worst part wasn't the larger guilt of inadvertently being part of the setup, the knockoff, but the bloody aftermath, the guilt of knowing they were dead but not being able to do a damn thing about it.

We'd made a pact of secrecy to protect each other and the Stabulas girls.

A handful of us. Numb about a murder. Bodies buried in Vaughan, Ontario.

Seven months since the killings. It felt like a decade of guilt.

And now there was a gangster, Lenny Cassel, who I tangled with in my last case, roaming the world free with Terrien's face, courtesy of plastic surgery. What ills was he performing with the face and name of another man, a guy, who really, deep down, was decent, a solid hockey player, a man who cared for and loved Lisa? "I think about it all the time. It's something I carry with me too."

She crushed her cigarette in an ashtray, her shoulders trembling.

I think mine were trembling too.

I ARRIVED AT SILVERWOOD'S SHORTY BEFORE 1 P.M. and none of the route drivers or managers were back yet from delivering milk and butter. Try around 2:30, a receptionist told me so I filled my 63 Galaxie with gas and wandered to a local bowling alley, had a plate of eggs and peameal bacon, and bowled three games: 133, 169, and 211. I was too tired to sleep.

And after a 211, I was feeling pretty damn good about myself.

And a little guilty about the bacon.

For the final game, I was rolling a big 16-pound ball, tossing it like a twelve-pounder.

Around 3:00, I met with Dad's boss, Bob Waterman, in Silverwood's garage. Yellow-and-blue trucks were all around us, with logos of bright yellow suns backlighting a pretty, smiling Scandinavian ingénue. Racks of empty bottles and product that didn't sell were offloaded. Bob nearly broke my fingers when we shook hands. He was wiry but had wrists the size of Popeye arms.

Some guys just have to assert their presence through a manly handshake. He was one of those guys.

And he was loud. When he spoke, he leaned back on his heels, his feet jet ailerons, appearing to want to lift off.

"So, what can I do for you?" Bob was a regular company man with his blue Dickies and yellow polo shirt.

"Wanted to ask about my dad, Ira Fuller."

"Ira? A fucking funny guy. Hilarious. Color of the day." He smacked his thighs. "Color of the motherfucking day!"

"Huh?"

Apparently, Dad had these shticks that his fellow workers found totally charming like *color of the day*. "He'd see a beautiful broad, right, and he'd say, blue. Blue is the color of the day. Cause she was wearing a blue dress. For the rest of the day we'd all be saying *blue, color of the day*." He laughed. "He made you feel good. One time, there was this chick with big knockers, I mean they were out to here, wearing a red sweater. But red wasn't the color of the day. No, sir. It was, get this, scarlet. Scarlet. Color of the day. Clever. Witty."

"Uh-huh."

"Because her knockers were so big. Red didn't do her justice.

Scarlet did."

"I see."

"I don't need to tell you, it was a shock when I found him." With the back of a heavy wrist, he wiped away run-off from his nose. "Can't wait for it to snow. Knock out these goddamn allergies." He wiped again.

"Any day now." We had a foot already in Montreal. I carried a shovel in my trunk to avoid getting stuck in grocery store parking lots and half-plowed side streets.

"How can you play for the Habs? You're a Leaf." He punched my arm. Playfully. It hurt.

I shrugged. "How did my dad feel about me playing for the Habs?"

"He loved it. Always rubbing it in when the Habs won and we lost. Go, Habs, Go. He'd just throw it in, in the middle of normal conversations. Just drop it right in. Right there. Like, 'How's the weather, Ira?' 'Oh, it's a bitch. Colder than a witch's tit. Go, Habs, Go!' Shit like that. Funny. He just made you laugh. Him and his Habs toque."

My eyes were raw.

"Wore that damn thing everywhere." His teeth were yellow, hair dry straw.

More small milk trucks arrived, backing into the bays along the walls of the loading dock, placing empties on conveyor belts to be cleaned. Water rushed over the bottles, creating an ongoing white noise.

"It must have been rough, finding my dad like that."

The garage smelled of gasoline and the heavy heat of truck engines driven hard in late fall. The heat in the room was awfully dry. No wonder Bob's hair stood straight up like pixie sticks.

"I'm really sorry for your loss."

I'm not sure how I feel about my loss. Really.

Bob assured me that when he was checking up on my dad, he wasn't trying to be nosy, *checking up on him*, you know, nothing like that, it's just that Ira hadn't reported to work in three days and he was always one of the first guys here to begin his route, 4:30 every day, every morning. "I think he really loved being a milkman."

"Yeah."

"I mean, it's like you're family." People let you into their homes, you see women in their pajamas and nighties, men fighting with their wives, children making a mess in the living room. "It's real. Not like the *Donna Reed Show*."

"That's for sure." When I was waltzing through puberty, Dad often bragged about how some of the women flashed him, just lifted the tops of their long T-shirts so they wouldn't have to pay their bills that week.

Bob suggested we leave the loading dock and talk in his office where it was quieter. On the way, I finally got to the point. I mean hearing about my dad's working relationships was nice and all, but I had a murder to solve and avenge. Could I see Dad's call sheets and was he having any trouble with any customers?

"No. Everyone loved Ira." He lit a cigarette and stood behind his desk, pulling out drawers and handing me four different call sheets. Customers differed depending on day of the week. One McGowan address jumped right out at me like an Agitprop fist in a Soviet poster, The People's Way to Christ.

"Dad delivered to the church?"

No wonder "Brother" Durgana knew how Dad felt about simplicity. Durgana and his goddamn auras, the goddamn phony.

It was a pretty big order. Every Thursday. Dad was found dead on a Tuesday. He'd been dead for three or four days. Saw the People five days before.

"Any trouble with any of them? Anyone call in to complain?"

"At the church?"

"Sure."

"No. No problems."

I wasn't sure how color of the day would go over with that crowd.

"He delivers just to the church or also the families in the ice-cubed Quonset huts behind?"

"Just the church." He pushed at and pulled up his dry hair. It made his head look like a set of drinking straws. "From what I understand they all ate their meals there. In the building." He leaned back, his aileron feet nearly lifting off. "I mean it was a big call. Thirty-five folks or so. Lots of milk." His lips twisted into a thin line. "No buttermilk though. Too much fat." He held up a hand. "I'm just reporting what *they* said. I like buttermilk. Silverwood's buttermilk. *Top*. *Top* of the line."

The guy wasn't wearing blue-and-yellow clothing for nothing.

"Sure." I pushed back my porkpie, wiped the edges of my mouth. His office, unlike the high ceilings to The People's Way to Christ, was low-ceilinged, crowded. If you were over six feet, you walked stooped. File cabinets nudged together in a far wall, a desk organizer was full of invoices, two phones were on the desk, a third off the hook on a filing cabinet, and the near wall was white cork board filled with hooks and round-tagged keys to the various trucks, I assumed.

"Any other problems, with anyone on the route?"

He gently lingered a wrist under his nose. "People took to your dad. He was funny." He pulled on his cigarette, offered me one. I took it. "Well, wait, there was one call. Mary something or other."

I spotted an address on the call sheet directly across from the church, Mary Hale. "Hale?"

I lit up. Exhaled quickly.

"Yeah. That's it. Widow. Saw him give a ride to a girl one day."

The sun kissing his window cut three gold bars across his desk.

"When?" I picked a sliver of tobacco off my lower lip. Everyone I know smokes unfiltered.

"I don't know. A couple of weeks ago. We have a policy. No riders. But you know, good old Ira. Marches to his own drum."

I handed him the photograph. "Is this the girl?"

"How the hell would I know? I didn't give her a ride."

"Did Mary mention what the girl looked like?'

"No. Indian girl, huh? Cute. No, no, the old broad just complained and wondered if we could start carrying margarine." He shrugged. "You know as an alternative to butter? We're a goddamn dairy. We don't do margarine."

"Right. Did Mary say if the girl came out of the church before she got a ride?"

He took another sharp drag. "Real pain-in-the-ass broad. I didn't really follow up on her story, to be honest with you. So, I don't know about the church angle. And I didn't talk to your dad about it. Figured what the fuck, you know? Good old Ira."

"Yeah. Good old Ira."

We quietly smoked for a few seconds. "You know, he did have one flaw, your dad had kind of a big mouth."

"How so?"

Every month the executives would come in and meet with the milkmen, go over their routes, suggest ways to put more business on them, and one Easter they were designing a new kind of pudding, not our usual chocolate but brighter, a vanilla to go with the pastel colors of the holiday, vanilla with bits of sprinkles in it. Ira thought the thing wouldn't sell, it was too girly, no, faggy he said. Too faggy. Anyway, that pissed off the bosses. How the fuck will you ever get promoted if you keep insulting the bosses' ideas, the company's ideas. "Ira just couldn't think like management."

"Uh-huh." I took a drag.

"But the fellas all loved him. He was a regular riot."

Those were the very words Tony De Luca had used. My father, the Jewish Jackie Gleason.

"Check this out—" Bob pointed at the cork board nearest to us. Next to the keys and posted invoices, and lithograph pin-up nude of Diane Webber leaning back in a canvas chair, was a big chunk of posted newsprint hanging crookedly with names, dates, and numbers on it. "You know what that is?"

"No."

"A pool. Like a lottery. A death lottery. Your dad started it. What day would Steve Smith, owner of the Leafs, die? You know he's got bleeding ulcers? The poor fuck." He flashed a mock smile. "We all picked a death date. The closest wins." He wiped at his nose. "So far the pool's up to $112. A riot, I tell you."

"Yeah, real regular."

I DON'T THINK MARY HALE WANTED TO TALK TO ME, but she let me in when I promised her an autograph for her niece and nephew. The latter was a Canadiens fan.

Before I could even open my mouth further, she handed me paper and a Bic pen, the cap chewed down. I scrawled my name and put a #28 under it. "You sure you don't want any extras for holidays or special occasions?"

That didn't lighten the mood. Damn.

She had a pie-shaped face with a crumbled-up crust. Her eyes were tired with crimped crinkles at the corners.

Her house smelled of wet wool and cat litter. Lots of cats. Tortoiseshell mainly. One oddball, a purple cat, Persian she said, rubbed against her polyester slacks as she spoke to me hurriedly in the hall. She didn't offer me a seat or direct me anywhere. We just stood in the hall by three cat litter boxes.

With her efficiency, she should be running General Motors.

Even her patter was efficient. She spoke quickly, with a slight lisp. Yes, she saw the girl come out of the church. Never saw her before or since. Just that day. Wearing a leather jacket and those stockings that look like fencing?

"Cyclone fencing? Fishnet?"

"Yes." Hopped in Ira's milk truck. And he gave her a pint of chocolate milk. "She didn't pay for it. I'm sure of that. And I'm pretty sure he didn't pay for it either." She wagged a finger at me as if I were Ira. "Pilfering is not okay. Where would this country be if everybody pilfered?" The wagging was still going.

The next day, Mary balled Ira out for giving the girl a freebie on the company's dime and a free ride. That's what the TTC is for: buses, streetcars, subways.

"I see."

"I order every Thursday three per cent milk, buttermilk, and chocolate milk. He never gave me anything free." The cat at her legs was still nuzzling, probably hungry. "I like buttermilk pancakes."

"Me too," I said.

"I told Ira, it's unsafe to pick up hitchhikers." She wagged her finger again as if Dad were in this very room, as if he were looking over me like Hamlet's ghost.

"You look a lot like him." She paused, eyes roving over me, up and down, as if she were about to buy a piece of furniture from Leon's. "You sure do."

"I get that a lot." I showed her the photograph of Ellen Reynolds.

We were still standing, my autographs in her left hand.

"Yup. That's the girl." She glanced down at the Persian cat, scuffling her legs, leaving thin slices of hair on her slacks. "I read she ran away from a white Mom. No matter how much we try to do the right things for those people we just mess things up. We should just let them be."

"Or not assume that we know better how to raise their children—"

She nodded.

"You saw her get in his truck?"

"Yes."

I snapped my fingers. "And that was the only time you saw

her, the day she hopped in my dad's truck?"

Her lips moved as I spoke, trying to guess my next word. She had an index finger lifting up her chin, her other arm, with the autographs, pushed across her chest. "Yes."

"But she came *out* of the church?"

"Yes. I told you that. Weren't you listening?"

"Not happening to just stand in front of it but came out of the doors of the church?"

"Yes. Absolutely." She nodded firmly. "With fishnets."

I quickly signed some more autographs for her. "Always good to have them on hand, in case," I said. "Unexpected guests?" I shrugged.

She laughed this time.

That's the way with comedy. Don't give up on a good bit, re-think it, re-tool, re-contextualize, and try again.

"What do you think of margarine?" Her eyes squinted and she leaned closer, almost conspiring in her spirited marketing plans for the company. "I've been trying to get Silverwood's—"

"I prefer maple syrup on my pancakes," I said, smiling. "With blueberries."

"Well, that goes without saying, young man."

"It sure does," I said.

And we both laughed.

STANA WAS PARKED UNDER THE STREET LIGHTS of a donut shop. A box of donuts on the dashboard. She was hunkered down the front seat, a Maple Leafs ball cap shading her eyes.

I tapped on the car window. "Some disguise." I pointed at the cap.

She lowered the window and placed a book next to the box of donuts. *Last Exit to Brooklyn.*

I rubbed my hands together. It was cold.

Across the way, in the Army Surplus store, people were buying up fatigue jackets, commando toques, and black boots. It didn't seem right to me to wear the gear if you haven't served. I guess I'm a little old-fashioned.

"This fella doesn't understand women at all—" She pointed at the book on her dash.

"Then why read it?"

"To understand you." Her words were full of light comic touches, but we all know what Freud says about jokes.

No movement so far on the Durgana front. She called the *Telegram*. At one time he was a broker, worked the floor at the Dow Jones, became a financial adviser, and left the business at thirty-five, three years ago. Other than that, his record: clean.

"Any religious piety in his background?"

"None." She smiled. "So much for the circular bed." He's no playboy. Doesn't mess around. She had asked. The whole afternoon had been rather quiet. Church business, I guess. A woman with a metal cart full of vegetables squeezed through the front door. That's it. "Shit, there's a passage in this here book about giving birth that's just pure horseshit—"

"Anything else?" The inside of her car smelled of cigarettes and the ashtray was full.

The families, those that were available to speak, appeared strange and aloof. And they walked weird she said, little half-steps.

"Half-steps?" I wrote it down in my yellow notebook.

"And two or three of them hummed that same damn song we'd heard in the sanctuary as they now went about their work. If you can call it work. She wasn't sure what they did all day but read scripture, weave baskets, make garments in their spare time, and walk in half-steps. "And get this, no one has a television."

"That's fucking sick."

"But there are surveillance cameras in their living rooms."

"Christ."

"They don't read newspapers, and I didn't see any books.

None. Everyone dresses the same, same kind of canvas clothes. Tops, pants. Hair cut short. Women too." She lit a cigarette. Stared at it. "And nobody smokes."

I reached for a donut and got powdered sugar all over my face. Donuts like Mexican food always add to my fashion statement.

Did they know the girl, Ellen? Had they seen her?

No, nothing, she said. No light in the rooms either, Hayden. Coleman lanterns, candles. Incense. No lights. No radios—

"Coleman lanterns? Army surplus stuff."

"Huh?"

I pointed to the giant store next to the church, red brick, large rectangles of stained glass filled with Canadian flags and Union Jacks.

"Come to think of it, some of them had Sternos in their rooms." She tapped her upper lip. "And one girl was drinking water from an aluminum canteen."

"Check into it."

"I will." She shrugged and tapped a set of fingers along the car's dash. "You know what was creepy? I swear. I felt like the cameras moved as I moved."

"Hmm."

"What the fuck's that mean? I've just finally figured out your uh-huhs and now you're throwing hmm at me."

"Hmm means hmm." I laughed, hands in pants. "It means I'm pondering."

"Well, just don't get ponderous."

That cracked me up.

She looked in the direction of the store. Someone carried out a cumbersome backpack and an oar for a kayak. "They have heating. The insides of those ice-cubes were very hot."

"The simple life, huh?"

"Yeah, but the people I saw, their emotions. Complex." She couldn't get them to say anything about the mass in two days.

Some denied it outright, but others just looked away, as if they couldn't lie to her, but wouldn't commit to a truth either. "There's a mass and it's happening in two days. I'm sure of it."

And that was the extent of her covert ops.

They ran her off.

She took another drag, slowly exhaled.

"Who's they?" For some reason when I ask key questions, I have a habit of pushing back my porkpie for emphasis. Now I had powdered sugar all over the brim of my emphasis. Damn.

"Thompson. Durgana." She shook her head, laughed, grabbed my hat, and dusted it with a forearm. "I mean they were polite about it. Even quoted scripture, but they weren't happy."

And I wasn't happy either. The autopsy report meant Dad would be buried on Saturday, but I had a game that night so the levaya would have to be early that afternoon. Aunt Miriam, my Mom's sister, was handling the details for me and I promised to pay my respects, drop in a few times for shiva over the next few weeks, but I wasn't missing the game in Detroit this Friday or the one in Montreal, Saturday. No way.

She wondered about my priorities, saying little, telling me we all mourn in our own way.

I wasn't sure I wanted to do a eulogy and all, but she said I ought to think about it, a few words might be nice, but she understood. The rabbi would deliver the kaddish.

"Dad wasn't a practicing Jew," I said.

Once a Jew, always a Jew, she said.

I didn't say a word about once a son always a son.

I told Stana all about Miriam and my meetings at Silverwood's and Mary Hale's.

"The girl was there?"

"In fishnets, apparently. Miss Hale mentioned that twice. Fishnets."

"Wow. What does that mean?"

Ellen was a follower, The People's Way To Christ?

Two women came out of the surplus store carrying a tent, the box the size of a large dog house.

"The people there—" She blew wisps of auburn from her eyes. "Hard-scrabble."

"Yes."

She smiled. All of the folks she interviewed struck her as the transient type, the lost, the homeless. "They wouldn't talk about their pasts. I asked. Believe me, I asked." But she didn't think they came from money.

"Then where does the money come from to run such an operation?"

"The surplus store?"

"The surplus store," I said. "Of course. See who backs it."

She'd check with the *Telegram*, their fact-checking staff, and find who owns the lease to both buildings. She also had a lot of the surnames of the church's followers. Check their money trails.

I leaned across the window and kissed her nose.

"What's that for?"

"I don't know."

She opened the car door and pulled me toward her, giving me a kiss that made a dark wing turn inside my stomach. "Maybe later tonight? Your place?" She handed me my dusted-off porkpie. "Sixish?" She smiled, her cigarette dangling. "You'll be done with your nap?"

"Yeah."

"Be careful when you go up against Thompson and Durgana."

"Huh?"

"Thompson's coat. It's carrying more than just pamphlets."

"His coat." I snapped my fingers. "Army surplus. Military issue. So's his aviator goggles—"

'Will you let me finish?"

"Sorry."

When Thompson escorted her from the cubes, his coat bumped up against her hip and she felt the hard edge of a gun, .45 most likely. “Like I said, he’s carrying more than just pamphlets in those pockets.”

BROTHER DURGANA WASN’T TOO HAPPY to see me. No grin, no talk of oneness, no pithy scripture passages to ruminate over, nothing. He didn’t even get up from behind his desk to shake my hand or share any of his food.

I couldn’t help but think of Jesus and the fish and the feeding of the 5,000.

Not that I really wanted any of Brother D’s food. It was all green, telephone lines of seaweed, and some kind of vegetable I didn’t recognize that had holes in it, like you’d find on a bass fiddle.

“Lotus root. Very tasty. Improves brain power.”

“Uh-huh,” I said. All that so-called simplicity stuff sure wasn’t on point in his office: famous paintings centered three of the walls, including a Renoir full of yellow green light and a girl looking away from the sun; from wood beams hung flowers in rust-colored ceramic pots; along the front of the desk clustered white plaster figurines, angels, kids on bicycles, ballerinas, dancers; and covering the floor was an expansive red and black Oriental rug. As was the case in the sanctuary, there were no windows. Only chalky, red brick.

“You lied to me, Durgana. Ellen Reynolds was here.”

High above our head twirled a ceiling fan out of a 1940s-film noir.

I hoped he wasn’t looking there, but at my blazer as it flashed open, giving him a momentary glimpse of my side-holstered .38.

I pushed down my porkpie and told him all that Mary Hale had spoken.

I left out the fishnets.

He wiped the edges of his mouth and smiled as if he were an ad man for Chrysler. We have a lot of transients, roamers, indigents, who fall into our building and discover our ways aren't their ways. She might have been a one-time guest. I told you she may have been here. We've had a lot of tribal people. His black eyes glimmered. "I see so many troubled, lost souls. I can check the visitor registers if you like."

I got a better idea, I said, check your surveillance tapes. "You got cameras everywhere. See if she's on those tapes." I pointed at the camera directly above me, waved. "I still got those tickets."

"I can't do that." He crossed his hands in front of him. "We only save the tape for a week—"

"Then let me see last week's tapes."

He whistled. It had a lot more bounce than the church's theme song. "Sorry. Privacy matters."

"Privacy matters." My tone was ironic.

I'm not sure he caught it.

"Only if you have a warrant—"

He caught it.

"Stana tells me a different story about your clients. They *all* appear to be former transients."

His ear was bothering him again, only this time it was the right one. He rubbed at the back of it, smiled shyly. "I assure you that is a mere appearance, part of the process of transition, not an ultimate reality. You see, a kind of confusion of the mind sets in, a vacuous expression that eventually fills with its new identities as the transition is completed."

"Bullshit."

"Excuse me?"

I placed my hands on my hips. "What's really going on?" *Were the people drugged? They were so listless, wandering without purpose.*

And the excess heat of the Quonset huts. Incubate their minds, keep them lethargic. Followers, indeed.

"We are a church. Nonprofit." His black eyes barely moved. "I can show you the paperwork."

"I'd rather see the surveillance tapes."

"I told you I may have crossed paths with her. The Reynolds girl. So many people visit our temple, asking for money to pay a water bill. Buy groceries—"

"Uh-huh."

"We have an emergency fund." He played with one of the figurines, a fisherman, getting him re-aligned, in step, with the angels. He didn't remember the Reynolds girl. That's all. "I was wrong." He shrugged.

"Your followers didn't remember her either, but Stana had a strong feeling they were lying. You see, you taught them well, some of the brothers and sisters can't lie at all, and it was their silences that told a different story. How long was Ellen here? Why did she leave? How is my father's murder connected to her and to you and this place? Enough bullshit!"

Brother Thompson, still wearing the long, akimbo green coat with all the buttons, including my main woman Emma, stumbled shoulders first into the room, the propeller in his beanie cap spinning randomly. His right hand gripped an upside-down broom like a cop's truncheon. His goggles were too tight against his face and eyes. The broom's handle was grimy and appeared to be covered with bed sores. "I heard loud voices?"

"Matthew 5:38–40, Brother Thompson. 'If anyone slaps you on the right cheek turn to them the other cheek also.'"

Thompson nodded, tap-tapping his broom handle on the floor, and then turned about in the opposite direction, showing me the other side of his face.

He was a pretty literal cat.

And then he started humming that dirge of longing and the walk of the soulless. The space between the notes was as unnerving as always.

I was feeling nasty, wanting answers, and I became abusive

like in Dr. Cohen's triangle. "She was here, and I'm going to find out what went down. My father was killed. That girl was with him before he died. And if you're involved, *Brother* Durgana, in my father's killing, you're going down," I pointed at the two of them.

Durgana played with his right ear.

Thompson was singing, again, and in mid-aria picked his nose. He didn't seem to mind that I noticed.

"My, my, such a temper. Fiery. Meditation would do wonders for your inner qi."

"My inner what, what the fuck is that?"

"The life force, and yours is spinning in all the wrong directions."

"Thanks. I'll buy a compass." I pushed back my porkpie. "Maybe from that surplus store next door." I turned to Thompson whose dirge-like notes continued to bleat bleat. "Is that where you got that coat?"

"We have an exclusive contract with them," Durgana explained calmly, fingers tenting twice. "We buy all our supplies there. Twenty-five percent discount."

"Uh-huh." I shook my head. "What about swords beaten down into ploughshares?" I figured the simple life would include a peaceful life, not one adorned with products of the war machine.

"I like army clothes," Thompson said absently, his singing and the propeller on his beanie now still.

"Sure. But if you enlist, learn to play taps, buddy. Please. If you sing for those cats they'll kick you out on a medical discharge."

That startled him. Suddenly, he swung the broom at my head and I ducked under it, grabbed the handle, turned right, and twisted him off the stick, toppling him into a book shelf of strange works of mysticism—Aleister Crowley's *The Book of Lies*, Francis Barrett's *The Magus*, Volume Two—and two gems of realistic, stylized photography: Weegee's *Naked City* and Robert Frank's *The Americans.*

Thompson sat on his elbows and stared.

One of the propellers on his beanie cap was bent like a frayed popsicle stick.

A book or two toppled off his shoulders.

"You read some pretty weird shit, Brother Durgana."

"There are many different truths."

"But just one god, huh?"

He didn't answer me right away. "Well, yes, of course."

"And no one else is privileged enough to read, huh? Stana said there were no books in your little ice cubes out back."

"They read, but they need to be guided in what they read."

"Where you the lookout for Gus's kill, Brother Thompson?"

He said nothing.

"Please, be gentle, Mr. Fuller—Brother Thompson is—"

"*Mr.*, now? I guess the brother bit wore thin. It had such a nice ring to it. *Brother Fuller.*"

"You're not nearly as funny as you think you are, Mr. Fuller."

"Really? Brother Ed Sullivan wanted me for his show just last week but he booked a bunch of Brother Russian bears instead."

"Please, Mr. Fuller. You're very droll and beginning to bore me."

"Brother Durgana, I insist. Call me Brother Fuller."

"You are a real pain in the ass—" He looked down at his hands resembling dolphins floating on their backs, the black glimmer glare of his eyes dissipating. "I apologize—my outburst was—unprofessional."

"Don't be so hard on yourself. I was being an ass." I smiled lopsidedly.

"I'm not the sensitive one. But Brother Thompson. Extremely." He leaned forward, one of the figurines toppling, whispered. "Don't push him too far. He breaks easily."

"Oh yeah he's real sensitive. Let me show you just how sensitive—"

I tugged on Thompson's lapels, pulling him up from the floor, then jacketed back the lapels over his shoulders, wrapping him in a Saran Wrap of cloth, making it impossible for him to use his arms, and removed the .45 from the left pocket of his coat. I popped the round from the chamber, slid out the clip, and tossed the works on Durgana's desk. It didn't land softly. Two figurines fell, one of them, an angel, broke apart at the knees.

I pointed at the fat, blocky gun. "Something else procured at your friendly neighborhood surplus store?"

Durgana said nothing.

"Why do you let a kid like this carry around that kind of heat? He's not big enough." I wiped the edges of my mouth. "Guns are dangerous." I pushed down my porkpie. "And if Brother Thompson's the sensitive type a .45 can sure take care of a lot of sensitivity in a hurry."

Brother Durgana looked at the .45 as if it were soiled fish. Three of the fingers on his left hand were covered in diamonds. He shoved the .45 into a drawer. Closed it.

"Thompson, you talked to me and Stana. For five, seven minutes. And then Gus was dead."

He was killed by a .45.

"I hear it was all about beef jerky. I assure you—" Durgana pointed at his plate. "None of us eat beef jerky. Or hotdogs." He smiled, a finger on his right hand rubbing at a diamond ring on his left. "And you really should eat fewer hotdogs, Mr. Fuller." The ways of the East. Berries, nuts, rice, and veggies. You'll live longer. Green. Could live to a hundred eating green. "Hotdogs? Dead at sixty-five."

"Dead at sixty-five," Thompson said, mouth full of tears. "I liked Gus." Thompson blubbered, hands covering his eyes. "He gave me milk. Bread too."

And then he let fall big spots of tears.

The leftovers, he said. The first will be last. Gus gave him the leftovers, the last, the stuff nobody wanted, stuff about to expire. More tears.

That got Brother Durgana off his Brooks Brothers ass. He comforted Brother Thompson and shot me surly looks.

"I wish he wasn't dead. He gave me bread." *The last shall be first.*

Thompson rocked, snot running down his mouth.

He cried and cried, his whole body shaking. Even the buttons on his green coat were vibrating.

Durgana held him and said something or other about a camel through the eye of a needle.

And then they sang. The same song, same pitch.

I felt like a total prick.

Their singing really wasn't half bad.

SHE WAS AFRAID TO LEAVE THE OFFICE.

It was 7:00 p.m., the city shrouded under a black asphalt sky. Her whole office was black: low lit, drawn dark curtains, darker shades on the lamp. Her professional ensemble matched the décor: black dress, tight black turtleneck, black-red lipstick.

"Someone's trying to kill me."

Her voice was low as if that someone might be in this very room.

Forty-five minutes ago, her phone call woke me from a power nap that had slipped into a deep sleep. I had gone back to my Houston Crescent home in North York, jiffyed up some spaghetti and marinara, showered, and fell asleep watching an Audie Murphy western from the couch. When I woke up, I showered again.

It was that kind of case.

Dr. Cohen called between the two showers. My second one was very, very short.

Dr. Cohen.

My therapist.

My friend.

I left Stana an apologetic note propped against a glass in the kitchen. "Gone to Doc's," the note said, with "love, Hayden," and a smiley face that looked like a forgotten Peanuts character. Next to the note, I left a Coffee Crisp, Stana's favorite.

Dr. Cohen reached into one of her lower desk drawers and tossed me a sheet of paper creased awkwardly in half, reminding me of those awful, unreadable teacher handouts that had stuttered and stuck across a ditto machine's drum. It smelled of duplicator fluid.

Damn. It was made on a ditto machine.

The artwork wouldn't give Andy Warhol a run for his money, but it was just as edgy: a blue, crude drawing of the Star of David, none of the triangular points matching in height or shape. It was off-balanced, a wobbly, drunken Star of David. Under the star was scrawled in an equally messy hand, as if the author were using his left instead of right, "We know what you said."

Oh, and the final touch? The star was splattered with brownish-red contours.

Fresh. Not ditto-copied.

"Blood?"

"I don't know." I smiled awkwardly. "You have any hydrogen peroxide?"

"I have a cabinet in the bathroom." She smiled politely and tugged at the cuffs of the turtleneck. The bathroom light flashed on, off, and Dr. Cohen screamed a subterranean howl.

I was by her side in seconds.

I turned on the light. The flash hurt my eyes.

But that was nothing compared to the hurt I felt when I saw what was in the room. Bloody Stars of David were wallpapered everywhere: on the bathroom mirror, the floor, the shower curtain, the ceiling, dozens of them. All duplicates, same quote, same crooked looking star.

But the blood patterns. All original. Different. Fresh.

"They've been in my office. Inside."

"Yeah. I know." It was an intimidation game, one of fear mongering. I grabbed her shoulders and hugged her. "Just stay with me. I'll keep you safe."

We stood like that for several minutes.

She didn't cry. She was tough.

From the cabinet, I grabbed the hydrogen peroxide and some Q-Tips. And several of the bloodied stars. Part of their intimidation was to hint at biblical-sized sacrifices, God said to Abraham kill me a son.

I spread the papers across her desk, uncapped the hydrogen peroxide. Dipped the Q-Tip in.

"What's that for?"

Blood contains an enzyme, catalase, which breaks hydrogen peroxide down into water and oxygen gas. If it's paint it won't bubble, but if it's blood, watch.

Two or three drops hit the reddish-brown stubble and bubbles popped and ran along the page.

And many other pages too.

"Shit," she said.

I lifted the sheet.

Where could you get that much blood at short notice? A blood bank; a recently executed corpse, from a host of zombielike followers at a McGowan Street cult.

What did We know what you said *mean?*

"I don't know." Her black bangs didn't move as she shook her head and sat down at her desk across from me. "I'm so sorry I called you, and I know you're dealing with your father's murder—but I didn't know who else to ask—"

"Forget about that. Friends ask friends for help."

She pulled her lips together. "They got into my fucking office."

I wondered if she'd said something in her past that she regretted.

"In Auschwitz?"

"No. Here, in this office with a client."

"I can't talk about my clients."

"Your life's in danger, Doc." I knew the rules. That whole doctor-client privilege thing was a myth. If lives were in danger, your life, your client's life, or if you knew about sexual abuse you had to report it. In this case I was sensing a lot of danger, alarm bells banging a death knell and Dr. No's island was about to go under.

Dr. Cohen didn't get the allusion. She reads *Scientific American.*

I leaned across the desk, placed my hands in hers. "Let me help you." Could any of this have anything to do with me? I too am her patient. Did we talk about something that made us targets for this hate group? It had to be a hate group, anti-Semites of some kind, or else why use the loaded symbolism of the Star of David? *And the blood. The death of first sons?* "When did this first note arrive?"

It was shoved under her office door when she returned from a late afternoon coffee break. They could be lurking now, waiting for me to leave, she said. That's why she kept calling my home, afraid to move.

"Why not call the po-lice?"

"After I called you, I did. I tried to call the police—" She picked up the receiver, held it out to me. "Dead."

I dropped it back in its cradle. They cut the line, outside. Professionals.

It could be Lenny Cassel haunting you, me, a murderer roaming the world with Brian Spinner Terrien's face. In my last case, Cassel killed a woman and fled Canada with the aid of plastic surgery as a new person, getting a new start. But Cassel knew that I knew that the real Terrien was no longer with us and maybe Cassel's Detroit mobster boys were taking matters in hand, making sure their boss would be protected from future exposure by a Toronto PI and Montreal Canadien hockey player.

I had also spoken, during several of our sessions, to Dr. Cohen about Terrien, my feelings of guilt over the secret I kept from his family in not revealing his death, the guilt I felt in knowing he was buried in a field in Vaughan, Ontario. I saw him die, beaten to death by Babe Migano and his men, one of Terrien's eyes hanging from its orbital bone, his last breath a blood bubble. Could it be related to that?

Terrien and Cassel.

Dr. Cohen didn't think so.

Seven months ago, when I told Dr. Cohen the story of my first case and the man I killed, blowing his brains all over the wall and across the face and hair of his daughter seated next to him, and the other man, Terrien, whose death I kept quiet about, she listened, nodded her head, and said that survivors often carry dark secrets with them to the grave. She carried several: the burdens of her patients, the burdens of her brutal past.

I know she survived Auschwitz. Saw her mother, father, sister and uncle die there. We all make compromises to survive abuse, she always says, but did she say something she shouldn't to survive in Auschwitz?

"I don't think they are Nazis." She smiled dimly, and I moved to the window, parted the curtains. On the street below, under a flickering street light were two men in long overcoats and fedoras, smoking cigarettes.

Hit men. "Then it has to be a client, Dr. Cohen. Someone's angry at you."

Before I closed the curtains one of the men looked up in the direction of the window. I couldn't make out his features, but his face was too long for his short, stubby body. "You can talk to me vaguely about your cases without mentioning names. Keep it general, but vaguely specific."

"I can talk. Violence is involved."

She smiled faintly, her eyes filling with a friendly light. "You know, since we have the hydrogen peroxide out, let's clean that damn cut. That adhesive tape on your chin has turned from white to off white to mud cakes."

I sat in a chair across from her and she gently removed the bandage. It pinched a little. She applied the topical antiseptic and it burned. "It's a little infected."

"So I hear."

She gently squeezed and gathered puss in a Kleenex. She applied a new bandage, new adhesive tape, her fingers almost soothing. I felt like a kid again. And I mean that in a good way. Seriously. I didn't have someone, like a mom, caring for me. Dad was often asleep on the couch, in a boozy freefall.

Dad's fingers were boxing gloves compared to Dr. Cohen's.

"Neither did my client. If it's the one I think it is."

"Huh?"

"Her mother died when she was three. Suicide," she said. Dr. Cohen looked down at her hands and let loose a deep sigh. "Those men were in my office. They have access to me."

"Was Ellen Reynolds one of your clients?"

I showed her the photograph.

"Ellen?" She recognized the name, not the girl. The same motherless client had spoken of an Ellen Reynolds and the church on McGowan she was a part of, a church the client found appealing and had, through Ellen, visited a few times. The client liked the church's philosophies because it was about letting go, finding inner peace, surrendering from a life of the seven deadly sins for a life of—

"The pearl of heaven?"

"Yes. And oneness. Those are the very words she used. Yes."

Ellen was one of the last people to see my father alive, he was taking her away from that church. Somehow she and Dr. Cohen's client were connected. "Did your client stay at that church?"

"Susan never told me that Ellen was—Métis, is it?"

"Yes." I rubbed the edges of my mouth. "Susan?"

"My client." Dr. Cohen didn't offer up the last name. Attended it several times, Susan did. Found it quaint, another word she used, quaint, and then she dropped out at the University of Toronto.

"Why?"

"She was pregnant. And wanted an abortion." Dr. Cohen discussed it over with her client through three sessions and because The Criminal Code of Canada views it as a crime to "procure a miscarriage," the client was seeking the help of a young medical student at the U of T, who performed such services for friends and desperate women.

"This doctor? Was he a friend of hers?"

"Yes. Part of her inner circle." She has a group of friends at the U of T; they call themselves the Defeatniks, beat-down hipsters of the nuclear age.

"The Defeatniks?"

"Yes."

"The law on abortion will change," I said. "Some day. Soon." I shrugged absently. "Her family was opposed, I assume?"

"They didn't know."

"And you suggested?"

"That she make her own choice."

"Those were your very words, that's what you said, 'make your own choice?'"

She saw where I was going with this. Someone connected to the client wanted the messenger dead. Maybe the family *did know* that the girl was pregnant, maybe a family member or one of the Defeatniks, or both, knew and wanted to *do something* about it.

"Yes, that's what I said." She picked up several sheets full of bloody Stars of David. "I'm a firm believer that we must be free to choose what we choose."

"I know." I kissed her on the forehead. She smelled of lilacs. "That's why I love you, Doc."

She leaned her head left, eyes smiling. "Don't—"

"I know, I know. 'Don't call me Doc.'"

She laughed.

"There's something else. I don't know what it means." She opened the center drawer to her desk, slid out folded-up blueprints to a floor plan. Ellen had given them to Susan for safekeeping. Susan passed them on to the doc. "'You can look into it,' she said."

I pushed back my porkpie. "Look into what?"

"I'm afraid my client was rather vague. It was her standard MO."

"Right."

I unfolded and smoothed out the floor plans. It was the McGowan Street church. I recognized the spacious sanctuary immediately, the fire exits, and the places were windows should be, now bricked up and covered over with neon kitsch. The basement to the plans was circled. Down there were laundry facilities, three or four separate showers, and something that looked like a bunch of condensers to a central-air system. "Why all the cloak and dagger? Why not just tell you?"

"She was into mind games."

"Another part of her MO?"

"Uh-huh."

That cracked me up.

"Why did Ellen take the plans?"

"My client didn't say."

"Swell." My palms were sore. "Speaking of cloak and dagger—" I smiled my lopsided grin. "I don't want to alarm you, but there's two men downstairs. Under a street light."

We crossed to the window together and she saw them, still smoking, their hats catching star points of yellow.

"Is there a back way out of here?"

She nodded.

"Susan have a last name?"

"I don't want to tell you, but maybe, for the client's safety, I should."

"Right now, Doc, I'm worried about your safety"

Susan had gone missing for over a week since dropping out of U of T.

"Do you know any of her friends, the Defeatniks?"

"No."

"Did she get the abortion?"

"I don't know. Haven't heard from her."

"Your case connects to my case—to Ellen—Ellen Reynolds, to my father, Ira Fuller, who wasn't a good man, but he was a man. His murder—"

"Susan Whitfield." She's the daughter of Mr. Franklin W. Whitfield, a munitions engineer, who made his fortune in WWII armaments. Family lives in Rosedale.

"Whitfield? Deuces' dad?"

"Huh?"

I filled her in, the stringer, the wannabe crime reporter.

Yes, the Whitfields, she said. Susan and her brother were close, two years apart. During their childhood they spent all their free time together, creating their own language that no one understood but them. Wrote a host of twisted fairytales where the Evil Queen wins and Cinderella's body is fed to the birds.

"Charming." I suggested we better find a back way out of here and head to my place where Dr. Cohen could hide out for the interim.

The door to her office kicked open, pulling from the wood, briefly hanging from the hinges, before falling.

One of the men had a long angular face, too long for his stubby body.

They were both holding machine guns.

And silence followed.

They weren't going to kill us.

Yet.

"Let's go tour the Bluffs," said the bigger of the two, his accent French.

I don't think they were about to offer us bus fare, motel accommodations, or a free continental breakfast with the tour.

Oh well.

Second Period

They weren't very talkative.

The bigger guy, red cowboy kerchiefs around his wrists, drove the car, the inside of his left wrist atop the steering wheel, twelve o'clock high. His right hand held a Gauloises cigarette, bobbing now and then like a baton. He wore a blue Cavanagh hat with a white band, Sinatra–style, Capitol Records, 1953.

The kerchiefs around his wrists hung down raggedly, broken bird wings. It was quite a look, somewhere between tough urban cowboy and folk-singing college kid. The fuzzy shadows filling his face like seconds of fabric meant he had probably started shaving last week. The poor bastard also had a cold. His eyes were red and his nose ran. I put him at twenty, maybe twenty-one, if that.

His partner, the stubby guy with a long face, didn't believe in deodorant. He gave off a gamey air, like that of a dog coming in after lollygagging in the grass in the rain. He gnawed on a chunk of beef jerky, its broken off shards reminding me of balsa wood.

Dad bought me a balsa wood airplane when I was a kid: thin wires, rubber band to spin the propeller, and red, plastic wheels. The plane's wings often broke on its third or fourth backyard flight. One time, Dad tossed me such a plane still in its packaging. "Don't get out of the car," he said, and entered a bar, the Highwayman, on Sherbourne Street. Three hours later he returned, having lost all of his paycheck on beer and darts.

His head collapsed against the steering wheel. On the way home, I prayed he kept the car between the lines.

This here now was a different kind of ride.

The stubby fella gnawed harder on his jerky. Every now and then he broke off a piece of balsa wood with enough flourish to resemble a toreador flashing a red cape.

At our feet, in the backseat, were twelve or thirteen beef jerky wrappers, eight or nine empty paper cups, and an assortment of pop bottles, including Orange Crush and Hires Root Beer. *Was Ellen Reynolds in this car? Ever?*

They probably killed Gus.

"Where you taking us?"

Dr. Cohen said absolutely nothing, her face a resolute mask, eyes ahead, faraway, lost in irretrievable memories most likely, hands politely positioned in her lap, the collar of her black wool coat up, shadowing her face.

"This isn't the movies, imperialist American horseshit," said the driver.

Definitely a college kid.

"We're not going to reveal secrets or reasons for our actions to help fill in the gaps to the story you're trying to decode."

"Right." Stubby smiled, his face full of beef jerky hash. "No Western storytelling here. That stuff's dead."

"Dead as a doornail," said the driver.

I wanted to tell him Rocky Sullivan said the exact same words in *Angels with Dirty Faces. Things are dead as a doornail around heah*. I couldn't stop laughing. "Dead as a doornail." James fucking Cagney.

"Shut up or you'll get it right here," said Stubby.

"You sure you guys aren't right out of the 1930s?"

"You guys killed Gus." Dr. Cohen's hands raised up from her lap and floated back down. She pointed at the wrappers filling the backseat floor.

"Like I said," the driver smiled. "This isn't the movies. No answers. No tying up of loose ends."

Streetlights danced over the hood of the car, ricocheting with comets of color. Loose ends. This case had several. *What did the note mean*, We know what you said? *What was said?*

"Too much, that's what was said." Stubby laughed and then the driver.

Big jokes all around.

"We're dismantling the universe," the driver said.

"What?"

"Shut-up. You talk too much," Stubby said to his partner.

"You worry too much. Don't worry. Those words mean nothing to them."

Dismantling.

The universe.

A gas station gleamed on the corner, its red-and-white sign a light buoy warming an empty street.

The stubby fella handed me college-lined paper and a Bic pen, the cap a broken golf tee. Write what I tell you to write, he said.

Streetlights fissured against the car's side mirrors.

A suicide note. That's what he wanted. Dr. Cohen and I had made a pact to end it together. We were going to jump off the Bluffs.

The plan, according to the driver, was to place the note on my father's kitchen table in Gradwell by a glass of warm milk and cookies.

"Like for Santa Claus," Stubby said.

"Yeah, like for Santa Claus," the driver echoed.

Big laughs. These guys should write for the Hemingway estate. They kept repeating themselves. Do that a few times and every utterance will take on a kind of helium-elevated gravitas.

They figured the cops being in and out of Dad's pad were bound to see the planted note and conclude that Dr. Cohen and I walked from there to the Bluffs and jumped. What these two PhDs of crime hadn't figured was in having me write the note now, instead of, say, at a table, the police would notice the rushed, uneven letters, the lopsided lines curving out of the page's inscribed lines, and deduce that the note had, in all probability, been composed in a hurry, in a moving vehicle.

"Okay, Hemingway, what do you want me to write, exactly?"

We rushed past a dull white and black-trimmed strip mall: a quickie Chinese Food restaurant; a flower shop; a Becker's; a donut joint; and a one-hour martinizing. My shirt sure needed to be pressed.

"I told you survival."

"Well, that's a little vague, Ernie."

"Just write."

"Sure thing, Ernest."

The driver chuckled. He had a better sense of humor than I initially gave him credit for. His eyes were gentle, full of apologies. "How about this, *Fitzgerald—*" He smiled. "Dr. Cohen couldn't take the guilty memories of Auschwitz." He swallowed, the broken-winged kerchiefs tapping the side of the steering wheel. "And you couldn't take the memory flashbacks of repeated abuses at the hands of your father. Just a kid: eight, nine, ten—"

Dr. Cohen shot me a look of sadness.

"Where did you get that information?"

If I had my gun he'd be dead. But they made me slam away the snub-nosed in a desk drawer at Dr. Cohen's before they shoved us into a 1957 Ford Fairlane, four-door, hardtop, orange and black, Quebec plates, white-wall tires, and rust slicing along the bottom of the passenger door.

"Our intel is pretty damn good," said Stubby face.

"We got it." The driver was unable to look at me in the rear-view. His voice quieted. "We got it."

"How?"

"Other people. In this case." He leaned his wrist harder atop the steering wheel. "That's all you're getting from us. Death to Western mythology and narrative storytelling."

Fuck, Durgana may have been an English major, but these guys were star pupils from the Philosophy department, and Marxist-Leninists to boot.

"Dismantling the universe? What's that about?"

"Think of it as the McGuffin, baby," the driver said.

"Oh, so you are into Western storytelling."

"He has you there." Stubby said, smiling, shoulders pulled up as if on a giant hanger.

"Who are you?" Dr. Cohen's voice was steady, the spaces between the words even. "Why the posters in my office?"

"I'm an art major," the driver said.

"McGill?" Quebec plates. And I had remembered the combination of letters and numbers.

"I told you, you talk too much," Stubby said.

"Leave him alone, Hemingway," I said.

"Will you shut the fuck up with that. That joke's getting old."

"Sorry, Jake Barnes."

The driver was chuckling again. He rubbed away, with the back of a hand, nasal drip from his upper lip. "I like art. I just go for it."

"Dr. Cohen." Stubby's voice revved like a Porsche. "This, this drive, in this, this car, is not a therapy session, seeking some magical rubber ducky moment that will explain everything. 'I kill people because I didn't get enough cookies when I was a kid' kind of thing, come on—"

"No, you kill people because you just don't get enough—"

"Is that a sex joke, Doctor? Oh witty."

"I thought it was pretty good," said the driver.

So did I.

"Shut up."

I guess I said the last three words out loud.

"You killed Gus," Dr. Cohen restated her previous claim. This time the words were rabbit punches to the kidneys.

"Yes. He was part of the, uh, dismantling."

"Now who's saying too much?" said the driver.

Stubby shrugged. "They'll be dead soon." Stubby liked words, the sound of words, how they filled spaces, but he wasn't going to fill our time with answers. Sorry. He smiled. The color of his bridge had yellowed.

"Soup cans," said the driver. "I want to do Pop Art but not with soup cans like Warhol. Donuts and beef jerky. That would be cool."

"Marilyn eating donuts and beef jerky that would be even cooler," Stubby said.

"Oh, that's good. Marilyn." He nodded his head with amped-up approval.

How did killing Gus help them dismantle the universe? What universe? Who's? What did this all have to do with Brother Durgana and the church and his goddamn neon fixtures and rooms without windows? How about Bob Waterman and Silverwood's? Was there something there I missed? What was I getting too close to? What did Dr. Cohen say that somehow involved me? We know what you said. *Fuck. Maybe they feared what my upcoming meetings with the Defeatniks might reveal? What about Ellen Reynolds? If she were alive, maybe she'd tell me something they didn't want me to know. How was Susan Whitfield caught up in all this? And how did they know my backstory, the lurid moments with my father? Did my father tell somebody? Ellen?*

"Enough kibitzing. Start writing." Stubby spoke with his gun, a .45 that not so gently nudged my face. Christ, I wish I had my .38.

I couldn't see too well in the dark, but I scrawled something about my unrequited love for the doctor and how I couldn't go on anymore. The fellas at *As the World Turns* and *The Edge of Night* would eat this shit up. The doctor wouldn't give me a tumble so I was willing to jump into the abyss. Doc had her own issues, the horrors of Auschwitz. It was pretty soapy. I hoped the cops who found the note could read through the suds.

Streetlight caught the top of the ribbed bench seat and a small, faint perforated line of white appeared, dots of confetti. I dipped a finger in it.

I expected it to taste like cinnamon, but it didn't. It was vaguely metallic.

I signed the note. Dr. Cohen did too.

And then I thought of Bob Waterman and his allergies, the constant nasal drip, the red eyes. Allergies. Uh-huh.

Stubby seized his pen back from me as if it were Tiffany diamonds or some damn thing. He quickly read the piece I had up for the writers' workshop.

"Which of you is the junkie?" I leaned back, arms crossed. "There's coke on the bench seat. I guess you don't get no kicks from champagne, huh?" I looked at the driver, propped myself up, whispered in his ear. "My bet's on you, Cavanagh Hat. Your eyes, red. Even in the dim light of the streets I can see your nose running."

Was Waterman a cokehead too? Instead of just finding my father was he in on the kill?

"It's not coke." Cavanagh Hat laughed.

"So, this is all about drugs?" Dr. Cohen exhaled sharply. "Drugs? That's why we kill people?"

Is that the universe they sought, a drug-addled one? Dismantle this one for that?

Stubby hit me hard with the side of the gun. I skidded back into the seat, blood dotting my chin, wind chimes jangling in my ears. A couple of stitches on my chin were re-opened. "What kind of a note is this?" He held up my barely intelligible scrawl. "It reads like an episode of *The Edge of Night.*"

"Cut the horseshit. Re-do the suicide note," the driver said.

Stubby tore off another sheet, handed me a different pen. Parker Brothers.

I'd try to put some $50 words into this one.

Drugs. Figures. Maybe Brother Durgana's McGowan Street crowd were doped up on something, maybe not coke but something, and that's why they mindlessly prayed, waltzing around in threadbare robes, giving generously, they were mentally brainwashed and physically beaten, and through drugs their resistances were lowered. They had no collective wills. They were the walking dead. Okay, makes sense, and Ellen Reynolds broke free from all that, used my father's taxi service to make a quick break. Did his helping her cost him his life? Did she set him up?

Is Waterman a member of this cult?

Or perhaps Dr. Cohen's client Susan Whitfield is a player in this little drama. What's her role?

She knew Ellen. Did my father tell Ellen about abusing me and she inadvertently told Susan who told these fellas?

"Write the note. Quickly." A wash of teriyaki jerky smothered my face. "Mention the abuse. Mention it."

I couldn't.

We arrived at the same park that was just blocks away from Dad's. Cavanagh Hat threw the car into park, killed the engine.

Damn. The new note would be clean, look like it had been written at a table instead of in a moving car.

How could I admit, to paper, and the world, to read what had happened to me, how I felt betrayed by my father, by my own body, the dirty residual guilt that covered me and my thoughts, fears of sex, for years? My skin's full of fish scales that won't fall away.

The sheet of paper remained a snow-capped iceberg weighing me down.

Dr. Cohen reached for the paper, pen, and wrote hurriedly, saving me from re-animated trauma, Dad's hands, boxing gloves, pushing down the back of my head as he grunts and comes between my thighs. I don't know what she wrote. I didn't read it. I signed it. I didn't read it.

Stubby read it. Three, four times. Slowly. "That's better," he said.

The driver wiped at his nose again, smiled dimly. "Much better." He couldn't look at us.

A pulse ran along the doctor's jawline.

"I'm sorry." Cavanagh Hat's voice was cake crumbles. He rubbed at his nose once more. "You know I'm Jewish?"

Dr. Cohen spat in his face. "What would Dr. Jayson Garfein have to say?"

He let the spittle trail slowly down one of the lines bracketing his mouth, his chin. "He wouldn't think I was representing my tribe well," he said. "He'd call me a closet anti-Jew." Spittle hung from his chin, dripping, forty pieces of silver.

"Anti-Semite not anti-Jew is what he'd say." Dr. Cohen smiled.

So the driver did attend McGill. Dr. Garfein was Dr. Cohen's professor of psychology years ago.

"I told you, you talk too much." Stubby picked away at a balsa wood chunk of beef jerky stuck in his back molars. He seized the note from the driver, waved with his gun. "Let's go."

The ground, cold gravel, crunched, and the sky was clear liquid black, as an even colder breeze blew off the lake and over the Bluffs, stenciling our faces with thin portières of mist.

Pinpoint stars shivered above and on white caps of tidal waves.

The driver mumbled something about how getting me out of the narrative would ruin his plans. The pronoun choice was a little fuzzy. *His? As in the driver or someone else. What plans? Who's plans?*

White caps shivered with light.

It was too pretty a night to die.

My heart was in my shoulders and the back of my legs shook as I walked. Dr. Cohen, the two hitmen behind her, reached for my hand with steady fingers, stilling my trembling. I was a real mensch she said. She loved me. Stay strong. Don't let them win, don't give them your dignity.

If only my father had ever spoken such words.

The driver, Mr. Kerchiefs, sniffed and sucked back nasal drainage, and I knew he was about four paces off behind me.

The gravel turned from cold slivers to bald grass and then dirt and blackness. The mist on my face and arms felt heavier at the Bluffs' edge. Below, blue-black waves capped with bits of white light. Seagulls lapped at the white.

"You know what I love about the Bluffs?" Stubby was revving up to give a soliloquy, his words elevated. "Natural. Not a product of monopoly capital but of nature. True beauty. No members of the proletariat died to create this splendor." He paused. "That's far enough."

Did Cavanagh Hat have a gun? He had a machine gun at the office, but those were locked in the trunk of the Fairlane.

In the distance, a floating buoy blinked.

I tried slowing my breathing. Don't hand over your dignity. Breathe. Pain left my shoulders. *Breathe. You matter. Breathe. My legs were no longer shaking. Vulnerability is your strength. Breathe.*

"On three you take a powder. Got it?" Stubby.

Take a powder. Right out of Gold Medal fiction. Jim Thompson.

"I'm going to count to three. If you don't jump, I'll shoot you in the head. One—"

Two shots, bleating like one, crushed the night's stillness.

White light danced on triangles of waves.

And I turned, because I wasn't dead yet.

I had just seen the white triangles dancing.

Both hit men had dropped with the gunshots. Stubby was in a three-point stance, and Dr. Cohen kicked him before he could assess what the fuck was happening. She nailed him a beauty, right in the middle of his face, lifting him by the nose, sprawling back, head snapping, gun dropping, suicide note still gripped in left hand.

He held onto the wrong thing.

Before he could pick up the fallen gun, I had it in my mitts, breathing calmly, not quickly, and with both hands tapped the trigger, twice, red blossoms spilling across his chest.

He fell back, panhandler hands opening, wanting loose change.

He wasn't going to want a damn thing in a few seconds.

I smelled shit.

Stubby's breath was heavy and shallow, a hollow rustle of leaves, as eyes filmed over, losing their target, the dark, black sky.

Cavanagh Hat hadn't moved since he slumped to his knees, and then he slowly toppled on his face, a crumpled heap, his hat twisting in the Lakeshore breeze, blowing clear off the Bluffs.

He died without a word. No epitaph. The back of his head, grapefruit pulp.

I looked for the source of the shots. Couldn't see a damn thing in the shadows of trees and black sky. "Sal?"

"It's me." Stana's feet padded quickly in the dark.

I sure have a knack for being rescued by women. Anne Chevalier of the RCMP in my last case. Now Stana Younger.

I crossed back down to Stubby, his breaths asthmatic.

I looked at him.

His last gasp was a slashed whitewall tire.

I rolled the suicide note into a ball and threw it into the night sky.

The Bluffs took it.

"He's dead," Dr. Cohen said, matter-of-factly. I don't think her heart rate climbed over sixty. "You okay?"

"Do I *look okay*?"

"Stupid question."

"No, no." I touched her left shoulder and smiled my lopsided lupine grin.

The watery mist from the Bluffs smelled of spawning fish and my mouth filled with tears. "How did they know all that about *me*—about *you*—how did they?"

She hugged me.

Did Dad tell Ellen and she someone else? Did they torture Dad before shooting him full of hop and he talked?

Why kill him?

Dismantle the universe.

Dr. Cohen whispered that I shouldn't feel ashamed. To cry is to feel, a good sign. She's the one who should feel ashamed for feeling no fear.

Stana emerged from the black shadows, carrying my .45, the one from the glovebox of my Galaxie. Her hair was sweat stained, eyes full of worries.

"Thanks," Dr. Cohen said. "You're one hell of a fakakta cavalry."

"I got Hayden's note. And the Coffee Crisp." She kissed my cheek. She feared I'd had a relapse of bad memories and was running to Dr. Cohen's office for a therapy session, in search of much needed love and support, and when Stana arrived and saw us escorted by the two McGill baby-faced killers, with one of the fine gents trailing too close behind me, his walk and manner reminiscent of a certain Brother Thompson of McGowan Street fame, and his green-padded coat with the .45 pressing against her hip, she knew we were in trouble, grabbed the .45 from my Galaxie, and followed. "I wasn't sure the gun was loaded." She had no idea how to pull out the clip, but thank God she knew how to kick off the safety and blast the thing.

Damn she was good, awful good.

She rubbed at her shoulder. The gun had a loud kick, she said.

"You're not supposed to hold your arm stiff, bend the elbow."

"Do I look like the kind of person who's at home on a target range?"

Then Stana moved in the darkness, crossing over to the man with the grapefruit head, her figure blending with patches of black, and I felt the most connected to her I had ever felt before. I wanted to just hear her breathe, talk, breathe, and talk some more.

"I killed him, didn't I?" She bit her upper lip. "Shitshitshit-shitshit. I killed him, didn't I?"

"Dead as a doornail," I said. "Dead as a motherfucking doornail."

Dr. Cohen laughed, throwing her head back. She smiled at Stana. "Dead as a doornail."

Her Cagney was better than mine.

AFTER THE POLICE BAGGED THE BODIES, the guns, the Tommies in the trunk of the Fairlane, stretched out more yellow tape, and asked enough questions to fill out the paperwork for a government grant, Top Cop Sal Lambertino and two lab guys followed us in Stana's car to Dr. Cohen's office. There I retrieved my gun from a lower-desk drawer and stood by the window as they dusted and Sal asked follow-up questions.

We showed him the posters, the Warhol-esque Star of David ditto run with artwork full of spots and comets of blood splatter.

"It's blood. I checked."

Sal lifted the bottle of hydrogen peroxide and handed it to me. "Your cut's reopened. You might want to clean it."

"Thanks, pal." I did so. Stana re-applied the bandage.

Sal told the lab boys take all the posters, run the blood through, see what we find. He sat in a chair across from Dr. Cohen. The room was high-key lit: desk lamp, two floor lamps, overhead fixtures burning brightly, chasing any shadows from the setting. For a moment, I thought I was in a goddamn Hollywood musical.

Dr. Cohen sat in her own chair, her wool coat snug tight, all but the very top button clasped. Maybe she was more affected by everything that went down than she let on. Her eyes were sharp points.

"So what they have against you, Doc?"

"Don't call her Doc," I said.

Dr. Cohen laughed. "And I have no idea what I allegedly said that I shouldn't have. *We know what you said.* That says nothing. I talk a lot. I say a lot." She shifted in her chair.

The lab boys dusted, took random photographs, and with a fluoroscope searched for traces of evidence in the killers' footsteps.

Sal wiped at the corners of his mouth, one foot pushed up against the edge of the desk, felt hat tapping out an errant rhythm on a raised knee.

He couldn't believe that Stana had killed a man tonight.

"I heard him count off, one, and I knew I didn't have much time to do anything else."

"Well, that's what you get for hanging with the likes of him." He pointed a stubby finger my way. "And I assume the other killing, yours Superstar, was self-defense?"

"Of course," I nodded.

"Sure."

"Hey, Chief. Check this." It was the heavier of the lab boys. He wore a dark suit, skinny tie, a homburg hat. He flipped a coin-size disc on Dr. Cohen's desk. It rolled up against an edge of the desk blotter. "The room was bugged."

"What?" Sal's slow rhythm hiccupped against his knee. The 2 and 4 hits shifting to 1 and 3. "Shit." He held up the disc, felt the pigeonholes. "Jesus Christ this is old. Prewar." He flipped it to me.

"Bugged?" I rolled the disc in my hand. It resembled a miniature mouthpiece to a telephone crossed with a diaphragm, a black bubble with ribbed aluminum ridges. *Shit. That's how the two hitmen knew about my past, my abuse at the hands of my Dad. How long had they been listening in on Dr. Cohen's sessions? More importantly, why were they listening? We know what you said suddenly took on a whole new meaning. They literally did know. They had heard it all. Who's they? Susan's family? Someone else? Someone connected to me? Did I reveal too much about Cassel and Steinmetz and Terrien and my first case and bodies buried in Vaughan, Ontario? Fuck.*

I pocketed the disc. They found two more. One inside a lampshade, the other behind a painting.

Dr. Cohen's face was absent of color. "My clients trust me," she mumbled, her eyes darting about, calculating, wondering how long she had been a victim of such surveillance. I thought of the cameras at The People's Way to Christ.

Sal didn't know what to say. Stana fidgeted with her handbag, lit a cigarette, blew smoke angrily in a corner of a ceiling.

Sal slapped his hands together, returned to drumming atop his knee. "So what have we got so far?" Let's quit worrying about what has taken place and do something to stop it, he said. They bugged the room. Who's they? What have we got, people?

The list was long. (1) My father was killed by drugs, perhaps for or over drugs, but the killers made a fatal fuckup: Dad was a lefty so the suicide wasn't a suicide. (2) A church/cult on McGowan Street, full of followers, people who have surrendered their possessions to allow their minds to be "possessed" by a charismatic charlatan, Brother Durgana, former stock broker turned all Elmer Gantry, is somehow part of the mix. The joint's crawling with surveillance cameras, there are no windows on the walls, and kitschy neon lights are everywhere; shit, surveillance cameras, people, hidden microphones: the two are related; I just know it; (3) Silverwood's Dairy delivered milk and butter to The People's Way to Christ. Were they delivering something else? Drugs? What's Bob Waterman's role, Mr. Company Man with his yellow polo shirts and blue Dickies and running nose? Allergies or fellow cokehead like Cavanagh Hat? Waterman found Dad. A coincidence? Or was he keeping company with somebody else? A woman? A cult? (4) Dad was seen by Mrs. Mary Hale taking Ellen Reynolds, a Saskatchewan runaway and member of the Métis, away from the church. Running from what? Toward what? What's Dad's connection to Ellen, the church, this case? (5) Ellen Reynolds befriended Susan Whitfield, of the famous Whitfields in Rosedale. The munitions engineer? His son, Deuces, is a stringer with the *Telegram*. Moreover, these floor plans—

"Shouldn't that be six—" Stana.

"Okay. Six." These floor plans. I unfolded the blueprints, spread it across Dr. Cohen's desk. It's of the church. The basement, as you can see, is circled.

"Is that an air-conditioning unit?" Sal.

"I think so. Maybe this has something to do with the midnight mass?"

Sal was no longer tapping his hat against his knee.

Stana jumped in. Her research this afternoon revealed that the Whitfield fortunes rested in armaments for the war effort, including an advanced form of creeping jelly, napalm in a grenade, that sticks to surfaces, climbs and burns.

"Where's this Susan now?" Sal's hat was pushed back on his head, a much better look than his bashing-about "Mr. Tambourine Man" pose.

"No fucking idea," I said. She's pregnant. Sought an abortion; (7) Is her father and his people the ones who know what Dr. Cohen said, bugged the room? Did they, after what they heard, want revenge on the good doctor? They're anti-abortionists? I don't know. Stana has a 4:30 p.m. appointment set up for us with the senior Whitfield, and his posse, tomorrow. A U of T medical student offered to provide the illegal abortion, but Susan changed her mind, after occasionally attending The People's Way to Christ with Ellen a few times.

"No shit." The brim of Sal's hat resembled a pug-nosed dog.

"No shit."

There's more. (8) Susan Whitfield hung with a group of Beat students at the U of T.

"Beat?" Sal wasn't getting the vibe. His beard said Hemingway not Jack Kerouac.

"You know, like the writer, *On the Road*," Stana said.

Nothing.

"It's pretty good," I said.

"Adolescent fantasy," Stana said. "The women in the novel are just fuck toys for the boys."

"Beat? Like bongo drums?"

"Yeah, Sal. Bongo drums." I shook my head and Stana laughed.

The U of T kids were atomic-era products, calling themselves the Defeatniks, figuring the clock was about to hit midnight and then all would go ka-bluey. I was going to track them down tomorrow at the local coffee shops along Harbord Street. I needed to understand their philosophies, get a profile of Susan.

Stana was next to me, curling a hip into mine, bending slightly so that she could nuzzle against my neck and clavicle. She smelled of sandalwood. One of her hands traced my chest. "You doing okay," she whispered.

"Comme ci, comme ca," I waved my hand slightly. It was shaking nervously, much more so than I cared to admit.

(9) Gus. Gus Carhart. Our two baby-faced killers copped to killing him, but it wasn't over cash and beef jerky. They killed him because they were dismantling the universe.

"Say what?" Sal's face looked as if he had just walked out of a darkened movie theater.

"I don't know. Those were their exact words—"

"That's all they said. Dismantle the universe." Dr. Cohen shrugged. Who's universe, what universe, I'm not sure, she said. I don't think they are either. "Call it a hunch." She smiled.

"Drugs maybe?" I mentioned the perforated line of coke on top of the Fairlane's bench seat, Cavanagh Hat's running nose, Bob Waterman's allergies, the church followers overall lethargy and lack of gumption.

"That's not a universe. That might be a gas station in a universe. But drugs isn't a universe," Stana said.

Nine items. How do they entangle, untangle, connect?

Tomorrow, and then tomorrow, and then Detroit. The Olympia. I was running out of time. *Dismantle the universe. How was Gus messing with their universe?*

"Ten." Stana extricated herself from my shoulder, stood straight. She wore a white blouse, black slacks, white low-heeled shoes. "The Army Surplus store."

"Oh yeah, ten. Army surplus." Pain returned behind my eyes and my empty stomach was full of coolant, my body trembling with air conditioning. "What about ten?"

The freckles in Stana's eyes danced. The lease for the building: Bolemac.

That was the name of the dummy organization of my first heavy case: the Stabulas girls, kidnapping, corruption, porn and gambling at Maple Leaf Gardens. Bolemac was where Smith and his potato-chip eating sidekick Bullard hid pots of money. Smith was now, because of that case, in serious trouble with the law: racketeering, gambling, extortion charges. He was also suffering from bleeding ulcers. Were his hands in more dirt? I couldn't quite figure the connection, but I recalled the cache of arms at his modern, post art-deco mansion in Rosedale: the room full of tear-gas canisters, potato mashers, Thompson submachine guns, and AK-47s. I wonder if he also housed bugging devices and some creeping jelly grenades. Let's just say, if he were into army surplus, I don't think it's for the camping gear or the joys of kayaking.

Sal sighed and picked up the phone. He asked for the boys in the lab.

Stana returned to nuzzling my chest, bending slightly, hair fine, sweat behind a right ear. "You look beat," she whispered.

"Maybe I'll read some Kerouac."

She smiled.

"You were good back there." I tucked a wisp of auburn hair behind an ear. "I never got a chance to thank you—"

"Redemption, remember?"

"I'm sorry I said that," I whispered.

"You're not going to fucking believe this." Sal dropped the receiver back in the cradle. It hit like a rim shot. He waited another beat. "Eleven. That was Anne Chevalier on the phone. RCMP." He held up a hand and spoke hurriedly. The two dead were college students at McGill: one Barry Kunz and one Ivan Sevrier. Believers in a free Quebec. Libre, baby. N'oublie jamais. Card-carrying members.

"Oh no," I growled, recalling their tossed-off comments on imperialism, monopoly capital, and Western storytelling.

"And let's not forget, 'Ode to the Scarborough Bluffs,'" Dr. Cohen said.

"Here we go again," chimed in Stana, shaking her head. My last case was full of so-called terrorists who ended up being posers, one of them from Kirkland Lake, Ontario, not Quebec.

But these two guys were the real deal, hardcore types dedicated to Quebec independence, Anne said. They were two of the culprits involved in dropping a few smoke bombs at the Montreal stock exchange last month. And when a multi-nationalist came to McGill to give a lecture, Kunz welcomed him in bare feet to protest a sweatshop the guy had opened in Peru.

"Twelve." It was Dr. Cohen's turn to hold up an authoritative cop-like hand. "Ivan Sevrier. Susan knew him."

Christ.

She had mentioned him, by name, in several of her therapy sessions with the doctor. "I remember the name because she made fun of it, saying one of her friends had a real commie name, that's how she phrased it, a real commie name, Ivan. As in the Terrible or the Bear." He was a part of Susan's inner circle and she liked him a lot, said he had integrity and spoke with his eyes. "They were always sincere."

"Uh-huh."

"He was also a member of the Defeatniks."

THE SKY WAS AN AMBER ORANGE and dust from a ribbon of road drifted into the car covering my hands, the steering wheel, the inside windows with silty chalk. Tall grass bent in the shape of curved, shadowy letters, Hebraic markings in a strange land.

The building, a block and a half long and shaped like a gold brick, glinted dark yellow. Instead of curtains, Hebraic letters draped in the long, angular windows.

I knocked on the door.

Sun on shoulders and neck, the sky above appeared to be crying. It was as if my body were under a blanket. I was a kid again.

A rabbi opened the door, his eyes wide-set, face, clean-shaven, even though he was sixtyish and I expected him to appear bearded.

"Things aren't always what they seem."

I smiled.

"Hayden Ira Fuller?"

Before I could respond, he handed me another Hebrew letter, and I wanted to spell something with all the letters I'd seen, but I didn't know what they meant.

With a hooked finger, he beckoned me to follow. He was dressed all in black, looking Medieval. Me, I was casual: black leather jacket, tan chinos, a chambray shirt, boat shoes. I never wear boat shoes.

But I was happy to be here, to come out from under the blanket into orange light.

Suddenly, I knew I had a lot of time left: life, hockey, love.

"You do." The rabbi followed my thoughts, eyes locked on mine.

"Is Dad here?"

"He is."

I was looking forward to seeing him, talking for a while about the past, about Mom's death, about the past twenty-four hours, about Ellen Reynolds, about my disparaging memories and how unkind I'd been in my heart toward him.

"He can't stay long," the rabbi said, handing me yet another letter.

I studied some of this stuff for my bar mitzvah. But that was years ago.

Another room. White furniture, walls, carpeting, Venetian blinds. Chandeliers hung from the vaulted ceiling giving off bright white light. A white coffee table. White glasses.

Dad sat in a canvas chair, one leg resting on top his knee, his face dotted with salt-and-pepper stubble, eyes weary but full of playful possibilities, jokes to tell. He was in his Silverwood's uniform but the blue-and-gold piping was now all white on white.

He wasn't holding any letters.

Hebrew or otherwise.

He stared, beaming at me, and I felt loved. No words. And then he was gone.

The room, white as ever.

"I told you, he couldn't stay." The rabbi rubbed together hands folded in front of him.

"Yeah, you did."

My voice was happy and content. I hadn't heard those tones in a long time. Something seemed meaningful about all this, attainable.

The white room turned dark green, and the grass outside was now inside, swaying.

The letter in my left hand became the Talmud; the letter in my right the Torah. And as the grass weaved about the room, lifting and falling, falling and lifting, we danced, the rabbi and me, dancing with the rhythms of the tall grass.

—

SHE WAS ON TOP, pushing my hips into couch cushions, lips

gracing mine. “Shh—”

“What about Dr. Cohen?”

“She’s asleep.”

Stana’s fine hair filled my eyes, lips, and I wanted to take all of her into my mouth, like Diego Rivera had wanted to do with Frida Kahlo’s ashes, dying and living, sex as death, as beautiful as death, as sad as living. Resignations of desire filled me.

My gun was on the coffee table next to the couch, watching over the two of them, allegedly asleep in my room, but now Stana was here, watching over me, wanting me. She arched back, breasts raised and I kissed her nipples, took in a breast, another, wanting to take in all of her. “She’ll hear us,” I murmured.

“I switched glasses.”

Dr. Cohen, knowing that Stana was upset over killing Sevrier, had mixed up a sedative for her, only Stana got Dr. Cohen to drink the one Stana was supposed to.

The tip of her nose glistened in the dark room, and I was hard in her hand.

I pushed against her hand.

“Easy, easy.” She guided me in.

She moved up and down, taking me quickly to the edge, and then just as quick that edge ebbed away, my body becoming grimy fish scales.

“Relax.” She pushed deeper, pressing arms into my thighs.

“I can’t. I can’t.”

I wanted to, and then I slipped out.

Hair in eyes, nipples under my chin, she reached for me, and said don’t worry about pleasing her, just have fun, and go when I’m ready to go.

My body just wouldn’t cooperate, I wanted to say.

I was struggling to breathe.

“It’sokayit’sokayit’sokay.”

She kissed the side of my neck, holding me, holding herself, holding on to us, what was left of us, of me, of my sexual self, holding, holding.

And then I came.

In her hand.

AFTER A FRIED EGG SANDWICH, black coffee, and an orange, I wandered around U of T's Registrar's office and asked about Susan Whitfield. Was there any support for such a troubled person, was she seeing a therapist? They didn't seem to know she had stopped attending classes. A young woman, a non-trad student and part-time secretary wearing a black pantsuit and leopard-spotted bandana, knew of Susan and her friends and gave a list of names and locations they frequented. I slipped her a ten-spot and followed the thread.

Sharon Dafoe was the first name on the list. A tall angular blond, whose hips entered the room before the rest of her, she was a barista at a local coffee shop at the corner of Bloor and Spadina, several blocks west of my old office. She wore a cashmere sweater, orange with black trim and black buttons, and tight-fitting capri pants. She didn't want to talk, but when I flashed my PI license and said it was me or the po-lice and their white interrogation room with bright lights on Bay Street she opened up.

Susan was, in a word, weird. Sharon's fingers stuttered as she spoke, and one leg under the table was crossed over the other. The sleeves of her cashmere sweater were pushed passed the elbows.

I sipped at my au lait and waited on significant details.

They weren't quite the flash of Sputnik's orbital arc, but they were pretty damn significant.

First off, Susan's brother was a real asshole. Just a jerk. And part of Susan's problem was listening to him too much. He guided her in everything from the fashions she wore to the lipstick across her lips to the books she read to the courses she took at U of T. And what he did to Colin Thompson—

Thompson. *Brother Thompson?*

I leaned forward.

She played with an earlobe, smiled thinly.

The coffee shop was full of Formica tables and along each wall were six or seven mannequins, mainly women, some naked, some wearing the latest hats designed by Coco Chanel, some looking on with approval, others with mockery. It was a little unnerving.

Thompson hung with the group, the Defeatniks, but he was a bit slow, okay, borderline, you know, retarded, and Franklin W. Whitfield II sets him up with a prostitute. Colin's, you know, twenty-four and never got laid, so Whitfield, the big-hearted guy that he is, lines up a rendezvous and you can imagine the failure that happened, the humiliation. She held a stiff arm in the air and let it fall straight down. On her pinky finger was a ring, green, with a bright yellow spot in the center.

"Was Whitfield in the room, dusting for fingerprints while Thompson and the woman fucked?"

One of the mannequins looked outraged over my f-bomb. Another one appeared to be smiling. She was the one that was naked.

But she had no nipples. What's up with that?

"Everyone knew about it, that's all I know, and Whit ridiculed Colin later that night and shit. The guy was a real dick. And that's all I'm going to say about him." She crossed her arms, bit her upper lip, and her eyes smoldered as she leaned back, worrying that she had already said too much. "Just a piece of work." She adjusted a feathered earring in the other ear.

How come Whitfield acted as if he didn't know Thompson when Stana and I first came upon the Gus kill? Why the subterfuge?

I flipped through old notes. Franklin had referred to Brother Thompson as a "nutter" but didn't claim any prior friendship or acquaintance.

However, he did tell us to investigate Thompson. To take him seriously.

Susan often talked about death. She was obsessed with it, because she believed that it held something better, something beyond the known. And she didn't like the known, her everyday reality.

"Her brother picking out her lipstick—"

"I guess." Sharon lifted a flutter of fingers to her neck. She was wearing a silver necklace that glinted every time she raised or lowered her chin. It was a philosophical position, Sharon said. Susan sought the spaces between the known and unknown. "She called it living in the in-between." Sharon tapped her fingers. The nails were chewed down.

"Hmm."

"Dimension V." As in the Venn diagram, you know, it's like living in the in-between, the space between the expected and the unexpected. "At least that's what she told me."

I sipped more au lait. The milk was just so-so. It wasn't Silverwood's.

Dimension V was for Susan a zone without judgment, without the restraints of social order. She didn't believe in monogamy. She believed in freedom of choice and the pursuit of personal pleasure without the fear of being policed by the look of the other.

"And yet, she allowed her brother to pick out her lipstick—"

"We're all full of contradictions."

Dimension V. Is that the universe Ivan wanted to dismantle?

Sharon's lipstick was a striking pink periwinkle. I wanted to compliment her on how it brought out the hazel of her eyes, but kept my mouth shut. It might come across as a pass, and I didn't intend it that way. I just *liked* her lipstick. Stana didn't wear much of that stuff.

I scratched at a pimple along the stitches on my chin. The couch cushions were a little rough last night, and there was a jagged kink along the right side of my neck and jaw. "How did that philosophy go over with the Defeatniks?"

"It was way out. We all believe in freedom but not to that extent."

"Monogamy?"

"Well, no. Not really." The entire group was about free love. "But Susan was about the right for targeted killing."

"Targeted killing?"

"Killing people who have nothing to give to society."

Two of the mannequins were shaking their heads.

"Like the homeless, the infirmed, the retarded?" *We're not The Third Reich.*

"Susan was outrageous. We didn't take her seriously."

"Well maybe somebody should have." I rolled my neck, the kink wobbling, a flexing saw blade.

Susan was an abstract thinker, she talked in the abstract, she never *did anything*. Theoretically speaking, she believed in "targeted killing." She wasn't into pragmatism, prudence, or utilitarian philosophy. You felt like it. You did it. "Outrageous, as I already said." Sharon lifted her chin, the silver necklace gleaming, and then she looked off in the direction of a full arriving pre-lunch crowd. It was now 10:57, between classes. "But she could be a lot of fun."

"A regular riot."

"She was sweet. I can't tell you how many times she stayed up late listening to me and my man troubles—"

There was a story there that I knew if I stayed long enough I would hear about. *Edge of Night*, revisited. "So, Susan Whitfield was a bit of a nut. Murder Incorporated wannabe by day; Dear Abby counselor by night."

"Please. I'm doing her an injustice if all you get from our conversation is condemnation and judgment."

"I apologize." I looked down into my near empty mug of au lait. I was being an asshole. Again. My third face, I guess. "What did you Defeatniks believe?"

The main slant to their manifesto was heavily influenced by France's post-World War II existential movement: to be responsible for every action, every breath you take, every moment of the day; to seek out and attain social justice; to make the world a better place by questioning the policies of NATO and the Soviet Union; and bringing about an end to the threat of nuclear war through protest, poetry, and poetic art. "Make a change, you know?" She shrugged, her left cheek in her right hand, hazel eyes full of uncertainties.

"Uh-huh." Did she know Ivan Sevrier?

"Red Ivan? Yeah." Susan and Red Ivan really hit it off apparently. They both liked Pop Art and wanted to make art even more relevant than Warhol, more committed to social change, and not to the aesthetics of parody, camp, and kitsch. "Ivan, however, was not gay." She raised her eyebrows as if recalling a passionate, personal rendezvous or interlude. "Most people who are into camp are flamers. Ivan, I assure you, was not."

"Were they lovers? Susan and Ivan?"

"No, No." Sharon covered her thin lips, trapping a laugh. Susan had little interest in sex.

"She was pregnant—"

"It's no big deal to get pregnant." She tapped false fingernails on the tabletop. I wondered if she chewed her nails down out of nervousness and wore the extensions to curb the habit. Susan, Sharon said, was only into sex to meet the needs of others.

"Needs of others. Like putting on red lipstick for her brother?"

"I didn't think of it that way, but I guess so."

Ellen Reynolds? I showed her the picture. Sharon knew nothing. Never met her.

I didn't quite believe her. Her nails were tap-tapping. "A little Indian girl, huh?"

"Who got Susan pregnant?"

She didn't want to say, but I assured her that I was worried about Susan's safety, and I needed to put the pieces of this puzzling case together so that I can help Susan, maybe Ellen, my good friend Dr. Jeanette Cohen, and myself: I needed to find the killer of my father. If I knew who got Susan pregnant that might lead to a lot of somethings.

"Okay, okay." Her head drooped. He was an older man, a non-trad student. Fortyish, fattish, hung around the Half-Life, buying up drinks for Sharon's crew. They quickly developed this thing because he was interested in Dimension V, was a follower of Jean-Paul Sartre, having read, not once but twice, *Nausea* and *Being and Nothingness*, and listened to Susan's ideas on the spaces in-between.

"The Venn diagram?"

"Metaphorically, of course—"

"Right, right."

Susan appreciated his appreciation and slept with him out of appreciation.

"Uh-huh."

"Her brother really liked this guy."

"Whit?"

"Yes." She raised her chin, hazel eyes darkened by the long eyelash extensions she wore. "Whit loved talking to Gus about everything."

"Gus Carhart?"

"I think that's his name. Yes." She nodded, fingers tapping. "Gus was a radio operator during World War II and Whit enjoyed hearing old stories about those radios they used, and how you could hammer nails with the walkie-talkies and they'd keep working."

"I see."

Christ. So Gus knew Beanie Boy too. And Gus knew Deuces. The three of them knew each other. This was too many coincidences and when there are too many coincidences that adds up to murder. Call it Fuller's law: coincidences equal murder.

And of course, Whit and Gus bonded over Dimension V. Franklin told him all about it and Gus wanted to live in that space, that zone. He was fascinated at the possibilities of leaving his boring life as a Becker's franchise manager. They were, well hell, fascinated with each other. They should have been dating instead of Susan and Gus.

"I thought Dimension V was Susan's idea?"

Well, it was hard to separate out their ideas from each other. They were so on the same page, you know, simpatico.

"Oh, so, Franklin wore red lipstick too?"

That cracked her up. You see, the two concocted the idea of Dimension V in fifth grade. Well, he was in seventh, she fifth. They always played together, after their mother died. Suicide. She had pneumonia, insisted on staying home, hated hospitals, and one morning they found her in her room. The windows wide open. It was December. She was dead.

"She had a separate room from her husband?"

She was English.

I wasn't quite sure what that meant.

Dismantle the universe. Dismantle Whit and Gus's universe?

Anyway, Susan was lost without a mom. And it was during one of their elaborate year-long narratives involving characters re-worked from classic fairytales that Dimension V was born. "They had their own language and everything. Dimension V became their central philosophy, their rules to run by." Sharon gently tugged on an earlobe.

"I see." I traced the lip of my empty coffee cup. "Did *Gus* want the child?"

"He was furious when she sought an abortion."

"How about Mr. Lipstick? Did he want her to have it?"

"I'm not sure."

"Hmm." I stared off at one of the mannequins on the wall. Its eyes appeared to be smiling. "Was Gus furious enough to hurt Susan when she sought out a doctor's help?"

"No." She looked over at the people crowding around the glass display case, scoping out the desserts. "I better go." There were only two other baristas working.

"Could Gus have got killed because of his fury?"

"Gus is dead?"

Her fingers quit tapping.

I reached for them. "Yeah."

Her eyes filled with tears.

Matt didn't like Gus, saw him as an infiltrator, an old-fashioned square.

"Of course. Matt, the doctor?" I was guessing.

"Yes." She sat back, uncrossing her legs. "How did you know?"

"I'm a detective." I smiled my lupine, lopsided grin. "He has one of those Scottish last names. Ogilvy or something." I snapped my fingers. Again, I was guessing. There are a lot of Scots in Canada.

"His mother was Scottish. Father English. Clarkson."

"Right. Matt Clarkson with the Scottish Mom." I smiled. "Susan appreciate him too?" I shrugged. "You know?"

Her wet eyes now mirrored sadness. She smiled wistfully. "No. He's married to Angie, but he has a thing for Susan. Weird, huh? Unrequited."

I nodded.

And I knew.

"The best kind of love," I said.

She couldn't look at me. "So they say." She smiled, face down.

Neither of us could look at the other.

Her fingers were quickly tap-tapping and mine countered with the same melody, in a slightly different key.

Matt Clarkson, between classes at the U of T, was home for lunch, a Shopsy's bag of corned beef boiling on the stove top, his one-and-a-half-year-old on his left hip. A pacifier daubed her mouth and the hair around her ears was matted with muddy cereal.

I assured Matt that I wasn't going to report anything to the authorities about his practicing abortions, that's not what this was about.

He nodded, his mouth firm. He had small, deep-set eyes, and frail hair with a high forehead. Look, I need your help, I'm working on a murder case and a missing girl case. And yes, nearly two nights ago, I lobbed a phantom grenade in the direction of Toronto Maple Leaf CEOs Cal Bullard and Steve Smith.

"That was great." He hitched his daughter Denise higher on his hip and flipped over the bag on the stove top. "Great." He was at the game last night, figured Bower was guessing pass on my two-on-one when I put it under the bar, stick side.

Water boiled rapidly. Behind us a shower rushed.

"Tell me about Gus."

"An interloper." Matt's lips pinched into a frown of afterthoughts. "No, that's too polite. A stalker."

Gus sensed a weakness to Susan and used her brother Franklin to get close to her. He listened to Franklin prattle on about Dimension V, his affection for radios, and all the goofy experiments he did in high school, including one gem involving mice in a controlled environment: he fed both mice the same amount of food, but one grouping heard only R&B and jump blues, Big Joe Turner, Louis Jordan, all hours. The other grouping heard only easy listening: Patti Page, Pat Boone. The jump blues mice grew much more stout, stronger. The easy listening trio of mice remained svelte.

"That's crazy."

"I know it. But who would you rather party to?"

"Turner and Jordan."

"Exactly."

So, Gus listened and listened, nodded at all of Franklin's talks and pontificating, and the next thing you know he's dating Susan. Franklin told her to.

"Hmm."

And Gus's hands were always all over her, inside the back pockets of her jeans, on her left or right shoulder, grazing on the fields of her ass or breasts when he thought nobody was looking. I saw. Sharon saw. Hell, even Thompson saw, and I'm not sure he totally gets sex. "Anyway, one time, Gus just touched her breasts when I was looking and said, 'look what's mine.'" Matt shook his head. Susan didn't seem to mind. "I think she felt sorry for him. Slept with him because she felt sorry for him."

Sharon had said something similar. Pleasing others. Into sex for the other.

Matt placed Denise in a high chair, snapped the plastic belt, and slid the tray tight. Susan was such an activist, into the rights of women to govern their own bodies, but when it came to herself and men—he shrugged.

Denise squeezed the plastic turtle and ducky in front of her. As the toys squeaked she squeaked.

Matt mixed up some dry Pablum with warm tap water.

"She's a cute kid."

"Yeah." He looked at the floor, stirring. It needed sweeping. "Looks like her Mom."

Something about the way he said those four words implied a subtext not to pursue.

He sat next to Denise, hands atop gray Formica. I sat down too, placed my porkpie on the side. Shit, I forgot to shave this morning. I could feel my face pulling me down. I was very, very tired.

Supposed to play on Friday. Years ago, Rocket Richard spent all day moving his family from one Montreal home into a newer Montreal home, and then played hockey that night, scoring three goals at the Fabulous Forum.

I'm no Rocket Richard.

I'll be lucky if I keep Howe from scoring three. Shit.

Matt lit a cigarette, blew smoke in the corner of the room,

and the Pablum was now the consistency he wanted. I hoped to be a dad someday.

"How did Franklin feel about the pregnancy? Toward Susan, toward Gus—"

"Deuces? What does he ever feel, really?"

"You call him Deuces too?"

"Anyone with a roman numeral after their name is bound to be pretentious. I'm just bringing him back to earth. Yeah, we all call him Deuces." He took another drag and then launched a spoon of cereal Denise's way, but she pushed her head left, clamping her mouth tight. "Even after the pregnancy, Deuces kept buying Gus drinks. He was the only one allowed to buy Gus drinks. Gus insisted on buying rounds for everyone else, ingratiating himself to us—the poser—since he had a job in the, so-called real world." The spoon became a rumbling jetliner and Denise opened her mouth. "Good girl," he said.

She chewed, pleased.

Off to the left was the living room, stocked with built-in walnut bookshelves, crowded with books. The floor was yellowed linoleum and along the west wall there was a velour chair and threadbare couch with towers of more books taking up all of the places to sit.

Matt made like a dive bomber this time and Denise smiled and opened wide, her face dimpled.

I asked if he knew Ellen Reynolds. Showed the photograph.

He did. Saw her twice. One time on campus. She arrived with Susan to discuss the abortion. They had become fast friends, I guess, he said, and Susan was worried that the baby would be born retarded. I told her we could do a test for that, but she was unconvinced the test would be conclusive. You see, she said, two generations back there was a retarded child on her aunt's side and she was so sure it was her turn. It was like a panic attack, her fear, and Ellen was holding her hand. They'd met at that church, The People's Way to Christ.

"Uh-huh."

I guess Susan went there quite a bit. Anyway, we talked and days later, he said, she decided to keep the baby. Ellen was maybe fifteen or so, troubled, and quoted odd scraps of literature, not scripture, but lit, *white* literature, and breaking down words, their meanings, you know, as if she were a walking Merriam-Webster's. He thought it was odd to read that shit. "I mean, the girl wasn't white."

"She was taken from her biological mom. Brought up white. What do you expect?"

He nodded absently. "Sure, sure."

"Yeah." I wiped the sides of my mouth. "You mentioned Thompson earlier? How well you know the cat? Eccentric fella, wears aviator goggles, a green coat."

"Back then he wore hockey gloves. Seriously. All the time with the gloves. Not joking. It was his thing. Hockey gloves. Made it hard for him to open doors for women."

I laughed.

"Guy wanted to be a hockey player. Figured that wearing the gloves would make it happen, and that wearing the gloves was the way to love. We all *love* hockey players."

There was some irony there. I caught it.

"A lost soul, really."

And then he told the failed sex story, the same one Sharon shared, only this time the girl Colin slept with wasn't a prostitute but Sharon.

"Sharon slept with Thompson?"

"Yeah." He fed Denise a half-spoon of cereal. Took another puff off his Player's Navy Cut.

"Why?"

"Because Deuces asked her to."

"Okay."

He's a charismatic guy, Matt said, people do what he asks.

"Were *you* in love with Susan?"

"Yes." He didn't hesitate for he felt no shame over it. You had to be honest with your emotions. "But did I fuck her? No."

"Would you have killed for her?"

"Gus?" He laughed. "Why should I want to kill Gus?"

A bright surreal splash of white dashed by my periphery, across a living room bookshelf. "You didn't leave me a towel in the bathroom, hon," the white slash said, the tone wobbling slightly.

"There's some."

"A *dry* towel."

He had taken a shower himself and forgot to replenish the supply, leaving a wet towel hanging on the rack. She reappeared in the doorway, small splashes of water gathered at her feet. He apologized.

"I'm Marie," she announced, walking naked through the kitchen to get to the hall cupboard. Seconds later, a beach towel was in her hand. "Is this all we have?" She held out the towel. It was nearly as big as she was.

"I better do laundry," he said.

Water dappled her hips and gathered along the curves of her upturned breasts and nipples. "Yes, you better."

She shook her head, returned to the kitchen, pulled out the Shopsy's bag, and then wrapped the towel around her body. Now she looked like a stout tight end for the Toronto Argonauts. The towel featured a girl with a bucket playing in the sand. The sun was a poached egg. "Would you care for a cup of tea?" Her back was to me.

I don't drink tea, too English. So out of politeness, I just asked for a cup of water, with ice, if you have it.

"Matt didn't kill anyone." She handed me a glass, three cubes. She stood in a wide stance, like Stana, perfectly balanced.

She had deep-brown eyes and coarse hair with Joan Crawford shoulders and eyebrows filled in with black pencil, a lot of black pencil. Apparently, she had put *that* on before finding a towel.

"I didn't think Matt killed anyone, really." I passed the wampum belt with my words.

She smiled. "You threw that grenade at Pal Cal and Steve Smith. Tuesday night." She'd watched the game on TV.

"That's right."

"They deserved that. The crooks. Loved it."

"Thanks."

She tightened her towel and slid a corned beef sandwich on rye with mustard and a kosher pickle to Matt.

He ate quickly.

"Susan was weird." Marie's eyes narrowed. "She might have killed Gus. She was always talking about death and—"

"Targeted killing?"

"Why, yes—"

Matt dive-bombed once again, and Denise opened wide, her hands bouncing with delight.

"Don't do that." Marie swatted at Matt's wrist. "She might choke. Don't get her laughing."

"She won't choke."

Marie took the spoon. "Let me." Denise opened without the requisite sound effects when Marie handled the spoon.

I thought Sharon said Matt's wife was named Angie. I flipped through my notes. *Angie.*

Maybe Matt took his *wife* to the game. Marie, I guess, watched it on the tube.

Susan's ideas were, well, disturbed. There was one man, Marie said, a fellow traveler, Jackson Grayson, C-student, that she suggested we do away with. Like for kicks. She had been reading up on Leopold and Loeb and liked the freedom exhibited by their killing choice. And Jackson, a fraternity fella, business major, fit the bill.

I wrote the name down. Jackson Grayson.

He died later at a frat party, fell off a balcony. Accidental the police said. "But I always wondered. His blood alcohol was three times over the legal limit."

"Was Susan at the party?"

"No."

"She was writing a paper on Prospero for an English Lit class," Matt said.

"Right. She liked Prospero. Thought he was a metaphor for her life. Anyway, Franklin was there, the ringleader, Sharon, Matt over here, and Tom Frieze, an artist friend who Susan liked." She smiled. "I was there too." She paused. "And Angie."

"And you all have alibis?"

Marie nodded. "Many of our alibis are contingent on the others we were with. We were with each other."

"Uh-huh."

Matt finished his sandwich, pushed his chair from the table, and said he had to get back to the U.

"Why did you want to help her, Matt?"

"It's a woman's right to choose, to govern over her body's reproductive—"

"Sure, sure, but why you?"

Denise was now making with the robust whoop-whoop noises, wanting Daddy's dive bombers to refuel and return.

"She might be weird, but there was a vulnerability to her, a gentleness—"

"You slept with her, didn't you? You said you didn't, but you did."

"Free love is a part of our—"

"Don't be such a square, Hayden," Marie chided. Love is love and monogamy is a social construct to control us and maintain patriarchal order. "Almost all of us Defeatniks are in open relationships."

I wrote that down too. I was afraid to look at her. Open relationships? Shit. Loyalty is what love is, love that changes as you change, love that learns to walk three paths: together, and two separate ones. Respect the differences. That's what love was about. Maybe I am a goddamn square. So be it.

After they made love, Susan cried against Matt's shoulder, saying her parents never loved her, and her brother too often controlled her, and she wishes she were never born; if not for her brother's love, she felt no love; her mom up until the day she died never hugged or kissed her; her father was cold and aloof and when she wanted to speak to him she had to make a goddamn appointment, in her own house, to see her father, an appointment. Dimension V held out the promise of a better place than here. Her whole life was a search to find it, to slip into it, and travel faraway.

"Anyone opposed to Dimension V, wanting to dismantle it?" I rubbed at the sides of my mouth. "Something Ivan said, about killing Gus. *Dismantle the universe*. Make any sense to you?"

Matt shook his head. "We all thought Dimension V was a little crazy, but it was their kind of crazy, you know? Susan and Whit's. Our philosophy in the Defeatniks is to let people be. That was their thing. Dimension V."

"Ivan Sevrier? Susan sleep with him too?"

"Yeah." He was the one man she may have truly loved.

"He was a student at McGill—"

Matt smiled, hitching his backpack to a shoulder. Ivan traveled here on weekends—

"Recruiting for N'oublie jamais?"

"Oh, you know about that, huh?" He laughed. "We called him Red Ivan or Frenchie or Vichy. The Vichy nickname he really hated."

"I can't understand why." I made a face. And then tossed out *11/14/65, midnight mass*.

"Midnight mass." He shrugged. It made no sense. Christmas was six weeks away. Susan's religion was art. Through painting she felt as if she were inhabiting the world of Dimension V, finding a portal between light and shadow, the known and unknown. She talked about this all the time with Tom, Tom Frieze. You should see him. Has a studio near Massey Hall. He let her share studio space with him. *That* was her church.

Tom Frieze. I wrote it down, had to ask for the spelling. "But she went with Ellen to that church on McGowan Street with Brother Durgana. Went there a lot from what I understand. I'd call Brother Durgana a Grand Wizard, but I didn't see any robes."

They have robes, Matt said. Susan showed him a photograph. Black robes. Hooded. They wear them for religious ceremonies.

"Really?"

Marie picked up Matt's plate; it was patterned with heels of bread that resembled a sad face. "Susan was full of contradictions. If she did go to the church regularly, maybe she was punishing herself, getting even with her father, who is a known atheist." Marie tapped Denise's nose and wiped cereal off her chin. "I don't think Susan liked herself very much."

What about Sharon sleeping with Thompson? Did she like herself?

Or Deuces telling Susan to sleep with Gus. Did he really like his sister?

I wondered if Thompson left his hockey gloves on while doing it. He wasn't sporting the goggles back then. That was a later affectation, a different mask to hide behind.

"The whole midnight mass thing just doesn't fit." Matt tapped me on the shoulder on the way out the door. "Got anatomy class to get to."

"Sure."

The fourteenth of November wasn't Christmas, he said. "And I don't think their church is Catholic—"

"It's not a typical church, that's for sure," I said.

And then again, nothing about this case was typical, nothing at all, I pondered, as Marie, and not Angie, directed a thumb-sized piece of crust into Denise's waiting mouth.

HANDS WERE EVERYWHERE.

Some were pointed, stretching to sky; others clasped together with thankfulness. One set was a boxer's fist, heavy, a knuckle caved in; but the biggest pair of hands, on a silver pedestal by the only window in the room, were a woman's, open, seeking alms.

Tom Frieze, prematurely balding, smiled at my appreciation of his sculptures, his head ducking slightly as he did so, embarrassed by my praise. About Susan, he held up a small hand and looked through my shoulder saying he didn't want to get too personal, she was a good friend, a great friend, but if he were about to reveal too much, for her sake, he apologized now, to her, in absentia. He respected private life, but he suspected, in the course of our interview, he would reveal things about her, himself, that he might regret. About her art, that he wanted to talk about and had a lot to say. Beginning last year he invited her to take up residence in his studio space, to develop her craft. She was a fine water-colorist. Her father did not approve of her journey in art.

"Why?"

"Impractical, he said. Get a real job. Make a difference."

"Social work?"

"No." He shook his head, his blue eyes bright pieces of jade. "Business. Make a difference in business."

"Sounds like an oxymoron."

Her father was one of the original Hidden Persuaders of advertising, playing on our fears, our desires, convincing us, after the war, to protect ourselves and our homes. We deserve it. We worked too hard to get what we got. We want to keep it, right? And to keep from losing it, to assure you are the protector your DNA wired you to be, be a man. Buy a monitoring system. Protect what's yours. From 1957, the era of Sputnik to the Cuban Missile Crisis, 1962, sales in his home security packages rocketed.

Monitoring systems. Bugs, microphones, in Dr. Cohen's office. His handiwork?

"I thought he was into weaponry, grenades full of creeping jelly."

"Yes, and guns." He half-smiled. "But monitoring systems too. Monitor, and then toss a grenade full of liquid napalm at your assailant."

That cracked me up.

"Recently," he said, "Susan tells me that her father was designing a fire extinguisher that's not quite a fire extinguisher."

"Huh?"

Instead of regular foam it fired some kind of advanced DDT, closing an assailant's pores, suffocating them instantly. "He's still working on the patent."

"Charming."

"A piece of work that family." He held up a hand and shook his head, his sandy-colored hair barely moving. "But I promised not to get too personal."

"Sure, sure."

I pointed at the sculptures, especially the glazed blue hands stretching for the sky. "You do good work."

"I'm obsessed with hands." He shrugged. Next to the eyes, the hands were the heart of expressions, revealing the root of our experiences, road maps to emotional truths. Hands, Mr. Fuller, can love, comfort; push away, threaten.

"Yeah." My father's hands were stubby, blocky, full of boxing-glove fingers.

One set of hands, on the far edge of a long white table, were saying no, the left higher than the right, warding off a possible blow. They were glazed yellow. "This is my favorite, I think."

"Yes." He couldn't look directly at me. Tom was quiet, withdrawn. For a fella in his late twenties, he had a much older face: heavy, fallen apple cheeks, blue eyes shadowed at times by a scaffolding of a protruding forehead and bushy eyebrows, and a nose that belonged on Emmett Kelly, the clown. He half-smiled again at my smile, and I felt a twinge of guilt for he saw that I saw that he was quirky, slightly goofy, but an intelligent, sensitive artist, nonetheless.

I meant no disrespect.

The problem with Susan, he said, was that there were three Susans: the outgoing one that hung with the Defeatniks spouting outrageous ideas in vain attempts to one-up theirs; the submissive Susan that followed alongside her brother who controlled and subdued so many of her natural impulses; and the third Susan, an insightful artist who shared his studio loft. That one was smart, vulnerable, introspective.

I wiped at the edges of my mouth and briefly saw the two of them in the space, working. Drop cloths on the floor, she quietly painting, he shaping a hand, dry clay on the outside edges of his own. Now, the sun filtered through the only window, the light turning a glowing white by the brightness of the nearly translucent walls, the cabinets, and the long, long table housing supplies. The room smelled welcoming. It was a relaxing room. And I felt like confessing, talking over things I had only told Stana and Anne Chevalier and Dr. Cohen.

"What about all the talk of killing Jackson Grayson?"

"Just talk." His hands hugged elbows tight to the white smock he wore. "Her first face. The one that tries to impress and push away others." That's the face she wore with her father.

"I heard about Daddy and Susan having to get appointments to see him. In her own home."

"Yes." He shook his head. "I don't think he ever wanted children. DDT in a fire extinguisher. That was one of his children."

"I get you."

"Do you?" He half-smiled again.

"But Grayson did die." Fell off a balcony or was pushed.

"He did." Tom pressed his hands into his thighs. The one window in his loft was tall, narrow, letting in the white light of the sun. Voices of children in a park on Queen Street diffused the room with a spirit of playfulness.

He noticed that I noticed and appreciated that together we liked the sounds. He was very aware.

"Children," he said. "Play is what art is all about. To push, to experiment, to take risks." To play with the same exuberance, the letting go of expectations that young children have, before goddamn puberty and self-consciousness sets in. An artist for Tom must be free of judgment.

"Dimension V? Is that why she wanted it, to be in that zone, free of judgment?"

"Dimension V? Drugs, sex, free love, rebelling against your father? That's not how you find it." He pointed at his heart. "It has to come from here. It's an inner peace."

I nodded.

"When I first saw you, you gave me that half-smile so many do, a smile that says I'm weird, strange, eccentric, possibly even a lightweight—"

"I don't see you as a lightweight, Tom." I took off my porkpie, studied the brim. "I'm sorry if I gave that impression."

"It's okay." He smiled wanly, eyes downcast, sad. "I'm used to it. Most people see me that way. I assure you, Mrs. Frieze does not, but most do. And in a way, I've courted that. I like people to underestimate me, and then I can surprise them with my art, my hands." He held them up and was about to say something, and then broke off his flow. "People can't surprise me, you see?"

"Yeah. I do." It was his armor against being hurt by the hands of others.

There was a long pause. But when he worked with his hands, on his art, all of his self-consciousness, fears and doubts were gone. "I suppose you feel something akin to how I feel as an artist in playing hockey."

That's why I took to the game, I think. Yes, I was very, very good at it. But I felt safe on the ice. The game has rules and patterns of improvisational behavior, movements that lead to a certain set of definable, agreed upon outcomes. I was looking forward to Friday night at the Olympia.

Miriam had the levaya under control. I had scribbled two sentences together for a possible eulogy, but my mind was on this case, and Howe, and Detroit, and not words I couldn't believe in.

"You're an artist of the ice."

That made me laugh. Tom had a way with *words*. He said "of" instead of "on". There was a poetry to that choice.

"I wasn't being funny," he said. Play created flow for him, and he was sure for me too, and flow created joy, contentment.

I was never more content than when I played hockey or lobbed that phantom grenade in the direction of Bullard and Smith. "Did Susan ever attain that in her art?"

"Rarely." She was good but almost always self-conscious. Sometimes she attained freedom to just be.

"Dimension V freedom?"

"I don't subscribe to the principles of Dimension V. It's—"

"Narcissistic?"

"Yes." He dropped one arm to his side, a hand still clutching an elbow. "The V for them meant Virtual."

"Not Venn, as in diagram?"

"No." He laughed. "Virtual. A world that isn't quite real but for them is." He smiled, resembling a wounded soldier after a fierce bout of trench warfare. Maybe the clay dotting the left side of his chin furthered this impression of a muddied man. Susan, he said, occasionally freed up a space for herself away from her brother, but too often his presence invaded her work.

"What do you mean?"

"Let me show you."

We crossed over a series of clay-dotted drop cloths to the long, low white table. He opened a large shallow drawer and pulled up a portfolio bag, unzipped it, and gently removed a host of water colors.

All were dotted with rain-drop splatters of blood. Some of the splatter were fat coins, others dots of confetti. I couldn't help but think of bloody Stars of David in Dr. Cohen's office: *We know what you said.*

"Oh." He smiled, his lips pinched in bemusement. "The blood. Her signature. Literally." Susan believed in completely giving of herself in her work and the dots of blood represented the life she'd given and given up to create.

"Her form of Dimension V truth, I imagine."

"Yes. One of their bullshit mantras: *Expect the Unexpected.*"

Christ. Deuces must have coined that.

"I told you her father was an original Hidden Persuader of the advertising age. It rubbed off on his kids. A lot of the finer points, nuances, to their project involved pithy advertising slogans."

"The pause that refreshes, huh?"

"I prefer Pepsi."

That cracked me up.

Her brother drew the blood from her arm, using a syringe, a vial, whatever, and from that small drawn amount, she'd "clip it" to her art.

"Her brother?" Always the brother, lurking. Drawing her blood. A regular Dracula.

He shrugged disapprovingly. Susan and Franklin had their own language, 100 or so words that no one else knew but them. Hell, they often completed each other's sentences, said what the other was thinking or said the same things on the exact same beat. Always in rhythm. They even had a self-invented sign language. Very quid pro quo.

"So Franklin told her to sleep with Gus. Who did she tell him to sleep with?"

"Franklin told her to sleep with Gus?"

"Yeah. That's what I hear. Gus. Owns a Becker's. Dead. Killed for beef jerky. Allegedly."

"He's dead?"

"Yeah." As a doornail, I wanted to say, channeling my inner Cagney.

"She slept with Gus?"

I flipped through my notes. Yup, that's what Matt suggested. "Wasn't he the expectant father of her unborn child?"

"She never said a word about Gus to me. She liked the doctor, Matt Clarkson. But Gus?"

"I thought Franklin liked Gus."

"Franklin liked Gus. Yes." He shook his head. "I didn't even know she had a thing going with Gus."

"Then who's the father of the unborn?"

"I think Ivan. That's who she loved." He shook his head. "Matt, she had a thing for, but Ivan—Ivan she loved."

"What about Thompson, the guy with the goggles—?"

"Thompson? He wore hockey gloves. Always. When I knew him." He smiled. "Hiding his hands, afraid to touch, to be touched—"

"Right. Thompson and Sharon Dafoe?"

A sordid thing really. Franklin set that all up and we all listened. Well, I wasn't there, but everyone else was.

"At the fraternity?"

"Yes." Franklin had talked Sharon into sleeping with Thompson, a kind of vestal virgin thing, I guess, I don't know, but it was all arranged, and Franklin set up a secret radio sound studio in the bedroom, one of his father's security systems, microphones under the bed, and they all listened in, in another room, listened to Thompson's struggles. I think he came really fast or couldn't come. One of the two. Sordid.

Microphones under the bed. Microphones in Dr. Cohen's office.

"They all listened in?"

"Yeah. Big joke, huh?"

I'd heard that Tom was there. From Matt. Or was it Marie.

Now he's saying he wasn't.

"Who's they?"

Gus, Jackson Grayson, Matt. Angie. Others, I can't recall all the names. "Anyway, I got the story from Susan so she must have been there."

"She wasn't. Shakespeare paper. Prospero."

"Oh, yeah. That's right." He half-smiled.

Grayson kept teasing Thompson afterward, calling him Short Dick. "How he knew the size, I don't know." He held up a hand. But Grayson wouldn't let it go, saying did you touch her tits with the hockey gloves, shit like that, and Thompson fled crying, and wasn't seen again by the group. Ever. He quit hanging at the Half-Life. A no-show. He quit hanging at the frat. He had been their mascot. He wasn't smart enough to attend the U of T, but he earned his mascot keep at the frat by sweeping floors, cleaning the kitchen, running errands for the fellas, buying cigarettes, condoms, that kind of stuff.

"Quid pro quo, huh?" I'm surprised the frat didn't make the poor bastard dress as Elmer the Safety Elephant. Rule Number Two: Don't Run out from Between Parked Cars.

"I guess so."

From frat mascot to gun-toting custodian at The People's Way to Christ.

"Sharon had no idea they were transmitting the escapades through speakers for all to hear." He shrugged. "She hasn't been a part of the group either, since that night."

Shit. I had to talk to her again. She pointed fingers at some, especially Deuces, and away from herself. There was no prostitute.

I turned to the water colors. Under the blood splotches was some really fine portrait work with the horizon line high or low in the composition. None of the portraits were T-framed. They were all off center, destabilized, giving an aura of urgency and uncertainties.

One man, with dulled red hair, stared openly beyond the

space shared by the artist, eyes vaguely brutal, face somewhat immobile, lips slightly parted.

"That's Jackson Grayson."

The guy who *fell* off a balcony. "You think Thompson came back and pushed him? Killed him?"

"Yes." He shrugged. "But the police interrogated him and let him go."

"Inconclusive I assume."

Another nod.

One canvas was blank except for the blood splatter.

"That's a self-portrait," Tom explained, his words soft puffs, a candle going out.

"There's nobody there."

"That's her. Invisible."

I snapped on my porkpie, adjusted the brim, unsure of what the blank sheet meant.

"What do you like about this one?" He gestured with an open hand to a third work.

A girl and Franklin W. Whitfield II waited by a bus stop, a brown bag on the bench behind them, the sun no longer visible, the street dusky.

"A lot of blue in the image. And yellow."

"Right. Look closer."

I did. The brown bag on the bench was actually a dark, almost earthen blue. It matched her blue dress, his blue blazer.

He smiled, eyes looking through my shoulder. "And?"

"Uh—the horizon line—"

"Forget the horizon line—"

The twilight's blue, the street's blue.

"Good." Notice, he added, the yellow tie, yellow belt, yellow hat band. Yellow shoes. She has yellow hair ribbons, yellow handbag, yellow sash to her dress. Yellow heels. "The accessories match."

Quid pro quo?

"He insisted on that. In real life."

Franklin was a controlling force, a regular Svengali. When they partied together, he insisted that her accessories correspond with his choices. "Hence the blue bag."

A sign of subconscious protest on Susan's part? A lunch bag is never blue.

Maybe, he said. "But in his world. In his sick world. A lunch bag is blue."

Franklin was two years older than Susan. He called all the shots. "Is it any wonder why she disappeared. Wouldn't you?"

"Uh-huh."

"See anything else?"

"The bus hasn't arrived. They're waiting. She's waiting for something, someone to take her away from all this."

"You've been there. Haven't you? Wanting to be taken away from all this?" His blue eyes probed, seeing the buried shadows of my heart.

"Yes."

"I have too," he said.

Could her escape involve the cult on McGowan Street led by the charismatic Brother Durgana and his promises of a simpler life?

"What about the hands?" He tapped his lower lip, returning our focus to the canvas.

Neither set were in a proper resting position. His index finger was sharply pointed at her, his thumb stretched at an adjacent angle, giving an imperative command. The fingers of his other hand were curled worms.

Both of her hands were snowballs, tightly packed.

"He's trying to tell her something," he said.

"I'm more interested in what she has to say," I said.

And we stared at the hands, and then I said something about the hands that he creates, the hands that once scared him, scared me, that we now have control over. "It got better for you?"

"Yes."

"Your father?"

He nodded.

"Mine too." I pushed back my porkpie. "Mrs. Frieze, the sex—?"

"It got better too."

"My sex life's not so good."

"It'll get better."

And then I pulled up a chair, removed my hat, and we talked, an hour, an hour and a half, about all that was broken.

SHE HAD BEEN A VERY BUSY GIRL. Those were her words, not mine.

We were rushing along the Don Valley Parkway, eating burgers, sharing French fries with gravy, and balancing cups of soda between our legs. Our meeting with the Whitfields had been pushed back from 4:30 to 7:30—big business meeting, teleconference for Whitfield Munitions with a bunch of CEOs or some damn thing.

First off, Bob Waterman's not a cokehead. Stana checked with Silverwood's. Two days ago, he'd taken time off work to get tested for allergies, his back a scratchy road map of various allergens: food, pollens, molds. Black mold was the one.

"Black mold?"

"Yup. He's going to get a new office."

"Cool. Good for him." I wiped gravy off my lower lip. "So, he's no cokehead. And it wasn't coke that killed my father."

Forty-five minutes ago I had called Sal from the burger stand and he said the blood results had come back on the Star of David posters: AB. I told him to run an HCG on it. I had a feeling the blood would reveal that it came from a pregnant woman, Susan Whitfield.

The autopsy results on my dad were also in. He had a massive seizure followed by a heart attack. In his blood stream were high levels of chlorpromazine, an anti-psychotic, better known by its brand name Thorazine. "Used on schizos," Sal said, calming them, taking away the highs and lows. *Does it taste metallic?* My sources have said so. *Does it affect muscular movement?* Yes, I believe that's one of the side effects that the lab boys listed. That and weight gain, cowboy. *The folks at McGowan Street walked with baby steps.*

"Thorazine, huh? Same drug used on the church followers—"

"Probably."

"Wow."

Now, Stana wiped gravy away from the corners of her mouth, licked the top of a finger.

Secondly, she said, Anne Chevalier called the *Telegram* and wanted to meet with us and Dr. Cohen tomorrow to talk over our case.

Chevalier of the RCMP. She helped crack my last case involving domestic violence, a possible terrorist threat, plastic surgery, and murder. Perhaps this case posed yet another threat to national security? N'oublie jamais.

Late this morning Stana had also surveyed the Army Surplus store, familiarizing herself with a kayak paddle, compasses, K-bars, and Sterno kits. Two men in wool coats, felt hats, and glasses bought some heavy rope and roadside flares. Nothing else or suspicious to report but those two fellas, wannabe secret service agents, or in all likelihood stage managers on the lookout for supplies for an updated *Hamlet*.

Oh, and in the back of the store, she said, the door, black, heavy with chipped paint and peeled-back strips, was stenciled in a florid fluorescent orange: "Keep Out." Rising up from the basement, low voices, and the rhythmic strum of a wonky machine. It had an inconsistent beat. Speeding up, slowing down.

"Like it was hand cranked?"

"Sure. Maybe."

"Like it was a ditto machine?"

I had to find a way into that room. Maybe it was full of guns and 1940s–era creeping jelly grenades to be run by N'oublie jamais into Quebec. Ivan was with N'oublie jamais. Was the universe he wanted to dismantle English and predominantly Protestant? Maybe. But I was beginning to feel that something else was going on in that basement and the French revolutionaries were a sideshow, a strange coincidence. This case wasn't about them.

Just a hunch.

But what was it about? A strange brother. A sister. A murder at a fraternity. The murder of my father. "A big mashugana, that's what this case is."

Stana sighed, and I changed lanes.

And remember Brother Durgana, how he knew so much about us, reading our auras? What if he had access to our prior conversations with Dr. C, what if he were behind, or at least involved with, the bugging of her office?

Another hunch, but they were adding up to something.

Stana's eyes expanded, her chin lowered. "Time for another conversation with the brother."

"Yeah." I laughed. "I'm glad he's not one of my relatives."

She wiped a spackle of gravy from chin, her fingers lingering over my cut, the dirty bandage. "How's the chin?"

"Okay." Sure the adhesive tape looked like a streak of heavy mud, but the pain was gone.

"Mashugana, that's like, what? A big storm?" She smiled.

"No that's mishagoss. This is like a storm, but of the mind. Crazy. Bizarre. Dimension V shit. And how does that damn cult fit in? We know Susan goes there or did. Does?" I shook my head.

"I didn't see her in the crowd I interviewed yesterday."

"Maybe she was in the church when you were interviewing?"

"Maybe."

"Maybe they're hiding her—"

"Maybe."

"Maybe I'm losing my fucking mind."

"Maybe."

That cracked me up.

The streetlights of the Don Valley glared above like the lights we stare into while waiting in a dentist's chair. Stana was turned sideways in her seat, huddling her shoulders closer toward me. The duct tape buckling against the broken part of the passenger window wasn't keeping all the cold air out. I had the heater on full but the air was just warm. I needed to add anti-freeze.

"There are so many loose strings. I can't tie it all together." *Gus and Deuces and Brother Thompson all knew each other and they had acted as if they didn't. Why?* I hit the steering wheel hard with my hand, and the car lurched left, then right. "Sorry." I apologized, biting my upper lip.

I filled her in on Colin Thompson and Sharon Dafoe, the recording, the ridicule, so many of the suspects present, listening in, and Grayson's later needling of Thompson and a fall from a balcony. Thompson could have got even, killing Grayson, pushing him off, or just nudging him. The guy was loaded. A woman could have done it. Sharon. I'd have to have a follow-up conversation with her—there were too many gaps in her narrative. If she'd made love to Thompson because Franklin told her to, could she also have been compelled to commit murder, nudging Grayson from the balcony?

And what about the microphones? The Whitfields specialized in home security systems. Deuces placed listening devices under Sharon and Thompson's bed; did he and the Whitfields also bug Dr. Cohen's office?

"I thought you thought Durgana bugged the office?"

"Maybe the good brother and Frank Two are in it together." With my left hand I felt the dimpled dome bubble in my pocket.

"Maybe."

Finally, there were a few other suspects: Matt, Angie, Gus.

They were there. Susan wasn't present, but could someone have done the "targeted killing" at that frolicking frat for her?

She was busy writing about Prospero.

"Angie talked to me," Stana said. This afternoon she visited her at the Free Clinic on Parliament Street. Angie worked there as a nurse, receptionist, doctor's assistant. It was a small, understaffed clinic.

"Sure."

Angie didn't give a damn about the Defeatniks. Thought they were self-absorbed posers. *Where's their fucking bongos?* "She must have uttered that refrain ten times during the course of our interview." *Where's their fucking bongos?*

"That's a gasser."

Now Susan. Angie hated that chick. Not just because she had slept with her husband (after all who hadn't? Sharon apparently), but get this, Stana said, when Angie slept with Susan, Franklin watched. Took pictures. Pentax. "She remembered the brand."

"Did he use a filter? I might have gone for some bounce light."

She punched my shoulder.

"I mean, who watches his sister having sex?"

Stana shook her head.

"Sick. Who does that?" *Quid pro quo. Did she later watch her brother fuck somebody? Gus?*

Stana reached for another fry, placing a hand under it to catch gobs of gravy that might add to her fashion statement. She wore a dark green dress, green pumps, and a big necklace full of white shells and smooth stones. Angie felt manipulated by the two of them. She swallowed the promised freedoms of Dimension V, resigned herself to Franklin's controlling charms.

"A common theme to Mr. Whitfield's escapades. Sharon, Brother Thompson, and maybe even Gus felt a similar vibe. He uses people."

"At the *Telegram*, you'd have no idea. He's so—"

"Obsequious?"

"Yes." She smiled. "I see our games of Scrabble have helped your vocabulary."

She always beats me at Scrabble. I hate Scrabble.

"That's his persona. His mask. His second face. His real face, his third, is on display away from the paper, away from his father, in the world of the Defeatniks."

"I guess so."

The duct tape buckled heavily with wind.

I still had to take care of my father's burial, and now the car window, and oh, by the way, suit up to play in Detroit on Friday. Shit, I needed a daily planner like the business cats carry around in their lapels.

Manipulation. Psychological abuse was Deuces' game. That was his will to power. And how about Susan's will to power? Isn't that the real reason she ran away? The pregnancy was the final push toward autonomy and freedom, a life outside the one brother and sister had created together, the fallen paradise of Dimension V. He was Adam to her Eve. She wanted to bite a different apple.

"Crazy," I said, channeling my inner 1950s Marlon Brando.

One night at the Half-Life, Angie recalled Franklin ordering Susan off the dance floor. Her green handbag didn't match the blue band of his fedora. "And get this, no one objected. They all agreed with Franklin. That's how *charming* he is."

"Suave." It was a similar story Tom Frieze told and the subtext to Susan's water colors. We hit the Bloor off-ramp. I couldn't believe a brother forcing his sister to fuck somebody else while he took pictures. Hard, lurid memories filled my head, me naked on the couch, forced at gunpoint to perform. Stana made to watch. My last case. Exposed before her. Weak. Inside. Outside. Ashamed. Survive, her eyes said. Just survive. And I did.

And then the other night.

"I'm sorry about—"

My hands were firm on the steering wheel as paper cups blew up against a curb in Jamestown.

She gently topped my hands with hers. Her fingers, warm; mine, pale white, the underbellies of dead fish. "We'll get it right," she said.

My eyes filled with appreciation.

"I think we ought to interview Angie again, with you there," Stana said. She felt Angie was holding back, she really hates that whole crowd, bongos and all. "Smith owns the surplus store. He wouldn't broker a deal with separatists, would he?" Fuck, his best friend was a munitions engineer, arms manufacturer. Could he be procuring guns for N'oublie jamais?

"I don't think so."

If dismantling the universe involved guns against the English, the Protestants, the United Empire Loyalists forget about it. Smith would never be a part of that program.

"Well, he's procuring something for himself." She gave me her smart-ass look, eyes widening with mirth, the tip of her tongue sticking out of the side of her mouth. After casing the surplus store and coming up a big zero, she visited Smith. He was talkative. Played with his glasses the whole time. Said the store was a tax break. "Called you an asshole about forty-two times."

"I'm glad he remembers me."

Following the interview, Stana drove her car down to a curving cul-de-sac, walked back, hid behind a long line of maple trees, and waited. Within twenty minutes a Ford Econoline van, white, arrived, off-loading two young women, fourteen or fifteen year olds, wearing padded jackets that resembled life preservers, big white boots, and fishnet stockings.

"Fishnets?" Like Ellen, the day Dad drove her away.

"Uh-huh." And, she said, these two girls were among the people she interviewed at The People's Way to Christ yesterday. They stayed about forty-five minutes. She handed me three photographs. "The blond in the white Bolshevik hat drove the van."

Sharon Dafoe.

Shit. She said she'd quit the Defeatniks over their sexual hijinks and now she was pimping for Durgana. No wonder he got such a good deal at the surplus store. I sifted through the photos. "You have been busy," I said.

"The church and Smith—and the midnight mass?"

I shook my head, confused, hitting the steering wheel, three quick taps. "I think N'oublie jamais is a dead-end street, a coincidence. A parallel world that has no meaning in the world of this case." Ivan Sevrier, Red Ivan, the fella you made into grapefruit pulp, was in love with Susan Whitfield. That's why he was in Toronto. Often. Sure, he did a little recruiting, but hell they called him Vichy. He wasn't making any inroads here. He was here for her. Not guns. He loved her.

"Then what did he mean with his toss-off comment, 'dismantle the universe?'"

"I don't know." I shrugged. "Maybe he wants to dismantle Dimension V? Maybe he hates Deuces?"

"Ivan's the father of the unborn child?"

"Yes."

"But what about the other fella, his sidekick?"

Neither of us could remember his name, the Marxist-Leninist cat who thought the Bluffs were beautiful because monopoly capital played no role in their being. Did it matter that he was forgettable? Once a side man always a side man. "A friend who made trips with his pal, occasionally."

"But why kill Gus?"

"For Susan?"

"Why?"

"I don't know." All I knew was I was holding the wrong threads; the surplus store was involved but not in the ways we suspected.

Sharon Dafoe was delivering girls from the church to Smith's home in Rosedale. Bolemac, Smith, owned the surplus store. What was the church, Durgana, getting in return besides a 25% discount to buy aluminum canteens and Sternos? "It feels like a dead end." Hopefully our meeting with Frank One and Frank Two would yield something new.

I felt the ribbed ridge of the microphone in my pocket.

"Frank One and Frank Two?"

"You know, like Dr. Seuss?" I said.

"That's good." She gathered up the photographs, looked away. "What about our case?"

"Huh?"

I could barely make out her eyes in the dim glow of the dashboard light.

"I took my vacation." She smiled awkwardly, pressing lips together. "Two weeks. I was thinking of going to Detroit. With you."

I smiled my lopsided grin. "For a vacation?"

"Yeah. And we'll work on your case—"

I wasn't ready to share what Tom and I talked about, but this was a giant step. "Detroit and then back to Montreal?"

"Yes. Detroit, and then back to Montreal."

She kissed my cheek, catching the side of my lips.

I tasted gravy.

It tasted sweet.

THE ROOM WE GATHERED IN was straight out of Tennessee Williams. *Suddenly Last Summer.*

It was part 1950s modernity with its tulip-shaped lamps, low-flung coffee tables, wide-flared chairs with metal triangular legs, and a hi-fi unit complete with Julie London records. And it was also part primordial ooze with a far wall that didn't appear to be a wall at all but a series of heavy plants, casting Neolithic shadows on all our faces. Its trees, heavy, stout, and full of elephant-trunk branches, weren't like any species of tree found here. A thin ribbon of water flowed inside this dense heat of green, and a slither of snake scarfed a rodent the size of a chameleon. On the table in front of us were three or four vases full of what I assume were orchids, a light bluish pink, giving off a fragrance that didn't quite fit in with the snake still slowly swallowing. Next to the vases were two black-cylindered fire extinguishers and a pair of sealed envelopes.

Temperature wise, the room was a goddamn blast furnace. My shirt was wet, collar stiff. I loosened it.

Julie London was the only nice touch to the joint.

Frank One sat back against a high, King Arthur throne, a clear break from the room's modernity and jungle themes, and a sure sign that he saw himself as special. He sat with assurance, straight, all angles and sharp lines, manicured fingers poised in front. His skin was the glaze of fresh frost, with a large cocoa-puff of a mole on his right cheek. Nothing bothered this cat. He wasn't sweating at all. And he had his jacket on. My jacket was draped to my chair, my Arrow shirt becoming see-through.

His son, Frank Two, appeared snappy in his freshly pressed charcoal suit, standing behind his father, like a member of the Queen's Royal Guard or some damn thing. He too wasn't sweating. Shit, his double-breasted jacket was fully buttoned.

At one of the table's short ends sat Steve Smith, Leafs CEO. His body drooped like a fallen leaf in *Macbeth* gone to sere. His Lombardis gleamed back images of trees and underbrush. I couldn't see his eyes.

Shaved off was the Errol Flynn mustache. I guess he wanted to strike a more innocent look for the jurors. Libertine of the Year, 1965, wasn't going to cut it.

"What's he doing here?"

"A family friend." Frank One smiled, his teeth very even. He and Smith belonged to the same country club. Whitfield had stock in the Leafs and "well, Steve came to me hours ago, saying that you, Miss Younger, were lingering about outside his Rosedale home—"

"I was spying," Stana corrected, shifting in her rattan chair, trying to get comfortable. She'd already downed the glass of water in front of her and the freckles of her face were aligned with the fresh dots of freckled sweat. Her green dress was a little darker, it seemed, than a few hours ago.

"Yes. So you were." He nodded. "I appreciate your honesty."

"I don't," Smith said. "I could have you arrested for trespassing." His security cameras had picked her up. Forty-five minutes of loitering. Apparently, he had purchased one of Frank One's monitoring systems.

Was he into microphones under beds as well?

Smith removed his glasses, wiped sweat off the stems, pushed them back on, shadows of trees filling his eyes.

"Those girls are underage." Stana leaned forward.

"Yes." He smiled. "You have a devious mind."

I reminded him of my first case: hidden cameras, a porn racket involving underage girls.

"And may I remind you, Mr. Fuller, that was Landover Leeds's peculiar obsessions. Nick Stabulas's sickness. The charges leveled at me involve blackmail and extortion, not sleeping with underage girls." He sighed. "And let me remind you further, they're just, as they say, charges."

"Uh-huh," I said.

The girls Stana saw were young entrepreneurs, working with Smith, in conjunction with their church, to market pies (blueberry, caramel apple, peach). He was giving them advice on a business plan on how to label and push their brand.

"Pies?" Stana looked skeptical.

"Pies. Blueberry, peach—"

"Yeah, yeah, I got it."

I was kind of looking forward to a slice of caramel-apple.

"Who goes to a business meeting in fishnets?" Stana tapped her lower lip. "Fishnets, really?"

"They're young. They'll learn appropriate attire—"

"These are a group of girls who usually wear canvas: tops, pants, dresses. Dull, canvas."

They also walk dully. Loaded with Thorazine?

Frank One held up his hands, tired of the banter. "I assure you, Mr. Smith has assured me that he has acted appropriately. He can show you their proposal—"

Smith reached for a briefcase by his feet, slid the locks open and pulled out folders full of pie photographs, pie recipes, and an assortment of memos and correspondences.

Stana flipped through the evidence and said nothing. Slid the stuff back across to Smith, his phosphorous fingers tapping together with victory.

"We done here? We cleared up our little differences of opinion?" Frank One's eyes were the brown of lentils, his face wide, Eastern European. I'm sure Whitfield, like Fuller, was a created name, an attempt to fit in. This guy wasn't a descendant of the United Empire loyalists, more like a member of the Balkan powder keg, 1914. "There were no underage girls involved in anything sordid."

I knocked back the last of my water, played with the brim of my porkpie. "Nothing sordid, huh?" I pulled the microphone disc from my pockets, tossed in on the table. "Three were found in Dr. Cohen's office. Three." I pointed at Frank One. "You're into monitoring systems." I pointed at Smith. "You're into voyeurism, hiding behind a two-way mirror while folks lap dance." I pointed at Frank Two. "And you. You're into planting bugs under beds and listening to people fuck."

Frank Two moved away from his father, bumping the edge of the table, his upper arms tensing in the sleeves of his sport coat.

"Now, now." Frank One held up a large hand. He rolled the disc between fingers as if he were about to do the Van Heflin coin trick from *The Strange Love of Martha Ivers*. "This isn't one of ours. It's inferior." He snapped the dome bubble from its ridged ribbing. Pulled out the transistor. "It doesn't even have meshing for noise reduction. No ambient noise filter." He smiled, lumped all the pieces together. "Our microphones are half the size of this and much more efficient." He saucered the lump back to me. I pocketed the mess. You better look into someone else, he said. All of us in this room use Whitfield products.

"Sure, sure. Brand loyalty, huh?" I wasn't buying it. "What about Brother Durgana?"

"What about him," Frank Two asked.

"He *loyal* to your brand?"

"He likes pies," Smith said. "That's all I know. Pies."

Frank Two returned to his proper place, standing behind his father's right shoulder.

"What about the floor plans? The floor plans that Ellen took and handed off to Susan?"

Stana pulled them out of her purse with the rings-of-Saturn handles.

I spread them across the table. Showed them the circled air-conditioning unit.

"That's where they're going to build the lab." Smith's hands flashed over the plans, a contrail of phosphorous. "That exact spot. Ovens, everything. Unfortunately the central-air unit blocks out the flow of ovens—"

Smith knew Ellen. She was one of the original founding members of the group to bake pies. It was her idea to make it into a business. "Who says redskins lack drive, initiative, huh? Bigots say it."

The irony was lost on Smith.

Why was Ellen wearing fishnets? The day she disappeared. Fishnets.

Something wasn't right about all this.

"How often did you meet Ellen?"

"Three, four times. At my place." He folded his hands in his lap. "And then she became disillusioned. I don't know why." He sighed. "Disappeared."

I folded up the floor plans. Handed them back to Stana.

"I have to admit. I thought your general demeanor the other

night, the lobbed grenade was in poor taste. On Remembrance Day?" Smith smiled when giving you a beat down. "Respect our troops, the men who served—"

I remembered Smith's father, the first owner of the Leafs affectionately labeled the Old Man, and his militia during World War Two and the guns and grenades and AK-47s in Smith's cubbyhole in Rosedale. "Point taken—"

"I thought my son's write-up, if I may piggyback on my good friend Mr. Smith's comment, my son's outrage in the *Telegram* over the event was extremely impassioned, well-written." Frank One smiled again, looking over his shoulder at Frank Two.

"Point taken back," I said.

"You don't have to be insolent." Frank Two's cobalt eyes were full of napalm.

"No. But I choose to be." I pushed back my porkpie.

Frank One held up both hands. He seemed to like doing that. Maybe he ought to moonlight as a traffic cop. "Head strong." He gestured again. "Steve? You're free to go. I think we've cleared up our little dispute with our guests. I have other things to discuss with them."

"Yes sir."

I never saw Leafs CEO Smith follow the orders of anyone so willingly. Maybe Frank One was paying his legal bills.

Smith gathered the folders, his briefcase, pushed himself from the table, and moved toward a large marble black door, feet faintly splashing with hollow echoes.

Frank One smiled awkwardly. "He's a little too enchanted with that church." He shrugged. "I appreciate him wanting to help the kids, be a mentor, but—I don't want him to hear my proposal to you."

Smith knew Ellen.

Frank One wanted to hire us to find his daughter. She was trapped in that cult on McGowan, he said. Steve thinks they're eccentric; I think they're a cult. He shrugged again.

Frank Two, his angular face with the aquiline nose, plunked a cassette recorder on the table's marble, pushed down a button and a woman's halting voice waltzed around the room, taking its time finishing sentences.

Daddy? Frankie? This is—Susan. I'm in the healing hand of our Lord—God bless his—ministry—his work—his healing power. I'm fine? Yes, fine. Love you. The monolog ended with a familiar scripture passage, Matthew 13:45–46.

"The pearl of heaven again." Stana tapped her chin.

"Pearl of heaven?"

She explained the passage to Frank One and he rose higher in his chair, his upper lip curling under the lower. "Does she sound okay to you?" Stana asked.

"No." She sounded as if she were reading from cue cards.

"Cue cards written in French," Stana added.

"The life has gone out of her voice," Frank Two said. "Like she's a prisoner of her mind."

A Venus fly trap closed slowly on a black bug the size of my first car. "How did you get this recording?" My tie was now in my pocket, my shirt three buttons undone. Sweat was even behind my ears. I could feel it. I sat forward in my canvas chair to keep from being stuck there like a fly glued to a strip.

Frank One wasn't shifting at all, his head didn't dip left or right. His chin was forever raised as if holding up a spackled crown.

"I recorded it." Franklin Two's lips slightly parted as he breathed.

The snake in the garden was still swallowing the rodent-lizard.

Frank Two had bought the gizmo from an army surplus store. It had a small suction cup on one end that sticks to a phone's receiver and the other end's jack slides into an RCA plug on a cassette recorder. He had applied this gizmo to the phone in his bedroom in case Susan called. She had been missing for over a week.

"An army surplus store or *the* store, the one next to The People's Way to Christ?"

A different one, he said, but I didn't believe him. Anyway, Susan called. Wanting money.

"Uh-huh." I rubbed at the edges of my mouth and flashed my lopsided grin. It's the same squirrely look plastered across my PI license. It's my don't-give-a-damn trademark. If I were a movie actor, I'd be the Robert Mitchum of the matzo-crackers set. "You've edited this, Prospero."

He grimaced, wanting to stay cool and loose in front of his dad. "I have. Edited it," he admitted, quietly.

"It plays like a soliloquy. Not a conversation—"

"For the sake of brevity, I thought—"

"That's right, Prospero, you thought. Yes, you thought. Mixing up the elements, using your hoodoo magic, removing the context in which the words were originally spoken, obscuring truths."

"I obscured no truths. I told her I loved her if you must know."

"Recording. Editing. You're good with technology, aren't you, Prospero? Placing microphones under beds and listening in with a host of friends—the Defeatniks—while a young man, a little slow on the ball cavorts with—"

"This isn't about my son or how he carries and comports himself with his so-called friends." Franklin One held up an abrupt hand. I'm surprised a scepter wasn't in it.

"You mock me again, I'll lay you out," Frank Two said, the twist of his Rolex gleaming.

"That gizmo, Mr. Whitfield? That part of your *brand*?"

"I've never seen it before," the father said.

"Right. And what's to stop Sonny Boy here from using microphones you've never seen before, bugging Dr. Cohen's office, writing anti-Semitic impulses on paper, paper with blood splotches on it, splotches reminiscent of Susan's signature on her art?"

"What splotches?" Frank Two.

"The design's the same, Deuces. On her watercolors in Frieze's loft and on the Stars of David found in Cohen's office."

"Susan's behind the bugging?"

I folded my arms and laughed and mocked his spin on things. "Sure, Susan's behind the bugging."

"Enough." Frank One spoke as if he *did* carry a scepter. They had a boxing ring in the basement, next to the bowling alley, and he invited us to take up our scrap at some other time, but right now petty differences had to be set aside. "Susan is lost. She has been lost from us for some time. She may be behind all of this." He sighed, his lips pushing together awkwardly.

Franklin Two and I said nothing. He untangled the twist to his Rolex. I put on my porkpie.

"Sharon Dafoe. That mean anything to you?" She was a member of the Defeatniks, slept with Thompson on your orders, and today was seen bringing girls in fishnets to Smith's home. All the players in this story mix and mingle in incestuous ways. What's your connection to her, today?

"Huh?"

I could see the retreat in his eyes.

Dafoe and you, Thompson and you, murder and you.

He prattled on about unfortunate coincidences, unrelated events, pies and fishnets, Sharon and Colin and Sharon and the pie girls, and his sadness over what happened to his friendship with Colin, the fraternity's mascot.

"Mascot? So what, did you dress him up like Elmer the Safety Elephant? Rule Number One: Look Both Ways Before You Cross the Street."

"Droll. Very droll, Fuller."

"And why on that first day, the day of Gus's murder, did you act like you had no prior history with either of them?"

I was waiting to hear this.

On top of the hi-fi unit were a series of framed family photographs. In one of them, a young eight-year-old Susan, in an orange swimsuit, sprinkled the plastic pool with water, the hose gripped with both hands, gingerly spilling. Ten-year-old Franklin, hands on hips, stood idly by. His skin was the white of cocaine powder. The tops of Susan's shoulders were sunburned.

"Look." Frank Two glared. "I've done some things I'm not proud of, things that I regret. I didn't acknowledge Thompson because I was sad over how I treated him. I denied him, okay. You want me to be biblical? *I denied him*." But, I'm still a man of integrity, a man of action, a doer, he said, playing with the flex band of his *prestigious* Rolex. He assured us that he had not been idle. Since his sister's disappearance, he had been asking questions of the police, Dr. Cohen, fellow Defeatniks, that chi-chi artist Tom Frieze who has a misguided thing for her, and more importantly he's been in talks with Tod X, a deprogrammer who recently left the US, the slums of Chicago, to emigrate to TO. Tod X had tackled the Moonies and other cults, infiltrating their ranks, finding lost men and women, and recusing them from these organizations' realms of brainwashing. Forty-seven cases so far. He was finishing up matters on a case in Northern Ontario and would be lending a hand to tackling The People's Way to Christ tomorrow.

Tod X was really a kind of secular priest, Stana said, performing secular exorcisms.

"You could say that," Frank One nodded, his face rippling with a patronizing smile. "You could. But I prefer to say he's a man of justice. Highly principled who frees people from their prisons."

Only to return Susan to another prison: her brother and Dimension V.

Tod X left Chicago after the assassination of brother Malcom, Franklin said. American Whitey, Tod says, has enslaved us for nearly 350 years, going back to 1619, but when we start killing our own, special visionaries, then it's time to start living elsewhere. Canada. Canadian Whitey's not so bad. "Those are his words." Frank Two now held up his hands like his father before him.

Uh-huh. What would the Indians say about Canada's human rights record? Ellen was taken from her home, in the middle of the night, by cops with guns on their hips, taken from her Indian mother and given to a white woman.

"How's what he's doing not kidnapping?" Stana shook her head, the white-shelled necklace around her neck a heavy pendant. "These *kids* are over twenty-one."

"Yes. But he has the permission of the parents. These kids are sick. Their minds trapped—" They're being *rescued*, not kidnapped.

What was Susan's life like with you? Filling swimming pools. For you. Following your orders, Mr. Accessories. A kind of internment camp, pally.

"Brother Durgana is a charismatic ne'er-do-well. A dangerous man. We know who the good guys and bad guys are here." Frank Two exhaled sharply. "Tod X will infiltrate and bring her back."

"Speaking of good guys and bad guys, pally, who would want to dismantle your universe?"

"Huh?"

"Dimension V. Ivan wanted to dismantle it." I was guessing, rolling with a hunch. "Why?"

Frank Two shrugged, looked away. "Everyone wants to be king." He smiled.

"So you're the king?"

"Of Dimension V. Yes."

"What about Susan?" Stana leaned forward.

"She's lost. In that cult."

"And you're sure she's there? In that church?" Sweat from her hair dripped small coins on the table, the lines of her clavicles were glistening. "We've looked into them. I interviewed several of their members, followers, excuse me, is the nomenclature they prefer. Followers." She wiped sweat from her brow with a chamois cloth of a hand.

"We're pretty sure she's there," Frank One said, his chin raised, the crown on his head straight. "Keep gathering evidence." When Tod X arrives tomorrow we were to share our intel with him and join in his pursuit of Susan.

Frank One handed me an envelope. It was heavy. $1,000 down for our efforts and expenses. 5K if we bring her back, alive.

Stana whistled when I handed her the money to put in her handbag the size of a milk crate. "What do you all know about Brother Durgana?" She lit a Parliament. If she tossed the butt over her shoulder, I'm pretty sure the whole place would go up in a blaze. She exhaled stiffly.

"A punk. A mediocre stock broker." Franklin One didn't pull punches.

"Knows his scripture," chimed in Frank Two.

"Oh?" Stana took another short drag, tapped the cig on the side of the ashtray. "So you've been to his church?"

"No." He laughed. "No way. But he's called here." He shrugged. "On Susan's behalf. Asking for donations."

"How much did he get out of Susan?" I asked.

"Bilked her for ten thousand, in securities, family trust stuff," Frank One said, his lips a hard line. "The balls of that man. The balls." He looked in the direction of Stana and waved apologetically. "Pardon my French."

"I like the French," I said.

"The balls," Frank Two echoed his father. "The goddamn balls."

"Now *you should* apologize." Dad pointed at Frank Two, smiling at Stana.

Tersely and somewhat reluctantly Frank Two did as he was told, eyes on the floor.

Stana tapped her cigarette against the ashtray's floor. She wanted to explore Susan's story, why did she leave the family, her life of privilege, access, and entitlement, for a group of marginal loners who wear canvas-cut clothes and meditated for hours every morning in threadbare robes. She was running from something to something else. "What are these two somethings?" She picked at a sliver of tobacco off her lower lip.

"I think you know, Mr. Microphones Under Beds."

Frank Two no longer smiled, but his voice was full of calm milkshake-smooth contours. "Susan was unstable. You have to remember our mother committed suicide when she was three. Susan didn't have a woman to guide her, to give her advice on lipstick and how to wear heels, how to talk to boys. Anyway, my sister was always temperamental. Flighty." He shrugged.

The speech was a total phony, rehearsed, so sincere as to be insincere, lacking urgent impulses.

One time, after watching a Frankenstein double feature with Karloff, Susan killed the family dog Ruffles. Poisoned him with anti-freeze and then sought to re-animate him, attaching electrodes to his paws and other extremities, and generating energy from a car battery. The car running, of course.

"Of course."

"I don't need to tell you how it turned out."

"No Zombie Jesus rising from the tomb, huh?"

"Zombie Jesus? You fucking Yid!"

Between breaths, I was out of my chair, across the table, and on him, tackling him to the floor. I hit him once with a left, and he turtled, covering his face. Stana screamed behind me, and if Frank One were carrying that damn scepter he'd be whacking me with it, but he didn't need a scepter. He had a gun instead.

The hammer cocked. I felt the edge of the barrel behind my ear.

"One more punch, Mr. Fuller, and I pull the trigger. You know I have a lot of friends in this community, friends like Toronto Maple Leafs CEO Steve Smith, who will accept my behavior, my cries of self-defense."

I climbed off Frank Two, stood tall, dusting off my suit.

Frank One nodded briefly, uncocked the .32, and returned it to an outside pocket on his jacket.

He ordered his son to apologize for the ethnic slur and me for the Zombie crack

Frank Two wiped his chin, the fraternity pin on the lapel of his suit jacket polished brightly with privilege. It had a gleam equaling that of his Rolex. "This is yet another one of his grenades. First at the Captains of Industry, now at the principles that this country lives by."

"We're not a Christian country," Stana corrected. "We're products of the Enlightenment."

"What about Susan's talk of targeted killings?" I snapped the porkpie tight on my lid.

We all returned to our chairs, none of us apologizing.

"I assure you my daughter never talked of targeted killings."

He sure liked that word: *assure* and making *assurances*. There was nothing sure about this case. "Uh-huh." I adjusted my sleeves. "And I suppose Jackson Grayson just happened to slip off a little old balcony after drinking too many Molsons."

"That's what the police report said." Frank Two.

"Hmm. I have at least three witnesses who can verify that Susan spoke of targeted killings. Sharon Dafoe for one. The girl you asked to sleep with Hockey Gloves. Matt Clarkson for two. And Tom Frieze for the trifecta. Win, Place, Show, baby."

"Susan targeted Grayson. She spoke of killing him," Stana said. "And then there's Gus." Stana was now standing, her white beaded shell necklace tossed over a shoulder. "Who you, Deuces, ordered Susan to sleep with, and did she order Red Ivan to kill Gus because she was so disgusted with what she'd done?" What was left of her cigarette vibrated, a hummingbird at her fingers.

"Susan talked murder but it was abstract for her. Theoretical. Never practical."

"Uh-huh."

"She also had to make appointments to speak to you, her own father, in her own house. Goddamn appointments?" Stana crushed the cigarette in an ashtray. Smokey the Bear would be proud.

Frank One pushed away from the Arthur chair and pounded a fist on the table. "I haven't been the best father." He shrugged. "Okay, damn it. I admit it. And I'm probably responsible for my children's eccentricities. My neglect. But Susan liked to push the envelope through talk, never action. Your Zombie Jesus utterance, Mr. Fuller, would have pleased her to no end, because it the kind of thing she'd say—disrespectful, unconventional, iconoclastic."

The ass-end of the rodent-lizard still protruded from the snake's mouth. Another animal squawked a death yawp. The ribbon of water appeared motionless, clogged.

"So. I failed them. Me. This—" He fanned his hand over the two black-cylindered extinguishers on the table. "This is my children." He held up one of them. It was a new weapon that he and his team had perfected, a modified version of 2,4,5T, a defoliant mastered in the Netherlands in 1963, and adjusted here into a foam spray. Spring a load of this on someone's face, and they'll suffocate to death in seconds, he said. Blocks the pores. He snapped his fingers. And. He snapped them again. And shrugged.

"Pillars of salt, huh?" I said.

"Yes. I suppose so. It makes people into pillars of salt. I don't know if we can market it that way—" He laughed, his Hidden Persuaders chuckle. "I might be an atheist, Mr. Fuller, but I know of the traditions on which this country was founded, Enlightenment or no Enlightenment." He smiled wanly. He had read the good book. "I never joke about Jesus." The Lord's aligned with power, he said.

"I've read the good book three times," his son said in the spirit of one-upmanship. Twice to get the nuances. A third time backwards, literally backwards from Revelation to Genesis, each sentence, backward. "That's the best way to memory retention."

He was serious. "Is that Dimension V logic?"

He said nothing.

"My children are very intelligent," Frank One boasted. Both scored off the charts on IQ tests, genius levels, 160 to 170. Sometimes, he ruminated, it was better to be only an ordinary genius, finding simple solutions to problems, making the clear direct choice. His children did create their own world for themselves, starting with the death of their mother, and perhaps even before that. Dimension V was part of that imaginary vision.

He lightly touched the extinguisher's nozzle. "My obsessions, shortcomings, are what should be on trial here, not my children." He smiled. "I love them. I don't model good behavior, what with the appointments to see me and all, but I do love them."

Stana sat down. "So what's next?"

"Wait on Tod X. He'll call you."

I gave them my home number and that of my father's house. I felt a need to return to Gradwell, to breathe in his scent to get the scent. My desire to find Susan was growing, but my desire to know my father was getting lost. I needed a returning, a countermovement. Gradwell might give that to me.

Frank One reached for another envelope leaning up against one of the cylinders. He undid the short clasp and slid two black-and-white photographs in my direction. Stana placed them side by side. The photographs were blurry, rushed by the circumstances of their shooting. The subjects wore black robes, triangle hoods with slits for yes. One photo, a long shot, showed followers meditating in the McGowan Street sanctuary. And very similar to what I saw on my first visit here, they were caressing the floor with their hands, silently praying. Neon lights and imagery surrounded them, and even in the sanctuary's dim shadows, the threadbare fabric revealed curves of breasts, patches of pubic hair, the dangled lines of manhood.

In another photograph, a medium close-up of two people, one had a hood, laughing behind it, eyes crescent moons. The other, hoodless, appeared to be wearing nothing. Wiry wisps of chest hair circled his nipples. Aviator goggles were pressed tight to his face, making his eyes amber. Colin Thompson.

A neon image of David glowed behind them. Too bad we couldn't see David's PF Flyers.

"Prepping for some kind of ritual," Stana said.

"Appears so." Frank One.

"Sacred or profane?" Frank Two.

"Both?" Stana offered.

"How'd you get these?" I turned the photographs over, checking the paper.

"They arrived in the mail, shortly after Susan's disappearance." Frank Two. "Four, five days ago."

Written on the back: *You will not harken to me. I will punish you for your sins*—Leviticus 26:18. The handwriting wasn't my father's; it didn't match what I found hidden in his switch plate.

Stana tilted her head right in conjunction with the lilt to the words. "The quote's not quite right," she said. "'I will punish you *seven times* or *seven-fold* is what it should say, modifying sins."

"Catholic school," I said, pointing at her.

"And Jesus was never a zombie," she gently scolded.

I apologized to her. To Mr. Microphones, forget about it.

Frank Two studied the back of the photographs. "She's right. The quote is wrong." He rubbed at the fuzz on his chin, his face grimacing.

A wrathful, vengeful God. Stana believed in the God of Love, the New Testament God. But these folks on McGowan were into fire and brimstone, Old Testament punishment, Sodom and Gomorrah, floods, Cain and Abel. Isaac and Abraham, kill me a son.

Is that what we had here? Cain and Abel, but instead of brothers we had a brother and a sister? Cain and April?

I flipped the photos back to the mass of black hoods. Anything else accompany these photos? Blackmail requests?

"None." Frank One held up both hands as if directing traffic. The only requests he had for money were from Susan, twice calling for donations to the church. And in both conversations, she mentioned becoming a part of heaven.

"That's what she said. *Becoming?* As in morphing into, transforming herself into?"

"Yes." He looked puzzled. "And?"

"I don't know." I pushed back my porkpie. The language was alarming. She was sloughing off her old self, leaving Susan behind, her life behind, her actual life. Becoming a pearl. In heaven. Now. In heaven. Dead. In heaven. Now.

"Has she ever been suicidal?"

"My daughter?"

"Yes." Frank Two said, looking at the cylinders on the tabletop. When she was seven she stabbed herself with a knife, trying to join Mommy, wherever she was. Two months before discovering her pregnancy, she had OD'ed on alcohol and pills and had to be rushed to the emergency room. After that stay, she started going to The People's Way to Christ temple. "Do they even call it a temple?"

"I know they call *it* a church," I said, looking at the black robes crowding the photographs.

"Tod X will be here tomorrow," Frank One reassured us. "He'll have a plan. Sit tight. By a phone."

We know what you said. Could it be these black-robed people with their vengeful gods?

Franklin Two placed the cards with my phone numbers inside the lapels of his crisp sport jacket as shadows of trees shrouded our table in the shapes of fighting dinosaurs, tearing away at one another.

My money was on the triceratops.

I SAT IN DAD'S CHAIR, my arms resting on the slick worn leather, a Rémy-Martin shot on the coffee table by my side, my head tossed back, taking in the ceiling's patterns, water stains resembling the Great Lakes. I was half-drowning in Lake Huron.

Dad's scent was all around. A mix of aftershave, beer, sweat, and Ajax cleanser. He always scrubbed away at his hands after each day's work, washing off the dirt of empty milk bottles, metal trays, and the truck's grimy steering wheel.

Next to my drink was a dog-eared copy of *Playboy*, featuring Maria McBane, and *More Joy in Heaven*, a sad gangster love story that Stana had me read three years ago.

When did Dad start reading?

Maybe they were Ellen's library books.

I wiped edges of grit from tired eyes. Two hours ago I had dropped Stana at my Houston Crescent home to watch over Dr. Cohen, handed her my .45, and gave her instructions to call if there were any problems. The Cerlons across the street and the Capetellis next door were good people. If you need help right away ask them.

I sighed, imagining going under, the water stain swallowing me, how easy it all would be just to let go.

Once I arrived here, an hour or so ago now, I called Anne Chevalier. Couldn't reach her. She was on a stakeout. Then I called Sal from Dad's chair. Lab results had come back: the blood splatter on the Agitprop work was that of a pregnant woman. HGC confirmed it.

Sal thought I sounded funny, asked if I were okay. Searching for memories or trying to lose a few I said. There was an awkward pause. "You're not in your dad's house?" "Yes." "It's a crime scene." "Yes." "We're not having this conversation." Another awkward pause. "Take it easy, Superstar. Rest."

Susan Whitfield. Dr. Cohen's client was possibly involved in harassing, threatening, ordering the good doctor's targeted killing. Maybe I needed to quit being so damn chivalric in my relationships with women, always seeing them as victims of bad male behavior, and maybe Susan wasn't merely a victim of her brother's Prospero–esque machinations, but a woman full of her own particular menace and desires to destroy others. She was a client of Dr. Cohen's. She could have easily planted the microphones.

We know what you said. Who's the we of that utterance? Susan and her brother? Susan and that black-robed cult on McGowan? Susan and her card-carrying N'oublie jamais boyfriend Ivan Sevrier (who with the help of Stubby Face killed Gus)? Susan and Gus whom she slept with because her brother told her to? Susan and Tom. Artists who shared a vision and a loft? *We.* Susan and Matt. He cared about her enough to kill for her? *We.* Two people or a club? *We.* A combination. Two people within a club: Susan and Brother Durgana and all the followers of The People's Way to Christ? *We.*

Did this we want to dismantle Frank Two's universe, Dimension V?

And what about Ellen and Smith. What really happened there? Too many pairs of fishnet stockings.

I pushed back my porkpie and swam to the shore, clambered out of Lake Huron.

Next to the Callaghan book was an even more worn copy of Hemingway's *The Old Man and the Sea.* I flipped, forward to back, deckle-stained pages. Dad loved jam and crackers before turning in, and this one had some red residue at the lower end. I flipped sticky pages, backward to front, and a folded recipe card fell out. It was full of writing.

Dad's writings.

I really love the style. Like reading a newspaper. Clean. And I can see the story. Like a movie. But I'm not sure about the whole fish thing. Sometimes you just got to let things go. The past is the past. To be a good fisherman is to know when to stop fishing. Move on. I wonder what Hemingway would of thought of Koufax? The guy wins game seven on two days rest. Arm sore and all. Complete game. I mean, DiMaggio was smooth, elegant, but nobody is as dominant as Koufax. And he's a Jew too. I don't think Hemingway liked Jews. It's in the prose. You can feel it. Couldn't finish The Sun Also Rises.

Maybe I don't like Jews either.

Maybe that's my problem.

But I didn't finish The Sun Also Rises.

So that should count for something.

I never liked myself.

I re-read the card twice and knocked back the two fingers of Rémy-Martin. Then I pushed myself off the chair, ambling to the kitchen. The milk was past its date. In the fridge: Kraft cheese, orange juice, Hebrew Nationals, and Hershey bars. I pulled a slice of cheese from an unsealed wax package. One of the corners was a little dry. I ate it, folding it in half first, like I used to do when I was a kid.

The dishes were still dirty in the sink and the ends of the curtain by the window were stained with smudged fingers. Dad must have used them as a makeshift towel.

I laughed.

That was so Dad.

No tea towels anywhere. No big deal. Use the kitchen curtains.

The cabinets housed a half-dozen plates and plastic cups. Yogi Bear was on one of them. Next to a tall angular cabinet full of dust mops, brooms, and cleansers was a dumbwaiter with a rope and pulley system. Dad had converted it into a makeshift laundry chute. I checked around inside its door and smelled cheese.

I picked up something that resembled a lemon slice of plastic. A piece of hardened cheese. It nicked one of my fingers.

Ellen was hiding in the dumbwaiter when Dad was murdered. He had stowed her there safely from the killers.

Christ. She had seen, heard, from her place in the dumbwaiter.

The phone rang.

I wandered away from the opened dumbwaiter and the glass of orange juice on the kitchen table to the beer sweat of the living room. "Fuller—"

"Hayden?"

Stana's voice was crisp and slightly elevated. An ice chest had just arrived at my front door on Houston.

"Did it just arrive or have you just now noticed it?"

"Both I think."

"It's an either-or question, Stana."

"It wasn't here before, when you dropped me off. It has arrived since then—"

"So in the last two hours."

"Roger that."

Her nervousness had somehow converted her into a member of the Royal Canadian Army.

She had nudged, all right, *kicked at*, the chest, heard water and chunks of ice sloshing about.

"Good. So that means it can't be a bomb."

We were on the same page. She wanted to open it, it might be an important clue, it might—

"It might also be something you don't want to see—"

"I'll risk it."

Always the reporter. Two-week vay-cay or not. "Okay." My heart was in my shoulders. "Be careful."

The lid unsealed with a long breath, and then pockets of silence, followed by a scream.

I couldn't make out what she was saying. She handed the phone to Dr. Cohen.

A pair of hands, Dr. Cohen said, matter-of-factly, hacked off at the wrists. Bones were exposed, bits of muscle, blood drained. The fingers, slender; the nails, pink; the pinky adorned with an emerald ring; the stone set inside the ring, yellow.

Sharon Dafoe.

"Jesus Christ, Hayden. Is this a typical couple of days in your line of work? A shootout on the Bluffs, a pair of hands on your doorstep?"

"No. I usually have time for some ballroom dancing."

"I better call Sal," she said.

"Yes. How's Stana?"

"She's been better." Stana was in the bathroom, tossing up the burger and fries we ate hours before. "Why Sharon?"

"I was going to ask you the same thing, Doc."

She was hesitant, halting.

"Susan? Your client?" The blood splatter was from a pregnant woman, AB blood. Your client was, in all likelihood, terrorizing you; she's a part of the "we" in *we know what you said*. Susan and Ivan were lovers. Sharon knew something. Susan had Sharon killed. "I'm guessing, of course. Or Susan did it herself."

"I don't know."

Tom Frieze, a fine artist, who specialized in rendering the beauty and horror of human hands in all of their complexities could have done this, but the symbolism, the hacked-off hands, was too obvious. Contrived. Yes, he shared a studio space with Susan, and maybe he was part of the "we," but I couldn't believe it about him, not after our two-hour conversation at his kitchen table. I preferred to think of this as but a clumsy attempt to divert suspicion on him.

I wasn't going to say a word about Tom's hand sculptures to Sal.

What if Ellen were a part of the we. Ellen and Susan? "Have Sal call me here."

"Right." Susan sure did love Sevrier, Dr. Cohen recalled. She thought he was funny, sincere, but to be a mastermind behind the killing of my father? No, Dr. Cohen just couldn't believe that about her client. No way.

Then I told her about Dad and the Thorazine OD and the church's followers and their baby steps.

"That's definitely a side effect of chlorpromazine," she said. "But I still can't believe that Susan could—"

"There's a lot of things that I used to believe in that I don't no more."

"Sounds like you're ready for another session—"

"Maybe." I smiled.

Her pause told me she could feel the smile through the phone. "My sessions with Susan were more about finding her own island of existence. That's what she called it. Her own island of existence."

"Dimension V?"

"Yes. I believe so." There was a long pause. "Don't give up on believing, Hayden. Please."

"Sure, Doc. Call Sal."

I dropped the receiver in its cradle and wandered back to the kitchen and the cup of orange juice waiting for me. It had got a little warm so I dumped it in the sink and poured another.

I must have sat there for an hour or so, holding what was left of my Yogi Bear cup of juice in one hand, smoking Dad's stale Rothmans with the other. I found the cigs in back of the silverware drawer.

I finished the orange juice, mind numbed.

Stubbed out the last cigarette.

Smokey the Bear would be proud.

Yogi the Bear would wonder where the fuck's the picnic basket.

I don't remember leaving the kitchen table.

—

IT WAS A DARK, DEAD SLEEP.

The kind you don't remember and wonder if this is what really happens when you just quietly slip away from it all.

Black stillness.

And then, thankfully, you wake up, free to listen to hardbop jazz, breathe in the warm sun.

But there wasn't any sun. It was black beyond the kitchen curtains, 10:17 by the clock over the sink.

A black sky.

I rubbed at my eyes, half-smiled at her face.

It was a nice face, a little heavy on the lower cheeks, nubs of dark hair peeking out from under her Montreal Canadiens toque, green eyes, a gap between her front teeth. The dent above her upper lip looked as if it were pressed there by an angel.

She half-smiled back at me.

"Ellen?"

Dressing Room

The kiss was just a little off, she said.

It was full of neon, bright and glaring with no real substance behind the kismet, puffed afloat with vapors and clouds of gas.

It happened on her seventh and final week at the church, three days before she jumped in Ira Fuller's milk truck.

For her first three weeks in the city, spring of 1964, Ellen Reynolds lived in a youth hostel, finding part-time work at Dominion's, stocking shelves late at night and later working in the bakery, making donuts, butter tarts, cakes, and pies. Only fourteen, she lied and said she was sixteen, and her supervisor, a heavyset man in thick glasses and a pock-marked face, believed her because he wanted to believe her and because she flirted a little, telling him he walked with confidence and wore way cool shoes. Wing tips, he said. Her foster father never wore such things on the farm in Melville, Saskatchewan. *Wing tips*. She wrote that down. She liked words.

Unfortunately, her own words were forgotten except a few like maybe, maashcoat, and the odd phrase her mother said, penepuea pchi feey, come to me my little girl.

Money was thin along the lakeshore, below minimum wage, and Ellen eventually left the hostel, finding shelter in a variety of abandoned buildings in Toronto's downtown hub around Front Street.

One night she met Scott Cameron, a pug-faced, freckled fella with lopsided ears, in a bus station diner. She was eating fries, drinking coffee. His approach wasn't subtle. "I got a fifth of scotch. You wanna go home with me?"

She had met a variety of such fellas along Yonge Street shoeshine parlors—a past she didn't want to revisit, now, with me.

"Why don't we just drink here?" she said.

"Why not?" He tilted his head left, banking on his elusive Paul Newman charm. He looked a little like Paul, the eyes a piercing blue, the hair curled, tight and sweaty. He removed the fifth from his beige jacket. It was a weird jacket. The collar curled up and opened into a tulip of a turtleneck. He topped off her coffee with two fingers, and they sat and drank for a while.

In the books Ellen was allowed to read, she supposed his smile would be labeled "rakish." There was a romantic aloofness to him, a sense of knowing yourself, how to be all the things Ellen wanted.

They walked back to his place, a long, narrow room above a pool hall. He had an athlete's glide and she felt a little dizzy, leaning against him, breathing in Aqua Velva and garlic.

Scott worked at an Italian restaurant and couldn't splash enough cologne to drown the garlic away. All day he found himself covertly sniffing fingers, wishing remnants of grease and garlic could vanish. They couldn't.

That made her laugh.

He was vulnerable.

In his flat, he watched TV while she read books, novels mainly written by whites, and together fixed easy meals: Shake and Bake chicken, mac and cheese, bacon and eggs. Occasionally, she brought home a pie she'd baked at Dominion's.

Twice a week they made love as pool balls thudded across tables downstairs.

She was fourteen. He, twenty-two and thought she was sixteen.

It wasn't really love.

She felt obliged to cooperate. Often, as he came, kissing her, he'd whisper, "I love you." She didn't believe in the possibilities of those three words anymore, so she responded with a tap-tap on the tops of his firm arms.

"Why'd you leave. Run away?" He asked one night, slowly lighting a crumpled cigarette.

Her foster mother had taken to hitting Ellen when she appeared less than thrilled completing a chore or errand. "It's in your shoulders, your eyes, all the times, the eyes. The devil."

I stayed with Scott out of convenience, a roof, food, she told me. "I feared going to the CAS—they'd probably send me back to Saskatchewan, and I didn't want to milk cows anymore." Her pattern was to run from trouble rather than confront it. She was aware of this, but inside, she knew, "I'll always be running."

So, one day after meeting Brother Durgana outside her Dominion's, Ellen decided not to return to Scott and to run somewhere else.

Durgana wore a long black leather coat and his hair was thick and curly, much curlier than Scott's, resembling a woman's wig. It was so full. He handed her a pamphlet to The People's Way to Christ. His eyes were blacker than coal, a description Ellen had probably first come across in an old 19th Century novel, and his eyelashes were long and lush. He was pretty. For a man.

"What a beautiful face," he said to her, "bristling with God's presence." He smiled, teeth perfect. "You have an old, old soul."

If you could have one wish to make the world a better place what would it be?

"For everyone to get along." She was surprised at how the words spilled from her. "For *all* to be okay, equal." *Mothers shouldn't have dominion over their adopted daughters.*

The latter thought she said out loud for he picked up on the theme. How do we seek and find such non-dominion?

He paused, tapped his chin, nodded, full of confidence and a non-threatening self-awareness that she found disarming. He was a spiritual man who felt no need to apologize for his particular disposition. Jesus walked into the desert with no possessions and fed the needy, helped the infirmed, gave comfort and advice to the lost, especially like the woman at the well. Remember her?

Ellen had read the bible only sparingly, because the mother who smelled of Avon products, insisted she read it. Ellen didn't recall the story of the woman and the well.

"How do you need to be fed?"

"With acceptance, appreciation, love." The words were just there, across her lips, all self-consciousness gone.

And then he talked about the pearl of heaven.

AT THE CHURCH, THEY HELD SERVICES eleven times a week, with three-hour meditations every morning, exercises in the afternoon, and evening devotions at night. On Thursdays, the women and men did their spiritual ruminations in separate quarters.

Once a month they washed each other's feet: an act of intimacy and humility, laying one's self bare before the Father and Son and Holy Spirit.

Ellen never felt more invigorated. The Word filled her with purpose. The people here truly believed and didn't use God to control her. She no longer hated her mother, herself. "I wasn't the devil's child." She couldn't quite look at me when she said that.

The only thing that was tough at first was giving up bubble gum. Since she was nine years old, she had enjoyed perfecting balloon-size bubbles, but at the church such practices were deemed extravagant, lacking in simplicity and a proper focus on the spiritual.

Within eight days, Ellen was baking the occasional set of pies for Friday night desserts, cutting back on the sugars for a tart flavor that fit with Brother Durgana's philosophy of simplicity and struggle.

Her cube, that's what the girls called their quarters, was shaped like an igloo and housed with three other transient runaways including Susan Whitfield, a rich heiress (do heiresses still exist, Ellen asked me, or was that simply a 1930s-word I'm using to describe a rich ingénue?). Susan, recently pregnant, was the leader of their dwelling. She taught Ellen the church's central hymn, a lament for a life left behind.

This Ellen could relate to as a Métis girl who no longer could recall her own people's words for bird, fish, deer. And because of Susan's privilege, she was allowed to leave the compound for day trips into the city, to visit doctors about her pregnancy or her therapist, Dr. Cohen, about her condition.

Ellen accompanied Susan on these visits.

On those days Ellen blew large pink bubbles that popped the air.

She felt a little ashamed for how much pleasure it brought her.

One time, at the Half-Life, a bar on Spadina, Ellen met Ivan Sevrier, Susan's beau, who spent the whole afternoon pontificating ("Does the root of this word, Mr. Fuller, come from that blowhard Pontius Pilate? To pontificate like Pontius Pilate?") about being French and what a second-class status it was to be so in Canada, for to be bilingual meant being French and having to learn English; it never worked the other way around.

She wanted to tell him, how do you think it feels being French and Indian and having a white man with a gun on his hip take you away to a woman who smells of tuna casserole? But she said nothing. Ivan's words, however, sounded forced to Ellen, like a rehearsed mantra, part of a manifesto. "Oh, Vichy, don't be so pompous," Susan teased, apparently agreeing with Ellen, but loving her beau nonetheless, kissing him on the cheek.

Ellen wanted to be loved like that.

Near the end of her second week, after baking pies for the tenants, Ellen met Steve Smith, CEO of the Toronto Maple Leafs and owner of the Army Surplus store next door. Smith was tall, angular, maybe even a little withered. He looked like Ichabod Crane, a story Ellen read in seventh grade, and he admired her pies and approached her about a business plan.

His bleeding ulcers made his breath bad, so he often pointed his words away from her, at a corner in the room, the ceiling, but he really liked her pies—the best he ever tasted—and sought a way to market them, creating what he called a brand. "Get the pies out in the world. We need a name." He snapped phosphorous fingers. "Something catchy."

"Melville?"

She was born in Regina but taken to the "suburbs" of Melville.

Melville Pies. He adjusted his glasses. That was okay, but not loud enough. Melville, huh? He snapped his fingers again. "How about the White Whale, the Whaler?" Eating one of her pies was like going on a quest, conquering Moby-Dick. *White Whale Pies.*

White? Was he aware of the irony? Was he not seeing her?

"Sure," she said.

The next day, at his home in Rosedale, they drew up a two-week marketing strategy, involving radio spots, billboards, newspaper ads. Smith, with a floor plan of the church spread across his mahogany desk, discussed converting the basement into a chef's kitchen, a row of ovens, sinks, refrigerators. The central air unit, which he had circled, would unfortunately break up the track of ovens, but we do what we can.

Susan, who cleaned Smith's Rosedale home twice a week, warned Ellen to look out for Smith riding his hobby horse: *Find your purpose in life. Your role.* He drops that little aphorism into every conversation. Susan laughed with a veil of smugness. Sure enough, that day Smith said it. "You are a nurturer, you give to others rather than yourself. Your pies are a gift of giving. Know your role."

It was all pretty cornball stuff, but she liked Susan's prior use of the word hobby horse. Ellen first came across it in Laurence Sterne's *Tristram Shandy.* And whenever Smith said the expected turn of phrase she tried hard not to laugh, or wind a family clock like Walter Shandy.

On the way to his car, Smith placed a hand on her shoulder. It was cold, surprisingly heavy and resembled glowing ash. "Next time you come, make sure you wear fishnets."

FISHNETS? ELLEN'S MIND WANDERED from the book Durgana forced all his followers to read: Norman Vincent Peale's *The Power of Positive Thinking. Fishnet stockings?*

"It's nothing," Susan said. "A fetish."

"What's that?"

"Guys who feel threatened by girls make them wear odd, sexy clothing to make themselves feel less threatened and in control."

"What?"

"Surely you've met guys who made you over into a fantasy. Ever put on a wig for a fella?"

She had. And she'd been labeled a cute little Indian girl so often she couldn't fix a number to the encounters.

Susan smiled, playing with the rough-edge collar to her canvas top. The lighting in the room was soft, a little foggy, making her dirty blonde hair turquoise. "It's a way of getting off."

Ellen was confused. How was this behavior part of a spiritual path? Why would Brother Durgana have such a friend?

Susan shrugged, played with the ridges of her canvas collar, and nonchalantly, as if washing her hands, said at the end of her Rosedale cleaning sessions Smith handed her a new pair of fishnet stockings and then escorted her to a back room, dark and cool, full of Toronto Maple Leafs memorabilia, classic photographs by Harold Barkley, and there removed his slacks, his briefs, and jerked off all over her netted legs.

"Gross." *And you allow that?*

"It's nothing." She tapped her lower lip, and once again played with her scratchy collar, while walking to a narrow night stand between their beds. A Coleman lantern sprinkled broken bits of light on a blond Jesus. Susan opened a drawer that took some work to budge. "And he gives me things."

Things? What did Susan need with things, Mr. Fuller? Susan had things when she lived with her father. Maybe her break from privilege wasn't as strong as it needs to be?

Maybe, I said.

But who am I to judge, she said. Shit. Sometimes while baking pies in the church basement Ellen subtly chewed Dubble Bubble, hoping the cameras wouldn't catch her or that Brother Durgana might not smell it on her breath.

The drawer was cramped with jewelry, bracelets, charms, including a horse with blue marble chips along its mane.

"You're not allowed to have this stuff." Ellen's voice quivered.

Both girls wore canvas clothes, sported short-cropped hair, no makeup: signs of foregoing the trappings of consumer excess for a life of spiritual simplicity and a quest for oneness.

"Oh, come on." Susan dangled the charm with blue marble in front of Ellen. "You want it. You do."

Seize it, her eyes said, seize it, girl.

Ellen did.

For several days Ellen kept the charm buried in the pocket of her canvas pants, fingers gracing its smooth surface, as if it were an element of the earth that one needed to live by.

Eventually, troubled over Smith and Susan's behaviors, she walked into Brother Durgana's office. I'm always available, he had told her when she first joined and took their covenant.

He wasn't pleased.

"You should knock—" He scrambled, inadvertently knocking over a figurine of a man fishing, and quickly reached for the small ear pieces in front of him. He quickly inserted them in his ears, a thin smile crossing crimped lips.

The room was dimly lit. There were no windows which always struck Ellen as odd.

She didn't understand his frustration. It was okay if he had a hearing problem. Why be ashamed? The church had taught her to accept all differences and to find your own inner qi, the life force, and to celebrate the beauty of each individual before God.

I'm part Indian and I'm beautiful.

He had taught her to say that. *I'm part Indian and I'm beautiful.* "But why only *part* Indian I wonder now, Mr. Fuller. It's as if there's a benefit in not being full Indian."

"Yeah, *part* cuts a couple of ways—" I struggled to say more.

"Anyway, back to the story—" She apologized to Durgana once again for not knocking, and a placid expression filled his face, a fresh coat of paint. "No harm." A shell on the beaches of Normandy, 1944, had punctured one of his ear drums. He had got pretty good at reading lips. He looked away, his eyes back on the bloody beach, as he picked up the fisherman figurine and placed it back in line with the others: angels, ballerinas, dancers.

One of his ear drums? But he had two ear pieces?

Yeah, I guess so, she said.

Hmm.

Anyway, Brother Durgana agreed that humility was central to a Christian life, and in this case, he wasn't very accepting of his own body's limitations. However, the hearing loss did encourage, in a small way, his stand to seek out a life beyond the body, beyond sex.

"Do you miss it?" she asked him.

"Of course." But his past loves weren't really about love. They were merely pursuits of carnal pleasures.

She nodded and spoke to intimate moments with Scott, her desire out of thankfulness to please him, but those encounters left her often feeling diminished.

"I understand." The coat of emotional pain had now firmed up his face, making Brother Durgana appear like the church leader she had come to expect. He smiled, placing the fisherman now at the front of the group, ahead of the angels. "How goes the pie campaign? Take lots of notes?"

"It goes." She had a folder full of marketing stuff resting on a mahogany table in Smith's home. She looked away.

"Good."

"What do you really think of Mr. Smith?" She spoke into her hands.

Smith was a weak man. Extremely so. His spiritual center was full of black haloes, but he genuinely cares about helping people, yes, the girls here. The light of Christ still walks with him, despite his darkness.

Ellen said nothing.

"We must learn forgiveness, Ellen. Forgiveness is God's love, it is the path to the greater good, outside of judgment. *He who's without sin cast the first stone.*"

"*Now go and sin no more,*" Ellen countered.

"Ah, you have been reading your scriptures." He wagged an admiring finger at her. "But in this case, walking in God's light, Susan has already forgiven him."

Apparently, Susan sought Brother Durgana's counsel over Smith some time ago.

Ellen smiled thinly, a hand on the smooth charm in her pocket, its chips of blue marble, feeling with reluctance that things had shifted between her and the church.

THREE WEEKS INTO OCTOBER, the shift became seismic.

Ellen was in the basement, mixing up pies for a special Friday night party, when through the vent, voices: Smith, Brother Durgana, and a third man.

Ellen wasn't trying to follow the contours of words, but when

Smith said let's do something "outside the boundaries of the acceptable" she wondered if the discussion were about her and Susan and fishnet stockings. She moved directly under the vent.

Brother Durgana, his voice barbwire fishing tackle, said, "Sure we can. Why not? As long as it's biblical." His voice was now cooling and full of distance. It was a timbre she had never heard before. "We can do it in a special service."

Do what?

"Biblical *and old.* A gesture," said the Third Man. His voice was full of stadium lights. He was clearly the leader.

"Can I watch?" Smith.

"Yes." Durgana, breathing naturally. "But you can't be a part of the service."

"This is my call," said the Third Man, reminding Brother Durgana of the church's hierarchy. "Yes, you can watch—from a distance."

"Sorry. I guess I didn't know my role." Brother Durgana laughed, Ellen was sure, in the direction of Smith.

Papers shifted, chairs scraped the floor, sliding up against the table's edge. "I have the perfect subject." It was the bright voice again of the Third Man. "Two subjects, actually, for such a ritual."

She could feel his smile through the words.

"A new chapter to the Book of Revelation. Our own Revelation." His tone was laudatory, self-assured, menacing.

"I'm not sure." Brother Durgana padded about the room, sighing. It was an unbalanced walk she recognized, the right steps heavier than the left. "It could be dangerous."

"Dangerous? Where's the fun without the danger?" Smith.

"Absolutely. Where's the fun?" The Third Man, his tone ironic, words full of quirky sideways glances.

Yesterday, Brother Durgana had kissed her, a neon kiss.

She had been tidying his office, dusting his desk with Lemon Pledge, when he walked in, right step heavy, left step light, seized her shoulders, and kissed her twice.

Did he feel he had a right because she's part Indian?

It was a neon kiss full of half-lived lives.

Her eyes were flames of forgiveness.

And then he left the office.

Now he was pacing, his left leg trying to lighten the right leg's load. "We have to be careful—"

"Agreed," The Third Man said, his voice a dark curtain closing the conversation.

WHEN SUSAN HEARD THE STORY from Ellen she laughed. "You must have read too many comic books as a kid."

"I heard them through the vents." *Two subjects, special ritualized service, a new kind of Revelation.*

"It's probably some kind of flashy sermon Brother Durgana is cooking up—"

"No. The tone was—"

"Conspiratorial?"

"Yes."

"It's nothing." Susan smiled vaguely.

It was a look Ellen had seen on her face all too often recently.

It was like she was becoming neon.

They, Durgana and Smith, had already approached Susan about it and the Revelation idea and she had agreed to do it. "I'd tell you about it, but I can't." She smiled again, face full of deferred feelings. "You'll find out. After Remembrance Day."

"Who's the third man?"

"The Third Man?" Durgana and Smith, there was no third man, she said.

"I heard three through the vents."

"Only two approached me."

"How long after? Remembrance Day. How long?"

"Shortly." She shrugged. "I have to do this for me. It'll take me where I want to go. Spiritually."

And then Susan hummed the hymn of lament, its discordant chords for the first-time filling Ellen with dread.

The fifteen-year-old hummed along, afraid to do otherwise.

THE FEAR DIDN'T LEAVE HER, she told me, voice heavy, and she slept broken dreams all night. In the morning, the women gathered in the sanctuary for three hours of devotions and silent meditation.

They were there without Susan.

Brother Durgana was vague about Susan's whereabouts, and as he tugged at his left ear chastised Ellen for listening in on a conversation, eavesdropping by the vents. "I saw you," he said, his black eyes full of the distance she had heard in his voice the day before. The cameras had captured her every gesture and attentive lean.

"You were also chewing gum."

Ellen's mouth was suddenly dry.

"The ritual you heard about you'll experience—soon."

"When?"

"Soon."

His aloofness alarmed her. She had lost his good opinion, and that turn of phrase made her face burn, thinking of Darcy in her favorite book *Pride and Prejudice*: "My good opinion once lost is lost forever."

Brother Durgana wasn't Darcy, and Ellen clearly wasn't Elizabeth Bennett.

Why did she care for this white man's good opinion?

But she did.

She hated having her good opinion lost.

"In the interim, as Susan prepares for the ceremony, you'll be cleaning Mr. Smith's Rosedale home. Today." He smiled, but it was like one of his neon kisses, floating in a mist of vapors. He looked through her shoulder. Smith's on the path of repentance, he said, help him find it.

He handed her a pair of fishnet stockings, quoted Luke 15:7: "There should be more joy in heaven over one sinner who repents than over the ninety and nine just persons who need no repentance."

FORTY-FIVE MINUTES LATER SHE STOOD WAITING in Ira Fuller's milk truck.

He made deliveries on Thursdays, often teasing Ellen, roughing up her shorn hair and telling her to stay in school, get an education, you're too young to surrender your life to God. And then, as his own kind of repentance, he'd hand her a pint of chocolate milk.

This particular day, he was wearing his Habs toque pushed so far back on his head that it looked like a red, white and blue yarmulke. A cigarette dangled in his mouth, smoke curving by his eyes. "What's with the stockings?"

"Fringe benefits and some bullshit about repentance." She looked away. "I gotta get out of here."

She mumbled, hesitating to form the words, about a ritual to take place after Remembrance Day, a profane ritual moving beyond the acceptable, and how the whole joint was giving her the creeps. *Should a fifteen-year-old be wearing fishnets?*

Ira knew to ask no further questions, threw the truck into gear, and pulled away from the church. His face was scruffy, he hadn't shaved that morning, and all of his fingernails were dirty.

Two calls later, empties rattling in the metal trays in back of the truck, she confessed she had nowhere to go. "Look at what *they want me to wear.*" She didn't trust the Children's Aid Society; they'd send her back to Saskatchewan.

"You hate farming?"

"No, my mother. Foster mother." She looked away. "Her. Her I hate."

She thought she had gotten over it, through the Word, but lately harsh feelings curled out from the shadows of her heart.

Ira didn't say anything, his upper lip curled under his lower teeth.

On the way to his next call, a series of apartment dwellings, she told him, a foster mother who tried to beat the red devil out of her with a leather belt, her foster father's. People around her, her minister, her friends, teachers, unable to ask about her sullen moods outside the home.

"Unable? Maybe they just didn't know how?"

"Or didn't want to bother—"

"I doubt that." He now gnawed at his upper lip, the sun creasing his eyes, one ear poking out from under the toque. "You don't need to go back to *that* or the church." He sighed. "We'll figure something out."

He lit a fresh Rothmans and offered her one.

Ellen was technically a minor, but Ira treated her as an equal. She accepted the gesture and lit her cigarette, careful to exhale smoothly.

That night they hardly said a word. He watched cop shows and she read. He asked her questions about the book and later ordered a pizza from De Luca's: half pepperoni and Kalamata olives (she liked that word and wrote it down—Kalamata. It took her some place beyond all this, a warm bleached bone of sand and sun and Dorian pillars). Her half pizza was pineapple and green olives. It seemed so boring next to his. She drank two orange sodas.

Afterwards she chewed three chunks of Dubble Bubble.

He asked her for one. It hurt his jaw so he stopped. Christ, won't this shit rot your teeth, he said. "They got a good dental plan at that so-called church?"

"I don't want to talk about that church."

"I'm sorry." He held up both hands.

"It's okay. It was kind of funny. So-called. That was funny."

He slept on the couch.

—

DURING SATURDAY'S HOCKEY TELECAST, he told her he wanted to read well; well, read better. He had dropped out of school after tenth grade and he always regretted that. As an immigrant, English wasn't his first language, and he often felt his mind didn't work fast enough, that contexts and situations took a degree of decoding, and he wanted to read with someone who, like her, studied and enjoyed the sounds, meanings of words, and maybe with Ellen's help, Ira could carry on meaningful conversations with his son who was an avid reader.

Ellen was embarrassed to admit that she actually liked white writers. She wanted, someday, to read words written by her own people, but for now her sense of selfhood was constructed by artists she felt aligned to in their fighting spirits and empathy for others. So, after a visit to the Public Library, she suggested they read *More Joy in Heaven* by Morley Callaghan.

Callaghan cared deeply for the people he wrote about and the irony of the title mirrored her own experiences navigating a space between the Indian and the white world. In her final conversation with Brother Durgana, he was quoting the *more joy in heaven passage* in Luke. This bemused her.

"I look forward to getting up to speed," Ira said, slightly smiling, looking away. "With reading comprehension."

"You don't need to get up to speed," she said. "You understand a lot." His empathy for her situation made her indebted to help in any way.

They read aloud during intermissions and for two hours after the game. Ira found the story moving: Kip Caley, a former gangster, can't escape his past. He serves eleven years for armed robbery, and then a priest, with the help of a group of civic leaders and reformers, gets his sentence commuted, and wind up, according to Ellen, using him as a symbol for their put-on charity.

"Kip's based on a real guy," Ira said, sipping a Molson Canadian. "A Norman, uh, Norman Ryan." It was in all the papers, in the 1930s, just before Hayden was born. A bank robber. Then he reformed, even had a heartwarming series on CFRB radio, celebrating his redemption and change, but all the time, get this, he was leading a double life, a gangster by night.

"A double life?"

"Yeah." Ira slapped the beer bottle on the table, harder than he meant to. Foam spilled over the bottle's lip. "Like me," he said, confessing to doing to Hayden greater cruelties than what the Government and Ellen's foster mother had done to her.

And then he cried.

Ellen wanted to forgive him but couldn't.

She quietly chewed her gum.

They sat, the TV turning to bumble bees.

Eventually they returned to the book, finished it, and Ira cried over the death of Kip's girlfriend (Julie reminded him of his own wife, Rebekah, and the sacrifices she made, her unconditional love for him, her death from cancer). Christ, I cry over everything, now, he said. A regular waterworks. Call Ontario Hydro.

Self-deprecating humor is charming. Self-deprecating. A kind of clever humility, really. She wrote that down.

The haphazard police busted in and shot Julie, in a crossfire. The police busted in and took Ellen, from her mother.

Unlike Smith, and his little aphorisms and promises of future moneyed privileges, Ellen felt that Ira was a real man of repentance, someone she was comfortable around. "I loved your dad," she said.

Yes, he had abused his son, but with him, now, she knew she was safe. He had changed.

They talked about the Jewish faith, suffering, and living in God's law.

Together they also baked pies—his favorite being blueberry—and she taught him how to make the pie filling less runny by adding three tablespoons of quick-cooking tapioca.

"I loved your dad, but not in a sexual way, but with affection, and love." He read with enthusiasm, wanting to learn, and when he pushed his Habs toque down over his forehead she knew he was really becoming the Old Man in Hemingway's novel. There was a vulnerability to his earnestness, a life of regrets.

He knew he couldn't take back what he did, and for this he was truly ashamed.

He owned it. She admired that.

Over three days they read *The Old Man and the Sea.*

On the fourth day, sixteen days after moving in with him, Ira was dead.

IT HAPPENED BEFORE DAWN.

She was asleep and Ira pushed her awake, yelling at her to hide *now*, in the kitchen, the dumbwaiter.

He gave her a slice of cheese, closed the door, and moments later was scuffling about in the living room, getting knocked over into the furniture.

Payback was the word Ellen heard again and again and again. Payback.

Susan's voice was hazy and full of doubts.

The other voice was French, Ivan's.

At gunpoint they forced Ira out of his clothes, and with what must have been a hand over his mouth, they shot him full of heroin, his last words mumbled murmurs.

Not heroin, Thorazine, an anti-psychotic. "Thorazine," I said. "Ellen, they ever make you take pills?"

Once a day. Vitamins, they said.

Uh-huh. *To keep you in line, slowed down*, I said. *Thorazine.*

"But I heard Ivan say uncut—can Thorazine be uncut?"

Maybe he thought it was H, but it was Thorazine, I repeated. Thorazine.

Ellen wanted to pull on the pulleys and sink to the basement but she scrunched inside the box wishing herself small, invisible.

It was over quickly.

Susan sighed and angled herself to the kitchen, leaning left. Ellen watched through a slit between the dumbwaiter's door frame and the door.

Susan ran a hand through what was left of her hair. She was buzzed, her hair now dyed a dark, dark black, licorice nubs.

Below the dumbwaiter, heavy footsteps trudged the basement, pulling an old bed's abandoned box springs from the wall, knocking over crates, kicking about old hockey gear. "She's not here," he shouted up the stairs.

Susan collapsed against the Formica table, her stiff arms anchoring her. She lit a cigarette, hands shaking. "Okay. Try the bathroom—behind the shower curtain."

Susan disappeared from view. Smoke filled the kitchen.

Ivan reached the landing and took his time getting to the bathroom. His steps were heavy Frankenstein feet. The whole house appeared to shake, and Ellen's heart pounded her neck, shoulders, chest.

The fridge door opened, closed.

"She's not in the bathroom." He was now headed to the spare room, Rebekah's "office," fitted with a Singer sewing machine, dozens of fabric remnants, patterns for old clothes, a rocking chair, and a lamp to read by. Ira hadn't changed a thing in that room since Rebekah died.

"That's because it was his penance of remembrance," I said.

Ellen nodded.

Susan stared at the dumbwaiter.

At the slit between jamb and door.

Into the slit between jamb and door.

Ellen's breath stopped, her heart punching away, the cheese slice dampening against skin.

Susan opened the door to the dumbwaiter.

Ellen said nothing.

Susan smiled and held a finger to her lips.

"Nothing here," a voice in the spare room shouted.

"Nothing here, either," Susan said, before closing the dumbwaiter's door.

Third Period

"I always liked this book." Stana and I read it together three years ago, in Mexico.

The hands on my father's clock stuttered as if each tip had been coated with fly paper. It was 11:07. I tossed the Callaghan novel on the table next to it.

"I need to take the book back to the library," she said. That and the Hemingway. They were signed out in her name. She smiled thinly. "That isn't why I came back, but—"

"Sure. Overdue library fines are a bitch." I smiled.

"You have your dad's humor."

I'm not sure I saw that as a compliment. *Color of the day* and all.

She gathered up the two books, stacked them neatly in front of her. She wore an argyle sweater. A weird choice: business-school conservative, not the look I expected.

Boundaries of the acceptable, post-Remembrance Day rituals, two subjects. What did all that shit mean and why was my stomach full of crumbling rocks? What do these things have to do with photographs of followers dressed in eerie black robes?

I pushed back my porkpie, poured us each another cup of coffee. It was strong and just breathing in its scent sharpened my own.

"Why didn't you report my father's murder?" I sat in his chair.

"Look at me. What chance do I have in a white world?" She

tugged at the sleeves of her sweater. "They'd probably find a way to blame me." Or send her back to her white mother. She had a history of running. Her first instinct is flight. "I just don't trust the system at all." So she ran and ran and ran. "I think I'll always be running."

I nodded.

"I really, really, really liked your father." She smiled awkwardly. "Loved him, like a daughter should love a dad." She never knew her own father. And her foster father? Forget about it. She shrugged dismissively.

"Sure." I tented my fingers together. "You ever see those black robes? At the church? Looks like a Klan rally without all the bleach?"

"I've worn those robes—"

"For what?"

"They're sacred. Special services. Rituals. Like Easter."

"On Easter you wear black?"

She nodded slowly, her eyes searching for something on the ceiling. Maybe she wanted to slip into Lake Huron too. The dark robes, she said, were a reminder to all followers that we can, at any time, slip back into our fragile pasts, allowing the darkness of temptation to return. Those robes are a plea, a kind of atonement, that we must be ever diligent about letting the dark sides of our nature win. We all walk in darkness and light.

"Uh-huh." I rubbed at the sides of my mouth. "Ever participate in a midnight mass?"

She laughed, a gap between her teeth, green eyes filling with light. "Midnight mass. Isn't that a Catholic thing?"

How many times had I heard that on this case? And yet "Midnight mass: 11/14/65" *was written* on an envelope.

She removed Dad's Habs toque and rubbed nubs of blue-black hair that resembled broken teeth on a comb. "We're not Catholic."

"What are you—exactly?"

"Multi-denominational. Of the way, but not the only way."

"Sounds like ad copy—"

It was. She smiled at her Buster Browns, dotted with spots of salt and sand. Smith came up with that, part of our brand. She placed air quotes around the latter word.

"The pie lover."

She rubbed at an elbow, adjusting the bunched-up lump of wool. "Yes."

"*Beyond the boundaries of the acceptable.*" I shook my head, played with the brim of my porkpie. "That sound Christian to you?"

"Not the way they said it. No." There was too much menace behind the words, leaking through the vent, the promise of the dark eclipsing the light.

I handed her the creased photograph I'd been carrying for two days, a portrait of her and her uneven bangs. "This mean anything to you?"

"I need a new hairdresser?" She laughed, deep and low, at her own joke. I liked it.

I pointed at the switch plate, told her how I found the photo.

"I didn't leave it there." She plunked a chunk of Dubble Bubble in her mouth. And the photo's so old, Mr. Fuller. Look, I have hair. It was taken by Brother Durgana when she first arrived at The People's Way to Christ. "I'm fourteen in this picture." She was now fifteen, fifteen and a half. "Look at all the pimples around my chin."

"That's my father's handwriting—"

"Is it?" She didn't give him the photo. How would he have got it? "You sure it's his handwriting? It looks like a prescription written by a doctor, and anyone can imitate that shit."

I rubbed at an itch on one of my elbows. A faint smile formed around my lower lip. She was right. It was an easy scrawl to imitate. "The Third Man. Through the vents. You didn't recognize the voice?"

It wasn't familiar. No. She blew a soft, small bubble.

Shit. So much of this case was pushing me into a dark corner. *Black robes. Biblical revelations. I couldn't connect the loose strings and time was running out.*

"Why did you take the floor plans, the blueprints of the basement?"

"Floor plans?"

"Yes. The one's to the basement—"

Ellen's lips crimped together. "*I* didn't take them."

"You didn't give them to Susan?"

"No." She absently traced a bulky triangle on her sweater. "Smith had the plans. Always had them."

"Uh-huh." *Smith.*

Susan must have got them from Smith. Why report something to Dr. Cohen that just wasn't true? Why drop Ellen's name off to your therapist? A setup, a false clue, a false lead. Why? Susan got them from Smith not Ellen.

"Did Susan ever say anything to you about dismantling the universe?"

"No."

"That phrase. You ever hear it spoken by anyone? *Dismantle the universe.*"

"No."

"Think. Think hard. Ivan say it when he was talking about being French and having to learn English?"

"I'm an Indian being forced to be white and I don't even say it." Hell, she noticed words, offbeat phrasings, she said. She would have wrote that one down. It had a rhythm, a poetry. And she'd never heard it until now.

"Sure."

"I've been circling the house for the last two days, hoping you'd return. To talk." She laughed, the crimp in her lips loosening. "And get the library books back to the library."

"Hmm." I smoothed out a crease on my chinos. "Where you

been staying?"

"Around."

"*Payback*. What's that all about?" She knew Susan, maybe she could guess at her motives. "Just give me your hunches. Like you did with the *doctor's scrawl*."

"I don't know." Her arms were bent at the elbows, half of each hand retracting inside the red sweater's cuffs. "She said it four times. At least four times." Ellen felt like Susan had to do it. She was being forced to do it.

"Payback? Not paying back my father, but paying back someone else, like a brother maybe?"

"Maybe."

"Just maybe?"

"More like yes. Definitely." She smiled, her lower lip a loose rubber band. "Most definitely."

"She ever talk about her brother?"

"I saw him one time. At the Half-Life, bossing her around for not wearing the right accessories. Accessories? We had to wear drab canvas clothes at the church, but still he thought her watch band should match the color of the canvas."

"Crazy."

"Susan often joked that she was in *retreat*. The church was a *retreat*. From *him*."

She flipped the photograph, a third time, as if it were a giant coin she was about to toss in the air and call tails. "Midnight mass. 11/14/65." She ran a thumb under her lower lip. "That's in forty minutes. Tonight."

"What?"

Midnight mass.

Ellen talked quickly, her voice falling dominoes. Look, you go to a Christmas service celebrating Christ's birth on Christmas Eve. You celebrate the 25th on the night of the 24th. Thus, if you're celebrating God knows what on the 14th, then the service, the midnight mass, would be the night of the 13th, today, not the night of the 14th. The 13th at midnight.

Fuck. I hadn't thought of it that way. Nobody on this case had.

Half dollars of sweat formed in my hands. Franklin W. Whitfield II told me to sit tight, he had hired Tod X, the great deprogrammer out of Detroit to rescue Susan from the prison of her mind, starting tomorrow, but what if tomorrow were too late and Franklin knew it, what if the whole Tod X sideshow was just that, a sideshow, a distraction to keep all of us at bay while he finishes, *tonight*, whatever he has planned to do to his sister, without Tod X's interference?

What if he never contacted Tod X?

Quid pro quo.

How many times had people I interviewed uttered those very words to describe a brother and sister relationship?

Quid pro quo.

Brother and sister had imagined a whole separate world, seeking a kingdom beyond all this: Dimension V. Brother and sister developed their own Semaphore codes of sign language, spoke a private language. Brother and sister were in the habit of finishing off each other's thoughts.

Quid pro quo.

Susan had suggested a targeted killing of one Grayson Jackson but couldn't make her theoretical proposition a reality. Franklin could, and did, shoving a liquored-up Grayson off a frat house balcony.

Quid pro quo.

A debt was owed. To pay back his targeted killing, Susan had to kill someone her brother targeted: my father. My father was but a set of accessories, another element in Franklin's control game. *I killed for you, now you must kill for me.*

And now at midnight something horrible was going to happen to Susan. She was about to become a voluntary victim that will take her beyond the boundaries of the acceptable and into

Dimension V's aesthetics of dismantling the universe.

Maybe she was suicidal and this was her way out.

I dialed my RCMP hotline, was placed on hold, and finally patched through to Anne Chevalier, one of their top agents in the field.

Her words were hurried, elevated, she was on a case. "Don't you have a game Friday?"

"I'll be back—"

"The grenade toss? That was five stars out of five."

I could feel the warmth of her voice. On my last case, we had faced death together, tackling a faux N'oublie jamais terrorist cell and sharing personal secrets (my abuse at the hands of my father; her closeted sexual orientation), and because of that a mutual respect and admiration embraced the words between us. We liked each other. We trusted each other.

"Listen—" I filled her in on this case, all about Ellen, what she'd heard, and how in less than thirty minutes I feared a black mass was about to descend on the cult on McGowan Street.

She was already on it and in position, surveilling the very The People's Way to Christ as we now talked. An inside follower had sent her photographs of people in dark robes and details of a possible black mass, Satanic ritual, tonight. Anne had three operatives positioned in the sanctuary, in stand-down mode.

"Careful. They have cameras everywhere. They'll see every move."

"We know about the cameras."

She apologized for cutting me off and spoke softly, giving directions to one of the operators inside. She was communicating with her team via radio transistors in their ears. "Look I have to go. Radio silence begins in a minute. I'm going to leave the car. Move to a position on the street."

"Right."

She said she was so sorry to hear about Dad. She knew my feelings for him were a mixed bag, but he was still my father.

"Yeah. It's a complicated bag."

And then she was gone.

I dropped the phone in the cradle, turned to Ellen, my mind floating away from all of this as thousands of camera bulbs flashed. "You ever see a control room in the church, a control monitoring hub?"

The Whitfields had made a bundle of post-war money specializing in security systems to protect families from burglaries, break-ins, home invasions. "The cameras? They're everywhere. Where's the control room?"

Ellen didn't have access to everywhere, just the basement, the sanctuary, her own cube, and Brother Durgana's office with no windows.

No windows. I snapped my fingers. "I bet reception is better without windows, without interference—"

And then I knew.

Dimension V.

Franklin W. Whitfield II was living it, in it. A watcher, he watched his sister fuck, listened in while Sharon fucked Thompson. And now he controlled the world through his Dimension V compound and its opticon gaze.

The Army Surplus store. The basement with a ditto machine.

"You ever see Brother Durgana rub at his ear, tug on a lobe?"

Her eyes creased. "Yes." Many times.

Yes. Me too.

Brother Durgana wasn't wearing hearing aids; he's fitted with radio transistors, like Anne's operators in the field. Brother Durgana is constantly being monitored by Frank Two, told what to say, what to think. "I always felt his words were too eloquent, refined." As if he were an evening news anchor reading from a teleprompter.

Ellen agreed. After all, his kisses were neon kisses. It was like he were a mask, a living mask.

"That's right. A mask. And the face behind the mask is Whitfield's."

The Third Man is Whitfield.

"Think back. The voice through the vent, the voice complaining about Susan's accessories at Half-Life. One and the same. Whitfield. Deuces. Frank Two."

"Maybe. Yeah. Maybe. The voices were very similar."

I pulled down my porkpie, called Stana; she picked up on the fourth ring.

"I wake you?"

"No. Just a little queasy. Slow moving."

"I'm sorry about the hands—"

"Yeah—"

"I have Ellen Reynolds here in Gradwell. I need to roll on the church. How long till you and Dr. C can get here?"

Fifteen minutes, she said. "And it was fucking horrible. The hands—"

"I know. I know." I'm going to leave in ten, I said. Watch over Ellen.

"On our way."

I smiled at Ellen, my lopsided lupine leer.

The RCMP had the church on lockdown. I was about to lock down Dimension V.

I don't think they knew about the Army Surplus store and there was no way to reach Anne.

I zipped my leather jacket, holstered my snub-nosed .38. "He'll be *watching the festivities.*"

"I want to go with you."

Her face was delicate, the dent above her upper lip, angelic.

I held her close. "It's too dangerous." She smelled of coffee and orange sodas and bubble gum. She was *only* fifteen. I leaned my forehead against hers. "Stana is a great gal." I lifted Ellen's chin. How horrible it must have been to be trapped in that dumbwaiter while my dad was murdered. "I'm glad you were a part of my father's life." I shrugged. "Dr. Cohen's a little stiff, but you'll like her. She's a fighter, a survivor like you."

"And you. You're a survivor too."

"Yeah." I played with the zipper of my leather jacket, setting it half-way. "Can I keep the book?" I pointed in the direction of the coffee table. "I'd like to read it again."

"It's due next week." Her lips crimpled together.

"I'll take it back to the library. I promise."

She separated it out from the Hemingway, slid it toward me. "Make sure."

"I will." I held up a hand. "Now you've got to promise me something."

"Quid pro quo?"

"Oh, God, don't say that."

She laughed.

"We have so much more to talk about—wait for me, please. Don't run. I'll be back."

"Why did Susan not kill me?" Her eyes were wet.

"I think it's a sign that she's not completely under her brother's control." I smiled again. "I think Susan genuinely liked you." I kissed her forehead. "*I* like you."

We separated and she walked to the far end of the coffee table. There she picked up the Habs toque.

The clock stuttered. 11:42.

"Promise to wait for me? Pinky promise?" I was still holding up my left hand.

"Pinky promise," she said, flipping the Habs toque, catching it by the inside. Ellen had wanted something to remember Ira by, that's why she took the toque, but she changed her mind, had to return it. Circled the house for two days. *It was meant for me.* He was going to give it to you after Tuesday's game at the Gardens, she said.

I held the toque lightly in my hands.

"Look inside—"

My face felt akimbo, a Picasso painting. Along the toque's

tag, in black magic marker, Dad had scrawled: "For Hayden, one tough Jew."

THE ROOM WAS BLUE, underwater moonlight.

He sat, his back to me, behind a long, hard table of black marble with blue lights burning, buried inside, casting indigo hues throughout the room. Above him was a row of eight monitors. Dark-hooded followers moved in a solemn processional down carpeted aisles.

A second camera, medium-long shot, captured a flash of gray-white centered on the carpet between curtains of black hoods. These two were without clothes. She, her breasts full, dimples along her hips, was probably about four months pregnant. They had shaved away her pubic hair. He, sporting amber goggles, walked without shame, his erection sharply pointed.

Susan and Colin.

The sanctuary's neon lighting was of one subdued, uniform color, fighting to match the underwater moonlight in Frank Two's lair. A giant headset covered Dimension V's King, a heavy crown. The headset had a Martian-like antenna and headphones resembling a pair of unopened Swanson's frozen dinners. Frank Two whispered words into the microphone curled by his mouth.

Brother Durgana, tapping at an ear shrouded by an oversized Ming the Merciless hood, repeated the maestro's words.

So, in this time of trouble, war in Vietnam, protests in Quebec's business district, people living outside of wedlock in our new, so-called advanced permissive society, we make this offering. Oh, Lord, keep us humble before you, keep us, through your grace, free from falling into the darkness of addiction and pleasure and violence. We are all eyes stuck in the needle. To be free we must become camels, innocent of sin, we must give something back to you, to crawl through the needle's eye, Oh, Lord. We must atone and make our covenant with you. We offer this sacrifice in the spirit of Abraham and Isaac. We are forever humble, your lambs, bloodied for you.

"Nice speech, dickhead." I pushed back my porkpie.

Frank Two's shoulders froze, locking into his neck.

Colin and Susan stopped at the edge of the sanctuary's platform. The Latin-filled curtain draped behind Brother Durgana, as he raised his arms to God, his black robe with a red cross on his chest, resembling the garb of a crusader. He shook his fists and bowed to his knees, before God.

Next to the podium was a bone-white pedestal. On it, two fire extinguishers, loaded up, no doubt, with the Whitfield munitions variant of DDT and 2,4,5T.

Brother Durgana rose, readying to make Colin and Susan into pillars of salt.

"Game's over, asshole."

The snub-nosed .38 was clamped in my hand.

Frank Two turned slowly in his chair, the size of something you'd find in the cockpit of an Avro Arrow fighter jet. A big Saran Wrap grin stretched across his face. "Game: a very apt word." He chuckled. It was a little wet. "But *asshole*? Really? My, my, my such language. So refined." He took off the headset, placed it next to him. "I think I preferred when you called me Deuces." He laughed, an empty rattle this time, lacking genuine enthusiasm. "You chose the wrong option, shamus. You let the pursuit of knowledge cloud your judgment. You bit the apple instead of following the Word. You should have gone to the church to stop this from happening, this mass. Not stop here to talk to me, the prime suspect, the genius behind it all." He beamed. "You want my knowledge." He beamed again. "And I'm glad. Because a genius likes to talk about what makes him a genius." He was still beaming.

It was pretty good, as far as beaming goes, full of conceit and glee. He must have been practicing that look in the mirror or something since he was five years old. "Oh, I'm not worried," I said.

To his left was a wall filled with a cache of arms: AK-47s; Thompson submachine guns; tear-gas canisters, and so-called grenades, liquid napalm really, his father's brand of creeping jelly, hexagonal, egg-shaped things with small broomstick handles.

A lot of ordnance for such a small room.

On the typewriter table to his right, by a pair of metal folding chairs, wasn't a typewriter at all but a ditto machine. Apparently Roy Lichtenstein lived here too.

I pointed at the ditto machine. "Why'd you have those bloodied posters, Star of Davids, posted in Dr. Cohen's office?"

"To throw suspicion on me and my family, of course. Or to throw you off. Or," he beamed again, "to fuck with you. I don't like Jews."

"Right. We played this act before. At your Dad's. This one ain't going to end well for you, pally."

"Words. Words. Words."

"Yeah, yeah, yeah."

He was awfully confident for a fucko who left the door to his basement hideaway unlocked. Sloppy. Nabbing him was far too easy. Frank Two never heard me coming because he was too absorbed in the show he was producing in the sanctuary. His addiction. The cobalt blue of his eyes matched the blue steel, technological vibe of this room and the one next door.

Blue.

Underwater moonlight.

On the white shelves were several closed cardboard tubs labeled C17H19Sin2S. I pointed in their direction. "Uranium isotopes?"

"Funny, Mr. Fuller, but you can do better than that." He smiled. "What killed your father?"

"Thorazine."

"Chlorpromazine. An anti-psychotic. Keeps our followers following. You get my drift?"

"I get it." Something to control *them* by. Blue is what *con-*

trolled him.

The primary color in Susan's art. They matched. He was living in Dimension V's blue; her art suggested a need to catch a bus, to get away from it.

"Dimension V, huh?" I pointed at all the monitors, the gizmos, the weaponry, the room's somber glow.

"What of it?" He crossed arms over his freshly pressed blazer. Underneath the blazer and his glistening fraternity pin was the collar of a new crew-cut sweater. He truly was in a celebratory mood.

"It's over."

He looked at his watch. The crystal too was blue.

"Over? Indeed, it is." He uncrossed his arms. "But not the way you mean." He couldn't stop beaming. "You can't stop it, now that it's started."

Durgana placed his hands on Colin's naked shoulders, said a few words, and then he moved to Susan's shoulders, mumbling similar words. He asked them to rise.

"Wanna bet?"

I knew about the RCMP, positioned, ready. He didn't. Fuck him.

"Put the gun down, Hayden."

That's why the door was open. CEO Smith came to watch and he now had the drop on me. Shit.

A hammer cocked. Jasmine perfume. *Not just Smith.* "I'll shoot in three—" A woman's voice.

I dropped the gun. Turned.

Sharon Dafoe.

Tall, angular, her blond hair curling up and back from a black beret, full of fashion élan and danger. She wore pink periwinkle lipstick, an orange wool coat, and white go-go boots right out of Christian Dior, topped off by a bizarre set of space-age hoop earrings that resembled flying saucers right out of Ray Harryhausen.

"It's Angie's hands your friends found. Not mine."

"She was getting too close." The Saran Wrap smile stretched even further on Frank Two's face.

Smith deliberately bumped my shoulder as he passed, trying some kind of macho assertion thing that just wasn't working. He was now rubbing at his shoulder. "You're a nosy fuck," he said, parking his bony ass on a metal chair in front of one of the eight monitors. He removed his Lombardis, cleaned the lenses with a thin square of cloth. "And now, shamus, you're going to be dead." He pushed his glasses back in place and leaned forward in his box seat to see the human sacrifice. "Angie always talked too much," he mumbled. "A real know-it-all broad." He dismissed her with a phosphorous swipe of a hand.

"I was the sawbones." Frank Two. On point. Always. "She was alive when I hacked off her hands." He smiled faintly. "Style points, you know? Like the etherized frogs we cut up in biology? Their hearts still beating?"

How long did it take her to die? "How do you sleep at night, Deuces?"

"Oh, it's Deuces now?" A faint chuckle slithered through his lips. "I sleep. I sleep fine, shamus." He glanced at the back of a hand, checking out his manicure. "I sleep fine. It's the other guy who stays awake worrying about what I'm going to do."

"Yeah, you're a real mastermind. A wizard of weird." I shook my head. "I understand how you could talk someone like Colin Thompson into being part of a human sacrifice—he probably figures he's going to a place where he can be playing hockey, but your sister, how did you convince her?"

"It was easy," he said. "She'd be done with me."

He didn't laugh this time. His tone, matter-of-fact, flat. *It was easy.*

And convenient. With Susan out of the way certain truths could be buried.

"Truths? Like you and Terrien and Steinmetz and their bodies buried in Vaughan, Ontario?"

My first case. He had been listening in on the goings on at Dr. Cohen's. He planted the bugs.

"Of course I planted the bugs. And you got really close to that truth. You're a worthy adversary." He pointed a proud finger. "Worthy. I admire you. Holmes and Moriarty. Only in my world, I'm Holmes." He laughed. "I win. Holmes always wins."

You see, he said, without an equal, all of this is no fun. He needed me. He heard of my exploits in Dr. Cohen's office, solving two prior sensational cases and wanted to lure me into his game. That's why he killed my father, to get the chess piece he wanted. Initially, he bugged Dr. Cohen's office to keep tabs on his sister, but when he heard of my cases against corruption and porn at Maple Leaf Gardens and terrorist threats and drugs involving a faux N'oublie jamais, he'd discovered his adversary, and what made me tick, and how to *play* me. "I need competition. And you gave it to me."

He arrived on the scene at Becker's, after the Gus kill, not as a reporter but as a psychologist, to see if I were truly committed and I was. He let me boss him around then, an act, a moment of humility topos. "I can only be as good as my opposition," he said. "And you're very good."

Sharon shifted the white purse on her left arm. It was heavy and resembled a large kidney. "You're such a fool, Hayden." She shook her head. "All a woman has to do in front of you is emote and your chivalrous streak kicks in. Everything I said fooled you."

"Everything you said fooled him because I was doing the talking." Frank Two's grin was now a twisting snake. "I helped write the script she spoke." Sharon was wired and had a transistor in her ear the day I met her at Half-Life. "I was in the room *with you.* At the coffee shop."

"How'd you know I'd interview Sharon?"

"I planted enough clues. You played the game according to

my rules." He inhaled, sniffed, shook his head.

"And I'm not a victim of unrequited love." Sharon adjusted her beret. "So touching when you held my hand." She laughed. It sounded like a whimpering animal caught in a trap. "I don't hate Franklin. I love him."

"Good for you," I said. "Where's the bridal registry. I'll send a gift."

"Let's not be too hard on him, Sharon." He raised a hand and clapped softly. "He's been a fine, fine challenge. I mean it, Fuller. You're good." For the third time, he looked at his watch. Maybe he was real proud of his Rolex portfolio. Blue chip stock and all. Me, if I had the money, I'd invest in Tim Horton's.

Without the aid of Frank Two in his ear, Brother Durgana now spoke some facsimile of Latin that was probably stats off the back of a hockey card.

A lot of hockey cards.

"The posters. That was me. Well, me with a delivery made by Kunz and Sevrier. God rest their souls. Good people. Sevrier had a real sense of humor. Anyway, the switch plate and the photo? That was me too." He held up the other hand, smiling with Saran Wrap blue. He swapped out Dad's oversized plate with a regular-sized one. I noticed the different textures of wall stains and found the photograph with the cryptic clue that Frank Two had planted. "I wrote that note. Me. The genius. You even solved the world play. 11/14/65. Tonight, on the 13th, not tomorrow, the night of the 14th."

"That was Ellen. You remember her?'

"Yes. A mousy thing." He had watched her on eight monitors, watched her in the sanctuary in her threadbare robes, watched her shower in the basement. "That was another one of my wonderful ideas." He smiled. "Showers—"

"Why am I not surprised?"

"Very sexy." He shrugged.

"She's fifteen—"

He shrugged again. "How old were the girls who posed for Renoir? I'm an artist."

"Bullshit."

"Let's not quibble. I was just beginning to *like* you."

Big joke.

"And the photos of the obscure black-robed rituals?" *He had sent those to* his father, clues to aid and abet the game. Tod X. Pure invention. Never called him.

"The game?"

"I invented it, Fuller. Me. All the rules. All of them." The church, its philosophies, teachings, all his vision. Everything Brother Durgana ever said of importance were his words, Frank Two's words. He was—

"A god? That's what Dimension V is all about isn't it? Becoming God?"

"*Vengeance is mine, sayeth the Lord.* And indeed, it's mine, oh brother, it's mine."

"Vengeance? Oh, you've been wronged, haven't you, poor boy. Mom's suicide—"

He dropped his hand with sadness. "That was hard—"

"Bullshit. You killed her. You killed your mother, left the windows in her room wide open, middle of winter, and her pneumonia worsened and she died." I was guessing of course, but my instincts are usually pretty damn good.

"You figured that out too." He chuckled to himself. "Damn, you're good. Bravo. Bravo." He stood up, applauding rapidly.

"I get by."

"Mother wouldn't let me be me, to fully be me." He shrugged absently. "She was always curbing my, shall we say, Dionysian impulses."

"Thanks, Nietzsche."

"Oh, you've read Nietzsche?" He sat down.

"Yes."

"I underestimated you."

"You also killed Grayson Jackson. Set up the Gus hit? Why? And don't give me this shit about testing my psychological mettle. Why'd you kill Gus?"

"Because I could."

"Uh-uh. There's another reason—"

"Could you two philosophers take your lecture notes outside? I want to watch this." Smith pointed at the screen, the couple sprinkled with holy oil or some damn thing. Colin's painful erection glanced across Smith's Lombardis. "Look at the boner on that guy—"

"Do you mind, Steve?" Frank Two pointed at Sharon who was opening her long coat, the gun trained on me the whole time. "Manners."

Smith bowed his head abjectly, raised a phosphorous hand. "Sorry."

"Why have Susan *kill* my father?"

Unlike Sevrier and Kunz, Frank Two was pleased to fill in this case's loose ends. If he could he'd *only* talk in paragraphs. After all, he was a genius.

You see, he said, he was losing his sister, he had to get her back under control, and that targeted killing did the trick. The death of my father was to lure me into the case. Sure, Ira had taken Ellen, but he wasn't being punished for that. No. He was being sacrificed to bring me onboard and Susan back to the fold. Quid pro quo.

"Uh-huh."

"Uh-huh, uh-huh, uh-huh. Don't play the laconic tough guy with me." He pinched his lips together. "Those killings are nothing compared to what I'm about to unleash. My greatest accomplishment." Another glance at his watch followed by a short lecture: two minutes ago, it started. You're a good dick, shamus, but you never figured out the floor plans, did you? Just a loose end? Something to do with ovens and baking pies? Wrong. Central air. It was all about the central air. "I had Susan give a big, big clue to Dr. Cohen. The floor plans. You missed it, dropped the goddamn ball."

He had planted cyanide pellets in the central air's cooling system; rigged to a battery and timer, the pellets were set to dissolve at 11:58, a minute ago, and now the room was filling with poisonous gas, in seven minutes, tops, following the ritualized sacrifices of Colin and Susan, everyone in the room would be dead, a black plague of biblical proportions.

Neon glass, faces full of boils.

His voice was elevated, like a poet hitting a rhetorical flourish.

It was a lousy poem.

Frank Two shifted about in his jet fighter chair. "Just sit back, enjoy the show, and then, I'll kill you." He sprinkled some powder on the back of a hand. Smiled. Inhaled it up his nose. "Consider this my Sherlock Holmes affectation." He laughed again. "You don't have much time before I kill you. Laugh."

"Like you killed Gus, because he knew. Knew the truth."

The chair stilled.

"Susan and Gus were intimate, pal. He figured it out." Gus wasn't the father of the unborn child, neither was Susan's real love, Ivan Sevrier. Susan was so afraid of the child being born with a mental defect that she contemplated an abortion, because you, you, pally, are the expectant father. Gus knew that. Gus died because he knew that.

"Yes, Gus did. And so I am the father." He smiled. "I told you, you were a smart guy, Bravo. Bravo. You're going to be dead in a few minutes but bravo, bravo."

Smith, eyes on the monitor, applauded in unison.

Sharon was holding a gun, so she applauded with her hazel eyes.

"*Dismantle the universe.*" I snapped my fingers. "Ivan wanted to dismantle the universe, your universe, kill me because he knew how important I was to you. That's why he took us out to the Bluffs. That wasn't part of your plan. That was his plan to ruin yours. He knew the child wasn't his and he wanted to get back, get back at you for what you'd done to Susan, dismantle your universe. Payback."

"Yes." Frank Two smiled. "Yes. His job was to scare Dr. Cohen, plant clues that were a part of the game, not kill her, or heaven forbid, you." He laughed. "A moment of excess. We all have them."

Brother Durgana carried one of the extinguishers as a sacred object, cradling it to his chest. The couple, he said, were granted a goodbye kiss, forming a dual covenant between themselves and our god.

He muttered some other words about Abraham and Isaac and Tinker and Evers and Chance.

I hoped the RCMP informant told them about the cyanide. My instincts told me she had.

"Go ahead and kiss," Brother Durgana said.

They did.

A neon kiss full of underwater moonlight.

"I think he's coming," Smith said. "Oh my god, he kissed her and just shot his load—" He slapped at an upper thigh.

"He's not a sophisticated man, Steven," Frank Two reminded the CEO. "Colin's a little, shall we say, slow."

"Slow. Did you see him jizz?" That cracked him up for some reason. He was now slapping both thighs.

Frank Two nodded briefly at Sharon with his eyes.

"God. Jizzed all over her. Christ. I remember what it was like to have—"

Susan shot him twice in the head.

His jaw and half his face were gone.

"Fuck," I mumbled, looking at Smith's crumpled remains slumped up against the monitor, his Lombardis resting on the lenses, a stem splashed with blood and bits of brain.

"He was beginning to bore me." Frank Two shook his head,

rubbed at the edges of his thin lips, removing traces of white. "This ceremony is about sacrifice, art, and beauty. It's an artistic statement. Poetic. A returning. Adam and Eve. Forgiveness for biting the apple, making ourselves naked before God, giving of ourselves to Him."

"So what are you, huh?" I stared directly into Sharon's dancing eyes, catching her with my glare. "He nods with his eyes and you kill a man. Does he give you the same kind of nod when he asks you to put on a skull cap so he can pretend to be fucking his sister?"

Her eyes exploded, and then I had the gun, her wrist with the gun, twisting it, sending her toppling into Smith's remains, the two of them commingled on the floor. She screamed at the brain matter now sloughed in her hair and stuck along the edges of her beret and orange coat.

I wasn't about to ask her for the next dance.

Frank Two, in the commotion, grabbed a pair of creeping jelly grenades and was readying to toss them.

"Drop that shit, or I drop you." I had Sharon's gun in my mitts.

He did so, they wobbled like eggs, the short broom handle sticks slowing their progress.

I picked my .38 up off the floor, re-holstered it.

"You can't stop the cyanide once it's started, shamus. It's taken hold. They'll be dead in seconds."

Sharon shrugged off brain matter, opened her coat further, adjusting her long skirt, and slapping away the crinkles of a slip showing through. "You picked the wrong building to come to."

"She's right," Franklin said. "You should have gone to the church."

"Uh-huh." My money was on Anne Chevalier and the RCMP.

I was about to say, you two are under arrest, or some such damn cornball-style thing, when commotion broke in the sanctuary, police whistles and screams filling the screen, as various voices yelled freeze, police, don't move, and Brother Durgana, lost without Frank Two in his ear, dropped the extinguisher, and glanced about, seeking an exit, wandering around the platform, lost, waiting on the rapture.

"They'd all be dead soon," Frank Two said.

Susan wasn't lost. Nimbly she picked up the abandoned fire extinguisher, rushed Brother Durgana, pointing the nozzle at his face.

Colin didn't try to stop her. He was enchanted by her, her bravery, her beauty. You could see it in his face. You could see—

I'm pretty sure he thinks he's married.

Durgana raised both arms, trying to keep a final curtain closing down on him.

Ropes of foam folded around his hooded face.

He died that way, arms yelling stop, a pillar of salt.

Operatives and police, not in robes, rounded people up. Sal Lambertino, in his Sloan Wilson grays, and a fellow detective carried Susan off the stage, pinning her arms. Thompson tugged at the police's arms, trying to free her, as Susan kicked with her legs and succeeded in getting a hand loose, sending coded signals through the closest camera, fingers jittering lightning bugs, signs, signs, signs. Her eyes were lean, full of unspoken screams.

But the fingers spoke.

I had no idea what the gestures meant.

But Frank Two sure the hell did.

"She told them about the cyanide, didn't she? That's what she just told you." They'd found it. 12:03 and everyone's standing.

Frank Two's face melted into a distorted twisted mask and his voice fell into reedy mumblings, murmurs, and backbeats. He was talking in tongues, running from Dimension V's lost possibilities.

Suddenly his hands were clamped with two hexagonal eggs of creeping jelly. Before he could toss them our way I shot him twice in the chest. He flopped back into his jet fighter chair, the napalm jelly catching fire by his feet, crawling up his body, skin burning, the top of his head full of Medusa flames, the backbeat rush of broken scat still jolting along, faster, faster, faster.

"No." Sharon couldn't believe I'd shot the sonuvabitch and was slapping my face, my chest.

I shoved her away and pointed at all the ordnance in the room. Get it together.

There were enough explosives to make Dimension V go up like Dr. No's island.

I prodded Sharon upstairs with my gun as the blue room belched red, yellow, and orange, Franklin's backbeat stumbling and falling to a coke-filled end as the flames towered higher.

Sharon's shoulders trembled with tears.

Halfway up the stairs it hit me.

Some lucky fucker at Silverwood's had won the Smith death lottery.

THE FIRE SCOWLED AND HISSED as water punched down on what was left of the Army Surplus store. Ten minutes since the last explosion. All told there were seven.

Followers of the church were gathered up and herded into police vans and immediately placed in quarantine for debriefing, deprogramming. Tod X had offered his services and would meet them at the hospital. Dr. Cohen was on the job now, traveling with one of the paddy wagons to Scarborough General.

Ellen was gone.

Stana and I leaned under a lamppost, the slick streets capturing shimmers of our reflections. By one of the church's brick walls, two cats stretched their backs in the night, odd sentries to an even odder cult.

Anne Chevalier, in a trench coat and black fedora, her face and ends of her hair damp, took mental notes while I rambled on. Sal, on my other side, pushed back his gray felt hat, scratching away at an uneven patch of his Hemingway beard.

"You ever go to a barber, pal? You're always playing with your beard."

"I can't afford a good barber, not on what I make." He laughed.

I don't have many friends. He was fun to tease.

When Stana arrived at Gradwell, there was no Ellen, only the lingering smell of Dubble Bubble. Against an orange soda bottle, next to the Callaghan book, she found a note, hastily scrawled: "On the run. I think I'll always be running. Thanks for listening—and understanding. Love, Ellen. PS, tell Hayden don't be mad at me. I wanted to keep my pinky promise, but—"

If not for the note, I'd begin to really wonder about myself. Did the girl ever really exist? She was the living embodiment of ephemera. Even in her Buster Browns and argyle sweater.

Under Ellen's signature was an infinity symbol, hard blue lines on a white page.

"She's a survivor," I said.

"So are you."

Anne always had the knack for saying the right things. Her gentle hands were on my shoulders, stopping my trembling.

"Smith's dead, what's left of the corpse probably brittle bits of Melba toast by now." Two shots to the head. I held up my hands. "I didn't do it. Sharon did. Run a paraffin test on her."

"Will do," Sal said, eyes calm, full of untold stories. But he knew the evidence was probably gone up with the explosions.

"Last thing I need is the NHL on my ass, saying I killed one of their *beloved* owners. I didn't kill Smith. Believe me."

"I believe you." Anne smiled, her lipstick gleaming in the shadows of rain and hissing smoke and a black sky turned light crimson.

"Yeah. But that Sharon I don't trust." She let Deuces do the thinking, the talking for her. She spoke, via a radio transistor, *his* words when we met. What words might she speak on her own? I rubbed the sides of my mouth. I killed her boy. You never know what she'll say. "She didn't hate him, like she told me. That was part of the game, to draw suspicion on him, to make me hunt him down. That's what he wanted. An adversary." I shook my head. "Hell, they were lovers. That's the real story." The girl with the hands? Angie. She was putting shit together, figuring out the names of all the players. Sharon helped take her out of the play, and that makes Sharon an accessory to murder. "Deuces confirmed it."

"Right," Sal said.

"She'll say I killed Smith. Run the paraffin test."

"We will, we will. We got your back." Sal smiled.

But what good would a paraffin test do really? She could say, "Yeah I fired a gun, but I missed the target. Hayden killed both of them." Shit.

Library book. Library card. Maybe I could get Ellen's address from the library, charm the librarian. No, Ellen probably gave them a false address, like Francie in *A Tree Grows in Brooklyn* so she could go to a nice school. Ellen was always quoting from books. I bet she's read that one. If she hasn't, she'd love it.

I hope eventually she can find stories written by the other side of her ancestral identity.

"I did shoot and kill Franklin. With Sharon's gun." I shrugged, my head thin and light as if it were inside a helium-filled balloon, floating. "Four bullets gone. Two by Sharon. Two by me. My two were self-defense. He was about to toss some creeping jelly my way. Or maybe at Sharon. Who the fuck can tell with that nut."

"Right." Anne was done with the mental notes. She was worried about me. I was talking too much and my tone was slightly elevated and wobbly.

"Don't worry about the bodies," Sal said. "Nobody's going to find nothing in all that. I counted six explosions."

"Seven," I said.

"Biblical, huh?"

"No. Six-hundred and sixty-six would be more appropriate

for that crowd."

"How did they get all those people to follow along, to—" Stana's eyes were full of wasp tails. "I mean, we're talking human sacrifices here."

"Brainwashing?" offered Anne. "Maybe they were drugged."

"They were drugged. Loaded up on Thorazine." I rubbed the edges of my mouth. "That shit numbs you a little, slows your reaction time, but not—"

"—Sponsoring human sacrifices?" Stana shook her head.

"Right. That can't hook you. No. Charisma was the drug. Frank Two's charisma via Brother Durgana. That's what they were hooked on."

Stana kicked at a Styrofoam cup wobbling up against her feet. "Charisma." She laughed. "Brainwashing in a way, I guess. That seems too easy. The intellectual in me wants to make them responsible for their actions. But their choices were somehow removed—weakened—"

"Your next story, huh?" I kissed the tip of her nose.

"No. I'll be in Detroit." She smiled. "Well, maybe when we get back?"

"Sure. Write the story when you get back."

"What about my going to Montreal? With you?"

"Write the story."

"I'm coming to Detroit."

"No, stay in Toronto. Write the story. Three, four days, a week of follow-up pieces, tops, and then join me in Montreal. Vacation. Shit, Stana, you're a reporter." I pulled her close. She smelled of sandalwood and sweat. "Write the damn story. It's important to tell."

"You sure?"

I nodded.

It was important for all of us. And tell Ellen's story, caught between two cultures, forced to follow a chalky white path instead of diversity's roads, roads I hoped she was now running along.

"We didn't figure on the Dimension V angle, the next-door hideaway," Anne said.

"Uh-huh. Your leak didn't tell you about it?"

"Apparently not. She told us a lot of other things. A lot."

They *did* get to the cyanide pellets with over thirty minutes to spare.

Sal shook his head. "Creeping jelly, huh?" He pointed a heavy thumb in the direction of the fire still scowling away. "That jelly sure has a lot of creep to it."

"Yeah." I shrugged.

Colin was all right, Anne said. He was by Susan's side, helping her, healing her, loving her.

"Poor guy." I shook my head, kicked at shallow splashes of water by my feet. "He had no idea what was going on—"

"His love is real," Anne interrupted. "So's his loyalty to the girl."

"And Susan?"

Anne scratched at a spot behind an ear. Susan was in shock, but she seemed to like having Colin around. She recognized him, kissed his cheek twice, I can tell you that, she said.

"Like this," Stana said, kissing my cheek.

I pulled her even closer to me, my leather jacket and chest cradling her. "Susan was the leak—"

Anne nodded and looked down at five or six shallow puddles around her. After Susan and Sevrier killed my father, Susan just couldn't play any further with her brother's schemes and plans to create a Dimension V here and now on Earth. When Susan refused to kill Ellen in the dumbwaiter she decided to, metaphorically at least, kill her brother. That's when she called the RCMP and their counter-espionage wing. She remembered Anne from a *Toronto Telegram* write-up on my previous case.

Yeah, but, she couldn't really kill him, even *really* metaphorically, I said. She told you about the cyanide gas, but she didn't tell you about his secret lair in the Army Surplus store. She was giving him a chance, a few seconds lead time, to get away.

"I guess she still loved him," Stana said. "He was her brother."

"Yeah." *And my father was my father.* "What's going to happen to Susan?" *Murder charge, charges reduced for cooperating with the—?*

"I don't know." Anne shrugged, ribbons of water falling from her shoulders. "I don't know. I suspect she'll be psychologically evaluated first. I just really don't know."

"I'm not looking for—the whole vengeance is mine thing isn't my thing." I nodded and the lightness filled my face, opening my smile, giving me a feeling of thankfulness. "She's messed up." I shrugged. "But a hell of an actor. I mean goddamn. The performance she had to give." Appearing naked before a large audience, acting all in on the grand gesture of the sacrifice, waiting things out, knowing if the authorities didn't move quickly enough, she could become salt. That's brave.

"Well, what's next, superstar?"

"Detroit. Later today, tonight. Much later tonight." I sighed, rubbed tired eyes.

"Let's go home." Stana kissed me again, her hand circling my chest. "I'll make you breakfast in the morning," she murmured, a flash of freckles in her eyes. "Before you go to Detroit."

She directed me by my elbow to her car.

"We all done here?" I shouted over my shoulder.

Sal and Anne nodded and wandered off toward the flames and firefighters. Anne assured me she'd take care of NHL President Clarence Campbell. "He won't fuck with you."

I like how emphatic she can be. "Thanks." I turned to Stana. "Breakfast in bed, huh? Soggy eggs and Carnation Instant—"

"I didn't say in bed."

"No, I did."

"And I don't make soggy eggs—"

"Yeah, you do. You do. The worst."

"All right. I'm a reporter, not a chef at the Waldorf. How

about half a grapefruit and a Carnation Instant Breakfast? That sound do-able, Mr. Food Critic?"

"Vanilla. None of that imitation chocolate shit."

"Okay. Imitation vanilla shit. Got it." She smiled, gave me a full, soft kiss on the lips. "Now that I can't screw up."

"No. You're a great kisser."

"I was talking about the grapefruit—"

I laughed. I just wanted to sleep and sleep and sleep or drown into the black asphalt sky for a while. I was tired, trembling, and yet I felt good, awful good, just floating away, up, up, up.

I hadn't felt this happy in a while.

I wanted to drown and live.

"I should be in Detroit by 2:30 tomorrow, catch Coach Blake, get the pregame plans, you know?"

"I know." She smiled, lips parted, freckles dancing. "What time do you want me to wake you?"

"In the morning." I plunked my porkpie hat on her head, pushed it back so I could see her eyes. "It's a four-hour drive to Detroit—so—I don't know." I smiled my lopsided, lupine grin. "Surprise me," I said.

"I shall," she said.

Day of the Dragons

1

I didn't see him until it was almost too late.

He stood in the middle of the two-lane highway, an X caught in the shimmering silver-white portieres of snow.

I hit the brakes, fishtailing into the oncoming lane before curling back and bump-bumping into a curve of a guardrail tented with snow.

He ran, a floppy looking scarecrow, trenchcoat splattering as if caught on a clothesline. Flecks of muddy snow dotted his thighs. His knit cap was pushed too far back to do any damn good.

I shimmed the Galaxie away from the guardrail and wedged open the passenger-side door. He slid in, hands under legs, lower lip a querulous tremble. The tips of his ears were pink and his close-set green eyes were curtained with fear. "They want me dead—"

They? Who's they?

Kraydon. He said. Kraydon. His words were vague and his eyes were now on his hands poised over the heat vents of the car's dash. He was working up at Lake Laurier with a group of scientists on a project outside Bannervile, pop 1201, small, perfect for such experiments.

I bit my upper lip. Who, what is Kraydon?

"It's a resurrection," he said. My brakes gave out. "They cut my brake line." A cloth of a cut covered his chin. "Crashed into a tree and ran to the highway."

I introduced myself. "The name is Fuller."

He nodded and reached into his trench coat for a crinkled envelope. "I need to see Dr. Bauer. Bauer built it. Back then, 1945." The envelope was blank. He slithered it under the passenger side visor. Bauer was at a science conference in Toronto— "Take me there," he said. "Please."

"Dr. Bauer? He's part of the US Space Program, isn't he?" *Worked for the Nazis during WWII, V–2 Rockets, atomic energy.* Now works for NASA.

"Yes. Royal York—" Hurry. He looked over his shoulder and to the sides of the road, to the inside of shadows of birch trees blurring by.

I wanted to tell him that I could take him as far as Peterborough, 85 miles north-east of TO. Hell, I was seeing my gal, Stana Younger, for a romantic getaway. Since last Christmas and the harrowing events the local papers labeled the "Neon Kiss Case" Stana and I had been moving closer to marriage. Neither of us had said the "M" word but—it's there, floating. The trouble? She has her career as a reporter in TO, and I'm playing hockey in Montreal. Scored a goal in our 3-2 win over Boston last night. I'm thirty. NHL expansion is a year-and-a-half away. Stana can't commit to Montreal if the Habs leave me unprotected and I wind up in St. Louis, or Philly, or Oakland. Who wants to live there, she says. Well, LA might be nice, she had to admit.

But now I had fallen into something—again.

Romance may just have to wait. I had to get this fella to Toronto.

"Once more, pal. Who is they, this Kraydon outfit?"

"A secret project." He wrapped his knit cap into a tight tourniquet. "Kraydon is to be feared." He didn't like what they were up to. Bauer might be able to stop them. *Them.*

"What are *they* up to?"

"Dragons," he said. Solitaire, he muttered. Bauer likes to play cards. "And Culpeppers. That's their—I wonder if he's playing cards right now?"

Culpeppers?

Suddenly bright lights filled the back window, haloes of high-beams.

A knock.

Another.

And what was left of my bumper was thumping behind me.

I fought the wheel and told the fella with no name to talk fast, goddamn it. What do they want with these dragons? "If I'm going to die tonight I want to know the shot."

I steered into the skid, picked up speed coming out of it, and was gaining distance on the lurching black sedan and their blinding beams. My Galaxie had a 427 engine.

An intermittent yak-yak-yak blew out my back window. Glass splashed, sharp nail bites.

"Talk—"

The left side of the car sank as a rear tire loosened from its rim.

Ahead, a four-corners, a single flashing light and a gas station that looked like a bleached white femur. My passenger chunked into the dashboard, his head grapefruit pulp.

The red, white, and blue Esso brand loomed closer.

Behind it shrouded a large corrugated triangle, like a boomerang, edge up, an extra garage.

Automotive parts were everywhere.

A conical light. Pumps closed.

The fellas behind fired a clatter of steel rain.

I shoved back my dead passenger, seized my .38 from the glove box, and his letter from above the visor.

Damn.

I floored it for the pumps, machine guns yak-yakking. I had never tried the stunt I was about to pull, but I had seen *Rebel Without a Cause* like twenty times. God love James Dean. I tucked in my shoulder, unlatched the door, and bodychecked the damn thing. It flung open and I hit the ground hard, rolling. The Galaxie cracked the pumps.

There was a calm tremble followed by a surprised punky pop, and then a full-on fireball.

I was still rolling, shoulders sore as hell, portieres of snow shimmering.

The trailing sedan, slid sideways on the service station's asphalt, before its blisters of high beams crunched into black flames.

The driver screamed. One of the two fellas in back staggered from an open rear door, his machine gun bending against the car's frame. He was all in black from his hat, to his wool coat, to his slick leather gloves.

I fired twice.

The door stumbled closed, with him behind it.

The fireball puffed and became a red fist.

Sometimes I think everything I learned in life I learned at the movies.

God love James Fucking Dean.

2

The Ontario Provincial Police serving Bannerville were more concerned about what happened to the goddamn gas station than to me.

It didn't help that our powwow was inside the station, Ernst Strehl, proprietor, wore a gray flannel shirt that looked freshly pressed, and had a vocabulary that rivaled many a hockey coach. I was the F-this and F-that clown that directly drove my heap into his F-in pumps.

"That's for sure," echoed Josef Ziegler. "Right into the F-in pumps."

The things we cherish about small towns. Friendly chit-chat.

"I saw it—" Ziegler and Strehl were playing black jack, heard the roar of gun fire and saw it all from an upstairs window. Ziegler's eyes widened with emphasis as he spoke and his nose was much too small for his face's lumpy mass. He was some maker and shaker in town. Ran a small press and owned the local restaurant—there was only one—Culpeppers—

I shrugged with sulky languor. "I hit a patch of ice, lost control." I raised my arms with mock surrender.

"Lose the attitude and get that kink out of your mouth, pal," Sgt Bob Frei said. "The act is stale."

I smiled, my lopsided grin.

Outside, fire trucks glowed puffs of red in misty air. Ropes of water hissed back the twist of flames

Inside, the gas station smelled of oil and cigarettes. Strehl stood behind the cash register with rows of candy bars and boxes of hockey cards parked in front of him.

Behind were hung posters for Champion Spark Plugs, Firestone Tires, and a pinup of a redhead rather strategically preserving her modesty with the aid of a basket of overflowing fruit.

"I reached for the brake and accidentally tapped the accelerator," I said.

"I warned you to get that kink out of your mouth," Sgt Frei weighed in with a left-handed smack. Blood dripped from my mouth.

"Easy, easy, Ernst, Bob." Ziegler tented his fingers as if preparing to address a jury. "His kind are full of wise-ass humor. It's part of their expression, right? Milton Berle, Henny Youngman, even that schwartze, Lenny Bruce—"

His kind?

Sgt. Frei, the lead cop, leaned closer to what his lanky partner was whispering in an ear. "Really, huh?" He rubbed at the edges of his mouth. He was heavy in the face, arms, and gut. A chunk of his right ear was missing. "We found a car a few miles back by Lake Laurier. Crumpled up in a tree. Belongs to Emil, Emil Gudegast." He gave a description.

"That's the cat," I said. He mentioned something about Kraydon.

His partner scratched at the line along his jaw and mildly chewed gum. Juicy Fruit mist filled the air.

"Kraydon?" Ziegler laughed, running a hand through his iron filings of hair. "Kraydon. Strehl worked for Kraft. Kraft, not Kraydon. Kraft. Maybe he had a few beers and was slurring his words." Everything Ziegler said had a light bounce to it, as if the whole world were a wry joke, and only he could see the truth. "He's a lab assistant at Kraft, a taste tester, finding new flavors of Jell-O. Pomegranate—"

"He also mentioned a Dr. Bauer—" And Culpeppers?

"That's my restaurant—the only restaurant in town—" Ziegler smiled faintly.

"Bauer, the NASA guy?" Strehl was now chuckling with a menacing undertow. "What would the king of rocketry want with a taste tester? Can you punch up the pudding? Put a little more Chiquita in the banana flavoring?" He thought that was a real riot.

I didn't dare mention our talk of dragons.

"I don't know how he walked away from that wreck," Frei said. "The boys tell me the engine went right up into the dash and steering column."

"At least we can ID one of the bodies," his partner said.

Who was he running from? "Those were real machine guns. They weren't firing rubber bullets."

"Well it wasn't alimony," Ziegler piped in, a querulous tremor to his words. He nodded in the direction of the red head with the strategically placed fruit basket. "That wasn't for him. Rock Hudson, dig? What do you people call it? *Fegele.*"

There it was again. You people. How did he know I was a Jew? I was getting pissed. "You expect me to believe that people from Kraft were gunning for him? What, Emil was giving away the secret recipe for Velveeta cheese sauce?"

"Now that's funny." Ziegler tapped Strehl on the shoulder. "That's real funny."

"I wasn't implying that Kraft killed him," Frei said. I was just saying this is a sleepy bedroom town. Most folks work in Peterborough. His face was limp.

Then who killed Emil and why?

Outside, ropes of water beat back flames, tongues of red dying down.

Emil Gudegast died in my car.

I owed him.

And I didn't trust these crumbs.

I said nothing about Emil's letter.

—

A GENTLE TOUCH ON MY CHEST and a star lifting.

"I like the look of this." Stana Younger smiled, eyes lifting with the star, filing with light. She kissed my Star of David, and then me. "It's kind of heavy—"

"Yeah." It wasn't a subtle Star of David. I guess, I wanted to be noticeable, to send a message, *this is me.*

It was something I had taken to wearing following the death of my father. Grades five and six he had abused me, repeatedly after Mom died, but in the end he protected a Métis girl, Ellen Reynolds, from getting killed, hiding her in the dumb waiter of his small home in Scarborough. He was tortured and shot full of a high concentration of thorazine, but he didn't give her up. I had solved his killing last November, involving a cult looking for the "pearl of heaven" on earth and led by a crazed leader who wanted to "dismantle the universe." While avenging Pop's death I discovered a Habs toque he had left behind for me, caught in the knitted folds of the hat's interior, a personal note: "For Hayden, One Tough Jew."

People are fucking complex.

Anyway, following that case, my faith was strengthened and the Star became a symbol of me and my people's history from the wilderness to the garden. I guess I no longer have secrets about who I am. Maybe one day, I'll go public about my abuse. Maybe that can help others to heal, others to forgive themselves, to no longer feel guilty about things they were a part of and yet had no control over. We were victims and yet our bodies also betrayed us in confusing ways. At least that's what my therapist, Dr. Jeanette Cohen says. Anyway, I love Stana, but when we make love, I feel the legacy of the past, my father's boxing glove fingers and alcohol, and I struggle to please her.

Sunlight dappled the edges of Stana's shoulders and made the eye closer to the window a lighter blue, an almost aqua green. She was on top, hair falling gently to her chest, my chest, as she leaned into a kiss. I bent with the kiss and then moved to the mole between her breasts, pausing to kiss it, before caressing her nipples.

The ends of her auburn hair tickled my chest.

She slid a little lower.

"Where am I?" I pointed to the pastel lamp shades. The room was awash in Impressionist blues and yellows.

"The Royal York—"

The wall clock, shaped like a star, read 11:12, I think. My eyes were struggling to adjust. Christ, I had slept and slept.

"Yes." She worked me down there.

After the OPP had dropped me off at a cheap cinder block motel at the edge of town called the Junction, Stana rousted me, saying Emil Gudegast had secrets worth dying for, and if friends of the guys toasted in the black sedan thought those secrets were passed on to me, then maybe I'd have some secrets worth dying for too. "Don't you see, Hayden. *You're* a target now."

On the drive to TO, I had muttered on about Kraydon, the dragons, and Dr. Bauer. She knew about Bauer. Her paper, *The Toronto Telegram*, was covering the upcoming science conference. Bauer was scheduled to give the keynote: "Faith of Science in the Face of an Uncertain World: the If God Exists Question."

She worked me down there some more and nibbled at my lower lip. "That motel they took you to," she murmured, "was something else. Flat coffee, yellowed road maps from the 1950s, and pizza coupons. But that wasn't the kicker. Brochures. About how the Holocaust never happened. It was, get this, an international conspiracy devised by the Red Cross to destroy and divide Germany into East and West—"

"Huh?"

"That fella you ran into the gas station with Strehl—"

"Ziegler."

"Yeah. The Reverend. He has a printing press. He's behind the brochures." And the Reverend moniker? A self-proclaimed title, she said. He didn't graduate from any seminary that I know of.

"A Nazi."

He was born in Canada. Raised in Bannerville. "Neo-Nazi I believe is the preferred nomenclature."

"Yeah—" I lost the power to speak, my lips numbing, as she slid me in.

"And get this, my contacts at the paper say Gudegast was one of Dr. Bauer's lab assistants, 1944–45." She pushed up, down, up, with her hands on my stomach slowing the rhythm. For the past ten years, he had been living in South America, she said. "You don't have to wait for me. Just go ahead—"

I gripped her shoulders, losing sight of the freckles there, as the world exploded.

LATER, WE SAT AROUND COMFORTABLY: me in briefs; Stana looking sporty in my pajama top, the cuffs covering her hands.

Papers were spread across the cedar top desk's blotter.

We had an appointment with Bauer at 2.

What is Kraydon? The dragons? Why is Gudegast dead?

Stana lit a Parliament while reading the tri-folded letter Gudegast inadvertently left in my possession. She quoted: "Both the man of science and the man of action lives at the edge of mystery, surrounded by it. The mystery shall rise on the 25th this month, February 1966, the day of the dragons. Can men of action stop men of science?"

She tapped her cigarette on the edge of the ashtray. The men of science are building something deadly, she said. Dragons. Some kind of weapon of destruction.

"Yeah." I pinched at a spot between my eyes that was suddenly throbbing.

The first part of the letter quotes Oppenheimer, she said. The Manhattan Project guy.

Stana's real smart. Kicks my ass at Scrabble. Got a degree in literature from the U of T, worked with Hilary "Chip" Hampton, a writer of children's books.

"The second part?"

"Flash Gordon?"

"So, what's he trying to say here? And why all the codes?"

"Well, we'll find out at two maybe." She took a drag off her Parliament.

"Hope so."

Gudegast worked on the V-2 rockets with Bauer. Maybe the dragons are some kind of rocket? She tapped my upper thigh, said she was going to wash her hair. "Let's eat and meet NASA's top braniac—"

"The whole space program is housed by ex-nazis," I mumbled.

"Not nazis. German scientists—"

"There's a difference?"

"Yes," she said. "Men *and women* of science are free thinkers. Just as it's unfair to accuse them all of being anti-God, we can't assume that anyone from Germany is an ex-Nazi."

"Oh, I can—"

She shot me a look and stubbed her cigarette.

"Okay, okay. I'll keep an open mind."

She shrugged, head tilting left, eyes lighting up. "Be ready in fifteen."

"Right." *Where was my shaving kit?*

She walked to the shower, tossing my pajama top over a shoulder. It slid down and away, revealing freckled shoulders and a bright back that resembled a sheet. Her curvy butt glowed in the dim glimmer of the room. "Why don't you join me in ten minutes," she said.

"How about seven?"

"Seven it is."

3

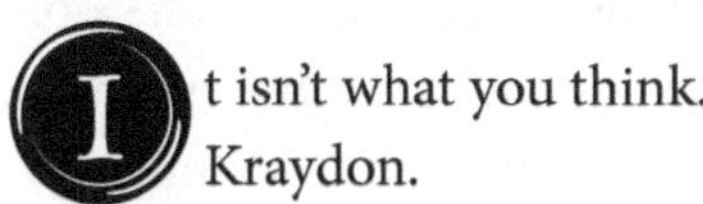

It isn't what you think.

Kraydon.

Defunct. That's why you can't track it, Miss Younger. Dr. Bauer grimaced slightly, wiped at the edges of his mouth and dunked a small portion of his English Digestive biscuit in a cup of black tea. I prefer the ones half-coated in chocolate, but he opted for plain. He took another dainty bite, savoring the moment.

There was some theatricality to this cat.

In front of Dr. Bauer were four solitaire games that he was playing at once, cards spread around like very important tangential notes. He was using six or seven decks for four games. I guess that gave him greater odds, chances to make a run.

I asked about the cards. He laughed. "Some say it's an affectation, but I enjoy it." When he first arrived at NASA, Friday nights were poker nights with him and several other scientists. "I won my fair share," he said, but it wasn't about the money, it was the fellowship, the fun, and trying to best your opponent through a combination of skill and chutzpah. Bluffing. I'm a good bluffer, he said.

I was surprised that he used a word like chutzpah.

Maybe I was being too sensitive.

Anyway, we were lucky to get to meet with him so early. He'd blown off the breakout sessions with fellow award-winning scientists to "convene with us," as he put it, in the Victoria Room. It was 1:16.

Outside, snow fell, heavier shimmers than yesterday.

His thirteen-year-old daughter Hannah sat next to him.

That's how he introduced her, my thirteen-year-old daughter.

Odd. Anyway, her wheelchair was pushed up to the table, a gray wool blanket covering her knees. She had white-blonde hair and nearly black eyes, a striking contrast. She was editing her father's keynote address, marking, scratching away words with red ink, writing fresh suggestions in the margins. She wore a pink blouse, no makeup, and had an ankh around her neck. Her hands were small, delicate, as were her facial features, fine bits of bone pushing lightly against nearly translucent skin. Her eyebrows were thin, and even her ears were quiet, little snowflakes hiding behind straight lines of hair.

Her father, by contrast, was big, burly, Eastern-European looking. He had a large nose, heavy lines around his mouth, and trenches across his forehead. His eyes were a dull blue, tired by the world.

Kraydon built planes and tanks during WWII for Hitler's war machine. After the war, and the splitting up of Germany into East and West, the factory, located in East Berlin, was taken over by the Soviets and eventually disbanded in 1959, shortly after Sputnik.

"Dis-banded or re-shuffled?" I asked.

"A little of both, I'm afraid. The factory and lab closed down but the work went on, in Moscow." And in South America, he said. Emil lived there for a time. The Soviets and their KGB and their NKVD and a host of other acronyms sent their scientists into Kraydon, focusing their attention on other worldly or wild pursuits such as nerve gases, mini-plutonium bombs, the kind that could wipe out a supermarket, not a city, and their big red-star agenda was working with sonic waves, and altering the speed of sound, to destroy standing structures and make airplanes fall from the skies. He laughed with derision. "They continue the work in Argentina."

And in Bannerville apparently. Pop 1201.

I wondered if the yak-yak-yak of machine guns was courtesy of a posse of KGB punk-asses.

"Sounds like something out of the Book of Revelation," Stana said.

"There was a kind of zealousness to it. Their program." But in Soviet Union you don't mention religion, he said. He held a pinky to his lips. The gesture was Zero Mostel–lite.

"Right."

The Reverend in Bannerville. He has zeal to spare. And a German Scientist from South America. Were there others, ex-Nazis roaming the small-town landscape? And where were they hiding? Where was their lab?

Dr. Bauer took another bite from the hard end of his Digestive biscuit, quickly playing seven cards, and then making a run, as one of the four solitaire games ended. This is just mindless entertainment, he apologized, pointing at the cards. "Got to keep the synapses firing." He gestured at his head. "Scientists lose their edge at the age of 29-30. I'm 65." He smiled thinly. "Lost my edge some time ago." He laughed again. There was something a little sad about it this time.

Hannah wrote another sentence, in thicker lines of red.

The Soviets wanted to scramble atoms— He shook his head, laying out another run, cards flipping quickly. Only two games left.

"Reverse the polarities. Atoms bouncing in ways they shouldn't." Hannah looked up from her father's manuscript.

Professor Bauer shook his head with disdain. A waste of energy, he said. The moon, space, is the next satellite system, a fort in the stars, *for war*. He flipped the cards three at a time, lips pressed together.

I nodded.

The Victoria Room had bright gleaming hardwood floors that you could see shadows of your shoes in. All around was wainscoting dotted with white roses that belonged on the trim of a wedding cake.

"It is possible, you know." Hannah glanced at Stana and me, her eyes moving quickly, darkening. "Polarities can be reversed." She believed that in the near future, through a process of atomic deconstruction, the shifting, or jumping of electrons, that free-standing structures could collapse in earthquake-like tremors.

"Pure science fiction," Dr. Bauer said.

Jack Kirby, she said. Marvel Comics gone real.

I pushed back the brim of my porkpie and smiled. I liked her.

"Dad—" Her voice was smooth glass. "I think your opening paragraph is a little strong."

"Pretentious?" He smiled in our direction, three cards in his right hand.

"No. Too stentorian."

"Oh." He played a card, flipped over the Queen of Spades.

"Leave some space for you and your audience to settle in. Set them up with a hook, and then several paragraphs later, state the issue." A spot on her aquiline nose shone. Tension and release. Like notes in a symphony, she said.

He quickly read her notes, eyes skimming, re-reading. "Good idea." The muddy part of his biscuit had broken off into his cup of tea. "Oh, damn." He pushed the saucer away.

He played a black four on a black five.

I acted like I didn't notice.

"Back to Emil—the note he left for you—" Stana leaned into the table.

"Yes, the Oppenheimer quote." He studied the tri-fold. I'm not sure why he's reaching out to me, he said. "Really. We had a falling out. He was into the science of destruction. I was into the science of preservation." He held up a curled finger, glanced over at his daughter. "There's a difference."

"Uh-huh." I rubbed at the edges of my mouth.

"Maybe he had a change of heart," Stana said and Hannah agreed saying most definitely he did.

Did? I wondered if she'd had conversations with him. There was strong, personal conviction behind her words. "Something about these dragons scared him," the thirteen-year-old said.

Okay, maybe, Dr. Bauer conceded playing another card. Maybe. In 1944–45 while we built V-2 rockets, another wing was working on other experiments, dangerous weapons of destruction. After the war, as I told you, Emil fled to South America. Perhaps he did reconnect with a consortium of German and Soviet scientists and didn't like where things were headed. But I'll never know for sure because he's dead.

He flipped a card, played it, flipped another.

Scientists in Bannerville. Pop 1201. Where?

Perhaps, an underground lab? He chuckled. "It's all so fantastic, I just—"

Stana's lips pressed into a straight line. "This isn't a game, professor."

He shrugged with indifference. "These dragons I have no idea what they are. And if they exist I'd have to see the designs to stop them—"

Maybe that was the next step, the designs were in Emil's head, and he was going to share them with you—I said.

"I cannot operate on if's, Mr. Fuller. Structured probabilities I prefer, but this is all speculative, narrative spinning."

Our small part of the world may end in three days, doctor, Stana said.

I highly doubt that. Emil had to undergo psychotherapy twice while on my watch. He was prone to paranoia and fits of fancy, imaginative leaps, he said.

"People don't kill you for imaginative leaps." Stana's eyes narrowed, her freckles dancing.

Dr. Bauer returned to Emil's jangled prose on the tri-fold.

"And he never loved Oppenheimer. I'm surprised he's quoting him. Thought he was a coward. Afraid to fully pursue knowledge." He made another run on a solitaire game, cards quickly flipping, and then collapsing the rows into one big pile. "One game to go. I miss Friday night poker." He smiled.

"Back to Oppenheimer?" Stana was no kibitzer. "The men of action versus men of science bit?"

The classic fight: science versus military, he said. The pursuit of inquiry versus the pursuit of utility, he said. "If you were in Eden today, and given the apple, right now, would you bite it?" You can live in blissful innocence, he said, or you can be burdened with the responsibilities of knowledge. What would you do?

His words were an eerie echo of my last case, and Franklin W. Whitfield II chastising me for making the wrong choice, pursuing the apple and the meaning behind Dimension V instead of heading to his neon church, his followers, and their possible demise through the spread of cyanide gas.

"I'd be like Eve in Milton's *Paradise Lost*. I'd want equality. I'd want power. I'd bite the goddamn apple," Stana said.

"Me too," I said.

"That's the dilemma for science, isn't it?" He laughed gently. Oppenheimer was afraid of the apple, at least according to Emil. I don't know why he's quoting him here.

"Maybe, as Hayden already said, as Emil got older, he became more like Oppenheimer. The more he became involved in the Soviet enterprise of scientific inquiry the more he feared the apple."

"I think that's it exactly." Hannah raised black eyes over the edge of her father's manuscript. "And that's why he wanted to see Poppa. He feared these dragons. I think he saw them."

"The dragons?" Dr. Bauer pointed at the paper, shook his head with heavy skepticism.

"No. He saw something." His daughter stood firm, taking on

the old man. Something scared him enough to want to see you. He knew a truth—

"He had to have seen something." I smiled in Hannah's direction. He was so insistent on doing something about it, that's why he was in my car, heading to Toronto. *Before the back of his head became grapefruit pulp.*

Professor Bauer smiled even more tightly and waved his daughter silent, two cards falling from his hand as he did so. "Maybe," he said. Maybe he *thought* he saw something, but the man was confused. I hate to speak ill of the dead, but the boy was unbalanced. Back then, when we worked on V-2 rockets, and later when he worked for the Soviets, he sent me little bits of communications, quoting Khalil Gibran, and *The Little Prince.* Strange mash ups of ideas.

James Dean loved The Little Prince. *It was his favorite book.*

Near the refreshment stand was Josef Ziegler. He wasn't in the background. He was the background, making himself present, known, noshing on a powdered donut. He wore a white seersucker suit and white top hat. The suit was dotted with white flecks of sugary snow. He was watching us, eating in slow-motion, trying to intimidate with his calculated deliberateness.

I pointed him out to Dr. Bauer.

Ziegler tipped his hat in recognition.

Dr. Bauer couldn't i.d. him.

Hannah could. "He's that idiot who thinks the Holocaust never happened," she said, flippng thin hair that resembled fish lines over a shoulder.

'Some people are still stuck in the past," Dr. Bauer said.

"Emil?" Stana asked.

"We'll never know." He shrugged.

And with that, Ziegler was gone.

Hannah busied herself writing a long paragraph on the back of a page somewhere in the middle of the essay, corners of her mouth drawn up with a slight smile. She had a soft spot for

Emil. "These transitions to your second point, Dad, need work," she mumbled.

"I don't believe a goddamn word out of his goddamn mouth." Stana's eyes were burning, hands in the pockets of her slacks. The smugness of the way Dr. Bauer mocked Emil pissed her off.

"I take it you don't like him."

That cracked her up.

We walked down a blue-carpeted hallway with hexagonal light fixtures glimmering by every other door. "His daughter's a braniac—"

"No argument here—" I said. *One thing was for sure, we were going to take a side trip soon to my office on Bloor-Yonge and get an extra gun, a .45, out of a locked box in a lower desk drawer. One piece wasn't enough against these scientists and their damn dragons.*

Stana thought something was a little off between them. Dad likes being the center of attention, and daughter's going to, real soon, push him out of the spotlight.

She unlocked the door. Our Queen bed was stretched clean, the sheets folded neatly over and tucked tight. The room smelled of detergent.

Stana dumped her purse on the other Queen bed, opened the blinds. Snow danced and flecks of auburn glowed in the snow's day-glo.

Something about that moment, Stana in the window, hair dancing with snow, the pulse line of her jaw, the strength of her back and arms, had me blurting, "Let's get married."

"What?" She turned.

I smiled my lopsided grin. What if I retire after this season?

"You just got back in the league."

"I know."

"You love hockey—"

"I know, but I love you more—"

That made her eyes water. She sat on the bed furthest from me.

The room wasn't as bright as it was before, and the snow no longer flashed with light.

"I want you. I want you there when I wake up in the mornings, and I want you there in the evenings as you tell me about, or read, your latest lead story. Every day I want to wake up next to you. I want to make you your morning cup of coffee."

"You make lousy coffee," she said.

"I do." But you make lousy eggs, so it's a push, I said.

That cracked her up.

Suddenly the phone directly across from her buzz squalled into a crackly crinkle.

"Stana—jump—now-now. Push yourself off—"

She launched toward me, spider webs of fingers stretching.

I tried to catch her, but my chin hit her cheek, and our heads knocked, and we tumbled across the room's second bed, powdered dust and chips of glass filling the spaces around us, as we crunched our tethered bodies down a wall.

I don't remember much of anything after that.

4

Bits of a head lamp and flecks of paint were splashed about the tree Emil had hit nearly twenty-four hours ago. Glass and chrome were on the hard, hard ground.

Both of us were cold, stamping our feet, and sipping from a thermos of coffee we had jiffed up in my office while I grabbed extra hardware: a .45 and a Leica.

We walked through powder-soft snow, narrow trees into denser trees, grateful for our winter boots, but our thighs burned from the cold bite to the black sky. Powder kept falling, little ellipses in the air. There was no open field, no structure of any kind, and after thirty minutes of searching, we staggered back to her big old Rambler. "Let's head that way, a little further north by northeast," she said. The Upper tip of Lake Laurier, shaped like a mitten.

I nodded, my face stretched with numbness.

When we had come to following the hotel explosion, the manager wanted to give us a year's comp. The police couldn't figure out the workings of the bomb. My sonic waves theory went nowhere. And Dr. Bauer was off giving his keynote and unavailable for comment. Ziegler was nowhere to be found.

Stana's car was warm. We sipped coffee.

A mile up the road we saw two squat cabins by Lake Laurier that looked a deep blue in the distance. Stana killed her lights and we coasted under a three-quarter moon.

No smoke trailed from the cabin's chimneys.

No lights flashed in the windows.

Stana parked. I checked the clip in my second gun, a .45, that I tucked in back, under my belt. My side-holstered .38 had been recently oiled and the firing pin re-aligned. Keep our breaths shallow, I said. Too deep of breathing and your lungs might freeze.

She nodded.

We crossed open ground quickly, zigzagging our way to the cabins. The Leica was a cowbell swaying around my neck. "Keep the flashlight pointed at the ground. If you raise it, we'll be seen."

"Right." She looked over her shoulder. "Smell the wood. Can you smell it?" She touched the outside rig of logs. "Fresh. These were built in the last six months or so. Maybe sooner."

She was right. The wood wasn't weathered at all.

The first cabin was empty and colder inside than outside. There was a pot-bellied stove in the room's center. It hadn't been fired up in a while. Inside: cool ashes, coffee ground, and egg shells.

The short conical blasts of our flashlights picked up a large oval rug, bindles of wood, one set of bunk beds and a small freezer filled with wieners, pork loins, and hamburger buns.

The room smelled faintly of cigarettes.

Someone *had* been here.

On a metal desk with a wooden inlaid top was a radio the size of a luxury car. You could pick up the BBC on this thing. Talk to people in Iceland. It had large luminous dials out of *Flash Gordon.*

I twisted the knobs.

Static.

Next to the radio were three monitors. I turned them on. Images of an open field loomed, backlit by glimmers of moon across the black of Lake Laurier.

Stana stood by an empty closet, hands on hips. "You know

what this is? An OP. The field work *is* here. *This* is where they observe whatever they're observing."

I nodded. The lake through the monitors: a black slash of velvet. Outlines of loons were barely visible. Pine trees swayed gently.

The other cabin was empty too. No smell of cigarettes. Four monitors. Different views of the lake.

Stana lit a cigarette. "I'm fucking cold." Our coffee was gone.

The lake? Why so many views of the lake?

And then I saw them. On the farthest left monitor.

Angular shadows moving rapidly across the open field.

From the lake's rim.

"Shit, look," I said.

Three folks, in heavy gear, parkas, mittens, thick boots, ambling. They were all carrying high-powered rifles and they were coming our way—

Our feet sank briefly into puffs of snow, followed by the zip-zip of bullets, tearing off bits of tree bark as branches splattered away. "Zigzag," she yelled. "Zigzag."

Bullets zinged. More branches fell, crackled.

And then a bright red ball glowed in the sky. It rose over the lake, darted right, left, and then hovered against the horizon line before dropping away.

We had found cover in some pines. Her Rambler was still two or three football fields away.

A rifle crack.

Followed by a second.

More branches crinkling to the earth.

The guns were a good way off. We had time to get to the car. But what the hell was that thing, that glowing ball?

"A UFO?" Stana asked.

A rush of red flight returned.

It was on top of us, white lights glowing, white heat.

As I looked up I was staring at the underside of something

out of Ray Harryhausen's *Earth vs. The Flying Saucers*. It was a smooth disk, with a rigid circumference.

It dropped lower, barely thirty feet above us.

We crawled backwards on our elbows.

And then it tipped forward, before rediscovering the horizon line; its facing, a 'head,' full of jagged brutal teeth, a long snout, and sharp triangles for eyes. A mechanical howl yawped from the head's mouth. The eyes were the red of the damned.

If it was a dragon it had no wings.

I snapped several quick photos with my Leica.

The beast rose higher and higher, shifting in the sky with a slow clumpy yawl, and then thrusting away from view, back across the black disk of the lake.

"It's not even the 25th," Stana said, as we reached the Rambler. "Who the fuck was firing at us?"

The scientists? Three of them.

"One thing's for sure. That thing had the face of a dragon." She started the car. "What the fuck was it, a different dragon?"

"It had no wings," I said. Maybe it's the brains of the outfit, the master control for the dragons yet to rise?

"Maybe," she agreed. "You think—is that what spooked Emil, the night on the highway?"

"Yeah, I do," I said. "It had the eyes of hellhounds."

"Book of Revelation." She snapped her fingers. "Or better yet. Ginsberg. Ever read *Howl*?"

"No." I had wanted to. Just never got around to it.

We spun from the field, Stana's snow tires kicking up ice, snow, and mud.

There were no more rifle cracks. I directed her to my home in TO. I had a developing lab there.

Her wipers stuttered across the window's thin, crispy wafer of ice. "Moloch. That damn thing is Moloch," she said.

—

HOURS LATER, ANNE CHEVALIER, head of the RCMP's counter-terrorist unit, squeezed past two police officers, shaking her head with mild scolding. It was hard to drag the lake with all that ice. They hadn't found anything so far.

The RCMP and Canadian Army had mobilized filling up the spaces around Lake Laurier. It was a presence Bannerville had never seen before. The three bodies in the black sedan? KGB, she said. Top Red agents. "And the pictures you took, Hayden, sure got the government men fired up."

I nodded and glanced over at the two regiments, one from Quebec, the other from Northern Ontario, setting up encampment in Diefenbaker Park.

"That floating head had to be the dragons' central intelligence," I said. "The brain."

"That's our thinking too," she said.

We were all huddled under a big green canvas tent, drinking coffee from tin cups. Stana had a wool blanket draped around her shoulders. Past her, I felt the heavy coordinated movements and heavy grumble of big half-tracks and anti-aircraft guns.

"We also inspected Emil's car." She sipped coffee. "The brakes were most definitely cut." She smiled a cool comfort of combat readiness.

I had known her for a couple of years. Anne was instrumental in helping me solve the "A Fourth Face" case, and I trusted her. She was in her mid-to-late thirties, curvy, edging towards plump, and her left eye rested a little higher on her face than her right. She had the three S's: style, sass, and sexiness.

And we shared secrets. She knew I was sexually abused years ago. I knew she was queer, and to keep her cover and avoid jeopardizing her career with the RCMP who saw homosexuality as a mental illness, she went on occasional dates with men. Outside of her secret, she was open, a great listener.

And she was listening now.

Ziegler. The dragons. Weapons of destruction. Neo-Nazi scien-

tists from South America. Where are they? Where's the lab? And what about Culpeppers, his restaurant, a front for activity?

I plunked my porkpie on a knee.

"They're all being investigated. Including Frei and Langhorne, the OPP—" *Lots of odd behavior the last three months.*

Tech installed communications: monitors, radios, satellite transmitters. The smell of propane was everywhere.

"We didn't find much in those cabins." You were right, definitely an OP, she said. But, she held up my photographs. "We've got these—Moloch."

I guess she had read Ginsberg too.

"What do you say we get a warrant for Culpeppers and go looking for a lab?" She glanced at her watch. It was 3:12 in the morning. Fuck Ziegler.

I liked her thinking.

5

Ziegler was playing chess. It was now 3:45 in the morning, Ziegler and Strehl in back moving pieces across a board, while the RCMP and the Army searched Culpeppers. They rummaged behind the cash register, along the row of beer steins on the shelves (it was always Oktoberfest here apparently), and deep in the shadows of a crowded utility closet.

Strehl's hair was parted in two even clumps that resembled a pair of shriveled navy beans. His index finger tapped the black knight, and then opted for a move with a bishop.

His eyes held anger but his eyebrows never moved. He pressed down on the boxed timer between them.

No lab in the basement, Anne shouted up from the basement. Just bags of onions and potatoes, industrial-size cans of tomatoes, veggies and mayonnaise, and a printing press and boxes upon boxes of BS brochures about how the Holocaust never happened.

One of them was curling in my hand as I flashed my lopsided grin and pushed back my porkpie.

"You won't find anything here," the Reverend said. The tin ceiling, like that found at Strehl's service station, slipped in places, tiles dripping down like half-torn flags. On the walls were a host of black-and-white photographs, circa 1920's-40's. The good years: segregation and lynchings.

Strehl and Ziegler, a couple of Beer Hall Putsch pals.

I rubbed at the edges of my mouth. "I'm onto you, *Reverend.* I got photos. A flying mechanical brain—the control center for the dragons?"

That got a response. Their shoulders straightened.

"Oh, I got your attention, now." I tossed the rolled-up, Holocaust-never-happened brochure across the chessboard. "A vast Jewish conspiracy, huh?"

Stana tugged at my elbow—

Ziegler smiled that short-round grin of his, a bullet that doesn't go all the way.

"I'm still standing, pal. That play at the hotel with sonic waves? Forget about it—" I yanked out my Star of David and flashed it before them. Earlier he called Lenny Bruce a schwartze. "I'm the white schwartze, motherfucker."

Ziegler deftly lifted the fanned brochure from the board and moved a knight to pawn six. The photograph behind him was Charles Lindbergh in jodhpurs, leaning against the Spirit of St. Louis.

There were seven or eight photos of Lindy. Around Lindy were several framed line drawings of white dragons with exaggerated bat wings, Gryphon claws, and a devil's tail. They resembled the designs found on the robes of a KKK Grand Dragon.

"I see you like the art—" He smiled briefly. "Images of purity, images of purity, my friend."

"I'm not your friend—"

"No. Your kind could never truly wear white—"

Another tug from Stana. Soldiers were looking behind beer steins.

The dragon is the angel's alter-ego, he said, faintly flashing that short-round grin. "The darker dionyssiasn side of all our psyches. It's the dragon that pushes the angel into the light, that brings about the purity of existence."

Strehl was nodding.

"Is that what the day of the dragons is all about: purification?"

Ziegler glanced at his watch. "How much longer are you all going to be? I want to catch the farm report—" He laughed at his little joke. "My parents were tobacco farmers." Another set of laughs. "It airs at four."

"Your scientists are hiding in this town. We'll find them. And that lab. Emil talked," I said. The RCMP and the army are here to stay. "Yours in Dresden."

Strehl rushed from his chair.

I splashed open my leather jacket, highlighting my side-holstered .38. Believe me, I wanted to use it but didn't. I ducked under Strehl's stiff-armed left and landed a beauty of a right haymaker on his chin. He toppled, crashing into a chair and bouncing on his elbows. Three or four chess pieces followed him down.

The Reverend rose majestically and held a steady hand, fingers spread. "Now is not the time," he instructed Strehl. His eyes narrowed. "White light, white heat. A future cleansing." Clam sauce was all over his breath.

I don't recall that being on the menu.

"Now, get out of his goddamn restaurant." A tiny tic flashed, a flicker under Strehl's left eye.

Stana tugged at my shoulder a third time, pointing with her chin at the photographs of Goebbels, Goering, and Strehl standing in a submarine's parapet, a swastika flag stretched to his left, firm hands on the metal rim of what looked like the casing for a shuttlecock. Same hair. Just more of it.

"U-boat commander, huh?" she said.

"I've been a citizen of this country since 1951," Strehl said.

"Hey, Anne," Stana shouted.

Anne had just returned from the basement, her hair had bits of fuzz dust along the part before the fall of her curtain of bangs.

"Check this out—" Stana pointed.

Anne waved at Strehl and the Reverend. "Let's go."

"Huh?" Strehl let out a sharp steam of disapproval.

Chevalier was going to question them on her turf, under the canvas tent at Diefenbaker Park. "I hear you wanted to hear the farm report? I'll have the radio in my car tuned to that station."

She ushered them from the restaurant.

The Beer Hall Putsch boys weren't happy.

Dragons hovered.

6

Hannah Bauer needed to talk—

She had buzzed my answering service six to seven times, and the sky outside was now pink with dawn.

The Victoria Room was empty. She drank orange juice and nibbled on a scone while toying with the ankh around her neck. Two days before the science conference, Emil had contacted her and they met up in Bannerville. He took her to Culpeppers and hoped through her to get a ticket to her father (Dr. Bauer and Emil's politics had separated them over the years). Emil's biggest fear: that his fellow scientists couldn't control the dragons. They're buried somewhere in Bannerville. Waiting to be re-born. "He thought my father could do something to harness their energy, stop them if necessary."

We shared our photos of Moloch.

It is the central hub, the brain the scientists built to control the dragons, she said, black eyes dancing. She lifted a compact from under the blanket and placed it next to her glass of orange juice.

"Are the dragons hollow husks?" Stana lit a Parliament and leaned upright in her chair, the cigarette waving.

Supposedly. But Emil feared they might have their own mechanical DNA beyond what the scientists imagined. "In other words, they could have free will. My father could have programmed them that way." Her dark eyes widened.

"Your father built the dragons?"

He has no memory of it, she said, straightening the blanket around her legs, and then breaking off a bigger chunk of scone. Emil worked for Dad. She toyed with the ankh, looked off, and then into the bottom of her glass of orange juice, bits of pulp floating like small grass cuttings. Dad's memory is—blurry—the past, a mix of what's true and what he wishes. He was always opposed to the pursuit of science for violence, but he was part of the team that made the dragons.

"So what, he's got convenient amnesia?" I pushed back my porkpie.

Hannah said nothing.

Stana took a slow drag off her cigarette.

Krylin-19, the dragons are loaded up with Krylin-19. "A nerve gas Emil told me about. More like a bacteria, man-made, that immediately freeze-dries your lungs and kills in seconds."

Kryklin-19. Kraydon. That's what Emil was trying to tell me and I misheard, misunderstood the words. Krylin.

Hannah tapped her chin. Moloch didn't fly straight, right? "It zigged and zagged."

"Yeah."

Stana nodded in agreement.

Outside the space/time continuum, she said, pushing back long, thin hair that glowed as if coated with phosphorus. "Every now and then science makes some kind of leap." Atoms are made up of protons and electrons and neutrons. If you can alter that arrangement you too can make leaps. She smiled tightly. "I'm not thirteen. I don't know why my father always insists on telling people that. I'm seventeen—"

I didn't know what to say.

"How did your father's keynote address go?" Stana asked, pushing away any awkwardness.

Hannah adjusted the blanket's edges once more. "Just all right." He stumbled about during the Q&A, struggling to directly answer challenges to the theoretical principles of his article. "I know the principles are right—" She tapped the compact before her. "They are sound." But he was lost. "He's been under a lot of pressure lately what with Emil's death and whisperings of Dad being a former Nazi. He hates Nazis." Her lips pressed together.

There was a paper she wanted to hear at 9 a.m., she said, looking at the clock across the way. She wondered if we could meet her here at 10:30 and take her to Bannerville. And she'd talk to Anne Chevalier and help in any way she could. But—

"The apple is calling?" Stana said with a wink.

"Yeah." Hannah shook her head. "Sometimes I fear all apples are full of worms."

THE FAINT SKY BLUE SUN of Houston Crescent dimpled through the blinds and along her freckled face. It was 7 a.m. and I was drifting into post-sex sleep.

Stana nudged me to stay awake. "I think we can grow together." I know that sounds corny, Hayden, but I feel we can bolster each other while appreciating each other's need for individual solace and growth. She smiled slightly. "Are you awake?"

"Yeah, yeah."

"You understand what I'm saying?"

"Yeah. We make a good team." I drew small circles on her arm. "And we can walk three paths: one together and separate ones for each of us."

"God, maybe you should write for the paper—that was good."

Our breathing synced together, and again I drifted off toward the gray wall of sleep.

She nudged me again.

Stripes of shadows on the ceiling resembled a dragon's tail.

"You don't seem as excited this time about playing hockey—"

I think that's what she said. I was kind of moving in and out of awareness.

I loved playing the game and hanging with my teammates,

especially Béliveau and Lappiere, and Montreal's a great city, but I missed TO. Montreal's loud and bright and bedazzling, I said. With its bistros, cafes, cool jazz, and feeling of outlaw status within the two solitudes of Canada. Toronto is workmanlike, humble, plain, right down to its right-angle, straight-lined architecture. I love both cities, but Toronto's home.

"How much longer do you think you'll play?"

"This season. And next." Maybe. The season started off great, 12 points in my first 15 games, named the game's third star upon my return to Maple Leaf Gardens on Remembrance Day, but soon after I struggled to score, and I was dropped to the third line, and then assigned to no specific line, just plugged into different configurations when Coach felt the team needed a jolt. I play the penalty kill, but I'm only averaging six or so minutes a game. But I had scored 11 goals, on pace for 15, respectable.

"Why do they have you wearing number 28?"

"I don't know." I didn't want to talk about it. The Habs have so many retired numbers and Talbot wears 17. "But, twenty-eight just feels like a marginal number for a marginal player, I wanted to say. I didn't.

And there was something else. After taking time off to solve my father's murder, things were never quite the same with Coach Blake. Or so it seems.

Tears collected at the corners of my eyes and I didn't know why.

"The goal you scored. Low stick side. A beauty."

"Yeah—"

The dragon on the ceiling was gone. "I wish we'd never broke up," I said.

She thought it made us stronger. In the time between the time together we learned to appreciate each other more deeply. And the deaths of Lisa and Spinner still hovered, a shared, secret history. Maybe someday we could make amends.

"I'm not sure how," I said.

"Yeah. I don't know."

Toronto's top gangster Babe Migano was building an amusement park over their bodies.

She traced warm fingers across my chest, lifted the Star of David. "If you want our kids raised Jewish, I'm okay with that." Stana was a woman of faith, but as she started pushing thirty, she became more and more anti-church hierarchy and anti-Pope.

"Whatever you want. I'm committed to you," I said.

"Me too," she said.

I HAD THE DREAM.

Again.

Ever since he was murdered.

Same dream with slight variations.

Dad and I are driving some kind of old, 1952 Nash out in the country.

He's guiding the top of the steering wheel with his right wrist.

The sky is a bright orange, marmalade, and tall grass outside my window waves, creating words that appear too quickly for me to remember. I'm twelve or thirteen, the abuse has stopped, and Dad has a cigarette in his lower lip, the sleeves of his white T rolled back. On his arms are several Chai symbols.

Dad hated tattoos, always saying they were for losers and sailors, but in the dream he has a sleeve worth of Chai symbols.

We drive up a gravel driveway and arrive at a rectangular two-storey building. The door opens before we can knock and two rabbi's smile at us, and let us in. Everything in the room is white, the furniture, the walls, the fixtures. Dad sits on a white couch and smiles, reads *The Daily Worker* as the two men nod me in the direction of another room. The door is slightly ajar, and I can see marmalade light glowing around the trim.

Dad isn't invited to join us.

From the couch, he smiles, pleased with me. One tough Jew, he mouths, but I'm not sure. I wonder why he can't join us.

This way, one of the rabbi's says, gesturing, smiling.

Bright amber fills the second room, and I feel accepted.

THE PHONE JANGLED US AWAKE AT 8:30.

Hannah.

"Poppa's missing—"

When Hannah arrived at his side of their adjoining suite, she discovered Dad's strewn clothes; a splatter of bloody dots on the carpet; two broken glasses; and the hinges of his briefcase torn away.

Also: his papers were gone.

But the biggest red flag: his playing cards. Six decks, including two unopened packs, were stacked along the far end of a coffee table, under a lamp. Poppa never goes anywhere without his cards.

"Kidnapped?"

"It appears so."

The police were dusting for prints and my pal Sal Lambertino, Toronto's Top Cop, was orchestrating the investigation, keeping the media from rushing the room and harassing Hannah. "He's a nice man," she said.

"The best." Sal had been my pal for nearly ten years, since my first year with the Leafs, 1957-58. I told Hannah how we had done several local charity events together, including Easter Seals. "So—" I rubbed at the edges of my mouth. "They took your father to help with the raising of the dragons?"

"Yes—yes—yes. That's the plan, I guess."

KGB? The Beer Hall Putsch Boys—Ziegler and Strehl's crew? If they wanted Dr. Bauer's help, why would they cut him? The splatter was the odd detail. And why not let him bring his cards? If you want him to have a clear head, let him have his goddamn cards. Something wasn't adding up.

I don't think they wanted him for science.

Her voice was collecting doubts. "The dragons? I don't see

how he can help."

"Why?"

His health is in decline, she said. For the past four years, Hannah had been covering up his increasing dementia. Yes, he has several moments of lucidity, where all appears normal. But the hard science? He doesn't have the brain for it. And several memories have faded. He doesn't even remember what his first wife looked like. He thinks she's his sister.

"He sounded lucid when we spoke to him."

"Yes," she said, "But he can't delve deep. His ability to theorize just isn't there."

"I'm sorry."

Hannah had even taken to bolstering his research papers in the last year, nearly writing 60% of the material under his name. She had written four-fifths of the paper for this conference.

"That's why he struggled during the Q&A."

"When they find out what's wrong, they'll have no patience. None."

Static click-clicked between us.

"I guess they should have kidnapped me, the cripple, the Easter Seals kid." She laughed until it broke apart, bits of blown glass.

7

Hannah curled near the rear window, dark eyes dancing. Stana floored her blue Rambler, pointing us toward Bannerville.

Hannah pulled herself upright, a shiny spot on her nose glinting in gray light. I told you of his failing faculties, she said. He doesn't believe he was ever a Nazi, or even worked for them. He thinks he worked for the OSS. The imagined versus the real, she muttered. "They'll kill him."

I was afraid he was already dead. First Zielger attacked me and Stana in our hotel room with his sonic wave surprise, and now his team (possibly a consortium of Nazis and KGB) had nabbed Dr. Bauer, hoping he'd provide the missing piece to the day of the dragons.

A huge shroud passed over the car, a deep black shadow, darkening our interior and Stana's instrument panel. Some bush pilot flying too close to the highway, probably, but there was no warning, no sound. I looked out the passenger window. Nothing. The shadow had lifted and disappeared.

The road thud-thudded under the Rambler's wheels.

Emil told Hannah that the Krylin-19 was scheduled to be installed in the dragons in December, 1944, but Dr. Bauer wouldn't let anyone near it.

"So he loaded them?" Stana asked, hands tight on the wheel, sun fissuring the windshield.

I guess. "He worked alone." Hannah shook her head. "Anyway, Dad programmed fail-safe mechanisms in the dragons. Secret codes and maybe Ziegler and friends haven't unlocked those codes yet, or need Dad to unlock the codes in order to unload the nerve gas?" She shook her head, full of uncertainties.

Hannah reached under her blanket. Today it was Aztec colored. "I've found a way to neutralize, to crisscross the dragons' wiring." In her hand was the silver compact we saw earlier that morning in the Victoria room, but only now did I notice the three push buttons at the edge of a curve. The whole gizmo resembled a guitarist's fuzz face pedal—

Hannah explained how it worked and I was completely lost.

She slowed down and spoke more directly. Apparently, the gizmo reversed polarities and caused an electron to jump in ways it shouldn't, shaking up atoms, collapsing molecular structures.

We reached the edge of Bannerville. Strehl's gas station was way off in the distance, to the left. The pumps had yet to be replaced, but the Esso sign was lit. He was open for repairs, I guess.

And then the rumbling returned, the whine of yesterday at the hotel, a heavy bandsaw whir—

A cape-like shadow covered the car, and then it was there.

Floating.

The dragon's head, Moloch.

Hellhound eyes burning, jagged triangular teeth. Bright lights glaring from the underbelly. A white heat, like walking into the sun, brightened the car's insides.

My hands hurt. So did Stana's.

A yak-yak-yak of aircraft guns thunked across our trunk, killing the car's engine and shattering our windshield.

My face itched from little glass scratches.

Stana tapped the brakes, but they pushed to the floor. Trees were everywhere, but there was an opening ahead, crumpeted pockets of snow.

"Brace yourselves," Stana screamed.

My stomach fell as the car rose, crunching through the guard rail, metal and glass scraping under us, as I hit the dash, and we plowed deep into the recesses of snow.

My ribs hurt like hell. I held my grimace.

The bright light all around us diffused into a final powdery blister.

And the dragon head floated up, up, up, and zigged left, and was gone.

AS WITH MOST ACCIDENTS, passing motorists stopped to see if we were alright, and the three of us were surrounded by a bevy of onlookers, mesmerized and scared by the floating red spaceship with a head, as one of them labeled it, that had briefly crowded the sky. Not just a head, a wild animal, like a boar or something, someone else said. A woman in a black wool coat with a fur collar asked if we were okay. She was a nurse out of Peterborough. Stana was bleeding from her upper lip and her face was bruised. My ribs made it hard to breathe. Hannah was fine. She was checking over her wheelchair.

But the car was totaled: the trunk was spotted with bullets, two front tires exploded from their rims, and a windshield splashed out.

Frei and his partner arrived five minutes later. The fifteen or so folks gathered clamored to tell the officers their stories.

Frei scratched at the flabby flap of his half-remaining ear.

It was a flying saucer with a head, someone said. Bright red. A second person. White light. A third.

Frei jotted down several notes, so did lanky fella. "We better get you guys into town—see a doctor." He directed us to his black and white.

"I think the girl may have whiplash," said the nurse.

Frei thanked her.

Stana craned her neck left. I handed her an Anacin. Sometimes I worry that I knock this shit back like candy.

She swallowed dry.

"It was a dragon without wings," said a fella wearing blue whose delivery truck was all green.

"Okay, okay, we got your statements, we got this under control." Frei rushed them off.

His partner radioed for a tow truck and scratched, now and then, at his face.

Hannah was tucked back into her wheelchair, Aztec blanket on her knees. She blew into hands covered with oven-sized mittens. "Christ, it's freezing," she mumbled.

After having helped situate Hannah in back of the black and white, Frei got behind the wheel. Rather than cross the busy highway, he turned right down a side street, passing Culpepper's, and then another right on Princess Street.

"Hey, the light's on," the Lanky guy said, voice dusky gravel.

Frei stopped in front of a ranch house. Hit the horn twice, and then quickly glanced over his shoulder at the three of us—

His partner scratched and turned around too. The lettering on his name-tag was chipped, faded.

A police-issue Smith and Wesson rested atop the bench seat, the barrel pointed right at us. "Don't try anything stupid." Langhorne smiled.

Some of his teeth were missing. Too much Juicy Fruit, I guess.

"The slightest bump and this baby goes off. Pop. Pop. Pop." He scratched his face again. "Your gun, shamus. Or I should say guns, including the .45 tucked in your back."

I handed him both.

Down the front steps of the ranch house came a sharp glow of white, set off like a cumulus cloud against a stretch of faded blue-jean sky. He wore a white tux, a white cumberbun, white bow-tie, and a white top hat. The only thing missing, a walking stick. In his right hand, a gun. It wasn't white.

Ziegler, putting on the goodman ritz.

Frei lowered the window and Ziegler walked to his side of the black and white, careful not to get dust and dirt on his duds.

"The girl. Not the cripple. The other cripple. The emotional one."

Frei yanked Stana from the car. Lanky fella rapped me across the mouth with a free hand for trying to intervene and Hannah screamed. "Come back for me in forty-five to an hour. I'll be done by then." Ziegler smiled, his short-round grin, and nudged Stana toward the house, as the black and white pulled away.

His top hat shook with every jaunty step.

She's not going to have an easy time of it, hero, Frei said, the window still down, his elbow sticking out. "The boss can't stand that she was making time with you and your kind. He's going to—what's the word?"

"Purify—" his partner said.

"Purify her—" Frei drove through the flashing red onto the gas station lot, pulling into an opening along the chain-link fence, deep in back by the old junkers stacked in flatbed rows. Rust, motor-oil, and heavy animal sweat, mine mostly, filled the air.

Ziegler had Stana, and I, like a sap, couldn't help her. I had no guns, and now we were shoved about and out from the car.

They didn't bother with Hannah's wheelchair.

I had to carry her.

Hollowed-out cars from the 40s and 50s surrounded us, testaments to death.

A barrel in the distance burned scraps of paper and bits of wood.

Snow gently scattered around us.

They ushered us deeper into the parking lot, away from the odd conical light, into a shadowy recess. In the distance flames jumped from the blackened barrel.

Our destination: a hole, complete with a rim of lye around the edges. The earth waiting for us—

"Why are you, why?" Hannah, still in my arms (she was light), struggled to find the words. *What does one say to traitors?* "Why are you putting in with them?"

"*Putting in with them?*" Frei's leer deepened. "We are them."

He turned to his partner and spoke Russian.

KGB.

Four weeks ago, they had been sent to Bannerville by the Kremlin. They liquidated the real Sgt. Frei and his partner Langhorne and assumed their identities.

"That's why your face itches—" I pointed at the Lanky Fella. "Plastic surgery."

He smiled. "I'm committed to my craft." He laughed.

Frei bent at the waist, joining in the hysterics. They should both be on Sullivan. "Climb in," Frei barked, motioning us to be swallowed by the dark earth.

I staggered in with Hannah, black dirt clumping to my shoes, and remembered reading stories of my people, members of my family, Jews in Russia, gypsies in Lithuania, dying in shallow ditches at the hands of the Nazis. And later having their jewelry removed from their corpses, sometimes a finger hacked off for a memento, a hard-to-get-at wedding ring.

Hannah smiled up at me faintly, and then from her coat pocket, pulled out the silver gizmo, pressed a button. A rambling wash of sonic waves scratched across the earth, and a red beam lit the two with a cold campfire glow.

Frei and his partner jerked and juked, mouths hanging loosely, hands at their sides, pissing and shitting themselves, guns falling, and my guns falling. As they tremored, eyes rolling, rolling, rolling, up, up, up, their faces scrunched into wrung towels. Smoke scuffed and puffed around their scalps, blackened, and then ignited with fire.

Frei was the first to let go—his head exploding, bits of pink matter, blood, and bone everywhere. The other fella's head burned and burned, turning to blackened charcoal, and then just puffed away in the wintry mix of air.

I helped Hannah from the pit.

Got her to her wheelchair.

"Let's get Stana—" she said.

I rubbed at the edges of my mouth. "I got a feeling the scientists and Moloch are here—in Strehl's corrugated garage behind the pumps."

She nodded.

I glanced at my watch. We still had thirty to forty-five minutes. "Let's check this building first. Then we'll get Stana—" I jacketed a round into the .45's slide.

Hannah never mentioned her father.

We both kind of knew he'd taken the long goodbye.

8

I pushed Hannah in the wheelchair. Flakes of icy snow dotted the shoulders of her down-filled parka, cold fish scales forming as the temperature rose. Fortunately the asphalt in the wrecking area had been recently cleared. The wheels of the chair spun a little but not much.

"I wish I could walk." Her words were streaked with defeat. "I'm slowing you down."

"Look, Hannah—" I bent over the top of her head. "I'd push you and this damn thing to Buffalo—" That cracked her up. "How's the gizmo?"

Not much juice left, she said. A little.

We reached the big corrugated building in the shape of a boomerang. The .45 was clamped in my hand. The .38 in its side holster on my left hip. Give me five minutes and then come on in.

She nodded.

My head was full of scorpions.

I slid open the iron door. I spotted four scientists right away, two exits in back, no makeshift weaponry, nobody appeared armed.

And no Dr. Bauer.

Strehl was there, however, standing in a glass cube with a scientist who had enough sideways hair to rival Larry Fine. The top of his head glowed from the fluorescent track lights.

Moloch hung suspended in a patchwork quilt of scaffolding, tension wires holding it upright within the scaffold's maze of metal squares. Its head reached the tip of the hangar's ceiling, barely fitting within the breakaway tin roof.

Three scientists stood atop the scaffolding, messing with the central computer system inside Moloch's head. They were tinkering with the wiring. "I told him not to fly it, the strain's too much," said a younger scientist with a receding hairline and more Brylcreem than a 1950s rockabilly trio. He was agitated, worrying his upper lip. A whole row of T-9 filaments were shot. He also said something or other about foggy pathways.

"Get some new energy cells. If this is going to fly tonight, we need to recharge the central capacitor." The other fella with a buzz cut was also young. He had puffy leeches for eyes. "We may need to re-encrypt. I don't think it's going to be ready for tonight—"

A third scientist, much older, with a goatee, stood off alone, studying a clipboard for answers. "It has to be. Clear the pathways? We don't have much time."

They were oblivious of me and my .45 and now .38, a regular Two-Gun Kid.

I was about to introduce myself.

Along the wall below the scaffolding were a box row of monitors surveying the area: Diefenbaker Park and Chevalier's crew with backhoes and pickaxes, digging up dirt all along Laurier Lake and in the open field with its remote cabins. Army personnel and anti-aircraft guns were securely in place. A third monitor showcased a room with bunk beds, a pool table, and a wet bar. *Must be the basement in Strehl's, the HQ for his crackerjack team of South American Nazis.*

The dragons were scheduled to appear. Soon.

A digital readout, a bulky makeshift scoreboard along a wall read: 8:37:22, 8:37:21; 8:37:20. Countdown to the dragons.

I fired a shot in the air.

The two young scientists, used to following orders, froze.

The older guy, used to giving orders, reached inside his lab coat.

I don't think he was about to handover a read out of Moloch's vitals.

I fired twice.

He crumpled, left arm draped over the scaffolding's edgings. The gun fell and clanged below.

A fourth scientist and Strehl came hurtling out of the glass cube.

I waved my guns in several adjacent directions. My meaning was clear.

Strehl smirked, his thin lips barely moving, his hair and eyebrows still. "We know you came alone. You and the girl. You must have bettered our men."

Your KGB buddies? Oh, they got bettered, pal. Hannah blew their minds, I said.

"Huh?"

"I did." She wheeled into the room, eyes stern, the gizmo riding high on her wool blanket. She said something about polarities and breaking down atoms. She glared at Moloch's head. "So that's the brain?"

She was inviting Strehl to talk, but he was reticent.

"Yes." He swayed gently, wedges of fingers by his hips, flexing, looking for an opportunity to strike.

"Where's my father?"

He said nothing.

Hannah raised the gizmo.

"Kraydon is a product of advanced science, a species that deserves—"

Kraydon. So that is what Emil meant after all. Kraydon wasn't Kraylin-19 but the name for the brain. Kraydon. "We're about to melt Kraydon down to Crayola crayons, pal," I said.

"The effort we put in—the months—you owe it to science to

save it—"

Somehow he was missing the very irony of what he was saying.

But I was going to aid and abet his narcissism, just for a little, because I wanted to know all about the floating dingus. So, I asked, and he talked and talked, saying something about Kraydon was there to guide the other dragons. His voice was breaking. So much time, so much effort, he said.

"Uh-huh." I rubbed at the edges of my mouth and pushed back my porkpie. "So, Bauer's dragons are too smart for you?"

"Maybe." They're too free, he said, unaware of his philosophical contradictions. Kraydon checks the dragons' impulses.

"And my father?"

He smiled a short-round grin, the trademark of his buddy Ziegler. "He was of no further use to us—"

Blue light beamed from Hannah's gizmo and Moloch winced at the waves and whir of feedback, a runaway band-saw buzz. The noise was so strong. I covered my ears. Moloch no longer had ears. The mechanical triangles had melted down to waxed metal nubs, and then the jagged teeth fell one by one, hitting the floor like metal stars.

The two scientists on high, ran down the scaffolding.

Smoke cycloned about Moloch's head, circling, circling.

"No—" Strehl ran toward the bigger and bigger, higher and higher, circles.

Moloch's head exploded and so too did Strehl's, bits of wire, blood, bone, metal, capacitors falling, pink matter bleeding.

I DROVE DOWN KING STREET TO FOURTH and then cut across to Princess. The repaired cars in back of Strehl's had their keys in them. Small town hospitality. The sky was brushed with coarse strokes.

Quickly I moved to the outside of the ranch house. It was one of those prefab jobs, built on a concrete slab, 950 square feet if that, no basement. I was looking for a quiet place to enter. Couldn't see a damn thing through the windows—venetian blinds were drawn.

I jacketed another round into the slide of the .45. Hannah had my .38. Her gizmo was out of juice and she was covering the rounded-up scientists until Chevalier and her crew arrived.

I gently popped a small pane of glass with an elbow near the side door, closest to the garage. Waited. Slipped inside.

The house was wet wool, mildew and mold.

Kitchen empty.

The floor was cold against my feet. I had taken my shoes off.

TV in the living room, brown threadbare carpet, no under padding, and pinkish-red frieze furniture. Studio piano along an interior wall.

Faint voices.

From above.

This is a goddamn ranch house.

The attic.

Of course, no basement meant an attic.

A small dining room overlooked the backyard. Snow filled the collapsed swing set confined within the small grape post-fenced patio.

Ziegler was talking about dragons and his voice was quite clear. There wasn't much of a subfloor above me. He was saying some damn shit about purity of essence and a day of atonement.

A slithery scratch across the ceiling and then a crack and a scream, far across the room. Stana.

On the other side of the room.

The sonuvabitch had a whip and he was snapping it at Stana.

The only way to the attic was through a plywood entrance in the ceiling, but there was no way I could slide it away and get up there without being seen—no way.

Ziegler's soliloquy marched on, something to do with Strehl bringing the dragons to Canada via U-boat in 1945 and burying them in Lake Laurier for this glorious day. He, Ziegler, was the real dragon, he said, the mechanical dragons are mere extensions of his will of triumph. This was his day of the dragons; he was the lead dragon. The cleansing rain was coming for all who live outside purity. The lion cannot sleep with the lamb.

His words were a mix of Old Testament righteousness and delusional grandeur.

Keep talking, Hamlet. The readiness is mine.

He was now right on top of me, the words louder than before.

The whip slithered and scratched.

I planted my feet and with two hands emptied the clip into the ceiling. Plaster chips and wood flakes showered down.

A groan, a gasp, followed by a thud.

I separated the plywood from the ceiling, sliding into the attic.

It was dark. I lit my Zippo.

Ziegler wasn't moving, a crumpled mass to my right. No bow-tie, no cummerbund, no jaunty top hat. No white tux. He was naked; his body powdered white; his face, a clown's greasepaint of white, as if his own skin color wasn't enough. *It was as if he didn't like who he was and needed to be* whiter *than white.* Harnessed around his shoulders, leather straps. Attached to the straps a pair of gigantic white wings, crooked, jagged lines, mechanical dragon wings. He was becoming what he was planning to unleash upon us all.

Four of my bullets had hit their mark. One of his eyes was a red hole.

I turned to my left.

Stana. She too was naked, arms cramped by the low triangle of ceiling, wrists leashed to a joist. Three or four perforated snake lines wound down her back; ends of hair stuck to the gooey glue spits of blood.

I went to her, ducking my head. I don't know how Ziegler was able to snap a whip in here. He must have used a side-arm motion. Anyway, I undid Stana's hands and she collapsed backwards, into me.

"I knew you'd come," she said. "I knew you would." She smiled faintly. "I knew—"

She's a good catholic girl, a woman of faith.

I brushed hair from her eyes, kissed her forehead, and draped bare shoulders with my leather jacket. "I love you," I said.

She mumbled imperceptibly and reached around my neck, lifting the Star of David.

She smiled once again and placed it around her neck.

9

The first dragon broke through the icy lake like scraps of egg shells and rocketed straight up, up, up into the air.

It was green, and its tail was as long as its wing span, but the body didn't have bumps and blemishes. Instead it was smooth titanium metal that resembled the sharp sheen of chrome, if chrome were green and on a new luxury car.

The first dragon did a series of barrel rolls in the black sky, turning, tumbling, before landing softly to the earth, and parking upright, legs crossed, wings folded in, tail a lighthouse.

It looked us over and over.

Its expression, pleased.

The Army, in gas masks, stood at attention. They had their orders. Helmets glistened in the soft cold light. The snow had stopped but a misty haze hovered. The mood was palpable. This dragon had no hellhound eyes.

It looked around and around at the mounds of black dirt dug up from the earth and wondered why we were here at his party, but y'all welcomed nonetheless.

We stood about awkwardly entranced.

Anne was talking softly into the headset around her ears.

Hannah dropped her hands, thumbs up, twitching about like flippers on a pinball game. I couldn't tell if she wished the gizmo were juiced up or not.

Cameras click-click-clicked—

The National Film Board of Canada was at the site, making a hurried documentary. CBC television was also there, broadcasting coast to coast every tense unfurling moment. A commentator wearing a Porkpie hat, without a bend in it, spoke quickly, his voice soothing but gently jangling with adrenaline. "Friend or foe?" he kept repeating.

"Could be playing possum," said a gavel of a voice bleeding through Anne's headset.

"We got this," she said. "It's under control. Your orders are to standby until I give the orders." Just hold your position.

A second dragon broke through the lake, egg shells everywhere, icy mist splashing the sky. It hit the ground with a series of somersaults, tail snapping behind. It too eventually sat up, covering its eyes with huge akimbo wings.

It removed the wings from its eyes.

Covered them.

Removed the wings from its snout, its mouth wide open.

A game of peek-a-boo.

If this dragon could laugh, it was laughing.

No fire.

Silent laughter, mouth opening, shutting.

And then it did four backflips.

Buster Keaton would be proud.

Nearly everyone applauded.

Dragon number two moved over to dragon number one and sat, little Tyrannosaurus Rex hands, reaching out in supplication of friendship, I think.

"No wonder we couldn't find them," Anne whispered in my and Stana's direction. "They were in the lake—"

The U-boat commander, Strehl, had buried them there some twenty years ago.

"Yes," Hannah said. "With some kind of time-delay device, and dragons waiting to come out of their eggs."

The third dragon walked out of the water, and quickly rushed to hide behind a tree.

The tree didn't hide him very well. He towered over it.

"She's shy." Hannah suddenly laughed. "And she's cute." Fat tears fell from her eyes. Something about this dragon, hiding on the periphery, living on the fringes, was her.

She stayed behind the tree.

Then, dry dust fell from its mouth and the energy portholes in its hands. More dust fell from the jointy tips of her wings, and a porthole that opened in the center of her chest.

"It's the nerve gas," shouted the bleeding gavel voice. "We're opening up."

None of us took cover. We were spellbound, I guess, or maybe we figured what was the fucking point? If it's Krylin-19, game over, man.

Anti-aircraft guns pound-pounded and the ground shook and there was nothing left of the tree.

Branches fell.

The third dragon hid behind another tree.

"Stand down," Anne barked into her headset. "Stand down."

The pound-pounding kept pounding.

Stand down!

It's not nerve gas, Hannah told Anne, and the Chief of Counter Terrorism relayed that to the general. It's potpourri. Dried petals. Spices. Dead flowers. Dust. It's not Krylin-19; it's dead flowers. That's all.

The pound-pounding stopped.

The ground still tremored.

But the area smelled of dust, bombs, and something nice, like visiting my grandmother when I was a kid.

The third dragon waited and waited and waited behind the little tree that couldn't disguise her location, and then ambled to the other two, sat, a little off from the pair.

TV cameras whirred and the guy in the porkpie had lost his porkpie saying something or other about nerves being frayed but everything is under a semblance of control, once again, right now, and we wait to see what else is in store. "Boy does it smell great out here."

We waited, sad and happy and hopeful. I pushed back my porkpie.

Stana squeezed my hand harder and I kissed her. She was in jeans, a sweater, a down-filled parka, and the Star of David. It was a great look.

Ten minutes late to the party, dragon number four arrived, walking out of the lake, with a sauntering, confident swagger. He carried twenty to thirty rocks in his small arms. There was a bounce in every step.

He was the badass. The leader.

He sat with the other three and handed out rocks.

They placed the rocks in stacks in front of them.

Chips for a poker game.

That's what that was. Chips for a goddamn poker game.

I laughed out loud.

The last dragon to the party moved his hands rapidly, shuffling an imaginary deck of cards. He asked the dragon to his left to cut the deck, and then dealt the hand.

They held up tiny hands, holding their imaginary cards.

One of the dragons waved a small hand our way, inviting us to join the table.

Many moved closer.

The second dragon threw in two rocks.

The third folded.

The fourth called.

The second dragon clapped and bounced on its tail. It was the obvious winner.

Dr. Bauer got the last laugh, double-crossing Hitler's war machine. He didn't load the dragons with Krylin-19; he loaded them with dead, dry petals and spices—flowers of love; he didn't design the dragons to kill; he designed them to have a childlike fun, an engagement with the world, and a joy for the very card games he found wonder in: poker, and I have no doubt, solitaire.

Too bad Strehl and Ziegler missed this final act.

The Beer Hall Putsch is patchouli, baby.

I dropped a hand to Hannah's shoulder. "Your father loved us, loved us all."

I felt the calm tremble of her body. "He was no Nazi," I apologized. "Never was."

"He wasn't." She held my hand firmly. "He wasn't."

It was a helluva legacy to leave a daughter.

And then many of us sat around the dragons' table, waiting for their energy cells to run down, gathering more and more rocks, and playing poker until dawn.

Shot, Reverse Shot

1

A weird-looking fella leaned with the sway of the door. His eyes were covered by a makeshift mask constructed from the inside reflectors of a car's headlights. I could barely see the person peeking behind long metal cones the shape of construction-zone pylons.

I was here to find the girl.

"Mordecai Zuger."

We shook hands, his was clammy.

"Fuller, Hayden Fuller."

"I know who you are. Played with Béliveau tonight—"

I nodded. I was a grinder, back in the NHL at long last, after a two-year forced retirement. Anyway, Rejean Bouldieu, my teammate and our flashy, high-scoring winger, called me, mumbling something or other about a thousand oysters and his girl being out of control, could I come and get her, she was making a scene, dig?

So, here I was at this party at Place Jacques Cartier in a converted warehouse at two-thirty in the goddamn morning. I don't drink so the fellas count on me to be their designated driver. Never mind that I had a post-game headache that two Anacin had done nothing to take care of—

Zuger ushered me in, smelling of gasoline. His clothing was of the limited costume budget variety—he was naked. "You must be here to get our Lucy."

He introduced me to the fella standing behind him sporting a gas-station attendant's shirt and nothing else.

"My makeup guy and DP, Marc Harris." Makes all those hockey cuts and stitches look real, he said. Zuger was filming his first ever mainstream film, *Firewagon Hockey*.

Harris, a big guy with wide-set eyes and a flattop, went on and on about Lon Chaney and his use of makeup. Something about fishing wire and putty. I feigned interest.

A haze of pot drifted from the ceiling like low-slung hammocks. Pale white bodies shimmied to thin jazz. Dots of pink powder and ashtrays of crushed cigarettes ran across a low-end coffee table. Marc drifted to the dust.

"Pink cocaine. That's a new one—"

"Cocaine?" Zuger laughed. "Cocaine? No, no. That's the latest in uppers." Another laugh. An inside joke, I gathered.

He pointed upstairs. Lucy.

Naked men with saggy chests and partial erections gathered around, placing specks of powder under their tongues. Young women jostled about like crashing white caps. Suddenly a woman with a blonde beehive, heavy lipstick, and a red dress lacquered across her body brushed high-riding breasts against my arm. It wasn't accidental. Barbara Channing. "Some party, huh?" She had green eyes and a voice of smooth scotch.

Zuger was her husband. No more grindhouse circuits for them, she said. This film is "downhome entertainment for the masses" and it has the backing of the Provincial government. But they still cut corners, filming with old stock, WWII seconds from the National Film Board. "That stuff is highly flammable, you know. But it keeps production costs low."

Across the room was their benefactor, a short fella with tight curly hair, bushy eyebrows, and a walking stick with figures, a man and a woman inside a glass hexagonal handle. "He was part of the church hierarchy under Duplessis in the 1950s. Gave 70K to jumpstart our project."

"Uh-huh—"

"Said what we're doing is culturally significant for French Canada." Their last grindhouse film was *Quasmo!* About a hunchback in a diaper looking to get laid. She shuddered good-naturedly at the ignominy.

The Duplessis fella, also in a limited-costume budget, scratched stick figures across the chests and hips of two girls: one had high cheekbones and appeared to be from the islands; the other had raven black hair and a cluster of moles along her back. "Seems he's got his own immersion program happening right now—"

That cracked her up. Henri Ducat, she said.

I had heard that Barbara and her husband were splitsville—

"Don't believe everything you hear—"

I nodded.

Her husband grew up above a service station. He lived for the mix of octane fumes with the tastes of breakfast: scrambled eggs and toast. Today, their film studio is a combination lab, where they edit the daily rushes, and an Irving station. "His own immersion program." She laughed again.

I wondered if she was putting me on.

2

Lucille was in the second room upstairs, wedged in a couch corner, hands and legs bound by hockey tape.

Falling lines of mascara scraped her face, and her powder-blue hair pointed like scorched grass. She hadn't been drinking, taking drugs, nothing. Her voice was helium-spiked.

"Cut the tape, now."

Reggie shrugged absently and smiled a squirrely grin. Too much pink candy, he said. "Out of control—some just can't handle the oysters, I guess."

Oysters. Again with the oysters.

He may have scored thirty-three goals last year, but he was pissing me off, and I decked him.

He bounced on his elbows. "I deserved that. I deserved that," he said.

We had a Cup to win for chrissakes and he was partying, taking drugs, and his girlfriend's fingers had turned a pulpy purple from a loss of circulation.

Barbara, finding scissors from somewhere or other, crossed to Lucy with short stabs from her spiked heels.

Lucy rubbed at sore wrists. She was in only a bra, panties, and Go-Go boots. I draped my leather jacket over her shoulders.

OUTSIDE, THE SKY WAS A BLACK DISK and Lucy's gray eyes crescent moons. She was quietly laughing. "Let's take Reggie's car.

That'll really piss him off." A set of car keys jangled. Where could she have been hiding them?

"We can drive in style—"

The car was a gold Lamborghini Miura, 1966. How Reggie could afford such a thing was beyond me. I was making $8,000 a year, him 12-5 with bonuses.

Grain Silo Number Two, a large slab of concrete columns, glowed like phosphorus as we made our way to the street. "I'm not sure about this—"

"Reggie's such an asshole," Lucy muttered. He—I'm not a sex machine, she said.

Our thighs bumped against the car.

"Come on, superstar—"

The harbor pinched at my nostrils. Seagulls splashed at the waves.

I don't know why: maybe I was pissed at Reggie for asking this favor; maybe it was the upturned nose and freckles that danced in Lucy's eyes like my girlfriend Stana's. I don't know, but we climbed in.

A truck with thick tires and side mirrors the size of toboggans drove past, and then pulled in front of Reggie's crate. The flatbed was crowded with corrugated drain pipes, underground tubing. Mayor Drapeau was transforming Old Montreal, into an upscale makeover for Expo '67. The truck's engine coughed to a stop and then the driver hopped out, hands in pockets. He wore leathers with a WWI aviator's cap, thick goggles, and a python-like scarf topping off his Knights of the Air ensemble. His colors were Northern Arrows MC: an Agit-Prop fist clutching a quiver of crushed arrows.

He quickly became sharp lines that slowly limned and then vanished under dim lights.

"Someone slipped me something," Lucy repeated. The guy with the walking stick, she said. He's the drug dealer. Ducat. "He messed with me before—"

The truck in front coughed to life. There had been two people in it, not one.

White light.

Reverse gear.

I yanked Lucy below the dash.

The car's front end buckled and crumpled, glass and metal bashing and popping. I shouldered open the driver-side door, pulling Lucy across seats to the street. Plumbing poles shattered the windshield, shearing away the Lamborghini's roof.

The second driver hopped out the passenger door, ran through the fountain and beyond Nelson's column to open ground.

I gave chase before my lungs exploded and I bent at the waist.

When I returned, the truck and its poles were wedged to the wreckage. Lucy was gone. She left a note on the remains of the car's window: "Henri Ducat used and abused me."

I called the gendarmes from a phone booth across the way. *He had messed with me before. Drug dealer.*

By the time they arrived, the party had busted up. Hell, you wouldn't even know there had been a goddamn party. The smell of pot was replaced with the electricity of Lysol. And nothing was there: no women with finger-painted hand prints on their chests; no naked men with their partial erections; and no ersatz jazz. But somewhere, I was pretty damn sure, Reggie was still searching for his damn keys.

3

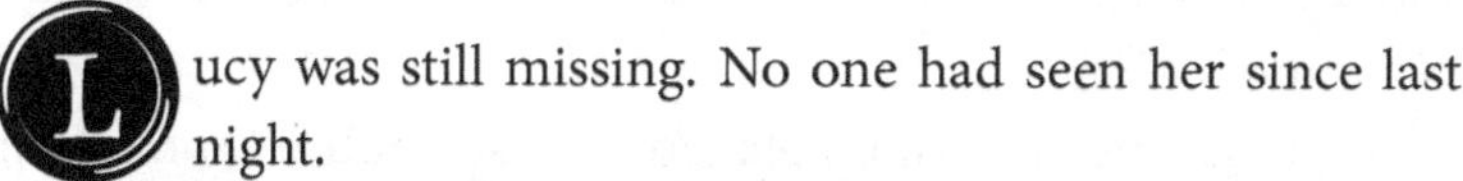

Lucy was still missing. No one had seen her since last night.

And Stana was pissed. She had been interviewing Lucy for an exposé to appear in the *Montreal Gazette*, and had grown attached to the kid. Anger and frustration darkened her pale blue eyes. “How could you have left her?”

I pushed back from the breakfast table, propped an ankle on top of a knee and absently played with my runny eggs. Practice was scheduled for 3. Stanley cup, game 5, was tomorrow, and now I was investigating a kidnapping.

And I had fucked up. Leaving the girl alone.

Stana sighed, flipping red hair behind her shoulder. When Lucy was a kid, she was taken from her Mom and placed in Rochefort Asylum, Duplessis era, 1952–53. Lots of “illegitimate kids” were falsely placed in mental institutions, government-sanctioned orphanages, to cloister away the fact that they existed. “It was a Catholic-led conspiracy to promote the nuclear family.” Stana shook her head. She was a wayward Catholic herself and had no problem talking so openly. I’m Jewish, so together we have a lot covered. She lit a Parliament and exhaled violently. “Anway, at fourteen, Lucy escaped. At eighteen she winds up an extra in *Firewagon*.” And now she’s a stand-in for Simone, the shot-reverse shot sequences.

“Shot, reverse shot? Lucille’s hair was blue—how can she be

a stand in?" The coloring would wreak havoc with a light meter.

"I don't know." Stana took a quick drag, blew smoke into the corner ceiling of my St Urbain's flat. "She said she was pissed at the director. Something to do with sins of the past."

"Hmm—"

Stana's fingertips tented. Ducat was the one-time director at Rochefort and according to Lucille performed strange experiments on the kids, even farmed some of them out, "sex slaves to rich parishioners." She flecked away a tobacco lash from her tongue, took another drag. "Some priests even took advantage. Nuns too."

I handed her the ribboned note I had found. "Something here's not kosher. Look at the writing—"

The words were in a smooth scrawl, even spaces between letters. "The words are too neat. Where's the urgency? Where's the fear?"

Stana slowly nodded. "What are you suggesting?"

"I don't know, but I'm not sure that Lucy wrote the note—"

She tapped her lower lip. "The story she was going to tell the *Gazette* would have blown the lid off the Catholic Church—" Stana shrugged. "I think Ducat has her—"

Drug dealer. Messed with me.

"Time to talk to Ducat," I said.

HENRI DUCAT NOW WORKED in a glass-walled building near the campus of McGill. He was the Minister of Culture or some damn thing since 1963, about the time Lucy escaped from the asylum.

His office was paneled with a walnut desk the size of a Buick. On the walls were photographs of young girls, 11-14, the Duplessis Kids, an underprivileged group from rural Quebec that the government had sponsored and helped place in expensive private schools. He was proud to have been a part of that program—

"Yeah, and what about that other program, trafficking young kids to priests and nuns and—"

"Miss Younger, be careful with what you say, or I may press charges of slander—"

"I have tapes, conversations, with Lucy Drolet—"

"The ramblings of—"

"In which she details deprivation experiments, electric shock therapy, and being traded about for sexual favors—bishops, cardinals—"

"—There is no truth. There are no witnesses—"

"—My witness is gone—"

Ducat tapped the edge of the blotter with square, bulky fingers. He pointed to the wall of coffee-cream file cabinets to his left— "In the case files, if you read them, you'll find she frequently heard voices—schizophrenia. This note you handed me. *Used and Abused.* A delusion. A frame job."

"She also called you a drug dealer—" I said.

"Lies—"

"And what about the girls last night at the party? They looked sixteen, fifteen. Farmed out from Rochefort—"

"What party?" His thin smile whitened the corners of his lips.

"You were there—"

"Witnesseses?" He laughed. "I was never there. Another delusion. I have a high-ranking MP that can tell you I was with him." Those girls were Channing's girls. Interns. Editing. Foley work. "And her husband assures me they are of age."

He struggled from behind his desk and limped to the cabinets. His left leg, from a war wound, was shorter than his right. The glass handle to his walking stick had shadowy figures inside, one hovering it appeared over another.

A cabinet squalled metallically. Ducat thumbed through a series of composition books. "Aww, here we are—"

He tossed them across the desk.

Clipped to one of the books was a 4x5 photograph of Lucy

at twelve, eyes full of sad knowledge that the world was full of hurt. Her sandy hair was in a pageboy cut that made her look sexually ambiguous.

Stana and I flipped pages.

Ducat's fingers tapped at the blotter's edge. "Those are Lucy's journals, around the time of the break. The images, surreal. The thoughts, incoherent. Observe the handwriting—"

We did. The letters appeared to be scribbled by a broken hand, lines leaning left. By contrast, the lines to the lettering in the note were upright, straight. Moreover, there were no bubbles in the tails of the D's to "Used and Abused," just straight, skinny downstrokes.

"Lucy did not write this note," he said. "She's a lefty."

Stana remembered Lucy popping cap bottles off Cokes at the edge of our kitchen's countertop with a left hand.

"I'm being set up," Ducat said. "Like I said, a frame job."

4

I pushed back my porkpie as elevator doors hushed open. The evening papers briefly mentioned a "Lamborghini Incident," but there was no mention of a warehouse party and powdered drugs. Simone Barrault, the film's female lead, was quoted as saying "quel dommage. Such a car, tres jolie." The article also went on to talk about her work in two Godard films, cited her filmography, and one columnist even listed her measurements.

Simone, now in a tight-fitting, terry-cloth robe, let us in. A cup of tea was in her left hand. The air: burnt toast and lilacs. "Sorry to run off last night and leave you holding the bag, mon ami." She smiled, little canine teeth. She had a thin nose and brown eyes that resembled coffee grounds.

I don't ever remember seeing her at the party.

On the breakfast table, a wooden basket was crowded with bruised fruit. A dark, discarded wig pushed up against it. There was also half a glass of orange juice, a red lipstick stain along the mouth. Simone's lipstick was mostly beige.

"Where's Reggie?" Stana wondered if he may have been the intended target of the "Lamborghini Incient." And this was allegedly his pad.

An appointment, Simone said. She had no idea with whom.

I glanced at my watch and mumbled, "You're wearing Chanel No. 5."

"Oui."

It was one of the few perfumes I knew. "But I smell lilacs. Two fragrances." I pointed at the cup of orange juice. "Two colors of lipstick—you can tell Barbara to come out of the back bedroom."

She wore a matching terry-cloth robe. Her hair was tousled up in a towel. She slid an ashtray to Stana. "You're very observant—"

"Why the wig?" I rubbed at the edges of my mouth.

"Guess—" She grabbed Simone around the waist and kissed her cheek. "I don't want the reporters knowing of my peculiar institution," she said, a faux Southern belle. She found that a real crack up for some reason. "Peculiar institution, suh," she repeated, lighting two cigarettes and handing her girlfriend one.

"Is your husband dangerous?" Stana exhaled quickly.

"We all have our dark sides." Barbara shrugged and turned to Simone.

The two women nodded in unison, the goddamn Doublemint Girls.

"What about the girls at the party? Your interns?" *That's what Ducat had said. Channing's.*

"Mordecai's interns. He has a thing for young girls." She held up a hand. "I mean, barely legal girls. Legal, but barely—" Okay, there had been an incident in the past involving a sixteen-year-old, but never mind about that. That was long ago—and Mordecai settled out of court, Barbara assured us.

"What about this?" Stana reached deep into her purse, the one that's the size of a milk crate with the rings of Saturn for a handle, and floated a ribbon of paper between the Terry-Cloth Girls.

"This just isn't true. You're saying Lucy wrote this?" A heavy crease formed between Barbara's eyes.

I played with the brim of my porkpie—

"You know Lucy's a chronic liar, right? Visions? Voices. She didn't write this." Barbara squeezed Simone's hand. "My husband did."

Barbara's index finger, the nail lacquered with black polish, traced the sharp vertical lines of the D's. Drolet's tails have bubbles, she said, these don't. She remembered Drolet's handwriting from the contract she had signed. Now, my husband writes like this. Always in an angry rush. "Never able to take it slow." She gave Simone a knowing wink. He hurries his fills, if you know what I mean. She laughed.

Simone joined in.

So if Mordecai Zuger wrote the note, why was he implicating Henri Ducat?

Stana thought the same thing. "Lucy had mentioned something about your husband and the *sins of the past*—"

"Sins of the past?" Barbara tapped her lower lip and glanced over at Simone. "Lucy, after she escaped from Rocherfort, and—well, you know she worked for us—well, she was the girl, the one Mordecai had slept with, underaged, but barely—"

"Barely, no, but—" Simone said. "Still wrong, yes?"

WE WERE TALKING AT THE COFFEE SHOP across from the Forum after the game, a 5–1 win. Well, I should say, Mordecai Zuger was lecturing and I was taking notes.

How could I possibly think that he would kidnap Lucy? Yes, they had a thing, a year or so ago—

"She was sixteen, seventeen, a year or so ago, asshole."

So was Donna Michelle when she appeared in *Playboy*, tough guy. Playmate of the Year. Nick Ray, director of *Rebel without a Cause*—great, great film—was banging Natalie Wood and she was like sixteen, maybe fifteen. "What's your beef?" He lit an angry cigarette, his hawk nose tucked in as if readying to receive a punch, daring me to take a poke. His dark hair was a threadbare placemat, a bad combover. "I was fond of that girl. But Barbara was fonder—"

"She had a thing for her?"

"A thing, yes. But nothing happened."

"Lucy wore blue hair to the last shoot before she went missing. She said something to Stana about the sins of the past?"

"That's more about my wife than about me—talk to her—"

"I did. She said it was more about you—"

"She would." He leaned toward me. "Look, who you gonna believe, huh? That's your worry—"

I rubbed at the edges of my mouth. "Ducat a drug dealer?"

"He's a businessman—"

"That doesn't exactly answer things—"

"We all had a falling out," he said. "Leave it at that." He took a quick drag. "She's a chronic liar."

"Barbara or Lucy?"

"Take your pick, pal."

Jumping Java, the coffee shop, sure lived up to its name. Framed hard-bop albums littered the walls: Sonny Clark, John Coltrane, Miles Davis, Art Blakey and his Jazz Messengers. On each Formica table were lamps with quarter notes cut in the metal shades. I smiled my lopsided grin.

He picked out three paper napkins from the placeholder on the table and clicked open his pen. "Ask me to write something, tough guy. Anything."

I mumbled something about the Jazz Messengers and he wrote, "Art Blakey's one *bad* drummer." He wrote that hurriedly, twenty times, and shoved the napkins toward me. A surly curve waved through his lower lip. "Does that look anything like my *used and abused* missive?"

It didn't. The handwriting was tiny crushed-down words with broken backs.

So it wasn't Lucy who wrote it. It wasn't Zuger. Could it be Channing? Ducat?

"She accuses me of writing a note that she knows I couldn't possibly have written. Bitch."

I was trying to figure out the alliances of this case, who was with who?

"She's a dangerous woman," he warned. "Are we done here—?"

We were.

He sulked off.

I slowly slurped a second cup of coffee.

5

The next morning, Ducat buzzed my St. Urbain's pad. He knew I had a plane to catch to Detroit, so he said he'd keep things brief. "Those stories Zuger and the girl Lucy are spinning—"

"Lucy may have told stories, but the note wasn't written by Zuger—"

"Then who?"

"I think Channing—"

There was a long pause. "Really?" That makes sense, he mumbled, his mind working quickly. "It all makes a lot of sense—" You see, Fuller, Lucy did tell the police things. Before she disappeared she spilled to the cop shop about my past, and Project LL.

"Project LL??"

Street name. LL. Long Lasting, he said. Cardinals, church hierarchy, the rich. They're my clients. "Mr. Boldieu was my, how shall I put it, bridge to privilege. Everyone loves hockey. He pushed the product in gated communities. For men with problems—"

A thousand oysters. An aphrodisiac.

More than that, he said. This makes you seventeen again. And the hangover afterward. He laughed. "Right now the drug's illegal, cooked up by chemical engineers in France. I have a connection with them through my Cultural Ministry office. You didn't hear this from me of course." Ducat figured if Channing's involved, then Reggie was playing both sides, a double agent, working for them and him.

"So who took the girl?"

"Them. One of them. Channing. Zuger. Boldieu." Another pause. "Or maybe she just took a powder to get us all in trouble." The police had been asking questions, a lot of questions. "It'll take some coins to quiet them. But I got the coins—"

I said nothing.

"I'll deal with Reggie," he promised. One final, long awkward silence followed. "After you all win the Cup, of course."

FORTY-FIVE MINUTES LATER I was at Zuger's, the basement of his small house behind the service station. We were huddled around a Steenbeck machine watching the raw footage for *Firewagon*. The room had cinder-block walls, a heavy smell of rubber cement, and a white cork board along a far wall, loaded with film equipment from reels to splicers. Several strips of film dangled from a shelf behind him, and along the corkboard were different outtakes, with little notes and numbers push-pinned by each coil. Ribbons of film were everywhere, resembling slick pieces of bent flypaper.

The basement matched the size of the ranch house, about 950 square feet. One section just over 280 square feet was a bulky box with a door. Its outer walls were paneled.

He noticed me noticing.

"That's my darkroom. That's where we develop the dailies—you want a tour?"

"No." I held up a hand.

"I run a shoestring, efficient operation—"

"Not aided and abetted by Project Long Lasting?"

"I told you, I have no idea about that—"

"No? Really, now. There was pink powder at your party; Reggie talked about a thousand oysters. Lucy told me she wasn't a sex machine. People were taking Long Lasting at your party. You said something about uppers. At *your* party."

Reggie brought it in, he said. I'm not distributing it—

Reggie, not Ducat.

"Your wife?"

Zuger shrugged. He was in hipster casual: white slacks, black turtleneck, chains around his neck. A stained-glass medallion rested near the porch of his barrel for a stomach. Some cat, his hair all askew and unwieldy, held out his arms, genuflecting. It could have been Moses carrying the Ten Commandments or John the Baptist after noshing all those locusts. My money was on the locusts. The fella genuflecting looked a little green.

"I can't account for what my wife does. She lives her life—but Reggie brought the drugs, for one-time recreational use—"

"And who brought the girls—?"

"I told you already. Interns—"

The camera placement for the *Firewagon Hockey* footage was incredible: at the blue lines, and center, and behind the two goals. The pace was fast, the movement fluid, the colors vibrant.

Let me warn you, pal, you're messing in Ducat's business and he'll mess with you, I said. When Lucy was taken, the people I saw around us were Northern Arrows. I saw their colors. You were a Northern Arrow.

Stana had done her research. It's good to love a gal with reporter friends.

"Emphasis on were." He admitted to being lost after the war, forming the outfit in 1949. But he quit in 1955. "Never looked back." He smiled. "Right after James Dean died. Seriously, the dream of the open road died when he did." He played with the edges of the medallion and that's when I realized the guy under stained glass was Dean from *Giant*.

He re-wound the film. The girls at the party were Barbara's groupies, he said. I may have slept with Lucy, but she and Barbara were lovers. For months. He flashed a thin, dirty smile.

"You know what I think?" I leaned forward, hands on my thighs. "That's not what you said before when I asked. Every time. The story changes. You're all playing me. You and your wife are partners and you're pointing fingers at each other to distract me—" I pushed back my porkpie. "You're both in a fight with Ducat for his drug empire—"

"That's good." He pointed a finger, and then shook a triumphant fist. "You should storyboard that. Make a helluva movie."

He handed me a ten-spot. "Put me down for a contribution—"

6

I had wanted to talk to Reggie, but at 28,000 feet and before game six of the 1966 Finals I wasn't sure if it was such a good idea. A dressing room and a hockey team is supposed to be a safe space. But I needed to know what he knew, if anything, about being a go-between with high society, a double-agent dealing a new drug, Long Lasting, and the disappearance of Lucy. And most importantly I wanted to warn him about Henri Ducat's vow to kill him.

Reggie was lost behind curtained eyes. Demoted to the third line, his face was painted with a sulky, wandering gaze.

"You got a minute?"

Surrender flickered through him. He was writing something with his finger on the window.

Quietly, I told him all I knew.

He winced.

I didn't take the girl, he said. He was pretty sure Ducat did. It's an old trick: point initial suspicion at yourself with an accusatory note, and then have us all doubt the validity of the charges. He smiled. Lucy was going to blow the whistle on the whole operation. Forget about what happened at Rochefort's, she was working with the Feds on the sex pill ring. "And so Ducat took her. Probably killed her, like he's going to kill me."

"Channing?"

She wants to take over his racket, he said.

"And Zuger?"

"I don't know." He shrugged. "Maybe—"

"They're going to kill you."

He couldn't look at me, his fingers tracing Lucy's name over and over again, in the glass.

WE WON THE CUP on a Thursday, 3-2 in overtime.

My shift had ended and Henri Richard rushed down center with Reggie on his left. A quick pass and Reggie caught it on his backhand and gave a perfect saucer return to Henri. He pushed forward, tangling up with Red Wings' D-man Gary Bergman, and they tumbled, sliding toward Roger Crozier, who was hunched, readying, and the puck hidden somewhere in all that colliding debris found shelter in the back of the net.

And that was it.

The referee pointed: goal.

Everything seemed far away. I was happy but I felt lost in a tunnel turning sideways. I watched myself watching a game as cool vapor spread.

IT WAS FOUR IN THE MORNING and nobody wanted to go home.

This was it. This group. The last time. Stanley Cup champs for 1965–66, partying in the lobby of the Fairmont La Reine Elizabeth Hotel. It was a lavish joint with high-vaulted ceilings and lighting that gave off a red watery shade. All of us felt an undercurrent of melancholy.

I had told Jean that I was retiring, again. Nobody else knew yet. Not even Stana. I thought I'd call her, tell her I loved her—

"Reggie, my man, that was some pass," Jean-Guy Talbot said.

Béliveau nodded. "Tape to tape, through Bergy's legs."

Reggie smiled, a laconic stubble of a grin. The winger was back in the team's good graces and he was happy.

He caught me leaving. "Hey, Fulls, where are you going?"

"Call my girl—" I was getting married in June.

"Sit down, have a beer—"

"He doesn't drink, Reggie—" Béiveau was always mindful of his teammates.

"I'll be right back," I promised.

"I'll come with you." Reggie brushed off his pants and pulled up close, his voice low. "I got an angle on where Lucy might be, if she's still alive," he mumbled.

He suggested we go to his hotel room.

"What about Simone and Barbara?"

There's a study on the same floor, he said. We'll go there.

I nodded and we got in the elevator.

We didn't say another word.

The doors opened with a hush.

A curvy woman filled the gap, leaning left with powder-blue hair, crisp gray eyes, and an upturned nose. The lighting was dim, but I saw the gun in her right hand, its filed-down sight. "You shouldn't have done it, Reggie," she said.

"Lucy—"

"You shouldn't—"

"Okay, okay. Can we—"

And that was it. Not much of an epitaph, really. *Okay, okay. Can we—*

Three bullets. Two tore through his chest and one caught his neck, splashing him back on the elevator's metallic walls, splattering their reflective sheen panels. He slid down as if a towel were slipping off his hips.

I figured I was next.

Lucy flipped blue hair over a shoulder and winked. "You're cute," she said.

The elevator doors hushed closed, and me immobile, as the car falls, down, down, down.

7

 waded through tall, uncut grass. An Irving station just ahead.

The red sun had slipped under the horizon.

Lucille Drolet was still missing. The papers thought she had killed Reggie. It didn't help that my initial testimony put the finger on her, but I was now re-thinking it all. Something about it just wasn't kosher.

When I emerged from the sea of grass, a black sedan was pulling away from the pumps. A fella in dark green pants, tan shirt, with a rag in his hip pocket approached me.

I brushed away dew and cattail fuzz from my legs. "Got a flat up the road. Need some help."

He asked about the spare, I said I didn't have one, and then he smiled. It was Marc Harris, the makeup guy and DP from *Firewagon Hockey*. I should have counted on that. I was bound to bump into someone who knew Zuger and knew me. And I had a feeling he knew all about the tire, what I had done with a buck knife.

He looked at his shoes, the toes and instep a lighter color because of gasoline spill off. High octane pinched the air and then it was joined by another, Chanel No. 5. Anyway, I had been fearfully expecting something like this. A gun jabbed my back.

It hurt.

"Don't turn around, Fuller—"

Simone.

LILACS. HEAVY, SWEET, BUTTERY.

"You couldn't just leave it alone. You just had to find the girl—" Barbara leaned forward in a hardback chair, wearing the same tight dress from our first encounter at the warehouse. It fit her like a bikini.

Simone stood behind Barbara's shoulder, left hand on the chair's back, right hand clamped to a .38. It was the same one that killed Reggie. It had a filed-down sight.

"Where's Harris, out digging a grave?"

Upstairs with the girls, Barbara said. He'll dig later. It's not dark enough, yet—

"And Lucy?"

I was parked in the basement on a threadbare divan, stuffing poking about like puffs of popcorn. Traces of rubber cement filled the air. Behind the two of them was the corkboard, Zuger's Steenbeck, and rolls and rolls of twisting film. Seconds from WWII.

"You're the connection." I pointed at Simone, pain behind my eyes. "Bringing the drugs in from France."

Simone nodded, the gun steady.

"Where's Lucy?"

"Boy you're persistent—" Barbara glanced over her shoulder toward the bulky box of a darkroom. "There's a cot in there, a small refrigerator, and Lucy. We're orchestrating a way for her to exit this narrative involving Ducat. "A clean little homicide/suicide scenario. Right, dear?" She smiled up at Simone.

"Right—" Simone's brown eyes brightened.

The last time I was here, Zuger had offered me a tour. That was ballsy. *If I had said yes.*

"Why kill Reggie?"

"He knew too much." Barbara looked at a fingernail, painted black. "And wanted in. Wanted too much. That's all—"

The strips of film along white cinder-block curled as the heater kicked on. It was cold for early May and the ends of the film rolled up slightly.

Upstairs, little wings of voices danced: groupies, escorts, sex slaves for Channing's business transactions. "Your makeup guy did a great job, Simone. With the upturned nose, higher cheekbones, and hair, but you know where you messed up?"

"Where did I mess up?"

"The gray contacts were good too, but you didn't pay enough attention to craft, the character's inner life." Lucy was a lefty, I said. You should have noticed it, known it. "She was your goddamn stand-in." But in this shot, reverse shot sequence *you* killed Reggie, not Lucy. "You with your right hand—that's what wasn't adding up for me—"

Simone handed Barbara the gun. "This fella bores me. Time for you to get your hands dirty, love." Simone crossed to the stairs, and winked over at me, a cover-girl smile before ascending.

"Did you ever care for Reggie?"

"He was a lousy lover—" Barbara weighed the gun.

I guess that says it all. *Lousy lover.* But I couldn't let it go. "You know what his last words were, *okay, okay. Can we*—does that seem like a fair summation of a life—"

The filed-down sight glinted.

Thuds upstairs. A faint murmur of broken wings, the crack-crack of handguns, followed by the steady strum of a Thompson.

Barbara staggered to her feet, but her balance was hinky. Spiked stiletto heels.

I rushed her.

She fired a ragged shot that somehow missed, and I hit her high with a crossbody block that sent her keeling into the table and cork board, stumbling and tangling up with several strips of seconds.

She grappled, mummified in tangled-up film, the gun stilled, tied tight to her thigh. She couldn't raise it and her eyes bled hatred.

I reached inside my leather jacket and touched off the films' ends with a tongue of flame.

They crackled, bopping and bashing.

I kicked the gun free and rushed to the dark room.

Lucy, her face nicked up from hard slaps, and who knows what the fuck else, ran to my side, blonde roots in her faded powder-blue hair.

Smoke billowed as we headed up basement steps.

Barbara's screams stretched with the links of flame.

She kicked like a beginning swimmer, staccato steps stuck in stilettos.

We climbed higher, a dizzy carousel spinning in my head, eyes hurting, as Barbara Channing became charred driftwood, a floating stillness, a rippling human flag of film.

8

A biker gang.

The fella with an aviator's cap, dark Ray-Bans, and a scarf full of Iron Crosses gave me the nod of a fellow professional. Tucked tight to his hip, a Thompson. "Don't think about it, hero."

My breath caught.

"Barbara?" Ducat, the short fella, now wore a gray Homburg with a thick plush band to make himself look taller. A tight curl or two peeked out from under the hat's brim. He waved his walking stick, the shadowy figures in the glass handle arm-in-arm. To his right, Simone. Against her hip, another Thompson.

"Celluloid flambé," I said.

Smoke curled around us. Wood, inside the walls, stretched with heat.

Ducat chuckled. "Put away the pea shooter, if we wanted you dead, Simone would have dropped you." His suit was charcoal gray, pin-striped, with an immaculate blue dahlia in the lapel.

Three teenage girls were huddled on the other side of the room, holding each other up. They were arrayed in pastel pajamas and fuzzy slippers. I recognized two of them from the Warehouse party.

I dropped the gun.

Dead bodies crowded the chairs.

What was left of Harris was sunk deep in a leather recliner, hand dangling over the side, a blood-spotted .45 in his lap. Half his face was gone. Makeup tips from Lon Chaney weren't going to do him much good.

Zuger lay on the floor sideways, hands cuffed behind his back, the top of his head grapefruit pulp. It wasn't clear if he was their hostage or had been participating in some kind of kinky sex.

Three other fellas I had never seen before said their long goodbyes in Irving attendant uniforms. One found a resting place at the foot of a green chair, a chunk of chin sitting upright on his thighs. Two others were X's on the Oriental Rug, vacant ceiling eyes, blood drizzle across lips.

"Okay, here's the deal." Ducat snapped fingers and the fella with the aviator cap and two of his lieutenants escorted the girls outside.

The whole house was bending.

Simone hefted her Thompson.

I asked about the cover-girl wink. Downstairs.

"Oh that—" She smiled.

Ducat bent gently with laughter, his Homburg slightly shaking. He lifted the walking stick, leading the band. One of the figures inside the glass handle was clearly him. It had tight, curly Brill-O pad hair. The other was a girl, I think, with short, short hair. "My beautiful double-agent." He kissed Simone's cheek.

Simone was a fine, fine actress. "Starred in a couple of Godard films, you know, and she can turn on the glamor and charm, and she turned it on with Reggie, Barbara, and Zuger." He pointed at Zuger on the floor. "Poor bastard. Thought he was in for a blowjob—" He inhaled the sparkle of his flower. She played them all and informed me that Barbara planned to muscle in on my business. "I made it my business to keep Barbara Channing out of my business, dig?"

"The wink?" Simone nudged Ducat's elbow.

"Go ahead and tell him about the wink—"

The gun she gave Barbara. Blanks.

My body, once again, filled with cold vapor.

"So, here's the deal—" Ducat held up his walking stick like a judge's gavel. "If Lucy keeps quiet about Rochefort and Operation Long Lasting all of your troubles go away. A phone call. That's all it takes. And Barbara will be charged with Reggie's murder. After all, she suggested the hit. Fair is fair." We can also pin her for the kidnapping.

"Who *did* the kidnapping?" I asked.

"Simone—"

"Figures—"

Ducat's stick shook with warning. "However, Lucy. You talk, Fuller dies. Bottom line."

Lucy pulled in closer to my side. "I'll say nothing." Her words wobbled like a sputtering clay pigeon.

"Nothing at all, pretty one, you hear?" He pressed an index finger against his lips.

"I understand." Lucy squeezed my hand.

"Good." He held out a sideways triangle of arm. Simone took it, and we followed their lead, out of the house. We stood in open ground, far from the gas pumps. In the distance a motley howl of sirens.

Minutes later, the house crackled and wood bent and snapped and half the roof caved in.

"Reggie didn't have to die," Ducat said. "I liked him. But he got greedy, wanting twenty percent for his role in procuring clients—" His eyes took on a faraway expression. "C'est la vie."

And with that he and Simone retreated to a bright silver car that was at least two blocks long. It purred gently as it slinked away.

The girls in their pajamas and fuzzy slippers curled near me and Lucy.

She recognized some of them.

Escorts, favors farmed out to CEO's for business deals.

Abused runaways.

I squeezed Lucy's hand. "Thanks," I said.

Stana had connections, social workers. They could help these girls. There had to be a better place for them and Lucy Drolet in the cultural mosaic of Canada. There just had to be. Anything was better than this—

Flames, red fingers, stretched through the black sky.

The sirens drew closer.

"Did you see the walking stick, the figures in the glass handle?"

"Yeah." I rubbed at the edges of my mouth. He was the bigger shadow, hovering, I said. I noticed the tight curls. "It was him and some girl—"

"Not just some girl," she said.

Simone, the chameleon; Simone the consummate actress, famous player of French cinema, I said.

"No, not Simone." She looked down at her Keds.

The short-short hair. The other figure had short short. A pageboy cut.

It was Lucy. Twelve years old. Lucy—

A Hayden Fuller Timeline

July 17, 1935, Hayden Fuller born in Cabbagetown, Toronto, Ontario, Canada.

March 17, 1955, Rocket Richard Riot in Montreal.

1957–58, Hayden's first season with the Toronto Maple Leafs.

April, 1962, wins Stanley Cup with the Leafs over Chicago.

Spring, 1962, begins a relationship with *Toronto Telegram* beat reporter Stana Younger and pursues a hobby in photography.

April, 1963, wins Stanley Cup with the Leafs; scoring the winning over-time goal of game two of the finals.

Spring, 1964, sent to the minors, the Rochester Americans of the AHL, for "moral turpitude." Spring, 1964, retires from hockey following the end of the AHL season. NHL totals: 458 consecutive games played; 107 goals; 318 points.

Summer. 1964 earns his PI license after taking courses at York University, Toronto.

January, 1965, Sarah Kerr murdered (Fuller's first case).

April, 1965, events of *Cheap Amusements* take place.

The novel introduces a recurring set of characters: gangster Babe Migano, reporter Stana Younger, and Toronto's Top Cop and personal friend, Sal Lambertino.

July, 1965, events of *A Fourth Face* take place.

The novel introduces more supporting characters to Hayden's universe: his therapist, Dr. Jeannette Cohen, and the RCMP's head of counter-terrorism, Anne Chevalier.

Summer, 1965, Hayden, reinstated in the NHL, with the help of Anne Chevalier, following the events of *A Fourth Face.*

November 7–8, 1965, Hayden's father Ira is murdered.

November 11–15, 1965, the events of *Neon Kiss* take place.

November 11, 1965, Remembrance Day, Hayden returns to Maple Leaf Gardens, wearing Montreal Canadiens colors and is named the game's third star.

February, 1966, the events of *Day of the Dragons* take place in Bannerville, Ontario, Pop 1201, a small town some 85 miles northeast of Toronto.

February, 1966, Hayden contemplates retiring from hockey for the second time.

May, 1966, the events of "Shot, Reverse Shot" take place. Hayden lives on St Urbain-Street, Montreal.

May 5, 1966, Hayden wins the Stanley Cup with Montreal, figuring prominently in the last three games of the series.

May 6, 1966, Hayden retires from the NHL for the second and final time, and returns to his Bloor-Yonge PI office in Toronto.

About the Author

In 2015 Grant Tracey turned to writing crime noir. Before that he had published nearly fifty short stories in small literary magazines and story collections.* The sensibilities of *Five Hard Bites* are in part indebted to the writings of Raymond Chandler, Samuel Fuller, Mickey Spillane, and Jim Thompson. Grant teaches creative writing and film at the University of Northern Iowa and edits the *North American Review.* In 2013 he received an Iowa Regents Award for Faculty Excellence. In 2021, he was a recipient of UNI's Graduate College Distinguished Scholar Award. Recent publications include *Winsome/Bend of the Sun*, a chapbook, "The Key Witness," a short story in *Tough*, and "Four on the Floor," a forthcoming Hayden Fuller mystery appearing in *Groovy Gumshoes.*

* Among Grant's story collections is *Final Stanzas*, available in paperback, digital, and audiobook editions from Twelve Winters Press.

www.ingramcontent.com/pod-product-compliance
Lightning Source LLC
LaVergne TN
LVHW041050080826
845145LV00007B/1520

* 9 7 8 1 7 3 3 1 9 4 9 5 2 *